Dear Companion

The Inner Life
of
Martha Jefferson

Kelly Joyce Neff

HAMPTON ROADS
PUBLISHING COMPANY, INC.

Cover design by Grace Pedalino
Cover art by Giselle Gautreau
"Deathbed Adieu" image from The James Monroe Museum,
Fredericksburg, Virginia

For information write:
Hampton Roads Publishing Company, Inc.
134 Burgess Lane
Charlottesville, VA 22902

Or call: (804)296-2772
FAX: (804)296-5096
e-mail: hrpc.hrpub.com
Web site: http://www.hrpub.com

If you are unable to order this book from your local
bookseller, you may order directly from the publisher.
Quantity discounts for organizations are available.
Call 1-800-766-8009, toll-free.

ISBN 1-57174-075-9

10 9 8 7 6 5 4 3 2 1

Printed on acid-free paper in Canada

Dear Companion

Books by Kelly Joyce Neff

Everyday Life in Two Worlds
Dear Companion

"If in the house of Hades men forget their dead,
Yet will I even there remember my dear companion."
— Homer, *The Iliad, XXII, 389*

Inscribed (in Greek) by Thomas Jefferson
on the gravestone of Martha, his wife.

Acknowledgements

A book such as this is never the work of one person. Many have contributed their information, insight, and enthusiasm, proof of the impact that Thomas Jefferson continues to have on our lives and psyches as a nation. They have my heartfelt thanks, for without them both I and this book would be the poorer.

At Monticello, Daniel P. Jordan, Lucia Cinder Stanton, Kristin Onuf, Dr. William Kelso, the entire docent staff; the Randolph family for their hospitality and kindness at the graveyard.

Peter Onuf of the Department of History, University of Virginia. The staff of Special Collections at Alderman Library at the University of Virginia. The staff of the Visitor Center in Charlottesville. Robert Coles and Virginia Valentine of Charlottesville.

At the Colonial Williamsburg Foundation: Mary K. Wiseman, Brenda LeClair, William D. Barker, B. J. Pryor, Don Kline, Graham Hood, Cary Carson, Mary Econemou, and Phillip Appleby. Barron Roller, Emily James, and the entire staff of the Foundation Library.

At the Jefferson Legacy Foundation: Sidney Stokes, Jr., Bud Leeds, and Camilla Rockwell. The entire staff of the Library of Congress, Sutro Genealogical Library, and the San Francisco Public Library.

At Shadwell: Dr Barbara Heath and the archaeology crew. At Tuckahoe: Mr. and Mrs. Tad Thompson. Nancy Carter Crump of Petersburg. Kristen Paavola and the entire staff of the Chesterfield Historical society for allowing me access to Eppington. James Madison Macon of Richmond for access to The Forest site. The entire docent staff at Berkeley Plantation. At Shirley, Nancy Carter and the entire docent. George Jones for his directions to The Forest. Wray Page of Rosewell.

Of scholars, I particularly wish to thank Natalie S. Bober for debates about Patty's medical condition and for her nurturance and special understanding. Jack McLaughlin for long conversations about Patty, Bathurst Skelton, the less-than-wonderful conditions of Monticello's early days and for his leads concerning The Forest site; T. B. McCord for his vast knowledge of John Page and access to Fanny Page's memorial sermon; Roberta Grimes for her debates about Rebecca Burwell, and Merrill Peterson for his shining example.

Many, many thanks to Frank DeMarco, Bob Friedman, and the whole staff at Hampton Roads Publishing Company, but especially to Frank for his insight, perseverance, and faith in a rather unorthodox manuscript. Thanks go to my family too for their patience, especially my children, who have grown up thinking Mr. Jefferson the Eighth Wonder of the World. Thanks too, posthumously, to Fawn Brodie, without the spur of whose book this volume would never have been written.

Contents

Contents

Contents

Publisher's Preface

Dear Companion is the second in our projected series of books about remembered past lives, following *Under the Inquisition* by Linda Tarazi and preceding *Northumberland Dreaming* by Mary Rhees Mercker. We call these books historical fiction, but really there should be a new genre for such books. Uncounted thousands of people are adding their testimonies about life in other times, other places by writing histories and biographies disguised as fiction. It isn't just Joan Grant and Taylor Caldwell any more.

* * *

Five full years have gone by since the arrival of *Dear Companion* on my desk in July 1992. I had received a phone call from San Francisco, from an unpublished author, a young woman named Kelly. Since Hampton Roads Publishing Company was located in Virginia, would we be interested in a novel about Martha and Thomas Jefferson?

Well, would we? Primarily we publish books in three areas: metaphysics, alternative medicine, and visionary fiction. A novel on the Jefferson family didn't offhand seem to fit. Plus, I'd read a good deal about Jefferson, including Dumas Malone's six-volume work and other biographies, so I didn't really expect to encounter something new. But I told her I'd look at it.

The book arrived, with a letter that said in part, "I have chosen, after much dithering, to call this work historical fiction, for while every bit of it is true as far as facts go, much of it has been drawn from widely divergent documents." Rereading that now, I smile, for a reason that will become apparent. "Widely divergent documents"!

I glanced at the manuscript—and wound up reading it day and night, fascinated, till I had finished. Never had I read anything that brought the life and time so vividly to life. But at this time Hampton Roads was still a small publishing house, able to do only a few books each year.

I wrote her suggesting that a mass-market house was the proper place for the manuscript, adding, "I went back to Fawn Brodie's book after finishing yours last night, and read a few pages around July 1781. I was impressed with how much more strongly you convey the sense of the Jeffersons as people. . . ." Kelly's manuscript described Thomas breaking his arm in a fall from a horse; told of Patty's inability to set it; even quoted the amount of the doctor's bill. Brodie's book merely mentioned that he had suffered from a minor indisposition. It was the difference between a first-hand account and a twice-told tale.

Then I offered a suggestion that had momentous consequences. "Think about pruning the ms. of some of the invented dialogue. I know why you put it there, and to a great extent it works; however, particularly in the more intimate scenes, it may work against you. For *this* reader, at least, sometimes the dialogue served merely as a reminder that this book was being written in the twentieth century, by someone who was not there."

Little did I know what an earthquake *that* bit of kindly, well-meant advice would set off within her (and without her). In a letter by return post, she said, in part, "Which brings me to. . .your difficulty with the 'bedroom scenes.' I can only say that their private life is my concern. . .and that for me such scenes are focal points of who they were. Here I speak not as an outside observer, but as one who lived with and amid Thomas and Patty. This is why Fawn Brodie's view incensed me; I always felt from a very emotional level that she was wrong. . . .

"I say this not out of vanity or to win kudos, but to explain the otherwise inexplicable. You might understand that I have been very cautious about going public with such information, for I have no desire to be taken for a nut, or to have my credibility as a scholar questioned. What I *know* does not invalidate my ability to sleuth out validations of it, but I doubt the public at large is ready to hear the truth. I am only telling you to assuage your mental qualms about 'did they feel that way about each other?' Acceptance of what I say is entirely up to you. You are free to think of me as a nut if you wish."

So she remembered being Martha Jefferson? "You are perfectly free to regard me as a nut, if you wish," she said. I knew that the paranormal draws fakes and self-deceivers, as well as the genuine article, and it's always priority number one to figure out which of the three you are dealing with. I didn't believe she was a fake or a crazy; the only alternative was that she was reporting what she thought was true. Certainly it would explain the vivid, sure-footed description.

I later learned that the decision to admit that the manuscript was based on past-life memories had come only after a serious struggle against fear of ridicule, and that her telling the truth to a stranger had had a liberating effect.

Even though I was convinced we would never do the book, I remained interested in it. In September I suggested that she rewrite the manuscript to be entirely from Patty's viewpoint, rather than alternating between Patty's and Thomas's.

By reply she said, "Man alive! I realized [that]. . .when I first thought of writing this story, I wanted to use only Patty's experiences. But. . .'who would really care about plantation life, who was doing what with whom, and how she [I] felt about it? After all I was only a woman doing what everybody else was doing. . .'

"Patty had a real problem with acceptance/self-worth. . .fears of abandonment, conflict between her essential nature and societal expectations; and once I really got into the life, all those old tapes started playing again. So what did I do? Caved in and wrote about stuff from Th's view because I felt otherwise nobody would be interested. Same old stuff."

After which a great deal happened, much of it recorded in Kelly's book, *Everyday Life in Two Worlds: A Psychic's Experience,* which we published in 1994. Several earthquakes later, it is with great pride and pleasure that we finally publish *Dear Companion,* a remarkable book about a remarkable couple, by a remarkable author.

Frank DeMarco, Chairman
Hampton Roads Publishing Co.

A Simplified Genealogy

The Wayles Family

John Wayles, Patty's father, was the fourth of five children. By Martha Eppes, his first wife, he had twins and Martha (Patty). By Mary Cocke, his second wife, he had Elizabeth, Tabitha, and Anne. By Elizabeth Lomax Skelton, his third wife, he had an infant who died. By Betty Hemings, one of his slaves, he had Nance, Critta, Thenia, Peter, and Sally.

Patty had one son, John (Jack) by Bathurst Skelton, her first husband. By Thomas Jefferson, her second husband, she had Martha, Jane, Peter, Mary, and two girls successively named Lucy. Of these children, only Martha (Patsy) and Mary (Polly, Maria) survived childhood.

Patty's half-sister *Elizabeth* (Lisbeth, Betsy) and Francis Eppes had eight children. Her half-sister *Tabitha* (Tibb, Tibby) and Robert Skipwith had one infant. Her half-sister *Anne* (Nancy, Nan) and Henry Skipwith had six children.

The Jefferson Family

Peter Jefferson, Thomas's father, was the third of five children. He and Jane Randolph had nine children: Jane, Mary, Thomas, Elizabeth, Field, Martha, Lucy, Anna Scott, and Randolph.

Mary married John Bolling and they had eight children. *Lucy* and Charles Lewis had six children. *Martha* and Dabney Carr had six children.

Thomas's and Patty's children are listed above. *Martha* (Patsy) and Thomas Mann Randolph had twelve children, Thomas's and Patty's grandchildren. *Polly* and Jack Wayles Eppes (Lisbet and Francis's son) had three children, one of whom (Francis) survived. Polly died from complications after the last childbirth.

Dramatis Personnae

Thomas Jefferson
Peter Jefferson—TJ's father, a surveyor
Jane Randolph Jefferson—TJ's mother
TJ's siblings:
  Jane
  Mary (Polly)
  Elizabeth (Lissa)
  Martha (Patsy)
  Lucy
  Anna Scott (Nancy)
  Randolph (Ran)

Martha Wayles Skelton Jefferson (Patty)—TJ's wife
John Wayles—Patty's father, a lawyer
Martha Eppes Wayles—Patty's mother
Patty's half-sisters:
  Elizabeth (Lisbet, Betsy)
  Tabitha (Tibby, Tibb)
  Anne (Nancy, Nan)

Their Children:
Martha (Patsy, Pats, Bat)
Jane Randolph (Janey)
Peter Field
Mary (Polly, Maria)
Lucy Elizabeth
Lucy Elizabeth (II)

Bathurst Skelton—Patty's first husband
John Wayles Skelton (Jack, Jackie)—their son

Elizabeth (Betty, Bett) Hemings—housekeeper to John Wayles
Her children:
  Mary
  Bob
  Martin, with a Negro father
  Jamey
  Betty Brown, with Matt Brown, blacksmith at The Forest
  Nance
  Critta
  Thenia, with John Wayles

Peter
Sally
John, with John Nielson, Monticello carpenter
Lucy, with a Negro father

Dabney Carr—TJ's best friend and brother-in-law
Robert Skipwith—TJ's brother-in-law
Col. Henry Skipwith—Robert's brother, TJ's brother-in-law
Col. Francis Eppes—Patty's cousin, TJ's brother-in-law
Peyton Randolph—Speaker of the House of Burgesses, TJ's cousin
John Randolph—Attorney General of Virginia, brother of Peyton
Edmund Randolph—son of John
Col. Thomas Randolph of Tuckahoe—TJ's cousin
Anne (Nancy) Cary Randolph—Col. Tom's second wife
William Randolph of Dungeness—Col. Tom's brother
George Carter—suitor of Patty's
Charles Carter of Shirley—George's father, an architect
Anne (Nancy) Carter—his wife
Landon Carter II—suitor of Patty's
Edward Coles of Enniscorthy—TJ's cousin
Elizabeth Coles—his wife
Edward Carter of Blenheim—TJ's cousin
Mary (Molly) Carter—his wife
Robert and Edward Carter of Blenheim—their sons

John Page of Rosewell—TJ's best college friend
Frances (Fanny) Burwell ("Burr'l") Page—his wife
Robert Page—TJ's friend, John's cousin
Mary (Molly) Page—his wife
Rebecca Burwell Ambler—TJ's first love, Fanny Page's cousin
Jacquelin Ambler—TJ's college friend, Rebecca's husband

Lucy Gilliam—Bathurst Skelton's sister
Sally Stewart—Bathurst Skelton's sister
Jenny Taliaferro ("Tolliver")—TJ's sweetheart
Mary (Maria, Polly) Willing Byrd—second wife of William Byrd III
George Wythe—TJ's law teacher
Elizabeth Taliaferro Wythe—his wife
Francis Alberti—TJ and Patty's Italian music teacher
Elizabeth Eppes Randall—Patty's aunt
Rev. James Madison—professor, astronomer, TJ's friend
Eleanor (Nelly) Madison—his wife
Charles Lewis—TJ's cousin and sister Lucy's husband

John (Jack) Walker–burgess, friend of TJ
Elizabeth (Betsey) Moore Walker–his wife
George Gilmer–TJ's friend/physician and cousin of Jack Walker
Lucy Walker Gilmer–his wife
Jack Jouette ("Jewitt")–captain of Albemarle militia
John Marks–painter, captain of Albemarle militia
Hastings Marks–his brother, married to TJ's sister Nancy

Phillip Mazzei–Tuscan vigneron
Mary Martin Mazzei–his wife
Margaret (Peggy) Martin–her daughter
Thomas Adam–surveyor
Elizabeth Adams–his wife
James Madison–TJ's friend, cousin of Rev. James Madison
James Monroe–TJ's protégé
Phillip Ludwell Lee–suitor of Patty's
Richard Henry Lee–burgess, cousin of Phillip
Arthur Lee–burgess, Richard Henry's brother
William Wiley–Richmond neighbor
Sarah Wiley–baker, his wife

Will Reynolds–Monticello carpenter
Elizabeth Reynolds–his wife
Thomas Garth–Monticello overseer
Mary (May) Garth–his wife
Stephen Willis–Monticello brick mason
Nancy Willis–his wife
John Brock–Monticello gameskeeper
Old Jenny–Patty's cook at The Forest
Jupiter–TJ's body servant
Sukey–his wife, Patty's cook at Monticello
Great (King) George–TJ's coachman (emancipated)
Ursula (Queenie)–his wife, Patty's pastry cook (emancipated)

Noted Visitors to Monticello, 1768–1782:

Prisoners of War:
General Baron and Baroness von Reidesel and daughters
Lieutenant Geismar
Lieutenant de Unger
Lieutenant d'Estaing
Captain Jacob Rubsamen
General Sir William Phillips and troops

Diplomats and Military Men:
Chevalier d'Anmours
Colonel Hugh Mercer
Marquis de Lafayette
General Thomas Nelson
Colonel Archibald Cary
Captain George Rogers Clark
Patrick Henry, Esq.
Chief Jean Baptiste du Coine, family, and warriors
Chevalier de Chastellux and entourage

Dear Companion

1

Governor's Lady

Governor's Palace, Williamsburg, September, 1779

Dearest Pattsey: The perceptions of our youth being so greatly different from those of our maturity, I will hazard that when you read this little journal as a young woman, you will not recall the circumstaunces under which it was wrote for you. So I will tell you that, being in indifferent health, and at some constraints to be useful in my enforced inactivity, I took to mind writing up some observations of mine, which may be helpful to you when you are grown.

I never knew my own mother. She died of childbed fever when I was a few weeks old. She was born at Bermuda Hundred, being an Eppes by birth, and I was called Martha after her. It is said that I resemble her, and by the miniature my father owned, it is so. She was small with reddish hair likewise, and musical. The spinet in the parlor at The Forest belonged to her, and she played excellently well, to credit my Aunt Randall, her sister Elizabeth. So I come by my small musical talent from her. Her family came from north of Williamsburg along the Tide water and made their fortune in shipping and receiving goods.

My father, like your Papa, was of Welsh ancestry. He came to Virginia from Lancashire at the age of seventeen years, being the youngest son of Thomas Wayles, of whom there were three. He apprenticed to the law with Mr. William Smythe and so began the practice of that profession. An inheritance enabled him to marry my mother and purchase land which he afterwards called The Forest. He was a man of above middle height, with a round face and broad frame. His hair must have been black in his youth, but I recall him ever as having grey hair, which he wore naturally. His eyes were large and round and kind, and this kindness showed in other parts of his sensibility as well, for he was never known to raise his voice or mistreat an inferior.

Of my childhood, I would say that I had no more anguish than any other child, and rather less, given that my half sisters and I were orphaned at tender ages. When Mother Elizabeth, my father's third wife, died I was not yet of marriageable age, being thirteen, and my sisters accordingly younger down to Anne, who was seven. We were very close, especially Elizabeth and I, being less than three years apart in age, and we spent much time together reading and sewing and practicing French and Latin. My sisters and I were taught to ride, but I was never exceeding fond of it, though of necessity I do to transport from one locale to another. I do not ride for pleasure. This must be viewed as a weakness in our country, where ladies are not unknown to enjoin the Hunt. Howsoever, I must say that I prefer less strenuous Pursuits. . . .

When I was sixteen, I went to Williamsburg for the Assembly with my father and sister Elizabeth and there met a kinsman of mine who had studied philosophy at the College of William and Mary, Mr. Bathurst Skelton, a lawyer. Mr. Skelton was the brother of Mother Elizabeth's first husband—Reuben was his name—and was at that time twenty-one years old. He read law along with several others, including Mr. Jefferson, at the offices of Mr. George Wythe in the town. His practice had begun some half-year before after admission to the bar by writ of Mr. Wythe.

Mr. Skelton was—

A knock sounded on the door opposite, and Patty put down the pen on the lap desk.

"Come," she called out. Nance entered with a tray of dishes and a pot of precious Jamaica coffee. Nance Hemings was one of the house servants she had brought from Monticello when she joined Thomas in Williamsburg two weeks ago.

"Thank you, Nance," she said to the girl as she removed the lap desk and placed the tray in front of Patty on the daybed. "I didn't think it was so late. . ." She pushed aside the curtain and glanced out the window that overlooked the gardens. The day had been warm, but clouds were gathering now, and the sky began to darken.

"It looks as if we might have a thunderstorm this evening," she said to Nance and spread out the cloth before her and the tray of supper.

"Yas'm, Mrs. Jefferson. Martin was saying so too." Martin was the chief servant of the house and Nance's brother, in charge of all the others' duties, excepting Nance and Thomas's own body servant, Jupiter. "He was saying them chickens is acting mighty peculiar, and he can always tell thunderstorms by the chickens."

Patty smiled at the homely story, for the Negroes were often right in such matters, and she lifted the cover of the central dish to find poached fish in milk gravy and her own black bean soup. Thomas liked both, being largely in disfavor of meat, and he usually joined her for these quiet suppers once his duties were over for the day.

She paused suddenly in her musing, holding the fork in midair, the unbidden thought stealing into her mind: *he was usually not so long in coming home. What if he had come to some harm?* Her heart pounded in her chest at the antique fear, and she felt cold in spite of the quilted coverlet surrounding her. Bathurst had been likewise late in homecoming on a September evening, and his advent only momentary before he was torn from her forever. No! She would not think it! Fate could not be so cruel twice. She averted the thought in a voice of hope.

"Is Mr. Jefferson in?" She asked Nance, who was straightening the cover.

"No'm, he's not. They's having some big ruckus at the Assembly today, I heard from Jupiter when he come back for dinner for the governor. He said he expected they all would run long today." Nance poured out a cup of coffee and topped it with cream, then took away the dish cover. "Is that all, ma'am?"

Patty sighed, distracted. "Yes. Go on Nance, I'll manage. If Mr. Jefferson comes in, tell him I'm awake." At least he was well. That was some balm. But Nance might at least have had the goodness to tell her when the message came. Nance was far more close-mouthed than her mother. Betty Hemings was ever nattering on about something, and mostly it was a mild annoyance, but now she longed for such an annoyance. Anything to distract her mind. But Nance went about her business, fluffing the pillows and doing other odd chores in silence. It was too bad Betty had not been able to come with her. Betty would have livened her dull hours while Thomas was away.

She found it hard to conceal her disappointment. Like as not, he would not be back until very late, and the day had been very long already. The only brightness had been the hours when Patsy and little Polly had been brought in to play with her. In her weakness, she had been confined to the rooms within the mansion the last two days, since the journey from Monticello had been so taxing. And she had only three months before fully recovered from Polly's birth.

The girls would be at their supper now. Off in the south end of the house, away from her. Thomas's well-intentioned edict that they should let their Mama rest was a bleak one for Patty. She fared better with folk about than alone. Not that Thomas had declared his will with any ill wish for her. She knew he only wanted her better as soon as may be. She knew her uncertain health was a weight upon his mind. Still, the company of the children would have cheered her, especially in the gloomy weather.

Her children were always a delight.

As she poked at the fish, she thought on the differences apparent already in her two precious-won little girls. Patsy was seven now, and tall, freckled like Thomas and possessing his temperament and iron constitution. Polly, at a year, was more delicate, darker in coloring and sanguine in temperament.

Patty suspected that her younger child could be more easily led than the tempestuous Patsy, and fretted over that. Polly was a clinging child, content to sit in her lap for hours, where Patsy had walked—nay, run—at nine months' age. She did not think the child lacking in wit, for she was animated enough with her or Thomas, or servants like Nance whom she knew well, but if someone unfamiliar came to call, she was often painfully shy, burying her face in Patty's skirts and crying. It troubled her greatly, but Thomas always reminded her, whenever she voiced her concern, that most of his life he had been shy in company.

It was true. Whenever he was called upon to address a large company, whether friends or strangers, or hold forth in any way, he would be nearly unable to speak, and what did emerge was so softly or hoarsely spoken as to call forth complaints from listeners of being unable to make out a word he said, which infuriated him into tears later. The eloquence of his mind and pen was stymied by the presence of potentially fault-finding outsiders. His friend in the Congress, Mr. Adams of Massachusetts, had teasingly once called him as "silent as a tomb stone". But did Mr. Adams, she wondered, discern the reason for his public silence? Likely not, from everything she had heard of him. At any rate, their Polly had nothing of her own vivacity.

Not that she had been particularly vivacious lately. Since coming to Williamsburg, she had attended only private functions as governor's lady, even though public evenings and visits wanted her presence also. She simply was not capable of public life. She poked at the meal with the long double tines of the fork, gazing distractedly out into the lowering twilight. Intermittent invalidism had become a pall, both within herself and with Thomas. With the war coming ever closer into their own sphere and other concerns pressing upon him as governor, they had little time for their old pleasures together. She was bored and he preoccupied, and they both missed their old quiet life at Monticello.

She ate the meal with little enthusiasm and poured herself another cup of the costly coffee, her gloom and anxiety increasing with the failing light. It was almost completely dark now, and the wind had begun to rise in the trees. She watched the mercury in the thermometer at the window fall steadily. It fell ten degrees in twenty minutes, and she saw a flash of lightning across the sky toward Richmond. She counted. One-two-three-four-five-six-seven. Thunder crackled and then crashed, shaking the window glass. It would be at Hampton Roads or Newport News, maybe going inland now. She opened the window to the heavy air and leaned her arm on it, her mind and heart an ache of worry. The spectres of the past had only abated, and not dissolved. They lurked in the corner of her mind, in the falling shadows about the room. *Oh Thomas,* she bade him silently, *where are you, my darling? What business keeps you so long from home?*

There was a discreet knock at the door, and her eyes flew to it.

"Come," she said, but it was only Nance, come to fetch the tray.

"What o'clock is it now, Nance?" She asked, putting her arm in from the window and leaning on the pillows. The girl went over to the Geneve clock on the dresser and peered at it on tiptoe. "Almost nine, ma'am. Do you want me to turn down the bed?"

Patty sighed, pushing away from the pillows with her hands. "You might as well. It looks as if Mr. Jefferson will be very late." She rose slowly from the daybed and replaced the quilted coverlet from whence it had fallen. She sat on the turned bed and pulled a hairbrush through her loose hair, which fell to her lap, letting Nance put her mules away in the wardrobe. It was thus she sat in her loose dressing sacque and rumpled stockings, yet uneasy, when the door opened without warning.

He filled the doorway with his height and the heavy black greatcoat he wore against the rain. Under the bicorne hat, his sandy hair was damp and his face haggard. She threw herself off the high bed, and on silent feet hurried over in relief, her dark auburn hair flowing about her. She launched herself on him, crying, "Thomas, you're home at last!"

His greenish-hazel eyes regarded her with kindly welcome, and he kissed her briefly before putting her away. "I'll get you wet," he smiled wearily. He divested himself of the hat and coat, laying them on a chair. She tossed her head.

"No matter that!" she exclaimed, taking his hands. She looked up at him. "What happened today that you are so late? Nance said Jupiter told her there was trouble. You look so weary! What were they gainsaying now? Come sit and I'll have Nance fetch you a plate." She scurried to the bell pull by the mantel and yanked on it. He looked up at her in amusement from where he had sat on the bed to remove his boots.

"You take good care of me, Patty," he said, putting an arm about her as she sat next to him. He heaved a sigh and put a bony hand to his forehead. "I have just spent the last six hours trying to convince this mulish Assembly to remove the capitol to Richmond. Williamsburg is too close to the coast, and within reach of British warships. I wore them down about it, but they gave me a most wretched headache."

"Oh my dear—" She put her fingers to his temples, wanting to soothe away the creases of pain she saw. Nance knocked upon the door and entered, carrying a tray of cold food for the master. He looked up at it in distaste.

"I'm sorry," he said to Nance. "Please take it away." Nance hesitated, glancing at Patty.

"Now Mr. Jefferson," she murmured, "you must keep up your strength.

Just a little. . . . a glass of canary. 'Twill ease your head. For me, sir." He looked at her askance from under the hand on his brow. "Very well. You may leave it then," he told the girl. "And you may retire if you like. I can attend to your mistress' wants."

Nance bobbed a curtsey. "Yassir." She left on silent feet, closing the door noiselessly behind her. Thomas rose and took the tray over to the bed where Patty still sat, and poured out two small glasses of canary wine from the decanter on the dresser. He gave her one and a wry smile.

"You are insidious, my Patty. You know just how to get your way." He put his hand under her chin and, lifting her face, kissed her again.

"I only want what is best for you. . . ." She took a sip of the wine, her dark eyes luminous, glad of his safe presence once more within her sphere, and put down the glass on the tray. She looked up at him again, considering now. "You should eat something, my darling. It is very late and I know you missed your supper. Would you like me to rub your head?"

He took her reaching hand. "Not if it is a strain on you." His eyes sought hers, a silent message written there, full of nuances. How many times had she heard admonitions from him that she overtaxed herself? They were countless. But now she could belay them earnestly. "Oh no," she said softly. "I am much stronger today. Let me, my dearest."

"As you wish." He finished the half-glass of canary he held.

She reached for her bottle of toilet water and applied it to her hands. Sitting behind him on the bed, she slowly rubbed his head while he ate the meal of cheese and common crackers. His tension melted under her fingers and she felt him relax. She wished he would not take public matters so seriously. Every concern that came under his eye, he took onto himself as a personal responsibility because he was governor, or legislator, or burgess. It was bad for him. He needed to laugh more, to potter about more in the garden, to lose himself in books or some scientific concern. There was little of that in the last three months since his investiture. All his time was taken up with matters of state or requisitions for the army. Dear God, the army! How would they ever feed them all? Even in Virginia, far away from the fighting, the war was making itself felt. A combination of high prices and bad harvests had taken its toll. Fruit was scarce these days and even apples were costly, but they had brought with them some of the produce from Monticello including peaches, which she had put up according to his instructions the summer before.

The matter of the war drawing closer preyed on her mind as she worked, and at length her fingers grew still. What if they were attacked before they could move? What would happen then to her little girls, to her sisters and their families, to Thomas? She did not want to imagine the fate of the governor of a colony in rebellion at the hands of the British. A question grew in her mind, bade to be asked else she burst.

Into the silence she asked finally, "When are we to move to Richmond?" She felt Thomas' shoulders tense, and he opened his eyes.

"Sometime around the New Year," he said, casually enough. "They complain endlessly about costs, but it will cost them more if they are caught here between the army and the navy."

"Is that possible?"

"It might be." He picked up another of their peaches with the long tines of a fork. "It will be good to be closer to home. And safer for you and the children. I have not had a moment's rest about your safety since this campaign began. But I could not bear to be away from you any longer. I'm glad you came."

She smiled at him placatingly and took the plate away, her auburn hair falling across his face. "So am I. Thomas—" She hesitated ever so slightly, for her fear and relief were mingled now, and she wanted his reassurance in a more tangible way that all would be well. "I am really very much better now. I was up the entire day. And I have missed you, my dearest. You were away so long."

He looked up at her, and his eyes were very green. "You know what the doctor said," he murmured, but she could see his heart was not in it, for the speaking glance he gave her that set her heart racing for another reason. She put her hands on either side of his face. "I do. I do." She kissed the aching place across his forehead. "But we needn't. . . It is not time in any case. I'm fine, everything will be fine. Thomas—" She lost herself in the warmth of his skin and the feel of his hands upon her tumbled hair.

He returned her kisses with equal savor. "Are you going to tell me, Mrs. Jefferson, that 'twill ease my headache, like the canary?" His voice was but a throaty murmur in her ear.

"I am not, sir," she returned, pulling apart the ties of the dressing sacque. "I'm going to tell you that 'twill prevent them. . ." He laughed and pulled her down into his lap.

"It's good to have you back, Pattycakes."

Thomas rose per usual at daylight the next morning and conducted his weather measurements and wrote his letters and journal. When Patty arose at half-past six, he was already bent over the middle of his accounts book, entering expenditures from the previous two days. She slipped her arms into the dressing sacque and climbed off the bed. It was still thundery, although the rain had stopped, and the day promised to be warm and humid.

"Another Indian summer," she said, going to open the windows over the daybed. "Good morning, Thomas." She kissed his smooth cheek and peered at the accounts. The last entry was for household expenses and paid to Martin. A reminder of her perennial failure as a housewife. She wrinkled her nose.

"Please God, it will not be an Indian winter in the west," he said, putting down the pen. "The British stir up trouble in the frontier by the day and the Indians—poor beleaguered souls—are played like trump cards in their hands against us. But let's not go into that; the morning is much too fine for politics." He put his arms about her waist, and she bent her head into his sandy hair. "I have written to Henry to send us a parcel of hazelnuts and figs. With any luck, they should arrive before we depart for Richmond!" He looked up at her. "Did you rest well? You look pale. You aren't worse again—"

She smiled, ruffling his hair. "No, sweeting, only tired. As for the pallor, I shall take the girls out into the garden today and sit in the sun, and then I shall be as freckled as you."

"Impossible," he insisted, for her skin, although fair, was free of the freckles he so generously owned. Her complexion was famous among the Randolphs, Eppeses, and Carrs for being the finest in the family.

"I thought it time Patsy embroider a sampler of her own and if it does not rain, the garden seems a pleasant place to learn. Then Polly will have someplace to sit and dig up the flowers again!" She laughed her tinkling laugh, for Polly at ten months had, in one brief hour of play, unearthed what had taken him a day of loving care to plant along the side lawn at Monticello.

He smiled, although it had not been humorous at the time. "And what shall you do with your sunbathe, my Patty?" The morning sun shone on his fair hair, glinting off the copper in it, and she wondered how his enemies found him unhandsome, for his visage was as pleasant and delicate as a cameo. She inclined her head. "Oh," she said airily, "I shall finish that tambour waistcoat I promised you. It only wants the buttons finished to be worn. Then you may wear it to the Assembly, and they will accuse you of purloining funds and aping the Royal Governors for grandness." He bent his head into the damask of her dressing sacque. "You know I treasure any work of your hands. . . Ah, sweet, would that we could be away from this coil, at Elk Hill or Poplar Forest, where no one could reach us but by a day's ride. . . ."

"And you would spend the time with your nose in books or worrying about what goes on in the capitol!" She teased, tweaking his nose.

"I never would," he promised, kissing her in return. "I would spend every day at my fiddle, wooing you with music and wildflowers from the woods."

She sighed. "Oh, Tom. . .that would be—" she flushed prettily. "But how the servants would talk!"

"We'd leave them all at home, and the children," he persuaded, weaving the phantasy. He caressed her dark hair from her face. She laughed and lifted her head. "And live on wild venison and berries! Oh my dear, how impractical you are!" She bent her head again and kissed him forgivingly.

"But I love you for it. Never change, Thomas," she bade him, surveying his countenance with an affection undimmed by ten years' familiarity.

"I will always love you so, you may count on it," he replied, folding her in his embrace and she found solace in the bergamot scent of his toilet water. It spoke to her of sunshine and virgin vistas, of the happy disorder of building materials and crates of books, of all the rare times they spent in utter privacy from the world at their Rowanty.

"I do," she murmured with her cheek against his fair hair, "I do every day." She sniffed with emotion and held herself away enough to see his face. "Now, would you like some coffee, my dearest? I daresay the servants are abroad by now!"

He laughed and let her go over to the bell pull to summon Nance. At Monticello they had their own private ember box for the brewing of coffee and tea, for they were often awake long before and long after the house servants. But it had been left behind, and here they were at the mercy of cock's crow.

She moved to the wardrobe in bare feet and pulled out a gown of Virginia cloth for the day, her dark hair falling over the sleeveless dressing sacque in ripples. It was fuzzy in the humidity, and she did not relish the battle it would be to tame it under a butterfly cap. The little girls could wear theirs flowing, but she had long since given over that privilege.

As she clambered into petticoats and shift while Thomas worked, she pondered what she would draw for Patsy's sampler, thankful for the semblance of normalcy in their lives again. Richmond doubtless would bring changes of its own, but for the nonce she had Williamsburg society, and that of her sisters at a half-day's ride, to amuse her. Now that her illness was again at bay she could attend to being the governor's lady, with all its demands. The management was not unwelcome, and she felt more like her old self than she had in a goodly while. As Nance brought in the coffee and laced her gown, she pondered, too, what to say to Patsy in her journal about Batt Skelton, and about her extraordinary meeting with Thomas.

2

Meeting At Randolph's

Williamsburg, Thursday, 8 June, 1770

She had come to Williamsburg at her father's insistence, ostensibly to play chaperone to her sister Tibb and her fiancé, but John Wayles was not the most subtle of men, and even Patty could see through the ruse. He had noticed her decline in spirits after the gaiety of the Christmas holidays and the christening of her friend Maria Byrd's latest infant at Westover.

"You ought to be dancing, Patt," he offered. "'Tis sovereign for blooming cheeks, and would save us all on carmine." She smiled at the teasing in his twinkling brown eyes as they stood in his office at home.

"Oh Pa," she scoffed. "I'm not that thrifty!"

He made a moue of skepticism, but did not argue the matter, rather saying instead with a shrewd glance, "Besides, what would Phillip Lee say if you did not meet him there?"

Phillip Lee! Among the Virginia beaus, he was known for his temper and his roving eye. It was an unhappy combination, which in truth alarmed her. He had as yet made no positive declarations, but had begun to grumble about other bees in the meadow. *Bother Phillip Lee,* she thought, but to her father only remarked, "He's not put a ring on my finger yet. Let him take his chances with the rest."

Wayles burst out laughing. "The rest? Oh my! What plot have I hatched, sending you as chaperone? Should I send Lisbet along to watch over you?"

So she had come. It was but a short distance from Charles City to the capitol, across their fields and down to the Chickahominy river. In little more than an hour she was in her Aunt Randall's parlor in North Henry Street, amid a flood of visitors, deluged by invitations, her quiet life of the last two years gone in a welter of conviviality. Forgotten were long hours of sewing, late nights of nursing, and the constant daily chore of managing servants, family, and guests. She was borne up in the rush of openhearted hospitality, giddy with the delights of seeing old friends again. No more did she feel the beleaguered widow, but young as she truly was, and a part of joyous life once more.

It was Mr. Skipwith, her sister Tibb's affianced, who suggested they take tickets to a ball at Peyton Randolph's. And though she had been invited to a supper with Phillip Lee, she wrote out a note of apology to him reneging her promise, feeling it not meet to abandon her avowed duty as chaperone. Tibb and Robert would be forced to come home much earlier if she did not go with them, and Tibb was mad for dancing, often lamenting her lack of opportunity to practice.

The dancing had already begun when they arrived. In the red oak-panelled hall was a crush of dancers in the first reel of the night. She paused upstairs in the passageway after changing her shoes and arranging her attire to greet her friend Martha Carr, who was just coming up. The last time she had seen Mrs. Carr she was waiting a child. But that was many months gone, and Patsy was now as slender and lively as ever she was. Her grey eyes were merry as she returned Patty's kiss.

"How are you, my dear?" She laughed. "You look so well! How long have you been in town?"

Patty smiled. "Just three days. My head's in a whirl. I haven't had two minutes to myself since I arrived. If it's not people at my aunt's, it's dinners or parties out. I feel like a new woman!"

Patsy squeezed her hand. "I'm so glad." She impulsively gave her a hug. "It's so good too see you! We must get together! You are staying with your aunt, in Henry Street?"

"Mm hmm." Patty nodded. "Come along to tea tomorrow, if you're not engaged."

"I will. You're an angel. Oh Patty, I will see you again; I want to hear all the news, but right now I have to change. Mr. Carr's down in the library if you want to say how-do to him." She kissed her again. "Bye now, honey."

Patty went downstairs, but Dabney Carr was nowhere to be seen, so she went instead to where her sister and Rob were standing together talking to Mr. Randolph by the entrance to the dining room. Peyton Randolph turned and made her an elegant bow in spite of his bulk, his piggy, narrow brown eyes crinkled further in a smile.

"Mrs. Skelton, my dear lady! Welcome. Our little town is so much the prettier when the flowers are in bloom, especially the biennials. I hope we may be graced with a long blooming?"

She inclined her head. "Aye, sir. I am here this month or so. But as to blooming," she blushed. "I am afraid I may be more inclined to wilt at all the attention."

"Nonsense!" Peyton cried. "Stuff and nonsense! It's good for young people. And you are still but a chit of a girl." She blushed further at that, and cast a furtive glance at Tibb. "Ah, none of that!" Randolph continued. "Pretty as it is. I am not so doddering as not to be able to recall the sway of a certain young lady in former days." He glanced about the room. "I daresay some of your young hotbloods may be susceptible to it yet. Make yourself at home, girl," he directed, "and no more of this retirement. We have seen too little of you."

She accepted these blandishments with some embarrassment, for it was discomfiting to be spoken of so by one who had known one since childhood. But she smiled as she had been trained to do, and thanked him for his hospitality, assuring him that she would avail herself of it.

She danced with George Carter in the next reel, feeling safe enough with him, as it was early and he not yet possessed of the sheen that told of too great an amount of claret taken. He was twenty years old, and a neighbor of hers in Charles City, his father having only recently taken over possession of Shirley once more. George was famous for his wit, his skill at cards, and his inability to hold strong drink. Last Christmas during their open house at The Forest he was sick all over their Turkey carpet, to everyone's mortification, for it was in the middle of a concert. But, being neighbors and moreover friends from childhood, such indiscretions were long since forgiven. She danced with him, and two other men in turn before she came to the third and glanced up as she took his hands.

He was very tall, with naturally curling reddish hair of a medium tone, high color, and laughing brown eyes. She felt a wash of shock as his hands touched hers and so looked up. For one eternal moment the room stood still around him, then whirled again, dizzyingly. She could not hear properly. Her knees went weak beneath her. Her heart stood still, and raced. No heroine out of novels could have been more overcome by a meeting with a lover than she was at that moment. Had it not been for the quick pace of the dance, her stumble would have made obvious to all the riotous state of her emotions. Mercifully, there was not time for her discomposure to be remarked. She watched the laughter fade from the man's face, and he turned pale. *Oh!* she thought in anguish as she moved on to the next partner, *I am leaving you forever!* When she glanced back, sought his form and eyes again, she found him looking too, with a face still pale with shock, his eyes burning, and she could not bear the glance. Quickly she averted her gaze and steeled herself to some calm. But she could not still the wild hammer of her heart and the giddy rush of pulse. Her stays were too tightly laced, and she seriously feared she would faint. Then she would be utterly undone.

She could hardly keep her mind on the partner before her. At every moment it was flying away back to the tall man in the russet coat. She did not dare look at him again—the contact was too disarming—but she was aware of him nonetheless, in the corner of her vision, behind her, every move he made and every glance cast her way. *Oh please, come to me!* she bade him, until she thought he and all the room must hear it in truth. *I would speak with you, dance with you, sit, stand, live, and die with you. Let it not be my own fancy only! Let me truly have seen what I saw in your eyes!*

When the dance was done, she abandoned George with a hasty syllable of regret and flew back to her sister, clutching her mittened hand in dismay.

"Sweet mercy, sister, I am undone!" she cried in low tones. She trembled still. Tibby looked over her blue silk gown in some alarm, plainly thinking a hem was caught up or that she was the victim of George Carter's unease. Finding no such emergency, her blue eyes posed a question.

"No, no, not me, goose!" Patty exclaimed. "There was a gentleman. . ." She looked up at Robert. "I know not who he is, but—"

"I do," Rob said, with an inclining glance. "And I expect you shall shortly also."

She turned quickly at that, to find the young man striding toward her little party, hand in hand with Patsy Carr. And she knew who he was. She had read of the loss of his house by fire some months back in the *Virginia Gazette,* and felt a spasm of pity, for her father had often before and since spoken of the brilliant young lawyer from Albemarle, admitting with delight that he was one of the few new young fellows at the bar who could outwit him. He was Patsy Carr's brother, whose lingering bachelorhood that lady had often lamented. Hero's meeting of Leander at the festival of Aphrodite could not have been more fated. If she could have run from the room, she'd have done it, would her legs have taken her so far; if she could have flung herself into his arms, she'd have done it, did propriety so allow. Thus she stood, speechless and terrified, yet mortifyingly compelled while he made them a bow and engaged in small talk with Rob.

"Skipwith, it's good to see you again. I heard you have embarked upon a study of the law. Not with my esteemed teacher, I hazard," meaning George Wythe.

Now Robert smiled, and looked at his blonde companion. "No, I am reading with Mr. Wayles in Charles City." Rob gave a sly smirk her way and said, "Thomas, I don't think you've met my pretty ladies. I know Miss Patsy has. Miss Tabitha Wayles, Mrs. Martha Skelton, Mr. Thomas Jefferson of Albemarle, one of our new burgesses, and his sister Mrs. Carr. Thomas, this is my affianced Tabitha and her sister."

"Affianced?" Mr. Jefferson glanced at Tibb before him, had her blushing with his warm gaze. "Well, well indeed." He took Tibby's hand. "Much happiness to you, Mistress Wayles. Skipwith is a dear old friend of mine, and so you must believe me that you could find no better man in the whole of Virginia." Tibb blushed again at this praise and smiled happily at Robert.

He turned to her then, and Patty mustered all her composure to remain still when he bowed over her hand. He must surely have felt its chill trembling. She wished fervently not to give away her excitement in such obvious ways. But she saw no mocking in his eyes. They were hazel, she saw now, not brown, flecked with green, and of the clearest amber color she had ever seen. His fingertips under her palm were rough. He played the guitar, or the fiddle. Fiddle. . .there it was! He had played at concerts with Francis Fauquier, the late Lieutenant Governor. His reputation that way was as illustrious as at the Bar. It would be well to hear him play—

"Madame," he murmured smoothly, with no evidence of such discomfit as she felt. "I was most sorry to hear of your bereavement. Mr. Skelton was an old school friend of mine, and his loss is sorely felt."

She felt a wash of delight that he had known Batt, and gratitude for his thoughtfulness, and smiled at him genuinely. "How very kind of you to say so, Mr. Jefferson," she murmured in low tones. He had not yet released her hand, and she realized that it was not only *her* hand that was cold. The knowledge was endearing. She had not been wrong! His discerning glance fell upon her person, and she felt the scrutiny with no little distress. Every little defect of her person was suddenly before his gaze. Was her hair in disorder from the dance? Her tucker come loose? Did he notice the small mole at the join of her neck? She tried to hide that, for there were too many memories of Batt for it to be on public view, subject to remarks, but this was a low-cut gown, and she had not worn neck linen because it was warm. She met his gaze with a burning blush, feeling her thoughts and fancies too obvious, and saw his own high color with relief. It was much to hope for, and yet by his face he felt the same as she. Rob made a small noise, and she became sensible that the silence between them had stretched out inordinately long, so she ventured, rather lamely, "I read of your late loss in the *Virginia Gazette,* and was most distressed. My father has spoken often of you. I hope you have begun to recover your law books and other documents? From a family of lawyers, I realize how much such things mean and how devastating their loss must have been." She looked up into his eyes again, willing that he know her sentiments to be sincere at least, if they were haltingly expressed, and was rewarded with his rare beautiful smile.

"Thank you for your concern, Madame," he said. "I have only this week received a shipment of books from Philadelphia which will rectify matters somewhat." His eyes changed, and with them the subject. He, too, had remembered the company. He dropped her hand and made her a bow.

"If you will permit me, Madame, I would like the favor of this dance. That is," he turned to Patsy, "if I might abandon your society for the duration."

Patsy waved her hand delicately, and teasingly rolled her eyes at him. "I can find my own way back if needs be, brother. It's good to see you, Mrs. Skelton. I hope we'll meet again." Her look was arch, and Patty laughed at the absurdity.

"As do I, Mrs. Carr. Now–" she turned her gaze upward and met Mr.

Jefferson's beautiful eyes. "I do believe I have promised this dance to a certain gentleman," she slid her glance to Robert and back again, "but I daresay he will not grudge it you." She gave him her hand and walked with him to where another reel was forming in the center of the floor.

The giddiness had left her, and she was not dismayed when they came together in the dance and he said, "I had heard Bathurst Skelton married one of John Wayles' daughters and that she was very taking, but I had no idea how great an understatement that was." In this he would find that she could give as good as she got.

"La," she laughed. "And I had heard Mr. Jefferson of Albemarle was charming, but they never said how very so." She released his hands and whirled away with the next partner. When they came together again, he replied, "It's no charm at all when the lady captivates at a glance." They were very close together, and he murmured only for her ears. "I was determined upon an introduction. My only curiosity is how we have not met before this. I could not have forgotten."

Her heart thudded at that. "I have spent the time since my widowhood in the country. This is the first I've come to town for the Assembly," she said rather breathlessly, and from more than the dance.

"And I was riding circuits for my practice. Do you believe in the Fates, Madam?" The words struck her like a dash of cold water. He let go her hands. The next was their last turn before the end of the dance. She struggled for composure against her thudding heart as she danced with her faceless partner. When she came to him again, she replied in her low voice, "Only if they are in my favor, Mr. Jefferson." She looked up at him sidelong, invitingly, that he might know that he, too, found favor with the Fates. Let him not think her yet a grieving widow! But by his lingering glance he did not.

Afterward, he guided her out of the crush of dancers toward the long hunting table where the refreshments were. Receiving a pair of lemon ices, he suggested to her, "Have you seen Mr. Randolph's garden? He has a very lovely arbor of wild grapes."

"No, I have not," she murmured, accepting the dish of ice from him. "I have only been in the house a few times. I should like to see it, though."

So saying, he took her elbow and led her outside through the French doors of the dining room. There were other people in the lantern-hung garden, likewise enjoying the balmy summer air and the lingering twilight.

They were silent together as they strolled. It was a loud silence, nonetheless, much filled with thoughts and hopes and abandoned avenues of conversation. How could she ever speak of that one moment in the dance? Unbidden, her whole mind and spirit had been changed—charged—with a glance. Cupid had struck well, and love was an ache in her bosom. But propriety demanded that a lady never say such things, even if the gentleman spoke them first. Any admission of the more boisterous passions was for the wed or betrothed alone, and then only in the strictest privacy. As she thought this, besought some way to speak her thoughts, she glanced down to find a bush of heliotrope beside her, and could have laughed. Heliotrope was by tradition the flower of eternal love. As it was, she blessed the gods silently and took stock of their offering, leaning close to enjoy the purple bloom and shy sweet fragrance. When she straightened again she found Mr. Jefferson regarding her with abstraction, and smiled in apology. Perhaps he did not know its significance.

"I have a love of flowers," she murmured. "And we do not grow this at The Forest." She ate some of the ice, now slightly melting.

"It is very difficult to grow," he admitted, "from the garden books I have read. And the winters in Albemarle would be too harsh for it. But is it not a lovely fragrance?" By the greening of his eye, she knew he did not mistake her. He bent his face amid the profusion of tiny flowers with an expression of delight.

"It is delightful," she said, and smiled at him. He took her elbow and led her to a bench which was surrounded by a trellis framework, and the air was heavy with the scent of ripening grapes. They hung down in great clusters from the vines, nearly black in color against a background of pale green leaves.

"Here we are."

They sat and ate the ices again in silence, thoughts again loud where words dared not venture. There was danger enough in such proximity and isolation. It was as a constant, high sweet note across fiddle strings, pulsing now and again, but losing none of its intensity to diminution. Strains of the music from within came to them, a gavotte, and it too hung on the air sweetly.

"Do you enjoy music, Mistress Skelton?" he enquired. She smiled and leant back into the shadows. "I do. I am better at chamber music than concerts. . ." she paused. "And better at Haydn than Mozart," she admitted ruefully.

He turned to her excitedly, his face suddenly animated. "Do you play? What do you play?"

"We have a spinet at The Forest, and there were both a harpsichord and a clavichord at Elk Hill when I was there." She smiled up at him from her dark recess. "And there is not a person in the Tidewater who has not heard of Mr. Jefferson's violin concerts with the old governor. Your fame walks before you," she teased.

He colored. "Not at all. Oh, do you like Mozart? I have some of his work with me. A sonata." He gathered his courage and plunged ahead into unknown waters: "Perhaps we might play it in duet some time. It is written for both." He was leaning forward, unaware, eagerly, imposing himself on her mind indelibly. She could not see his face clearly, turned as it was from the light, only the outlines. But his presence was unforgettable. It was not merely that he was larger than she, it was the way his shy, passionate soul reached out to her from unseen eyes in enthusiasm.

From that first moment in the dance when he held her hands and looked down at her, laughing, with those drowsy eyes of his, she knew he was extraordinary, for nothing could compare with the jolt of recognition she had felt. Not even with Batt Skelton had she felt so compelled to be with him again. Could Mr. Jefferson guess that she had hoped and even prayed, nay, willed, that he come to her and make her proper acquaintance? From the look he had given her, shocked, recognizing, she suspected that he might. "I would like that very much," she said, quite seriously, and moved from the shadows.

They were very close, and she could see his face now, all its lines and planes, and its aristocratic delicacy. His coloring was similar to hers, but fairer. He was all awkward grace and shyness, full of revealing words and speaking silences. He shared her loves, and her reticences. Looking at him was looking at a mirror of her own soul and self. Oh, yes indeed, she wanted very much to play with him, to share his passions, and shew her own to him. She wanted to know him and be a part of him. He had but to ask, and she would follow. Later she could say with certainty that he had won his suit at this one moment in the garden, even though it had not properly begun. She was overcome, made giddy by his sudden presence in her life, as though he was someone looked for and at last found. But she had not searched for him, had she? Her mind was in a whirl, and she could not sort out her feelings.

A bell was rung from the house, signalling the supper interval. He moved away from her and stood. "Will you sit with me? I am without a partner tonight." He held out his hands for her to rise. She stared at them a moment, reorienting herself to Peyton Randolph's garden. They were long white hands, faintly freckled from much outdoor life.

"As am I," she managed lightly, shaking herself from her bemusement. "I should be most pleased to accept, Mr. Jefferson." She took his hand and rose with her skirts rustling. They walked from the arbor into the house together, each bearing cheeks flushed with the new passion of friendship.

3

In the Library

Williamsburg

The supper was buffet-fashion, allowing for friends to gather where they would. They had found a seat together in the library, and chatted about sundry things before Mr. Jefferson playfully challenged her initial remarks to him.

"How could you have known, Madame, that I was a lawyer? Do you divine? To my knowledge the notice in the *Gazette* remarked only to my standing as burgess for Albemarle."

She glanced at him sidelong, and chided, "It was no mere courtesy of mine to say my father speaks of you often, sirrah—" she saw his flush at the word, "—and often with admiring deprecation for your talent."

"I know your father, also," he remarked, his color subsiding a little. "I meet him in the courts on occasion. I must say that another more industrious man is not to be found. He outdoes even my old teacher in that regard."

She smiled. "Papa is very busy," she agreed. "I am never quite sure whether this is because his business is good or bad, for he defends the accused and accuser alike. What would you say, sir? Do you have any traffic with the wicked?" It was an impertinence to speak so, but not too great. Many's the time she had played such word games with beaus, to a lesser or greater degree, depending on their wit. She was a-dying to know whether the wit she discerned at first in this man was true, but she did not have to wait long for satisfaction.

He countered in kind, leaning forward in the chair, his eyes frankly engaging. "Only if you assume the general wickedness of mankind. Or, do you not believe that man is essentially an holy creature, destined for better worlds?" He was enjoying this as much as she.

She drank sherry punch. "I believe, sir, that man is as his situation warrants him, and doesn't think much about loftier things until the need arises. Is that not dissenting of me?" She took a broken morsel of buttered bread.

He laughed outright, and the sound echoed in the room. "I would not like to stand before you accused in the courts, Madame, for fear my life would come forfeit. Such mercy as yours would find no patience with pleading false innocence!"

She leant forward over the punch-worked footstool, so that she was hardly a handsbreadth from him: "I am not so harsh a judge as that, sir," she said softly. She saw him catch his breath. "I fear that stood you in my docket, I would be quite moved to mercy, warranted or no." If he had not understood her in the garden, he assuredly did now. His eyes kindled green, and the tension between them, so shortly quelled, was alive again. He met her hazel eyes with his own, and there was a stillness in the room wherein the beating of one's heart could be heard.

"Such a quality of mercy," he murmured in a voice scarce above a whisper, "is likened to the Divine." His hand came up, and his fingers were under her chin. She melted. "As—"

"Jefferson!" John Page burst heartily into the room and stopped at the door, his narrow face reddening when he saw the scene, and made a bow while they composed themselves. "Oh, I beg your pardon, it will hold," he mumbled, about to retire. Mr. Jefferson dropped her hand as if he had been burned and removed the other from her chin, rising quickly. She leaned back in the chair, pulling her feet under her, endeavoring to arrange her face in something like ladylike calm.

Of all people to come in now, John was the last she wanted to see. She and John Page had had their moments of fascination with one another before he settled on Frances Burwell. There was the Christmas party at Colonel Harrison's when she was fifteen, where they had celebrated their success at pantomimes in kisses stolen in the dining room. Before that, there was a barbecue at Shirley, when a hunt on the slopes of the creek for a swamp rose had yielded a not-so-chance encounter. She heard her pulse thudding in her ears. She had not forgotten how close they came to courting, nor her bewilderment at his sudden and unexplained defection. He had caused no little anguish to her afterward in her friendship with Fanny, playing the lover in unguarded moments, and sending her into agonies of love and jealousy. But he was wed these five years gone. Did he yet remember those days?

She took in John's discomfited face, and realized, seeing the two men together, that she had met Mr. Jefferson before. The scene came with a rushing sense of horror. It was John's wedding to Fanny, and Mr. Jefferson had been one of his bridemen. He had not grown into his face then, for all he was twenty-two, and was at that time head-over-ears about Fanny's cousin Becky, and his mind had been plainly elsewhere.

Becky Burwell was now Mrs. Jacqueline Ambler, and smugly secure in a burgeoning pregnancy. She had never liked Becky. She was every thing good and bad that their society could produce in a young lady. Oh, butter wouldn't melt when Becky was surrounded by beaus. She was pretty, blonde, charming, witty; she sang well, danced gracefully, and made up to every man until he thought he was love's messenger incarnate. But to other girls she was mean, slighting, spiteful, and not above starting nasty rumors if one of her favorites appeared to be casting his eye in another direction. Howsoever, she was Fanny's cousin; for the sake of that friendship, it behooved Patty to be nice to her.

She had heard that Mr. Jefferson had once been amongst Becky's swains, and this she heard from Fanny. At the wedding, she had felt sorry for him, that he should have been made the victim of such disdain. But by that time she had taken up with Batt, and her mercy was impersonal.

But John Page! The terrible irony was reeling. Vaguely, vaguely, she recalled Batt's remark about the friendship between Thomas Jefferson, with whom he studied law under Mr. Wythe, and John Page. It was along about the time Mr. Jefferson was admitted to the bar, and Batt had done some writing in a case which was eventually won by his colleague. Briefly, he had waxed nostalgic about college days, and some of the antics Page, Jefferson, Walker, Ambler, Fleming, and others of their group got up to. It made her look at the two men before her anew, with a more discerning eye. Indeed, they were not nearly as proper as they seemed. Or, at least not so in college days.

Mr. Jefferson was hastening John into the room.

"Come in, Page, and stop fussing," he said. He looked down at her. "You intrude upon nothing that may not be shared." Patty cringed inwardly, but the next was worse, "Do you know Mistress Skelton?"

She looked up at him, wondering if he would betray them to his friend, now or later. He had never done so to Fanny, to her knowledge, and she had no reason to think that he would to Mr. Jefferson. But there was always the chance. Her faith in him was justified, however, for there was not so much as a twinkle in his brown eyes to give anything away.

"Aye." He bowed in her direction. "Madame, it is good to have your society again. You have been too long from Williamsburg." He came into the room properly, leaving the door ajar behind him. She moved the plate of food from its place on the arm of the chair and extended her hand.

"How kind of you, Mr. Page. It is well to be remembered when one is long from society." She smiled at him a little, unable to help herself. The past was always between them, and now there was this, too. "How does your wife? I saw her last at the Byrds' christening." Her manner was as smooth and amiable as any could wish.

Mr. Jefferson was staring at them in amazement. Page glanced at him and saw his expression, and his eyes twinkled merrily. *Oh*, Patty thought in a panic, *he'll tell him! I know he'll tell him! I should not have asked about Fanny!* But he only came forward and took her hand, making the proper grace. In that moment, bent near, his eyes promised words to her later.

"She does well, Mrs. Skelton, thank you. I will give her your regards." There was laughter in his tone. She had had a letter from Fanny not a week before. Yet they must continue the ruse.

"She is not attending tonight?" she enquired.

"No, alas," he answered. He was ever still an excellent actor, as in their days of pantomimes. "She is still in the country until next week. Her sister lies in."

"Ah. Well, please do extend to her my invitation when she arrives."

"I will indeed," Page bowed again. "Jefferson, I leave you to your revels with the lady. I am in town this month. . ." He paused, and cast one wicked glance in Patty's direction. "I dareswear I shall not see much more of your company this evening!" With a whirl of his coat skirts, he was away to the door, closing it behind him noiselessly.

Patty looked after him, and in that one departing glance, knew that John had not forgotten their past. It was as alive to him as to her. But here was Mr. Jefferson, regarding her bemusement. She endeavored to put him at his ease, to steer him away from awkward questions, and laughed a little.

"Poor Mr. Page! He looked quite undone. Have we caused the scandal of the age, with the door closed, Mr. Jefferson?"

He sat down beside her again, shaking his head. "He shall hear me long after this for not introducing me to your society ere this. It seems you are known to all Virginia save myself." He gazed at her frankly, with a blush, and her face softened immediately from its merriment. It was plain that her friendship with his sister, and now John, made him feel foolish.

"Nay, sir," she said in earnest. "As I said to Mr. Page, I have been long away from this place in the country, and have not frequented others' houses overmuch since my husband died. Do not be vexed with him. His wife I knew from before my marriage, and not seen but once or twice since. I would not have you wroth with him. Come, Mr. Jefferson, I hear the music starting up again." She rose, holding out her hands, "And I have a notion to dance. You have liberated me, you know. I was quite the wallflower all alone with my sister and Mr. Skipwith." Her expression was entreating, and he gave over his glumness in the face of it. He rose and tucked her hand in his elbow.

"You would never be that, Mrs. Skelton, were you in a room of handpicked virgins," he replied, and looked down at her. Oh no, he missed nothing! He touched the mark on her neck lightly. It was better than all the stolen kisses of maidenhood.

"You flatter me overmuch, sir," she said breathlessly. "But pray, do continue, for I am most taken!"

He laughed and led her from the room into the hall.

They were in time for the Highland reel and hurried in to take their places at the end of the line. As the music began, Patty raised one hand gracefully above her head and picked up her skirts with the other. She wore a cherry-colored petticoat beneath the quiet blue silk of her gown. She saw that he noticed and flashed him a little smile of devilment. Then the dance commenced, weaving and turning, and there was no time for speech or thought.

The set ended and the dancers dispersed, leaving them standing together with Patsy and Dabney Carr. The latter bowed neatly to her. He was a slender man of medium height, with dark hair, worn powdered this night, and dark eyes. Since his marriage to Martha Jefferson he had largely given up rich laces and other finery, for they had an ever-growing family, but tonight he was splendidly turned out.

"Madame," he said, giving her his respects. She made a neat curtsey.

"Mr. Carr. How good to see you again. My father will be sorry to have missed you." Her eyes twinkled merrily.

"I espy a wit," Dabney said. Laughing, he turned to his brother-in-law. "I have but lately met Mr. Wayles in the courts, and my client's cause was roundly trounced by his efforts on the floor. But he consoled me after with Malmsey wine and the hospitality of his house." He turned back to Patty.

"He does not attend tonight?"

"Nay sir, he remains in Charles City. I am here with Mr. Skipwith and my sister," she added, sotto voce, "playing chaperone." Her glance strayed to Mr. Jefferson wryly.

"They are to be married in the spring, I understand," Patsy Carr said, taking her husband's arm. Patty smiled. "Yes, and we are all in a ferment at home. You would not think Papa had married a daughter away before this."

Patsy shook her head, laughing, as though it were understood what helpless domestic creatures men were. She patted her husband's arm.

"Come, Mr. Carr, I see they have set out more refreshment, and I am perished after that reel!" As they bowed politely away, Patsy glanced back. She knew something. She had been speaking alone with Mr. Jefferson in the interval between the dances. A little tea, a little cake, and on the morrow she would know what Patsy knew. She felt Mr. Jefferson looking at her, and raised her eyes.

"I espy a contrivance," she murmured, echoing Carr. He laughed out loud.

"So it would seem! But I confess I am most willing to comply with it." He walked her over to the table where the drinks were and poured out a lemonade for her.

"You are pink," he said. "I would not have you expire by neglect." He touched her hand as he gave her the glass, and her color rose anew. This was aught but neglect, and he knew it as well as she. She wanted that touch again, any little thing: his hand under her elbow, an embrace of fingers in the dance, whatever John Page had been about to interrupt. . . They were staring at one another, and she could hardly hear the music though they were standing in the hall.

"I make an unpardonable chaperone," she admitted. "Mr. Skipwith and my sister can have eloped by this point with no notice from me."

"They are by the wall," he inclined his head in their direction, behind her, by the staircase, "and most decorous of demeanor. Shall we join them?" His eyes did not leave her face.

"It would be seemly," she remarked, with a note of self-deprecating laughter welling up from under the surface, "until the dancing begins anyway!"

It was past midnight before she and Tibb and Rob were in the carriage and on their way home. Even Tibby was yawning, casting her speaking glances from her pillowed corner. For over an hour, she and Rob had endeavored to get her to the door, but for the first time in years Patty was not willing to quit a happy society until torn away. She was tired herself, but at Aunt's house she could sleep past breakfast if she wanted, with none to reproach her seriously. She was tired but would not sleep. How could she ever sleep with the memory of their parting in her eyes and ears?

"I would meet you on the morrow," he said, holding her hand in the relative privacy of the deserted library. She had promised Patsy tea, but she would scorn even Patsy for him.

"When?" she whispered. He smiled a little.

"After breakfast."

"Aye." *Before, if I had my way. We'd never part again if I had my way.* She saw the answering sentiment in his eyes and sighed. Well, she could see him, and then hear from Patsy what her heart already knew.

Tibb was making desperate signals at her from the door.

"Your sister grows anxious," he said. "So this must be farewell."

"Aye."

He touched her lips with a finger, and she went weak in the knees. *Sweet mercy!* she thought fervidly. When she opened her eyes again he was smiling gently. *She could not say good-bye to him, not now, not ever—*

"Until tomorrow," he murmured.

She smiled too, and nodded. "Until tomorrow."

4

Town Ramble

Williamsburg

Patty was in the drawing room of her aunt's house in North Henry street when the housemaid Pippa came in bearing a posy and missive on a tray. She put down her sewing and rose.

"They's a sarvant outside from the gentleman, ma'am," the girl said.

"He's to wait if they's a reply."

She took the slip of paper and the heliotrope from the tray. "Thank you," she murmured distractedly, breaking open the seal on the note, and went to the window. Her hands shook to see his writing on the page. It was small and round and even, with the d's curving back like her own, and his signature a large scrawl.

> "and i will make thee beds of roses,
> and a thousand fragrant posies_"
> Th: Jefferson

She did not miss the reference to Marlowe's passionate shepherd. The very words of the poem and the scent of the blossom brought his face to mind: earnest, aristocratic, delicately featured. She put the flower to her cheek, stood musing in the warm sun. *Yes, Mr. Jefferson,* she thought, *I have not forgotten.* How could she have forgotten? She had not slept until the small hours, and then he filled her dreams; and his name was on her lips in the morning. Since then, she had recalled to mind every instant of their meeting last evening for signs of his interest and intentions. What if it had all been a dream, or his supposed attentions some fancy of her lonely imagination? She could not bear that! And now, oh now, he had made her all the promises she could hope for.

A noise in the room brought her back, and she remembered the servant waiting. Oh dear! She gave a fleeting smile of apology to the waiting Pippa and flew to the table where the writing goods lay for her use. She wrote hastily,

> Α ωελχομεδ ρεχειπτ οφ μεμεντο γρεετ
> ψουρ βλοσσομ οφ τηε μορν.

Σχορν νοτ το μεετ ὠιτη κινδρεδ σῶεετ
ανδ τηου σηαλλ φινδ νο τηορνε.

Martha Skelton

and folded the paper once, knowing it could not be read by either of the servants.

"Here you are," she said to the girl, "for the gentleman's man." Pippa bobbed a curtsey and went out, her cap lappets fluttering. Patty flew to the window and watched Mr. Jefferson's servant until he was out of sight.

It was not to display her learnedness that she wrote her couplet in Greek letters, for she would hardly do that with a beau, but it was a subtle test of a man's mettle and she could hardly wait to see what his reaction would be.

An hour later, she had her response in the person of Mr. Jefferson himself. She was upstairs putting the flower, in a posy bottle, into the neckline of her gown and adjusting her neck handkerchief of Brussels lace around it when her sister Tibb opened the door.

"Oh Patty, he's here–Mr. Jefferson!" When she saw the flower she broke off with a sigh. Tabitha was a girl of great sensibility. "Did he send that?"

"Mm hm," she nodded and took the pin out of her mouth and affixed her outdoor cap with it. "This morning after breakfast." She could not stop the slow creep of color that came into her cheeks. It was exciting to be paid court to in such a fashion again. Others had done so since her coming out of retirement, but none so vigorously as this. Marlowe's shepherd!

"How kind, how thoughtful," Tibb rhapsodized, the blonde curls about her face bobbling as she clasped her hands. "Oh, I hope you shall be married. I hope you shall be as happy as Mr. Skipwith and I—"

Patty laughed. "Tibby, I've just met him! What if he turns up a toad?" But she did not believe that Thomas Jefferson would turn up a toad. She shook out the folds of her striped chintz gown, adjusted her sleeve ruffles minutely with nonchalance. Tabitha's face paled, and she looked shocked.

"Patty, how could you, he's such a nice gentleman!"

She picked up her tan and green sunshade and tweaked one of her sister's curls on the way out the door. "Silly," she murmured, and went downstairs.

From the lower half of the stair she could see him standing before the spinet in the drawing room as she came down. She stood for a moment at the bottom, her stomach all a knot of sudden anxiety. He had not seemed so large last evening. His height was intimidating. She watched him as he read her music notebook, turned as it was to exercises of trills. What if she was wrong? Had her exuberance put her into a difficulty again? Then she saw his hand and fingers move in accord with the music before him, and heard a low singsong "ba da da da da da dum. . ." and her heart melted in relief. She came forward in a rustle of skirts.

"Good morning, sir!"

He straightened suddenly and turned. Clearly, he had not heard her entrance in the hall.

"Ah," he smiled. "Mrs. Skelton." He came forward. "Your note was very amusing. I am grateful to be received without thorns." Her note had run:

> A welcomed receipt of memento greet
> your blossom of the morn.
> Scorn not to meet with kindred sweet
> and thou shall find no thorne.

"As I was to have been promised a bower of posies, Mr. Jefferson." She looked up at him as he stood before her. "Your offering is very welcome. I had begun to think my last evening a dream, and just when I was convinced," she touched the flower lightly, "this came. How did you convince your cousin to part with it?"

He grinned. "I told him it was for a worthy cause." He took her hand and made the proper grace. "The most worthy, I believe." His eyes were gold and green, perceptive, missing nothing of her face or person. A giddiness overcame her, powerful and sweeping, and she dropped the sunshade on the floor with a clatter. Her throat was dry, and she felt like a young girl with her first beau rather than a widowed mother. She could not credit the physical effect this man had on her. All her carefully correct reserve went for nought in his presence. He let go her hand and retrieved the parasol with a glance that made things seem all right again.

She took her sunshade and was able to laugh. "It is said that heliotrope is for clarity of the mind, but I think it is a wives' tale."

"Even Aphrodite needs beauty rest, and I detained you overlong last night," he replied gallantly. His hair shone copper in the sunlight, gleaming like the helm of a prince of ages. But she had recovered herself and was not bemused. "Not overlong," she said provokingly, and gave him a sidelong glance.

"Have you met my aunt?"

He nodded. "Yes, when I arrived. She is a most kind and gracious lady."

"Yes. She has always been a second mother to us, though she is my mother's sister only."

"As she said." He looked toward the window. "Would you care to walk? The day is fine."

The graceful invitation to more private conversation was not missed. If they stayed here or in the garden they would be heard by all the house, but if they walked it would only be by passersby, and he was plainly bursting with things to tell. They would not go far nor be gone long, but her status as a widow meant they could walk unchaperoned, an unbelievable freedom. Even Tibb and Robert had a servant trailing behind on their daily walks after dinner.

"That would be most welcome," she agreed. "It has been too long since I was in town." They moved toward the front door.

"Have you been to the new theater?" He enquired as they went out. The old one had burnt down the year before. The sunlight was brilliant, and she put up the sunshade against it.

"No, I have not." She laughed. "I've been to a party every night since arriving!"

"I hope you would come with me, then?" He opened the gate and let her pass.

"I should enjoy that," she said, and meant it.

She walked with her sunshade poised so against the glare, and Thomas put his right hand behind his back in courtier fashion. They turned from North Henry Street, breathing in the humidity of the morning.

"I see you are a student also of Signore Alberti's," he said. They wandered in the direction of the windmill and the chamomile lawn there.

"Yes. I take instruction from him when I am in town. As you know, he is quite in demand for. Are you his violin pupil?"

"And the cello," his voice was soft and quiet, with a fine timbre, and a melodious drawl. He seemed a man for quiet conversations and not the raucous brawl of taverns. "I tried the flute for a time but wasn't very good at it," he admitted ruefully.

"I have heard," she said, carefully standing aside as a black and white dog passed by, "that those who are robust do well on wind instruments. They seem to have more breath." They walked on again.

"That is logical. . ." he paused and mused. "Perhaps I should entice my cousin Randolph to the flute, then, and complete our musicale!"

She laughed, for Peyton Randolph was of generous girth, and the thought of him piping away at a slender flute, to the company of dancers or before an audience was very funny.

"I seem to find," Mr. Jefferson said, shaking his head, "that we travel in the same circles." He looked down at her briefly," And yet it is only now I come across you. I might have met you once at Maestro's, or any of a dozen places. I feel I have wasted time, if that is not too impertinent, but I must be candid." His hand sought her elbow to cross the road, and she felt herself blushing. She could not bring herself to say that they had met before and not remembered.

"You asked me last evening did I believe in the Fates," she murmured, unable to look at him, for her heart was thudding, and she could not add the intensity of his gaze to her state of excitement without some loss of decorum. "Perhaps they had this time and place forethought. . ."

They walked for a few paces before he said, somewhat hesitantly, "I should like to meet you at Maestro's, now, while you are in town. I am not ever pettifogging, and we might find a piece of music we esteem in common."

She smiled. "Aside from Mozart?" They came to the meadow beyond his cousin Randolph's house. "My lessons are generally before dinner," she paused and gave him a sidelong glance, "if you should happen not to be pettifogging one afternoon." She let her hand slide down into his as she stepped up the raised edge of the field. It was large and warm and soft, but the fingertips were much callused from fiddle strings. It was bold enough of her to do so, though it could not actually be said indiscreet. Her heart was fluttering again. If he knew the riotous state such contact caused—but as she let go his hand she saw by his high coloring that her turmoil was not solitary. "Here we are," she managed pleasantly, as they came to the bench.

All about them along the east boundary road was meadow, filled now with wildflowers, and their summer colors—gaudy pinks and bright yellows, brilliant oranges—stood out pleasingly from the grasses and the woods beyond. The town proper might be in the midst of its busiest season of the year, but here all was whirring locusts and the quiet rustle of grasses like a lady's skirts down a staircase. She was glad he had chosen this walk and not one in the town. The sun beat down upon them languidly. Near the windmill was a seat built several paces from the road, for it was a favorite courting spot. It was discreet enough, for the millhouse keeper could see anyone who sat there, but beyond those and the watchful eyes of God, they were utterly alone. They came to the chamomile lawn, and the odor of it hung apple-scented in the heavy air. Patty lifted her face to it in delight.

"When I was a very small boy at Tuckahoe, Mrs. Randolph kept a chamomile lawn," Mr. Jefferson said, gazing across the meadow at more than twenty years past. "Not as large or as fine as this, but we used to roll in it down the knoll, Thomas and Will Randolph and I. We would come back itching and sneezing, and the dogs would lick us. I hazard they found us very sweet."

He smiled at her. "But I have ever after loved this fragrance. It speaks to me of childhood and those endless summer days that seemed to stretch on for years."

"I envision a wild country there," she admitted, leaning to pluck some of the flowers rippling against their knees. "I have been no farther west than the Point of Fork. I am sensible that it is not all painted Indians and log huts out there, but such romantic notions still intrude now and again, against my better judgement." She began to pick apart the stems and weave a garland of the small, daisy-like blossoms. Thomas stretched out his long legs and leaned his arm on the bench, watching her progress.

"There used to be—Indians, I mean. My father brought back trinkets from them when he was surveying, and I met a great chief one night. His name was Ontasetté, and he was a Cherokee. He was our guest at Shadwell while he and his people were on the way to Williamsburg, and he brought for me a canoe paddle he had made with his own hands, which I still own. He and my father liked each other well. . . . I heard him speak the evening before he went to England to petition the king. It was Mr. Carr's fancy. I have no notion of what he said, but theirs is a most moving and beautiful language. I will not forget that evening, tho' I live a hundred years," He paused, and she saw that his eyes were tear-sparkled. She wanted now to take his hand in earnest. He went on, "They are fascinating peoples, of great dignity and stillness. It was a pity that they needs must have been stirred up against us," he referred to the recent French and Indian War, "for I believe that we could live in harmony together. Oh!" He leaned forward, heedless, in excitement. "There is a view from the back of my hill, where I am planning my house, that I wish you could see! It is more than an hundred miles distant to the farthest mountain of the Blue Ridge, and it rolls like the ocean waves, back and back until there is only sky. It is sublime! In the mornings when the dew has not yet lifted it's as tho' you are alone in the new-created world."

"A pilgrim come to his heaven at last," she murmured, smiling benignly on his enthusiasm.

"Now you are mocking me," he chided, although from his tone she knew he was not wounded.

"I most certainly am not! It is only that too few men have been able to choose out for themselves such a spot as yours. Most are encumbered with the house of their forebears in whatever situation was convenient at that time." Her own father's house was pleasantly situated amid poplar and Virginia pine trees, and she was glad for that, for Elk Hill's main house looked down into the muddy sludge of the Point of Fork in summer and dreary ice floes in winter. It was neither raised nor lowered enough, but at the whim of river navigation for the transport of tobacco down the James.

"Tell me about your house," she asked, beginning again on her garland. She sat and listened for an hour to his talk of the Italian architect, Andrea Palladio, of Doric and Ionic columns, of balanced proportions and fitting a house into a landscape. She asked questions, as any good housewife would do, about practical domestic arrangements, and did not find his ideas wanting in that regard, although she did think that underground kitchens and other outbuildings were rather impractical for hard mountain clay, to say nothing of the likelihood of fire. What could be more horrible than to be trapped in a burning kitchen underground? Any concession to the sublimity of view she would willingly sacrifice to health and safety. But she gave him none of her doubts on the matter, hazarding that he would find out the difficulties himself without her interference.

5

Over Tea

Williamsburg

The morning wore away into afternoon unnoticed while they talked, and she was surprised to hear the bell of Bruton church ring out one o'clock. It seemed they had just sat down. Dinner would be on the table at her aunt's house in one hour, and as in most Virginia households, it was a gathering not to be missed by resident or guest. Thomas walked her back to her lodging and refused her impulsive invitation to dinner by the garden gate. It was as well. She had forgotten about Patsy.

"But it is kindly received," he said, quoting her verse of the morning. He took her hand and kissed it. "Thank you for coming with me today, Mrs. Skelton." He held her hand gently and she did not move it away.

"I was exceedingly pleased to do, Mr. Jefferson. Time wastes too fast, tho," she smiled, seeing his face light up with the snippet from Sterne.

"I will see you on the morrow?" Sunday church was as much a social occasion as a religious duty in the town, just as it was in the country.

"Perhaps we may share a prayer book," he agreed. He let go of her hand and made her a bow. "I count the hours, dear lady, until then."

"Good day, Mr. Jefferson, "she said fondly, wishing that she did not need to say good-bye. His hazel eyes were warm as they regarded her, and she hoped that his was a similar emotion.

"Good day, Mrs. Skelton," he returned. She turned and went up the step and into the house. He watched after her until she closed the door, and as she hurried to the window in the parlor, she saw his jaunty step and heard him whistling merrily as he walked away. *Oh, Mr. Jefferson,* she addressed his retreating figure, *how dear you are to me already! O, let it be as Tibb said, for if you petitioned I would not gainsay you.* All her melancholy and loneliness since Bathurst's death melted away in the recalling of Thomas's lively conversation, his quick mind, his sensibility, and friendliness. In her passionate heart she knew that it would be very easy to fall in love with him, and that there was no bar to it.

She went in to dinner when the bell was rung, and found her aunt, sister, and Mr. Skipwith all assembled. The table was set in huckaback linens, it being a private dinner. When there were guests of any sort, the table was set in damask and crystal. She marvelled at how alert the servants were, for she had not been asked whether her beau would be staying. It was a reminder that there was nothing private in their houses, whether in town or country. Discretion was a prudent watchword. How little of life was one's own! Every movement, every scrap of paper written upon, every urge of the body was, if not espied, then noticed later in its after-effects, by the servants or by family members. Guests were somewhat removed, but only by virtue of the custom of public and private rooms.

The door of the dining hall was opened to the entrance hall breezes, and the ceiling fan swished above their heads, its cord being pulled by a pickaninny who sat in the corner. Patty removed her napkin from the plate and sat, spreading the volume of the rough cloth over her lap. Mrs. Randall passed a pitcher of cider about the table, then enquired pleasantly,

"How was your walk, my dear?"

"Very fine, Aunt, thank you." She told her sister, "We walked out to the windmill and back."

"He is a cordial young man, is your Mr. Jefferson," Elizabeth Randall said. "I spoke with him before Tibb went up to you. A most solicitous and gentle-mannered man." She paused. "His mother is of the Isham Randolphs?"

"Yes, I believe so." She had not enquired all too closely, truth be known. The tally and tangle of who was related to whom was most important to ladies of her aunt's society and age. During her days as a young matron she spent many a house party listening to the litany of families and relationships. There were disagreements about third cousins, and what became of so-and-so, but the memory of those women was remarkable in its detail, particularly given the custom of common family given names which confused matters further. For herself, Patty could cite her own family and those back a generation on either side, but she knew she would never be the chronicler those ladies were. It was fatiguing to contemplate. She drank her cider, and in so doing missed her aunt's shrewd and thoughtful look.

"Are you coming to the races with us on Monday, Patty?" Robert asked. Patty looked up from the dish of greens.

"No, I have a music lesson with Mr.—Signore Alberti that day." Her sister and Robert exchanged glances, and she felt herself blushing. "But I will go on Tuesday if you do."

"Fair enough," Robert agreed. "If I can pry Mistress Tibby from the shops, I mean." His blue eyes were fondly teasing and Tibb took the bait, protesting. "But Robert, I only come to town twice in the year, and we must have wedding clothes!"

"It is well for your father that it's so, else he'd spend all his income at the draper's." There was no malice in his words, for the money was patriotically spent on Virginia cloth and such necessities as needles, pins, and wool for embroidery. Tibb had a fair hand at crewel work, and had already presented Robert with many small items she made and embellished herself, from garters to covered buttons, and he wore them with pride.

Patsy Carr came to tea, bearing a sponge cake and a voracious curiosity. But Patty, far from being offered illumination about Thomas from his sister, found herself induced to telling all about the evening before, and the walk today for Patsy's avid hearing. At the end of it, she sat tired and anxious, for all Patsy's enthusiastic nodding, and clasped her friend's hand, enquiring desperately, "So, tell *me*! What has he said to you? What were the two of you whispering about at Randolph's? How does *he* feel?"

"Oh, my dear!" Patsy exclaimed. Her dark curls bounced in her excitement. Her eyes were shining. She shook her head. "I was never so amazed as when he came away from you in the dance. I thought he'd seen a ghost. I have never seen him so with any girl. I first could scarce believe that he didn't know you, and then—" She shook her head again and glanced toward the hall door, lowering her voice. "My dear, I have seen my brother in love twice in his life—"

Patty broke in. "Oh, who, with who? Tell me!"

"Oh," Patsy shook her hand in a gesture of dismissal, "Jenny Taliaferro, and that awful Becky Burwell." Jenny Taliaferro, Mrs. Wythe's niece, was married now to Col. William Steward, and lived mostly out on their plantation in Henrico. She had been sweet as a girl, a better friend than Becky. They had once sung harpsichord duets together. As with all of Thomas's favorites, she was little and finely made, with a lovely soprano voice, brown hair the color of Mrs. Wythe's, and startlingly blue eyes.

From without this reverie, Patty had her hand taken up again. "But don't you fuss about them. Oh, Jenny's all right, but it was nothing to this, I have never seen him like this! Why, Mr. Carr tells me that he wrote straight—" she paused a moment, and her face changed, like flitting clouds across the sun—"he wrote straight home about it, which he never has done. Oh, Patty, you are so right for each other! I could see it right away; so did Mr. Carr, and he's known Toms longer than most anybody outside the family."

Toms. A baby name. It gave her heart a pang to think of him so. There was so much she did not know, so much she wanted to know. Every little thing he ever did or thought. More than anything, she wanted to be part of that magic circle of his family, who knew his every mood and fancy. If he asked for her tomorrow, she would answer him yea. But none of this was the answer to the one question she wanted most to hear. She asked it at last, taking Patsy's arm as they sat together like schoolgirls on the sofa.

"But Patsy dear, tell me: do you think he loves me?"

Patsy looked at her with a very queer expression. "Why, Patty darling, of course! Haven't I been saying that?"

When she told her aunt about it later, Elizabeth remarked, "Randolphs." And shook her head.

"What d'you mean?"

Elizabeth looked over the top of her spectacles as she sat sewing. "Nothing, dear. Suffice to say they are a breed unto themselves." She was not to learn the meaning of those words for some time.

In the cool of evening, Patty took herself a chair by the open window in the back drawing room, and on a lap desk wrote to her father in Charles City.

> Williamsburg. June 9, 1770
> My Deer Papa,
> We have arrived safe and well at Williamsburg and are installed at Aunt's House. The town is uncommen full this season, tho the Weather be unusually Warm. I cannot tell you how glad I am that you are away with little Jack in the country, my deerest Papa, for I fear the Crush would prove too much for him. I have been able to practise my music all Day if I choose, which is a grate treat, and Tibb and I yesterday went to Prentis's store and relieved you of some of your Bond. Howsoever, I dout not that you will be pleased with the Purchase, for we Procured a gown-length of silvered damask at a very good price, being £4/5/0. Tibb has said she wishes to compleat the Trimmings herself, ribband and Such, from the blue Taffety, so we shall spare you any further expense in that Regard.
> Last even Tibb and Mr. Skipwith and I went to a Dance at the house of Mr. Speaker Randolph, and staid until passed mid-Night, for which I know you will chide us, but not if you knew the Circumstaunce. Oh Papa! My heart overflows, I can scarce put the words to paper. I met there Mr. Thomas Jefferson of Albemarle, who sais he has met with you in the Courts. He is here for the Assembly, being a burgess for his county, and for the General Court assizes also. Public aprobation will say all that needs be said of him in that sphere, but privately he is no less. We walked together to day to the Windmill, you will doutless recall that Place, and it was very pleasant. He is building a House near to Charlotsville on land by his father's House, and has a goodly many unique Ideas concerning Domestick Arrangements, all of which I dare say have not been seen in this country at any Time.
> I inclose a letter under this Cover to my deer little fellow, and bid

you kiss him for me, for I miss him grately. How I shall endure the Month apart from him is to be guessed by Providence alone. Believe me, my beloved Papa, that I am ever

> Yr loving and ob'd'nt Daughter,
> Martha Skelton

She wrote out a little note to Jack, that he could read himself and have read to him, so that he would not miss her so much. She disliked leaving him, even with her father and Mammy Bett, Elizabeth Hemings, both of whom loved him dearly. She had not been apart from him so much as two days together in his whole life, and while she was enjoying herself, she worried that he was miserable in her absence. So she wrote,

> Deerest Son,
> I write you this from Williamsburg to let you know that I am well and that I love you. Aunt Tibb and I will have many lovely Toys for you when we return. I hope you are being a good Boy and are minding Bett and doing well in your Lessons. Say your prayers just as when I am there, and know that I am always
> Your loving Mother,
> Martha Skelton

6

Echoing Holy Songs

Williamsburg

On Sunday she, her sister, Robert, and Aunty Randall set out in the post chaise for Bruton Church. It was largely a matter of formality, as Mrs. Randall was in no way infirm or incapable of walking the quarter mile to church services. The show was necessary for her station, as it was for anyone of consequence who did not live directly adjacent to the church. Mr. Wythe, for instance, whose house bordered the churchyard, was never so ostentatious as to take out his coach for the few paces to the church door. It was unlike him foremostly, and unseemly secondly.

She had dressed carefully in her pale sprigged silk gown and the posy from yesterday, which had not yet faded, in the hopes of seeing Mr. Jefferson, and in this she was not disappointed. As the chaise stopped before the church she spied his tall form among the neighbors gathered in the churchyard for gossip. Although his hair was powdered and his coat white like many, she could not mistake him, for he was taller than any man there save for Richard Henry Lee. But Lee was older and heavier, and was far more volatile in his conversation.

"I see he is waiting," murmured her aunt in a low voice, and Patty flushed scarlet. She laid her hand on Elizabeth's arm.

"Oh, please, Auntie, don't say such things!" she begged. "I would die of embarrassment if anyone guessed how giddy he makes me!"

"Aye," Tibby laughed as Robert helped her down. "She went through four gowns this morning and unpinned her hair twice!"

"So that's why you were late to breakfast," Elizabeth tut-tutted. "And you never are," she squeezed her hand to relieve her of the burden of all their teasing. "Come you, my dear, and we'll not say a word."

They got down and went into the churchyard, where she was immediately set upon by Elizabeth Wythe.

"Mrs. Skelton, my dear, how good to see you!" Mrs. Wythe kissed her cheek, and over the shoulder of the former Miss Taliaferro she saw Mr. Jefferson looking at her. Did he have the same sensations then, as she, whenever they were in proximity? That prickling sensation down the spine that said 'there he is'? She smiled at Mrs. Wythe.

"Thank you, Madame. I hope you and Mr. Wythe are well?"

"Oh, quite, my dear. Quite, thank you. How does your young son? Gracious, he must be all of three years old now." It had been that long, at Jack's christening, since they had seen one another. Elizabeth and her husband doted on children, but they had never been able to have any of their own. They did host several of their nieces and nephews and were favorites with the students of the college.

"Yes, in November. He grows fine, although we have to guard his health carefully. He is nearly ready for the infant school in the spring."

"Really? How delightful! Where are you sending him?"

She looked up as Mr. Jefferson came up behind Mrs. Wythe. She was too conscious of her creeping blush, but was saved from humiliation by Elizabeth, who turned to see who she was staring at.

"Mr. Jefferson!" Mrs. Wythe cried fondly. Thomas took her hand and made her a bow.

"Good morning, ma'am." His smile was sunny, and his ruddy coloring belied the sober tone of the hair powder. "It was my intention to call upon you before this and give you my regards, but other matters detained me."

She was not fooled, and waggled her finger at him. "I can see what other matters, young sir," she replied in mock fierceness. "But you are both welcome for tea if you are free today. Mrs. Skelton has not seen our garden, I believe, have you, my dear?"

"No, ma'am, I have not." She looked up at Thomas for confirmation. "But I should be delighted to do," she said at his nod.

Behind Mrs. Wythe the rector was trying to herd people inside for services. The bell had ceased to ring for some time. His green ribbon vestments fluttered in the brief wind, and he looked anxious. Lateness now would mean polite restlessness later.

"You look fetching this morning," Thomas said to her as they were going in. "It's a fair thing to see the bloom has not withered." He took her elbow proprietarily and led her along to her aunt's pew box. But she knew by the timbre of his voice that he spoke not of the flower alone.

"And never shall under a merciful heaven," she murmured as they came to sit. He was on her left with Tibb beside her and Aunt Randall and Robert on the far ends. They held the hymnal together with their fingers just touching. He smelled of some clean, spicy toilet water. . .bergamot. When they began to sing the opening hymn, his voice was fine, a good rich baritone, not always even, but certainly on key.

Together they sang, she in her lilting soprano and he in his soft baritone, through the entrance hymn and the collect, to the communion. He rose for her aunt to pass, but knelt again after, and did not take communion either. They were alone in the pew while the others were away, softly singing, blending voices in holy praise. His arm and shoulder were pleasantly hard against hers, and she enjoyed this proximity, exulted in the scent of toilet water and hair powder, his husky voice, and the gentle touch of his fingers near hers on the hymn book. It was an innocent pleasure, born of a sensuous nature, but even in this holy place, she was not unaware of a tension underneath his mild demeanor.

They moved apart when the other returned and sat again in their former places, listening to the parish news politely. When finally the last note was sung and the books closed, and they made to depart, she told her aunt that they had been invited for tea at the Wythe's next door.

"Ah." Elizabeth said, as though she had remembered something. She gave Patty an appraising look. "I shall expect the both of you for dinner, however, so be advised." She relented and gave her a kiss on the cheek.

"Good-bye, my dear." She said into her ear, "Be happy." She turned to Mr. Jefferson. "You will take good care of her, I trust?"

"The best," he assured. "Between myself and Mrs. Wythe, we shall see that she is well entertained, and home on time for dinner!" His rare smile was all light in the late morning sun.

"Good-bye, Aunt." She walked toward the gate with Thomas.

They had not come to the corner yet when he said to her in a detached sort of way, "You did not take communion with the others?"

Neither had he, so he could hardly be fault-finding. She paused to consider. "No," she said judiciously at last. "I find my communion elsewhere these days. The song is one place. I find it much more elevating to the realm of saints than a piece of biscuit." She looked down the expanse of the Duke of Gloucester Street, holding her breath inwardly for his response. For her words could be taken by some as sacrilege.

"You do not fear public censure?" Again, his manner was detached, as though her answer one way or another was of the purest disinterest. She felt by his tone that she could be frank without fear of his censure.

"I would not refuse if it were specially requested," she explained earnestly as they rounded the corner. "I would not wittingly give offense, but as it is not actually required that we partake regularly, I do not." She met his gaze candidly. His greenish eyes under their prominent brow were benign as a parson's.

"I enjoy the hymns as well," he admitted. "What does it say about making a joyful noise?"

"I hope one's singing may be referred to other than as noise," she commented drily. He looked at her and laughed aloud. She liked the sound of it, and wanted to provoke more of it. If his attentiveness were any indication, she would have ample opportunity.

They spent the afternoon strolling in the Wythe's garden, looking at flowers and herbs, and in gossiping indoors over "tea", which was in Mrs. Wythe's case, a brew of huckleberry leaves, mixed with sarsaparilla, for actual black China or East India tea was quite forbidden the patriotic since the tax against it had been levied the year before. But the name and custom remained, no matter the beverage served. They were joined afterward by several students, and Thomas and Elizabeth conducted her on a tour of the house. When they came to a small back room overlooking the flower garden, Thomas said, "I could lead her through here blindfolded."

"This is where Mr. Wythe does his tutoring," his wife explained. "When Mr. Jefferson was my husband's student they very nearly lived here."

"But every moment was fondly spent," he assured them, with a wink.

7

First Names

Williamsburg

Elizabeth Wythe had a fine herb garden, and Patty took some cuttings of different varieties she did not have: lemon basil, orange mint, and silverweed. They would keep in wet rags at her aunt's until she was ready to return to Charles City.

On the walk home, Thomas carried these treasures in a willow basket for her and amused her with a tale of some of his planting disasters on his mountain. Her laughter was in complete sympathy, for she had her own failures as well, but these mutual agonies only cemented their friendship further.

They enjoyed a pleasant dinner with her aunt and two guests, Tibb and Robert being away after church also, and afterward sat together in the parlor. He turned the pages while she played the spinet, and thus they idled away several hours together. The other company came and went, but Thomas remained, sitting beside her with eyes full of dreams while she played, and full of unspoken words when she did not. The words lived between them, making playing difficult (for they intruded on her concentration) and intervals worse. She thought of his sister's words, "Why, of course, haven't I been saying it?" and wished he would say something of the thousand things that rent the air. Her limits of self-control, after some five hours, were beginning to be reached. Every glance that he gave her hair, her brow, or the turn of her neck, every brushing touch as he moved to turn a page was an agony. At length she pled with him in living air, *Do something, say something, or I shall run distracted!* It was not his silence that upset her, but everything behind it.

In answer, he turned to her directly, away from the keyboard and the music. Her fingers faltered on the keys and grew still. There was a pregnant silence in the room, now that the echoing of the spinet had ceased. He took her hand, and the world dissolved around them.

"Mrs. Skelton—"

"Patty," she murmured in a voice too low for servants to hear. Her hand trembled in his, and he clasped it. His voice was husky as he continued.

"I would. . ." He met her eyes and faltered with a groan. He closed his mouth again and lifted his left hand, tilted her chin gently, leaned forward, and kissed her mouth.

Patty closed her eyes. She could not still the trembling that came from deep within. The world dissolved and there was nothing else but him. His fingertips under her chin were rough, hardened from countless hours at the fiddle. Her fancy gave way to imaginings of forbidden things. . . She wanted him to go on kissing her, to feel his hands caressing the hair from her face, to— Dear God! Her eyes flew open in alarm and she let out her breath.

"Mr. Jefferson—"

"Thomas," he countered, even as she had done.

"Thomas. . . I—" She looked down at her keyboard, striving to control the tremor in her voice. "I think it very unsafe," and she met his eyes that he might know that she meant herself and not the servants' listening or spying, "to so continue. Not that I think it unseemly, but I cannot answer for myself if we do." He made to speak and she forestalled him. "It was not unwelcome, believe me, but I am a weak creature, so I beg of you—" She sought his hand again, warm and comfortable as it was. "Let us play again, or be at some other sport!"

His fingers caressed her hand, and even that was too much in her agitated state, but she did not remove it for fear that he would take it wrongly.

"I would never wittingly cause you distress, my angel." He smiled, "Sweet Patty, what you perceive as weakness might be called else by another." Thomas took her hands and lifted her to her feet. He was none too steady himself. He smoothed her hot cheek with the back of his hand.

"Indeed," he smiled, "I am gratified to produce such a response." She smiled ruefully. "There, sweetheart. Patty. Patty, I could say your name from now till doomsday and its sweetness would never pall for me. There are other things I wish I could say, but those must wait. For now: will you come to the play with me tomorrow night?" He looked down at her, and she sighed, grateful for the distraction. She would manage her emotions tomorrow when the time came. For now they were safe.

"Aye," she said simply. He touched a tendril of her mahogany hair where it had come loose and curled in the damp. Behind them, the clock on the mantel struck half-past eight.

"Good." He did not kiss her again, but brushed her lips with a finger. "I must go now," he said with regret. "I look forward to the morrow, only for its reunion with you." He kissed her hand, properly. "Good night, sweet Patty."

She nodded, grateful too, for the chance to sort herself out. "Good night, Thomas, thank you for today." He went out then, closing the door noiselessly behind him.

She ran upstairs to fling herself on her bed. That she was now wholly and completely in love was plain to her, for what else could have possessed her to grant him use of her private name on two days' acquaintance? For no other suitors had she, as Tibb said that morning, changed her gown four times before a meeting. For no others had she allowed such a kiss without so much as a by-your-leave. And yet, she had not only allowed it, but encouraged it. It would have been easy enough to refuse.

But how could she refuse? He had but to look at her with his drowsy eyes and she melted inside. She was no tame virgin, unknowing what such looks meant. She did not hazard him a libertine, but he would not wait forever either. This to be no casual courting which could be let off at any moment with no rancor on either side. She had had plenty of those, and they were pleasant enough. This was not pleasant. It was soaring and sweet, anxious and absorbing, and she had thought herself beyond such wrenchings of the heart. Since her widowhood, she had resolutely put away all memory of love's revels, for such memories were invariably painful for their loss. But Thomas had brought them to the fore again in a few short days, and the impact was frightening.

They must go more slowly; they could not be wildly heedless of conventions or they would be undone. It would be so sweet to give over to their desires, but he was plainly not of that sort, and it was as well. He had honor and dignity and a fine sense of decorum. Some had little or none, and she was beginning to think she had little enough. Oh! She didn't intend this when she came here! She put her fist into the pillow and made a place for her head. She was not a wanton, for all her sensuous nature, and the riot of the afternoon was disturbing. It could be many months before he would even ask for her hand, years before they married, and here she was, stirred up in a most provocative way over a little kiss she wouldn't generally trouble over. It would not do at all. She turned on the bed, casting about Aunt's quiet room for some answer, but none came. Slowly, her anguish gave way to exhaustion, and Tibby found her asleep thus when she came up not long after.

8

The Music Lesson

Williamsburg

The next day was her music lesson with Signore Alberti. As she walked down the Duke of Gloucester Street toward his house, she did not seriously anticipate meeting Thomas there, for today was the opening day of the Governor's Council, and it was likely that he would be too busy to engage in a piece of whimsy for sentiment's sake. Thus, she walked along, with her music notebook being carried by Pippa, who walked behind her, smiling to acquaintances and enjoying the unseasonably warm weather.

At the Courthouse there was an overflow of men going in and out and crowds standing near the door to hear the outcome of cases. Felony cases were not tried here, but in the Governor's Council, for they were necessary to be dealt with dispatch, as the accused were held in the gaol until such time. Civil causes went on much longer, as she knew from her father's circuit, and could often drag on for years before being heard. If the agenda of the day did not allow a case to be heard, then client and lawyer had travelled for nought. Yet they must come to assizes in the hope of having their cause heard. This was the reason that she rarely had seen Bathurst during their brief marriage, and was likewise grateful that her father was able to take time to be with Jack while she was away from The Forest.

She came to Signore Alberti's and went inside the open front door. He held his lessons in the parlor, and it was comfortably situated with chairs suitable for musicians. His harpsichord stood in the center of the room, facing away from the door. Presently, he was finishing instruction to a young man from the college on the cello. She sat down in one of the chairs and took her notebook from Pippa. Maestro looked up from his marking time and nodded to her abstractedly.

When the time came for her lesson, Maestro came forward and greeted her warmly, taking her hand, for they had not met since the summer when he came out to her father's house.

"Madame Skelton, it is good, good to see you, buona." He shook her hand with enthusiasm. Francis Alberti was a Florentine who had come to Williamsburg in 1763 as a player and liked it so well that he allowed himself to be induced to stay and teach music. He was now forty-three years old, tall and spindle-shanked. He was swarthy of complexion, with dark eyes and hair, now worn curled and powdered. His manner was always courteous, friendly, and ebullient. It could truly be said that he was fondly regarded by students and neighbors alike, for he had never been known to have a cross word for any person.

"Good afternoon, Maestro," Patty returned in kind. "You will see, I have been practicing every day since we last met, and I believe am improved in dexterity. The partita comes much easier than it did."

"Very good, very good." Maestro said. "Shall we sit then? Come, come" (he waved his hand, leading her to the bench), "and we will see how you have improved." They spent the next hour going over old pieces and discussing new ones. He gave her a new sonata by Domenico Scarlatti and worked with her on it for half an hour. He sat to her left and nodded along with her, his fingers moving in time, his voice a gentle, insistent correction now and again.

"No, Madame, pianissimo, issimo, buona, good, yes. . ."

At length, she worked through the piece while he finished writing out another from Albinoni for her to work on alone later. That was an adagio for organ which he was transposing quickly for her harpsichord, and which she should have no trouble with herself. Just before her two hours were up, she played for him the Bach partita. She was so engrossed in the intricacies of the music that she did not even hear the entrance of his next student.

Patty started to hear the air of a fiddle behind her but did not turn her head from the keyboard. Her heart thudded quickly, and she could but guess whose fiddle it was. He had come after all! She went on with her playing, feeling a different tension in the room. The music built to its conclusion, and her pleasure in the piece was unmatched in soaring delight at the richness the fiddle added. The last notes from the harpsichord came tinkling, and the song from the violin finished the piece in perfect harmony. She took her hands from the keyboard and turned to her companion.

"Good afternoon, Mr. Jefferson," she murmured. "This is quite a surprise."

"For Maestro, too, I see," Thomas said of Signore Alberti who was staring at them in puzzlement. "Good day, Mistress Skelton. Maestro, the lady and I are new friends this season," he explained. "She invited me to join her lesson today, but I was not able to come earlier." He came forward and gave their teacher his hand.

Alberti rose, shaking his head. "When you began to play, I confess, I didn't know what to think. Why didn't you tell me, Madame?"

Patty had risen also from her bench, and the two men looked down at her. "I wasn't sure if he would make it—" At Thomas's raised eyebrow, she continued. "He is, after all, very busy with far more important matters." She smiled. "But I'm glad you did. Maestro, do you have a moment to spare that we might play something else together? Mr. Jefferson has told me he has a piece of Mozart we might enjoy, and I may well never have another chance to catch him at leisure. May we, sir?"

Alberti, still bewildered by the unexpected turn of events, acceded with an uncertain nod. "Of course, of course," and he ushered Patty back to her bench.

"Minx," Thomas whispered in her ear, and took his place beside the stool Maestro had vacated.

When he closed the door behind them, Thomas bent to murmur, "What if I had not carried the Mozart with me today?"

"Just because I am without expectation doesn't mean I am without hope, Mr. Jefferson," Patty said archly over her shoulder as she walked up the street toward the college. "I can say that I hoped you could be there, but didn't demand it of you." She smiled at him devilishly, and he took her arm aside.

"Wait." He dug in his pocket. "I wanted to give you this." He held out his hand to reveal a ribbon knot of turquoise lute string. It was finely embroidered in gaudy colors, in a tiny pattern of rose and trellis. But more than the handsome work, she valued the sentiment behind it.

"Oh, thank you, it's beautiful! Why," her brown and green eyes were mischievous as a recollection came, "I have a pair of garters just this color!"

He was brought up short by her audacity, turning white, then red, and stood speechless for a moment in the path. "Have you," he managed lightly at last, and steered her in the direction of her aunt's. She laughed at his discomfiture. Conscious of the servant walking behind them, he added, "What a charming coincidence." He was answered by the revelation of a dimple.

"Perhaps you would like to win one?" She offered of the garters. But this did not perturb him. He was not so very innocent after all! This was a game he had played before with others. They crossed the street at Market Square and went up Palace Green.

"Perhaps," he pretended unconcern. "What would be the price?"

She considered. "A piece of poesy—" he raised an eyebrow, as if to say 'is that all?' "—from my favorite author."

"Ah," he frowned, and then sighed. "I shall do my best."

"It's easily done," she said, and laughed.

The play presented that evening was Middleton's *A Chaste Maid in Cheapside*, which was listed as "a pleasant conceited comedy." Once they were settled in their seats and the play had begun, however, Thomas covered his face with his hand and shook his head, glancing at her from under his hand in watchful embarrassment. She laughed at this and settled down to watch the play. It was a delight, though quite bawdy from start to finish. Maudline inquired of her daughter, Moll:

> "Have you play'd over all your old lessons o' the virginals?"
> "Yes," came Moll's reply.
> "Yes?" gasped her mother. "You are a dull maid o' late, methinks; you had need have something to quicken your green sickness–do you weep?–a husband! Had not such a piece of flesh been ordained, what had us wives been good for?–to make salads, or else to cry up and down for samphire. . . ."

"It was a goodly play," Patty said as they were seated in their quiet booth at the Mrs. Campbell's tavern. He raised an eyebrow sardonically. "You didn't find it bawdy?" He stared at her intently, visibly noting how her hair blended into the dark of the wood behind her and the way she had it dressed, in loops and curls.

She affected not to notice his staring and shrugged a little.

"'Tis no worse than Mr. Yorrick in the tavern," she said, making reference to Sterne, "and besides, I had read it before."

He leaned forward with his elbow on the table. "I thought I detected a fancy for Sterne the other day. I knew it could not be happenstance."

"I used to read when Mr. Skelton was away from home," she confessed, toying with the ribbon knot on her bodice. "Mostly novels, to my discredit. I had better spent the time improving my circumstance than idling away with Smollet or Fielding, but alas!"

"I wouldn't call the like of that idling." His gaze flickered over the picture she made. "There's much instructive to be gained from novels. Tho' how it is taken is entirely up to the individual." This banter was interrupted by the waiter bringing their tray.

Over the oysters and Rhenish they discussed their favorite novelists. She preferred the sentimental and moral: Swift, Defoe, Fielding, Marlowe, Smollet, Richardson; but she had also read Dante in both Italian and French and was as well versed in Chaucer as he.

"How did you come by such a breadth of reading?"

She picked up a common cracker and adorned it with a piece of strong green cheese. "My father has an extensive pocketbook," she smiled. "I order what I like, and am indulged. . . ." and was delighted at his good humor at her foxing. "Quite truthfully," she went on, "I read from an early age, and he thought it important, as he had no sons, to train his daughters as he would have an heir. Unfortunately, we all are as enamored of romances as French or Latin sermons." She nibbled daintily at the cracker and crumbly cheese. "So you see what I mean by wasting my intellect. Papa taught us Latin and Greek as ciphers, and now I bog down in *Pamela*."

He leaned back in the seat. "So that's where you got the impetus for the note you sent!" He laughed. "It was very clever. I enjoy ciphers myself. Between us, I think Page and I have dreamt up half a dozen or so, but none of them ever live very long. One of us loses the key, or interest, or both."

"Well," she intoned, drinking of the Rhenish. "I shall have to continue my notes then, shan't I? It's a pretty amusement."

"Aye," he agreed softly, coming forward again. "I believe I would have more tenacity than with Page."

Her eyes sparkled. "I would so hope, Mr. Jefferson."

When they parted that night, it was in the quietude of the entrance hall of her aunt's house. It was but ten o'clock, and Rob and Tibby were out also, leaving only the hall boy in lonely vigil. The child had the good sense to make himself scarce, and Thomas answered her expectant gaze with a very chaste kiss. Her aunt could not have complained of it.

"Ah," she murmured in protest, taking his hand. He sighed helplessly. "Patty, I—" he began. She kissed his hand and laid it against her face, reveling in the warmth he radiated. One might call her under the influence of too much wine and oysters, too long a celibacy, or a sharp infatuation, but she couldn't have cared. For this one moment, she was in a welter of longing. There was no one about, no one expected, and it was not too much to ask that he give her a proper kiss. It was not so great an indulgence. She looked up at him again, from under her lashes, and in response he gave her the embrace she sought. She learned then how very great was his own desire, and how marked his self-control. They dithered between the two for some time before propriety won out, and he stepped away. When he did, she was trembling from head to foot, as shaken as he by what they had uncovered.

"Well," his voice was husky, and his eyes very green. "This won't be easy," he told her ruefully.

She raised an eyebrow, mimicking his expression. "At least, you are not alone in that. That should give some small comfort. . ." All the emptiness of the last years and the promise of those to come filled her mind and heart, and she could not bear to let him go. "Oh, Thomas," she burst out at last, "I don't want to say good night!"

For a time she was embraced again, rocked in his arms fiercely, his hands tumbling her hair while she listened to the racing of his heart. She could feel the struggle in him, and she needed no one's reassurance that he loved her. At length, he moved enough from her to see her face. Swallowing, he traced her temple and cheek with a finger.

"I would fain say good morrow, too, sweet," he murmured hoarsely. "But all that's away yet, and the hour grows late. I pray it's enough to know that tho' we part, I am never absent from you in thought, for I love thee, Patty."

Overwrought as she was, the words were too much. She burst into tears.

"Oh!" she cried, burying her face in her hand.

"Here," he said, lifting her chin. "What's this?" He took in her pale face with its wet eyes and spiky lashes. "Is it so unwelcome?"

She tittered then, not on an even keel, wiped her eyes, and shook her head. "No, no. I'm sorry. It is most welcome, Thomas." Her eyes searched his face with tenderness. "I am simply overcome. It was almost too much to hope to hear after. . .after Batt's death and such awful melancholy. I thought I could never love again." She did not continue that vein, but hastily took up another. "I hoped, for I have been the same since Randolph's ball, and was mortified that it mightn't be requited. I do love you, Thomas, though it's bold of me to say."

"The truth is always best boldly spoken," he said. "And sweetly when they are such words as those." He kissed her lightly." But I have kept you from your rest, and would not wish my blossom to fade on my part."

"I am not so frail as that," she murmured.

"Howsoever, I would not wish to tire you." He kissed her forehead. "Adieu, sweet, dearest Patty. I do not live until I see love's sweet face again. Good night!"

She nodded and held his hand until he moved too far away, letting her fingertips touch his in one final caress.

9

The Winning of Garters

Williamsburg

The weather turned cooler in the next week, to the relief of everybody. She spent the time playing the spinet and receiving callers, some of the gentlemen of whom were rather put out at her defection. Landon Carter, when she came downstairs, charged across the hall at her, took her by the arms and declared, "Miss Patty, since you have forsaken me, I have no course but to order my pistols and shoot myself." But he was only nineteen years old, and she did not take his perturbation seriously.

"Now Mr. Carter," she said mildly, disengaging herself. "Where would all your lady friends be if you took such an action? I daresay we should all go into mourning. Now come, sir, and sit with me. I'll hear no more of such talk from you. Fancy you should think I'd give up a fine friend like yourself!"

But he was not a serious suitor, as some others, whose offended vanity she was put at constraints to soothe, while at the same time not playing false Thomas's and her own feelings. At one dance, Phillip Lee stole her away for an hour, begging, cajoling, and threatening her not to continue her cruel torment of him, only desisting when she burst into genuine tears at the distress of being thought cruel or selfish, as he had called her. She wrote to her sister Elizabeth Eppes at Eppington.

> "... so you see, Lisbet, to what a pass I am come, at the one hand quite happy in my friendship with Mr. J_n, and at the other plagued on every side with being labelled pert by those whose esteem I value. Yet none have been in such earnest as the one. Je suis melancholique tout á fait. ..."

Yet she was not entirely unhappy. The Phillip Lees and Landon Carters could not damp her forever. During the long carefree days, she was pleased to sit and embroider or read, or stroll in the town with her sister, enjoying the balmy air and summer color of the trees. In the evening she went to dances, suppers, musicales, or theater with Thomas. Life was pleasant away from her ordinary cares of household management, as she had no duties at her aunt's besides occasional chaperonage and receiving company, and those were no hardship.

She realized over and over again how much she had confined herself in the past two years. It was against her nature to be so cloistered, for she was at heart a sociable creature, and too much time alone made her morbid. Here she truly bloomed in the convivial atmosphere. It was made all the better by sharing in Thomas's old friendships, and becoming part of his circle. She was embraced by all his friends, received in such openhearted hospitality and genuine warmth that she lamented having been so inward. How much of life had she missed!

Of all his friends, they spent the most time with the Pages and the Wythes. In that first season in Williamsburg, the latter were preferred for the simple reason of her discomfort with the proximity of John Page.

He had done nothing to ease her circumstance in the last fortnight. In the midst of her turmoil over Thomas, he remarked to her one night in a minuet at the Palace, "You look very pretty tonight, very happy."

She looked up at him quickly, cautiously. "I am." They moved apart and came together again. John's gaze wandered across the room. "My friend is in agonies over you." His brown eyes were sharp, and he left her no doubt as to his meaning. "Would that it were I who had inspired such passion, for I can see the answer in your eyes."

He had not forgotten. He would not let her forget. It brought her a shudder of dread. It was he, after all, who had not pursued that course! And how dare he come now, when she was so happy with his friend, and make such remarks? She could not complain to Fanny, nor Thomas neither. Even a letter to Lisbet could not be trusted. There was no one to whom she could unburthen herself.

She knew by instinct that if Thomas ever found out, he would be devastated. John was his best friend next to Dabney Carr. He had already been thrown over by one friend. She doubted he would tolerate even the hint of another such betrayal.

The matter preyed on her mind for days, and she thought too of Bathurst. She would not deny, even to Thomas, how she had loved Batt. It was quieter than the love she had for Thomas, but no less real and warm for all that. Finally, on the day they were due at the Wythes' for a musicale, she prevailed upon her aunt for advice.

She had spent the day drawing in the back parlor, listening to the low song of the laundress as she boiled linens in a large cauldron in the yard. The smell of soap permeated even here, although the window was open only a crack. Mrs. Randall sat hooking net for a canopy for her niece's bride chest while Patty sketched her in charcoal and watercolor. The clock in the hall chimed at intervals, but for that there was nothing to mark the passing of time. Tibb had gone visiting, and Rob was away at the chancery office, so the two women were alone.

Neither had spoken in some time. Finally, Patty broke the silence, venturing, "Aunt. . ."

"Yes, dear?" Elizabeth looked up over the tops of her spectacles, never missing a stitch in the net.

"Tell me again of my mother and father, and why she married Papa, and how he was with her over Mr. Eppes."

Mrs. Randall looked at her with affection. "Are you worried, Patty? You needn't be." At Patty's pleading look, she gave over and sighed.

"Very well: it was in 1744 that my sister Patsy came home to Bermuda Hundred from Eppington. Llywellyn had died of the smallpox, and Patsy herself had been very ill of it. But we brought her home and nursed her better. It was not until she was so that we told her Mr. Eppes had died, for we feared the shock would send her off again. She was very low for a goodly while. But in the spring, your grandfather Eppes had a visit from a young man from up the country, who had just become the agent of Lidderdale and company of Bristol, through whom Papa sold his crop, and his name was John Wayles. He was not thirty and had recently come back from England where his father had died.

"Howsoever he was Papa's guest. Patsy and I did our best to make him comfortable, for he stayed with us several days. He saw our pretty Patsy, and how low she was, and enquired of me privately the reason that such an handsome young woman should be so dispirited, and I gave him the reason. My dear, don't you know that he pressed my hand and said to me with sorrow in his eyes, 'Mistress Eppes, I am beholden to you for saying it to me, for I esteem Madame Eppes greatly, and it pains me to see her so.' Dear man! He spent the next six months drawing her out. He called very often, though his business took him far afield here, until in the autumn my sister confessed to Lucy and me that he had asked for her hand.

"They had to wait until her mourning was over properly, and by that time he had purchased several parcels of land, and he gave her the choice of where to build her house. She chose The Forest, and so he built there. He loved her greatly and made her happy every day, never shrinking from a passing mention of Mr. Eppes' name, for he was not jealous. She said to me, when she knew she was sick enough to die, that she had never had a better friend in all the world than he—" She sniffed, and continued her netting, and Patty wiped her own eyes with the back of her hand before any tears spoiled her work.

"Thank you, Auntie," she murmured in a choked voice. She had heard this story, or versions of it, from divers relatives through the years, and it never failed to evoke compassionate tears. Her own father spoke of her mother to her privately, always saying, with a hand to smooth her hair, how much she took after her. He was modest enough to omit his own hand in her mother's transformation, and she had only heard this from others.

She loved this story, for Martha Wayles had died when Patty was only three weeks old, and her memories of mothers ran to harried, busy stepmothers, indulgent black mammies, and this one aunt who, being herself childless, was always welcoming to her nieces and nephews. There was a sense of rootlessness in her that was borne of never really ever having had her own mother, for, loving as her father was, he could not be there always as a child needed. It was only when Jack was born that she had felt a true connection to her mother, in the endless chain, back and back through dim time as a daughter became a mother herself.

But now she had wanted the story for a different reason, which her aunt had so deftly surmised. For her mother, too, had been a sudden widow at a young age and had lived to love and marry for love. She had not forgotten Mr. Eppes in her happiness with John Wayles, but continued to think and remark on him now and again, at the indulgent understanding of her beloved.

"Auntie," she began. "Do you think. . ." She paused to shade her piece further. "Do you think Mr. Jefferson such a man as Papa? Do you think he could bear with me and Jack? I should hate to think that it would cause him a private misery that there had been someone before."

Elizabeth regarded her from across the room, and her mouth softened. "I am not the best to ask of him. I would expect you'd find Mrs. Wythe or young Mrs. Page more knowledgeable."

The thought of asking either of those ladies such a question mortified her, and she colored up. "Oh, Aunt, I couldn't ask *them*!" she exclaimed.

Elizabeth smiled. "Well, I wouldn't discomfit you." She shook her head. "From what I have seen—" she paused here delicately, "Bathurst and young Jack are no bar to him. It appears he would have you if you were wed half a dozen times and as many children from each!" They laughed, and Patty blushed, her curls falling over her shoulders. So the ardor hadn't gone unnoticed. Well, folk did like to talk. She tossed her hair out of the way and held up the sketch.

"What d'you think?" she asked. She presented the picture of a slender, brown-haired woman back-lit by the window, her hands daintily upon her work, her face a study in tranquil absorption. Elizabeth raised her head and looked down her nose through her spectacles. "Much too flattering!" she declared, pleased. She waved her hand. "Come here, my dear, and let me give you a kiss."

Patty put down the sketchbook and came, kneeling before her aunt. Elizabeth kissed her forehead and she laid her head in the taffeta lap.

"You are deserving of happiness, my dear girl," her aunt said, touching the lace of Patty's cap, "and if I were a wagering woman, I'd wager you'll find it with your young man, even as your mother and father did."

The words brought stinging tears, and she squeezed her eyes against them. That it should be so was her fervent prayer in the night beside Tibb, when she lay awake unable to sleep for thinking of him. She clasped the hand in hers and raised her head.

"Thank you, Aunt," she whispered.

Thomas came to call on her promptly, as he always did, that evening. When she came dancing down the stairs she saw him waiting at the bottom, an animation to his manner beyond the ordinary. He was positively quivering with excitement over something.

He kissed her hand and then said, as though he could contain himself no more, "I found it! I found your poet! This afternoon, it came to me like a thunderclap when I was sitting in the house. I had to beg a volume of Mrs. Wythe, but I found it!" He dug in his pocket and produced a folded sheet, sealed in wax and bound up in blue ribbon. "Here it is, here it is," he caught himself and glanced about. Seeing no one, he rocked up on his toes once, pressed her hand in enthusiasm and gave her the note. "Here it is," he said sotto voce, like Jack when presenting her with flowers or worms, or the squashed remains of his breakfast. She giggled at his infectious spirit and untied the ribbon deftly.

When the seal was broke, she unfolded the piece to find Donne in his small, neat hand and caught her breath.

> *Deare love, for nothing lesse then thee*
> *Would I have broke this happy dreame;*
> *It was a theame*
> *For reason, much too strong for phantasie,*
> *Therefore thou wak'st me wisely; yet*
> *My dreame thou brok'st not, but continued'st it,*
> *Thou art so truth, that thoughts of thee suffice*
> *To make dreames truths; and fables histories;*
> *Enter these armes, for since thou thoughtest it best,*
> *Not to dreame all my dreame, let's act the rest.*

"Oh," she cried, "Oh, Thomas!" This last came in a low voice. "Oh, my very favorite poem; oh, how did you guess? Oh!" Heedlessly, she flung her arms around him, kissed his cheek. "You guessed it, and no one ever has before."

He smiled benignly on her delight. "I only followed my heart as to the poem. There's nothing said but 'tis an echo of my own feeling." Her aunt had been right about him this afternoon. How could she have worried?

"Oh, my dear," she murmured. "I'm so glad you found it."

"Well, I did have some help." He raised her chin and his eyes were fondly chiding.

"But it was oblique enough," she defended. "Only one with a sharp memory could have recalled such a remark."

"I savor every concourse we have," he said, "and everything by you spoke." He caressed her hand. "Your words are my dreams, and your image my star. How could I disremember?"

Thomas had recently been made by Governor Botetourt the Lieutenant of Albemarle County, and Commander of all His Majesty's Militia, both Horse and Foot, of that county, so the evening at the Wythes' was celebratory, as George had been one of the witnesses. Thomas's father Peter had held the post from the age of forty-two, and while it was largely ceremonial in peace time, it was nonetheless an honor and a mark of his esteem in the colony. His health was drunk in a new pipe of Madeira and he was wished, in great jocularity, all success upon the field of battle. Thomas had affected not to mind the teasing.

The evening's entertainment was a musicale, in which they were joined by that man of the hour, Mr. Patrick Henry, on his fiddle. Patty had never met him before and found him a boor. He seemed as like to wipe his nose on the tablecloth as make a lady a proper address. He was loud and histrionic, much given to interrupting other people, and played the fiddle with vigor and not much delicacy. He was reputed to be quite a fellow at house parties, but she couldn't see it. She strove to ignore him as far as was polite.

Later, as they were returning in the Wythes' coach, she mused on Thomas's duet of Pachelbel with Henry. With the first strains she had been struck by a welling joy, soaring and unique, and the most indelicate sense of knowing as she watched him play. She looked down to where his hand rested innocently on her knee, not far from the promised garter. He had fine hands, and their delicacy never failed to move her anew. She recalled to mind their sensitivity at the fiddle that evening, how deft they were and gentle. There was promise there. . . . She shook herself from such thoughts— they would only torment her—and spoke instead of the prize, "I'm sorry I cannot give it you now, but I fear it's still serving its natural use—" Thomas raised an eyebrow at her, and she hastened on, "—but I can deliver it on the morrow."

"I call that soon enough," he answered. He glanced out the window, then turned and kissed her. "You know, my dear," he murmured into her hair, "I find it hard when you do deliberately provoke me." He moved away and searched her face seriously.

"That time it was not deliberate, I swear to you," she said feelingly. "I would not torment you and myself in that way."

"But you do. Every day, with every sidelong glance I am tormented that I may not own that which I love—" his voice caught huskily, "—and desire." His sharp eyes roved over her face and shoulders, their hazel turned dark and dappled green.

"Thomas," she protested. He put a finger to her lips. "Think you that I did not hear your thoughts tonight? The very air crackled with them. I heard because we are attuned together. Why do you think it was so easy to play at Signore Alberti's? Only two such as we are could achieve such harmony at first course. I promise you, my sweet" (his lips brushed her temple, fervent, burning, and she closed her eyes against the warming thread of fire it kindled), "that when our course does run to its fitting end, we shall neither of us come away disappointed. I know that as I breathe. But not yet. It cannot be yet." He held her closely against him and she felt the telling trembling of his arms. She buried her face in his neck cloth, the measure of his pulse keeping time with her own. They spent the rest of the short journey home thus in silence.

10

Homecoming

The Forest

A week later her father came to town on legal business and to affix his signature to the amendation of the previous year's nonimportation agreement.

John Wayles was fifty-five and was variously a planter, lawyer, merchant's agent, and miller. He was well loved by his neighbors and accepted by them since his arrival in the county in 1744 from Goochland. He had buried three wives, two sons, and a daughter, so his four daughters remaining were especially dear. He was not without contact with his brothers and sister in Lancashire, but mail travelled slowly from the interior, and often six months went by without a word from the home county. He had grown stoutish in the last few years, not unduly so, but befitting his status, and his embrace was warm and comfortable.

Now, their father held out his hands to them in welcome. "My dear girls, how pretty you look. All the dancing I expect." His eyes twinkled at them.

"Oh, Pa, we didn't spend all our time at parties!" Tibby cried.

He inclined his head. "That is not what I hear from Aunt Randall and others," he paused, "but no, I suppose you strolled about the town and used up my next tobacco crop at Prentis's and other shops. The important thing is that you've had a good time. You did, I trust?"

"Oh yes," they said in unison.

They were home before dinner. Jack came running out to meet them, the skirt of his white frock flying. She had not mustered the courage yet to cut his curls, and they sprang from his head, bouncing as he ran.

"Mama!" He bounded into her arms, knocking back her calash hood, and nearly toppling them both. She hugged him tightly as he wet her face with kisses.

"Oh, Jackie, it's so good to see you," she cried. "Mama missed you every day, and worried over you. But you're fine." She smoothed back his blond hair from his face, looking into his green eyes, assuring herself by his pink cheeks that he was indeed fine.

"Did you bring me toys, Mama?" He was bouncing up and down. "Grandpapa read me your letter and said you was to bring me toys."

Patty laughed and took his hand, rising from the dusty ground. "Yes, sweeting, Auntie and I brought you many toys, and I have one for you now. Why don't you run and tell John that it's in the brown trunk for you? Mama and Auntie Tibb will be along in a moment."

"Oh huzzah!" Jack cried, and dashed up the steps into the house behind the house servants who were carrying in their trunks. Tibb shook her head.

"He'll have them all out in a trice," she said.

"I know," Patty laughed. "But Pa's probably been filling his head with wonders this month gone!"

"I protest!" their father said, not very effectively. He was as indulgent as they. Patty put her arm about Tibb's waist. "Come along," she said with a backward glance at Wayles, "and let's see what mischief they've made together."

They went into the house and down the hallway to the office, for letters that awaited them. As they unburdened themselves of tales of their month's holiday, Wayles remarked, "So my young ladies are glad to have taken my advice for the visit?"

Patty kissed his cheek. "You know we are, Pa. Thank you."

"Good," he replied gravely, "because things have been in an awful coil without you all to smooth things over. The food," he made a face, "was terrible. I didn't realize how you worked over Jenny to put a decent meal on the table. I even begged Betsy to send us one of her cooks, but no avail. Oh, and Patty, I'm to tell you Leah's Mary had her baby the other day, a boy. She wants you to go down and see them."

It was back to work already. Patty nodded a bit glumly, for she had hoped to spend some time alone with Jack. "I will. Just as soon as I can change my gown."

"Wait," Wayles dug in his waistcoat pocket, "I have your keys." He went to a casket that stood on his desk and unlocked it, producing for her a large ring of many keys. There were keys to every conceivable door, drawer, chest, and box on the plantation, and this ring of keys, symbol of her office as mistress, had passed through the hands of her mother and stepmothers before being turned over to her at the age of fifteen. There was no loaf of sugar broken or sip of rye whiskey taken that she did not know of, or had unlocked its storage place. When she retired at night, the keys lay upon her bedside table, and she was light enough a sleeper that any movement of the large jangling iron circlet would be immediately heard. Not that this had ever occurred. She accepted her offices resignedly and turned on her heel, about to go upstairs. Her father detained her.

"Oh, Patty, there's a letter for you in your stillroom. It was sent to me by a young gentleman via George Carter the other day." He rolled his tongue in his cheek. "You may find the contents of interest to you."

She frowned at the mystery, for she had seen him almost every day in Williamsburg. He could have given her the letter then to give to Papa.

"Thank you," she said distractedly, and went out.

She went upstairs and found Jack sitting in the middle of the floor in their room, amid a welter of toys, boxes, and paper. Betty Hemings, who was minding him, stood shaking her head. "I tole him to wait for you," she said.

Patty laughed. "It's all right, Bett, I told him he could open one." She knelt down beside him, glad to see his pink-cheeked delight. "But my young fellow got all excited, didn't you dumpling?" She rumpled his hair. "Now what's there left for grandpapa to open with you? Silly."

"I can wrap this one back up," Jack offered, holding up a carved horse and wagon. She kissed his head. "You're a good boy, Jackie, and Grandpapa would like that very much." She rose again. "Papa tells me Mary laid in," she said to Betty. "How is she?"

Betty frowned. She was a tall woman, thirty-six years old. Her father had been an English sea captain, and she had admixed in her features the grace of those English forebears and the strength and intuition of her mother's Ghana tribe, for her mother had been full African. She was efficient, cheerful, and very fruitful. To this point, she had borne ten children, and the next was due in a few weeks. She was, by virtue of her special position in the house (having been raised by John Wayles as "an experiment") given extraordinary freedom, her only duties being the light ones of a lady's maid and sometime mammy. She was always, even in advanced pregnancy, majestic in her bearing. She stood like a queen now, recollecting the fate and condition of Mary and her baby.

"Well, Miss," she said, "she was fairly poor the first couple of days, and we's all thought she was gone to milk fever, but she turned right around and 'em's doing fine. Big fat sassy baby he is. You shore can tell Rob's his daddy, he's got ears on him like an elephant!" They laughed together. Rob's big ears were an old joke.

"Maybe they'll get smaller as he grows," Patty suggested, not too hopefully. Betty shook her head, still grinning.

"Not them jugs of things. No ma'am, Miss Patty, he's stuck to them for life." She tossed her head, setting her earrings jangling, and looked down at Jack, who had tied the paper back on his horse. "Not like our boy here." Her hand strayed upon the curly head, fingered the gold locks. "Him's a fine man growing, like his Papa."

"Yes," Patty said shortly, taking off her hood. As long as she had Jack, she would never forget Batt's face. They did not think Jack was paying them any mind, but he piped up in a growly voice, "I ain't got no Papa, Betty!"

The words tore her heart. It was not merely that they were true; it was the fierceness with which they were said. She turned away so he might not see her distress, kicking off her shoes. But Betty's green eyes were sharp.

"Jack!" she snapped. "Look how you hurt your poor Mama." Jack looked up curiously, for his intention had not been so. His cherub's face was troubled as he sought Patty's gaze.

"Mama?"

Patty turned. "Yes, dear." She unhooked the front of her gown from its stomacher, not looking at him. He put away his toy and rose, to come and lay his head on her thigh. "I'm sorry, Mama. I love you, Mama." She looked down at him, then, with his big solemn green eyes. He knew well how to get round her, and could get his way with a few well-chosen words, but she saw this time that his sorrow was genuine. She knelt down and embraced him, smoothing his hair. "I know, baby. I love you too. Look here," she lifted his chin. "Why don't you go give Grandpapa the horse and ask him to open it for you. Would you do that now? He's waited as long as you to see your new toys."

Jack's little face brightened, the momentary discourtesy forgotten. "Yes!" he cried. He wriggled out of her embrace and scooped up his toy, running down the hall and stairs, shouting, "Grandpapa, Grandpapa, I haf a toy for you!"

"You're too soft on that chile," Betty said disapprovingly. "He knows how to sweet-talk you too well."

Patty rose. "Oh, I know, Bett, but. . . . Well, I would feel dreadful if something happened to him, and I'd been harsh or mean with him. He's so confined of necessity, is it any wonder he misbehaves now and again? Poor little dear." She sighed. "Well, I've got to get down the row. Could you fetch me the blue Virginia gown from the trunk? It's in the banded one, I think."

"Yas'm." It was plain by her thinned-out mouth that Betty had much more to say on the matter but would not. She fetched the gown and helped Patty into it, talking of other things.

When she was dressed again, with a working apron covering her plain gown, Patty went out the back of the house, past the kitchen where her distillery was, through the garden to the path down to the cabins. It was a far piece, half a mile from the house to the Negro quarters, and Rob and Mary's place was on Guinea row in the new section, not immediately accessible from the main road. As she came to the cabin, Rob's grandmother was sitting outside, dozing in the mild day, a white cap over her equally white hair. She was ancient, and had been so for as long as Patty could remember.

"Hello, Lila," she said loudly to the old woman. "How are you feeling today?"

Lila opened one eye and looked up at her, for she had not really been asleep. She cackled. "Well, Miss Patty, I 'spect I'se doin'm jest fine," she said, and cackled again. "I'se a great granmaw now. . ." She trailed off, as the old were wont to do, and patted her hand.

"Yes, I know dear," she replied, speaking up again. "I'm just going to see Mary and the baby now."

She stepped up over the stoop into the dimness of the little house and paused. The smell of cooking and birth and dark bodies assailed her, and she had to steel herself against it. It was always this way. She'd rather have died than let them know that the smell of their houses nauseated her, but it always did, and she was always glad to get out again into the fresh air. Luckily, because of the darkness, this pause could be taken as allowing her eyes to adjust, especially on a bright day such as this. She hoped fervently that it was, for she was not personally disgusted by their Negroes, even the great big men at the end of a long summer's day in the fields, and it would not have been taken well if they thought she disliked their proximity.

"Hello Mary," she said to the dim figure in the corner on the low bed.

"It's Mrs. Skelton." Mary was fifteen and this was her first baby.

"Oh, *ma'am*," Mary's voice crackled. "You's back! And did ye come t' see my baby an' me?"

"I surely did," Patty replied, coming over to where the girl was lying with the baby. "Hello Leah," she said to Mary's mother, who sat on the stool.

"How does it feel to be a grandmother?"

Leah waved her hand. "Sha, Miss Patty, it don't feel no different from before, 'cept now I git to hold a little one of my own again."

Patty smiled. "But without all the work, eh? Well," she turned to Mary, "so when did you have him, how did it go?"

Mary paused to recollect. "Well'm, 'twas Sunday afore last, cause I member the bells ringing over to 'Muda Hunnerd and Sharley. He came along about midday, ma says." Her eyes sought Patty's in understanding. "It was hard, ma'am. I never did no work harder in m' life, and I allus thought myself a hard worker."

"I know," Patty murmured in sympathy. "But at least you had your mother and the others here. That always makes it better. How are you feeling now?"

"Oh, better ma'am, but I git so tired."

"Mmm. It's the suckling, makes everyone sleepy." She looked to Leah, who nodded. "You have another week, don't you, before you go to work again; I'd spend it just as you have. Let your mother and the others see to your needs. I'll bring you some tonic myself that I have put away. May I see the little lad?" The baby was asleep in the low cot, and Leah picked him up and handed him to her.

"What's his name?"

"Denny," Mary said, and grinned, for she was plainly proud of him. He was a sweet, fat baby, with little cherub cheeks, and as Betty had said, Rob's ears. But he was a man child, so prettiness did not matter so much. She moved the clout to inspect the stump of the navel-string and found it soft and enlarged.

"Now Mary." She came over and knelt on the floor by the girl, showing her the place. "You see how the string is all wet? That's bad. You must tie his clouts below it and let it dry out, otherwise it'll go putrid. Air's enough for it. Jack's went the same." She wanted to reassure the girl that her inexperience was common, and not limited to Negroes. Mary nodded.

"Yes, I see, ma'am. Jest air. Oh thank you, Miss Patty for yo' help. I was fretting over it." Patty smiled and gave her back the baby.

"He's a fine bonny boy, and you'll do just fine. Listen to your mother, she's had—how many?" She looked at Leah.

"Ten," Leah said, "an' raised all 'em." Leah looked at her daughter. "See honey, I tole you she'd say the same as me; Miss Patty knows all that panjangle." They looked at one another as women of experience.

"Just so," Patty said, rising. She clasped her hands before her. "Now, I'll go and fetch to you that tonic I'm in mind of, and you have a rest. Good-bye now."

"Good-bye, ma'am. Thank you, ma'am." Mary said from her corner. Leah walked as far as the door.

"It's shore good to see you back, Miss Patty," she told her. Patty turned back, looking into Leah's face. It was sincerely meant. A plantation without a mistress was a less friendly place to all the blacks. She smoothed things, ordered things in a hundred small ways every day that the men had no inkling of.

"Thank you, Leah, it's good to be back," she said feelingly, and went. Rob's old grandmother was genuinely asleep now, her mouth hanging open in the sunshine. Patty walked up the road again to her distillery, breathing in the summer air in great gulps.

The stillroom was a wall-partitioned space to the back of the kitchen with a connecting door, and one of its own towards the garden. It was only eight feet by ten feet and had a tiny window over the dry sink, but it was her haven. A working office where she wrote up her household accounts and made medicines, poultices, and all manner of herbals needed by black and white, it was also from whence she directed the day. If she was not to be found in the house, then she was generally here, overseeing outside tasks and cooking, settling disputes, and handling all the other duties that fell to her. The room was outfitted with a small brazier; various pots, jars, and measures; a tall stool under the counter; and an old battered chaise longue that had come from Bermuda Hundred and had definitely seen better days.

Its stuffings were lumpy and the upholstery faded to a dull olive green, but it suited her purpose for tending to the walking infirm, as well as the occasional nap.

Now she unlocked the door and took a jar of nettle tonic off the shelf. The liquid was thick and dark green, almost black, and was just the thing, now that the young nettle tops had matured too far to eat as a salad. She was about to go out again, when she saw the letter her father spoke of on the counter. Picking it up, she set down the tincture with a thump. It was from Thomas Jefferson to her father.

Turning it over, she opened the letter and saw that it was dated the ninth, the day after they'd met, and the same day she'd written her father about him. It ran:

> Williamsburgh. June 9, 1770
>
> Dear Sir,
>
> Having previously made your acquaintance in the courts, i now turn to as personal a matter with you as delicacy permits. while here in town, i have lately been introduced to your daughter mrs Skelton. finding her a most agreeable and sensible young woman, I wish to advise you of my design to pursue this friendship further. in fact, sir, i mean to say that i herewith desire your permission to pay court to that lady, should she be also so inclined. i look forward to your word on this matter at soonest opportunity and assure you that i am,
>
> Yr humble an o'b'd'nt s'vt, Sir,
Th: Jefferson.

She let out the breath she had been holding and stared out the window, stunned. *Upon not a day's acquaintance* he had written to her father and formally asked to court her. Dear God, if half the swains she'd played at parlor games with in the last two years had done so, she'd have been married ten times over. Had she needed any further indication of his earnestness, it lay before her. The letter waiting inside her stays burned suddenly to be read, but she had promised Mary she would deliver the tonic herself. Then there would be dinner to get through, and all afternoon and evening. . . . Oh! She jumped down from her stool and picked up the jar, wishing all the hours until bedtime away as quickly as extinguishing a candle.

At dinner Nancy and Tibb and she were all seated at their usual places, awaiting their father. When he finally appeared, he took his place at the head of the table, withdrew his linen solemnly, then enquired to Patty, after a great wink at her sisters, "So, did you enjoy the letter?"

"Oh Pa!" She could have thrown the napkin at him. "You mean thing!

You told Nancy and Tibb and let me fall on it unawares! How could you?"

"Then you are displeased?" Wayles's brown eyes regarded her benignly beneath heavy eyebrows.

"Yes— No!— Papa!" She spluttered, exasperated. Her father laughed.

"If it smooths your feathers, I gave him my consent," he chuckled at last.

"I would think, the way they were going on," Tibby enjoined. "You'd expect they needed chaperonage. Landon Carter threatened to shoot himself, and Phillip Lee nearly challenged Mr. Jefferson to a duel."

"Did he?" Nannie exclaimed, "Tibby, you didn't tell me that!" She leaned on the table, her round face all excitement. Wayles raised a skeptical brow.

"It wasn't as bad as that," Patty said coolly.

"No," Tibb conceded, "But he did have you away in the Cary's closet for over an hour, begging on bended knees."

Patty shook her head. "I don't think we were in the same place at all. He did a lot of hollering, to my recollection. But I soothed him over about it," she looked pointedly at her sister, "and he never promised to call him out. He's never so silly as that, for all his pride."

"The Stratford Lees are certainly a proud breed," their father agreed. "Well," he said to Nancy, "it seems we missed out on all the excitement, sitting here playing whist and patience."

The girls all groaned, but he was not abashed for his low humor.

Later, when Jack was asleep and she had only the candle for company, Patty took up the letter that had been waiting all day. It was somewhat squashed for having been in her stays, but the seal was unbroken and it was readable. How nice it was to open up a letter and see his hand when he was now so far away. She was glad she had kept her promise to read it when alone. When she broke the seal, out tumbled a carefully folded pair of cardinal red garters, beautifully embroidered in silk.

> Williamsburgh. June 30. 1770
>
> My dearest love,
>
> i hope the enclosed will amply replace the loss of your generous gift. i cannot call it a prize by great effort won. i shall treasure it nonetheless. i especially like the little bird, he put me to mind of a jay we have at Shadwell who returns every spring and summer. now i have two rememberances, for i shall never see or hear him again without thinking of you. how i shall endure this last separation, only providence may divine, as i have grown all to used to brief partings only, but i trust my sweet blossom shall not forget its sun and moon, but will, like friend jay, long for summer when the sun may touch again its face with warmth.. i could run on into hundreds of pages

with small things to you, but these i shall save until they may be shared together de facto. until then all i wish to say is that i love you. Every morning and night i send a kiss to you upon those stars. i count the hours until we may be together, and they are as years. i love you, and will love you thus for ever, my beautiful, darling Patty remember me often, read this and every letter often, I pray you, that you may be assured that i am ever your devoted,

She was glad he had encoded the last of the paragraph—for she certainly wouldn't want that to fall into the hands of the idly curious. Even with Betty, who could read, she did not wish to share this most precious of missives. She held the china silk of the new red garters against her face. How like him to pick red, and silk! They must have been dear since the agreement of nonimportation. Smuggled or hoarded, they told her more truly even than the letter how highly valued she was to him.

11

Amongst Primroses

The Forest

Through July, Thomas wrote to Patty. He never missed a post, and penned letters four and five pages long, rambling, adoring, scattered with love poetry and classical verse. As he had asked her to do also, he wrote every detail of his day, of the bloom and fade of summer flowers, of music he was playing, how the work progressed on his big house, and his preparations for the county courts. At the end of July, before he was due to go off to Charlottesville and Staunton, he copied out for her an Italian sonnet from Milton, secure in its being understood without translation.

> *Beautiful lady, whose fair name honors*
> *the green valley of the Reno and the famous ford,*
> *truly he is devoid of all worth who does not*
> *love your noble spirit, which is sweetly*
> *expressed in the unfailing bounty of its*
> *gracious looks and the gifts that are the*
> *arrows and bow of Love, in that place where*
> *your high virtue blooms.*
>
> *When you in your beauty speak,*
> *or give forth happy song that could move*
> *tough mountain-trees, let every*
> *man who finds himself unworthy of you watch*
> *well the portals of his eyes and ears.*
> *Only grace from above can avail him to prevent*
> *amorous desire from rooting itself in his heart.*

She received it four days later. She was in her stillroom writing up her household accounts for the week. Jack was asleep on the chaise longue behind her, and a pot of carmine paste was brewing for Nancy on the brazier. John, her father's steward, brought her the letter with others from her Aunt Randall, from Lisbet, and from Lucy Gilliam, Bathurst's sister, saying that Sally, another sister, was doing poorly. Would she write to cheer her? She saved Thomas's letter for last, as she always did, and when she opened it to find a page of Italian in his even hand she laughed out loud. Only he would think to quote her Milton in Italian! Since she had pen and ink at hand, she withdrew a sheet and wrote across the top:

> Forest, 2 August, 1770.
> My deerest Thomas,
> Since you wrote last my sister Nancy has come home from Eppington, and bids you greeting from Mr. Eppes, whose letter herewith I Enclose to you. I am sorry you were not in to receive Mr. Skipwith's Brother, but I've heard he's gone out to Louisa now, so mayhap on your way here you might chance upon him. He lodges with Mr. Martin there, if you know that gentleman.
> Yes, our R. moschati and R. eglanteria are well into bloom. They began about a Week prior to yours, if that is any help to your charts. I dont no what to do about the Bugs, save from spraying them, the Plants I mean, with soap. An Admixture of two Part water to one of soft soap if you have any or a quarter Part grated hard soap should suffice. Take then a watering can and when the Mixture is glossy, sprinkle it at the roots. As to those already on the blooms, I can only suggest Hand-picking them off, which is grately tedious.
> My darling, I am always ready to be of aid to you in any way I might, but to write to you of modes of garden pest removal strains my pen. I would fain write rather how very much I adore my sweet friend and what a pain it is to endure yet another fortnight's separation. I have read every letter of yours to bits, and sleep with them under my pillow. They are now quite a pile, so you may imagine the lump it makes, but this only sweetens my rest for how could I be othwise when so near to my Beloved knight! Let Justice be swift, tho fair with you, for there is one who waits upon your Decrees of several matters. May this Supplicant not languish long awaiting Trial, as some are suffered to do, unto years. Papa says hoc age was never the Rule of the Courts, but may God grant it so in Augusta that I may be with my Friend the sooner.
> I am playing from Memory now the Mozart piece which was sent, and Practise it every Evening. That it may please both sender and receiver to hear it played is my fondest Wish; for my part I will do my endeavour that it please, the rest lies in the hands of Providence and the mercy of my Judge.
> The Milton sonnet is entirely too undeserved by me, but so sweet, I must remarque it. Such devotion and fine sentiment from my own darling makes my love grow the greater, and I know that time and distance mean nothing when compared to such regard. I am more

than flattered, I am overcome, and can but blush to think of the time spent devising it in my honour. A suitable companion needs must be found for it. deerest Thomas how delightful you are! Surely there was never a lady better serenaded by a cavalier than I and thou.

We too have many fine Walks about the property, which, like yourself there at M__o, I long to share. Away in the Woods, even the sickly Months are pleasant to pass, for one is completely sheltered from such malignant Influences. We have wood violets and evening primroses up to neerly September, and I relay this only to entice you to hurry, for I do so long for your Companionship on my evening walks in our wood, even if it be for but a few Days. Write to me next week, tho you be in Chottsvle. Any scrap will be welcomed. I treasure every word, and remain until then and always, your loving

Martha Skelton.

When he did come, a fortnight later, she was upstairs in her room, reading a story with Jack. Elijah had just fled the king's vengeance when Poll burst in, skirts awry crying, "He's here, Miss Patty, he's here!" Now, Poll was an impressionable girl, just fifteen and newly posted as Betty's surrogate for a few weeks, so Patty didn't think much of her alarums. She thought her to mean her father, who had gone over to Shirley earlier that afternoon. She looked up calmly from the book. "Who, Poll?"

"Mist' Jefferson! Pete saw em coming up en road—" She switched her skirt agitatedly.

"What?" He was not due until the morrow, and there was nothing prepared in the way of house room for him at all. She pulled aside the curtain and looked down into the yard, and sure enough, there he was, bouncing down from Fearnought. Jupiter came trotting up behind, and she saw Thomas start toward the house with his long, easy stride and her heart skipped a beat.

"Oh dear!" She pressed the book upon Jack and leapt up from the chaise longue. "Stay here, both of you, I'll be right back!" she cried, and went running down the hall to pound on Tibb and Nannie's door. "Quick! Come downstairs! Mr. Jefferson's arrived and Pa's not here!"

Nancy opened the door, with her fair hair hanging down. "But he's supposed to come tomorrow!" she protested, drawing the dressing gown she wore about her shift. Her hand went to her hair distractedly. "Tibb's asleep—I, let me dress and I'll fetch Kikey to the linens. I'll be down as soon as I may—"

Already, they heard his voice in the hall, talking in low tones with John, their steward. Thank goodness she and Jack had not been sleeping too! She ducked into her own room and told Poll, "Bring Jack down in a quarter of an hour." She kissed Jack's sleepy face and hurried out of the room and down the stairs.

John had the presence of mind not to leave a guest, sudden or otherwise, standing in the hall, and she found Thomas in the front parlor, running a finger experimentally over the keys of her harpsichord.

"Hello," she said quaveringly. "I'm sorry I wasn't down to receive you, but Jack and I were reading." She smoothed her hair with one hand, realizing that her cap was crooked. His face broke into its rare smile, and he came over, taking her hands.

"It's all right," he told her with amusement. "I know I am early. . .but I couldn't bear to keep away longer." He kissed her fingers.

"Oh my dear, I did miss you so!" She exclaimed, delighted now that the shock of his sudden arrival had subsided. She led him over to the sofa.

"Come sit, you must be fatigued. Even from Tuckahoe it's a long journey."

He smiled at her sheepishly. "I didn't come from Tuckahoe."

"What? What do you mean?"

"I came from Varina," he said simply. "I left before breakfast."

"Thomas!"

They looked up as Nancy came in with Jack, who was still blear-eyed, and not his usual lively self at all.

"I sent a note over to Papa," Nancy told her.

Thomas rose and Patty introduced them. Jack looked up and mumbled gravely, "How do you do, sir." Thomas made him a bow with equal gravity and decorum and replied, "Very well, Master Skelton. I trust you are well?"

"Yes, sir, thank you. Mama and I were reading a book," he volunteered.

Thomas gave her a sidelong glance. "Oh yes? And which book was that?"

"Elijah, sir. I can read," Jack assured him proudly, "but not that. Only little words."

"I see. That's *most* admirable. Do you know all the numbers as well?"

Thomas was in grave earnest with the child, kneeling now to his level, listening carefully to the reply.

"Aye, but sometimes I get confused past a hunnerd." Jack said solemnly. He was becoming more his engaging self and moved away from Patty's skirts. "Are you staying for tea?"

"If you like," Thomas did look up now at her smiling.

"Mr. Jefferson shall be here for a day or two," Patty told Jack. "So you may show him all that you know." Thomas rose again. "Why don't you go find Jenny and see what she has for tea? Auntie and I must show Mr. Jefferson his room."

"Yes, Mama." He made a neat little bow to Thomas. "I'm pleased to meet you, sir," he said crisply in his piping voice and ran out into the hall.

Her father came home during tea, smelling of tobacco and brandy, and it was evident that he had been unable to disentangle himself from Col.

Carter's hospitality and talk of horses and crops. His face was flushed from the brandy and the ride, and he was in high spirits.

"Well, Mr. Jefferson," he said as he sat down to table. "'Tis good to see you again. Augusta went well, I trust?"

"Indeed, sir. All cases concluded that were on the docket with two days to spare."

"By God, a miracle! You should see Charles City Court! Babel and then some. And what the racket don't confuse, the inertia kills. I've had young clients die before their cause was heard." These complaints were made in the greatest good humor.

"That seems the general run of matters," Thomas agreed. "I can only hazard that the fates knew my impatience to be away and felt benevolent. It's never happened before. I usually leave in the midst out of ennui, else someone had set fire to something at home, or other domestic emergency. But you have none of that." He regarded the three women. "Your house is as well-run as an Admiralty vessel."

"Thank Miss Patt for that," Wayles said. "When she and her sister were away at Williamsburg, Nancy and I were more like founderers on a raft adrift in an angry sea."

"Pa!" Nancy exclaimed, blushing.

"It wasn't really so bad as that," Patty murmured, to soothe Nan's ire. "But they were glad to see us."

"Only because we had the key to the sugar chest in our trunk by mistake," Tibb said.

Wayles shook his head. "You see how they torment me," he said mournfully. But his eyes twinkled.

"I should live in paradise were I so tormented by ladies such as these, Mr. Wayles," Thomas replied gallantly, and all three of them exclaimed.

"See, Papa," Nancy teased him, "how much you should appreciate us?"

"Oh, but I do, Nannie," her father said, "every time I write to Farell and Jones." He addressed Thomas: "When I went away today, one of my purposes was to deliver a letter from that agency, and my good neighbor assures me that he is besieged every month by requests from his ladies for gewgaws. I will admit to you sir, that mine do admirably for themselves in most regards that way." He looked across at Nancy again. "So you see, Nan, I do appreciate you, because you do not depreciate me."

"Oh, Pa!" The ladies groaned. Thomas shook his head and laughed.

"Your family are delightful," he said later when they started off for a walk. "Are they always so jolly?"

She thought of days that had not been so happy and put that memory by. She would not burthen Thomas with it. Not yet. "Nearly," she said, instead. "I believe Papa began his comraderie with us to make up the lack of a mother. I certainly know of few families in this area whose paterfamilias is so engaging with his children." She looked out toward their woods, grateful that her hat hid her eyes from his view. The dark days of Elizabeth Skelton were not a time she wished to share, and he would ask, did he see her upset.

"My father was," Thomas said, "when I was there and he yet alive. He always took an interest in our lives and opinions."

"You are very lucky, then."

She took up his hand as they came to the path through the wood. "This way. We have evening primroses not far up this direction." She picked up her skirts and stepped over a fallen branch. "Tell me about your family," she entreated.

He paused for some time, gathering up what he chose to say. She began to wonder, taking in his haunted face, what situation there was at home to distress him so. Her aunt's warning about the Randolphs came ringing.

Those that she knew—Mr. Speaker Randolph; Peyton and his brother John, the Attorney General; and Richard, her father's business partner at Bizzare—seemed normal enough. What did it mean, that they were "a breed unto themselves"? She could not ask Thomas that yet.

He took her hand, and began, "There were eight of us altogether, though most of the girls are married away now. Mary, she's the eldest, was married the year I went away to college, and Lucy's at Buck Island. Patsy you know. Elizabeth's yet at home, though she's two years younger than me. Nancy's coming up a young woman, and my brother will be readying himself for William and Mary before long."

She made a mental tally and pressed his hand encouragingly. "You said there were eight," she murmured gently, looking up at him. It was plain by his face that there was more to tell. She wished his confidence, that he should feel safe with her unburthening his secrets.

"Yes," he said slowly, musingly, and stared out through the woods, his eyes far away. "My sister Jane was the eldest of us, and named for my mother. She was tall and fair-haired, and possessed the quietest, most gentle spirit I have ever known in man or woman. . . . She was the friend of my childhood, a second mother, a confidante." He paused, surveying the woods. "We used to walk together, like this, at Tuckahoe, at Shadwell when I was home. She knew the name of every flower and bird that passed and was a fine hand at coaxing some shy bloom to live in our garden. She played the spinet with beautiful feeling, far surpassing my mother, and it was she who encouraged me to take up the fiddle and the cello." He paused again but she remained silent, listening intently with grave encouragement for his continuation.

He pressed her hand and went on: "She owned a fine voice and used to love to sing the old hymns from the English prayer book. A beautiful soprano, without a tremor in it. . . It was like a lark's song. . . When she died. . ." he heaved a sigh, "I was away from home, at Williamsburg, and the letter sending word did not come until a week after she was buried—" his voice broke in anguish. "They said it was a consumption, that she had languished not a month's time. But I was not sent for! Even though later my sister Bolling told me that she had asked. That I was not there is my eternal regret, for I loved her well."

He closed his eyes against tears that welled up, and Patty stopped beside him, her hand on his sleeve, her heart in her throat for his grief. He stood for a long time, not looking at her, but away into the past, at his own Albemarle woods, and upon the memories of a dear sister whose loss he yet felt with a pang. If he was in Williamsburg, then he would have been at college most like, or studying law. That was five years gone. He too, carried a long memory of griefs, for it was plain that it was not healed over. Because of him, her own had begun to do, and she wanted more than anything to assuage the hurt she saw in his countenance.

"Thomas?" He came out of himself. The tears that had threatened he had conquered with a strong will, and she was awed by it. He covered her hand with his free one, and smiled a little.

"I'm all right, dear. But bless you for your concern." He put his arm about her. "Where is this primrose patch of yours?"

They came to an avenue of yellow, sweet-scented blossoms just beginning to open their petals in the tranquility of early evening, and knelt together, exulting in the velvety petals and honied fragrance. He gathered flowers and tucked them about her, into her hat, her hair, and the neckline of her pale, striped gown. As he placed the last flower there, all the gaiety of the last moments of childish play vanished between them. A stealing warmth crept over her and she was mesmerized, unable to move. In the weeks of his absence she had once envisioned such a moment in this place. And now that it had transpired she was helpless with dread and longing. She was still as a deer caught out, scarcely breathing, watching him with her great dark eyes, with her heart beating under his finger. He raised his eyes slowly to her face, and she knew he was under the same spell. Sympathy was there, and yearning. Diana would deny him nothing now that he had made his offering. She had no power against his advance.

He leaned and kissed her once, his willing goddess in this natural rite. A pilgrim's kiss, a holy kiss. The contact was electric. Galvanized now, Diana would claim her quarry. Anacteon had torn the veil, Virbius had laid the offering, and Endymion had awakened to her love-struck gaze. Her hand was on his face, soft and coaxing, but he took it away with a kiss, murmuring softly, so as not to disturb the gathered Muses, "I promised you a bower."

"Aye," she whispered fervidly. He would not retreat this time, as he had done in Williamsburg. She was her father's child now, not her gentle mother's, and her glance was full of mysteries. "And I wished us here this way. Every day, I wandered the path and wished this here." The green came alight in his eyes, as her arrow struck the mark. Endymion was hers, and she would hie him away to the secret cave. But there was more than compliance in his gaze when he spoke his next words, "And what else did you wish?"

A querulous jay overhead broke their spell at length. Not as untried as she thought him to be, she was doubly regretful for the suspension of their dalliance. It was growing dark behind them. Cold reality intruded in his disordered glance, and the enormity of what had nearly occurred struck her like a blow. And now, coming in disheveled and hasty after dark, none would think otherwise than but they had in fact been lovers. She sighed in dismay and looked up at him.

He smiled at her benignly. "Nary a word, sweetheart, but I would defend you with my life." He held out his hands. "Come. The sooner left the sooner put behind us."

She rose and brushed off her skirts.

"Can you run?" he asked, challenging. "I'll race you."

She laughed. "Watch me."

Hand in hand they ran back past their course, to be in before the midges came swarming out, and fell upon the bench outside the house heaving breaths and laughter.

"You're quite a runner," he said admiringly, his hands upon his knees. She laughed shortly, still out of breath.

"I have to be, with Jack. For an invalid, the child is a whirlwind. He keeps us all on our mettle from dawn till dark."

Thomas leant back on the bench, appraising her.

"What?" she asked, fanning herself with her discarded hat.

He paused a moment, and leant forward again. "You've referred to his state before."

Aye, and she had, obliquely. He must know, if they were to marry. But she did not relish the telling. If he should scorn her for it, she would lie down and die here and now.

"If you do not wish to speak of this," he hastened, "I will not press." She stayed him with a hand.

"No, no," she replied. "It's right that you know, for it may affect matters." She paled and took a deep breath. "Jack is, has—," she faltered and sought his eyes. How to tell him calmly, in a few words, all the anguish she had borne on Jack's behalf, all the many times in that last two years she had been in fear of the child's life?

He took her hand. "It's all right, my love."

She shook her head and spent some moments collecting her thoughts. When she finally spoke, it was in a great rush, words tumbling over one another, to get out the awful truth. "When he was an infant, crawling about, we noticed how extraordinarily he was prone to bruise. The bumps which caused no trauma to other babies left him with great black swellings. When he began to walk after his father died, he would stumble as they do, and if he happened to scrape himself in some way it would bleed for hours. If he cut himself he bled a river. The smallest scratch could send him off. Nothing, nothing I or the doctors could do would staunch the flow. It was just then that we realized that he had the bleeding disease." Her voice rose a little, anguished. "Oh God, when I knew! I was afraid he would die in the night." She looked down into her lap. "He shares my room still; his bed is in the dressing room, so that we might hear him if he calls." She looked away toward the river and its lazy meanderings.

"From that time we have kept him restricted. He rarely plays outside. For what havoc would a tree branch work upon him!" She shuddered. "But he is a very active little boy. He loves to run and jump and all those things. But he must be watched constantly. We are always running after him, in case he should fall. He has never ridden a horse, or climbed a fence—" She smiled a little, "—or rolled in a lawn of chamomile. He cannot. To save his life he must not." She looked at him now, tears welling, and she marshalled the stern resignation she had put over her tender heart to shield it from too painful rumination on what must inevitably come. "You wondered why I was unknown to you before. This is why. If it is too burthensome to you, I will understand."

He looked at her a long moment, and she knew not whether it passed through his mind to disdain her. *Please, please understand!* she begged him silently. I could not bear it! Anything, I may endure, but not that!

To her great relief, he put his arms about her and gathered her into an embrace. "It is not too burthensome, little one," he said into her hair. "We shall bear this together, you and I."

12

Concerto Alfresco

The Forest

In the morning while she was hastening Jack to dress, Patty started to hear the sound of a fiddle in the house. She looked up at Betty, who shook her head with a comically hopeless expression.

"He'ms been out sin' it was light, your pa says," she remarked. "An John seen him going off down toward the creek like someone light a fire under him." She bent her a teasing glance. "What kind o' man d'you got here, Miss Patty, that he don't eat nor sleep on your behalf?"

She blushed. "Oh hush up!" she cried. But Bett only laughed.

"Oh, he'ms got it bad," she nodded sagely. "Near as bad as you. I never did see such a to-do."

Patty glanced at Jack, who had left off playing mittens with his stocking and was staring at them.

"Never you mind," she said coolly. But she sent Thomas a note by Jupiter, his servant, nonetheless, before she went down to see to breakfast:

> ev'ry thing that heard him play
> even the billows of the sea
> hung their heads and then lay by—
> in sweet music is such art

Jack was fractious during breakfast, and from the moment it was concluded he was up from his chair, racing about the hall, with Nancy and Tibb following after him. Thomas kindly offered to occupy him, so while Patty was down in the kitchen overseeing the day's chores, he sat with the boy in the sunny parlor and played naughts and crosses with him on a piece of slate.

She was in the kitchen with Jenny, in the midst of reading out a receipt for Banbury cakes, when the thought came to her that they should have a picnic. It would require extra work for Jenny and her helpers, and she broke off to ask, "Jenny, would you be willing to make up a picnic for Mr. Jefferson and me?"

Old Jenny looked up from the table where she was weighing out flour, her small dark eyes watchful and shrewd. She was a large woman, and the warmth of her eyes was shrouded in a mass of wrinkles and round cheeks.

She had come to The Forest with Patty's mother when she married, having lived her whole life before at Bermuda Hundred. She was not young, having been in her prime those twenty-five years ago, and now had a string of grandchildren ever clamoring about her. Jenny was Patty's first introduction to the love of servants. She was more than a mere cook; she was a motherly bosom and solacing word in troubled girlhood; sharer of joys in bridals and births; and trusted partner in domestic management. She could be truculent betimes, for she knew her own mind well, but they rarely clashed as Patty had with Naomi, the cook at Elk Hill, for affection lay between them. Now she said,

"What were you thinking on, Miss?"

Patty shrugged. "Whatever may be had. . . Oh, maybe some of the strawberries that came in yesterday! And cakes. . . Some of the chicken, sallet greens, whatever you think best. Oh, could you, Jenny?"

Jenny smiled. "I s'pect I could, Miss. If you wish."

Patty could hardly contain her excitement. She clasped her hands over the book, her finger marking the page. "Oh good! I'll fetch a basket down, and some wine. . . Let's see. . ." She fiddled with her keys, taking stock in her mind of the contents of the wine cellar. Rhenish. He liked Rhenish. There would be a bottle left maybe from the Christmas parties. . .

"Miss—" Jenny's voice called her gently out of her reverie. "I'm ready for them cakes now." Patty blushed. "Of course. I'm sorry!" She opened her receipt book again.

She went into the parlor later in her plain working gown and cap to find Jack and Thomas, and the child came running into her skirts headlong.

"Did you have a nice time?" She asked him.

"Oh yes, Mama, an' I won!"

"Good for you!" She ruffled his hair. "I hope you were kindly to Mr. Jefferson about it." She smiled up at Thomas.

"Oh aye," Jack said offhandedly. "Mama, may I play with Joe?" Joe was one of Jenny's grandsons and helped with small chores about the kitchen: pulling weeds in the kitchen garden, chasing the chickens from the doorway, kneading bread. He was only four, and the work was more to occupy him while his mother was busy than to make him useful. But he thought himself a great helper. He and Jack were fast friends.

"If you like, but only in the kitchen."

"Yes, ma'am." He turned and made a bow to Thomas. "Thank you, sir, for playing with me. Good morning!" With that he turned and ran down the hall toward the back of the house, yelling all the way.

"It's nice of you to let him win," Patty said.

"But I didn't," he protested. "He's very bright. What he won was by his own efforts. You should be proud of him."

"I am." She ducked her head. "I have a fancy," she admitted.

"Mmm?"

She raised her head, and her eyes showed their flecks of green and orange. "I thought instead of dinner we might have a picnic down by the creek." Thomas came and took her hand, saying softly, "I think it's a splendid idea, and you mustn't be shy about proposing things. I'll not think you forward." It was not fear of censure that way that made her blush, but the memory of their last sojourn in the woods. It was sweet that he yet thought her shy. He kissed her fingers. "Shall I bring my fiddle?"

She looked up at him with the roses in her face. "Oh, yes, I was hoping you would!" It was heaven to hear him play.

"I will gratify your every wish to the best of my ability," he said sincerely. "How fortunate that this one is so simple."

She smiled. "Thomas. . . . Well, give me leave to change my gown, and I'll be with you directly."

"Please don't," he entreated.

"What?"

"Change. I think you look charming, like a milkmaid." He meant her little round mobcap and tucked up gown. "And I am jealous of further time spent from you on such a fine day. Come, the birds are singing and the bees droning. All we need is a switch and a berry and we shall have perfection!"

She laughed at this. "Very well, sir, you argue too well. Away then, to sylvania!"

The creek ran to the southeast of the property, one of the many small springs that fed the Chickahominy and James Rivers; it lay behind the house athwart, among the pines. Its murmur was soft and could only be heard from close-by. It was a narrow little causeway, lined in moss banks and graced by wetland flowers and cress. Called Herring Creek on surveys, it entirely crossed John Wayles's lands and joined to the Chickahominy on the Carter lands farther southeast, so they referred to it as Carter's or Shirley Creek among themselves. In midwinter it was but an icy trickle, giving way to its present ebullience in the spring thaw. Under the shelter of trees, it was a fine picnic spot, cool and peaceful. Jupiter carried out the hamper and whitework coverlet for them and then departed, with instructions to return after the house dinner. Left alone, they put out the quilt and laid aside the hamper, sitting down together on the white nest.

"If we were a country song," Thomas said to her in amusement, "they would leave out the next while."

Patty settled her skirts about her and looked up. "Shall we?" She folded her hands primly.

"I asked for that," he admitted. "But I suppose it depends upon one's expectations. . ." Already, they were treading on dangerous ground.

"As I've said before, Mr. Jefferson," she drawled casually, picking at a minute piece of lint on her petticoat, "I have no expectations where you are concerned, only hopes." Her eyes flickered up, laughing, daring, enjoying the verbal fencing as much as he.

He drew nearer, leaning. "And what do you hope?"

Her gaze took in his face, a thread of fire quickening her pulse. They could not turn down that road. Not so soon. But there was another avenue: "At the moment, that you would play me a song on your fiddle."

He bowed his head in courtly assent. "Your servant, ma'am."

He took his fiddle from her case, admiring momentarily how the sun dappled on the wood, drew a single note across the strings to test their humidity against the air, and made a correction in tone. Then he began an air that sent her melting against the tree behind her. They were attuned together indeed.

The "Heather Isle" slipped slowly away beneath his fingers, speaking of mist-covered glens, hardy warriors in feudal majesty, and a link with a time long gone. "The Highlander" came and went, and the "Queen of Argyle," before MacPherson's "Lament" brought his Scottish concertino to a close.

She came out of herself and smiled a little. "I like Scotch music," she said. "I always have. There's something. . .evocative about it with me." He laid his fiddle aside and covered her hand with his own. "It's why we like Ossian. There is music in those words." He had written to her, rhapsodizing about MacPherson's translation of the ancient bard, and had been mortified last evening to find a copy of the book on her father's shelf. He broke off now with a disparaging glance. "Why did you let me run on in that way in my letter, explaining him to you? You might have told me that you knew of him."

"It is rather difficult at an hundred miles distant to say, yes dear, I esteem him also. Besides—" she traced the trimming on his sleeve with a finger, "—you'd soon enough discover a mutual passion; I saw no reason to discomfit you." She looked up at him. The creek beyond ran in time with her blood. He was too near, and knew as well as she her reason to discomfit him. They regarded one another a long moment.

He returned, softly, "Such natural kindness is frequently sought, but seldom found."

She blushed. "You flatter me. I am as mean-spirited at heart as the next person. I merely hide it well."

"Never," he avowed, then ventured, "Would you sing me a song? You have a lovely voice, which I can't hear properly when distracted by my own buzzing in my head. Won't you?"

She laughed. "I can't very well refuse when you played for me so kindly."

She sang for him the Nightingale song, wherein a pair of lovers are seen walking beside a river, waiting to hear the bird's evensong.

"O come, said the soldier, 'tis time to give o'er
O no, says the fair maid, please play one tune more
I do like your playing and touching of the long string
And to see the pretty flowers grow, hear the nightingales sing

"Now, said the fair maid, come, soldier marry me
O no, replied the soldier, how can that be?
For I've a nice little wife at home in my counterie
Two wives in the army's too many for me."

"That's a dim view of love," he remarked dryly. "I hope it's not an indication of feeling."

"Certainly not!" Patty exclaimed, alarmed. Then she saw that he was in jest. "My family's influenced you, I see," she murmured darkly. "No, 'twas chosen for the part unspoken. You made me think on it, and a few others, with your remark." He was not looking at her, but at the way the sunlight dappled on her shoulders.

"Do you know," he said, touching the linen of worked muslin she wore, "I noticed first your eyes, and then how graceful your shoulders were. They are not bony or stout or stooped or rigid, but curving like a bow." His fingers travelled lightly along her collarbone, to where the hollow was at her throat. "I found it most appealing, and I still do." He dropped his hand to take up hers, making a proper grace. Her hand trembled.

"My dear," he said, and leant to kiss her. They were treading again into dangerous territory and he was mindful of it this time, not carrying things farther than either of them could refuse. Of what lay beyond the border of that country he had admitted not owning her experience, but he was nevertheless no stranger to its terrain. There were maps aplenty.

He touched the thread lace of her cap, smiling. "My milkmaid. My charmer, how dear you are to me." He leaned back again and pulled her over to sit with him against the tree. They said nothing more for some time, spirit communicating to spirit where words failed. There was enough in each other's company, to be alone and unrestrained by polite observances. They sat, listening to the water's course and the song of a linnet nearby, until at length they took their leisurely meal together, with tiny wild strawberries and Rhenish. They collected cress and forget-me-nots from the sloping creek banks, and wondered in delight to find a single plant of swamp rose growing close by. This cousin of the primrose in their woods was rarely seen at this spring creek, and they could only surmise together that it must have come from upstream.

When Jupiter came to fetch them they gathered up the day's hunting and lay it in the picnic basket atop the empty wine bottle. When they returned to the house, they found Robert Skipwith in attendance from dinner, and Patty went upstairs to change her gown.

Jack was asleep in his sleigh bed in the dressing room, and Poll was nowhere to be seen. It was like the girl to be off, fingering the house linens or daydreaming among the passageways. She was very flighty in that way. She was a good girl, not belligerent or sour, but she took some prodding to get about the ordinary business of life. Patty rang the bell and laid her house gown away in the wardrobe. By the time Poll's puff-capped head appeared in the doorway, she had completed an entire change of toilet, save for the gown's lacing. Her good humor was stretched.

"What took you so long?" she enquired in exasperation. It behooved the lady of the house to be prompt, and by this out those downstairs had probably thought she'd expired. She hated waiting on the incompetence of servants. Betty would never have left her adrift in this fashion. If she could have laced the gown herself or discreetly called one of her sisters, she'd have done it. But the former required such contortions as were impossible in tight-laced stays, and the latter was indiscreet, to say the least. The girl shrugged.

"Well, you must do better. If we are in a hurry or have a guest without a body servant such sloth would never do. You're lucky I can dress myself. Here, lace this up." She turned round, dusting the powder off her lace with a flickering touch. In a moment she was into her shoes and hurrying out the door. "Stay here with Jack," she commanded, and was down the staircase in a trice.

Thomas and Rob were confabulating in the corner by the harp, Tibb and Nannie sat on the long sofa nearby, choosing music, and her father had just closed the adjoining doors from his office as she came in. The bowl of flowers gathered by the creek stood upon the table behind her harpsichord, their soft blues and pinks a gentle counterpoint to the cream draperies. She went over to the two young men.

"Hello, Mr. Skipwith. I had no idea we'd be graced with your company this evening," she said smoothly. "You'll pardon I was late, I hope. You know ladies and toilet, or soon will. 'Tis never perfect."

Rob was gallant. "I never saw such feminine perfection as the ladies of this house, ma'am." Tibb turned her head and smiled at him across the curved back of the sofa. "Do you not agree, Mr. Jefferson?"

"I do, most vigorously," Thomas smiled. He looked a trifle sunburnt now, about the tops of the cheeks. He'd said he took it easily, and she saw now how so. But it didn't take the polish off his manners. "No wait is overlong that results in such graces."

"Then I should be tardy more often," Patty said, and went over to the sofa. Leaning over the back, she asked Nancy, "What are we playing for our musicale?"

"Purcell, mostly." Nancy threaded her fingers through the ribbons on her guitar. "I have the continuo."

"Mr. Skipwith has brought his oboe," Tibby said.

"A solitary woodwind among strings." Patty rose again. "I say, Mr. Skipwith, that you are a solitary woodwind among strings this afternoon. Papa plays a fife—" her glance flickered to her father across the room, "—but won't. But Nancy has the continuo she says, so you shan't be entirely alone."

"I shall be as a thrush among the linnets," Rob assured." If you'll pardon me, Mr. Jefferson."

"Either has a song worthy of note," Thomas said, and they all groaned. He went to fetch his fiddle from the table.

They took Jack out for a stroll later, through the gardens proper behind the house. Amid the annual border, Thomas asked suddenly, "Is he very like his father?" His face had been brooding, and she'd thought him contemplating weightier matters than Jack's behavior. "I knew Mr. Skelton slightly, as a boon companion, but never as a friend as Page or Carr."

She hesitated only a step. "Yes," she said shortly. She didn't want to talk about Batt now, not in this way. She looked over to Jack, gamboling about the rosebushes yonder, on his fair ringlets and jovial little face. Her mind ran to that plumpish young man, who'd so swayed her with his ingenuity at the Assembly ball. She known him for years, but he had never been so attentive before. And it was all without the swoop and polish of the gallants. He was an earnest young man, and it had won her heart.

He came to her mind, amiable, hard-working, loving of graces. He had been so proud of his little family, so delighted when in its bosom. A hundred small things half-forgotten flitted past, unspeakable things which would lay buried forever, even to Thomas. How could she tell? She remembered also the terrible day in Williamsburg when they brought him home, gasping, ghastly, weak and grey, too weak to sign a hastily drawn will. Run down by a carriage. . . Dear God, and she had not managed to tell him that another pledge had come to them. In the end that hadn't mattered, and Jack was as solitary as she.

She looked on her son, with his father's dancing green eyes and cherub's face. O Batt! His name was an ache. He had not lived to know the truth of Jack, either. But she knew that if he had done, he would have taken it as blithely as Jack.

"Yes," she repeated. "He is like his father. I can't. . ." she felt dim and faint, shook her head. "Please, I must sit down."

When the greyness receded she opened her eyes again to find the world still spinning in a ringing vortex. The light was whiter than it had been before, and she blinked against it.

"I'm sorry," she said, "That was very foolish of me."

"No." Thomas was all worried gentleness. "You're very pale. Do you want some water?"

She shook her head. "I'm sorry," she said again. "I don't know if you recall, but Mr. Skelton died very suddenly, very unexpectedly, and the details of it are still painful to recall. . . . I have never fainted before. It is very strange. I feel as though I've been under water." She took in great gulps of air, feeling her face cold and stiff, and her hands none too steady. She gladly accepted the proffered one.

"I am a dolt." Thomas muttered. "I should have recalled, should have guessed. . . ."

"No." She turned to him. "How could you know? You said yourself you were not close. You are not to blame. I am only being foolish. I'm fine now. I only need to sit a moment more."

"You're certain I can't get you water, take you inside? Something? I feel helpless," he admitted.

She bore him a candid gaze, designed to disarm, for she was feeling better now. "Well, the sovereign remedy is to remove one's stays, but I believe we should have a scene if we tried that." She delighted in his shocked face, satisfied that she had convinced him that she really was fine now, but the matter of Batt's demise was not broached again for a very long time afterward.

13

The Ruling Lady

The Forest

In the evening, Thomas went up with her and Jack at the child's bedtime. Bathed and tousle-haired in a fresh nightshirt, Jack was all too happy to sit quietly and listen to his favorite story read by their friendly, quiet-voiced visitor. Patty sat on a stool on the other side of the bed, listening also to the familiar tale from Stanyan's *Græcian History*, and was pleased at how well they got on together. Jack was not famous for his politeness to any suitor who looked as if he might be getting too familiar, but he liked Thomas. They had played marbles on the floor in the office before Jack's bath.

When Alexander's history was concluded, Jack gave a great yawn and sighed, eyeing her. Every night it was the same. He listened rapt to hero tales, but when the time came for his simple prayers, he was too tired. She bent him a speaking glance, however, to say that a visitor was no excuse, and he obediently folded his hands and announced with comically tight-shut eyes, "Dear God, thank you for your bounty. Bless Mama, Grandpapa, Auntie Tibb an Nannie, Joe and Mr. Brown, Jenny." Here he screwed open one eye, "—and Mr. Jefferson, who read my book. Amen."

Thomas flushed. She hazarded that children's routines were a foreign enough thing to him, but Jack's unorthodox prayers he certainly had never heard the like of.

"Jackie," she shook her head. "You are a very silly little boy. And sweet." She rose from her seat and kissed him soundly many times. "Sleep well, poppet." She tucked the sheet and brown coverlet between the hair mattress and the bed. Jack flung his arms around her neck.

"Good night, Mama." He turned to Thomas then, and asked solemnly, "Would you kiss me good night, sir?"

Her heart thudded heavily for a moment, and she felt the color rise in her face. Not from shame, but from sentiment. She couldn't gainsay him, or say anything, for the ache that clogged her throat. Thomas smiled.

"I certainly will," he said huskily, and rose from his chair a little. He kissed the boy's forehead. "Good night, son." He received Jack's strangling embrace graciously.

"Good night, sir." Jack snuggled down into the covers, happy now to go to sleep.

"He doesn't do that with anyone," she said, as they passed through her room to the stairs.

"I gathered that," Thomas said.

They sat in the parlor that evening, listening to Nancy and Tibb read from Fielding. The first breach had just been tried against Pamela's virtue when Poll came in.

"Miss Patty," she whispered furtively, from behind the sofa. She had made her small self smaller still by attitude. "They's trouble. . . ."

"What, Poll?"

"Rob an Mary senned me to fetch you. They baby's got some terrible gripe—"

The words rolled over her like a shock. The summer complaint was the dread of plantations, of childhood particularly. It always seemed the little ones and the aged bore the least well against it. Her mind was ticking along a list of the herbs needed against the disease. Scarcely a minute in time had passed, but her focus was entirely shifted onto the emergency at hand, for an emergency it could well be. A gross outbreak of *cholera morbus* could last weeks, take a dozen lives. She needed to marshal all her forces, and she was cool now, directing, "Tell them I'll be there directly. Fetch me a lamp."

Thomas looked over at her now, just noticing that something was amiss. She stayed him with a hand and whispered, without panic, "I must go, excuse me. Good night." She slipped her foot out from under her and rose, hardly making a stir in the room, but once out in the hall her movements were quick and sharp. John came with the lamp lighted and her light tippet against the evening breeze. Thank God she had an efficient house! She took the lamp in hand and was halfway down the hall before a quiet voice brought her up short.

"Patty."

She looked back at Thomas's tall form. "Can I do anything?" He'd have built her a ladder to the moon, did she ask. Across the hall, in the flickering light, she wished him a thousand mercies. He was a good man. She picked up her skirts. "No, dearest. Everything's in hand. Thank you!" She turned and fled.

In her stillroom she gathered up necessary items in her sailcloth bag with its shoulder strap. It had labored once as a store for seed broadcast, but was now retired for her humble medicinals. She ran, ran down the pitch-black road unaided with the lamp toward the fevered house. She was not afraid of the dark, nor of what might lurk there. Her person was sacrosanct in the place, and she knew every rock and gully of the road from babyhood. The long mile was longer in the dark, but she reached the cabin shortly. In the doorway she flung on her apron, hastily taken up in the distillery, and accepted the small welcome of the worried family.

The two-months child, Denny, lay on the bed, writhing and kicking and crying in a sharp, intermittent way. His belly was distended farther than merely that of a new baby, and the room reeked of fever. He was not too far gone, but with a small baby things could turn for the worse in short order. They'd had the wits to call for her at least.

"How long has he been this way?" she asked the mother.

"Sin' afore sundown," Mary said. "He'm's had some straining jest the last day or two."

"Well, he would do." She said shortly. She gave the bag to Rob and took off her tippet. "I want you to boil some water, Mary. Do you have any?" She looked around for the bucket in the dim house.

"I'll fetch some more," Rob said, putting her bag down by the bed. He took the half-filled bucket and emptied it in the one pot, then went outside, lighting his way with a sputtering, smelly candle of hog dripping.

Patty went over to the baby and laid her hand on him, gauging his fever. The coolness of her touch sent him howling. She raised his head up under her hand, and crooned to him.

"There now, little one, it's all right. We'll soon make you better." Please God. She picked him up and turned to Mary. "His fever's not so very bad. I believe we might get it down. Do you know what ails him?"

"Well," Mary said uncertainly, "I 'spect tes the summer disease, ma'am."

Patty nodded, pleased. "And you'd be right." She gave the girl her baby.

"Now, we shall do our best for him. But we must be diligent, watchful. If he turns this night, you must be very careful of him and keep him away from others for a while. Now I know that'll mean a hardship on you, but I'll speak with Mr. Wayles and impress upon him the urgency of your confinement for a few days, so as not to spread the contagion. Do you know of anyone else come down with this?"

Mary rocked the whimpering baby in her arms, her brown eyes full of fear. "No'm."

Well, that was a matter for debate, but she wouldn't argue it at the moment. Rob came back with the water, and Patty set the herbs to boiling in the pot. It was a slimy mixture, but sovereign for drying up the flux. All through the long night and into the small hours they worked together, forcing the herbal on the baby at intervals, alternating massage with liniment and applications of linting dipped in the steaming herbal on the child's belly. Finally, when the cock's crow was heard in the lane, the child slept peacefully and was cool. He had not had an eruption of the bowel in well above an hour. Patty drew a hand across her aching brow, for the damp, hot closeness of the house had given her a terrible headache, and she was exhausted. But the child was improved. "I think he's turned," she said to his parents.

Shortly after, Rob set off for the field, and she and Mary cleaned up the debris of the night. When the lintings, spilled bottles, and fetid clouts were all disposed of, Patty took up her tippet, her bag, and the lamp and started the long walk back up to the house. In the kitchen, she took up some water to wash her face and tidied her sagging hair. Breakfast was well under way, and she gave out to Jenny and her helpers the menu and instructions for the day. In the piece of looking glass in her stillroom, she realized that she was hardly a fit sight for company, let alone Thomas, with dark circles under smoke-reddened eyes and hair screwed up anyhow, but it would have to do until after breakfast. When she would sleep, she did not know. The day would go on, as it always did. She had not the luxury of sleeping all day. There was flax to be broke and dressed today, and the last peaches to be put up. They needed more soap, and the dairy wanted scrubbing.

She was subdued at breakfast and once caught herself before she spilled her cup of coffee into the plate. Her stays were murderously tight, but she had not after breakfast the privileges of deshabille to do without them. She was conscious of being a bad hostess and worse lover, but she could hardly bring herself to lift the fork from the plate; conversation was impossible. She gave monosyllable responses to enquiries of the health of the child and explained shortly that Mary needed to be excused for three or four days. Her father simply nodded.

"I'll tell Raiford," he said. "Two of the others can make up her work." Mary was a laundress.

In the upper hall afterward, when she was going to change, Thomas caught her hand. "Are you all right?" His eyes were green in the morning light. She smiled wearily. "I will be. This happens oftener than not. Someone's always coming down sick or dying or bringing a baby. I'm used to it."

He shook his head, raising her chin with a calloused finger. "You are not a convincing one for untruths, sweet."

"I suppose not," she admitted.

It would be sweet to lay her head on his chest, to feel his solicitous embrace, to rest there knowing the world could not intrude. She blinked to clear her focus, for she was weaving on her feet. The coffee had not been vivifying.

"What shall you do this morning?" she asked, in an attempt at hospitality. It was a custom in their houses for guests to be at liberty in the mornings while the work was done. Yesterday's picnic was only due to putting off the work until today, and her sisters' good natures. They had done all the mending in her stead.

"I thought I would take a ride about the place." Thomas said. "And get me in readiness for the afternoon." After dinner, he was to ride to Williamsburg and Rosewell, and then back to Albemarle.

It struck her suddenly that he would be going away, and for an undetermined time. It was too much in her state. "Oh," she cried in distress. "I have so much to do, that I must do, but I would fain leave it all and ride with you, or sit with you, or do anything with you that we may not be parted sooner!" She clasped his hand in both of hers and laid it against her cheek.

"I know, sweet," he said in tender sympathy. "If love holds any authority, I would enjoin you to sleep rather than work, for you are overwrought." His hand smoothed back her sagging hair. "Won't you, Patty?" He was right, and she had no will to argue with him.

"Aye." She nodded and let him steer her to her room and close the door.

At dinner, her father addressed to Thomas the question she could not ask, "Well, I hope we shall see you soon again, Mr. Jefferson. Before the next sitting of the house, perhaps?" He glanced at her, sitting at his elbow. "I know that Miss Patt would want me to ask, and frankly, your visit has been too short."

"With which I would concur, sir." Thomas said. "It is only pressing business that drags me away, otherwise I would make myself a nuisance."

Wayles waved his hand. "Never. We welcome the diversion you bring us. Such friendship is never a pall." He leaned back in his chair. "I hear you were out riding also, today. I believe our crop here is some weeks ahead of that in your country, if the intelligence of Col. Carter serves me rightly."

"It is. Our drying season had just begun." Thomas looked over his wine glass at her. His advice to sleep had been well taken, and she better able to cope with his leaving than she would otherwise have been.

"Does that not put you at a disadvantage, sir, in English markets over those farther downriver?"

"I have not found it so." Thomas put the glass down. "Although I expect it is so with some smaller planters in the back country. But that will change. I have a plan to open up the Rivanna to navigation." He broke a piece of bread.

Wayles squinted appraisingly. "And how it that?"

"It would require a deeper channel," Thomas explained," but after that it would be navigable to any barge or other light craft suitable to tobacco trade." He smiled a little. "It would also leave us up-country folks less stranded from civilization. There could be a dependable post, for instance." Patty did not miss the glance that fell her way.

"You aren't worried that doing so would open the country up to speculative dealers?" Her father was a good lawyer, diligent, exploring every avenue.

"They already have tried. My casebook is full of such claims. Making the river a better roadway appears to change that prospect very little."

They went on with their talk, but the ladies listened only politely, until Jack got too noisy in his singsong play even for them. Patty slipped from her chair.

"I'll take him upstairs," she said. "Excuse me." She held out her hand to the boy. "Come along Jackie, it's time for a nap."

"I don't want a nap," Jack said fiercely, busy commanding his forces.

"Yes, I know," she replied patiently, "but it's time." She took his hand. "Come have a story then." She led him from the room.

"I want 'Zander!" he shouted down the hallway. He went to climb the stairs. "Zander Zander Zander Zander" he sang.

"Hush, Jack, I'll read it to you. Be a good boy now."

When he was finally asleep she came out again and went down the hall to the opposite door and knocked.

"Come," Thomas said within. She entered and he turned, about to say something, then closed his mouth again. "I thought you were Jupiter," he said.

"Not by a long stretch." She watched him pack away his brushes carefully. He was remote from her, absorbed in the common task.

"Jack is asleep?" he asked, without turning.

"Yes, thank goodness. I love him, but he wears me out." She leaned on the desk with her hands behind her. She hesitated. He seemed not to care at all that he was leaving, and had not set out any time for his return. Had she put him off with too much knowledge of her self and situation?

"Thomas—"

He turned. "Yes, sweet?"

The endearment undid her. "When shall I see you again?" She couldn't keep the desperate rising note from her voice. She loved him so much that the thought of another separation of months' endurance was unbearable.

"Oh, Patty." He came to her then and embraced her briefly. "As soon as may be, I promise you. Two or three weeks. Not a month. My dear," he smoothed her hair from her face, "don't fret. Look you: at the end of a fortnight you will be so inundated with letters that you'll wish us together just to staunch the flow. And there's the Assembly. You are coming?" His fingers were under her chin. "I couldn't face the theater without you, and all those dances. I would pine for my blossom. Say you're coming."

She smiled, feeling foolish for her fears. "I'm coming," she promised, though she hadn't considered it. What else could she do? He had asked, desired her to be there. That was enough.

He kissed her lightly. "Good." There was a knock at the door. "Now that ought to be Jupiter. Come!" He called out. Jupiter entered with a pair of newly cleaned boots.

"Well," she said shyly, not wanting to disturb his business with his servant, "I'll just go now. I'll be downstairs when you're ready to leave."

He smiled at her from across the room, the rare smile she loved. "I'll be there."

They made their good-byes before the family, out on the lawn before the house.

"Expect a flood!" Thomas called to her, as he and Jupiter started off down the avenue and she laughed.

"What does that mean?" Nancy asked, staring after the departing riders.

"Paper," she said gaily. "A deal of paper."

"Paper's on the list," their father said, with a twinkling eye. "But I don't suppose that will hold the tide at bay."

"I sincerely hope not."

Despite the best precautions she had taken with closeting away Mary and her baby, the dysentery spread among the cabins, sweeping rows like a river. Denny himself grew well again, but Rob's aged grandmother succumbed, hardly a week afterward. It spread from the new section first, ribboning its way along through the little village of houses. It seemed to be worst near the well. Of the eighteen who died, fully six came from that area. Her sister Lisbet came to help, and Patty wrote to Thomas in Albemarle not to come.

"It is beyond our control at the moment," she wrote in the middle of the second week, when he had told her he would arrive in six days. "And as grately as I desire your company, I cannot put you at risque for this complaint. I beg of you, for our and your own sake, to stay away. Those are difficult words to pen, but I know you will comprehend the spirit in which they are written. I shall not fail to give you notice the moment the danger has passed. Until then, believe that I am, Yr loving, Ma. Skelton."

The letter was put on a west-going horse and reached him, by his reply, in three days, remarkable in itself. But it had come in time: he had intended to leave in the morning.

Lisbet's presence in the midst of calamity was more welcome than an angel's, for she was an excellent nurse and a capable apothecary. For three weeks, they worked together, trading duties with Tibb and Nancy in a round-robin. In spite of long nights and strain, the work of the plantation continued smoothly in the hands of the four sisters. There had always been much cooperative feeling among them, and as children they had rarely quarrelled. Now, four pairs of willing hands and stout hearts dosed the sick, directed the house, and prepared the dead. Even Nancy, who was squeamish, did not shirk the last duty. At the end of a month, an abatement was in sight and after dinner, Wayles gathered his four ladies together and praised them soundly.

"I was never sorry for a lack of sons," he said, looking round their circle of faces. "And never more grateful for you all than now. You have done a monumental task, and each and every person on this place, not the least of whom myself, bids you a heartfelt thanks."

Lisbet laid her hand on his arm. "Thank you, Papa." She had left her own husband and small son at their plantation in Chesterfield on the Appomattox to shift for themselves, and it was she who lost the most in this ordeal, being tired already in the early stages of another pregnancy. Yet she came without a complaint.

Later, Patty embraced her sister fondly. She was her best confidante and dearest friend.

"You're an angel," she murmured into the soft brown curls at her sister's ear. "Mr. Eppes has a treasure, as we all do." She moved away. "Dear Lisbet."

"I've only done what you yourself would do," she said mildly. "After all, you came when Richard was born without hesitation."

"I was not putting myself at risk when Richard was born," Patty chided. "You cannot modestly deny this one, Betsy. You are our true heroine."

14

The Gift of a Rose

The Forest

Thomas wrote from Monticello:

the flooring is now laid in the north wing of the house and the joists are going in for the salon next to it. . . . work has progressed much more slowly than i had anticipated, due to an unexpected shortage of planed and cured timber, which causes me no little anxiety. i had hoped by the summer's end to have both floors in and erection of the walls begun. . . . but the plaister in the out-chamber is dry at last, and i have chosen, after much consideration of your remarks on the matter, the filigreed pattern wallpaper, for i agree that it will reflect candle or firelight handsomely. i have as yet no curtains, but being as you discovered an early riser the sun is my clock, and am, I hope, not in such immediate need of adornment.

. . .i wish you would write. i know you are very busy in looking after those struck down with the summer complaint, βυτ I μισσ μψ δαρλινγзσ ηανδ. any little token would be cherished. please write to me! i am in a ferment of anxiety lest i should hear that you too, have fallen victim. take care, my sweet. . . . i have been on a visit to my sister Lewis at Buck Island these last two days. she speaks only well of you and sends her regards. . . . i had wrote to Rosewell, from whence intelligence comes that both our friends shall be in attendance at Williamsb. this season had you heard that also of mrs. Page? i enquired of you to them, hoping that they had heard something of your circumstaunce, and received that they had no ill word, but that mrs Page would write. . . .

. . .law occupies me much, but you are no stranger to that. . . . in the garden we have the last of the raddishes come to table, and late beans. i put out straw on the squashes yesterday. could you send to me another copy of the receipt? the original has vanished into the greater mass of papers on my table, i suspect in dismay at keeping company with such lofty extracts from Littleton and Black- stone. . .the militia meeting concluded well, with our Lieutenant Dr

> Gilmer breaking up the men in his usual manner, that is to say, at Fouette's ordinary down the road apace. . .have at last finished the bookcase. . . .

Patty, in the middle of September, deluged with letters from his friends and hers to write, sent him word.

> We are all safe and well, and my sister Eppes has decided to visit across the river at Bermuda Hundred with Mr. Eppes's family until the Assembly, at which we shall be joined by Mr. Eppes and the heir. I do not bide with my aunt this time, but in Nicholson street. . . . But enough of such trifles, I may give them to you in person and spare you the tedium of being told twice. Do come, my beloved! Tho' we are but to shortly convene in Williamsb, I am desolate at the thought of waiting that long to see my dear again. Three weeks! 'Tis an eternity!

In accordance with her wishes, he headed for Charles City the next day, sending a note ahead from Tuckahoe to announce his arrival.

In Charles City summer was delayed, and the last roses were still in bloom. Patty had a visit before dinner from Landon Carter and Reuben Lee who was visiting him from his place on the Northern Neck. She opened the doors to the parlor where they waited with a pretty smile set upon her face, giving no indication that she had been in the middle of overseeing the starching and ironing of clothes. Upon word of their presence she rushed upstairs, narrowly avoiding them, and hurriedly changed her sodden gown for the pink one she wore now.

"Mr. Carter, Mr. Lee, how good it is to see you! I was just wondering what had become of you both. I haven't seen you all summer." It had been before Thomas' visit that she had seen them, but that was July, and seemed a summer away, with the intervening sickness. She came into the room and accepted their obeisances graciously.

Landon took this pleasantry as a rebuke. "I'd have come, ma'am, but I was away with my brother to Annapolis. I've only just arrived. But I hope," he nudged Reuben Lee, who held something behind his back, "that this small token will affect a close of our breach." Mr. Lee presented her with a beautiful deep red rose in full bloom.

"'Tis the last lonely inhabitant of our garden," he said with a bow." Carter here said how you esteemed them."

She took the flower with a soft exclamation. "Oh I do," she murmured, testing its fragrance. "It's beautiful. Thank you. Were there any breach to close, this would most assuredly close it." She held out her hand. "Come, sit, and tell me all the news."

They stayed all morning and through dinner, at which they were the sole gentlemen, her father being away trying a cause. They passed a pleasant afternoon, gossiping, but she needed to wash her hair before Thomas came, and she began to wish that they would be on their way, that she might get to it, or it would never dry. She gave no sign of restlessness, being trained to politeness, and endured cheerfully all their talk until at last Reuben looked at his watch.

"I don't wish to be rude, ma'am," he said. "But Carter, you and I were due to George's half an hour gone."

Landon took out his watch also. "Damme, so we were!" he exclaimed. "Pardon, Miss Patty," he said, coloring. They rose. Reuben bent his brown head over her hand. "You will excuse our haste, I hope, Miss Patty, and know that is not due to a desire to be gone from you."

She smiled. "I do understand, Mr. Lee, and I thank you for your offering." She touched the rose which she had put in her hair behind her left ear.

They walked to the door together, and she watched until they were gone from sight toward the stables. She would never get her hair dry now before evening! She turned and ran through the house and out to the kitchen for hot water. On the way upstairs she collided with Nancy.

"What's the rush?" Nancy enquired.

"Oh," she exclaimed. "I'm sorry, but they just wouldn't leave, and now I have only an hour or so to get ready! Is the bed made up?"

Nancy's blonde curls bobbed with her nod of assent. "Betty told Lily before dinner to make it up. I put out fresh linen myself."

"Good." She pressed her sister's hand. "Thank you! My goodness, what he would think, to catch us out twice together! Where's Bett?"

"I don't know." Nancy turned to look up the hallway. "She was putting away Papa's linen the last I saw."

"Well, I can't wait for that. Fetch me if he comes before I'm done, won't you?" She had to do her washing in the kitchen, as her hair was too long for the basin in her room, and there wasn't time to draw a bath.

"You know I will." Nancy continued on her way downstairs.

Patty fetched three towels and on her way outside remembered that she hadn't made up another rinse, so made a detour to her distillery for her scissors to cut some rosemary. She pulled the pins from her hair, but left the rose, intending to give it to Jack, took up her willow basket, and hurried outdoors again. She had just begun her examination of the bush when she heard a voice behind her.

"Good afternoon!"

She turned towards the path beside the kitchen and saw Thomas striding toward her in a white linen coat. She put down her basket and ran over to him, her hair flowing behind her like a veil.

"Thomas!" There was no one about, so she raised her face for a kiss. "I didn't expect you till this evening."

"I trust I am welcome nonetheless," he smiled and bent to kiss her briefly. When he straightened again, he touched the red rose secured by her ear. "This is lovely," he murmured. "Is it from your garden?" His eyes scanned the distance to the flower garden, whose rose bushes were yielding up their last offerings.

She took his hand in hers and began to walk back to her rosemary bush.

"No," she said companionably, "Landon Carter and Rueben Lee were here for dinner and brought it. It's from the garden at Stratford." She picked up her scissors and began on the sprigs before her. Thomas took the basket and held it for her.

"Yes," he said abstractedly, "I saw them on my way up."

She put the first sprig in the basket and looked up at him. Something in his voice puzzled her, and she saw his quick flush.

"Thomas? What's amiss?" She laid her hand on his as he held her willow basket. His expression was one of consternation, and she feared that some disaster had befallen him.

He cleared his throat. "They come frequently, it seems. I would venture to say more than I, living closer as they do." He would not look at her, but fiddled with the basket. Patty breathed a sigh of relief.

"Is that all? Heavens, I thought you had come to some grief." She went back to her culling. "They spend about as much time here as anyone else. They mean no harm." She put another sprig in the basket.

"But you haven't sent them packing, either. . ." His voice trailed off suggestively, and she turned back to him.

"What do you mean? Why should I do so? They have committed no offenses against hospitality or friendship." She looked up at him, bewildered, as the breeze lifted a lock of his coppery hair. Why should two such harmless friends as Messrs Carter and Lee upset him so? They had no claim on her affections beyond that of friendship. Surely he knew that?

But it was plain by his face that he did not, for he looked quite unhappy. There was a line etched suddenly between his brows that had not been there a moment before and he looked pale, in spite of the close warmth of the day. He laid the basket on the bush and took her forearms in his hands.

"Patty. . .sweet, I wish you would." He was struggling for a calm demeanor. "You say you love me, and it is highly contradictory to that to still have queues of beaux hanging about the place. By your letter, I was given to think that you missed me, and yet I come to find the house filled with errant lovers. I would have thought you'd have gotten rid of them ere this."

She stepped back from him in astonishment. "But I can't!" Her whole being revolted at the thought of being deliberately rude to a guest. She went on quickly, her mind in a whirl, trying to fathom why he should ask such an impossible thing of her. "I *do* love you my darling, you know that! But I cannot simply brush off these men haughtily! They are old family friends, and we must meet with and treat with them in society ever after. How would it look if I sent them packing willy-nilly with no thought for their pride or families? I have not seen them as often as before, and accept many fewer gifts, and those only of a very neutral nature! I thought to leave your very presence and the talk about to let it be known that I am no longer to be beaued about so. Thomas! Why, if even Mr. Skelton should appear I would be as kind to him, though I love you!"

The rose fell from her hair onto the path, and he bent to pick it up. He gave it to her silently and straightened to his full height. She gazed at him, beseeching him to understand, and felt a cold fear at his expression: it was icy and closed, more terrible than other men's angry rages, for it left no room for feeling. In his eyes there was no mercy. There was no sympathy that could touch him. He had removed himself from her. If she could have taken back the words, she would have, but he gave her no time to speak.

"Were he to appear," he replied coldly, "you would have no business loving me, and I no business here—as perhaps I do not—" he turned on his heel and walked away, and she saw her world shattering about her.

Helplessly, she dropped the rose and buried her face in her hands, weeping, not for sympathy, but because she had lost the one person in all the world whose love mattered most. She could not live without him and she had lost him. Thomas, my darling, I meant you no offense! Ah! She was alone as she had never been before, for he lived still and she was forsaken. She had driven him by not seeing his possessiveness of her, not understanding what she should have about Rebecca Burwell.

His strong arms were about her then, and she buried her wet face in his coat, sobbing and trembling. Her hair stuck to her face, spilled about them, and he smoothed it away. She felt his cheek against her head, and she was rocked in his arms like a child. "You should know, you should know—" she hiccoughed and went on—"that I love you and how I love you, and that there will never, and could never, be anyone else! How can you think it, Thomas? I love only you!" She could not go on and cried, not caring who on the plantation saw.

"I'm sorry," he cried, and his voice had the rough edge of emotion. "I'm sorry, my darling, my Patty, don't cry! I'm sorry! It's just I love you so much, and the thought of that pair of dolts being where I should—I'm sorry! Patty—" He lifted her face, but she would not look at him, for she was never able to cry prettily and knew she looked terrible. "*Please,* look at me!" his voice was husky and agonized, and she raised her wet eyes reluctantly.

His hazel eyes were full of tears. She stared at him wordlessly while he put his hands on either side of her face. "The moment I saw you, I swore you would be mine. I love you Patty, more than any person I have ever known. I would do anything for your sake. I swear to you that this will never happen again!" She nodded mutely, shuddering with relief that she had so narrowly avoided such a terrible tragedy, and his arms came about her tightly. She laid her head against the smooth linen of his coat.

"Come," he said after a while, and he let go of her to gather up her things, leaving the troublesome rose where it had fallen. "You need to sit and rest yourself; you are shaking. Come." He led her by the arm to the door of her stillroom, and she let herself be deposited on the chaise longue by the wall.

He brought her a cool wet cloth and a beaker of water, there being no other vessels to drink from. She sat up and took the water.

"Thank you," she murmured, and gave herself to his care while he wiped her face with the cloth. When she had drunk the water she gazed at his face at a level with her own, ruefully, and pushed back her long hair. "I must look a sight," she mumbled.

He put aside the beaker. "Nay, sweetheart. Beauty may not be destroyed by such a tempest." He took her hands, caressed the backs of them with his thumbs and forefingers, then looked up at her again.

"Patty, we can have no more of this. We both have known our course since Williamsburg, but from whatever hesitations, have declined to set it." His eyes held hers and his face swam before her, the only point of light in the dimness, for she was still not collected. "We have intimated and taken for granted our destination, but obviously the time has come to mark it clearly. So, I want to ask you properly—" There was a pause and she caught her breath, "Martha Wayles, I here do humbly petition that you would do me the honor of being my wife."

She felt her heart thumping in her chest and swore he could hear it also. It was as though she had waited for those words her whole life. She swallowed against the thrill that went down her spine and stared at him with wide eyes that were brown in the darkness of the room. She opened her mouth and sealed a destiny long ago foreset as she spoke the correct words: "Yes, Mr. Jefferson. I will."

She saw in his eyes the same peculiar feeling that had washed over her.

"Well," he said softly, not breaking the spell, and moved his hand to caress her face. "So it is done." He leaned forward and kissed her, binding them both to their pledge.

He sat back on his heels, then rose, holding out his hands to her. "Come, we should not stay here," he said of the intimate space, and she stood with care, following him out into the sunshine.

It was a different garden she looked upon and a different kitchen path they trod back to the main house, for it belonged not to her any longer. With a simple exchange, she was no longer the mistress of this place, but acting so. Her place now lay far away to the west, unseen but not entirely unknown. She knew it as it was intended to be; she knew the orchards and the infant garden, the deer park and the grove full of statuary; she knew the rolling vistas of his childhood and the wild turkey that roamed his woods. With her few words, she had pledged herself not only to Thomas, but to all that magical, genius-touched world he was creating upon his mountaintop.

Her father returned from Henrico the next day, and in the morning after she had a visit from the overseer in her office. He wished more hands at the upcoming harvest and wanted to make use of her dairy maids. While she agreed that harvest was certainly a time for all hands to be in the field, she had no liking for his timing, for they were in the midst of soaking indigo from sugar paper and she was full of the dye, having put her hand in with a cloth to test the strength. It was a common process, for the dye was readily leached and required no mordant to be used again.

She spoke to him rather sharply. "Mr. Raiford, if you please, I am quite engaged at the moment. If you could come back to my office in an hour's time, I should be pleased to accommodate you."

He reddened and looked uncomfortable, not used to dealing with kitchens or sharp-tongued lady manageresses. There was no love lost between them, for he had made it plain he thought she was stepping out of her place to run things in her father's stead. But, sweet mercy, how did he think houses were managed? They hardly ran themselves, and Papa had no one else but her. He could never ask Betty. That would set every tongue in three counties to wagging.

"Might I speak with your father about it, ma'am? I need them today—"

She held her temper with difficulty, betraying her agitation in not the smallest wise. She put her hand on the table and spoke to him in her cool, directing voice, that which she used with slow-minded servants. "Mr. Raiford, I am sure that Mr. Wayles would say no differently than I in this matter. I am likewise certain that he is at this moment engaged in legal work, for he spoke to me his intention to be so engaged not an hour since. However, if your needs are so urgent that they cannot wait until I have seen to this, then I will put off my work this instant and go to him. Does that suit you?"

Dislike shone in his eyes briefly as he stood across the room. "It would, Mrs. Skelton, if you please, ma'am," he managed.

"It does not please me," she muttered, too low for him to hear, and swept past him out of the kitchen. She was still fuming when she got to the house and went into the office without knocking.

"Papa. Mr. Raiford wishes an audience, and I told him I'd see if you were bus—" Thomas sat with her father at the desk, and by Papa's expression she could guess their subject of discourse. Warm color fanned up in her face, and she was ashamed of her apron and dye-stained hands, all her ire at the overseer forgotten. "Oh, I beg pardon." she murmured. "I'll tell him you're unavailable." She took a step backward. They rose.

"Nonsense, my dear," her father said. "Come in." He looked at Thomas. "We were just concluded, were we not, Mr. Jefferson?"

"Aye." Thomas smiled at her and she came over, her hands hidden in the pockets of her skirt. He saw the smudge of dye on her forearm, and across her cheek. She looked at the two of them and blushed again.

"I've been informed," Wayles said cheerily, coming from around the desk, "that I'm to lose you again."

"Yes, Papa." She looked at Thomas, and he reached out for her hand, which she gave him, blue as it was.

"Well, I couldn't wish for a better match," Wayles said. He came and kissed her forehead.

"Thank you, Papa." She bowed her head.

Wayles clapped his hands together. "Now, since I have business wanting attention, I will leave you both. Where is Raiford, my dear, that I might speak to him?"

"In my office," Patty said.

"Good." He made them a little bow and strode away with a springy step.

"I've just gotten indigo all over you," she remarked to Thomas, looking at his hand. He examined it also.

"So you have. Well, it's not a blood pact," he teased, "but I suppose it will suffice." He turned to her, smoothing the blue stain on her cheek. "We shall have to consider a day, you know."

"Tomorrow!" she cried, and he laughed. "Tibby would be rather put out at that, stealing her fire."

"I know," she said fondly.

"Seriously, my dear," he told her, "we should pick a time with the greatest leisure following," he lowered his voice, "because I intend to spend the entire time discovering all about you."

"Oh?" It was difficult to maintain a light tone, with the close intensity of his eyes.

"Aye," he said softly. "Every facet. And at the end, I shall know you better than myself."

"Hmm." She was smiling her secret smile. "That's a tall order."

He laughed, undone by this. "Patty, what a wanton you are!"

"I?" she protested. "I only follow your lead, sir!"

"Nay, nay. You lead better than any general, and I have no will but to follow." He searched the contours of her face with a loving glance, from the widow's peak to the barely clefted chin. "But I follow gladly. No tempest can sway me, no battle discourage. So I'm afraid we're comrades in arms until the end."

"Beyond that," she promised gaily, tossing her head a little.

"And what is there beyond the end?" he asked, amused.

"Only the endless summer country where heroes drink the wine of their past glories, and parted lovers are forever in their first youth." The echoed images from Ossian rang in the stillness of the room.

"Then so shall we also be," he murmured. "My woaden one." He took up her hands and held them before him and she laughed.

"I shan't get it off for a week," she cried, "and now neither shall you."

He shook his head. "Such a fate, such a fate. But I could not think of a better."

15

The Chosen One

The Forest, Williamsburg

Lisbet came from Bermuda Hundred for dinner. This favorite sister was superficially like Patty but without her dash. Her hair was chestnut, her eyes brown, her face speaking her Welsh forebears in its roundness, and where Patty had mischief, Lisbet was all mildness. She was three years younger, at nineteen, but by her mien seemed older. She was not a dampe, for she smiled as often as her sisters, but she lacked their spriteliness. Her husband Francis was Patty's first cousin, and had been a student at William and Mary a year behind Thomas, and he knew him, but like Bathurst, not well.

After dinner Patty and Thomas retired to the parlor, where he took out his violin, and they played several airs from Purcell, an adagio from Boccherini, and a chorus from Spenser's *Faery Queen*. This led to the singing of several songs, the first of which was the tale of a highwayman and his ladylove:

> Come unto my bosom, my own stricken deer
> Tho' the herd have fled from thee, thy home is still here
> Here still is the smile that no cloud can be-caft and
> the heart and the hand all thy own to the laft.
>
> Oh! what was love made for, if 'tis not the same
> Through joy and through torment, through glory & shame
> I knew not, I ask'd not, if guilt's in that heart,
> I but know that I love thee, whatever thou art.

They played several more in this vein, from Rowe, from Spencer, and from Clark, before she stopped and smiled up at him with mischief in her eyes.

"What now?" He asked, warily.

"I have one you might like," She said, and turned her music book upside down and backwards and began searching the pages in reverse. At length she came to a song and began to play. The unmistakable notes of a Scottish tune came forth, even with the harpsichord's distracting echoes, and he laughed as she sang:

> As soon as I got married,
> a happy man to be,
> My wife turned out a sorry jade
> we never could agree,
> for what I thought my greatest blifs
> is grief without compare and
> a' the cause of my complaint she's mine
> forever-mair
> for she's aye plague plaguing and she's
> aye plaguing me
> she's aye plague plaguing and she never
> lets me be.

Before dark they all—Patty, her sisters, Thomas, and Jack—went out for a walk in the woods. Jack and Lisbet ran ahead, gathering up huge armfuls of seed-sprung grasses to tender home; Nancy and Tibb walked together hand in hand, their blonde heads of a height and a fetching sight in their light gowns and India shawls. Thomas caught her hand to linger for a moment near the primroses, where they had lately played Virbius and Diana; and while there he took out his penknife and inscribed their initials in the tree with two intertwining circles and the year between.

On the way back to the house, Patty took up Jack's collection of weeds because he was complaining of tiredness, so Thomas offered to carry him, which the boy accepted. She was glad that he had so quickly won Jack's trust, and was touched when he carried him upstairs and laid him in his little bed. He would soon be guardian for this child, and she hoped for all their sakes that they would come to love one another. It would be unbearable if they resented the others there had been before or would inevitably be after them. She had no wish for Jack to remain solitary, but neither could she erase the fact that Bathurst was his father. And she knew from hard experience how the difference felt. That she would never wish on Jack.

She and Lisbet tidied up their toilet together after Thomas retired. As she shook the hay from her petticoats, Lisbet said with a candid glance, "I should tell you, Patty, that James Leach and Nicholas Cary were here earlier."

She looked up through the mirror. "When?"

"While you were playing with Mr. Jefferson." She threw down her petticoats over her hoop and picked up the skirt of her gown from the bed.

Patty put away her comb. "I never heard them. Why weren't they announced?"

Lisbet was struggling with her arms over her head, pulling the yards of skirt about so that it fastened at the sides. "They left," she said, muffled in cloth. "John showed 'em to the dining room, they sat there for a while, and left. I wouldn't have known except I went to the back parlor to fetch my sewing and saw them departing. You two were singing something, so I'm not surprised you didn't hear. Oh," she gave a little sigh of frustration, because her skirt had caught on the open top edge of her loosened stays. "Would you untangle me?" she begged. "This is wretched." She stood with the skirt about her armpits, unable to move. Patty laughed. "Poor little Mama," she said, jumping up from her chair. "Here, let me help you." She went and smoothed out the gown. "Just think, in a few months you shan't have to worry about this sort of thing."

"Months?" Lisbet said skeptically, with a hand on her thickening waist. "I was never so far out with Dick this soon."

"They say that's how it runs," she remarked, then ventured, "I hope soon to find out for myself if it's so." She fastened her sister's skirt, and Lisbet turned around with a glad cry.

"Oh my dear, I'm so pleased for you!"

"Shh. They'll hear you in Williamsburg," Patty giggled.

"What's the secret? Pa hasn't said no—"

Patty waved her hand. "Oh nothing like that. I just want to savor it a while before the crush. You know."

Lisbet squeezed her hand. "Yes. Come then, let's go down or Pa'll come looking for us, crying for his dessert."

They went down the stairs arm in arm, like the old days, and Patty was glad she had told her. Lisbet was fine for the sharing of secrets, for she was close as a grave.

They ate sponge cake and preserved gooseberries and laughed over their father's renditions of neighbors at pantomime. They always had a good time when Lisbet came home, and with Thomas next to her on the long sofa, she felt her circle was at last complete.

In October the governor, Norbornne Berkeley, Baron de Botetort, died, and was laid out in state in the Palace. At the funeral service at Bruton church, Patty sat together with Thomas and Fanny Page while John, as head of his family, spoke extolling the merits of that genial man. She found it difficult to believe that so much time had gone by in their lives. Only yesterday they had all been romping together at Shirley, and now John was the representative of his vast and influential clan. Gone in such a solemn moment was the giddy young man who doused lamps at the college with Thomas. He bore in his slender frame all the dignity of generations, in his face all the cares of his family, and in his words all the religiosity and profound compassion of his soul. She wept, and was grateful that it could never be known that it was not for the governor.

He gave her another reason to weep that evening. At Archibald Cary's open house afterward, he took her arm as she was about to go upstairs behind Fanny.

"I would speak with you," he said. His brown eyes were grave, and they quailed her. She could only nod dumbly as he steered her away to the corner bench beneath the stairs.

"Please sit." Bewildered, she sat as he bade her, settling the black woolen skirts of her mourning gown about her, furtively glancing beyond his coat for Thomas. But he, thinking her to be engaged upstairs for some moments, had disappeared.

She looked up. "Mr. Page," she managed through her dry throat. Thomas's absence suddenly took on a more sinister meaning. Her hands clenched on the gown. *Oh, God, if he had told—*

"I would speak with you, Mrs. Skelton, concerning our friend, if I may be so impertinent. I have received many letters from him that cause me great concern." He paused.

"And which friend would that be, sir?"

"Don't be coy," he said shortly. She wished he would sit, or allow her to stand. She felt like a naughty child being delivered a lecture. He went on: "I would have you know that I love him very much, and the turnings of his mind or wrenchings of his heart mean no less to me than to you—" She began to sense that this was but a preamble—"or so I should like to hope. I know this is neither the proper time nor place, but having received no word from you yourself on that head, I am uneasy as to whether certain measures about to be undertaken are prudent."

Thomas must have told him their news.

"You must recall," John was saying, his face harsh amid its surrounding black, "the situation concerning my wife's cousin." She nodded, about to speak, and he held up a hand. "I will say nothing against that lady, here now or at any other time, but to admit that he was afterward as unhappy as I have ever seen him." He looked at his shoes a moment. "I cannot profess to know the ways of every woman's heart—" his eyes met hers, piercingly, and he dropped his voice; "I had once entertained the hope of knowing yours—" She felt the room sway around her. "—But that is all so much dross now." He raised his voice once again to a conversational tone. "But I would know yours regarding him, if only that I may advise him truly and with a clear conscience. You must understand, Madame, that I would not be the instigator of another such shipwreck of my friend's hopes." His voice cracked, and through her own misery, she saw John's real anguish. "Once was bad enough! I blame myself to this day for my part in it, for not issuing him a sterner warning of danger, or a truer chart of the sea. So tell me, if you please, whether or not you love him as he so plainly does you?"

The question, amid all her anxiety, distress, and ambivalence, was undoing. In public or not, she burst into tears before him, laying her head in her hand.

He groaned and sat beside her, shoving his handkerchief into her hand, shielding her from the view of the room. "Patty, I'm sorry," he whispered wretchedly. "I had to know."

She looked up at him through her blur of tears. "Know? Know! John Page, how dare you? Know? Have you heard nothing I've told Fanny; are you blind? Have you no thought for what I've suffered, and how glad I am that he loves me? Know? It would be obvious to a blind man!" She was angry now, to have been compared with Rebecca Burwell. "That you should think—" she spluttered, aghast. "And the ill breeding to throw up the other to me when it's you who—" His face was a knot of pain, and she could not hurt him further, no matter the humiliation she had suffered at his hands. She gave a sob. "I love him with all my heart!" She struggled up from the seat, though he put his hand on her arm. "Let me go," she whispered fiercely, and tore herself from his grasp.

Upstairs, Fanny turned white when she came in tear-stained and sobbing, and hurried over to her.

"Patty darling, whatever's the matter? What's the matter, are you ill, what's happened? My dear! Oh, come here and sit with me," Fanny put her arms around her. The love, amid the irony, was unbearable. She could never tell Fanny, and she did so desperately want to.

"Please," she sobbed, "I can't! It's— Oh, I can't! Please, I think I shall be sick—"

The next day John wrote her a sealed letter of apology, delivered by his body servant. She put it on the fire.

16

Deliverance

Williamsburg

Her birthday was two days later. She and Thomas were due for the theater that evening, but he stopped by on his break for dinner to deliver to her a rosewood box tied with a ribbon. "Happy Birthday," he said.

She looked up at him in excitement. "May I open it?"

He smiled, rocking a little on his toes. "Please do." They went into the parlor where the light was better and sat down before the fire. She opened the box, which was lined in velvet, and found a silver and garnet necklace resting inside. She uttered a cry of delight, her face suffusing pink. "It's beautiful!"

"It belonged to my grandmother Randolph," he said, as she took out the delicately filigreed piece, studded and dangling with its dependent purple-red stones. "Grandfather saw it in the collection of an Indian trader and bargained dear for it. It's over an hundred years old and was made as a wedding piece, but the bride died shortly afterward, and its owner couldn't bear to have it about, so he sold it. Somehow, the trader came by it—plundered, I suspect—but it took my grandfather's fancy for his wife. She gave it to my mother on her wedding, and now—" He took the ends of the necklace and fastened them about her neck as he spoke. "—I give it to you. My mother bade me tell you how it was come by, for she has cherished it these many years, and especially since the fire." He kissed her forehead and dropped his hands to her shoulders. "It's beautiful," he said, admiring the rich stones against the tone of her skin. "As beautiful as you are."

"Thomas," she cried, overcome, flinging her arms about him. "Oh, I love you!"

"So I am to tell my mother it's appreciated?" he enquired, smiling at her.

She laughed. "Yes! Most appreciated. Tell her that I shall cherish it and later give it to a child of ours." Her eyes were dark, all their fire gone a quiet brown.

"Ah," he caressed her face. "That's a sweet sentiment."

She wore it that evening with the blue gown and cherry petticoat he had first seen her in.

Francis and Lisbet were among the household in Nicholson Street that fall. He was a small man, hardly taller than his wife, brunet of coloring, bearing the same heart-shaped face as Patty, so common to the Eppeses. They all went to the races together, the sisters, Thomas, Francis, and Rob Skipwith, who had brought his brother Henry along. Francis lost twenty-three shillings and laughed about it, calling spectacle of wind-driven horseflesh a value for the price. He and Thomas played chess in the evenings against her father and Rob, and won equally cheerfully. He was, like Lisbet, of such a temperament that little could sway him from his basic kindness.

As before, Patty and Thomas spent their evenings and the weekend together. For the two weeks she was in town they were constant companions. They went to dances and suppers, musicales and the theater. They took long walks on Sunday afternoons in the tranquil woods about the town. They wandered far afield on botanical expeditions, sometimes with Jack, but oftener alone. One Sunday they borrowed a rowboat and went as far as Jamestown. Past them on the grassy banks of the placid James ran barges from upriver, taking their cargoes of tobacco, hogsheads, wheat, and cotton to waiting ships at Hampton and Newport News in the lower end of the broad Chesapeake. Thomas lay with his head pillowed in Patty's lap as she sat patiently weaving a long rope of dying grass, carefully piercing each piece with a fingernail before conjoining it to the next.

Presently she grew bored with this game, and looked down at Thomas as he lay scowling into the distance. She took up a piece of grass and tickled the crease in his brow.

"Such a frown," she chided. "Whatever could be its cause, I wonder?"

He smiled a little and took the leaf from her fingers.

"Nothing worthy of the company," he said. He sat up beside her, facing inland from the river, and looked over her face and hair with an expression whose meaning by now she knew well. He touched a curl of her hair that had come loose and blew about in the breeze.

"Let us always take the air in autumn," he murmured. He was not a hand's space from her.

"Why is that?" She asked breathlessly.

He kept his voice low, hardly above a whisper, for these were words for her alone, not the barques on the river, nor the birds in the field.

"Because in autumn all of nature contrives to match your splendor, and fails." Her answer was a throaty murmur, and he slipped his hand down so that it rested just below her ear, along the line of her jaw. Her pulse beat strongly against his palm. A curlew cried overhead, and it was the last thing she heard. He kissed her and she yielded as she always did, coming into the circle of his arms. There was nothing and no one in this place to gainsay them, and she lost herself in the fire he kindled between them.

To those upon the passing barges, who might have chanced to view them, it was a common scene, not remarkable, certainly not untoward. The sloping knoll above Jamestown was a favorite spot for a quiet idyll. They might have been any young man and his sweetheart, for rank or race did not tell from a distance. Such complete anonymity was the sought-after prize of the place. Therein lay the danger.

Some time later, stretched out in the grass, he raised himself from her, and she saw the hard decision brewing in his green eyes. They had come to the critical point. She knew the path that lay ahead and was happy to show him the way, as she knew it, but she saw that as great as his desire was, he yet owned some fear, if not moral qualms. But she loved him; he loved her; they were soon enough to be married; they would not be the first in Virginia to adjourn to a hasty wedding, if needs be; it was not the right time for that, in any case. So they had no reason to stop save his fear. And she could conquer that.

He smoothed over the lace of her neck linen that had come loose in the fray, hardly daring to breathe.

"Patty."

"Aye," it was an affirmation, not a question. "Aye, my dear. It's all right." Her sleeve lace fell back as she raised her arms about his neck. Insidious as ivy, she moved but a little, yet was suddenly beneath him, where every curve and hollow could be felt with an agonizing sweetness. He would not refuse her now. Nor did she want him to. *Oh, kiss me, dear. Yes. Yes.*

He bent and kissed her once, softly, and was about to do so again, when of a sudden he tore himself from her and jumped back. "Good God!" he exclaimed, sitting up.

Patty sprang up also, all the color drained from her rosy face in alarm. "What's the matter?"

"It's only a barge man," he said in relief, his hand against his heart, which beat visibly, "having a lark on us." He looked at her. "Are you all right?"

She giggled now. She had not heard the horn. But shock had taken them away from danger.

"Yes." She laid her hand on his cheek. "You look ashen."

"Well, it was a bit of a surprise," he said ruefully.

"Yes," she agreed wickedly, with a glance, "a rude one. And providential. Thomas—" The enormity of it struck her, and her voice emerged shaken, "how can we endure thus another nine months?" Tibb and Robert were to be married in June, so they had planned a wedding for July, leaving them that month and most of August, barring a few days, and September together.

"I don't know," he told her frankly. "But obviously providence has designed that we should in some wise, by our own efforts or not." He sat on his knees, facing her again.

"Should we then trust in providence to keep us from our folly," she asked with some irony, "letting our own natures dictate our actions? I think not. I, for one, do not trust providence that far. No, we must devise us a plan whereby we may satisfy both virtue and soul's requirements enough to live in peace."

"That is the order of mankind," he said, smiling.

"You mock me," she pouted playfully.

He shook his head. "Not at all, madame. Find the answer there and you have the deliverance of the ages. 'Tis admirable. I wish I'd thought of it myself."

"Thomas," she chided.

He lifted up her hands. "Come on. We should get the boat back before it turns dark. The nights grow longer by the day."

She groaned, "Oh, that was really very bad. You and Papa. . . ." She rose, shaking out her skirts.

"I like your father's puns," he protested as they walked down to the shore. "Mind your step here," he cautioned, holding her hand carefully over a slippery patch of stones.

"Yes," she agreed. "But you don't live with them. He's incorrigible."

"Like his daughter," he said with a backward glance, as they made their way to the boat.

"What shall our plan be?" she asked, with her forearms on her knees when they began their journey up the James. His reply was gruff. "I haven't a notion."

Perhaps she had offended him, offering no resistance, nay encouraging him, leading him. He would think her fast now.

"I'm sorry," she mumbled. "I didn't mean to be forward."

"What?" He looked at her, away from the glittering water in the middle distance. "How were you so?"

"My. . .enquiry," she explained lamely, with a blush. He reached across and took her hand briefly. "Oh no," he said, gently. "Is that what you thought? Then 'tis me should apologize. No sweet, it was not a rebuke." He shook his head. "I honestly have no idea, never having had this problem before, and there's no one I would ask."

There was one name that came to mind, though not without some bitterness. "What about Mr. Page?" She would like to see the look on John's face if Thomas asked him how to keep one's continence, especially since he would know that she was the subject! But that was unkind. He had never really promised her anything, nor led her to expect more.

He paused to consider, rowing awhile. . . "No," he said at last. "I would do but for the fact that we differ in one regard: Page is deeply religious, and I don't believe such notions as ungovernable passion have ever entered his head, at least not in this instance. Don't mistake me: He and Mrs. Page are quite well attached, so far as I can see, but he never has intimated a dilemma such as this."

I would not have you know the truth of that, my dear, she thought. "My father would be an excellent man for such advice," she began, and he shouted with laughter. "No," she insisted, "let me finish: he is very forthright and sensible, and by his tales of his youth he was, shall we say, less rigorous than a divinity student in his demeanor. But our relationship rules that out. . . Besides," she smiled a little, "he owns a copy of *Les Engarements de Julie.*" This was a rather blue novel of the Viscomte D'Estraing's that had come out in 1756.

"*Does* he?" How he could not have suspected as much of her father ere this, she did not know, for there were gossips aplenty abroad. Thomas's face was thoughtful. He leaned forward now to pull the oars, and when he straightened again he asked, "Have you read it?"

She colored. "Well, yes, now and then." She blushed farther. "It's really not as bad as it's made out to be. No worse than *Moll Flanders* or *Tom Jones.*" She paused until he came forward again. "Or certain passages of Sterne's." She traced the line of his nose with a fingertip, her eyes dark and luminous. He did not miss the reference. Slawkenbergius's treatise on the length and qualities of noses was famous innuendo.

"You do have a very interesting reading list," he murmured, and she laughed. This entire discussion did nothing to illuminate a plan, in fact it further obscured it, but the heady autumn day was too fine to care for such matters. Time would be enough when he was away again at Monticello, or some other necessity-driven place.

They came back to the chaise all too soon but it was providential, for the wind came up howling around them, harrying them on their journey back to town. Even with the lap robe it was cold, and by the time they were arrived Patty's teeth were chattering.

"Oh let's hurry!" she cried, flying up the step into the house. "There's a fire, I can smell it." He ordered the chaise away, and followed her. In the hall she asked for coffee, then turned to him, dancing-eyed and red-cheeked. "That was fun!"

He smiled on her enthusiasm. "Even with the cold?"

"Oh but, sir," she said archly, "getting warm again is half the fun." He glanced into the parlor doorway to be certain they were not overheard, and taking her hand, kissed the palm.

"There's a start," he said, watching the orange flecks come alight in her eyes.

"Who's there?" Francis said from the next room, and came round the door. He nodded. "Oh I see, back so soon? It's only first dark." He smiled as he spoke, a willing conspirator in their Sunday escapade. He had secured the loan of the boat.

"It was cold," Thomas said, taking her arm.

"Yes, I can see that," Francis murmured, and went back to his chess game with Rob.

Henry and Nancy were reading *The Pilgrim's Progress,* and Tibb sat winding yarn with Lisbet on the settle before the fire. Richard, the Eppes' baby, and Jack were long since abed, and Papa was carving a new reed for his recorder with a pen knife. He looked up when they came in, over the tops of his steel-rimmed spectacles.

"Ah, the young people." He pushed up the glasses with the butt of the knife. "How was the day?"

"Delightful," she said, going to warm her hands at the fire. "It got windy on the way back, tho', and nearly put us in the river. But Mr. Jefferson was a good pilot." She smiled over her shoulder at him.

"She's being kind," he said. "Rowing upstream against a strong north wind took a bit of doing." He rubbed his shoulder briefly.

Wayles laughed sympathetically. "Well, it's good to see you're as able at steering through troubled waters *de facto* as you are at the bar." He said to Patty, "You should have seen your young gallant here in court on the Friday. He was magnificent, even against his old tutor."

Thomas made him a bow. "Thank you, sir. That's the highest of compliments."

"Yes," Wayles said, affixing the reed in his instrument and screwing it back together. He glanced over at Robert and said loudly, "I hope one day to be so defeated."

"I'll do my best, sir," Rob called back gaily. He moved his king against Francis's invading forces. It was of little avail. In a sweep, Francis captured the queen and won the day.

Robert rose. "I stand defeated, sir," he acceded. "Well done."

"Another?" Francis was gathering up pieces.

"Nay." He held up a hand. "Two futile charges at the ramparts are enough for one day. I'm going to retire to the ladies and unskein yarn."

"I'll stand in," Wayles said. "At my age to charge the ramparts at all, futile or no, is an achievement." He put down his recorder on the table. "White or black, Frank?"

Francis rubbed his hands together in Machiavellian fashion, and said, "Black!"

Rob came over to where Patty and Thomas were sitting by the fire. He let go of her hand, and she leant to stir the fire with a poker. "My condolences," he said. "Francis appears unvanquishable."

"Thanks," Rob said dryly. He scratched his forehead. "Um, Jefferson. I meant to ask you before: would you be willing to write up a list of books for me?"

Thomas nodded. "Certainly! What sorts of books?" He rose.

"Oh, a general run," Rob said, gesturing vaguely. "History, philosophy, that sort of thing." He lowered his voice. "I feel something inadequate in those respects, if you must know."

Thomas shrugged. "No harm in that, if there's a will to remedy. I'll make you one up and leave it when next I'm at The Forest."

"Oh, thank you," Rob said, shaking his hand. "Now, I was thinking twenty or twenty-five pounds for a common lot of books, but I'd be willing to pay more on some items in a fine binding."

Patty rose and went to them, and Thomas took her elbow behind the cover of her sleeve. "I see," he said. "Well, I'll get to it. I don't think I'll be there again until about the end of November. Is that acceptable to you?"

Rob nodded. "Most. Thanks, Thomas. I appreciate the trouble taken."

"Not at all," he replied. Patty stifled an exhausted yawn behind his shoulder, but he saw it and steered her over to a private corner. It was colder here than before the fire, but they could have a word or two without being overheard. The hall was out of the question; it was frigid.

He traced the violet shadows under her eyes. "You're very tired," he chided. "You should have said something."

"I am," she agreed. "It's all the air taken." She smiled up at him. "But I wouldn't send you away, not so I could *sleep*."

He shook his head. "No, just fall asleep on me. Ah, sweet, it was nice today—" He touched her cheek with the back of his fingers, "dalliance and all. I will think of a plan, but I can't when I'm with you. Any sense just runs out of my noodle." He raised her chin and kissed her forehead. "But you are tired, and I'm keeping you up, no matter—" He held up his hand against her protest, "how welcome it may be. So good night, my beloved." He bent over her hand, and pressed a kiss upon the palm. "Dream of me?" He asked, below the hearing of the nearest company.

"I always do," she said fondly.

17

ℒikenesses

The Forest

In November, Thomas wrote from Albemarle:

. . .of my dear friend mr Carr then that. let me describe to you our journey together over the mountains to the Augusta court; for surely the trail we followed may be yet no different from when my father and mr Fry tramped over it. it certainly felt so to us, belabored as we were with extra horses carrying our packs. . . . we had just arrived at the summit of the pass, the air in that place being very thin and cold, and so clear that you could see the stubble blowing on the next pass. . .when oh, what a thrilling sight we beheld! a large silver buck come out of the trees before us. his height with horns measured eleven feet, by my calculation. thankfully he stood long enough regarding us for me to remark the measure, else no one would have believed us henceforth, rather consigned our stories to those of wistful, enthusiastic anglers whose fancy outranges their good sense.

. . .it was easy to imagine ourselves in our fathers places, for so we used to do since we were at the Latin school. but how much better this reality than our childish imaginings of what it must have been like to trod ground which as yet had never been touched by the foot of a white man.

. . .there is one story of my father's which came readily to mind when we saw the buck, which i will share with you. it was when he made the survey for the source of the Rappahannock river. the commissioners from Williamsburgh had turned back at the foothills of the Blue Ridge, not finding themselves hardened to a travel across what was then trackless mountain, and took the easier route along the valley to the Shenandoah. the mountains at that time had been a tangle of blackberry, and Father came home much torn, bruised and stained. one divide was particularly difficult. they spent the better part of the day in gaining the summit of the hill, and when they had come down a little from the other side, hot, tired, exceedingly thirsty, the only water to be had was, as Thomas Lewis complained, "a puddle", wherein were rolling several large black bears. they decided not to drink. they were beset by a lack of forage several times, and one of their horses died from eating mountain laurel in its extremity of hunger. but in the end, they reached their goal, carving their initials and the year—1746—into several trees. i would hazard the marks are still there. i some times think how fine it would be to go and find them. i own a certain envy of his prowess and his daring, which has not been transmitted to me. for who could but be thrilled at the notion of being the first of one's race ever to set eyes or foot, upon a place? they were bold men, my father and his ilk, and blessed. howsoever, when they returned a few weeks later Father bore the visible marks of their hardship; he was bone-thin, ragged, dirty, with a wild beard and a bandaged arm which had just been saved from turning septic. it was not the first time i saw him so. but posterity knows the source of the Rappahannock from that early time because of his bravery and that of his compatriots. thankfully, our journey was something less hazardous. we arrived at Staunton in two and an half days, despite winds and frost, tho' we did have a brief snowfall on the return. it was not long lived, and not hardy enough to allow us to capture any of it in earnest, but for a short time we were solitary revellers in a crystalline world. . .

. . .you may expect me this sennight. i do have some business in Williamsb. to conduct, but i shall be at charles City directly. . .

At The Forest, they had celebrated Jack's birthday by outfitting him in grown-up clothes. Patty tried to contain his wriggling while she cut his hair, leaving only the back long enough for a queue. When she had tied up his hair in a length of black ribbon and showed him the effect in the mirror, his swagger was great. He stuck out his chest in its new brown Holland shirt and swaggered about in his brass-buckled shoes in imitation of the gallants, bellowing and swearing. It was difficult not to laugh, for he had his grandfather's art for mimicry, and still more difficult to chide him for swearing. Betty had no trouble, however, and threatened to cuff his ear if he continued. Jack scowled at her darkly, from under his fair brows, and made an impudent little turn on his heel.

"You won't let her, will you Mama?" he said.

"Not if you are more polite," she told him. "You must not be so with Betty. You are a great boy now, and should behave a gentleman—" She held up her hand at his grin. "Not," she cautioned, "as you were, but really. You don't see Grandpapa going on in that way, do you, or Uncle Eppes?"

"No," he said, with reluctance. He turned to his old nurse. "I'm sorry Betty, I was rude."

Betty smiled broadly, bending down and holding out her arms. "Now, they's my little man!" she cried, and accepted an embrace from him. It was a small victory, but one which Betty had been waiting for for a goodly while. He was rarely rude to Patty, but with Betty he seemed to sense an inferior quality to the relationship, no matter that she was far more likely to tell him out or box his ears than his mother, and he took advantage of it. Where he had gotten such behaviors, Patty didn't know, for he was not in daily view of poor treatment of servants.

He tried very hard in the next few weeks to live up to his new clothes, whether this was because he wanted to be thought more grown up, or because of the Christmas holidays, they didn't question. He was easier to live with, and as time passed, only occasionally flew about in his infant frenzy. He was more careful of his escapades, without being nagged at it, and overall showed fine promise.

At a Christmas party at the Byrd's Patty met Lucy Lewis, Thomas's sister, and her husband, who sported a lovely miniature of his wife. She asked him where he got it.

"A fellow in our neighborhood, Mr. John Marks," Charles Lewis said, drinking rum punch. "Came by for a few days and this was the product. I could almost be jealous."

Lucy smiled. "Now, Mr. Lewis, what will Mrs. Skelton think?"

"That we're fond, I hope," he said.

Patty asked them, "Do you think he might do one for me? I have a design in mind."

Charles shrugged. "Ye may as well write and ask 'im. He's at the Hardware."

Lucy patted her hand in its lacy mitt. "Send it by us and we'll see he gets it." They looked at one another. Lucy could guess the reason for her enquiry even if her husband could not.

Thomas came up behind them, having been detained by Robert Page.

"I espy a conspiracy," he said, giving her a glass of punch. "One should always be suspicious when the conversation draws a hush upon one's entrance. What are you two plotting?"

"A surprise," Patty said, with a sidelong glance.

"Oh dear, am I to be safe in the carriage?" He caressed her elbow behind her back, out of sight of the company, above the sleeve of her shift where it was sensitive. Payment, she supposed, for that glance.

"That depends," she murmured, but did not elaborate, drinking sherry punch instead.

"Ah, beware," Charles cautioned. "There's mischief ahead where a lady does not disclose her plan."

Thomas made him a small bow, and gave her a smiling glance. "Thank you, sir, but I am well apprised of this lady's mischiefs."

"I believe I'm being maligned," Patty said to Lucy.

"Deprecated anyway," Lucy agreed.

Thomas took her hand at that. "Come along now, Madame, before my lady sister and you have me roasting over coals." She laughed, waving an airy farewell to the Lewises as he led her from the hall.

"Now," he said, leaning over her as she stood against the doorway inside the dining room, "what was all that?" His arm was on the jamb above her head, and she was encompassed. He smelled enticingly of bergamot.

"You'll see," she said lightly.

"You are a most provoking creature," he murmured.

"So I've heard. . ."

"Please," he entreated, "no more of your wanton glances, miss, or you'll have to answer for them."

"Oh?" She felt a quick racing of pulse. "And how's that, sirrah?"

He moved his hand down, so that it was beside her ear. "I think you know that better than I. . . . Now tell me, what dread surprise have you planned out with my sister for me?"

She shook her head. "Not dread at all, sweet," she said, tracing the line of his cheek with her closed fan. "Merely agreeing upon a birthday gift for my dearest love."

"Ah. Well, I shall tread carefully on that day, then." He rose, letting his hand rest a moment on the bare part of her shoulder as he did.

"Thomas," she chided. He raised an eyebrow. "I am not the only wanton."

"I don't know what you mean," he said innocently. "Shall we take in the house?" He relieved her of her fan, carrying it for her, and tucked his hand underneath her elbow. From his coloring and demeanor she knew the wine had gone to his head rather, for he would have ordinarily not been so daring in public, but she didn't mind. It was high time that the world saw that they were seriously courting. The new year would soon be upon them, and the announcement made.

On Twelfth Night, they exchanged the gifts they had been hoarding and hinting about all week. For Jack, Thomas brought several books and toys, including a paper model Grecian barque, with which construction he promised help. For Patty, there were two pairs of embroidered gloves, a scent bottle, a rosewood needlecase embellished with frescoes, and sheet music. In return she gave him a delft-handled penknife, an engraved pewter casting bottle, a set of violin strings, and sheet music. In two instances, the music was identical, over which they had a good laugh.

"Well," Thomas said, "at least we know our tastes run in the same direction."

At the revels that evening, when the toast was made, her father made the addendum to the gathered company, "As you all know, my daughter

Tabitha is shortly to be married to Mr. Robert Skipwith, who after this next query at the bar shall no longer be my clerk. However, you may not be aware that I shall soon lose my other daughter as well: Patty has accepted Mr. Thomas Jefferson. I believe I would not be amiss in hazarding their general feeling as to a date to be the sooner the better." The company laughed, and both of them blushed, standing as they were together nearby. Wayles raised the bowl. "So here's to a long and happy life to them, and to us all!" He drank from the bowl and passed it round.

"Our year," Thomas murmured, as he passed the bowl to her. She took only a small sip of the strong punch and handed it on. "This—" She slipped her hand in his behind her skirt, "and every other, for the next forty years."

"Forty, is that all?" he asked, his tone intimate. "Madame, I intend to celebrate a centenary at least with you." He disentangled their hands from her hoop. She laughed a little, and accepted the token kiss he pressed upon her hand.

In February she wrote to John Marks in Albemarle, in care of the Lewises, to enquire the possibility of his painting a miniature. He wrote back laconically three weeks later that he would be pleased, if she would but send him passage in advance. This smelled to her of extortion, but she wanted the portrait done by April, and since he had taken so long to respond she had little choice but to accept him, as finding and courting another miniaturist at this late date would be difficult. She sent him four shillings along with a note apprising him of the urgency of the matter. He did not arrive for two and an half weeks. When she greeted him in the parlor, she was not a little dismayed. He was bony and stoop shouldered, with his most remarkable characteristic being the brownness of his visage and clothing. He was, in a word, dull. This lank-haired, spindle-shanked cracker was the artist for which she had paid, and whose work she admired so? It couldn't be!

But he sat her down immediately before the window and started sketching, making pleasant conversation of the most proper and yet diverting sort, that she forgot her ire with him entirely. Despite his unpromising appearance, he was erudite and charming, full of graceful wit and a certain elegance of speech. He had gone to William and Mary briefly, before the turn in his family's fortunes caused him to abandon that venue. He then, as he said, travelled a little, farmed a little, and poached a little before he discovered a talent for drawing that won him some small revenue, so that he managed to succeed in keeping body and soul together. He was still cash poor and took his pay in kind, which was why, he explained brazenly, he had asked her for passage fare; it was difficult to carry chickens or barrels of preserved fruit as payment to ostlers.

By the end of the afternoon, he was sufficiently pleased with his sketches that he could "go along and paint now." How did she want the colors, and did she wish the material to be of wood or ivory? It would take him longer on the ivory, as he had but a small store, but it painted better. She chose the ivory, fetched him half of his six pounds price, and sent him to spend the night with their overseer. Entertaining as he was, she would not chance an infestation of their bedding on him.

The resulting miniature was delivered to her two days before Thomas's birthday and was a grave disappointment. Oh, in its lineaments it was all very correct; it did look like her, but there was some essential quality missing from the portrait that disturbed her. The soul was lacking. She could have been any lady *en deshábille*. Yet she had no choice but to give it, and hope it would be well received. She encased it in its pewter frame, wrapped it in velvet, and furtively prayed some magic might bestow the wanting sparkle.

Thomas came to Charles City for his birthday, as he had promised, though his stay would be short, as he had to prepare for Albemarle court. He came in the middle of the day and found her and Jack in the herb garden, gathering nasturtiums for tea. She smiled up at him from under her chip hat and murmured secretively, "Happy Birthday."

He laughed. "It's not until tomorrow; or is this an April Fool?"

"No," she said, "the fool is not till tea. It's orange."

He shook his head.

Jack came up to her, holding a snail. "Here, Mama."

She waved her hand. "Oh Jack, take that away. I can't abide snails." She shuddered in disgust. "Put it in the dung heap by the shed, where it can do no harm." He looked wounded and went off with his prize toward the outbuilding, but she was watching him sharply and spoke up when he pocketed the creature, "Jack!" she cried. "I will not have that in the house, do you hear? Put it down."

"Oh, very well," he muttered resignedly, taking it out. He laid it on the compost and walked away, rubbing his hands on his trousers. He wrinkled his nose. "It's sticky," he complained.

"Well, it wouldn't have been if you'd not been holding it by a death's grip," Patty chided, laughing. "Go in to Jenny and wash your hands." She picked up her basket of flowers. "This ought to suffice." she said to him. "Let me put these in the kitchen and I'll be right with you."

They stayed up until past midnight, reading Sir Phillip Sidney. When her father retired at half-past eleven, he came and kissed her. "Not too late," he admonished, and disappeared. They were trusted utterly to be decorous, and were, even later when they lay on the floor before the fire. Sydney verse and a world of fancy was between them, and they partook of its delights innocently. The clock in the hall chimed one o'clock, and Patty looked up at it. It was after midnight. Thomas's birthday. She could give him the portrait now.

"Oh!" she exclaimed, and rose quickly. Shaking out her skirt and caraco jacket, she turned and ran upstairs, returning a moment later with a parcel of velvet.

"What's this?" he enquired, sitting up. He took the proffered package from her fingers.

"It's your birthday," she said simply. "Surely you won't torture me into waiting longer." She waved her hand. "Open it. . .please!" She sank down with him and gazed at him with expectant eyes while he untied the green ribbon from the dark velvet.

"What is it?" He held the box in his hand. It was small and of some weight. He tested it in one hand. "It's not a book," he said, grinning.

"Thomas!" she pleaded.

"All right," he conceded, and lifted the lid. He was silent for so long that she feared his scrutiny of the work.

"You don't like it," she said in disappointment.

He looked up. "Oh no," he said tenderly, "that's not it at all. My dear," he leaned forward and kissed her, "it's beautiful. I shall keep it as my dearest treasure. Thank you." He pressed her hand, and she smiled again.

"A neighbor of yours did it," she told him. "John Marks. Mrs. Lewis and I conspired upon it for several weeks. Do you recall at Christmas—"

"At Westover," he finished, shaking the portrait at her. "Lucy had just had one done. She showed it to me. I should have guessed."

"Then you really were surprised?" She clasped her hands together.

"Really," he assured her.

"I'm *so* glad!" she exclaimed. "Truth to tell, when I first saw Mr. Marks, I was quite dismayed, and then when it was delivered, I was so disappointed. But it does have a certain charm that grows on one."

He kissed her again. "You needn't explain," he said. "I love it. What more could I wish than a likeness to carry of my sweet Patty? It could be by Botticelli or a tinker, it's all the same to me. Now when I am away, I may see your sweet face in more than my memory." He touched her cheek.

"Ah," she murmured, fondly. "Then it's worth ten times its planning and fretting." She came forward and embraced him. "Happy Birthday, my darling. May this be the first of an hundred."

He smiled, remembering those words, and their occasion. "May it be," he confirmed. In the morning it was her delight that he had found she had engraved upon the back: *MW to TJ, in aeternum tuo.*

18

Jack's Accident

The Forest

In May, the Rivanna and the James rivers rose to flood levels unrivalled in an hundred years. John Wayles alone lost at Elk Hill several hundred pounds worth of cattle and sheep, the carcasses being piled, when the waters at length receded, six deep in some places. The crops were ruined and the stench was unbearable. One of his best farms was in effect made barren for the year. Shadwell fared somewhat better, though the grist mill, just begun, was carried away.

Thomas was in Williamsburg for the sessions of the House and the General Court. Patty came, but for a week, because they were in a ferment at home over Tibby's upcoming wedding late in June. While they were in town together, they went to a musicale at the Palace, whereat the newest acquisition was a fortepiano, and Patty fell in love.

It was a small instrument, no bigger than a regular harpsichord, but its internal mechanism was vastly different, the strings being hammered rather than plucked by quilled jacks. The effect was remarkable, and they had both been struck by the deep rich tones and pure clarity of the notes.

After she was home again, Thomas came out at the weekends and they made plans for their own wedding. When he was away she sewed on gowns, her own and the finishing touches on Tibb's, and began to be nervous. Early in June, he came for three days before going back up to Albemarle to settle his affairs and arrange to bring his family down the country. His visit was pleasantly uneventful. They walked, played and sang, and read poetry; he played too with Jack, and promised to teach him fishing on his next visit, forgetting the danger that could ensue from an errant fish hook. She did not disabuse him, but let be, willing to foster such companionability. Had she been able to read the future, she would never have let him go.

She had given Jack permission to play with Joe, Jenny's grandson, down at Brown's forge by the creek, first directing him to be careful of himself, but trusting that some person would oversee their play. He came home later at tea time, tired, dirty, and a little dispirited. When she enquired as to the cause of his troubles, he sighed hugely in his comical, endearing way, saying, "Oh, nothing. I've just had a long day."

He did not eat much that evening, though by rights a rare day of romping with his favorite friend gave him a tremendous appetite. He was content with a cup of gillyflower tea and corn bread, and climbed down, quietly, to go and read one of the books Thomas had given him. She felt his cheeks and throat, but he was not warm, so she let him be for a time and went about finishing the day's mending. When it was his bedtime, he had obviously recovered some of his spirit, for Betty came downstairs to complain that he was being intractable about having his hair brushed. She tried coaxing and scolding, she said, but he wouldn't let her do it.

Patty frowned a little and rubbed her brow, for the long day of close work had given her a headache. Untucking her foot, she laid aside the sewing.

"I'll see to him, Betty," she said wearily. "You go on."

"Yas'm," Betty said, with obvious relief. She had struggles enough with her own children, Patty reminded herself; she did not need Jack's tempers added to them. She went upstairs. Jack was sitting listlessly on her small sofa, kicking his feet against the bottom. She sat next to him.

"Jackie, what's wrong? Why are you giving Betty such grief over a little old thing like hair brushing? Come now." She made to gather him to her and smooth his brow, but he shrank from her with a cry.

She sat up. "What—" She really looked at him, and felt all her vitals go to water. "Oh, my God" She could not help the panicked little moan that escaped her, for high on the child's left temple, partly hidden by his hair, was a purple-black swelling the size of a goose egg. The thing she had dreaded for two and a half years had transpired. She felt cold, numb; her stomach was leaden and the room began to look grey. *I must not faint,* she told herself sternly. *I must not faint!*

She struggled up from the seat and stumbled to the door. Wrenching it open, she shouted as she had never before done in her life: "Papa, where are you? Pa!" She trembled against the door frame. Nancy came running down the hall.

"Patty, what in heaven's name's the matter?" she exclaimed.

"Fetch Papa," she said in a strangled voice. "Jack's had an accident," she finished weakly.

"Oh, dear God," Nancy went white. "He's outside. I'll go—" She flew down the stairs two at a time, and Patty closed the door.

Jack was sitting dully where she had left him. She gathered him in her arms, crying shakily now, trying to avoid the terrible swelling on his head that grew steadily larger.

"Oh, my baby," she crooned, rocking him. "My Jackie, my sweet boy. What happened to you?"

"I fell down," he said simply, lisping into baby tones. "I'm tired, Mama."

His head drooped, and she shrieked at him, "Jack!" He opened his eyes. They were dull, but the pupils not unequal or unduly enlarged. "Jack, you mustn't go to sleep baby, you mustn't– Oh, Papa, where *are* you," she cried to the door. She broke down and wept a little, hysterically, trembling and cold though the day was still warm.

He came at last, flinging open the door. She had regained some of her composure, although she was still shaking, and was taking off the child's shoes when he arrived. He put a hand on her shoulder.

"It's all right, girl," he said, to steady her. He bent down and peered into his grandson's face.

"What's the trouble with our laddie, now? Bump yourself, did you? Let Grandpapa have a look at you." He knelt beside her while she stripped Jack of his stockings. "Where does it hurt, eh, *'y machgen?*"

The boy made a gesture toward his head, and Wayles moved the blond curls aside gingerly. "Oh, I see," he said gently. "That's some bump." He turned to Patty.

"When did you notice it?"

"About ten or fifteen minutes past. Betty came down to say he wouldn't have his hair brushed. Well, I shouldn't wonder! Papa, it was the size of a goose egg when I saw it first, and now–" She waved her hand at the contusion. The skin over it was stretched and shiny now, and the dark stain was spreading. Her father caught her hand. "Hush, you'll frighten him. We must send for the surgeon. Where's John?"

"No!" All her instincts revolted at the idea of some lancet-happy surgeon having his way with Jack.

"We must," Wayles muttered quietly. "See how he is!" Indeed, Jack was hardly conscious.

"No, Papa, please, I beg you!" She entreated, but he rose and stalked to the door, bellowing through the house for his servant.

The surgeon, Mr. Harwood, was sent for, and in the meantime they got the child into bed. Various endeavors to keep him awake were marginally successful, in that he would sleep but was easily roused. He was fitful, though, and tossed against some nightmare she could only guess at. Mr. Harwood arrived and was shown up. He was a relative of their doctor, William Carter, and at the moment plainly disgruntled at having been called away from his evening's leisure.

"It must be lanced," he said pompously upon seeing the trouble.

Patty nearly fainted. "You can't!" she said hoarsely, still holding Jack's hand. "He has, he is–"

"He's a bleeder," her father said plainly. The surgeon looked discomfited.

"He bleeds upon little or no provocation." Wayles said, mistaking the blankness for ignorance. Mr. Harwood was offended.

"I know the term, sir," he replied disdainfully. "I have never dealt with a case such as this." He went over and looked at the boy's eyes. They were no longer clear. "Mmm, mmm." he muttered, shaking his head.

At length, he said abruptly, "Well, I still say do it. It may relieve some pressure on the brain. If not," he shrugged a little. "I don't give him the night in any case. That tumor is enlarging before our eyes. There's no way of knowing what has leaked into the brain case."

Patty gave a cry. Oh Jackie, Jackie, my little one! I tried so hard to protect you from this! She leant on the coverlet and wept. Tibb and Nancy came and put their arms around her.

"Give us a moment," Wayles said to the surgeon. The man obligingly stepped from the room. Her father closed the door, coming over to kneel behind her, speaking softly but firmly in her ear, "Patt, I think we should let him do it. He's right—you know it and I know it—Jack is going to die." He waited through the fresh outburst of grief, smoothing her hair. "Now, my dear," he continued, "if we can ease his sufferings somewhat—" he paused "—or hasten a merciful end, I believe it's worth it. But it's up to you. I am only his guardian. You gave him life; his last end should be your decision."

She raised her head within the circle of her family and looked at her small boy. How small he looked now, in his great bed with his cheeks gone a sickly pale grey. Her baby. She recalled his birth, and the joy they had in him, for though it had been harrowing, he was sound and beautiful. She thought of all his important days: his first tooth, his first step, his first word. He was a dear, sweet, funny, bright little man, and he was fading from her. She could feel him going. He would live with his Papa, which is what he had always said would happen if he injured himself so. She stroked his forehead, avoiding the swelling, and wiped her eyes. Take care of him, my love, she said to Batt. Take care of our boy. He's all I have of you, but if your need for him is so great, I will not gainsay you.

"Do what you will," she said to her father. He took her hand. "Are you sure, girl?" She nodded, sniffing, and passed the heel of her hand over her eyes. They laid the bed in clean towels and called in the surgeon. Because of Jack's condition, he said he didn't see much point in giving him laudanum. She and Tibb held his arms and head while Nancy and their father held his body and feet, and the cut was made. They were covered in black blood, which quickly turned fresh and red. Jack screamed and was silent, lapsing into a coma. Patty, with his blood soaking her clothes and hair, felt like a murderess.

It was impossible to staunch the flow once the barrier had been breached, and he bled steadily for twenty minutes. No amount of pressure on the wound could lessen it, and they soaked every towel in the house. At length, the child turned grey, the flood lessened, and he breathed his last. Her grief was uncontrolled. Never before a stranger had she behaved with such abandon. Even when Bathurst died she had managed to contain herself before the gathered witnesses. But something within her snapped, and she wept and keened loudly, clutching the little body of her beloved boy, his head against her breast, the terrible wound hidden from the world, but not her heart. She had killed him, her baby, her darling. She should never have allowed it to be done. His father would never forgive her this. But she had done it from love! She didn't want him to suffer! All his life, she had protected him from this lurking evil, only to hasten his end by her own admission.

At length she collapsed and was carried from the room. When she awoke she was fuzzy-headed. They must have given her laudanum, or some other drug, because she felt leaden in all her limbs and was assaulted by a coppery taste in her mouth. Tibb was dozing beside her but awoke when she stirred. She saw her sister's stained clothing, and turned over into the pillows. It was a black day.

She wrote to Thomas later, a disjointed and incoherent note, begging him to come. It was smeared and blotted, but she sent it, not having the heart to write another. It took a week to reach him, and another several days for him to arrive. In the interim, they buried the child, and received the story of his mishap from Matt Brown, who was distraught at his part in the tragedy.

"They'm was skipping stones in em creek, him an Joe and my boy," he said as he stood in her office, twisting his cap in his hands. "Davy was keeping eye on 'em. 'Fore God, Miss Patty, we dint leave 'em to 'emselves!" His cow-brown eyes besought her understanding. She patted his arm.

"I believe you, Matt," she murmured. "Just tell me what happened. I need to know."

"Yas'm." he paused. "Well, they'm was hollering an carrying on, having a good ole time, and pretty soon they was quiet, so I fetched out t' see what trouble was, and Mast' Jack was sittin' on the ground.

"'What's wrong wi' you, boy?' I ast em. 'Nuthin,' he says to me and gets up and dusts heself off. 'I slipped,' he says, and that was that. He dint say no more nor act quare 'r nuthin, so I figured he'm was all right. They'ms played til they was fetched home. I sware 'tis the truth, ma'am. I'se no cause to lie to you."

She nodded. "I know." She sighed heavily. "And we can't expect you to divine things either." She clasped her hands. "Thank you, Mr. Brown. I'm sorry I had to call you from your work for this." She gave him a ten shilling piece for his trouble. She had lost her boy by a simple fall that was commonplace in the life of every child, unremarkable. If it had been by some extraordinary feat—falling out of a tree, for instance—she could have borne the injustice better. But to die by a tumble that he himself thought nothing of was wickedly cruel fate.

When Thomas arrived she was upstairs, and she saw him coming up the long road from the river. When he was near she ran outside, and heedless of Jupiter beyond or anyone else, flung herself into his arms the moment he was off his horse. She wept afresh, relieved in the safety of his kindly embrace, and clung to him. In the last few days of waiting it had come to her, too, that they must now put off the wedding. He would not be unaware of it himself.

"I'm sorry I wasn't here," he said into her hair, "sorry I couldn't get here sooner. My dear girl," he let her go enough to lift her chin. "We should go inside." His hand slid down to hers. "Come, we can talk there."

They secluded themselves in the privacy of her father's office, and there, with the outer shutters closed against the heat of the day, she poured her heart out to him, not only about Jack, but about Bathurst as well, for the loss of her boy was inexorably bound up to that earlier grief. She sat on the floor at first, with her head in his lap, giving him the details of Jack's misadventure. By the time she came to the decision that was made, her hair was falling; so gently, as she spoke, he removed her cap and pins and set them aside, smoothing the coil of her hair into a river that touched the floor. He spoke little, encouraging only, and she was grateful for his attentive silence.

". . .I knew immediately that it was the wrong choice," she said. "I should have allowed him his slow way. He was slipping from us, anyway. He might have lived until the morning, I might have spared him the pain of that instrument. . ." She shuddered. "When he died, all I could see was Bathurst. There was the same fading then." She looked back into the past.

"He too, had come by a sudden injury and was to shortly die." She gave a little moan. "Oh, God, that day! And that I should lose the son as the father—"

"Tell me," Thomas coaxed quietly, his hand on her hair.

"It was in September. We had gone to Williamsburg for the courts. I shall not forget the day. It was Indian summer yet, and we had rented a house in Francis Street. Josiah Harris came in a chair on the run to tell me—" She closed her eyes and held her breath a moment before continuing. She had never revealed to a living soul what had transpired that afternoon. "He came to tell me that a pair of carriage horses had shied in the Jamestown road, and taken flight. Batt was crossing from the college, and didn't see them until it was too late. . . . He was reading a book! Ah!" She wept a little, and Thomas held her hand fast on his knee.

She sniffed. "He was in a very bad way. The wheels had crushed his chest and broken his leg. He didn't live above half an hour after they brought him back—he was so weak. Christopher Manlove signed the will." She sniffed again. "It's here someplace. We haven't put it through probate yet. I suppose we should." She looked up, around the room to the cabinet where her father kept his files. "There's not much to be had, but now that Jack—now that things are changed, it should be put through, for the effects will come to us, and we should have matters tidied up." She looked at him, not caring how dishevelled she appeared, and clasped his hands. "But oh, my dear, the most awful end to all this is that now we must wait for the wedding!" Her eyes flooded tears again. "When I realized *that*, it was as bad as losing Jack. . ."

He smiled at her in tender sympathy, and rose up with her to fold her into an embrace. The callused tips of his fingers brushed her cheek as he held her, rocking soothingly to and fro. His combination of strength and gentleness was calming in itself, but the warm smell of sunshine and horses and bergamot he emanated was the greatest balm she had ever known. No woods, no church, could bring her such peace as that homely combination of fragrances.

"Don't fret, my sweet," he said to her. "I will own to disappointment as great as yours in this." He moved away a little, gazing at her. "But it shall not be forever. It is only six months in a lifetime together. We can bear it. We shall bear it, you and I." He kissed her forehead. "And I will see you happy again, my Patty. I'll do my endeavor to make it so. For the nonce, you must come to me if you are sad; or if we are apart, I beg you write to me and tell me your heart, for I care for every thought that passes with you, and I swear you shall never find a more bosom friend than me. Will you?"

She smiled at him a little. "Oh, you know I will!" she cried. With Thomas at least, it was certainly true that sorrow shared was sorrow halved, and she was further evinced of his loving concern when in the morning she found a note slipped under her door that ran: "*Sed levius fit patientia, quequid corripere est nefas.*" "—But through resignation, even that grows lighter which heaven forbids us to remedy."

Whether he meant by this Jack's death or the postponement of their marriage, she was touched by his optimism and encouragement, and tucked the note away among her treasures of his correspondence.

She was surprised, however, at the receipt of a letter from his mother. It was the first notice she had been given by that lady. In a backward slanting script, indicating left-handedness, Jane Jefferson wrote:

> Madame, These are perhaps not the best of Cercumstauncis under wich to commence a Correspondance with you, but my son has letely informed me of your recent Loss. Having suffered such Slings at the hand of fate myself you will Apprisiat with what sincerity I take this time to Condole with you in this matter. May God lighten your burthens, my childe, and bring you to his peace.
>
> I am, Y'r respectful servant, ma'am,
> Jane R Jefferson.

19

Ten Shillings

The Forest

During the week, while Thomas was away in Williamsburg searching through patents in the land office, Elizabeth had her baby across the river at Bermuda Hundred. Francis sent a note in the morning when it began, saying that Betsy had asked that she come if she felt equal to it, and so Patty went. By midafternoon, young Richard had a brother, in the person of Francis Cocke Eppes, his second name in honor of Lisbet's mother. He was a small gnome of a child with dark hair and a crabbed little face. Lisbet had some trouble with milk fever, but was well enough to come over to Tibby's wedding, though she spent most of her time sitting down.

Her father would not allow Thomas his plan to stay in Williamsburg during the wedding. No matter that the house was overflowing with guests and he had the pick of several rooms in town, Wayles insisted that he should continue his usual *habitué*. Of necessity, the room was shared for the first day, but after that, when the crush of guests lessened somewhat, he had it to himself again. Nancy slept the two weeks with Patty, as Tibb and Robert had her room; and even Patty's dressing room, tiny though it was, was made use of for extra beds.

On her wedding day Tibby was a picture of beauty. The shot silver and blue accentuated her fragile blonde loveliness, and the carefully preserved bluebells she and Nancy and Patty had patiently sewn onto the gown were the very color of her eyes. She wore her hair unpowdered, as for the last three months she had been washing it in chamomile to increase its brilliancy, and hair powder would have only detracted from its glistening beauty. She carried a small nosegay and her mother's handkerchief, the same one that Lisbet had used when she married Francis, and was told by their father that she outshone even her mother on her wedding day. Tibby blushed and wept a little, thanked him, and bent her face in his coat.

"Oh, Papa," she said. "I love you!"

"Let's go then, and have you married," he said, taking her arm. "Miss Patt—"

"Yes, Papa?" Patty was adjusting the train of her grey-blue gown.

"Are you ready?"

She looked up, and into her sister's shining eyes. "For my Tibby? Oh yes! Good luck, my dear." She leaned over and gave her little sister a hug, careful not to disturb the carmine or powder they had carefully applied that morning. She went out into the upper hall before them, carrying a lighted candle in her mitted hands.

Down in the hall, where Rob waited, there was a sea of faces, but she did not miss the one whose smile reached out to her. When her part was done, she moved aside and sought him out, slipping her hand into his behind the cover of her hoop.

"The next is ours," he murmured. She did not reply, but pressed his hand as Tibb gave her pledge, and thereby became Mrs. Robert Skipwith.

Later, in July, after the rounds of visiting had been completed, Robert remembered the promise Thomas had made earlier in the year for a list of books, and so sat down while at The Forest briefly to write to remind him of this. He gave the letter to Patty, who was expecting him the next week, and she delivered it duly.

Thomas brought with him his latest completed elevation of the main house at Monticello, for Patty's perusal and commentary. He had brought rough sketches with him before, but this was the first proper rendering she had ever seen. He laid it out on the top of the card table after tea, and they sat poring over it and the plan for the cellar rooms and terraces, while he explained the position and use of each room. She was greatly relieved to find that the kitchen was not after all to be in the cellar and said as much.

"What do you mean?" he asked.

"From what you said before, I had the idea that it was to be entirely underground, and not, as you have here, coming off the slope of the hill. I envisioned fires in a concealed building, I'm afraid." She could feel herself blushing.

"I do have some common sense, Miss Patt," he teased. "Even if I don't cook my own food, I know what's required of it. Good grief, Dilcy would lay siege to me if I ever suggested putting her kitchen underground. She's wary enough of the kitchen not having a window now." Dilcy was his cook at Monticello, and her kitchen was directly beneath his one-room out-chamber, with its only source of natural light coming from the door on the south wall, as most of it was dug out from the hillside.

"What's this?" she asked, pointing at a space in the basements under the house. It was not marked.

"Nothing yet." Thomas shrugged. "Do you have something in mind?"

"Yes. . ." she said, picking up an apple and cutting a slice from it. "We shall need some place to ferment beer."

He looked at her blankly. "Beer?"

She laid down the apple. "My dear, with the growing of wheat or barley it is eminently practical to brew beer as the common drink, as you say your well is not yet established as reliable. Especially with the men working on the site. What do they drink now?"

"Cider, mostly."

"Beer would be cheaper, and more readily had." Her mind went to her household ventures in that direction here and at Elk Hill. He seemed convinced by her surety.

"Very well," he said, taking up a pencil. "Beer it is." He labelled the empty space as a beer-room, and thus her first supplication as the mistress of Monticello was made and successfully obtained.

The house as planned was a graceful combination of rooms, balanced front to back by large central chambers opening onto porticoes, with smaller rooms at either side. An unusual feature was the placement of the main bedroom downstairs, rather than having a ballroom or library as in most houses. Another missing feature was a central staircase, with its complementary upper hall. When she had enquired the reason for this, he replied, sensibly enough she thought, that another room could be gained by placing narrow stairs in the wings of the house. The library, indication enough of his future plans, was fully the size of the parlor downstairs, and could not be reached by either of the upper bedrooms.

Palladio's buildings, from which he had taken his design, had been crafted in stone, taking advantage of the local materials. The same was to be at the house at Monticello, for it was literally being made from the earth upon which it sat. Thousands of red bricks, carefully measured from those at Rosewell, had been and continued to be manufactured from the soil of the mountain. From timber cut upon its slopes came the wood for joinery and fascia. Already, adaptation to local conditions had been made, for the walls of the out-chamber were two feet thick, to provide insulation from the disparate summer and winter climes.

With his first sketches, he had told her of the lineaments of his little house, preparatory to her seeing it, for it and the dining room were the only rooms even near to finished on the place.

"Now, mind, it's not very large, but it needn't serve for long," he'd said. "Not greatly above six months, certainly not a year. It's cozy for all that, and with the kitchen below, there's space that would be ordinarily taken up with cooking. It's rather like a suite of rooms at an inn, although the bed space is not as crowded," he added, rather provocatively.

She smiled and gave him her sidelong glance. "That would depend upon other factors," she said. By the way he'd colored up, he had not missed her meaning.

Now, she glanced again at the draught of the out-chamber and recalled how she'd stood in her kitchen and inspected it with fresh eyes, for they were of a piece.

"Could I live in a space like this only," she wondered nearly every day since, "for an entire year, with Jack and maybe an infant?" Truth to tell, it was an appalling proposition, but she held out hope for the narrower estimation. They had no longer to trouble about where to put Jack, and for some time she had seriously considered proposing a nook in the kitchen for him, so her only concern was that they would have room enough to conduct the affairs of daily life without stepping on one another continuously. The plan for the dependences looked promising, and she breathed a little easier.

Before Thomas came again, Patty broached to her father the subject of Bathurst's will. He sat at his desk, and as she spoke, pushed his spectacles up on his head and tossed down his pen.

"Well, you know, Papa, we have never probated it, and I'm not certain, with the present lay of things, how much longer it would be valid. . ." She spoke only from what she had gleaned by careful, if discreet, listening to table conversations through the years.

Wayles smiled, folding his hands. "And what did you have in mind, by the present lay of things, Patt?"

She sat in the chair. "Well, Jack's death for one, and for another—" she blushed, "the wedding."

"You still have another four months before that may be accomplished," he said judiciously, eyeing her. He was teasing her and she knew it. "Where's the rush?"

"Papa," she complained. He held up a hand.

"All right," he laughed, rising. "What say we set the wheels in motion at the beginning of next month?" He went to his cabinet and withdrew the document she had last laid eyes on three years before, almost to the day. "That should give us plenty of time to have everything appraised before the wedding." He turned to her. "Have you decided a date?"

She colored again. "Not yet." She accepted the will from his hand and glanced at it, feeling a cold chill at the script. It was written in Bathurst's neat round hand, dated the day he died, but written earlier. Chris had filled in the date, and signed it, after reading it out to him for its correctness, because Bathurst was so weak. When she came to the words, "Whereas my wife Martha will be intitled—" her hand trembled. Saved in a rosewood box upstairs, she had a packet of letters in his hand, mostly beginning, "My dearest Wife." She had not read them in over two years, but the sight of his hand brought back their happy courting days, and their untimely parting. The document before her was straightforward, made out after Jack was born, as Bathurst was always travelling the roads in pursuit of his career, and meant to be enlarged upon later. She braced herself and read through it to the end:

> . . .Whereas my wife Martha will be intitled to sundry slaves at the deth of her father by virtue of a marriage settlement made betwixt him and her mother, all which slaves I give to her and her heirs forever in case my son dies under age or unmarried, but if he attains to his full age or marries, then the said slaves to be equally betwixt them, my wife and son. . . .

He had little property on his own, some deeded him in his brother Reuben's will, in Goochland and Cumberland counties, and divers personal effects, including books, which presently rested on a lower shelf by the window in this same room. Even without the list attached, she could have told the titles by heart:

> *Furguson's Astronomy; Boyer's French Dictionary, abridged; Johnson's Dictionary, abridged, 2 Vols; The Perceptor, 2 Vols; Furguson's lectures in Mechanics, etc; Milton's Paradise Lost of Newton, 2 Vols; Patter's Mathematics; MacLauren's Algebra; Ward's Algebra; Ladies' Geography, 2 Vols; Terrence Delphini; Boyer's French Grammar; Rollin's Ancient History, 10 Vols; Dryden's Virgil, 3 Vols; Cotton's Virgil; Table of the Bees, 2 Vols; Roderic Random, 2 Vols; The World, 4 Vols; Telemaque Buckingham's Works; Spectator, 8 Vols; Swift's Works, 8 Vols; Pope's Works, 10 Vols; Prayer book, French.*

The latter, the French prayer book, was on her bedside table even now, inscribed with his initials and the date, "Decr. 22 1762." Before he died, it was his request that she read to him from this the prayers for the dead. Those pages were ruined with her tears, for she had but gotten halfway through when he expired, yet she continued on to the end as one last link to the young man she had loved so dearly. She could not look upon his staring green eyes and mangled form, covered even as it was with the blanket, so she had read, in grief-broken French, the supplication for the repose of his soul. If there was a God, she had thought in her lonely days of early widowhood, surely he had heard that heartfelt prayer.

In the first week of September, she, her father, and Francis went to Charles City Courthouse and probated the will, giving, in joint, a bond for £6000 as surety. She signed her name as Mrs. Bathurst Skelton for the last time. The inventories were made shortly thereafter. Portable objects not already brought back came to The Forest, including her wedding saltcellars. The entire estate, including thirty-three slaves and ten horses, was valued at £ 1591/ 18/ 4 1/2, without the land at Elk Island.

When Thomas came after the Assembly, both Patty and her father were most anxious that they now set a date. After all, her father reasoned with a wink, the holidays were coming up, and they didn't want such an important decision to be lost in the rounds of affairs. So on the tenth of November, at long last, she and Thomas made the date for the wedding. After much bargaining, for she wanted Christmas Eve, they decided upon another symbolic day: January 1st, 1772. When he left for Monticello the next day he gave out to all the house servants every bit of monies he had on hand, so great was his elation. The servants were agog.

On the twenty-third of December, Thomas rode over to Charles City Courthouse with Francis, who, along with Dabney, was one of his bridemen, and wrote out the marriage bond. Francis and Lisbet had been at Bermuda Hundred since early in the month, as was their wont, and Patty was grateful for her sister's constant presence in the days before the wedding, although Francis was his incorrigible self. He told, that evening and long afterward, a tale on Thomas that set both her and Thomas blushing.

"We were standing in the records office, right you, and the clerk chafing his hand behind the counter, looking as if we had interrupted his jar of flip, and Thomas writes out the bond. Well, he gave it to me to look over, see," Francis continued, "and I notice he's written our Patt up as a spinster, not a widow—" he grinned at Thomas. "There's wishful thinking, boyo." Patty hid her head in a pillow while they all laughed, and did not dare look at Thomas. "So I tell him, 'I have an ammendation, Jefferson,' but does he see it? Not for worlds." Francis laughed, and Thomas shook his head as he sat next to her.

"Ah, my friend," Francis murmured, to soothe his dignity, "I told you then, and I'll say it now before all, when I wrote up ours— mine and Bet's—" his eyes strayed to Lisbet, who smiled, "I was hard put to write my own name and mucked up the damned thing twice. So you're a sight better off than me. I tried to bribe the clerk to hide the copy, but he was feeling scrupulous that day."

"You're a true-born Welshman, Frank," her father said, standing up from where he was poking at the fire.

"Eh?" Francis enquired. " How's that, Uncle?"

"Insult a man and leave him loving you." He looked over the tops of his spectacles.

Thomas stirred beside her. "I'm not insulted, sir." He bent Francis a stern glance. "I only wish he'd not made it such a matter of public notice." He looked down at her apologetically, and she pressed his hand. It was not so bad that he had wished to think of her as his alone. Batt would understand that.

Thomas's family were due to arrive on the twenty-eighth, coming together from Tuckahoe and Christmas revels with the Randolphs. On the morning they were expected, Thomas took Patty aside a moment after breakfast before the hurly-burly of the day began. In the hallway under the stairs he sat on the edge of the cherry table holding her hands and said, "As you may have guessed from things I've said, my mother is very proud. What may be taken in her for haughtiness is not always so."

Patty smiled. "Like her son. You needn't worry, dearest. I shall do my utmost to charm her into ease." She inclined her head briefly. "She wrote me a kindly note after Jack died. I had hoped," she looked up at him, and her great dark eyes were glistening, "that this indicated an acceptance."

"Did she?" he asked, surprised. "She never said anything to me on the matter. When I told her we were delaying the wedding she made no remark." His voice cracked. "She never told me that. I thought her indifferent!"

The words tore her heart. What mother could be indifferent to her child?. . . But what indeed? Mary Cocke's face rose before her. No true mother, then, no mother of her own child. "Perhaps she didn't wish to seem interfering," she murmured hopefully.

"Perhaps," he agreed. "Ah, and there is the subject of my sister Elizabeth." He paused, trying to think of words to succinctly convey the trouble. "She is. . . ."

"Simple?" she concluded gently. He stared at her. "Lucy told me as much by indirection last Christmas."

"You knew and said nothing?" He shook his head. "You are a vixen, Mistress."

"Nay, sir," she continued in the same vein. "'Twas but prudence, for where's the good of gossip and speculation? There's naught for it, to hear Lucy tell it."

"Not these twenty-odd years," he agreed. He leaned his hands behind him on the table, bumping against her bride-box. "But she is not entirely hopeless, as you'll see. And she does have a certain childlike innocence, even if it is cloaked betimes in the Randolph temper." He was distracted by the box, and picked it up.

"What is this?" It was a small casket with a hinged edge, three by five by three inches, carved of rosewood with Jacobean designs.

She smiled at him, clasping her hands before her like a girl. "My bride-box," she said, her eyes smarting tears.

He looked it over, puzzled. "What's it for?"

"Open it," she said. For inside were several shillings, a half crown and a sovereign. "They're gifts," she explained. "Contributions from visitors to the house," she blushed, "so that we needn't want for cash our first month or so. You've never heard of the practice?" Her dark eyes showed their orange and green as she gazed at him.

"Never," he admitted. "It is an eminently practical notion." He examined the carvings on the box in greater detail. "And every bride has one?" he ascertained.

She nodded. "Everyone I know. Of course," she smiled briefly, showing her dimples, "I have two. That is unusual. But one of our carpenters made this for me, and I couldn't refuse it, even though I'm not supposed to have another. . . ." She paused for effect. "It's for virgins."

He passed over the implications of that spoken by her bright dark glance.

"What did you do with the other one?"

"I gave it to Nannie." She rocked a little on her toes as he did, feeling the color slowly fading from her face.

"Well," he said softly. "I shall have to see about this tradition." He put the box away and took her hands again, rising from the table. "I am learning all manner of things about you," he said as they went into the parlor.

His family arrived *en masse* shortly before dinner. Mrs. Jefferson was not the termagant she had feared, but a little woman hardly taller than herself, with a fine English complexion and lively brown eyes. Patty came forward and extended her hand in welcome, kissing his mother on both cheeks in the English manner. Jane Jefferson's eyes came alight.

"Mrs. Jefferson," Patty said warmly, her dark eyes mildly brown, "welcome to The Forest. And thank you so much for your kindly letter. It was most thoughtful of you."

Jane made a brief curtsey. "Mrs. Skelton," she said. Her voice bore a trace of an English accent. "I wish you every felicitation, my dear." She clasped her hand.

"Thank you, Madame," she said sincerely. "Won't you come and meet my family. . . ." She led her over to where Papa stood with Nancy and Tibb and Rob, relieved that their first meeting had passed off so smoothly.

She greeted the others in turn: Randolph, Nan, Mary and John Bolling, Patsy and Dabney Carr, Lucy and Charles Lewis. Between her and Patsy and Lucy there were genuine embraces all round. Both were in circumstances, although Patsy more visibly so, and Patty felt a pang. *Soon,* she thought, *oh soon, we shall all dandle our babes together.* How she looked forward to Patsy's company! And Lucy was vivacious and talkative, if she wasn't bright.

She would have women friends in Albemarle, or near by.

When she came to Elizabeth, after such emotion already, she had to steel herself to calmness. This poor affected sister of Thomas's was half a head taller than she, with the stooped carriage of a slightly wilted lily. She was brown-haired as her mother, and indeed that seemed to also be a consistent Randolph trait. What in Mary Bolling was rare beauty, and in Patsy and Lucy vivacious charm, was in Elizabeth a mockery. She had the same coloring, the same features, only coarsened, roughed, distorted by her affliction. She had a very fine skin, and had the left of her face not dragged down in that peculiar way, or her eyes been quite so heavy, she would have been beautiful. She looked at Mrs. Jefferson and back again. It must tear that lady's heart to see such an unkind mirror of her own youth's beauty.

"Miss Jefferson, welcome," she said in her low country drawl, taking Lissa's hand, not at all certain of how much would be understood. "I have heard so many kind things about you. Did you have a pleasant journey?"

Lissa nodded. "Yes," she said in her distorted way. "There was snow. It was—" she paused, trying to get out the word, and Patty waited patiently to hear, "lovely!"

"How wonderful!" she cried, glad that the girl possessed such sensibilities. "I hope it will snow here before Wednesday."

"So do I," Lissa's eyes shone in delight at having found a new friend.

"Well, come," Patty said, taking her hand and arm. "You must meet my family, then our John will show you where you may put your things. . . ." Thomas turned away from the company, toward the parlor, and when he turned again, she saw how affected he was. Later that day on a solitary walk through the frozen woods, he said to her, "You pleased my sister Elizabeth no end. She'll be your friend for life."

She looked up at him from under the warmth of fur-lined and knitted hoods, and slipped her gloved hand about his arm, her breath blowing white plumes before her.

"How could I treat her otherwise than as an honored guest? I would be most remiss if I neglected her."

"That's precisely what I mean. It does not occur to you to shrink from her because of her affection. Most people are not so patient, and write her off as entirely stupid, which she is not." He paused. "She has flashes of brilliance in certain regards, particularly mathematics," he explained, "and all the wonder of the world of a child. . . . As Jane and Patsy and I were drawn to the woods and to growing things and music, so too was Lissa. She cannot play, because of her incoordination, but she shares our enthusiasm. . . . So you see what I mean about your welcoming her, little one."

"She isn't a leper," she said, deeply moved by Elizabeth's fate. Though she be not a leper, it was true, her affliction could be borne by others of the family, including children of theirs. But Thomas laughed at her observation, diverted as she intended him to be, the sound echoing in the empty, crystal-touched woods.

He stopped on the path and turned to her. Her cheeks burned with the cold, though she was wrapped in grey and red woolens. "I don't believe I've told you this in the last twelve hours," he said, "but I love you very much." He bent to kiss her, and even through all their layers of clothing, the contact was electrifying. Warm color replaced the cold in her face.

"Oh, my dear," she said breathlessly, leaning her head against his shoulder. "How dear I love you! How I wish Wednesday were here! Three days is an eternity. I burn."

"Oh Patty," he murmured, and she raised her face at his tone. He kissed her properly, revelling, and had it not been for the cold they might have come to some business. It had been a long six months for them, and for her an even longer four years. She might as well have been a spinster, as he called her in their bond.

In the evening, after she'd retired, he sent a scrap of verse to her by Jupiter:

> *Where to live near,*
> *And planted there,*
> *Is to live, and still live new;*
> *Where to gain a favour is*
> *More than life, perpetual bliss,*
> *Make me live by serving you.*
>
> *Dear, again back recall*
> *To this light,*
> *A stranger to himself and all;*
> *Both the wonder and the story*
> *Shall be yours and eke the glory;*
> *I am your servant and your thrall.*

On Monday, Mr. Coutts, one of the ministers, arrived, and as he had the cash on hand, Thomas gave him his five-pound fee, only having to borrow twenty shillings of it back in the afternoon. As they were coming out from dinner, he stopped with Patty at her box on the cherry table and dropped in a ten-shilling piece.

"What's that for?" she asked in surprise.

"Insurance," he said, smiling. "And I warn you, I charge interest."

She leaned her hand on the table. "Is that so?"

"Indeed." He waited until his mother and sister Mary passed by, and continued sotto voce, "and I intend to collect in full."

"Am I to have no mercy?" she asked, hopefully. Her eyes were languid under their dark brows. He took her hand and kissed it.

"None whatever," he said softly.

"Oh my," she breathed.

"Such a picture," Patsy said, as she came up with Dabney.

"Like an engraving from a novel," Carr agreed.

"Oh, go away," Thomas bade them good-naturedly, flushing. Patty laughed and ducked her head.

The next morning in his account book, Thomas wrote simply, "Dec. 30—Loaned Mrs. Sk 10/ . . . ."

20
Nuptials

The Forest

It was Betty who roused her at the late hour of half-past seven. For the rest of the house breakfast was in half an hour, and Nancy was already downstairs, capable in her capacity as hostess. But Patty herself was not allowed downstairs until noon, when she would walk with Lisbet and Patsy down the stair to their holly-and-ivy-bedecked hall. Now Betty leaned down in her bright saffron jacket and brighter indigo and green head scarf and jangling earrings, to murmur in her ear, "Coffee, Miss Patty."

She raised her face out of the bolster, and the first thing she saw was her wedding gown spread out on the sofa. Nightmares came back to her, and she sat up with a start.

"Oh my goodness, what time is it?"

Betty laughed. "Goin on for near eight o'clock, I reckon. You hain't missed it," she said fondly. She pulled the tangle of hair from her face and accepted the cup of coffee.

"Is Mr. Jefferson abroad?" She poured cream into the cup.

"For more'n two hours to hear your papa tell it." She pulled a slip of paper from her pocket. "His man sayed to give you this."

Written in Greek characters were lines from *A Midsummer Night's Dream*, "I know a bank whereon the wild thyme blows, where oxlips and the nodding violet grows; quite over-canopied with luscious woodbine, with sweet musk rose, and with eglantine, there sleeps Titania, some of the night, lulled in these flowers with dances and delight." Such a fancy did not require a reply on this day.

Later after she had eaten several biscuits at Betty's insistence, she was set upon by the ladies of both families, her sisters and Thomas's, and so began the ritual that every bride and bride maiden knew well. It took nearly the full four hours for the combined group of ladies to accomplish all the bathing, perfuming, coifing and toileting required, but at length, with her hair powdered and dressed in the loops and curls that Thomas especially loved, her face a discreet mask of carefully applied paint, they were lacing her into the gown that had lain now unworn these six months.

It had belonged to her mother, although she had not been married in it, and after some alteration to suit her figure and the current mode, she was well pleased with it. It was of corded silk that had once been cream sprigged with tiny yellow blossoms like elder, but it had since darkened to buff. She had cut the neck away and split the front, adding fine ruching and a petticoat of matching dark green taffeta, and palest yellow silk flowers she had painstakingly cut and sewn by hand. The sacque back was looped up with green cords and flowers, and in her hair were pinned more of the same silk blooms, for she'd made many more than the gown required. When she looked at herself in the pier glass they brought in, it was as though she was looking at another woman, some faery-tale creature instead of the person she knew. Before she was allowed to put on her left shoe, Lucy Lewis laid in a sixpence for luck, and she was called readied. Already, they had tidied up and laid out her evening gown. There was nothing left to do but be married.

When her father came in, she was alone in the room with Lisbet and Patsy, and her heart started hammering. When she reached out her hand for her French prayer book, it trembled. Lisbet took her arm.

"Don't swoon now, silly; the best is yet to be."

She smiled gratefully and gazed at her father with round eyes.

"I hear we're supposed to have a wedding," he said jovially, "and by the crush in the hall, it must be so. But who's the bride, I wonder? It must be this ravishing creature here. Can this be our Patt?" He came forward in his mulberry wool and flowing neck cloth.

"Please don't tease me, Papa," she begged. "I'm like to collapse."

"That's what I'm here for," Wayles said, taking her arm.

She swallowed. Her throat was dry, and she was shaking so that a fine sift of powder came raining down from her coiffure. "Is Mr. Jefferson down?"

"And waiting expectantly," Patsy said, laughing. "He's utterly dumbstruck, poor boy. I don't know how he'll make his pledge."

"Oh, I think he will," Wayles said, eyeing her fondly. "This is the last time I'm giving you away, Miss Patt, so make it do."

"I will," she said quaveringly. She shifted the prayer book to the other hand.

"Tell them we're ready," her father said. Lisbet went to the door and gave them the signal.

The music played was one of her favorite Scottish airs, but she barely recognized it. As she walked down the stairs, she could not have told who she was looking at. When she turned the corner of the newel post behind the two ladies she saw him standing there by the minister, and his eyes shone with such love that the tears welled up and slipped over. Her father's hand was firm under her elbow, and it was a good thing, for she never would have made it the ten feet required unaided. He was so handsome! Her gentle, sweet, dearly beloved darling. Thomas! Her tears fell unheeded until she came to stand beside him and gave her prayer book to Lisbet, who blotted them away with her handkerchief.

The ceremony was short, just over half an hour, and most of it was a blur, but she would remember till she died his face and the timbre of his voice when he spoke his pledge and bound himself to her with all that he was and owned. The Reverend Mr. Coutts' voice was a mumble, "In the name of the Father. . . ." Thomas' hands were cold when he slipped the little gold ring on her thumb. "And the Son. . . ." As the ring came to rest on her middle finger, she looked up at him and he met her gaze. She was the only one overcome, for his greenish eyes were glittering. "And the Holy Ghost. Amen." He smiled a little and clasped her hand, before they turned to the Reverend Mr. Coutts. She now was Mrs. Jefferson in truth. Under the cover of the chaste kiss he gave her to seal the bargain, he murmured, "My wife." She choked on tears and reached up on her toes to return the kiss. The fiddlers played and there was cheering from the crowds in their hall and dining room and parlor.

Before the wedding breakfast they toured the crowd, receiving congratulations on all sides, but he was never farther than a few inches; and whenever there was a respite from the handshakes and bows and curtseys, his hand sought hers, openly now, with a caress that spoke his love for all to see.

The wedding breakfast, as the first one, was wasted on them. Champagne and toasts flowed around them but they were cocooned in the aftershock of actually having accomplished the deed. Thomas sought her hand under the table and held it, his own palm up, on her knee. She leaned over to him.

"I'm wearing your garters," she said in low tones, and moved his hand to where the lump of one was.

"I see," he murmured into her hair.

"You shall," she laughed, with her sidelong glance. She slid her hand so that it rested along the inside of his knee.

"Vixen," he chided, plucking the garter playfully. She gasped, and he laughed a little in deep tones. The company were but a sea of faces and a humming drone.

Dabney, sitting on the other side of Patsy on the left, leaned over, grinning. "It's nice to see this isn't a marriage of convenience."

"On the contrary, my friend," Thomas replied, picking up the fork again, "I find it most convenient." He smiled at her, and she shook her head and drank some of the champagne.

They were separated in the mingling company afterward, for there were people who wanted to see her after long absences. They never lost sight of each other, and she was always looking back to make sure she knew where he was, delighted when she found him.

John Page came up with Fanny. "Do I get to kiss the bride?" John asked, with a rueful sparkle in his eye. On this day she could forgive anything. "Only if you're a good boy," she countered, and embraced him.

It was Lisbet who took stock of her longing glances and saw fit to remedy matters. She came up with Patsy and took her by the arms bodily. "Come along, my dear," she said. "Excuse us," she said to Anne Carter and Mary Bolling. "Enough conviviality for you. Mr. Eppes and I have hatched a more comely plot, and you are bound to comply."

She tried, with both her elbows held, to pick up her skirts so her flowers would not be crushed. "Betsy, what are you doing?"

"It's time to throw the stockings," Patsy said. She didn't argue anymore after that.

In her room, they took apart all their careful work of the morning, from unlacing and laying away her gown to washing the powder out of her hair and off her face. An hour later she was bathed and only slightly damp, being put into her best silk shift with the tissue ruffles and heavy pale green dressing sacque. They sat her on the bed and Patsy went to call in the men.

"How do you feel?" Lisbet said.

"Scrubbed," she complained. Her sister smiled. "Nervous."

"Don't be nervous, goose," Betsy squeezed her arm. "You've done this before!"

The words brought tears to her eyes. "Not with Thomas!" she cried.

"Oh, sister," Lisbet said, as she had when Jack was coming and Patty wept for her mother. She found herself embraced. "Hush, sh." Lisbet rocked her in her arms, leaning over the bed. "Don't cry, sweetheart. It'll be all right."

She nodded, sniffling. She knew it would, once he was here, once they were alone. But between then and now lay memories of Batt, and she was afraid. What if they should interfere?

Patsy came in and saw the scene. "Ah, what's amiss here?" she said gently, coming to smooth her hair. "Is our lovely bride upset?" She gave her a hug. "It's good luck to cry, you know," she said nodding, as if talking to a hurt child.

Patty flung her arms about her. "Oh, Patsy, I love you! Lisbet, come here! Kiss me, won't you, and tell me it'll be all right." They complied. "It really will, you know," Patsy said. "Dab says Tom's in a state. How do you think he feels? They're over there filling his head with wonders and rude remarks. He wouldn't even look at me!"

She laughed at that. Her poor darling, beset upon by his well-meaning friends. They'd been ragging him to marry for years, and he had less experience in these matters than she. Poor Thomas! She should be mindful to soothe his unease.

"That's better," Lisbet said. The door opened. "Oh," she cried, and hastily wiped the tears off Patty's face.

He came in, blushing, with his determined look on his face, ahead of Francis and Dabney, and sat on the bed, his wadded dressing gown gathered around him. "I feel perfectly silly," he muttered to her. She took his hand.

Their clothes had been folded up on the chairs, with the stockings on top, and Lisbet went now and gathered them up. There were several more pairs than necessary.

"Oh, wait," she said, pulling on one, "it's stuck."

"This is unendurable," Thomas complained. Patty giggled beside him and touched his arm. "Shh," she whispered. "They have to."

"But why?" He hissed back. "Why can't they just go away?"

"I heard that," Francis said, taking two or three stockings in hand.

"He's impatient enough now," Dabney said. The ladies giggled.

"I'll get you for this one, Currus," he promised. Dabney only laughed.

They took a long time about aligning themselves, facing away from the bed with the ladies opposite Thomas and the men opposite Patty. There was a deal of furtive commentary and snickering going on, but at last they were ready.

"Please try to hit the mark," Thomas said.

"It's you should be worried about that," Francis replied. Thomas hit him with a pillow in the back of the head, and the company broke up again.

"Do let's get on with it," he entreated them, desperately. "Or we shall be at it till cock's crow."

"I thought that was the idea," this from Dabney. Their bridal party was dissolved again. Thomas shook his head, and said to her, "This is hopeless." She smiled and put her other hand on his.

Finally, they counted three and half a dozen pairs of hose raining down, falling in all directions.

"Well, there's good luck," Patsy said.

"And stamina," Francis added. Thomas wadded up one of the stockings into a ball and hit him in the nose.

"So he can make the mark," Carr commented. "I suppose we can leave now."

"Please do," he said. But there was good humor in it.

Lisbet came around the bed and gave her a hug.

"Good luck to you," she murmured.

Patty kissed her, beaming. "Thank you."

Francis stood up, and in his capacity as chief bridesman, gave them a blessing. "May you have good health, long life, and great endurance." With that they departed.

Thomas leaned back, disentangling himself from the stockings. "It's about time. I thought they'd never leave."

"Me too," she said, shy now. She put the stockings she held into a little pile on the table. The time was truly here, and now she was frightened. She hadn't been this nervous the first time. It was just. . . . She had wanted him for so long, and she wanted it to be perfect. She looked sidelong at Thomas.

He tossed the stockings aside and took her hand, only to leap up again. "Oh wait," he said, and got up to yank the bed curtains closed. When he came back, he knelt before her. "Now we really are alone. For always." He cradled her face in his hand. "Sweet Patty," he kissed her, softly. She trembled, and tears welled up. "Now there but remains a promise to keep."

A promise to keep. In Williamsburg he had promised her that when they did come to this, neither of them would be disappointed. All the love she bore him rushed to the fore. She shifted her position, for she had been sitting taylor-fashion, and came to kneel with him, as they had done long ago in the woods.

"I thought you'd forgotten that," she murmured, touching his hand upon her face.

"I shall always keep my promises to my dear girl," he said, putting his hands under her hair. Her answer was a wordless murmur as her arms came round him.

> *Tell me, when th' appointed Hour*
> *Calls us to the secret Bower*
> *Blushing trembling, why I run*
> *Early as the rising Sun?*
> *Gentle youth, O tell me true,*
> *Is it then the same with you?*
> *Gentle youth, O tell me true,*
> *tell me, tell me, tell me true,*
> *Gentle youth, O tell me true,*
> *Is it then the same with you?*

It was well dark in the room when they were awakened by Betty Hemings's loud whisper, "Miss Patty, Sir, I come to tell you the dancing's about to begin."

She pushed her hair out of the way and raised her head enough to be heard. "Thank you, Bett, we'll be along directly." She turned her head and found Thomas looking at her, perfectly awake.

"Will you need help, ma'am?"

"No," Thomas said, smiling. She pushed herself up and sat up. "We'll manage," she called to her servant. "Thank you, Betty."

"Yas'm." A moment later the door closed quietly. She could not suppress a giggle.

"Shh," he said, laying a finger to her lips. "She'll hear you."

"She's gone," she said. "Besides—" she kissed the hollow place in his throat, "it's ridiculous to think of her standing out there, trying to discern whether we are occupied or not."

His look was sardonic. "I think she would have noticed. Between this infernally ancient bed and a certain lady—" He traced the line of her collarbone with affection.

"I heard no complaints at the time," she murmured provocatively.

"Save about the bed," he corrected. "'Tis a poor joke, if joke it be."

She shook her head. "It's quite in earnest, I'm afraid. This bed is a castoff of my grandfather's."

"Then God bless Francis Eppes, because I do not." He reached out his hand to smooth back her fallen hair. "What say we get dressed?"

"I'd rather stay here with you." She touched his hand, where the nails were long and the fingertips callused. That texture had been strange, for otherwise his skin was as soft as a girl's. His drowsy eyes kindled a darker amber-green.

"As would I, but we've said we'd come." He took her hand and kissed the palm. "So we are bound, Mrs. Jefferson."

"In truth and deed, sir," she agreed.

He shook his head. "Patty. Sweet Patty, what a caution you are! Come!" He kissed her briefly. "We must away. I hear a gavotte calling us."

"Very well."

She pushed her cast-off dressing sacque away and opened the curtains into the candle-lit room. The draperies had been drawn, and there was a low fire in the hearth. All was cozy for their nuptials, and it brought to mind the lines from *Paradise Lost*:

> *Nor gentle purpose, nor endearing smiles wanted,*
> *nor youthful dalliance as beseems Fair couple,*
> *Linkt in happy nuptial league. Alone as they__*

She laughed a little.

"What's so funny?" Thomas asked, coming up behind her.

"Nothing," she murmured over her shoulder, "if you want to get downstairs. I'll tell you anon," she promised.

21

Wedding Journey

The Forest, Monticello

They spent the next two weeks visiting, though the continuous snow was something of an impediment. It necessitated their staying over two nights at Rosewell with the Pages and one at Shirley, although the latter stay was mostly due to the rear wheel box on Thomas's phaeton giving way. Shirley was well worth the extra day whilst it was being mended.

Back at The Forest they made ready for their journey into the mountains. Sundry items of Patty's from Batt were packed up, and Thomas duly catalogued them in his memorandum book. They included above two dozen-odd spoons, marked in their initials, a pair of saltcellars, a gold watch, surveying instruments, bottle stands, service waiters, and books. The latter would be sent on when the weather improved. Thomas noted in the back of his little journal, where he had set aside a page for the *estate of Bathurst Skelton, dec'd: by sundry European goods on hand at the death of B. Skelton and taken by me.* It was the eighteenth of January, and they left that morning.

It was snowing when they left, and by the time they reached Tuckahoe the snow was a foot and a half deep. They spent four days with Thomas Randolph and his family, including his old mother who was Jane Jefferson's dearest friend. They had to wait again for the phaeton to be repaired, as the opposite side of the wheel box had let go. One late night when the wind was howling around the sills, brewing another snowstorm, Thomas said to her in the cozy warmth of their high-piled bed, "Did I tell you that my first memory is of coming here?"

She stifled a yawn, for it was long past midnight. "Oh excuse me. No, when was this?"

He leaned his head back against the wall, adjusting the bolster behind, musing. "I was two. Lissa was just born and we came here because my father was named as guardian to Mr. Randolph's children. 'Twas springtime and the woods were full of flowers. I remember being lifted up onto a horse by my nurse. Jupiter's father had a feather pillow before him, and I sat on that. We wandered for days and days and finally we came to this great white house, and that's all I can remember." He looked at her. She was half asleep and trying vainly to keep her mind on what he had said, and whether or not she had made her reply.

"That's amazing. I don't think I can remember anywhere near that far back. . ." There was a long pause. ". . .Certainly not as specific. . . ."

He smiled and gathered her into the curve of his arm. "Good night, sweet," he murmured, and snuffed out the candle.

At Blenheim, Carter's place in Albemarle, there were snowdrifts three feet deep. They arrived in the afternoon, but the house was deserted. They walked around to the back and the overseer, John Hill, came out of his little house briefly, ushering them indoors.

"I thought you'd a known they was all gone for the holidays," he said, pouring out rum into his leathern cups. To this he added water, sugar, and a knob of butter, and scalded it with a fire poker.

"No," Thomas said, handing the cup to her. "I thought they'd be back 'ere this." She didn't take off her gloves. Her teeth had been chattering earlier, and since coming indoors her feet began to burn with cold. The warmth of the toddy through her gloves was painful, and the fire was making her sleepy. The men talked around her, and she hardly heard what they said or understood it.

"Well, I expect the weather's kept them away," Hill was saying. Kept who away? she wondered. She had forgotten where they were. They had stopped. . .because it was cold. . .but it wasn't cold now. She was burning all over.

"Ma'am?" She looked up slowly. A man. Who was he?. . . . Overseer. . . . He held out the battered common-ware plate bearing cornbread and salt pork.

"Oh thank you," she said stupidly, and accepted the meal. The plate slipped down to her lap and remained there. It was too heavy to hold. Her feet were burning.

"You're surely brave, coming way out here in this," the man said. She did not reply because she couldn't tell if she was being spoken to. Her ears were ringing, and she could not keep her eyes open.

A cup of tea was pressed into her hand. It was strong and sweet, liberally dosed with brandy. It calmed her shivering and quelled the fire in her head. She drank some more, and began to come awake again.

"You're welcome to spend the night," Hill said. "It ain't much, but it's here." She ate a piece of cornbread, only to find it was gravel in her mouth. She could not spit it out, so swallowed some more tea. They had put more brandy in it. Ordinarily she would have protested, but it kept her ears from ringing, so she drank it.

Thomas was beside her chair now, asking in low tones, "Do you want to spend the night?"

She looked at him, up at the room, at Mr. Hill. He was not prepared to deal with them, for all his kindness. "Oh, no," she said quickly. "You wrote we would be there today and it's not far." She clasped his hand. "It would be well to spend the night in our own house." From Milton, where they'd had to ford the Rivanna because there was no ferry in this weather, that had been her hope and prayer. Tonight in our own house. No more strange beds and travelling.

"We could easily wait," he said, with a worried frown. "It would not be difficult to heat a room in the house and lay up a bed. It's early yet. You could take your rest, and we could go up to the house in the morning when it's light." Already, daylight was beginning to fail.

She smiled. "But I'm not tired," she insisted. The tea and brandy had begun to take effect in good earnest. "And truth to tell, the thought of another night in a strange bed brings me no comfort, however conveniently located."

"It would mean a journey on horseback," he cautioned. "I cannot trust the phaeton to this snow. That back hinge is still weak."

She turned to him fully, putting down the cup in her lap next to the uneaten food. "I can ride! O, do let's, Mr. Jefferson. It's only a few miles. Katie's a strong little horse, she'll do." She spoke of her iron grey filly. "I should so like to spend the night in our own house."

He looked at her dubiously. "If that's what you want—"

"That's what I want," she insisted.

"Very well." He sighed.

The sun was just setting over the Blue Ridge when they packed up only their most necessary belongings on the two horses and mounted the track for Monticello. Carter's overseer bade them good luck and good night and handed over the lantern he held.

"You'll need it," he said.

"I know." Thomas replied shortly.

They rode across black and wooded country. Once into the valley between Carter's plantation and Monticello their bright full moon availed them nothing. It was impossible to see two feet beyond the lantern's light. Even here in the gap the snow was deep, and though Thomas obviously knew the way even in this weather, Patty felt lost and blinded in the dark. Her petticoat was soaked up to midthigh from dangling in the snow, and the cold wore through her boots and two pairs of woolen stockings. She could no longer feel her toes and had begun to wish, as the night lengthened and the effects of the tea wore off, that she had accepted the offer of a bed at Blenheim. Her horse was stumbling under her in the rocky terrain, made deceptively smooth by the blanketing cover of snow.

At length, they turned their horses into a track veering off to the right. "This is it," he said, pausing a moment. She looked dubiously up the steep path to the vastness of dark wood on either side.

"How far is it up to the top?" She could hardly see him as his face was all shadows in the cavernous dark.

He hesitated. "About a mile. . .a little more. We're nearly there." He looked back at her. "Ah." He brought his horse over and put a reassuring hand on her shoulder. "You'll see," he said. "Come along," he said to his horse Fearnought, who, if he regularly had to make it up this narrow treacherous path in all weathers, was worthy of his name.

They began their ascent. Holding the lantern aloft Thomas made his way before her, but there were so many stumbles that, after only a quarter of a mile, he got off his horse, took her horse's bridle in the same hand, and walked them up the mountain. In the gleaming grey-tossed darkness it seemed that his lantern was the solitary light of the world. Their bright moon was not visible for the overhang of thick trees, and though he was but a foot in front of her, his figure was dim.

It was forever that they climbed, upwards along the winding, snow-covered path, the loose rocks underfoot making the horses' steps uncertain. Her hands were utterly numb through her gloves, and the muff on her right hand did no good. Her feet were beginning to ache with the cold, the two pairs of woolen stockings only serving to insulate the cold within. Her wet petticoats and pelisse were frozen now in the wind. Her nose began to run, and her teeth were chattering again. If there was ever a misery of existence, this had to be it. Why had she not let him talk her into staying at Blenheim? Even if they'd have had to sleep in the overseer's cottage, they'd have had a fire and could have been abed long ere this. She had no idea of the time, but it felt like it must be past midnight. She swayed drowsily, overcome by the cold, and then her teeth would rattle again and start her awake into the lurking dark. She clenched her teeth to stop the noise, but that only made it worse. Thomas glanced back at her.

"Almost there," he said, breathing hard against the exertion. She had to trust that he knew his way, for she could see nothing but the lantern.

After what seemed an age they reached the top of the summit. In the moonlight, clear and strong, she saw a lone out-chamber, hardly the size of her kitchen, clinging to the far edge of the hill. Before her stood a single structure (their dining room it was to be; she knew it from the plans), and the pilings of the middle room rising lonely sentinels against the vastness of the sky. Her despair was utter and complete. It was black, save for the moon, with not a single candle's light to welcome them, weary travellers.

"Here we are," Thomas said, still heaving breaths. He spread out his arm and let it drop, indicating the scene before them. "Home." She slid off her horse in a crunch of snow.

Some of her dismay must have shown on her face, as Thomas came over and put an arm about her shoulders. She looked across at the dining room. The pilings were still up, for the roof was not complete. Two small rooms, no bigger than slave quarters. It was all there was. Oh, and he had told her; he had warned her it was small, but even in the cramped space of her kitchen she had not imagined it would be as bleak as this. She should have reckoned on it, she told herself sternly; she should have seen that it was a building site with few amenities. But gracious, since the levelling of the hill there weren't even any trees save those down the slopes of the mountain—and the orchard he had planted, but those were barely discernable beyond the out-chamber to the south. She shuddered, unable to speak, as much from disappointment as cold. If she could have cried she would have, in spite of its effect on Thomas, for she was wretched, but she had no tears. She caught herself in the rebellious thought: *I want to go home.* But this was home, now, for good and all. All the bright dreams and grand plans were nothing to the drear reality, and her despair was sharp. She turned to him wordlessly, not wanting to hurt him with words or tears, and his mouth twitched a little.

"It'll be better in the morning," he said quietly. She nodded.

He kissed her forehead and turned her toward the dark little house on the edge of the wilderness of trees, saying, "I'll let you inside and go put up the horses. It's warmer than waiting out here."

"Yes." She could hardly speak. Her face felt numb. She knew he was hurting and wanted to reach out to him, ease his wound, but she had little enough energy to make it across the white expanse of lawn. He unlocked the door on the north side of the out-chamber, and she stumbled inside while he laid her travelling case on a chair. Inside it was worse—cold, crowded, without a welcoming landmark.

"I won't be long," he said, and closed the door. She turned around but he was gone, passing by the window, turning up the collar of his greatcoat.

A sob of misery tore from her unbidden and then she was silent again, like a babe newborn. She stood in the middle of the dark room as if she had been dropped there, trying to get some bearings. Her pelisse—the fine fur and heavy wool of the coat ruined in its sodden and frozen state—and petticoats weighed on her like an anchor, and the place where she had stumbled only now came alive to the sensation. Her feet burned with cold. She put her muff over her face and cried a little, in short fitful sobs. When she raised her head again, wiping her eyes and nose with the back of her gloved hand, she began to discern the lay of the room in the moonlight.

Before her, on the west wall, was a fireplace, surrounded on either side by alcove nooks with tall standing bookcases. Beside her was a small table with three chairs with high curved Windsor backs. Opposite to that was a wing chair. Behind her was the bed. She could make out now her white quilted counterpane, brought up by Jupiter after the wedding. There was some small comfort. There were two chests, a wardrobe, a stool, a standing desk, and books. Everywhere were piled the gifts and acquisitions of books the last two years since the Shadwell fire and whatever of their wedding gifts Jupiter had managed to fit on the cart. *God preserve us,* she thought, though from this out she would do her best to conceal her disapprobrium. She shivered in her wet, thawing clothes in the cold, dark room. It was better, in any case, than standing outside facing into the unknown reaches of mountain and forest.

Thomas came into the house with the lantern and put it on the table. His arms came around her shoulders from behind, and she leaned against him, feeling less dull. He had had the exertion of his walk to keep him warm, and the damp wool of his garments radiated a steamy heat. He let go of her and took off his hat.

"There's tinder here somewhere," he said, searching through chest drawers. He came up at length with paper twists and tinder and knelt down at the hearth with his flint and steel. The spark glowed in the dim light, and twice the paper caught; but it was damp, and twice it failed before it flamed up and the tinder took light. He laid a good deal of wood on the andirons and set the burning tinder about them. The fire was a lodestone, and she came to sit on the floor next to him while he worked. Before long, he had a tidy little blaze encouraged and sat back on his heels.

"We need to get you out of those wet things," he told her decisively. She stared at him stupidly. All her clothes and goods, save for the travelling box, were at Blenheim.

"What do you mean?"

"I mean," he said shortly, with a grimace, "that I don't intend to have you die of exposure because I was too vain to listen to my own common sense." She began to perceive that his manner was due as much to self-deprecation as her reaction to the place. He rose and went to the chest by the bed, and from the second drawer pulled out two shirts at random, one ruffled and one plain.

"These should suffice."

He came to her, untying her hoods and unfastening the clasp of her pelisse. It fell to the floor with a sodden thud. She felt much lighter already, although the cold was more noticeable. She took off her fur-lined riding gloves and laid the muff aside. They were gifts from Lisbet at Twelfth Night. Her teeth chattered betimes as he helped her out of the weighted clothes and tossed his shirt over her head. It came down to her knees, and she could put her hands through the closed sleeve bands, but it was dry, and by the time he had wrapped her white coverlet about her as well, she was quite comfortable, so long as she sat before the fire.

He would not let her help him lay out their clothes about the room to dry, insisting rather that she sit and sing him a song.

"What should I sing?" she asked, feeling silly. Here she was, sitting in a quilt and her husband's shirt in the middle of the night on top of the world, and he wanted a serenade! He'd do better with tree frogs.

He shrugged, tossing his breeches over the bookcase. His loose hair hung damp and curling about his shoulders. In the firelight his skin had a golden cast. "Anything," he said. "Anything to bring the blood back. Something lively."

Lively. The humor of their situation struck her as the warmth from the fire began to seep into the coverlet. It was all such a complete absurdity, sitting here this way. And they would not have, if she had not insisted. Well, it would be something to laugh over in times to come. "As you wish." A bubble of laughter came up. She sang him "The Ill Wife." When she was done, he was smiling again. "You must be feeling better," he said, coming to sit. "Sing me another."

She plumbed the depths of her memory and came up with one of her father's songs from Vauxhall Gardens. She sang in a somewhat crackling and warbly soprano:

> . . . Come Lads and come Lasses be Blithesome and gay
> Let your hearts be open'd and your pipes full of glee
> The Highlands shall ring with the joys of the day
> While thro the wood happy, we dance sing and play. . . .

"Your turn," she said. The fire crackled and then snapped between them. He thought a moment, and then his face brightened.

"Oh wait," he said, scrambling up.

She watched as he skirted the table and went to his alcove of books, and rummaged through the titles. "Ah, Swift," he said, and pulled out the book. But instead of the volume, he came back to the fire with a bottle of Malmsey wine that was about three-quarters full and a pair of glasses.

"This ought to warm things up," he murmured, pulling the cork from the bottle. He poured her out a measure of the sweet, amber wine and took one himself, stretching his legs out on the lee side of her.

"So what did you want to hear?" he drawled, his hair falling in his eyes. She laughed. "Surprise me."

He did. He sang "Robin Hode," and "The Northumbrian Poacher," "Thomas the Rhymer," and "Tam Linn." They drank more of the wine. She returned his songs with "Colin and Phæbe," "The Kind Inconstant," and "Sally in Our Alley." They finished the wine and ended their singsong with drinking songs and bawdy choruses from Shakespeare, giggling over nothing and leaning together giddily on the floor. Their lack of a decent supper sent the wine to their heads. It was no longer cold, at least. She took off the coverlet.

"Do you know what I want?" she asked, looking up at him.

"I can hazard a guess," he murmured.

"No, really," she protested. She was still sober enough to be coherent of thought.

"All right, what?"

"I want you to play for me." She reached for his hand.

"I don't know if I can," he admitted.

"Please?" She kissed him and saw the kindling of his eyes.

"You do beg prettily, Madame." He rose, his ankles creaking, and fetched his violin.

"Did you have anything you especially wanted to hear?" he asked, testing the strings. He sat across from her again, on his knees, and the firelight shone on the fiddle with a warm glow.

"Oh yes," she murmured. "The Canon by Pachelbel. . . ." It was her favorite piece that he played, for the first time he played it was in Williamsburg at the Wythes' house. He inclined his head, briefly, his greenish eyes frankly engaging, and then he gave himself over to the piece.

She watched him lovingly as he began to play, his fingers moving over the strings deftly and with delicacy. And O, the soaring beauty of that gentle crescendo! He was absorbed, his loose hair falling across his cheek. The bow lifted on the transporting melody and she was undone. She closed her eyes against the tears that welled, listening, revelling, feeling him play, feeling a part of the music, of him. She opened her eyes to find him watching her, looking through her. He was beautiful, and she loved him so that her heart could not contain it all. He met her eyes once and then was absorbed by the final notes. When the piece was done, he sighed.

"Oh. . . ." she cried softly, still in the thrall of the music. She reached out her hand, and he took it, his drowsy eyes dark. "Come," he said, rising with her. He laid the violin away on the table, safe from the fire in its case, and picked up the quilt from the floor, but left the wine bottle and glasses as a silent testimony. He tossed the cover on the bed.

"Welcome home," he murmured, and she went into his embrace.

22
Mistress of Monticello

Monticello

In the morning it was breathtakingly cold, for there had been another snowfall during the night. At half-past seven it was twenty-three degrees of Fahrenheit inside their chamber. Last night's fire was but embers, and the hearth too far away from the bed to admit much heat. It was a pot clattering on the hearth downstairs that woke Patty. She started awake in alarm, her heart thudding in her chest, before Thomas laid a hand on her shoulder.

"It's all right, it's only Dilcy banging about," he said. She moved her face out of the bolster and squinted at him sleepily. He sat with his thumb in a book, washed, shaven, and wrapped in his wadded banyan. Such industry put her to shame. She was hard put to keep her eyes open.

He smiled. "Good morning, slugabed. Did you know it's nearly nine o'clock?" She sat up, her fingers measuring the length of a lock of hair that fell in her eyes.

"Mmm." She peered at the clock on the mantel. "Why didn't you wake me?"

"I'd have woken the dead easier," he teased. She made a moue. For the last fortnight he had worried her unmercifully on this score. "Besides," he said, laying a hand on her hair, "it was a long day yesterday, and a later night, and I thought it best to let you sleep."

"Ah," she said, and kissed him. "You are good to me."

"We but aim to please." He closed the book and laid it by.

She groaned. "Oh, not so early! I don't have the wits to pun with you."

He raised an eyebrow, eyes sparking green. "Your mind does run in strange directions, Madame."

Nothing loath, she moved aside the heavy blankets and closed the narrow space that lay between them. The rough nap of his dressing gown was vivifying. "Some would say I had encouragement," she said lightly, and slipped her hand along his back under the banyan.

He gasped. "Your hands are cold," he complained, closing the covers about them.

"Not for long," she murmured. "I know a remedy. . ."

"Some would say you don't need encouragement," he muttered, and kissed her. She laughed, for it was the last of his complaints, and this one was not in earnest.

Dilcy came up later, though they had not yet opened the shutters, and knocked on the door. Thomas looked at his watch on the stool by the bed.

"What time is it?"

"Nearly half-past ten." He looked her over with an appraising eye. "Should we let her in?" Her dressing sacque was on the floor in the corner. She did not miss his point and leaned over to fetch it. By fingertips, she managed to reach it and pull it up by one corner. Being silk, it was icy, and she did not relish putting it on. She sat up and twisted her hair back on her neck in a loose knot, glancing at him under her upraised arm. "Must we?"

"We shall have to, sooner or later."

"Later," she laughed.

He raised an eyebrow, and got up, closing the buttons on the banyan.

"You know," he said as went to the door, "she's going to be utterly scandalized." He ran a hand through his disordered hair.

"Good," she shrugged. He opened the door to his servant.

Beyond the door, she listened to the embarrassed exchange.

"Good morning, Dilcy," he cried, extra cheerily. A gust of frigid air blew into the room.

"Good morning, sir," she mumbled.

"We gave you all a bit of surprise this morning, I'll warrant." There was a rattle of crockery. What in heaven's name was he doing? She leaned across the bed and peered through the open crack of the door. *Counting spoons, sweet mercy! Just take it, Tom, and close the door, it's cold in here!* She pulled on the dressing gown.

"Yassir," Dilcy was saying. "Jupiter went down stable and saw the'm horses, and 'twas the first we knowed of it."

"Ah, Jupiter," he murmured. "Tell him I wish him in about an hour's time, won't you? Mrs. Jefferson will be abroad then, and you can meet her."

As if this were not meeting enough! She'd never be able to look the girl in the eye!

"Yassir."

Oh dear! She rolled on the bed, trying not to be heard laughing. And there he was conducting all in the most cool and businesslike manner, clad only in a dressing gown. . .

Thomas closed the door, and she took her face out of the pillow.

"It's not fair to laugh at poor Dilcy," he said, "she's not exactly bright." Which only made her laugh harder.

"Oh," she had a stitch in her side. "Oh, my dear, oh how ridiculous! How shall we ever face her again? Oh," she laughed again. "Here is the mistress, Dilcy, you remember her: she's the one who kept you waiting outside half the morning long, wondering if it was safe to knock—" He was laughing too now.

She waved her arm. "Oh, bring that here, before you drop it." She lifted a dish cover weakly. "Is everything gone stone cold? Let's see. . ."

They were collapsed on the bed in tears. "Oh, here," she said, wiping her eyes. "Have a muffin—" She handed it to him, but it only made him whoop, and she dropped it to fall on the bed again.

Now she felt like she was truly home.

They bundled on several layers of clothes before they went out, and as Patty had no servant here, the task of helping her dress fell to Thomas, but he never complained. Patiently, he would lace her stays and hook or lace her gown with the greatest attention. He had early on fretted over the mold of her rib cage, with a worried frown and a kiss. When she shook her head in wonder at him, he remarked that it was unnatural, and tut-tutted. But it was natural enough to her, for she'd been wearing stays since she could remember, and said as much. How else could a lady hope to have a fashionable figure? She could hardly be expected to look like Jenny! So he ceased to argue with her about it, but rather used the opportunity to play love games.

He tied the strings off now and threaded them through the lattice above, kissing her neck when he was done. "I like this part," he murmured in her ear. She raised her hand to caress his cheek. "You like all the parts."

"'Tis true," he agreed, and swatted her.

It was still very cold. At noon, the mercury had only risen to twenty-eight degrees, but it did not deter them from their ramble. When she stepped outside and looked up at the burgeoning house beyond, she was stunned. The view was magnificent.

"Oh!" She cried, clasping her hands. "Oh, Thomas, it's beautiful! Oh, look at the view!" She turned around several times, taking it all in, before she looked up at him again. "Oh, my dear," she exclaimed, and meant it, "I love it here!"

He took her on a tour of the house and kitchen garden, explaining painstakingly where everything was or would be. It was too cold to walk down, but he pointed out the place on the north side of the mountain where he told her the garden would be. This would have a grotto with a basin fed by the nearby spring, and this would be covered with moss, spangled with translucent pebbles and the beautiful iridescent shells that rested on the shore at Burwell's ferry. Springwater was to fall into a shell basin in this haven, and a statue of Diana would recline upon a couch of moss. Near her would be carved lines from Pope's translation of Horace:

Nymph of the grot, these sacred springs I keep,
And to the murmur of these waters sleep;
Ah! spare my slumbers! gently tread the cave!
And drink in silence, or in silence leave!

The whole would be surrounded by beech, poplar, honeysuckle, and jasmine, and through the rest of the garden, their informal English landscape, would be inscriptions from classical and modern verse. She did not miss the inference to Diana, and it moved her to tears. How much of the soul of this place had been crafted in her honor? It went far, far beyond the new little dairy and the washhouse.

On their way back to the little house, they stopped by the kitchen so she could meet Dilcy, who, when they entered, appeared to be industriously preparing dinner, but in reality to her practiced eye was simply moving from hither to thither, and accomplishing no real tasks. Patty began to suspect that she did not know how, and queried her as to the routine of her day.

Punctuating the nervous explanation, filled with stuttered incoherences and lame silences, Patty glanced about the room, noting its organization—or, in this case, its disorganization. Supplies were scattered about the room in no particular order, and in cupboards were mixed cooking utensils and table ware, so that it was a wonder anything was found when wanted. The hearth was arranged in an inconvenient manner, and a complaint about the temperament of the baking oven yielded a coating of ash thick enough to make soap from.

All the while her eye lit on a large crate in the corner opposite. It was large enough to be a sofa, although she couldn't hazard if that was so, why it should be stored in the kitchen. At length, bored and exasperated with Dilcy's witlessness, her curiosity got the better of her. She turned to Thomas as he leaned with his arms crossed on the door. "Mr. Jefferson, what *is* that enormous crate?"

He smiled and threw himself off the door, clasping his hands behind his back. "Go and read the label," he said.

She went over, the hood of her pelisse falling back, and leaned to peer at the stamped plate on the end. Her face paled.

"Oh my," she breathed in disbelief. "It's a piano!" She could hardly contain herself before the servant.

Thomas was grinning. "Indeed?" he said lightly. "Fancy." He came over and laid his hand on her back above her stays. "It's been devilish to keep it out of sight, especially since it was on the cart with your trunks."

She stared at him. "Jupiter brought it up here with our things?" She examined the crate again, shaking her head.

"Aye," he said, "and covered it in your blankets. That was Mr. Wayles's idea."

Of course Papa would be in on the ruse. He loved to play such games. "You all conspired against me," she murmured in mock-woundedness, but her eyes were shining.

"To a worthy cause," he assured.

She was a-dying to see it, to hear it, to sit and play. The fortepiano at the Palace had been heavenly. A thousand bells ringing holy songs could not have been sweeter to her ears. She clasped her hands, conscious of Dilcy's goggling stare.

"May we uncrate it, sir?" she pleaded ". . . and take it upstairs? Oh, please!"

He laughed. "Let me have Jupiter fetch some of the men."

It was a beautiful instrument. It retained the shape of a regular harpsichord, with the strings running crosswise in the sound box. Of dark polished mahogany, with a fine spruce soundboard, not larger than a moderately sized desk, it was delicately inlaid with fine scrollwork and flowers of ebony and holly. The keys were mother-of-pearl, with the sharps solid ebony, not painted wood. It had a fine, rich sound in the lower registers that was matched by a perfect bell-like clarity in the upper. She loved it unreservedly, and Thomas too, for being so extravagant and thoughtful. It put her half-dozen embroidered waistcoats to shame! Now they could have their own private musicales while secreted away in these winter quarters, for who would come to visit in weather such as this? They put it at the far end of the bed, under the window.

They had a visitor after dinner, in the person of Col. Carter's son Robert. Coming home in advance of his family, he had heard of their plight from John Hill, and taken it upon himself to deliver their phaeton and clothes. His advent was quite a surprise, and they ushered him in to a glass of mulled cider and a warming fire. Robert looked about the room, crowded as it was now with the piano and new large bed, for Thomas's own had been a narrow cot not requiring much space, and said, "You certainly are well outfitted to set up housekeeping."

Patty blushed at his interest and laid aside the poker, where she was mulling cider. Rising, she poured out a measure for their guest. "Mr. Carter," she murmured.

He raised the mug in respect. "Mrs. Jefferson. Welcome to our country." She blushed again and made a curtsey. "Thank you, sir."

He had the good sense not to stay too long, and by the time dark had fallen he was gone, down the mountain on his bay horse across the gap towards home.

He was hardly out the door before she was out with her keys.

"Oh, now I can change!" For she was yet wearing her travelling costume, and it was somewhat worse for wear, due to its wetting and hasty drying last night. She unlocked the first trunk she came to and pulled out a dark silk evening gown. Thomas laughed.

She turned to him as she was unhooking the front of her jacket. "What's funny?"

"It's a bit rich," he said. She paused and bent him a loving glance.

"Not for us," she said; "not for you. . ." He gave over teasing at that, and they spent the evening drinking wine and reading from Thompson:

> Oft let me wander o'er the dewy fields
> Where freshness breathes, and dash the trembling drops
> From the bent bush, as thro' the verdant maze
> Of sweet-briar hedges I pursue my walk;
> Or taste the smell of the daisy; or ascend some eminence. . . .
>
> And see the country far diffused around
> One boundless blush, one white-empurpled show'r
> Of mingling blossoms; where the raptur'd eye
> Hurries from joy to joy, and hid beneath
> The fair profusion, yellow Autumn skies.

In the morning she began her housekeeping in earnest. They still rose a trifle later than was each their former habit, but after breakfast she was down in the kitchen in her plain gown and apron, bundled in a caraco jacket and extra petticoats, rearranging the kitchen furniture to suit her convenience and trying patiently to teach Dilcy a better hand at pastry than the leaden, soggy crust of the rabbit pie of yesterday's dinner. This would simply not do. She recalled all of old Jenny's light, perfect pastries and wondered how Thomas could have eaten such swill as they had been served for the last fifteen months. Granted, he was on the road a good deal of the time, but it cannot have been much of a homecoming at any time, with looking forward to such meals. Dilcy was better at vegetables and roasting meats, she discovered, but gravies left much to be desired.

She had in two strong young boys, moving heavy cupboards and storing the pots and trivets and skillets she had brought from The Forest, while she enquired of her cook how she usually made paste.

Dilcy rolled her eyes, uncomfortable. "Well, ma'am," she said in her squeaky voice, "I d' just usually take a mort o' fat and mix it up with 'nough flour to make it stiff, and then pour some water on and work it out."

Patty put her hand on her hip. "What sort of fat?"

"Hog, mostly."

"Well, there's the trouble," she said. "'Tis better to use suet, for it's lighter in its way. Here, I'll show you." She went over to the cupboard on the north wall and took down two of the stoneware bowls the boys had just put up. They were glazed in bright blue, and nothing stuck to them. She tucked up the ruffle on her shift sleeves and called for the suet, milk, flour, and her kitchen scales.

"The proportions are most important," she said, weighing out the pale, pinkish chunks of suet. She indicated a blob of bloody gelatin with the knife. "And none of this." She cut off the spots and proceeded. "Half a pound of fat is good for most double pastes. If you use more, then it goes grainy like a short crust, and we don't want that." Dilcy nodded, frowning a little. "Now, watch." She took up a pastry blade, cutting through the suet until it was the size of cheese curds, no larger than an half-inch in diameter. "You want the fat very fine; otherwise there are gaps in the paste when it's cooked. The flour should be just over half again as much as the fat, a pound and a quarter here." She measured out this amount on the scale, calculating for the weight of the bowl, and looked round the kitchen. "Where's the salt?"

Dilcy moved with speed. "Here it is." She went to the sack that was stored against the opposite wall.

"Well, bring me about half a teaspoon." The salt was ground fine in the mortar and laid in with the flour and fat. These she mixed together with her bare hands until they were crumbly and fine as coarse meal and added a half-pint of milk. "You shouldn't work pastes too much," she said as she kneaded, "or they go heavy. Just enough to amalgamate."

A space was cleared on the table, and Patty strewed it with the soft flour and rolled out first one ball of paste and then another. She was in the midst of the second when she heard an unfamiliar voice call from the doorway.

"Mrs. Jefferson."

The title was new enough to produce a blush in her, and she looked up quickly, hoping that in the dimness of the room it would not be noticed. In the open half of the door she saw two ladies, dressed as she in plain clothes.

"Good day," she returned, though she had no idea who they were. "Please come in." They entered and she pushed back a lock of fallen hair with her forearm, only to realize that her hands were full of flour and paste. She rubbed her hands on the towel and told Dilcy, "Finish this, if you please."

"I am Mrs. Garth," announced the woman who had addressed her. "My husband is the overseer. And this is Mrs. Reynolds."

She bowed to them, saying to the latter, "I have met your husband, Madame, this morning on my way outdoors. I'm pleased to meet you both."

"We came to welcome you," Mrs. Reynolds said. She was a tall woman, even without the pattens, with brown hair and a round face. She reminded Patty of Lisbet. Mrs. Garth was smaller and dark, and in spite of her narrow, pretty face and porcelain complexion, she gave one the sense that she was not frivolous. "Mrs. Willis would have come, but she has a cold."

Mrs. Willis's husband, Stephen, was their master bricklayer. Three-and-an-half years ago, Thomas had tried a case against him for Edward Lee for a job poorly done, but he had been perfection itself here on the mountain. Mrs. Reynolds produced the basket she was carrying. "She did wish to send you this pudding, however, and extend her welcome and best wishes to you."

Patty accepted the gift. The odor of nutmeg wafted pleasantly from under the cover. "Why, thank you, both of you. This is most kind. Please do give Mrs. Willis my regards and hopes for her recovery." She put the pudding on the table, out of harm's way, and gave the ladies back their basket. There was no coffee ground but there was plenty of water, and she could have some blackberry tea brewed in a few minutes. Though the chairs were rough, it was warm in the room and pleasant for a friendly chat. She indicated the hemp-bottomed chairs. "Won't you come and sit a while?" She was, in truth, glad that there was some hope of female companionship, for aside from their Negro women, she was hopelessly outnumbered.

Mrs. Reynolds looked over longingly toward the chairs and seemed about to speak, but her companion shook her head.

"No, indeed, thank you, Mrs. Jefferson," Mrs. Garth said in her clear voice. "I've left my servant with the baby, and she's a stupid girl. I wouldn't wish to leave her longer than necessary."

Patty clasped her hand. "Oh, why yes, of course," she cried. "You must not leave your baby! Please, don't let me keep you."

Mrs. Garth turned to her tall friend. "Shall we go, Elizabeth?" Patty's heart swelled that this new friend, so like Lisbet, should share her sister's name.

"I believe I'll stay, thank you," Elizabeth said quietly. "That is, if you don't mind, Mrs. Jefferson?" Patty smiled. "Oh, not at all! We are not terrible busy." She said to the overseer's wife, "Would you like for me to fetch you an escort? 'Tis a steep way down the garden, especially with the snow."

Mrs. Garth shook her head. "Nay. I'll manage, but thank you the same." She made a curtsey, which Patty returned with a bow, for she knew the requirements of her station. They went to the door.

"Next time you must bring your baby," she said. Mrs. Garth turned, and for the first time she saw a thawing in those sharp eyes and a genuine flicker of friendship. If this woman had been expecting her to play the haughty lady of the manor, she was much mistaken. There was a glimmer of a sweet, dancing-eyed belle in the black eyes on a level with her own. Patty wondered what had occurred in her life to make Garth's lady so defensive. Her guest smiled briefly and murmured in low, emotional tones, "Thank you. I will."

"Good day," Patty said, opening the door.

"Good day, Mrs. Jefferson."

"You must not mind Mary," Elizabeth Reynolds said when Patty came into the room again. "She has a good heart, but is ill at ease in expressing it oftentimes."

"Well," Patty said, taking down her tin of blackberry leaves from the shelf, "I dareswear it cannot be easy for her to be usurped in her privilege here." For in absence of a mistress, the overseeing of household duties fell to the overseer's wife, if he had one. She put three teaspoons of leaves in the pot and took it over to the fire.

"I'll do that, ma'am," Dilcy said, lifting the kettle off the hob with a towel and pouring out the water.

"Won't you sit down?" she said to her guest, indicating one of the chairs. "I won't be a moment, but I have a dumpling that wants putting together."

"Oh, of course." Elizabeth sat, taking off her pattens and shaking the snow off her skirts. Meanwhile, Patty buttered the bowl and laid in a layer of paste. Dilcy poured in the filling she had been cooking of mutton, onions, carrots, and the sauce and watched as her mistress covered the whole with the other round of paste, sealing the edges with deft fingers.

"Now," Patty said in a low voice, "the most important thing is that the water must not seep inside to the crust, or it shall be ruined. The cloth must be sealed very tight. Where's the cotton?"

"In the cupboard."

"Well, fetch me about a yard of it," she directed. When Dilcy had done so, she wrung out the cloth in hot water and dredged it in flour, covering the bowl. This was to ensure that the cloth didn't stick to the delicate paste beneath. She tied the cloth at top and bottom with clove knots and handed it to her cook. "That should do," she said proudly. She had learned what she knew from old Jenny, who could accomplish the entire maneuver of wetting, wrapping, and tying in less time than she, Patty, could wring out a cloth.

She poured out the tea in her china cups and took it, with a lump of sugar to her guest.

"That was most impressive," Elizabeth murmured. "I wish I could get my servant to work like that. Without a single reprimand."

Patty blushed and sat, breaking up some of the sugar with the tongs. "I believe she is overcome," she said. "Our arrival was rather a surprise, and she is yet in awe of that."

Elizabeth stirred her tea, and said judiciously, "Yes, I'd heard you'd arrived very late." So the story was known. Well, they would not know the half of it, how despairing she had been; enough to think that she had made a great mistake. But when Thomas had played his fiddle, she was charmed, and lost any lingering doubts the wine had not yet dissipated. She could feel herself blushing again.

"Yes," she said bemusedly.

"'Tis a hard road up here," Mrs. Reynolds drank tea. "And I have not been down since the snowfall. It must have been exceeding treacherous."

"How long has there been snow here?" She asked, taking up her cup.

"Since before Christmas."

Patty saw what those words meant and the regret behind her guest's brown eyes. "Oh," she said in sympathy. "And you did not travel to see your family these holidays? I am sorry."

Elizabeth smiled gratefully. "How kind of you to say! Oh you are a sincere friend, Mrs. Jefferson."

"I hope I may be, Mrs. Reynolds," she said invitingly. "May I tell you? You put me much in mind of one of my sisters, my favorite sister. Her name is Elizabeth, also."

"Ah." Elizabeth clasped her hand warmly, and she was glad she had ventured to be so bold. They whiled away the morning in magpie chatter, ranging over divers subjects both domestic and general, and at the end were friends indeed. It grew nigh onto dinner time, and Patty called Charles and Quash, who had been working outdoors clearing snow from the path, to escort her new friend down the treacherous path to her house on the south side of the mountain. They waited shift-footed, chafing their cold hands in the warm room, while Mrs. Reynolds bent in her chair to tie her pattens on her feet once again and stamped the snow off them; for though her boots were sturdy, they would never withstand the snow and mud of the yard. At the door, she and Patty kissed in the English manner.

"Good day, Mrs. Jefferson," Elizabeth said fondly.

"Good day, Mrs. Reynolds," Patty returned, smiling. She stood at the door until her new friend and her escort were out of sight.

Thomas came up. "Waiting for me?" he said lightly, so as not to be heard within. She laughed, taking his hand. "Yes!" she cried, opening the door again. "Come see our miracle," and she led him into the tidy transformed kitchen. The flags were sparkling clean, having been scrubbed with sand and lye water, and the cobwebs had been chased from every corner. The cupboards and tables were orderly and efficiently organized. Dinner was moments from being served. And it had all been accomplished with two gawky boys and a simple but well-intentioned girl, whose last job had been weeding the kitchen garden. Dilcy now was outdoors, so they could be frank with one another.

"I should have married you sooner," he teased, looking round at her work.

"You'd have eaten better, anyway," she said.

Later, over the pudding, when he was marvelling at the difference in the cuisine, she ventured, "My dear, something really must be done about Dilcy."

He looked up from the chestnut-stuffed pud. "What?"

She sighed. "Well, she is amiable enough and works hard, but she lacks direction. I daresay that if she had no one to oversee her, she would be utterly at a loss as to how to conduct herself so as to accomplish everything necessary in a reasonable amount of time. You say she is not bright, and I believe that if she had some quick-witted soul working with her who could organize the day she would do well, but as it is, she's near hopeless. I cannot spend all my days directing her every move as I did today."

She poked at her beautiful crust with the long tines of a fork, hoping he would not take her criticism wrongly.

He was silent for so long that she feared the worst and looked up at him from under her lashes. He was watching her, and now burst out laughing.

"If you aren't a lawyer's daughter," he cried. "Well-spoken, my sweet." He leaned and kissed her. "And I can hardly argue with it. But truth to tell, I had never thought about it before. Of course you are right. Perfectly right. I'll ask Jupiter if he knows any of the girls or women who would be suitable to the post. His stomach has never been wrong."

She smiled again. She didn't wish to be seen as domineering or without her rights, but the kitchen was her one undisputed place of domain, and she could not have it in disorder. "I'm so glad," she said. "I was afraid you might be angry at me, deposing your servant from her place so hastily."

"Not when the product is as good as this," he replied. "It makes me wonder how I've survived thus far without you."

She laughed her bubbling laugh. "You only love me for my cookery," she teased. His hand sought her knee, and his hazel eyes kindled a greener hue.

"You know better than that," he murmured, in an intimate tone. She felt the rising color in her face, and a thrilling warmth. Yet another meal was left unfinished. They shuttered the windows and didn't give a hang for what the servants thought.

> *I had beheld, e'en her whole sex, unmov'd*
> *Look'd o'er 'em like a Bed of gaudy Flowers*
> *That lift their painted Heads & live a day,*
> *Then shed their trifling Glories unregarded:*
> *My heart disdain'd their Beauties, til she came*
> *With ev'ry Grace that Nature's Hand could give.*

23

Enlargements of Circumstance

Monticello

The next day Patty reckoned up her cash on hand, £ 4/11/3, and wrote it out on a loose sheet of paper which she enclosed in one of Thomas's casebooks, for she had begged a book for her accounts and it is what he produced. There were blank pages at the back, so as was her wont, she turned the book upside down and backwards and began her journal of housewifery, as she had done before at The Forest and Elk Hill.

On Thursday she called for Jupiter in the morning, and he met her in the house where she was tidying up.

"Yas'm?" he said. For one who purportedly liked to eat so well he was amazingly thin, even more so than Thomas. His wrists and knees stood out in relief through his clothes.

"Oh, Jupiter," she said, turning from the chest. She skirted her fortepiano and came to him purposefully. "I was wondering if you would be so good as to ride down to Fouette's and procure for me a small cask of cider. Our supply is low, and I shouldn't like to run out."

He bowed his head. "Yas'm Missus, I will."

"Good." She went to her bride-box and took out Thomas's ten- shilling piece.

"This ought to suffice." She gave him the money, and then remembered that Thomas was supposed to have asked him about a woman to cook. He was shy with her still, and she didn't want to press but her need was great. She'd spent most of yesterday in the kitchen again.

"Did Mr. Jefferson tell you my request?" She tried to ask conversationally.

He ducked his head again. "Yas'm, he did," he said, and looked at her askance. "I can think but one gel 't would be well for you, tho' she a mite young. . . ."

She smiled. "And who's that?"

"Her name Sukey, and she but thirteen or little more now," he said, and by his nervousness she perceived that he was rather taken with this girl. She nodded soberly. "I see."

"But she a fine hand, ma'am, and smart, too. She make the best cakes I ever ate."

She laughed. "Well, that's the best recommendation I could hear!" she said. "Next time you see her, won't you send her up to me that I might meet her?"

Jupiter was beaming. "I will, shore, ma'am, thank you ma'am." He was practically dancing with pleasure. "I'll go for the cider straight," he assured her, hurrying out the door.

When she told Thomas at dinner of their exchange, he shook his head.

"You have won him over, I doubt not, pleasing his appetite and his heart. He's been mooning over Sukey since she came here. Very clever of you, my dear."

"It was entirely selfish of me, I assure you," she remarked. "I wished him to run an errand for me and saw no better way of winning him over to it. I had no idea his heart's delight was involved."

Sukey arrived on her doorstep the next day, a fresh-faced sweet young girl who was not above fourteen years. But, as promised, she was quick and clever, and once trained, made their lives run the smoother for her presence in the kitchen. Dilcy was put out, however.

The second week of February came, and Patty began to have reason to think her courses would not return at the usual time. The day passed; Mrs. Jefferson came for a visit with Lissa and Nan, and she said nothing. She went about her usual business, opening a barrel of Colonel Harrison's flour, sent as one of three for a wedding present, bought eggs and potatoes of the Negroes, made notations of the livestock killed for table, and waited.

By the end of the month, when Thomas was getting ready to go to the courts, she was certain, but said nothing, expecting that he would notice and remark upon matters, for he was most observant; yet he did not. Surely he would have remarked the lack, even given her long course, for the last time had been a week after the wedding. Most men—even husbands in her experience—were notoriously blind to such intimate details, but Thomas was not most men. She bought butter from one of the workmen's wives, paid Robert Page's wife for sending her a ewe lamb, brewed a cask of beer, and took inventory of her house linens:

> a list of the house linen
> 6 diaper table cloths
> 10 ditto damask
> 12 diaper napkins marked   T I 71
> 12 ditto towels T I 71
> 6 pr of sheets 5 pillow-cases   T I 71

"I'll be back in two weeks," Thomas said, when he kissed her farewell before his journey.

"Two long weeks," she said, glumly. It was very early and they sat on the bed, she yet in her dressing sacque. He smiled and caressed her face. "At least you know I'll return in haste," he murmured. Her heart gave a leap, and she knew she must now tell him her news or forfeit until after his return. Then they would be occupied with packing for the Assembly, and she would probably be sick. She was already sick. She didn't want him to think something was wrong, if he came home to suddenly find her retching. He felt badly enough about the little cold their journey here had given her, and it but a trifle.

"Thomas," she paused, and her courage failed her. Why was it so hard to tell him the greatest news of her life? He kissed the hollow place behind her ear, and her mind wandered.

"Yes, my sweet?" His voice was a throaty murmur.

"I—" she paused again, distracted. "I fear things may be more crowded here when you return. . ."

He left off kissing her. "What do you mean? Is Betsy's journey delayed?" For Lisbet had planned to visit while he was away.

"No," she said, quaveringly. Her heart thudded in her ears. "I—" She looked into his amber-green eyes, and a wash of calm came over her. "I am with child," she said simply, that he might not mistake her. He stopped dead still and his face paled. He stared at her for a long time.

"Oh, my Patty," he murmured at last, a slow-dawning flush of elation coming over his face. "Oh, my dear girl, my beauty—" He embraced her and then held out her hands, looking her over. "Well, I should have known," he said, and she blushed. "When did you know?"

"For certainly about a week ago," she said, and then in a rush, "I thought you would notice. . . things. . . but you said nothing, and every day it was worse and worse. I wanted to tell you, and wanted you to discover it on your own."

He shook his head. "I didn't think— I wasn't thinking at all—" he looked her over again. "Yes, I can see now." He paused.

"Oh God, and we. . . ." His oblique gesture made reference to their frequent closeting themselves away from the world in their little haven. "We haven't hurt anything, have we?" he asked anxiously. She laughed.

"No, and if you leave off, I shall be most sorely vexed." He smiled.

"There's my vixen." He embraced her again, the heaviness of his coat scratchy through her shift. He was trembling. "My dear girl," he murmured in delight into her hair. "Oh!" He rocked her a little in his arms, his happiness making her cry. "Oh," he said again and kissed her soundly, "we're going to have a baby!" His enthusiasm was utterly endearing. She laughed and cried and tumbled with him on the bed, giddy and glad, her earlier nausea ignored.

He was late going because of her news but didn't mind. He bade her a tender good-bye and promised to be back the instant the major cases were done in Augusta. When he was gone, she sat on the bed again and wept a little, happily, and sat musing over their rosy future before the nausea that had earlier threatened sent her scurrying to yank the pot out from under the bed. She had hoped she would not be sick as she had been with Jack, but it seemed the way of things with her. It was all worth it, though, and she was glad that Thomas should miss the worst of it. He would fret.

She dressed then and went down for her breakfast. There was no point in having them tote it up here just for her when she could do it herself. She would not be alone long, for Lisbet was due in a few days. She could manage until then, and looked forward to the novelty of being utterly alone for the first time in almost five years.

In the interim before Lisbet's visit, she was wandering the bookshelves in their little house in search of something new to read, and came upon, to her delight and amusement, John Floyer's *History of Cold Bathing,* printed in 1706. Though this practice was supposedly a preventative to ill health, inuring the practitioner to all weathers, she was not unaware of the other virtues of cold bathing, namely the cooling of one's passions. By her knowledge of him and certain rather telling remarks he had made in their courtship, she was sure that Thomas used this method for other purposes than the author of this treatise intended. She thumbed through the book, reading his marginal remarks about the efficacy of various courses, and decided, for a small joke, to leave it on his reading desk for his return. She was in no wise actually suggesting that they give over the privileges of their marriage bed, for she was quite in earnest when she said that she would be sorely vexed without. There was nothing in her experience that would cause harm, even late on. She simply wanted to see what his reaction would be.

When Lisbet came she was down the kitchen garden, picking out herbs with Dilcy for dinner. She heard a voice call out from up by the house, "Sister!" and she looked up.

"Lisbet!" she cried in excitement, and waved. She pressed the chives on Dilcy and hurried up the slushy plank steps beside the paling fence.

"Oh, Betsy!" She flung open her arms and embraced her sister, more glad than she thought she'd be to see an old familiar face. Even with her new friendships, the sheer isolation of the mountaintop had told on her. Visiting was not so easy here as taking a barque across the river.

"You look splendid," Lisbet said when they parted, pushing forward her travelling bonnet. "The air up here certainly agrees with you," she teased. Patty felt herself blushing.

"That isn't all," she said, taking her sister's arm and walking toward the house.

"What?"

She nodded. "Come inside," she said, "and I'll tell you."

"No!" Betsy said when she'd told her. "When?"

She smiled as she set the small kettle of water to boil on the fire. "Some time in the middle of October."

"Well, we won't see you at the Assembly." Patty turned from the fire and came to sit at the table.

"How are Francis and my little nephews, and everyone at home? I've not heard the least news since we came. We had a dreadful snowfall, and I expect it's kept letters away."

"Francis does well. He spent last week at Winterpock installing the new overseer. Dalton simply indulged the whip too much, so he released him. He was much put out, as you may imagine." Lisbet said.

"Who's the new man?" She rose again to pour water in the teapot.

"A Mr. Crothie, a Scot, I think. He's not as young as Dalton was, and one hopes, more experienced at getting the people to work without inciting an uprising." Lisbet's voice was dry.

Patty turned in alarm. "Had you an uprising?"

"Very nearly." Lisbet picked a minute piece of lint off her sleeve. "One of the corn cribs burnt down very mysteriously. No one seems to know anything."

"Oh dear." The news was quite sobering.

Betsy changed the subject. "Young Francis is walking now—"

"*Is* he?" She asked in delight, for he was only nine months.

"And Dick is become quite bossy and obstinate. But we bear with him for the greater part. Oh!" Betsy took the teacup she was offered. "Tibb is in your way, also. They anticipate it sometime in the early part of August, I think."

"She never said a word!" Patty exclaimed, breaking off a piece of sugar for her tea. Lisbet frowned.

"Well, I believe they wanted to wait and make certain, since she had such a poor outcome last time."

"Yes." Tibb had lost a child shortly after her marriage at two or three months forward. "Papa must be pleased no end," she said.

Lisbet laughed. "Aye and will be more so when I tell him your news. . . or have you told him, yet?"

She shook her head. "'Twould take longer for a letter to get down there than yourself to bring the news," she said. "Besides, we've just known these two weeks certainly."

Her sister smiled. "And what does Mr. Jefferson think?"

She blushed, remembering his delight, and inclined her head. "I believe it took him somewhat by surprise, but he was very glad." She looked up, putting a hand to her warm cheek.

"You'll do just fine," Lisbet assured. "Have you engaged a midwife?"

"Lisbet!" she laughed. "It's seven months yet!"

"Never too soon." Betsy drank her tea.

"Besides," she continued. "I don't know of any hereabouts."

"Well, I dareswear that his sisters could aid you in that regard. Didn't Mrs. Lewis just lie in?"

"Aye," she said. Lucy could tell her of the women in the area trustworthy enough.

"And there's always his mother—"

"*Please,*" she entreated, setting down her cup carefully.

"Oh dear," Lisbet said quietly. "That doesn't sound good at all. What's the matter?"

Patty shook her head. "It's nothing really. It's just that she isn't. . . well, warm; do you know what I mean?" She looked up. "I try to count it off to her age, that women of her generation are more formal than we, but I remember Aunty Randall, and I know it isn't so. She's a cold woman, his mother. I do my best to be engaging and friendly, but she won't admit my advances in that way. It's most distressing."

She scolded herself for silly tears that sprung to her eyes as Lisbet took her hand. It was her circumstance, she knew, for she had been weepy too with Jack, but it looked badly.

"I can see that," Betsy said softly, caressing her hand.

She shook her head. "You don't understand," she amended, waving her hand. "This. . . weakness is only me. It's not as bad as that. She isn't cutting or cruel. She's just cold."

"Well, your news should clear that up." Betsy picked up the teapot. "I never met a woman yet whose heart didn't melt at the thought of being a granny, especially by her son. Do you want some more tea?"

Patty shook her head, sniffling.

"Don't worry, Patt, she'll come round."

The way she spoke, anyone'd thought it was Lisbet was the elder sister, but she always had been steady. They sat and drank tea, and then Patty showed her the fortepiano. They played a few tunes, went for a walk in the mild spring air, then retired for their dinner in amiable companionship. She was glad she'd taken Thomas's advice and invited her to come up. It showed how well he knew her, for though she had not spoken of being homesick, he plainly saw that she was. Lisbet was good medicine, and at the end of her visit she had but two days to wait until Thomas came home. By then her spirits were much improved.

Would that the same could have been said of her health. The morning he was due she was laid low with a violent bout of nausea and sickness, cramps, and fever. She lay on the bed all morning, trying to read between periodic spasms of these combined agonies, worrying that she might lose the child. But there was no sign of a flux, so she remained where she was, in utter dissipation, until she heard the harness jangles and shouts down by the stable herald his arrival. She rose then and quickly put on a house gown and brushed some Spanish papers over her cheeks to hide the pallor. He mustn't think she was languishing, or he wouldn't ever go away again; and he had neglected his law practice and other duties shamefully.

He opened the door and she turned, for she was poking at the embers of the fire. He seemed taller, thinner, and, when the mask of his reserve melted on sight of her, livelier than she recalled. His complexion was ruddy and showed signs of sunburn. So he hadn't spent all his time in court! That was good to see. She laid down the poker and came over, waiting for him to remove his hat. He closed the door behind him, and his smile made up the lack of light.

"Hello, Mama," he murmured, with a kiss.

She kissed him back. "Hello, Papa."

"I missed you," he said. She laughed, touching his face where the sunburn was. "I can tell."

"No, really," he insisted.

She raised an eyebrow in imitation of him and let him go to put his things away. She sat on the high bed, swinging her muled feet idly while he retrieved the books from his saddlebag. She watched as he went over to his book alcove and began methodically shelving them in their proper places. He turned and noticed the book lying on the stand, picked it up. All was still silence for a moment. She held her breath.

"Where did you find this?" he asked, turning to her, his head bent with an eyebrow raised sardonically.

"On the shelf," she tittered, dimpling.

He smirked at her. "You minx!" He flung the book away and came rushing at her, swooping her up, and tickling her unprotected middle in the loose gown. She squealed, shouting with laughter, crying, "Stop, stop!" but he continued.

She endured it as long as she could then cried, "Forfeit!"

They were still laughing together. He lifted back his head. "I name my price?"

"Oh no," she said, holding up a hand. "I know your prices, sirrah, and they are highway robbery."

"In that case—" He made to tickle her again, and she gasped, laughing, "All right, all right! Name your price."

"A kiss—" he said.

"Is that all? In truth sir, 'tis but small potatoes."

He bent her a wicked glance. "Yes, but I didn't say what the conditions were."

She caught her breath, softly now. "I guess you did miss me after all," she said. He was very close, his arms about her properly. "Don't you want to hear the conditions?" he murmured.

"Surprise me," she said, and kissed him. They were interrupted by a knock on the door.

"Go away," Thomas called, not very loudly. The knock came again.

"Oh hell," he muttered, and went to the door. It was Jupiter with his trunk and pack.

"Your timing is exquisite," he said, allowing him the house.

"Sir?" Jupiter enquired, blankly.

Thomas shook his head. "Never mind. Thank you. Put them over there." He gestured towards the other alcove beyond the fire. As Jupiter was going, she said to him, "I believe Sukey's baked a cake today, Jupiter."

He turned to her briefly, his cheeks darkening. "Thank you, ma'am." By his demeanor, she adduced that he had now some idea of what he'd interrupted, for he stumbled out hurriedly and did not look back. Thomas came to her again.

"How's my blossom?"

"Well enough," she admitted. She was still cramped.

"And our dear pledge?" he asked softly.

"Fine and strong," she said. It had to be, for that was the wives' tale about nausea. It also foretold a son. It must be a son, as even gooseberry jelly could not cure her uneasy stomach.

"Good." It was lucky that the pot was on the other side of the bed, or he'd have seen that she was not fine. She managed to move it again while he was busy emptying his pack, and when they went for a walk she had a quiet word with Dilcy. When they got back, all evidence was removed. The spring air was warm and heavy with the scent of burgeoning fruit trees. Life renewed itself, and Thomas was, to her knowledge, never the wiser of her unease, for she never mentioned it; and luck was with her that the worst of her indisposition was over.

24

Sundry Visits

Monticello, Williamsburg, Rosewell, The Forest

They built a granary house that spring before they left for town, and a sheep pen, for Mrs. Wythe had promised her two ewe lambs when they came. In addition to the one she had from Molly Page, she would have a nice little stock begun. She made more beer, and from the grease saved from a mutton killed late in the month, she had enough fat to make up forty-six pounds of soft soap for laundry and other household washing, and twelve pounds of hard for their personal toilet.

The roof was put on the dining room and the parlor floor was laid, although it would not be finished until the weather improved, when the nailing and varnishing could be done in open air. At least they were no longer subject to living in the tent-like atmosphere of the canvas roof. It was so low and depressing that it made her want to catch her breath every time she sat down there. The oilcloth on the windows was bad enough, admitting no natural light. They had George Gilmer and his wife Lucy to dinner and ate turkey. Shortly thereafter, they packed up their trunks and goods in the wagon and began the journey down to Williamsburg, anticipating a stay of at least two months.

For part of this time, they rented rooms in Nicholson Street in the house the family had secured before in October. Thomas went about his business in the General Court and Governor's Council, and she spent her days visiting: with her aunt, her sister Tibb who was in town, Mrs. Wythe, and Mrs. Speaker Randolph. She began a pillow for the baby, drawing out fanciful designs of birds and spring blossoms in her receipt book. She purchased a suit of childbed linen and the stuff for a new petticoat, as she had given away or refitted those maternity petticoats she had had before. In the evenings she and Thomas attended the theater, musicales, or supper parties, and there was always dancing.

She did not dance the country dances that season. In the first place it would have been unseemly at formal parties for her, as a married woman, to dance them. In the second place, she was feeling quite heavy in the belly these days, not enlarged yet, but gravid, and it was uncomfortable to jog about so. She was pleased to take a turn in a minuet or quadrille, if it was with Thomas, but for the most part she sat with the married women or strolled about, making up conversations with people she knew or watching the men play at faro or billiards. Thomas played neither of the latter himself, but many was the time he was engaged in a private conversation in which she had no part, and she must needs find her amusement elsewhere. She was not put out, for she had her own friends and knew his private sentiments anyway. They were hardly expected to go on as they had when courting.

After two weeks she retired, going to stay with her father at Charles City, having had her fill of town life. Her retirement was at Thomas's insistence, for he declared that she was looking peaked, and she did not protest overmuch. She saw him at the weekends, and the rest of the time he occupied their rooms in town, riding out between Williamsburg and Charles City on Friday evenings as he had done when they were courting.

They spent four days with the Pages at Rosewell. John and Fanny had had four children, tho' one had died in infancy, and were anticipating another's arrival in the winter. Fanny was as lively and bright as John, and she was dear as a sister, for they had been friends since Patty was ten or eleven years old. Though not a bluestocking, Fanny was learned and well read; though not a belle, she was charming and gracious. She managed her large household staff with admirable calm, for such great numbers of house servants (they had forty in all from bottom to top) would have sent a lesser woman running distracted.

Rosewell had been rightly called the finest manor on the Virginia shore, and the best example of what colonial architecture could produce. Vaulting for three storeys plus an attic into the clear space on the rise of the hill above the York river in Gloucester, it was a great rambling house, rectangular in shape with the outbuildings turning away in columns at the back. In the main hall between the borders of the grand staircases there were two magnificently carved mahogany fireplace mantels, bearing two equally impressive French gilt-looking glasses. All the best workmanship was evident in the gleaming joinery, in the cornice moldings and ceiling decoration, in the India and Turkey carpets, and in the appointments in the private rooms. They had the best collection of silver this side of the Carters that Patty had ever seen.

Amid all this opulence they lived with the noisy, happy clutter of parents, children, cousins, guests, dogs, and servants in an atmosphere of genteel disorder. There were as many books as in their little house at Monticello, and an even greater collection of music, games—for Page was fond of cards, parlor boards, and billiards—hunting trophies, and assorted oddments and mementos. The Page, Mann, and Carter ancestors gazed down from the walls of the hall and upper gallery as in any English country house, portraits dating back to that of Page's namesake John, who emigrated from England more than an hundred years before.

The family had an easy grace that only came from such long association with the land and a single place. Jane and Peter Jefferson had not been able to duplicate that at Shadwell, despite her proud Randolph heritage. But hopefully, she and Thomas would be able to found such at Monticello. It would be wondrous fine to look in old age, as Page's stepmother Anne did, upon an increasing flock of grandchildren, or great-grandchildren, and know that life would continue here just as it always had. They had all the right ingredients, with the Randolphs and the Eppeses, and even her father's family running far back in England and Wales, all commingling in a single, new line. There was value in the Jefferson blood, for its newness—Thomas knew back only to his great-grandfather for certain—was its greatest asset. There was a pioneering, adventuresome spirit there that would carry them far into the future.

That future spoke for itself while they were at Rosewell. She and Fanny were walking in the knot garden in the sunshine, each with a shade raised against the brightness, when she felt the first fluttering herald of quickening, as of a butterfly caught in a net. She was so surprised that she stopped and gave a little cry. Fanny turned.

"Patty?"

She looked up. "No, no," she said, holding up a hand. "It's nothing, just. . . our stranger making his presence known. . . ." She blushed and dropped her eyes again, sorry now for her outburst.

Fanny came over, tenderness in her blue eyes. "Is this the first time?" she asked softly.

Patty did not look up, hardly daring to believe the sensation. Their baby! Oh! Her eyes flooded with tears. "Yes," she nodded.

Fanny smiled, taking her arm. "Well, there's a cause celebre!" she said, and gave her a hug. "I'm so pleased for you!" Quickening was always taken as a good sign, for misbirth was less likely after that.

When she had collected herself somewhat, they began to walk again, talking of babies and confinements. Fanny looked up at a movement from the house. "Oh, look, there's Joan with our Sally." She called out, "Sally, come here to Mama, dear!"

The Pages' daughter was just over two years old and was fond of running. The child came as bidden, her soft brown curls bobbling. There was no mistaking that she was John's child, for she bore the strong familial resemblance. Fanny laid a hand on her head. "There's a good child. Say hello to Mrs. Jefferson," she prompted.

Sally stuck a finger in her mouth and curtseyed shyly, afterwards hiding her face in Fanny's skirts. Her mother shook her head. "She is usually most animated with company," she said. "And since she's learnt to talk it's difficult to hush her."

"It must be she's tired yet," Patty volunteered, for the child had been sleeping.

"Indeed," Fanny said, and let the child go along to her nurse. They continued their walk.

"John tells me your building proceeds apace at Monticello," she said, gazing out upon the woods beyond the garden gate. "I wonder how you manage, with building going on about you, to run a household."

Patty smiled. "'Tis true, we have a real roof now, and the floors are laid in the middle room. But as to the rest, it is only because we have our kitchen below the house that I own any discipline or convenience at all." She paused, blushing a little. "One hears everything, so there is not a domestic crisis I am unapprised of. I will admit to you that it's not always easy. I ended up one day with sawdust all over my freshly washed laundry because the wind shifted, and was picking it out of my petticoats for weeks, but I haven't had so many failures as to dishearten me entirely. My sister Lewis is much more unlucky in that way than I, and she has her own mother with her and an established place."

"I remember when I came here," Fanny mused. "My mother Page was then not suffering from rheumatics as she is now, and I was quite young and untried. I'm afraid 'twas not a good combination. But," she sighed, "she took ill shortly, and I was forced to make a go of things on my own. I have since come to value her advice greatly. And she is such a boon to me with all the sewing that I don't know what I should do without her."

"It does not trouble her fingers to cut and sew?" she asked.

"Not for short periods or in fine weather," Fanny said. "But you never had that trouble. Widowhood has the sole advantage of granting one experience."

Patty sighed, passing over the subject of widowhood, for though it was a wound, it was an unintended one.

"I was lucky enough also to have my father's confidence as mistress of his house." She shook her head. "What I should have done otherwise, I cannot say, for Elk Hill was difficult as it stood. They were not pleased to see my installation and plagued me grievously." She meant the house servants who, in absence of a mistress, were almost entirely at liberty. "So we all have our fire, you see." She smiled at her friend.

Fanny patted her hand. "But all that's past, eh? We old married lot. We could give those spring chickens a well word!"

"Someone should," she said, looking down at a planting of lad's love. "Heaven knows their mamas do not! Even a copy of Bradley's book would not prepare some of them." She meant *The British House-wife,* printed two years ago.

"'Tis sadly so." Fanny agreed. She leaned close, laughing a little. "But some are better served by hard experience! Maria Byrd, for instance."

"Oh, shh," Patty hushed her, looking about. "If it ever got back to her. . . ."

"Back to her," her companion scoffed. "My dear, her own sisters gossip about her so. She's legendary! I never saw a woman wear out a servant as I once did Polly. It was a perfect scandal!"

"Perhaps she had just cause," she said. She'd been angry and frustrated enough herself before to beat a servant, although she never had.

"Patty Wayles, you're too good to be true!" Fanny exclaimed. "You know how she carries on. Admit it!"

"Yes," she said reluctantly. Such gossip always made her wonder what was said about her in *her* absence. She was therefore unwilling to indulge in it to any degree. Only with her own sisters was she perfectly frank. "But as with some others, I hope that by granting her indulgence I might also be so graced in my worst moments, for I am far from perfect that way."

"Tut," Fanny said shortly, "I don't believe it! I've never heard a word against you."

"By mercy only," she said dryly. She looked up, and saw the men coming back from their ride.

What a picture they were together, John and Thomas! In frame and countenance they were similar, differing slightly only in coloring. They might have been brothers. They went on as though they were. Last night they had played chess and oiled guns together after the company had grown weary of cards. It had been hard on Thomas, growing up in a houseful of sisters, and John's friendship—more than friendship—supplied him what his boyhood had lacked. They were like old Mr. Jefferson and Joshua Fry together. Mrs. Jefferson had complained of it, though with what cause Patty wouldn't venture to say. For her part, she knew that she had Thomas's heart and a place in his life that John could never supplant. She watched as they went into the house laughing and was glad now they had come.

In spite of a vow made by Thomas and John to the contrary, the dinner conversation ran to observations of the weather here and in the west, and she and Fanny were reduced once more to idly listening with amused patience. It was impossible to get these two together without the discussion revolving about heavenly spheres or the latest design for a pivoting desk chair or whatnot.

"Did you see," John was saying, "that Mars is now come in within conjunct of Venus?"

Thomas was lounging in his chair, leaning on one elbow as he commonly did, so that one shoulder was more raised than another. It gave him a comically boyish look and drove his mother distracted. She was ever prodding him to sit up straight, as she had in his childhood, to no avail. Patty found it endearing, and a measure of his stubbornness against that woman's rule. Sometimes, she knew, he did it willfully, as if to say that he was long since a man and would do as he pleased in his own house, but it was ingrained habit also, and he did it now without thinking. Now his eyes flickered over to her briefly.

"No," he said. "I've been too busy for many observations. When did it appear?"

"This last week," John remarked, looking toward the window. "If it's clear we could go up on the roof later to view it."

"Oh aye," Thomas said, leaning forward now. "What a pity we shall not see the trio of those and Jupiter again for some years." For the year before there had been a convergence of the three planets which occurred only once in an hundred years, and he had missed observations due to hazy skies and rain.

"Did you manage to see that here, Partridge?" The latter was a nickname, after the Scots almanac writer, because of his enthusiasm for astronomy.

"I did!" John enthused. "Though only on one night clearly."

"And the rest rain," Thomas said, shrugging. "Would I had my equipment near then, but it was at Monticello. I did have a spyglass, but it wasn't strong enough to—"

Fanny made a noise and rose from the table. "If you two gentlemen are going to be thus engaged long," she smiled at her husband indulgently, "I believe we ladies will retire. Please do put out the lights before you come to bed." She laughed, and John with her. "Won't you come, Mrs. Jefferson? I am sure we can find other amusements more suited than a drawl with our heads in the clouds." She picked up her fan while Patty rose likewise.

"Good night, John," she said to her husband. "Thomas," she nodded. He rose and made a bow.

"Fanny," he said. His eyes strayed in Patty's direction. "We won't be long," he promised. She said nothing but rolled her eyes and followed Fanny to the door. John laughed heartily as Thomas sat again. "She knows you better than you do yourself," he said. "Good night, Patty. I shall see he finds his way to bed."

She made a mocking curtsey. "I am obliged, sir," she murmured, and went from the room.

It was sometime in the middle of the night when he came to bed, to judge by the way her eyeballs hurt when she wakened. She turned over and leaned up on an elbow. "Hello," she murmured, kissing him. "Did you have a good time?"

His hands sought her in the dark. "I'm sorry. I didn't mean to wake you."

She smiled a little. "I can never sleep when you're away," she said, settling into his arms. His lean warmth was comfortable. "Did you all go up on the roof?"

"Aye," he said, musingly. "Mars and Venus in conjunction. . . . You know what that means—"

"Mercury?" she teased. He laughed shortly and she sought his hand. "I had a message from our own increase today," she said, laying his hand upon the small rounding of her belly.

"Did you?" he asked lightly, in delight. "How appropriate!" She basked in his soft caress. "So all is right with our fair friend." His other hand came down along her back, the callused fingertips tickling, and she drew up.

"Sorry," he said abstractedly and embraced her firmly, with a groan. "Ah, my sweet, life is good. All I want for is within my reach. . . ."

She could not see but felt his eyes, dreaming bright dreams in the dark. A devil moved her, and she murmured, shifting a little, "How convenient that we agree!"

He gasped, surprised, and complained in a low tone, "Your hands are cold."

She laughed and kissed his throat. "I know a remedy. . ." He bent his head and kissed her, and she did not need to elaborate.

In the middle of May they were back in Williamsburg, and she went to see Dr. Brown about a prurient discharge she had had now for some weeks, and would not go away. While at Monticello she had tried all her simples from her receipt book appertaining to the problem, using those ingredients she had on hand, to little avail. It had become quite painful, to say nothing of annoying and distressing, for it required constant washing, and her skin was already raw without that.

With great blushes she sat in his consulting room, her gloved hands clenched on her bag, and explained the trouble, haltingly at first, but in greater detail in answer to his searching and most embarrassing questions. Bad enough that she must explain to Thomas why she required a doctor's visit, but to relate to this stranger the intimate details of her marriage bed was unendurable. When he requested an examination, she wished the floor would open up and cover her over. In the end, he told her with a sympathetic smile that her trouble was not at all uncommon to either new brides or women in her situation, and gave her a receipt to an apothecary which would clear up matters.

"And meanwhile, Madame," he bade her in grave tones, "I would recommend you to abstain from the usual felicities, as it only exacerbates it." He paused, then muttered, as if to himself, "It cannot be any too comfortable, anyway." He was perfectly right, but she would not say so, as it was none of his business. She thanked him and went out into the receiving rooms again, under the watchful eyes of waiting clientele. His revolting nostrum and gentian salve, purple and messy as it was, righted things in a few days.

The last day of May found them at The Forest, where it was their plan to loll for a month. In Williamsburg she had purchased the stuff for the baby pillow she designed, and along the way she began to stitch the first of many flowers on it, in red silk. A blue-purple spray of heliotrope followed, and gaudy yellow primroses. Then they were arrived.

She bought cherries in Williamsburg and took them along when she and Thomas went for a walk in the woods. When they came to their former bower, they found the primroses just beginning to put out buds, and sat in companionable silence, listening to the creek gurgle and whisper beyond. She leaned against him, feeling his chest rise and fall beneath her head and the warmth of his hand upon her now plainly rounded belly. It came to her, drowsily, that their days of such idleness were short indeed. How good it felt to sit in the dappled woods this way, without a care for duties or the tides of the great world's fortunes! Would that it could ever be this way—peaceful, mild, and lazy.

After an hour or so he stirred, not getting up, but leaning forward to murmur in her ear, "And of what is in your basket, my pretty maid?"

"Cherries, sir," she replied in kind, "be my fair wares."

"And what, pray, be the cost?"

It was hard not to laugh. "Thre'pence the pound in coin they be, or may be half a crown."

He shouted with laughter, not missing her bawdy allusion, for their evening readings of the Bard and others were speckled with half-crown tarts.

"You are a wanton piece," he said. She took the cover off the basket and fed him one of the cherries with a smile, quoting, "'Julia and I did lately sit, Playing for sport at cherry-pit: She threw, I cast; and having thrown, I got the pit, and she the stone.'" He nearly choked and sat her back to see her face. She leaned in his arms, giggling, watching the color come back into his face.

"Where did you learn that?"

"In a book my father has," she said offhandedly.

"It's very bad," he said, with mock seriousness. "Does your father know you read such things, Madame?" He sounded for all like a Wesleyan minister.

"No," she said softly, "but happily my husband doth–" She reached up, twining her arm about his neck under his hair. "We are unobserved, sir," she said silkily, "and my complaint is no more. . . ." She watched his drowsy eyes come alight. "Would share with me a game of cherry-pit? "

He swallowed and she saw the flush come into his face. The arms that held her trembled. When he spoke his voice was husky. "If we may not disturb my lady wife," he murmured, taking up one of the red-and-yellow fruits. He returned the favor.

"Oh, no," she breathed. "I think the lady is much agitated." She took out the stone and tossed it toward a nearby rabbit hole, not aiming very accurately. "Oh dear." She turned to him and gazed into the depths of his greenish eyes. "I missed."

"Well then," he intoned, and she felt her heart quicken, "I claim my forfeit."

25

Family Matters

The Forest, Monticello

Henry Skipwith was there when they returned, for he was earnestly courting Nancy now that she was out in society. She had bloomed in these last months, and her childish prettiness had become beauty. But Nannie had other recommendations beyond a pretty face. As Patty had done before, she ran the household and played hostess to Papa's clients and divers guests, and with a placidity that Patty envied. Yet Nan had never been subject to her own passions, as neither had Tibb or Lisbet. They were as easy in the world as a leaf on a stream. That did not come from the Wayleses, as much she knew! Perhaps her recollection of Mary Cocke was awry, but she didn't fancy it coming from that quarter either. Her sisters' grace was one of the enduring mysteries of life.

Papa seemed less lively than usual and that troubled her. It was nothing that one could remark on precisely; he was not debilitated save for an occasion complaint of rheumatics, and yet he was not himself. When come upon unawares, he appeared more bemused than was his wont, and Betty complained that he spent too much time reading old letters. He admitted to having begun a fresh correspondence with her Uncle Waller and Aunt Margaret in England after a lapse of a year on either side. But when Thomas came back from a fishing venture with him at Chickahominy river quizzing her for details of the stories Papa had only touched on, she became seriously alarmed.

She was sitting in the parlor beside the window, stitching and looking out across the James toward Bermuda Hundred. The day was warm and fine, with little humidity to discomfit her, and while she stitched she thought how very nice it was that they should be out together angling. Papa had always been a mad fisherman; and Thomas drove her distracted, going on about flies and lures, and tying up things with little bits of thread filched from her sewing basket. Let them stand in the river all day, scaring the fish with their talk. Supper would not depend upon them, and perhaps the release of action would garner her a little peace at home.

She looked up as she heard the door open. Her father went upstairs, and a moment later Thomas came in, sunburnt and damp. When he leaned to kiss her, he smelled of fish. She wrinkled her nose.

"I trust you caught something?"

He laughed. "It's not so bad. At least we didn't fall in." He shook his head and pulled up a chair to sit beside her. "Your father outdid me, I must say. But then, from some things he said, he had plenty of practice at it, and other leisure occupations."

She looked up from her sewing. "Pa's been telling tales, I see." She smiled. "Did he tell you about being read out from the altar with his brother?"

"He did. But in broad hints only."

She shrugged. "'Tis no wonder. His brother Thomas met a bad end thanks to his capricious ways."

"What happened?"

He was frowning in puzzlement. The moral dilemmas of people always held his interest, but this struck rather close to home. It was a common thread among their family, and one of which she was not proud, especially as it affected her. But, she sighed, they were wed now, for good and all, and he must take her skeletons as she did his.

She regarded him candidly. "He was killed in a duel after having been caught in flagrante with his captain's wife."

"Good God!"

She held up a hand, shaking her head. "He was in the merchant service with the Dutch East India Company, and being gregarious, ingratiated himself much in the captain's house." She stitched a little. "He called once when the captain was not at home and was entertained by his lady. Unfortunately, she was young, and they developed a rather strong passion for one another. . . . My uncle could never be said to have been prudent, but for this lady he lost all self-esteem as well." She looked up. Thomas was pale beneath his sunburn, and when he spoke his voice was hoarse.

"When was this?"

"1743," she said shortly. "He was twenty-nine years old." She looked up, out the window toward Bermuda Hundred. "The shock and the shame of it killed my grandfather; at least that's the story my Aunt Braxton tells. . . ." She paused, thinking on the old story. It was yet a wound to Papa, for he had loved Tom, and spoke of him still. After the funeral there was an awful scene with his sister Margaret, with Papa defending him, and having his own past thrown up in his face. "My father went home, of course. And when he returned, he came to Bermuda Hundred and met my mother." She looked at Thomas.

"But it isn't all. I don't know that I should tell you this—" She hastened at his frown, "because I think it would be decent of me to keep silent until. . . Papa dies." The words were a knife. She knew he must eventually, but she did not want to look on that day soon. "But it bears upon us, or did—" she blushed, "and so you should know." She glanced up, around him into the hall, to make sure there was no one about to overhear.

"Papa came here in 1732, at the age of seventeen years. He had been at Lincoln's Inn, studying law—" He was nodding. "Yes, he would have told you that!" She shook her head and took up her pillow again. "He and his friends much fancied, by his admission, bear-baiting and cockfights to dull old study. But they were not without their visits to Vauxhall Gardens and the Bartholomew Fair.

"At Vauxhall Gardens he met a young lady—I do not know her name—and I expect he loved her. Howsoever, she was an Earl—or Viscount's—daughter, and there was some trouble. When it was discovered, her father threatened to hang Papa, and I'm sure it was taken earnestly, for he was in Virginia in a matter of weeks." She looked up and smiled a little to quash Thomas's drawn expression.

"There is one piece of goodness in all this moral depravity. Let me tell you a story. When Papa was that young, his friends fancied he looked rather like the Reverend Donne—" Before that he had been simply Black Jack to them. Beside her, Thomas was shaking his head and she could not suppress a grin as she spoke. "They found it a great joke, given him, and called him John Donne, as much as you all do call Page Partridge. Howsoever, when the time came for him to leave, they presented him with a farewell copy of the Reverend's poems and elegies. . ." She paused and saw him begging her silently not to speak the next words, but she could not resist ". . .to dun him."

He groaned in agony at her terrible wit, and she laughed, glad in her heart to take the edge off her father's sad tale.

In July they were home again, and now there was need to make haste in securing a midwife, for by George Gilmer's assessment, they might expect their newcomer some weeks early, for he was larger than should be anticipated at this time. Patty penned up her new sheep, sewed on her pillow, finished the petticoat she now had great need for, having outgrown everything else, and spoke with Lucy Lewis about the midwife.

She engaged Mary Bradley, an Irishwoman who lived near to Charlottesville. Mrs. Bradley was a widow and had come to Virginia on an indenture, her skills being highly prized. Missing in the rolling hills of the Tidewater her own native mountains, she had come westward, settling in Albemarle. She had, she said, an idea to go farther west, but only once the frontier was better settled. She was a tiny little woman of above middle age, with a crabbed face that was lightly lined and coarse black curling hair only threaded white. She concurred in Dr Gilmer's opinion of the child, and asked her how large her last had been.

Patty shrugged. "The usual size, not overlarge, about six pounds or so, I'd hazard." There was suddenly no comfort in the woman's warm hands upon her belly, and a ribbon of fear ran through her. "Why?" She asked quickly. "Is there something wrong?"

Mrs. Bradley gave her a friendly pat. "Nay, lady, 'tis naught wrong, as such." She peered at her with penetrating grey eyes. "By my faith, I would guess your first husband was much the same size as yourself, was he not at all?"

She nodded. "Yes, more or less—" She saw where the conversation was leading and paled. It was not something she had ever considered before.

"Then there's good reason for the difference," the midwife said complacently, "and no cause to fret. I would ask your lady mother, if she is willing, how great large her own were, for there's most often a similarity there."

"My mother is dead." She said bluntly. "She died when I was born."

"Ah." Mrs. Bradley crossed herself. "God preserve her." She nodded. "You must ask your husband's mother, then. . . if she be living?"

"Aye, and heartily," Patty said, though she doubted Mrs. Jefferson would be willing to relay such intimate details to her.

Mrs. Bradley gave the baby a fond pat and helped her up again from the bed. "There's no cause for alarm, deary. Them's a fine strong babby there, and you look a healthy girl. Did you puke much?" Such forthrightness was less embarrassing with a woman than the doctor in Williamsburg.

"Yes!" she said strongly.

"Ah, 'tis a grand sign." She patted her hand and went to fetch her basket where it lay. Patty gave her five shillings. "Mind, now," she said at the door, "you call for me before you've great need, Ma'am, for I've aids aplenty to get you through." She looked her over sharply, leaving the obvious remark unspoken. "Take yourself some air and sunshine," she advised. "Rest as you may; work a little. Foremost, be cheerful." She bowed her head. "Good day, ma'am, bless all." She turned then and was quickly gone.

Patty turned back into the house, and in spite of the comforting words, fear was a cold hand clenching in the pit of her stomach. It had never occurred to her that the disparity of their statures might cause the child to be too large to be born, and yet it should have been obvious that this was possible, or, if the opinions of doctor and midwife may be credited, likely. She paced the floor, recalling to mind the difficulties she had endured with Jack, especially once the actual birthing was under way. If it was as bad as that with Jack, how much worse would it be with this one, and he larger still? They would not tell her how much more so, doubtless not wishing to frighten her, but she was already frightened and would have welcomed a decent estimate. She bit her thumb, her anxiety making her sick, and tried to remember how large she had felt with Jack at this same point, but could not. Those days were all a blur.

"Oh, God!" she cried to the four walls. "What am I to do?"

Mrs. Jefferson came to call the Saturday afterward, bringing Nan and Lissa with her. Thomas was away down the mountain, watching the hay cutting, and Nan declared that she and Lissa were for a walk.

"Don't be overlong," their mother cautioned, "and put up your hats, or you'll take a sunburn."

"Yes, Mama," Nancy said. They went out. Mrs. Jefferson called to her servant, "Bess, fetch to me that bag there and you may go. I'll send for you if I need you."

The bag was brought and the servant departed. They were alone in the house. It was as neat as Patty could make it with their lack of storage space and many possessions, and the clock ticked peacefully on the dustless mantel. Her mother Jefferson sat in Thomas's encompassing red leather arm chair, the best chair, and she pulled over one of the Windsor-backed chairs nearby, sitting on the edge of it, as it was difficult to get out of otherwise.

"My dear," Jane said as a preamble, opening her bag. That title did not necessarily connote soft feelings, for she used it with everyone. "I have brought these to you, as my daughter Lewis informs me you have need of them, lacking any of your own." She produced half a dozen infant bonnets, finely wrought. "I regret that they are new, but what has not been used by my daughters was destroyed in the fire. . ." Her face grew soft, wistful, and her brown eyes lost their customary sharpness. "I had a lovely one made by my grandmother, which all my children wore, but it is gone now. Gone." She bestirred herself and looked up at Patty. "But I wish you to have these, for your use." She paused, and an emotion washed across her face briefly. "May the same be said of them someday."

Patty accepted the gift, exclaiming over the excellence of the work.

"Oh, Mrs. Jefferson, they are beautiful! Did you make them?"

Jane smiled a little, wryly. "Lucy made one, and Polly and Patsy, but the others are mine." She accepted her embrace with grace.

"Thank you, my mother," she said. "I shall treasure them!"

"Good. . . Patty." She was awkward with the name, but the effort was made.

Patty got up and laid the bonnets on the table. Thomas should see them, and see that his mother was not the ogre he feared. She had a twinge as she sometimes did when she moved too suddenly, and laid her hand upon it. Jane asked quickly, "Are you well, my dear?"

She nodded. "Yes, ma'am. 'Tis just a spasm I get betimes. It passes quickly." She paused and sat again with care. Since they were on the subject of her health, she ventured, "Mrs. Jefferson, I am curious, for the doctor and midwife both cautioned me as to the size of this child; were any of yours very large?"

"Oh, indeed," her mother said, without hesitation. "They were all well above average, save for the twins and Field. He was quite small, poor babe, and weakly. But you have no cause to worry–" She looked her over. "You look about right for the eighth month." The words took her aback. Whether this was sheer miscalculation or malice, she didn't want to speculate, but murmured instead, "It is the sixth." She folded her hands upon her belly.

"Oh." There was a worried silence. "Well, I am sure you'll do fine." That was everyone's commentary, and was not reassuring by its frequency.

Thomas came in later in shirtsleeves, for it was a warm day, tossing his coat on the bed, and immediately poured himself a draught of cider from the pitcher. He looked sunburnt and squinted at them from where he stood.

"Hello, Mother," he said at last, when his eyes had adjusted. "I thought I saw Lissa and Nan down the garden. Welcome." He came and kissed Jane on the cheek. "Hello, my dear," he murmured to Patty, and kissed her. She did not miss the change that flickered in his eyes. It was from more than the dimness of the room.

Mrs. Jefferson nodded her head. "Thomas. You look winded," she said, as he threw himself into one of the chairs. He reached out a hand and Patty took it. "Aye," he said shortly, "I ran up here from the stable."

"That was foolish in this heat," his mother said. It was, but she would not have put it that way, not with Thomas. He didn't take kindly to such bluntness. She saw the mask come down over his face: the closed, cold expression she dreaded. Before he could speak, she rose and went to the table, gathering up the bonnets.

"Mr. Jefferson," she said, bringing them over, "look what your mother was so kind as to bring us. Aren't they beautiful? Now I shan't have to push myself to finish those I cut." She met his gaze, pleading silently for peace, and he smiled at her a little.

He picked up one of the garments, examining it closely with his chin raised. It could not be said that he merely looked at it; scrutiny was a better word. Such close attention was not directed ill against his mother, for he often did the same with any sewing, plain or fancy, she was working on. Sometimes she thought that if she gave him thread and needle he would do as good a job himself.

"It's very fine," he pronounced, putting it in her hand with a minute caress. He turned his gaze to his mother, and his visage changed. "Thank you, Mother. It is very kind of you."

"It's the least I can do now you've made me a grandmother," she said drily. The small attempt at humor failed.

"You are already a grandmother," he said. *Oh my dear,* Patty begged him silently, *yield a little. She is making such an effort!* For she felt sorry at that moment for Mrs. Jefferson. It was painful to watch their interchange.

"But not of our own name," that lady said, in a softer tone. "That is a different matter entirely."

Please, Tom, Patty prayed, *please, show her a little kindness! She cannot have wounded you so that all tenderness is gone forever!* He showed no change of expression but said somewhat wryly, "At this out you may have had to wait for Randolph!" It had been a sore point between them that he had waited until he was nearly twenty-nine to marry. Like his father before. It was an attempt, anyway, Patty thought, though his mother didn't seem to appreciate it as such.

"That never troubled us. . . . your father would be pleased," Jane said, and there was no mistaking her now. That was clearly an olive branch, and it broke through Thomas's reserve.

"Aye," he said huskily, and rising, went to the open door. "Aye," he said again, after a long moment. "He would." He put a hand to the bridge of his nose, briefly, and turned again. He was wearing his genial host's face now.

"Would you like to come and see how the work progresses on the house, Mother?" Jane laid aside her bag.

"I would," she said.

Thomas came to help her rise, although she didn't require his, or anybody else's, assistance. He said to Patty, "Will you come, my dear?"

"No," she said quickly. "I— must see that dinner will be on time. I'll meet you there." She pressed his hand, and he nodded, smiling genuinely. "Just so."

It was a beginning; feeble, fragile, perhaps not destined to last, but it was a beginning nonetheless. She breathed a sigh of relief and put on her outdoor shoes to go down to the kitchen.

26

Miss Pattsey

Monticello

She had nightmares after that. Nightmares wherein she was trapped with a monster within that refused to quit growing, refused to be born. It came at least twice a week, startling her awake, causing her to lie sleepless for hours. Thomas always noticed when she wakened, for he was a very light sleeper, but she said nothing to him of her dream, or her fears either, hoping that he could not detect the differences of her now normal frequent waking and this other. She did her best to conceal its effects, for she would not have him fretting over her, but towards the end she dreaded going to sleep, and it was only because of his lulling presence that she did.

Life continued apace, making no allowance for her fears, her tiredness, or her sincere wish to have this confinement over and done with. She made casks of beer, gathered summer's bounty from the garden, played hostess to their never-ending stream of guests, and waited. She was very large now, her skin changed to a golden tone and itchy, but she bore none of the marks others complained of and dreaded. She felt pendulous, ponderous. Her feet ached or were painful upon walking, and her eyes troubled her some, especially as time went on. This last was a trial, for she could read only with difficulty. But she said nothing. Not to Gilmer, whose social visits were frequent, nor to Mary Bradley, who visited her again in August.

At the end of August they had word from Lisbet that Tibby had had her baby, a boy, and about a week after this they had a letter from Rob, informing them that both had died. Of her sister, they supposed it to be milk leg, and of the baby they had no idea; he simply died. Coming as it did so close to her own time, the death of this well-loved sister was very hard on Patty. She'd not seen Tibb since the wedding, and as the burial had been held before Rob wrote, she was deprived even of the chance to say good-bye. It put her in a funk for several days.

She had wanted to write to her father, to condole with him, but couldn't bear to write her sister's name. She crumpled several sheets and then gave over entirely. Throughout her mourning Thomas was very kind and solicitous, and she was grateful, but he could not bring her sister back nor quell her fear that it was an evil portent for herself. She woke herself one night with the nightmare, weeping, and turned instinctively into his embrace.

His hands smoothed her hair while she cried, and his murmurings were gentle as a mother's. When she was calmed somewhat, he lit a candle and gazed at her with grave concern.

"This all is not merely for Tibby," he said, and she shivered. He raised her chin. "Is it?" She could not lie to him, not with those penetrating eyes and loving heart. She gave a sigh and shook her head, coming to rest again upon his bosom.

"I'm so afraid!" She said, from the safety of this place. He did not scorn her.

"Why?" he asked gently. "Of what are you afraid?"

She choked on a sob. "I'm afraid it will happen to me!"

"Ah, no, love." He held her closely. "No, no, not us, my girl." He kissed her hair. "The world doesn't work that way, sweet, no matter what vicious old crones may tell you." His voice was disturbed. She sat up. "But they haven't! It's not that! Why should I be so foolish as to listen to such evil slander? No—" She broke off, her courage quailing for a moment. "I have a better reason than that to fear—"

He frowned, shaking his head, not understanding. She sighed desperately and admitted at last in a fierce, low voice, "Both Gilmer and the midwife have said they are concerned about the child's size. . . . They think he's bigger than he should be."

Thomas turned pale. "How long have you known this?" he asked at length.

"Since July," she said reluctantly.

His voice was sharp. "Patty, why didn't you tell me? Mercy, no wonder you're having nightmares!" He gathered her into an embrace again and he was trembling. By the pounding of his heart she knew his agitation. He was worried, angry with her now too for having said nothing before. She wished in truth she had not at all. "Do you trust me so little—" he said bleakly, "so little that you would conceal such a danger from me? Dear God, would I have had no warning to such an awful shock?" He sighed quickly, turning his head. "And I should like to know what the devil George is about, not telling me either—" She struggled up to face him again.

"Thomas—" She wiped her eyes with the back of one hand. "Thomas, don't! I'm sorry! I didn't mean to *deceive* you, my dearest. Oh, you know I would not!" She laid her hand upon his pensive face. "I didn't want you to fret," she said gently. "After all, it may come to nothing! Why should I want to grieve you needlessly? You would ever after think me full of alarums. It may come to nothing," she said again, quietly, and he met her eyes. "I love you. I would never be so cunning as you describe."

"Yet you would endanger your own safety and peace of mind by not sharing your fears with me," he accused, wounded still. His anger was hard to bear, but it was better than that awful coldness. He was well-nigh unreachable then, and she thanked her lucky stars that it had only been directed against her the once.

"To spare you only, my dear," she pleaded. "You would not seek to fill my ears with rumors and suppositions if they were evil! You would not needlessly distress me so! Neither would I do with you, my own. Ah, you must believe me, my Leander, that I was silent only because I love you so!"

That love-name had some effect on him, for the hardness left his eyes, and they were once again gentle. "Sweet Hero," he said with a caress of her face. "I would lay me down upon your bosom and disclose to you the whole catalogue of my soul, hopes and fears alike, for your blessing and your balm. I had thought we were alike in that."

She caught his hand. "Fears of outside things, yes, but not that which may cause my darling grief. I would not lie that upon your breast."

"But you should know I'd take it all, Patty." She nodded and dropped her eyes, feeling duly chastened and failed in his trust. "I'm sorry!" she murmured in a crackling voice, before the tears came.

"Ah, love," he said, embracing her again. "Don't cry! I didn't mean to make you cry. Patty! Sh, hush sweet." He stroked her tumbled hair, and soon she had control of herself again. "You must always tell me any of your concerns," he said gently. "Let me decide if they trouble me or no." He paused and his voice changed subtly. "For such omissions become a wall. And I would have none of that between us." He bent his head to look at her. "As we have no boundaries here, so should there be none within our hearts. . . . Thanks to them," he referred to his parents and their situation, which he had often related to her, "I require it." He met her eyes again. "Bear with me, sweet."

"I will," she promised, and meant it sincerely. He put out the candle and they slept again.

On the morning of the twenty-sixth Patty was in the kitchen, having just removed a pair of loaves from her sugar stores, and began to walk across the room when without warning the child's waters broke, drenching her and the floor. The activity in the room stopped, Sukey and Dilcy and the turn-spit boy all staring at her as if she had grown another head. She put a hand on her belly and stared at the floor in surprise.

It was a fortnight yet, by her calculations, before her time was due, and she had had no other signs that birth was imminent. Yesterday she had a long backache—the whole day—but it was no more severe than her usual intermittent one. She had no pain now, only an uncomfortably sodden feeling. The ripe smell of the waters brought back memories of other births, her own and others, and she tried to recall the course when the waters broke first, but her mind was numb.

"Do you want I fetch the master, Ma'am?" It was Sukey. Dear, quick-thinking Sukey. She came back to herself with a start. "Yes, if you would. Send Joe." She indicated the turn-spit boy, sitting on the floor by the hearth. He was all of six or seven years, but he could run. She lifted up first one foot, then another, and stepped out of the puddle. Her shoes were ruined. She gathered up her petticoats a bit, so that they wouldn't get muddy as well outside.

"Do you need help, Ma'am?" Sukey asked.

"No," she said, with assurance. "I can manage."

Upstairs she got herself into a clean shift and her dressing sacque, and found that some of the membranes had come away also. This was most surely the day. She still had no pain, and when Thomas arrived half an hour later, anxiety written on his face, she was sitting in the chair on an old towel, calmly reading a book. She smiled at him.

"You heard what happened, I trust?"

He stopped short. "I did." He looked confused. "Are you all right? I expected–"

She laughed. "Nothing's happened yet, except the flood." She held out her hand. "Come here, my dear. You look shocked. "He came and knelt beside her.

"I am. They said–" He gazed at her anxiously, as if she were a lighted keg of gunpowder. "Shouldn't we send for the doctor?"

She laughed again and rumpled his hair. "It'll be hours and hours yet." At his look, she relented. "If you like." She kissed him and he went to the door, hollering for Jupiter. "Don't forget the midwife," she said.

The child was born at nearly an hour past midnight. In her relief to have the ordeal over, she was not seriously disturbed that it was a girl. She recalled already little enough of the long hours, except at one time reaching out her hands for Thomas and Mary Bradley, crying, "Help me!" George Gilmer came in the evening and stayed through till the end, and she was grateful for him. Between them–he and Thomas and the midwife–they were able to effect enough pressure to get the child born, although in the midst of it she was certain they would break her bones trying. But oh! When that cry was heard, gasping, angry, filling the autumn night, she forgot her exhaustion and the stinging pain, and wept for joy.

"A girl, a girl," Thomas cried in delight beside her as she held the baby upon her breast. He reached out and laid his hand upon the little wet dark head, coming to tears when the baby opened her murky-dark eyes and looked at him. "Oh, she's beautiful! Our baby, oh Patty–" He broke off and kissed her face, sodden as it was with loose hair sticking to it. She wept a little, overcome, and laughed and cried again, laying her hand upon his on the back of their little daughter. It was the sweetest moment of her life.

She had some bleeding later, but not enough to trouble her, and by the time the sun arose, they were alone again, tucked up in the bed with the grunting, well-fed sleeping baby. Ah, she would be sore tomorrow, but right now all was bliss. She was drowsing in Thomas's arms, almost asleep, when he asked, "What name shall we call her?"

She forced her eyes open again. "I don't know," she said sleepily. "I hadn't given it a thought." It was bad luck to name a child before its birth. Even idle contemplation was not encouraged.

"I know one—"

"Mm?"

"Martha."

Her eyes flew open. "Oh, my dear," she cried. "My sweetest dear! But we couldn't."

"Why not?" He looked down at her.

"It would be confusing."

"So, we'll call her Patsy," he said, shrugging. She smiled. "Very well, Papa," she murmured. "I would not gainsay your right to name your firstborn."

Thus Patsy she became.

27

Storm and Strife

Monticello, The Forest

The next day she felt so well that in the afternoon she was up for a visit from Mary Garth and had word of the offices from her. There had been a beef killed, but the weather was not cold enough to set it up to cure, so that it was merely laid in salt to be eaten fresh. They divided it between them and wrote up a tally of distribution. Thomas had gone riding out over the farms, for it was harvest time, so they were alone. May brought a ring for the baby, of pewter, and examined her with interest as she lay in her lap. Patsy was a greedy baby already, and was presently snuffling in exhausted sleep from a surfeit of milk.

"Oh look, she has such dark hair!" May said, peeking under one of Mrs. Jefferson's lovely caps. "She hasn't that from Mr. Jefferson, I vow." She looked up.

Patty smiled. "No. My father had such hair in his youth." She looked over Patsy's still-red face and squashy head. She would be pretty soon. She was peeling now, about the hands and feet, and the nails on the little hand that peeped over the edge of the blanket were long. There were mittens about somewhere; she must remember to put them on her.

"You must see her when she wakens," she said to Mrs. Garth. "Her eyes look as though they may be dark. They are not blue."

"One would hardly expect it." May said. "Not when both parents are brown-eyed. Yours are brown, aren't they?" She peered closely, and Patty colored at the scrutiny. "Why!" May exclaimed, "they are hazel! And so beautiful—there's orange there. I never met a person with such eyes as yours, Mrs. J!"

It was mortifying to be stared at. "Please," she begged, "don't!" Her whole life long she had borne such scrutiny and amazement, and she never liked it. Folks exclaiming when they noted her hair was not chestnut but auburn, and making remarks; or her eyes a peculiar hazel and not brown, and making remarks; or asking what she did to keep her skin so fine. She sometimes wished to be plain or poxy merely so they would leave her alone.

"I'm sorry," May mumbled, drawing back, and she winced at the tone. It was unkind of her to rebuke her when Mary had been so helpful, especially last night.

"No," she said, laying her free hand on Mary's mitted one, "'tis me who should be sorry. I am simply cross, and too irritable. You have been so good, Mary, and I return your kindness in such a fashion. Forgive me."

Mary waved her hand. "Pish, 'tis naught but a fit of the mother. I was ten times worse with my last babe." She leaned forward a little, peeking at Patsy again. "Do you know what gave me ease? Gillyflower tea! I will bring you up some if you wish it. That cook of yours is a dolt."

She smiled. "That would be fine."

She had other visitors soon after: Liza Reynolds and Nancy Willis, Mrs. Jefferson with Nan and Lissa, Lucy and Patsy and Polly Bolling, Lucy Gilmer and Betsey Walker, Elizabeth Coles and Mary Carter; in short, all the neighbors, but she missed her own sisters—and letters did not suffice.

She was under orders from George Gilmer to remain abed a fortnight, but by the end of the first week she was bored to tears being so confined. She was perfectly healed, felt perfectly well, and there was no reason to lie about when she could be up and doing. She could only read so many books! Besides, she wanted to be abroad for the christening, so dunned Thomas for two days before he agreed to send for Dr Gilmer and have her out of wraps.

Once the bindings were off and George's careful sutures snipped away, she wept bitterly for the result. She was soft and doughy and far fatter than she had recalled being after Jack. The gown she had hoped to wear for the christening would not fit, for she could not lace her stays tight enough, and there wasn't time to let it out. She'd have to cut it all apart and put on a stomacher in front, and there wasn't time. Her stays were murderingly tight, and just when she felt about to explode from an apoplexy, Patsy began to wail and she dissolved in a heap of tears. So she sat nursing the baby, perspiring and yet despairing in the mercifully loosened stays while Thomas went to see to what he called "an urgent matter."

She was annoyed at this, wondering darkly what could be so pressing that he would leave her in such a fit of melancholy. . .and was ashamed for her annoyance and suspicion of him when he returned from Charlottesville not long after with a lovely pink gown that would fit.

After this her temper improved and she went about her household tasks in good cheer. The christening went off splendidly, and the next day she saw Thomas off to try his cases in Williamsburg. He insisted that there was nothing pressing in the House of Burgesses that his attendance was utterly required to it, that he would not stay the month, only long enough to see the major items passed on the docket, and he would be home again.

She laughed at this and kissed him. "We'll be fine, Papa. There's no cause to be so anxious." She ruffled his hair. "So tend to your business with all attention, and don't fret about us."

But she had spoke too soon. He was not away three days before she was laid up with a cold, which quickly became a pleurisy. In his absence she could not spare the time to pamper herself and soldiered through, with Patsy becoming more fractious and colicky by the day. When he came home he was wild to find them at such a pass and blamed himself.

"I should have been here," he said, running a hand through his hair. She and Patsy had been at contretemps for two hours since, and she had little patience left, but the idea that he abandon his practice and other duties for them was too much. If he coddled them thus, how would they all get on?

"Nonsense," she said shortly, over the head of the screaming baby. "It's just a colic. She's fine, we're fine— Oh, hush baby, shh, sh." She bounced the baby. Her voice held an edge. "As for the other, it's my own fault, going out in the wet. I should have known better." She paused and coughed some, which only startled Patsy into further howls.

"Here," he said, coming over. "Let me take her a while; you rest." He took the baby from her.

"I can manage—" she said.

"Go," he said firmly. She handed over the baby, not really needing much convincing. She sat on the bed and coughed while he walked Patsy up and down with a worried frown. But he did not chide her, and for that she was grateful. She could not have borne it if he had.

Late in the month they had letters from Francis and Lisbet, who were expecting another child, informing them sadly of the loss of their young Francis to a teething fever; and one from Papa to Thomas that brought back her earlier worries of him, for he wrote without any connecting remark, "I have heard nothing of dear Patty since you left this place." She told herself it was not untoward, given the loss of Tibb and her baby and Lisbet's young Francis, for him to fret over her; yet the disjointedness of it disturbed her. She wrote to him:

> . . .I would endeavour to ease your mind, my dear'st Papa, on my and the babe's behalf. we are well and sound—Patcy begins to lose her Hair now, and I espy some new beneath that is quite of a different Colour— and you must not in any wise desturb yourself over us. . . . we have hopes of introducing you both during the xmas Holidays. . . . I have missed you, Papa, and i am minded not to forget to Thank you for your kind Token on my Nativity, tho' I should think i shall not find excuse to avail of it 'til we meet again. Adieu, sweet deerest Pappa. You may thus be assur'd by this of enduring Esteem and affection from your loving Daughtur
> Martha Jefferson

Despite her assurances to her father that all was well, Patsy was as disturbed as ever and was not gaining well. She was weighed once a week on Thomas's assay scales, but Patty did not need a scale to tell her what was before her eyes. She thought perchance the child had worms, so dosed her, but that accomplished nothing. They had the doctor out to look at her, but George could find nothing certainly wrong and bade them to endure as best they could.

When the weather turned in November and they were much indoors, Thomas planned a walkway around the hilltop and down the mountain, and took note of the progress before the ground hardened too much for digging. He sat ciphering and remarking to her one night, while at the same time noting in his garden book:

> . . . 3 hands would make 80. yds in a day in the old feild, but in the woods where they had stumps to clear, not more than 40. & sometimes 25. yds.

In November, she noted in her own accounts that she:

> 1 used the last of the coffee
> 4 bought 3 bushels of what of Robrt Page
> 11 brewed a cask of beer
> 13 bought a quarter of beef weighd 72 lb a 6/
> 18 bought 2 lb of coffee
> 21 bought a quarter of beef
> 23 bought 2 bushels of wheat of Robrt Page

On the twenty-fifth, she went down to the kitchen on a rainy afternoon when Patsy was finally asleep and made an experiment of coffee while her beer was cooking, trying to find the most economical use of their supply, for they seemed to use far more than she had planned for. She wrote into her accounts book later:

> Experiment of Coffee
> 2 oz of beans Troy weight made a pint
> 12 oz 1lb wd made 6 pints
> the Troy lb is to the Averdupoize lb as 14:17:

Patsy was no better tempered now than she had been six weeks before, and she began to despair. It was Thomas's mother who pointed out that her evil temper might be due to some lack in the milk she was taking; and this was no comfort, as she suspected it was true. But what to do? There was not a wet nurse on the place, nor a woman among the workmen's wives at a time of childbearing suitable to ask, for Mary Garth's child had long since weaned, and Betsy Reynolds's child was not due for another two months. It was a knotty problem with no solution. They did not go away that Christmas, but spent it at Buck Island with the Lewises and gathered family.

In February, a solution of sorts appeared in the person of a slave owned by John Fleming. Fleming was willing, for a sharp price, to part with his carpenter George. Now George, called Great George because of his girth, for he was very fat, was married to Fleming's pastry cook, Ursula. There was no greater news to Patty than this, for Dilcy was yet impossible, and Sukey still had to be watched over, and sometimes her results were less than desirable. Oh, to have a decent trained pastry cook who could manage without every step being criticized! It would be heavenly. Ursula also was expecting a child in April. George was already bought when she set out to convince Thomas to buy Ursula as well, for she knew full well he didn't like to break up families, and though they could in truth ill-afford the further purchase, she was firm in the notion now that they could kill several birds with this single stone.

"Think of it!" she said, sitting up in their bed and disturbing his reading. "We'd never have to worry again whether what came to table was going to be edible or not! She being older could offset Dilcy and Sukey's fighting, and we would have peace in the kitchen! And you wouldn't have to break up the family."

"He's asking two hundred and fifty pounds," he said, putting the book down.

"For the woman and her children," she reminded him. "She's soon to have a child as well. It's a bargain, my dear! Besides, you're a persuasive men, you can talk him down. . ."

He laughed, shaking his head. "If you aren't persistent! What if Fleming doesn't really want to sell?"

She kissed him. "Why wouldn't he? What good will she be to him moaning and moping because she's lost her man? She'll make his life a misery, I'll warrant you."

"We really can't afford it," he said reluctantly. "Not before the next crop goes to market."

She kissed him again, moving nearer. "Oh please, say you'll consider it? It would make things so easy! Please?" She traced the line of his throat with a fingernail. "It would please me so, and we can always find some way to get the money. . ." She was being deliberately distracting, and he leaned his cheek against her hand.

"You're being unfair," he murmured.

She smiled a little. "I just want to soften you up. Is that so bad?"

His eyes kindled. "It's bad politics," he said.

"Don't petitioners generally offer a few bribes to the right people?"

He kissed her. "Is that what this is?"

She caught her breath. "Oh no! I—" She lost her train of thought. "Tom—"

His voice was low in her ear. "Anything, sweetheart. . .anything you want."

Not long afterward he bought Ursula and her two boys, and once she was delivered of her child they came to Monticello, to become an indispensable part of the household; for she offered to suckle Patsy of her own accord, and the child immediately recovered her good health. For that, they owed her more than she ever did them in work, love, or loyalty.

In May they were at Williamsburg, where Thomas was much engaged in the Assembly's dispute over a spate of counterfeiting and the ramifications of the news from the Rhode Island colony that criminals of theirs were being transported to England for trial. The new governor, John Murray, Lord Dunmore, so lately toasted and heralded up and down the Tidewater, proved himself no friend of Virginia's when he—incensed at the measures against such trials so eloquently put forth by Dabney Carr—prorogued the Assembly.

They were on the advent of their journey home when they had urgent word from Francis that her father was ill. It was supposed to be a cancer. They hurried to Charles City behind the servant in a welter of alarm. The horses could not go fast enough, and even stopping for ferriage at Chickahominy river was for Patty an eternal agony.

I knew it, she thought to herself again and again as the carriage bounced along the narrow road from the river. *I knew it a year ago. Oh, Papa, I should have paid more heed, should have cared for you better!* She was afraid of what she would find on arrival. What if he was already expired? She clutched poor Patsy so tightly that the child wailed and struggled away. Papa had not even seen her yet. Oh! She buried her nose in Patsy's mass of curls. *Please, Papa, wait for me!*

Francis and Lisbet were already there, she just out of childbed, helping Nancy to cope with the duties of the house and sickroom. Poor Nancy, due to be married to Henry in a few months, was worn to a shadow with grief and worry. When they arrived, her father was telling Francis he wished to draught a letter to his brother.

"I've tried before this, but I cannot hold the pen," he said.

"You tell me what to say, Uncle," Francis murmured, patting his hand, "and I'll write it for you."

She was appalled, despite her grim imaginings in the carriage, how wasted Papa looked. How can he have declined so in just a few short months? When last she'd seen him, he was hale and vital, with his old devilish sparkle dancing in his brown eyes. Now he was an old man, tender, pathetic, and greeted her with an outstretched hand that was blotted with age spots. She clasped his hand and fell on her knees by the bed.

"Papa, oh my dear Papa!"

He smiled a little, painfully. "Miss Patt. Such a good girl. I can always count on my Patty. . . . Where's that granddaughter of mine? Bring her here, girl, and let me see her."

She sniffed and nodded and took Patsy from Betty's arms. She was going on eight months now and could stand with small help. She showed every sign of early walking. Her black hair had fallen out, to be replaced now by a dark, burnished auburn that sprang in curls all over her head. Her eyes were most definitely hazel, but had her own color and not Thomas's amber. But for all that she was his child. In every line of her face and body the resemblance showed. She was large for her age, and fat now, with great rolls of flesh on her sturdy legs. She had his Randolph nobility of profile; unfortunately she also had his nose. Now, it was not a bad nose, on Thomas; in fact she rather admired it, but he was six-feet-three and a man; and it was bad luck that it should have been passed on to a girl. She would never be a beauty; striking, yes, and handsome, but not a beauty. None of that mattered now.

"Come here, darling," she said to the baby. "Come meet your grandpapa." She held the baby on her knee, balancing her fat legs on either side. "Say hello, Patsy. Say 'hello, grandpapa.'" She waggled her fingers and Patsy did likewise. It was her new trick and her Papa's delight.

Her father laid his hand on the little curly head with a wistful look.

"Ah, she's fine, fine," he said, and tears sprang to his eyes. "A bonny *baban*."

The old Welsh word was undoing. She buried her face in Patsy's hair, against his trembling hand.

"Oh, Pa!"

"Now, my Patty," he said, in an equally emotional voice. "How do you expect me to get on if you collapse? I need my Patty's strength, and courage–" he lifted his hand to her cheek and she looked up at him– "to help me endure." Her throat was aching and she could not speak, so nodded fiercely.

He sighed, tired out, and with difficulty withdrew his hand and laid it on the covers. She picked up the baby, gave her to Poll, and went outside into the hall to speak to Betty. Betty was again waiting a child, her first since Peter three years before, but she had none of her queen-like carriage now. She was dull and dispirited, made unhappy by the sinking of the man who had raised her, taught her letters, welcomed her into the bosom of his family.

"How long has he been this way?" she asked.

"Nor 'bout a week or more," Betty said bleakly. She took her hand. "Miss Patty, what'll we do without him? Us old folks and Miss Nancy. Poor Miss Nancy! She want'd call off the wedding but he wouldn' hear of it. Says he wants to know she safe married before he passes on—" She pulled out a turquoise handkerchief and covered her face, weeping.

"Oh Bett." She patted her arm in distress, and when that provoked greater grief, she accepted the tall body into her embrace, Betty bending her head upon her shoulder, as she had so often cried upon that bosom in her lonely girlhood. She wept for her old nurse's grief and patted her consolingly until Betty raised her head and wiped her eyes.

"I expect I'll have to leave now," she said.

"Oh no," Patty said. "Why should you do that? Papa would want you to stay here, where you were raised."

Betty looked at her as if she did not know her. "But it's coming sold, Miss Patty, the whole place; I thought you knew'd that. For debt. Your Papa, he's in great debt. I heard Mist Francis and Henry saying—"

The words rolled over her, and she was numb. Sell this place? For debt? Papa was in debt? How could he be in debt, when he was an agent to Farell and Jones? They wouldn't let him get into debt. The whole security of her early life drifted away from her, and she gave a cry, turning her face to the wall.

Thomas came out from the sickroom, and heedless of the company she laid her head on his chest and sobbed. Not genteelly, but great choking, unladylike sobs that wracked her whole frame.

"Come," he said, and steered her toward her old room, now a sitting room. He closed the door and sat with her on the sofa, patiently waiting through her torrent of grief. She told him Betty's news. He scratched his forehead.

"I know. I had a talk with Francis and Henry. Patty, it's the only way, we agreed. It'll clear most of the debt and leave the rest of the land to divide up."

"But it's my home," she said miserably.

"I know, sweet," he said, still caressing her hand.

She drew a trembling breath. "How much of a debt is there?"

He shrugged. "About eighty thousand pounds."

"Dear God!"

"But the balance of property is worth far more, so he is hardly destitute."

She shook her head, quickly. "I can't. . . I don't want to talk about this now! It's too cruel, too mercenary. He's not even dead yet."

"As you like." Thomas smiled a little, his face all sympathy. "Come here, sweet, you're trembling." She hadn't noticed that she was. "Come here, my Patty."

She went into his arms, her safe haven from all the world's cares, and was soothed there as if she were Patsy, discomfited by some hurt, until she was collected again. He did not gainsay her grief by telling her all was well, but let her have it as her right. It was for such great sensitivity that she loved him, for he was like no other man she had ever known. When she rose up again, she felt that she could be brave as her father needed, thanks to Thomas's loving care.

28

A Pledge Fulfilled

Spring Forest, Monticello, The Forest

They stayed as long as they could at home. She spent her days in a round-robin with her sisters of nursing and household chores. Lisbet being least able to work, the bulk fell to her and Nancy, and when she was occupied with Patsy, Nancy did more than her fair share with nary a complaint. Patty gladly did anything that fell her way, from changing beds to brewing simples, but she best loved the hours she spent reading to her father.

When she was a child, he had taught her to read aloud, not from the Bible or ladies' gazettes, but from hard history and works of philosophy, much to Mary Cocke's despair.

"You'll make her a bluestocking, fit for nothing," her stepmother had complained, "and then we shall never see her married!" This did nothing to endear Mother Mary to her, for she took the implication that she wanted to be rid of her, and in rebellion she redoubled her efforts to please her father. *We'll see,* she had thought then, *who is unfit to be wed!*

It was shameful to admit even to herself how much she had loathed Mary Cocke, whose only benefit in Patty's mind was her giving birth to Patty's dear sisters; even more shameful was the lurking resentment of her father's continual absence which threw her continually upon the woman's bad graces, for the absences certainly weren't Papa's fault. He had a family to provide for, and they were not great wealthy. She remembered the terrible day of Elizabeth Lomax's funeral when she had, at the age of thirteen years, confronted him in his office in a fit of childish pique, declaring, "You'll not bring in another, Papa; I'd rather die!" How sorrowful his brown eyes then! "I won't, Patty, I swear it," he had promised. And he did not. He took up with Betty after that and their household was peaceful.

Her unorthodox reading stood her in good stead with Batt, who was philosophically inclined. It was pleasing to be able to discuss Diderot and Descartes, Voltaire, and Montesquieu with him intelligently, and not to be dismissed because she was a woman. He had liked to tease her of her forays into novels and bawdy plays, but the most exquisite memory of their early marriage was reading Moliére with him in flowing French.

With her father she read Bolingbroke, as he requested, and Shenstone for the same reason. When he asked for Donne, she sensed a pattern to his queries and looked at him in sorrow.

He squinted at her. "Do you not have it, girl?" However it was come by, his copy of Reverend Donne was precious, and had been given to her with that proviso when she was sixteen. Her eyes blurred with tears.

"Of course I do, Papa!" she exclaimed. "I carry it with me everywhere!"

He raised his hand and gave a feeble wave. "Well, read it to me then." She nodded, and the book was fetched.

"What would you have me read?" she asked, when she took it up. She expected from him one of the sunny poems or songs, and was therefore unprepared for and unnerved by his answer, "The Relique."

She looked at him a long moment, her throat aching with tears, until he returned her gaze with mild impatience. Taking her courage in hand then, she opened the book, and read,

> *When my grave is broke up againe*
> *Some second ghost to entertaine,*
> *(For graves have learned that woman-head*
> *To be more than one a Bed)*
> *And he that digs it, spies*
> *A bracelet of bright haire about the bone,*
> *Will he not let'us alone,*
> *And thinke that here a loving couple lies,*
> *Who thought that this device might be some way*
> *To make their soules, at the last busie day,*
> *Meet at this grave, and make a little stay?*
> *. . .First, we lov'd well and faithfully,*
> *Yet we knew not what we love'd nor why,*
> *. . . Comming and going, wee*
> *Perchance might kisse, but not between those meales*
> *Our hands ne'r toucht the seales,*
> *Which nature, injur'd by late law, sets free:*
> *These miracles wee did; but now alas,*
> *All measure, and all language, I should passe,*
> *Should I tell what a miracle shee was.*

He was sleeping now, and she closed her eyes against the truth: there had been no wrong done to the girl he had loved. Out of love and respect for her honor he had fled, changing his life forever. She owed that unknown girl her very life, for in staying or going, were it not for her, she, Patty, would never have been. The painful memory and the row with her Aunt

Margaret had caused in Papa a desire for respectability. Were he not so determined, he might not have pursued her mother's affections, for Mama had been a broken-hearted widow when they met, and he by his kindness healed her griefs.

She looked across at the aged form on the bed, tears slipping heedless down her cheeks, and whispered to him, "I love you, Papa."

When they returned from Charles City on the nineteenth, they stopped at Spring Forest, the Carrs' place, only to be struck with greater tragedy. Mrs. Jefferson and the twins were still there, having buried Dabney a day and an half before. And poor Patsy, just up out of childbed not a few weeks.

When Thomas heard that news he went livid and utterly still, only closing his eyes briefly. For one terrible moment she thought he would faint, and took his arm. He looked at her as if he did not know her and turned to his sister, asking after not a few false starts, "When? How?" He shook his head, as if trying to shake out the awful truth, and looked up at Patsy again.

"It was in Charlottesville," she said bleakly, and her eyes filled.

"He'd gone to see to a case. There was some contagion in the town. . . . He died in two days." Her voice rose a little. "The doctor could do nothing!" She came to tears, and he went and embraced her. Patsy sobbed into his coat. "We had to. . . bury him straightaway, for fear that the disease would spread. . . . My poor dear!"

Patty took the baby away into the next room where Mrs. Jefferson was and closed the door.

They did not stay the night, but continued home, their depressed spirits damped further by the latest tragedy.

"I told her I would look after them all," he said, heaving himself into the carriage with her, "that they should want for nothing." She nodded dumbly. It was rare that he did not choose to ride on their journeys, but she feared, looking at his ashen face, that he was not equal to it. He leaned against her with his foot on the opposite seat and a hand over his eyes. He would have a headache; she knew that posture on him. When they were home, she went about her business without remark, bringing him reliefs for his head and taking away the untouched supper in respectful silence but alert for some sign that he wished to talk. He did not. She put Patsy to bed and took up her mending nearby him. It was a still night, with only the cricket's song to disturb the peace, and the four hours they sat thus were an eternity.

At length, past midnight, he reached out for her hand and she gave it, warm and soft and comforting. She could bear his misery no more and said, entreating, "Come to bed, my dear. It grows late."

He roused himself at this from his reverie, sat up in the chair. "Aye," he said absently. He made no response to her advances in aid of comfort, and with a sigh, she settled herself against him on the bolsters. She had been up since half-past five and the day was wearying. She was leaden, half asleep, when he cried out in the darkness and sat up, fumbling to light the candle again.

"Thomas?" Her heart was thudding in her ears.

"I know what evaded me all this evening," he exclaimed, and looked at her, shaking his head. "He did not mean to be buried at Shadwell!"

She frowned. "What d'you mean?" It seeped into her foggy brain that he was speaking of Dabney.

"We had a compact, he and I," he said, fixing the bolster behind him. She breathed a sigh of relief. By his exclamation, she'd thought the room was on fire, at least. She sat up with him, and he put an arm behind his head, staring back into the past. "You know where that tree is—the oak I showed you, where we used to sit?"

"Mmm?" She thought a moment. *Tree, tree.* He had shewn her many trees, each to a different purpose. . . . *Ah, the one down towards the Thoroughfare road!* She focused her attention again on what he was saying.

". . . .When we were about seventeen we were up here one summer night and were laying out our plans for the future—" He paused, with a bitter smirk. "And we agreed that whichever of us—" He paused again and he caught his breath. "Whichever of us should. . . die first—oh God!" He put a hand over his eyes and after a moment continued with difficulty: "would . . . bury. . . the other. . . there—" He shook his head violently and lost his composure entirely.

"Oh, my dear," she cried in sympathy, and put her arms round him. "Hush sh, ah, there, my love!" He gave himself up to grief and her tender mercies and wept without restraint upon her bosom, as he had once promised he would, until he was exhausted with it. And she did not sleep all that long time, but kept watch with the solitary candle, vigilant until the first dim light of morning seeped through their shutters. They were equal now, the debt of solace met and paid.

On the twenty-eighth, her father died in Charles City. She was more peaceful with it than she thought she would be, for she knew that he was ready and accepting of whatever lay beyond. He was buried in the graveyard down beside the Chickahominy, between her mother and Mary Cocke, at the head of the small stone that marked the grave of the twins that had been born and died the year before her on Christmas day. With Francis and Lisbet and Nannie, she pored over the wording of the plain granite slab he had desired:

Here Was Buried
John Wayles

Native of
Lancaster, England
b. 31 Jan'y. 1715
d. 28 May 1773
aged 58 years
by his humour & good works
he was known

Nancy and Henry's wedding was, of necessity, a small affair. Had not mourning proscribed such, good taste would have. Being a younger daughter, moreover the youngest daughter, meant that by custom her wedding would not have been as lavish as Tibb's or Lisbet's, or Patty's to Thomas for that matter. It was unseemly to make such a grand show so many times. The primary difference in the scale of these weddings was in the numbers of guests invited, for each person was allotted about the same amount of food and drink, and the festivities continued for the same amount of time. But in this case, since they were in mourning it was smaller than it would have been otherwise, and Nancy's gown, a beautiful red shot with blue so that it shimmered mauve in the light, was the sole ornament among soberer hues of greens, browns, and blues.

It was her father's last wish for her that her wedding continue as planned, for he truly loved his Nannie and wanted her to be happy. There was a practical side of this, too. Nancy was just shy of eighteen and delaying the wedding six months or more would have entailed a good deal of legal trouble in having her made a ward under someone's guardianship. Her Cocke relations would have been the likely choice, but a fair number of them were in Goochland, and Nan was not amenable to the move.

Francis gave her away, and Rob stood, as he promised he would, as brideman for his brother. Lisbet did the offices as bridesmaid, and no one complained that the wedding was all so very in the family. They had the usual wedding breakfast and two days of parties before all departed.

Just before they were due to depart, Betty had her child, this time a girl. Nancy claimed the privilege of naming it, and she was called Sally. Before the inventory was done on the property, Betty and four of her youngest children repaired to Elk Hill and remained there for over a year. The rest would come to Monticello after the settlement.

They did not see much of Rob after the wedding. Rumor had it that he was courting a Louisa girl, and doubtless he may have felt somewhat embarrassed in their presence, though not one of them grudged him his happiness and were very glad to see him. He was thinner than he had been before, testimony to the trial he had undergone, but when he spoke on parting to travelling to Louisa his entire countenance revived. *God be with you,* Patty thought, as they waved him farewell. I know my sister would wish it so.

Once they were home again, towards the end of July, she had reason to rejoice, to hope that at last their long spate of sorrow was over: it was now fairly certain that they were to have another child. She would give it a few more days, until after the twenty-fifth, and then speak. But she knew the flux would not come, for she had that heavy feeling again and the course was more than a week late. Life from death, and joy from grief; it was fitting that it should be so. She made a cask of beer and wrote up in her accounts that a loaf of sugar had been broke and a barrel of flour opened in her absence. They ate the last of the peas, new cucumbers, and the first of the watermelons. Then she told Thomas her news.

It was one of those rare evenings they were without company after dinner, so they had retired to the little house to enjoy the cool there, for it had been near the century mark on the thermometer for five days. The windows were opened and the shutters drawn, including the new one over the door, so the house was cool and dark, lighted only by two or three candles. They had about as much space as before, even with Patsy's crib, for the pianoforte had been moved, along with several shelves of books, into the dining room. They desperately needed a clothes press, but there was simply not room, and now with another child their space would be even more crowded.

She laid aside her sewing and rested her arm on the clear space on the table. The rest of it was sprawled with books and papers, as Thomas was writing up his notes for the succeeding court in August. He sat in shirtsleeves, rolled up, and his waistcoat undone, for the air was close, and his hair was rumpled from leaning on his hand. It astonished her how dapper he could look sometimes, on court days and other occasions, for this useful deshabille is how he always appeared in her mind. The other was a foreign creature not wholly belonging to her; a public figure, not wholly himself either.

They knew only the effect of his industry and his skill, not its mechanics. Nothing came full-blown into life perfect with him, for he was extraordinarily critical. He wrote and rewrote, tinkered and fine-tuned, seeking always the most precise words, or if of an object, the purest and most practical form. And he was not averse to excising much to gain a felicity of expression or a smoothing of line or movement. His idealism was painstaking, radical; its effect was borne out by his intermittent headaches. He would have one now, squinting so in the light he had. She rose and brought him one of the candles. Patsy knew her way about well enough not to require such illumination. She placed it beside him, and he raised his head from his hand.

"Thank you," he said absently, and looked around. "I hadn't realized it was so late."

"I know," she smiled. "I should be getting Miss Patt to bed." It was nearly eight o'clock and he had been working for three hours. He laid his head against her hip, stretching his neck, and she tried to think of a casual approach to her announcement. At length it came.

"Do you think we have room for a trundle in here?" She asked, inspecting the clear space beside the table. Patsy stood there now, her woolly knitted ball in her fat hands. She had only just learnt to walk, so standing and playing was her new game.

He frowned. "What for do we need a trundle? Pats isn't that big yet!" He smiled up at her.

"No, but she will be shortly." She paused for a heartbeat's moment, then plunged in, "—will be when the new one arrives."

He was about to speak, stopped, frowned a little, looked at Patsy standing on the rug, and then at her. "You're joking?" he asked. She shook her head with a little smile, for his expression was not one of utter horror. He straightened and leaned away from her a little, looking her over. "Well, I'll be!" He laughed then. "It's a good thing we're coming along on our building then. At this rate, Dabney may be right—"

She shook her head, not understanding.

"Oh!" he nodded. "I didn't tell you. Ha, when we were in Augusta the last time we had such news, he said that we'd be catching them up in no time. . ." His face sobered with the bittersweetness of that memory, for Patsy Carr was now left with six children to look after, and the youngest but an infant.

He rose and put an arm about her. "I'm glad, just the same. Patsy needs a playmate besides Bagwell and Archy." These were Great George and Ursula's youngest and were fixtures in the kitchen, and Patsy's fondest playmates.

"She has the Garth children and Sally Reynolds," she reminded him.

"Aye," he said, "and they're the ones who dumped her out of the wheelbarrow." They had been playing with it in the kitchen garden, pushing the babies back and forth, when James tripped up, tipping their makeshift cart over. Patsy had rolled out onto the grass but was not seriously hurt.

"They didn't do it on purpose," she said. "And Pats wasn't injured, after all."

"No," he agreed, "but what if she'd fallen down the hillside? Purposeful or no, she'd have been hurt then. They are not careful."

They'd been over this road before. It was his contention that only luck had saved their little one from a sudden arrival in the peach orchard.

"He's only seven," she reasoned. "And children have mishaps. 'Tis the way of things, how they learn. You can't protect them from everything." Goodness knows, she had tried with Jack, and that had availed her little. She did not intend to wear herself out that way over every child. She looked up at him, the memory of Jack's mishap full in her eyes, and he let the matter drop.

"Aye," he said quietly. "I suppose you're right."

"Are you very busy this evening?" She asked him.

He looked down at her speculatively, smiling a little. "Why?"

"I thought we might take a walk."

He laughed shortly.

"'Tis a fine night," she said.

"We'll be eaten alive with bugs," he said.

She tossed her head. "I don't mind. . . Can you spare the time?"

"I might," he said in amusement. "What'll we do with Miss Patt there?" Patsy looked up from her ball singing, "doe-doe-doe-doe," and held out her arms. "Pa pa pa. . .up!" She came over, toddling with her sailor's rolling gait, and Thomas picked her up, smiling.

"I thought we'd take her along," she said, laying her hand on the baby's head.

"As our chaperone?" he asked, and she laughed.

"If you like," she said, quoting his favorite assent.

He made a little bow. "Very well, Madame, put on your walking shoes and the three of us will away."

"Four," she corrected, and he looked at her.

"Aye," he said, "four."

It had cooled off somewhat by the time they were outside, and the twilight was just setting in. All the earth had a damp, green smell of leaf molds and the ripe blossoming of summer. The air was heavy with life. The cooling trend had indeed brought out the lightning bugs and gnats, who swarmed or flitted over the tops of the grasses, the former setting off intermittent signals to their kind like a thousand tiny lanterns. As a child, she had caught them in a net, imprisoning them for the evening in jam jars, but now she was content to let them conduct their evening ritual in peace. They walked among the woods on the northeast side of the mountain, with Thomas carrying the child, and betimes they would stop to shew her some woodland flower whose petals were just closing. And Patsy would reach out her fat hand and try to eat it, to their amusement.

At the end of their walk it was full dark, and she lit their lamp inside the house before putting the child to bed. The cicadas whirred outside, and the crickets sang their song through the shuttered windows. Lazy summer was drifting on, and they were safe on their mountaintop from the evil humors of the low-ground air. Not a single soul had developed the summer complaint, either among the Negroes or the workmen's families. They were blest that way. She took up her sewing of shirts as Thomas went back to his notations, feeling at balance and peaceful for the first time in months.

In August before he left, Thomas was busy with building, for the middle room was nearly ready to have a temporary roof placed over it, and he also catalogued his growing collection of books. As compared to the thousand-odd he had at Shadwell before the fire, he now had twelve hundred and fifty-six, with more anticipated in the next London shipment of goods. In this regard, having no more bookcases, they were reduced to using the packing crates as temporary shelter for the books, even as they made do with the little house for themselves. But there was hope; if the building schedule continued according to plan, they would have the brickwork begun for the hall and the bedroom. They could not expect more than to have the bare bones—no more than the first three feet—completed before the building season let off in September, but at least they could work up the dimensions and make necessary adjustments. The chimney was already raised for the middle room, the parlor, and the foundation for the fireplace in the bedroom was laid out. They ate peaches and yellow plums, and she made a conserve of tomatoes before it was time for Thomas to leave.

It was a fortnight of the worst heat of the year. She stopped looking at the thermometer, even though Thomas had asked her to. Where was the point? It was hot, too hot, and it was depressing to see the century mark day after endless day without relief from heat or humidity. That was the worst of it, the heaviness of the air. It did no good to bathe oneself in spring water or cologne to be ten minutes later as uncomfortable as before. She stayed inside with the windows half-closed and shuttered, dressing Patsy only in a clout. Poor little baby—her cheeks were red all day long, and she drank constantly, always asking for water, and at night she thrashed out in her little bed, unable to bear the weight of even a sheet.

She was not utterly alone with the child. Every day Mary Garth or Elizabeth Reynolds or Nancy Willis would come by with buttermilk or some other treat and their sewing to while away the time. Nancy was hooking a rug; Liza was sewing baby clothes; and May was always mending something, for she had three children and a husband to look after. She also helped with the sewing of clothes for the Negroes, a never-ending task. Patty had stitched this spring and summer until her fingers were sore, and she wouldn't have completed the task without May's help. It was lucky that they had a month or so of respite before the winter clothing ration needed to be cut, or she would have given up in despair. She had a dress to finish for Patsy before she outgrew the ones she had, and she was fairly sick of plain sewing and fancywork alike. And they yet only had fifty slaves. There would be more whenever Papa's will was proved; she didn't know how many. Thank goodness they would not all be here!

She was sick again with this baby but not as badly as before, and once again Thomas managed to miss the worst of it, though this time he did not miss it all. He was most distressed when she told him that, yes, it was always this way, at least with her. His concern was touching, but there was not really much to be done about it, save endurance, and he couldn't help with that. That she had to find on her own, and after four pregnancies she had become expert at it. By the time autumn came she was done with it and glad she'd not made a fuss.

29

Vinetum

Monticello

Governor Dunmore had prorogued the Assembly until November, and when November came, until the following May, found disfavor in the actions of the Burgesses last March. But his decree did not mean they were utterly without action, for they had visitors in November in the persons of Mr. Thomas Adams, Thomas's London agent, and his Florentine friend Phillip Mazzei, who were on their way westward to seek land for a viticulture experiment. They proposed to grow Italian wine grapes in Augusta or beyond, in the fertile, virgin valleys of the Shenandoah.

They arrived after dinner, their entourage jangling and creaking up the winding mountain road, for aside from themselves and their pack horses, they had a wagon of goods and several servants. It was their surveying expedition, after all, and they could hardly manage it with less than full equipment. In food alone they had enough for several weeks.

Thomas put down his violin, and Patty and Eleanor Madison (Mrs. Reverend Madison) looked at one another. Patty rose from the piano seat as Thomas went to the door. When he entered again, he had with him Mr. Adams and another man unknown to them, a smallish man with a narrow face and swarthy features. By the cut of his coat he was foreign. He bowed to them all with exaggerated elegance that was at once courtly and familiar. She did not like the look she received; it was too appraising, as if she were some common orange hawker. She gave him a cool nod.

"Mrs. Madison, Mrs. Jefferson," Adams exclaimed. "Reverend, sir." They bowed to one another. "I have the honor to present to you Mr. Phillip Mazzie, or however the devil he says his name"—Adams and his companion exchanged a droll glance—"late of London, but earlier of Firenze, Italy. Mazzie, these are Mr. and Mrs. Thomas Jefferson, and the Reverend and Mrs. James Madison." To the company he said, "We're on our way in search of land—" he paused silkily, "for a project."

"How do you do?" their foreign guest said in his heavy accent. It was not so much that his English was overborne with Italian as his manner of intonation was deliberative. His glance had a watchful quality, and she began to perceive that what she mistook for impudence was in fact the mark of his observant nature.

"Come come," Thomas said quickly. "Please sit. Will you have some wine?" She went and took the glasses from Jupiter who was standing in the corner by the buffet. This article of furniture stood in a nook which was to eventually be a doorway but was now sealed off until the parlor was finished. The wine was poured out and she went to sit at her fortepiano again, due to their lack of chairs. She could have called for one from the house but did not. Thomas looked rather flushed, and she expected that the proximity of one more or less fresh from Italy was the cause of his excitement.

"I understand," he said to Adams, "that congratulations are in order."

Adams colored happily. "Oh, indeed. I hadn't realized the news had travelled so far as this."

"I had it from Colonel Carter, who was in town then." He was still standing and crossed his arms, balancing on one hip more than another.

"Mrs. Adams does not travel with you?" he asked, though this was evident.

"No, alas," Adams said with a sigh. "She preferred to remain in Williamsburg."

He was a furrow-browed, middle-aged man with once-blond hair, now darkened and greying at the sides, somewhat stout of body and particular of dress. His clothes were, if not the latest mode, then a modest version of them. His coat sleeves were above the wrist and narrow, but by the cut of the back the coat fitted. It was a strange fashion, to look as tho' one's clothes were too small. He wore a yellow-and-white striped waistcoat that was entirely unsuited to travel. Their foreign visitor was better equipt, in dull-colored clothing of a fine worsted that would repel dust and keep him warm at once.

"How long are you to journey?" James Madison asked.

"I have some property in Augusta I wanted Mr. Mazzie to see, or if not that, then speculations in Fincastle. A month at least, sir."

"I should be quite jealous," Patty said, "were I Mrs. Adams, sir, to lose my new husband for a month's time. She must be an extraordinary woman."

He smiled. "She is, ma'am. She was Elizabeth Miller before. Perhaps you know her."

She had heard the name, but that was all. "I know of her, Mr. Adams. You must bring her with you next time." She glanced at Thomas, who sat now, and he nodded his assent. "We should make her most welcome."

Adams bowed his head. "Thank you, ma'am."

Mr. Mazzei turned to Thomas. "Mr. Adams tells me that you are a student of Palladio, Mr. Jefferson, and that you are. . ." he sought the word, "designing your house yourself on those principles." His accent was heavily Florentine, in spite of his travels, and Patty caught herself several times expecting to hear Italian from him, for the cadence of his speech was much closer to that than English. Thomas colored and leaned forward some in his chair.

"That is high praise indeed," he said. "And while I don't think I deserve the title of student of Signore Palladio, I have followed his rule in my design. . . albeit, adapted to our local conditions, namely brick." He made an oblique gesture towards the window, for the yard was hazardously full of bricks and lumber, especially in the dark.

"You are too modest, sir," Mazzei said. "From what I have heard from my friend here and seen of your Virginia manor houses, your Monticello—" He paused, savoring the name, and Thomas smiled at the pronunciation—"is unique to your country. Most of the houses I've seen sit in the river. Bad, bad. In Italy, we never do this. Always situate them on a hill. Keeps the bad humors away."

"What of Venice?" James said.

Mazzei waved his hand. "Pah! Venice!" he said in disgust. "'Tis a—" He scratched his cheek. . . "how I say, with the ladies. . . a privy pot?" He waved his hand again. "Stinking, stinking. Bad air. Toscana, Monticello, they are much better." He laughed, a bit loudly, and winked at Adams.

He turned here to the Madisons. "You must not misunderstand me, I admire your country, your Virginia. Everyone is most kindly welcoming. The men at the college—" He shook his head. "You are lucky to have such men among you, such freedoms. Such a liberty to write and speak, we have not in my country." He colored. They would discover only later that he had been exiled for importing Rousseau and Voltaire into his native province.

After a time, the forgotten music was returned to, at Adams' insistence, and their Italian friend was much pleased with their rendering of Corelli. He talked all through the breaks in the music, pausing only to listen with a savoring glance, to resume precisely where he had left off. He was most diverting, but at the end of the evening when the Madisons made to depart, Patty excused herself also to make provisions for beds and then retire. Their guests would have to sleep here, unless they wished to sleep amid the roughness of unplastered walls in the parlor next door. The only other place was with the Garths in their loft, and that would be insulting. So, late or not, she ordered beds made up, handing the linens down herself. She did not hear when Thomas came in, and when she woke in the morning he was already out. Mazzei had claimed him.

They returned when breakfast was well under way. She had just poured out Mr. Adams more coffee, and that gentleman, not deigning to take the cup, looked up from his plate of ham and biscuits and put down his fork, leaning back in his chair. He rolled his tongue in his cheek and said to Thomas, "I see by your expression that you've taken him away from me. I knew you would do that."

She looked up as well. Thomas bore a beaming countenance. *What mischief has he done?* He only smiled at Mr. Adams and raised an eyebrow, but to Mr. Mazzei he gestured towards the table with a courtier's bow. "Shall we have breakfast, sir?" he said. He was plainly in a teasing mood, and she would not riddle the mystery out until he had tormented them all with hints and clues. She poured out coffee while Jupiter fetched up serving dishes. Sukey generally waited at table in the mornings since Dilcy had been sent to Elk Hill, and there was no one yet trained up in her place, but Thomas had murmured to her covertly last evening that it was offensive to the sensibilities of their foreign guest to be tended by a female servant. She wondered at how he was so versed in the table manners of Tuscans, as he had never been there himself. But to ask that of a man who had taught himself the language with no more occasional help than their music teacher was perhaps to get an answer no less foxing than one deserved, so she demurred.

"What would you say to having a houseguest?" he asked her later when they were alone in the little house. She looked up from changing the baby.

"Lie still dear—" she said to Patsy, with her mouth full of pins. "Mm—"She took the pins out. "Who d'you mean?" though she knew well. She finished pinning the child's clouts and set her on the floor again. He said nothing but waited for her to guess. She stood up.

"Not Mr. Mazzei?" she said. He nodded, rocking on his toes. She shook her head. "Oh Thomas! You are incorrigible! Poor Mr. Adams comes all this way, only to lose his buyer to us." She folded her arms and inclined her head. To her alarm and astonishment, he swung her up in his arms and around in a circle as if she were Patsy.

"But, Pattycakes, you don't understand!" he cried with a face of joy. "He wants to grow grapes here! Oh, think of it!" His eyes were shining. "To have the society of Florence in our own backyard! Wasn't I just saying how I wanted to buy John Brady's two hundred acres down the gap, and how bad it was we could not afford it? Well, they're still for sale, so Mazzei can buy them! He has workmen already down in the Tidewater—Tuscan men, Patty! So all he'd have to do is go down to fetch them before beginning. What do you say, tell me what you think?"

It was impossible to resist his enthusiasm. "Where shall we put him?" she asked with a little smile. "In the parlor with the wet plaster and sawdust; in the cellar with the beer? I know, he can live with the Willises down the mountain. He should do just fine with Nancy always sick and all the babies crowded in the lean-to." She gazed at him frankly. "Have you asked him?"

"Good Lord, no!" he exclaimed. "I thought I'd ask you first, as you're the one who's likely to be most put out."

"I am not at all put out," she said lightly, smiling.

He shook his head. His eyes were very green. "You know what I mean," he said. "I wouldn't want you feeling taxed by a houseguest in your confinement because you said 'yes' to please me."

She looked up at him under her lashes, her eyes dark and challenging. "Now, why else would I say 'yes' but to please you?" she asked, and saw his flush. "Every thought I have, every movement of my day is to that end ultimately. Why should this be different?" She raised her arms about his neck. "You are set on it, I can see, as clearly as Mr. Adams. . . . How long would he be here?"

"A month or two—"

She raised an eyebrow with his own skeptical expression. "All right," he amended, "more reasonably 'till spring. March. After the first thaw. Before the baby."

She laughed at this and reached up to kiss him. "If we're lucky," she said. "Maybe his house will take as long as ours."

"I hope not," he said sincerely. "I like Mazzei. He's a good man, correct, methodical, amusing. . . but God, does he talk too much!"

That was entirely too much! She laughed again. "This from my chatterbox who can't be pulled away from Page before the middle of the night," she said fondly.

"No," he protested. "Really! Page and I at least have some silences. You saw him at breakfast! He was that way the whole time we were gone. I don't know how I managed to get enough words in to advise him of my plan, let alone convince him. He is never quiet."

"Poor Thomas," she sighed, shaking her head, "trapped with an erudite Florentine man of letters for an entire morning. La, how'd you shift?"

"Vixen," he murmured, giving her a kiss. "So, what is the verdict to be, sweet? Do you say me nay or yea?"

She closed her eyes a moment as he leaned his forehead against hers, and when she spoke again it was softly, "I say thee yea, sir. As always, in this and everything. Tell Mr. Mazzei he is our most welcome houseguest, and I'll fetch to him his own towels and a regular place at table. . . on your side, where he may pester you."

He laughed and let her go. "I suppose it's the price I must pay," he said, and went to his file box and began rifling through it for the plan of the house.

30
Discontents

Monticello

Mr. Adams had to travel out to his own land, in any case, and Phillip Mazzei accompanied him there and back again to the Tidewater where his Tuscan workmen were shivering in the Virginia winter. He there succumbed to the persuasions of his friend, quite reluctantly, to marry the widow Martin, whose husband he had known and whose estate was now governed by him. He did not in truth like her much, for he knew her too well for that, but he was brought round to the idea that a wedded life would yield him greater comforts than a single one. So when he returned to Albemarle after Christmas it was with a wife and stepdaughter in tow. He had written ahead to inform them of his change of status, and they yet extended their open invitation to all. The housing was arranged somewhat differently than originally planned for, but it would not be impossible to accommodate them. Three more guests more or less amid their constant flux was no hardship.

In the time since his departure they had killed several of the hogs, and she set up the hams and bacon for curing in the cellar, put by the good lard and cracknels for soap and candles, and divided up the low parts among the servants.

The Reynolds had an unexpected tragedy before Christmas; their Sally took a fever which lasted a week before the child developed the bright red rash of scarlet fever. Their boy Jack had it also by that time. George Gilmer was sent for, but it was too late for poor Sally; she died the next day. For a time, Jack's life was feared for also, but he was older and stronger, and he recovered with no ill effect. She had gone down to help in the days before the cause of the trouble was known and was anxious that she would be taken with it also or some harm come to the baby, but George looked her over and pronounced her fit in that regard.

"However," he cautioned, waggling his pinard horn at her, "you have been less than frank with me about your old complaint. I can see we shall have the same trouble as before."

She looked at him, with his round green eyes in a face surrounded by a shock of curly brown hair. There was an intensity about him, perhaps due to his Scots forebears, even in such a professional capacity. She flushed and dropped her gaze.

"I wouldn't trouble yourself to engage the midwife," he said. "Not that she wasn't excellent at her art, but what you need she cannot provide." He meant instruments, and she knew it. It was part of the division of services between a midwife and a doctor; the midwives, no matter their skill or age, were disallowed by law the use, or even to gain knowledge of the use, of forceps. He went on, "How are your eyes now? They look clear, but that is not always an accurate indication. Do they pain you?"

"Sometimes," she admitted. "But only when it's late and I've pushed myself to some task."

"Well, stop," he said bluntly, in his lilting way. His voice held a bare trace of a Scots' burr, the relic of his father and his Edinburgh days. "You are not yet at the third trimester, and as you *should know*," his voice grew sharp, "the greatest trial of endurance is yet before you. I don't like that this one is again so large this soon, tho' it seems a pattern with you. How's he moving about?"

"Fine," she said.

"Does he keep you awake at night?"

"Yes," she said reluctantly.

"Then you should rest more in the day. Let the servants mind Miss Patt, and the steward's wife, Mrs. Garth, take some of the work. She looks a capable soul. You'll do yourself no good, Mrs., gadding about working yourself like you were not in circumstances, nor this little one either. And mark me, I shall tell that husband of yours so as well, so don't think you may get by that way."

He smiled a little. "I know how strong-willed you are. I will not say stubborn, as I don't have that privilege, but I warn you, I shall enforce you to bed rest if needs be, so go easily on yourself from this out. You'll be less tired, in any case." He put his things away. "Don't fret about the scarlet fever. If you haven't shown signs of it by this time, I doubt you will." He rose and put on his hat. "Good day to you, ma'am. We'll see you at Twelfth Night. Lucy's made up her pud already."

She smiled at that. "Give her my regards, won't you, George?"

"I will." He turned from the door. "Bed rest!" he said, shaking his finger, and departed. She sighed, glad that she was out of danger from contagion, but she had a shiver of apprehension for another difficult birth. Thank goodness, for her sake, that Lord Dunmore had prorogued the Assembly further until May! She could be assured at least that Thomas would not be called away. She would not like to die apart from him, and that was a not-too-indistinct possibility.

She rose from the bed and was about to tidy up the room, when she remembered George's admonition and rang the bell instead. She picked up a book, curled up in the red leather armchair, and settled in to enjoy the blustery afternoon with guilty pleasure.

The Mazzeis took up quarters in one of the vacated workmen's houses down the south side of the mountain. It was a log house, not great large, about the same size as the little house up above, but it had among its amenities a ladder loft so that young Miss Martin—Peggy was her name and a sweet girl she turned out to be, taking more after her father than her imperious English mother—could have a space of her own. She was just about twelve years of age, a tall, willowy, brown-haired girl with a fragile prettiness that could be plain or lovely depending upon her mood. She took to the small house in the woods and her place in it like a duck to water, but her mother was more difficult to please.

In many ways the new Mrs. Mazzei reminded her of Thomas's mother but without that lady's wit or essential nobility. One had the feeling with Mrs. Jefferson that, in spite of her forthright speech, there were actions and words that were beneath her ability to undertake. It was not so with Mrs. Mazzei. Mrs. Jefferson may be aloof, but Mrs. Mazzei was plainly hostile, not merely to the enterprise her new husband had undertaken, but to every aspect of life in the colonies or colonials. She did not hold a very high opinion of "this backwater," as she referred to Albemarle, and refused to see any of the sublimity in the sparkling winter woods or the spectacular view, claiming that the whole place merely gave her a headache. Now, this was not the sort of headache that had assailed Thomas when first he climbed up to the top of the Natural Bridge, a wondrous rock formation on the other side of the Blue Ridge; it was not that awestruck insensibility he had described to her, but the nagging, droning perpetual sort of the perennially dissatisfied.

"She could meet with Jesus Christ in the road and he'd give her a headache," Thomas remarked of her acerbically. Between him and the wife of his friend there was no love lost, although he was at pains to be cordial at all times, as behooved his behavior toward a guest, welcome or no; he also did so for the sake of Mazzei and Miss Martin, who were most dear.

They rang out the old year with their household thus considerably enlarged, for Mazzei had brought his Tuscan workmen with him. Those men lived in huts on the property Mazzei had bought from them and christened "Colle," and they regularly sent over pleas for blankets or provisions which were readily filled, for they always received prompt repayment for the articles.

There was a light fall of snow on New Year's Day, just to crown the memory of their particular New Year and subsequent arrival at this place. They toasted the day in a bottle of Madeira and managed a quiet hour alone together before dinner to savor their changes and how far they had come. Thomas played the Pachelbel Canon for her, not forgetting, as she had not. It was hard to believe that it was just two years they were together. The rhythm of their lives were so completely intertwined with each other and this place that she felt she had been a part of it forever. There were inconveniences; she would not deny that—sometimes she despaired of ever having a finished house—but the tenor of their life was right for her and peaceable, and she could say that at heart she was truly happy. On that one day she flung away all of her concerns and cares for tomorrow's fate and lived utterly in the warm eyes and tender love of her dearest beloved, secure that nothing and no one came before her in his heart.

In the middle of January 1774, her father's estate was at last divided amongst the heirs, with the debts assumed likewise. It had been his wish that the lands remain in common until the debt to Farrel and Jones was paid, but this was not possible. Of the eleven thousand acres deeded her from her parents' marriage settlement in the will, they would end up selling half, retaining the Elk Island property and Poplar Forest in Bedford County. Of the slaves, all were kept, and Thomas very carefully delineated their whereabouts as of that time. They were dispersed between The Forest, Dun-lora, Crank's, Wingo's, Elk Hill, Judith's Creek, Indian Camp, Angola, Guinea, Bridge Quarter, Liggon's, and Poplar Forest.

Betty was presently out at Guinea with her younger children, but they moved her to Elk Hill that she might be closer to her family, who had come to Monticello. They'd have brought the entire family there, but they needed time to knock up more housing for their servants and Elk Hill was better than Guinea for visiting. Old Jenny was yet at The Forest, and she was accepted into the kitchen at Monticello with gladness. She could serve as a supervisor to the younger girls at their work while Ursula and Sukey carried out the large chores. They would need the extra pair of hands soon enough, as Jupiter had made his intention clear by his perpetual presence at the kitchen door that he meant to take Sukey to wife as soon as she passed her sixteenth birthday later in the year. If they lost her services temporarily to pregnancy, they would at least have a young girl to replace her for that while, if Jenny carried out the training.

When they returned from The Forest they killed twelve more hogs and dressed them, and she made jelly from the last of the apples in the cellar, as they had begun to brown, and for this enterprise had to borrow about half the sugar from Mrs. Jefferson. She promised her part of the preserves as well as the repayment of sugar for the kindness. She made butter and small beer, and they slaughtered several hogs to take advantage of the cold weather while it lasted. The snow was not deep, and it looked as though they would have a forward spring.

At Colle the workmen were delayed in their building, shivering in their makeshift huts in the cold weather. Mrs. Mazzei, living uncomfortably in her log house with a fire, wondered aloud what on earth was taking them so long, until it was patiently explained to her that the ground was frozen too solid to dig the cellar, and even if it had not been, the mortar was in no fit state to use in the cold. Another week or two and the house would be under way. As it was to be a frame house with only a half-cellar, it could be raised and habitable, if not entirely finished, in a single building season.

Even this did not satisfy the lady. As if to prove her point about unfinished houses, she managed to turn her ankle on one of the unnailed boards overlaying the open floor in the hall and ended up with a nasty sprain. The doctor was called, and thankfully George, with his University of Edinburgh credentials, was good enough for her. He recommended ice for the swelling and that she stay off her feet. She then had to be carried—*carried!*—down the mountain through the woods along the narrow turning path by two strong young boys to her house and complained of that. They had bruised her, she claimed, wrenched her ankle worse purposefully, and in any case she didn't think much of blackamoors; before God did no one have any white servants in this country? She had sold the indenture of her waiting maid when in Williamsburg to come out here, assured that there would be plenty of willing and quick girls. No one had told her that they would all be black. Peggy did her best to soothe her mother's fretting and quietly went about setting things in order and brewing a precious cup of real black tea.

Thomas was not so forgiving this time. In a single afternoon, by her meddling—she was not to have been nosing about the hall in the first place as she had been warned it was dangerous—she had managed to insult everything and every person on the place in the name of garnering herself some much undeserved attention. In a rare display of anger, he came into the house and slammed the door behind him, rattling the windowpanes. He was livid, trembling, and she feared he would have a seizure, he was so agitated.

"That. . . *woman*," he exclaimed, pointing off in Mrs. Mazzei's general direction, "is the greatest bitch it has ever been my misfortune to know!" He shook his head. "I have never met a single person so contrary to the warmth of human sensibility as she. Good God, she outdoes my mother and Polly with her spleen! Does she truly think that we, that I, should apologize to her because she was too vain of purpose to listen to fair warning? I will not! I've had quite enough of her airs and haughty glances to last me till hell freezes. If she doesn't find our country suitable to her taste, why doesn't she damn well go back to Williamsburg? Why hell, she can go back to England and good riddance for all I care!" He paced the floor, his hands shoved into his overcoat pockets, and she went on with her sewing, declining to interrupt him to try to mollify before he was willing to it, lest his wrath be turned upon her.

"Did you hear the way she went on? After we've offered her every hospitality, every cordiality, that could possibly be wished, she has the gall to complain because the house is not finished—our house! Bloody hell, does she think we are only living thus to discomfit her?" He sighed quickly and shook his head. "I honestly don't know how Mazzei lives with her if she's that way all the time, or why he married her in the first place. He apparently knew what she was like."

She spoke now. "Loneliness will make strange judgements on matters of the heart."

"He'd have been better off without her and keeping the loneliness," he said acidly, taking off his coat and putting it on the chair. He went over and looked at Patsy who was asleep in her crib at the end of their bed. The child could sleep through anything.

"He didn't know that at the time," she murmured, taking minute stitches in the mending of the shirt. "Perhaps he hoped that wedded bliss would soften her. It often does other women."

"Perhaps," he agreed, not very convinced, and paced again. His face was pensive, and she put down her sewing. Pushing herself out of the chair, she caught up with him on his forward travel and took his hands down from their folded pose on his chin.

"Thomas," she said shaking her head. "You'll not find peace with her; there's no use seeking it." He met her gaze and smiled a little. "The best we may hope for is that she has the grace to keep the worst of her opinions to herself."

"That could be a vain hope."

"It could," she nodded. "But is it worth wearing yourself out for? Let her go! What is she to us? We have endured worse and more constant annoyances, and we can weather her. They shan't be here very long. We shouldn't let her spoil the venture or the society of Mr. Mazzei or Miss Martin." She laughed. "I have it! We can ignore her, since we colonials are beneath her notice anyway. It may improve her temper, rather than trying endlessly to please her."

He was regaining his good humor, smiling now and putting his arms about her shoulders. "And what if she worsens?" he asked in amusement.

Her manner was offhand. "If she worsens, we can send her to Colle to live with the workmen until her house is finished. She may then appreciate better our luxurious appointments here!" Her dimples showed, and she was rewarded by his sunny smile.

"You are remarkable," he said, shaking his head.

She bobbed a bare curtsey. "Thank you, sir. It's nice that you notice."

He laughed, his ill humor forgotten for the nonce, and let her go. She took up her sewing again and he went to the bookshelf on the south side of the fireplace, coming up with several volumes. They spent the time until dark at their occupations, peaceable once more.

Mrs. Mazzei's were not the only discontented grumblings. One afternoon late in February they were gathered in the dining room, the cloth only just having been removed, when the windowpanes began to rattle, almost imperceptibly at first as if moved by distant thunder. It continued, however, and grew with a vague roaring noise until the house itself began to pitch. They looked at one another for one frozen moment, and Mrs. Mazzei cried out. Poor Peggy was white, staring stricken at her mother as if she were suddenly a mad woman. "Outside!" Mazzei cried, and rose with alacrity.

They gave no thought for the precious china or glassware but scooped up the baby and hurried outside for the relative safety of the yard. By the time they were all out, the earthquake had abated. They were left staring at one another, wondering awfully if it would happen again.

Patty took the baby, who was whimpering, and wrapped her in a close embrace. "Baby, baby, shh shh," she murmured into Patsy's hair. "Husha baby, it's all right now." But her own heart was hammering, and she had no idea whether it was. She looked up at Thomas. He was pale but watchful, scanning the grounds and the sky with a penetrating eye. The inhabitants of the kitchen were likewise out on the lawn, with the two skivvies snivelling and Ursula trying to hush them. She had her baby under one arm and the hand of the turn-spit boy in the other. She was calm even in the face of this unprecedented event, her countenance betraying no fear, though she had her two boys down the mountain. Sukey still had a rag in her hand.

"Well, my friends," Mazzei said, recovering his humor. "That was an earthquake! Tho' I was given to understand that you did not have them here."

"We don't," Thomas said shortly. ". . .Didn't."

"We have them in my country," Mazzei said peaceably. "I've been through three." He paused. "There are generally aftershocks." *More!* She and Mrs. Mazzei gazed at him in fear. His wife was speechless. "I only say this to warn you fairly that this may not be all. I do not wish to alarm."

"It appears all right at the moment," Thomas said. He put an arm about her, and she nodded. They were all safe, it was true, and the house had not fallen in. They had fared better than the Pompeians. She said as much. Thomas laughed sharply and Mazzei made her a bow.

"Just so, Madame," he said, smiling.

"We ought to check on things," Thomas said. He turned to her. "My dear, if you could look after the ladies, Mazzei and I'll have a look about and see if all are present and accounted for. Are you up to that?"

"Aye," she nodded. She shifted the baby to the other side and said to Mrs. Mazzei, "Won't you come with me, Madame, and I'll fetch you a chair and a nice cup of tea." It would be sassafras or huckleberry, but she doubted the lady would mind, or notice, in her state.

She went with the two ladies across the lawn to the kitchen. Ursula was still standing out front. Archy by this time was howling.

"Is anything broken?" she asked.

"Well, ma'am," Ursula began. Patty glanced at her in dread and went inside, moving aside the two girls who stood in the doorway. Inside the kitchen most of the cupboards were ajar and the contents awry or on the floor. The table, strangely, was overturned, although nothing else heavy was. The room was disordered, but not impossible.

"What happened to the table?" she enquired. Ursula was standing behind her.

"Them two eejits," Ursula said in contempt of her two young girls, "knocked it over getting out the door."

She sighed. "Well, they're young, and I was frightened enough myself." She turned to the girls. "Nell, Scilla, start cleaning up this mess so Mrs. Mazzei may have a rest in peace, and be quick about it. Peggy," she said to the lady's daughter, "I think if we put a chair by the door it would be best. Does that suit you, Madame?"

Mrs. Mazzei nodded. She had still not recovered her color.

Patty put Patsy down with Archy on the floor away from the fire and went to the dresser. Thanks to the plate rack, nothing of the everyday ware was broken, and she took down three cups and saucers, quite surprised when her hand trembled. She was less steady than she thought.

The clock had stopped in the disturbance, so she had no idea what time it was. But Mrs. Mazzei had regained some of her animation by the time that the men returned. The kitchen was cleared, although it would have to be reorganized later, and there was at least a semblance of order.

Their chamber upstairs was another matter. Everything that could be thrown about was on the floor, with several pieces smashed, including the looking glass. Books lay everywhere in heaps, and the tester, curtains and all, had come down from the bed. One of the posts showed a large crack. The bed itself had moved several feet into the room and lay at an angle to the wall. But ironically, Thomas's violin, the one for which he had paid five pounds in Williamsburg and had survived the fire at Shadwell, was safe on the table, having moved only a few inches, though the table was against the door. "I am cursed with this blasted thing," he said.

They cleared away the books and clothes and broken glass as best they might. There was no hope immediately for the bed, and the tester was stowed against the wall. They put Patsy to sleep when it was dark, then went over to see how the work had progressed in the dining room. No one slept very well that night, there being a constant undercurrent of anticipation of further disturbance.

It came in the next afternoon, about the same time as the previous day, and the disorder and confusion caused by the first earthquake were nothing to this. This one was sudden and sharp, rising in a pitch that was greater than yesterday's. She had retired to put the baby down for her nap and was standing on the far side of the bed by the window. There was no support to be had from the cracked bedpost, and she landed on the floor with a thump. Patsy was howling, as her safe warm bed was scooting across the room. Thomas was yet up at the house and must have run outdoors at the first sign, for the room had not stopped moving before he was there, throwing open the door to stumble over and snatch her up.

"It's all right, Baby," she heard him say. He must have turned to look for her, for he called suddenly, with panic edging his voice, "Patty, where are you? "

"Here," she cried, muffled, as her head was in her arms on her knees as she sat on the floor, "behind the bed."

He came and helped her up, and they made their way outside before another set of shocks disturbed them. But these were small.

Thomas's face was white. "Are you all right?" he asked, looking her over.

"For the moment," she admitted shortly. She was greatly shaken. "We shall see for the rest." She knew what he meant, for she was now going on for the eighth month, and the dangers were greater from her fall than a mere bruise. It would be all they needed, trying to get George Gilmer up here in the middle of an earthquake. They both knew she could not have the baby without help.

31

Revelations

Monticello

But there was no disturbance that way. They lost more goods this time, in crockery and china and likewise breakable items, and had a crack in one of the dining room windowpanes. There were other losses, less replaceable. In the afternoon Mrs. Jefferson sent a frantic note to Thomas: "We cannot find Lissa, and are afraid she has wandered away somewhere. Please God not by the river! Would you send some men over as quickly as may be had?"

He sent half a dozen, and Charles Lewis had the same number from Buck Island. They searched the woods and along the river through the afternoon and evening. When night fell torches were lighted, but this enterprise was nearly useless, for it was all but impossible to see beyond the fire's light. They gave up and would try again in the morning.

In the morning he went over and combed the woods with them. They presumed that she would go, if anywhere, in a familiar direction, that is to say near to Buck Island or Monticello, but she did not. When they found her at last towards evening of the second day, it was in the opposite direction two or three miles, in sight of the river. She was unconscious, fevered, and damp from having passed the night out of doors. Poor lost soul, lost in truth now. The thought of that poor simple girl wandering the woods in fear that the world was ending moved Patty greatly. She wanted to go over to the Lewises, to help look after the sick girl, for Elizabeth was fevered and delirious for nearly a week, but Thomas would have none of that. As they stood debating it in the house, his face was mottled with patches of high color.

"You're eight months gone," he reasoned. "I will not risk you to sickness or a troubled journey."

"It's two miles!" she exclaimed. "I could walk as far." That was not quite true anymore, for her feet had become painful again, and walking very far or standing very long was an ordeal.

"The river is swollen," he insisted. "What if there was some mishap in ferriage? What if things should start while you're there?"

"George knows where Shadwell is," she said, with a touch of humor. Thomas was not amused. He shook his head several times.

"No," he said shortly. "No."

She gazed at him a moment, then sighed. "And you say that I am the stubborn one! Tom," she entreated. "Your mother is an old woman. She can't be expected to bear the burden of looking after a sick woman all on her own."

He raised an eyebrow. "I have three grown sisters over there at this moment helping her. You are not necessary. No."

"But I *want* to, and it's right that I should be there! How does it look that your own wife does not come to help? They'll think I scorn them! Please?" She took his hand.

"No," he said, with an edge in his voice. "And I don't care how it looks, to them or anyone. They know your situation; they'll not require it of you." He sighed a little. "Patty, I know you speak from only the highest motives; I know how you are moved by my mother's plight, by Lissa's, but I cannot—I *will not*—agree to let you go. I don't mean to say that it's frivolous, but between them they can manage, and you have other, more immediate concerns. Or should."

She took her hand away, her temper flaring at last. How dare he imply that she didn't have the proper concern for her child? His high-handedness annoyed her. Why should he dictate her every move? She was not a child, or a fool. She knew the limits of her capability. But she also knew her duty and the pull of family ties. She should go; it was her place to go. The burdens should not be left to his sisters and mother solely. Good grief, Lisbet had come to them from Chesterfield when with child in the midst of an epidemic! Surely it wasn't unreasonable for her to travel two safe miles to aid his poor sister? She gave a sharp little sigh and turned away from him, lest she say something she would regret, but her anger boiled. He was the only man who had ever said to her, "You will not." She went to the window beside the door.

"You're angry with me," he said, behind her.

She stood with her arms crossed above the great mound of her child. "Yes," she admitted evenly.

"I'm sorry." He drew near, put his hands on her shoulders, but she did not turn round, for she knew he was sorry that she was vexed, not sorry for his decision or reasoning.

"Not enough to change your mind," she said quietly, looking out at the view beyond the house.

"No." He was more stubborn than she, and when pressed on a principle would not yield. What was admirable in public life, in the Assembly and in the courts, was a thorn in private. If he was willing to something or undecided, she could sway him, but never, once his mind was set, rightly or wrongly, on an issue, had she been able to change his mind. "I only want what's best for you," he said.

The words broke through her anger at him, and tears smarted her eyes. "I know," she said miserably, staring at the blur of the house. "But you make me feel so helpless! It's not fair I should be treated as Patsy. I am not without reason or the capability to foresee possible danger. Good grief, I am not a child and it is irksome to be treated so! 'You will not'!"

He turned her around. "I never said that," he told her quietly, lifting her face. "I said I would not allow it."

She shook her head, trying to shake herself of tears. He would think her cozening him, and it was not so. Her throat ached. "'Tis all one to me, no matter the fine point you put on it. I am dictated to, as a child or worse—" She was choking on tears.

The hands that held her arms changed their grip almost imperceptibly. When she looked up at him again his face was white. His eyes were burning, the green plainly evident in their mild amber. His voice was raw when he spoke.

"I will endeavor to forget you said that," he said shortly. "I suggest you do the same. I can only assume that your sense of compassion has got the better of you to go so far." He let go of her, took up his hat, and went outside. She stood dumbstruck. Where in heaven's name was he going? What had she said? What had she said that upset him so? She could not fathom it. Oh, where was he going, and what if he did not come back? He must come back! She loved him, loved him so, and needed him. Thomas! When she heard hoofbeats on the road she wept afresh and flung herself on the bed, shaking in a fit of grief. . . . *I have lost him forever!*

He didn't return until it was dark. By this time she was thoroughly miserable and had made herself sick. Ursula sent her up a cup of tea made from raspberry leaves, and she felt better after that. They no longer had a looking glass, so she could only guess at the blotchy swollenness of her eyes and face, for she had been weeping all day. When he came inside his face was quiet by the light of the single candle she had lighted. She flung herself on him.

"I'm sorry! I'm sorry!" she cried. "I didn't mean a word of it! My darling, I'm sorry! It was selfish of me and wrong to berate you so. I'm sorry! Oh, don't be angry with me, Thomas, please, I can't bear it!" She wept afresh, all the misery of her day coming back at her.

"Don't," he said gently, and held her away a little. He kissed her face, remorseful. "Don't, sweetheart. Patty, don't take on. I'm sorry, too. I should not have been so harsh." He smoothed away her tumbled hair, endeavoring to get her to look at him but she could not. She was a sight and miserable into the bargain.

"I thought you were not coming back," she said in a small voice, into his waistcoat.

"Come," he said, and took her to sit on the bed, took her chin in hand and raised it so that she was forced to look at him. The penetrating scrutiny of his gaze was worse than misery. *Don't look at me now!* she begged him silently. *I don't want you to see how bad I am!* For despite their occasional differences, they had never had a serious altercation before. She had not before spoken the small unkind remarks and wounds that lingered in her heart. Heretofore she had been only loving, but she had never been gainsaid by him in a matter that meant much to her. Heretofore, she could always follow her heart, get her way to put it meanly. And now, oh now that he had seen how she really was, he had fled from her in horror. Hot tears welled up again and slipped over, and her throat ached with them.

He gathered her into an embrace. "My sweet Patty," he murmured, "don't you know that I love you? I will always come back to you, my dear, no matter what disagreements we may have had. Always. Oh, darling, little one, I promise you that." Against his shoulder she nodded but could not believe it. Hadn't she been told her life long by stepmothers how bad, how inadequate she was, how much she must endeavor if she was to be deemed lovable at all? Even with Bathurst there had not been perfect accord, perfect love; she had been small in her concerns, and it brought him grief. And now Thomas. . . She felt a rising panic. Oh God, oh God, I love him so! Let him not leave me, too! She choked on tears and wept afresh.

Much later, when the candles had guttered down he sat with her in their companionable bed caressing the hair from her face, endeavoring to soothe her aching head. She leaned against him drowsily, calm now, and listened while he spoke in hushing tones.

"I left because I was afraid, dear. Not because I did not love you. I was angry, yes, but more afraid of what you would think of the truth." She looked up at him, feeling a cold thrill down her spine. *What truth?*

"About my mother," he said, and she didn't know if she had asked the question or not. He shifted a little and put his arms about her. "You see, my dear—" He paused and laid his mouth against her forehead. He was silent some while. ". . .The Randolphs are a peculiar people. Some of them are quite brilliant, as my cousin Peyton, and as genial and amiable as one could wish. Others are volatile, as Col. Tom, given to rages but essentially harmless. . . . And there are the rest, whose inheritance is rather chancy at best. . . . Someone back there must have liked to gamble! You see," he kissed her again. "There are those like Patsy and my sister Jane—gentle, vivacious, brilliant—while in the same family are cast those like Lucy and Nancy, who are, shall we say, giddy of brain. . . . And then there are those like my mother and Polly—you are not unaware of Polly's dark moods." She nodded at this, for at the party last Christmas Polly had thrown a Bedlamite fit that shocked her. "Well," he continued dryly, "my mother has those also. When I was growing up we were never certain when she would be subject to mania and so learned to be cautious. She would throw things or strike out, as Lissa does in a fit. Once she set the draperies on fire; and it was only by luck that Father was home, and we managed to put them out before there was much serious damage—"

Patty shuddered. An ugly possibility was before her: had Mrs. Jefferson set the house afire? The circumstances were certainly peculiar. Thomas had been home for dinner, then went back to Charlottesville to try a cause. He was not there above two hours when Jamie came out to tell him the house was gone. Only the house. Not the kitchen, nor the smokehouse, nor the laundry, nor any other place at which there was likelihood of a fire. . . Thomas went on, seeming heedless of the turning of her mind though he tightened his embrace.

"I believe it was the strain of such an existence that kept my father much from the house. They had such awful scenes. . . She would rail at him with the vilest, most abusive language and strike him. . . . and he never said a word against her," his voice broke, "but bore it all in silence until she began to calm down. And he would call to her then, 'Jane, Jane,' as to a child in a nightmare." He gasped and she realized he was weeping. "I believe that he loved her. But he had to shield himself from the pain her affliction caused, and the only way was to remain aloof. . . . Ah." He leaned his head back against the wall, struggling for control, and she heard him murmur under his breath, ". . .Father. . ." She kissed him fiercely.

He sniffed and wiped his eyes with the back of one hand. "Thank you! You are so dear!" He shook his head. "I have told no one this before, not Dabney, not Page. . . How could I tell them?" He sniffed again. "Howsoever, lest you wonder how I could love him save from pity, I must tell you that he was always most affectionate with us children, as I told you at The Forest. I was not dissembling."

She took his hand and kissed it. "I believe you, love." He clasped her hand at this, and smiled a little.

"I know. . ." He sighed, settling down with her again. "So you see now why I did not want you to go. I couldn't put you at risk if she happened to have a fit in distress at Lissa's condition. She has worked so hard these last years looking after her all alone. . . . I could not risk your safety, or the baby's—My God, Patty—" She was smothered in a fierce embrace, and his heart pounded beneath her ear, "I love you more than my life! If anything should happen to you, I would die!" He lifted her face and kissed her as if he were drowning. At the end of it her head spun with the intensity of his passion and the knowledge he had revealed to her. Even with Polly's extraordinary fit, she would never have guessed his mother was similarly afflicted.

They lay together in silence for a long while. Beyond the bed, the clock struck two, yet neither of them could sleep. How would they ever face the morning?

"It was really very bad of you, calling me a dictator," he said, with some humor now. "You made me sound like Cardinal Richelieu."

She smiled. "A benevolent dictator, then, with our best interests at heart."

"Am I so bad as that?" he asked frankly. She saw the fear behind his eyes.

She considered. She could not lie to him but had no wish to hurt him either. "Sometimes," she admitted at last, and turned to him. "But it's not unbearable," she assured him. "I know from whence it comes, most of the time."

He touched her face. "You must tell me if you are wroth with me, and not let it burden you."

"I never have been truly," she murmured, taking his hand, "until today. And I shall endeavor not to be again. As for telling you so. . ." She looked down. "Do you earnestly believe that I would risk your affections by telling you every little time I am cross?" She looked up. "Nay, sweet. I would rather swallow my ire and let time and distractions dissipate it. It's generally undeserved anyway. Only my own mood. And I did admit it to you today, if you'll recall, so fear not." She smiled a little. "I'm afraid I may be called too outspoken in that way. Ask the kitchen or the laundry girls." She sat up more and turned to him fully. "I love you, dear, better than any person that breathes. I would never risk that on folly. I am sorry. I said some dreadful things today, wide of the mark, and I apologize. By what demon I was possessed I cannot say. But I beg you, when I am thus, remind me how I love you. Not because I am apt to forget, but it will spare me doing or saying anything to hurt you."

He swallowed, with eyes as round as a child's, and she could not bear his haunted look. "I will," he promised, "if you'll but do the same."

They had found their means of coping with the ordinary irritations of a married life in that pledge, for neither's will to quarrel could stand against those three words spoken by the other. For the rest of their lives it could soothe any hurt, balm any sense of disadvantage between them. For her part, Patty vowed that it would.

32

Ends and Beginnings

Monticello

Lissa died of her fever on Sunday, the sixth of March. She had spent a long night and almost two full days in the woods, and the effects of such exposure could not be overcome. Thus a pathetic life was brought to an equally pathetic close. She had had moments of intelligence, one could almost say brilliancy, especially with regard to mathematics. Some part of that idiot's brain was finely tuned, for she had been able to understand the most complex algebraic equations. She had a fine appreciation of music and a childlike love of animals and flowers. Yet all that could not compensate for her basic lack of ability to control herself or care for herself in any way. She had not the manipulative ability even to dress herself or write the simplest line of words. She was gone now, to whatever heaven God set aside for simple creatures.

They had no little difficulty transporting the body and mourners over from Shadwell for the service, for on the day Lissa died the Rivanna, already swollen from the spring thaws, overflowed its banks throughout the neighborhood and as far as the Point of Fork, once again engulfing low-lying parts of Elk Island. This was not the disaster it had been in the great fresh of '71, but it was bad enough.

It was late in the day before those from Shadwell could gain ferriage at Milton or anywhere else along the river, and the Reverend Mr. Clay, come to conduct the services, was kept amused by reading matter and the purchase of two bookcases which were tendered him as part of his fee. At length, as evening was setting in, Lissa was buried.

They went back to the house and Patty had beds made up for Mrs. Jefferson and the twins, as there was no hope of getting them across the river tonight, and it was more convenient for Thomas's mother with her rheumatics to stop here than to be carried to Buck Island in the damp. Their unfinished parlor was not as elegant a chamber as one of the bedrooms at the Lewises, but it was warm, and it was here.

The Mazzeis joined them for supper, and Mr. Mazzei remarked to Thomas, with a twinkle in his eye, "This is certainly a mild country you have here, Jefferson: snow, freezing weather, earthquakes, floods. Most amiable indeed." A mild climate was necessary for the culture of grapes.

Thomas was lounging in his chair, wine glass in hand. "Just wait until the summer, Mazzei," he said, admiring the color of the Italian wine that gentleman had brought along. "Wait until summer!"

She glanced at Mrs. Mazzei, who bore a face of dread, and smiled. "Yes sir," she agreed, "then you shall bake or have thunderstorms alternately."

"With luck," Thomas continued, his expression full of silent laughter, "we might even be struck by lightning. That would be a novel entertainment, would it not?"

Mr. Mazzei laughed, and the company stared at them as if they'd gone mad.

Shortly afterward, their house guests were able to move over to Colle. They yet had one room, and it not much bigger than the little house at Monticello, but at least they were on their own property and out of her sphere. Oh, not Mr. Mazzei, or Peggy, but Mary Mazzei's complaints had begun to wear on her; and the workmen were everywhere, making up to her laundry and dairy girls, distracting them from their work. Thomas thought they were wonderful, and they had shared many tokens back and forth: they were flattered that he spoke their language and gave him garden bulbs and seeds to accompany Mr. Mazzei's wine; Thomas, for his part, copied off their tools and garden implements and had her take a pattern of their coats as a hunting jacket. When he laid out a permanent vegetable garden that spring it was full of transplants, and all the little sticks bore the plant names in Italian. She didn't mind herself, but when Mary Garth took over the household duties during her confinement, Mary said she'd like to run distracted, seeing as she could never tell one thing from another even when they were in English.

Her labor began in the morning on Thomas's birthday. Because it was his birthday and she didn't wish to spoil it in having him fret over her, she kept her counsel as long as she was able. But by the afternoon she could no longer stand when the pains came. It was more difficult than Patsy's birth already. She leaned on the kitchen table and made the most undignified, cow-like moan.

"Bagwell," Ursula directed her knee-baby, who was six and did odd chores in the kitchen, "you go tell your daddy fetch the master. You tell him go quick, Go on, boy!" She shooed the wide-eyed child out the door.

Ursula was an immense woman, sturdy and strong, and in her largeness there was comfort now, for though she was thirty-six she was still bearing children, and neither her knowledge nor her skill was forgotten. She came over now and took her shoulders, not about to stand by uselessly and watch her lady suffer.

"You hang on t' me, Ma'am," she said in low easy tones. "And when it git bad you let Queenie hol' you up."

She gave in to the direction, to the warm bosom that smelled homily of flour, when the pain came again. She sank into an abyss of red-blackness, and let herself be dangled by the armpits. It was such a relief not to have to hold herself up! *I should never have been so proud and foolish. I should have gone to bed an hour ago, two hours ago, when I could walk, instead of trying to do every last little thing. . .* Ursula's voice came back to her,". . .and we go slow, Ma'am, up the'm stairs."

"What?" She looked up. "I'm sorry Queenie, I didn't hear what you—" She cried out at a sudden sharp stab that came without warning and was breathing hard after it. "I think we should go upstairs," she said slowly. To her own ears she sounded as though she were talking under water.

"Jest so, Ma'am," Ursula nodded. "You, Suke," she said to Sukey, "leave that here and give us a hand. They won't die for the'm pudding."

They got upstairs, and after a long time she was at last lying curled in the embracing bed. Ursula said, "I go and fetch you some of the'm hops, Missis. That'll set you right."

She looked at Sukey, who stood at the foot of the bed with her hands clasped and her eyes as round as saucers. She held out her hand to Queenie. "Oh, please don't leave me!" she cried. "Send Sukey!"

Queenie glanced at the girl. "You go, Suke," she said, "and fetch it here. You know where the chest is. In the beer cellar—" There was another pain coming. "The key—" She gasped, and continued when it was done. "Take the key and bring it back with the tea." She pulled the key off the ring and gave it to her. Sukey bobbed a curtsey. "Yas'm."

When she was gone, Patty turned to Ursula. "I'm so glad you're here! Her standing staring made it worse."

"Well'm," Ursula drawled. "She ain't never had no baby nor been at any birthings sin' I been here. I 'spect she scared, ma'am."

"She'd be more so if she knew what to expect," she said, more to herself. Ursula said nothing.

It seemed a long while before Thomas arrived, but he came on the run. She had drunk the vile hops tea, and its sedative properties had indeed made her sleepy, taking some edge off the pain. It also made it difficult to concentrate on what he was saying.

"I sent Martin off for George—" The rest was lost.

"Who'll serve dinner?"

"It's past dinner, Patty."

". . .Oh." She drifted awhile, endured more of the pains, and came back again. ". . .Thomas?"

"Yes, dear?"

"I'm sorry this had to happen today."

He was smiling and let go of her hand to replace the warm cloth on her head with a cool one. "You let me worry about that, sweetheart."

There was someone else in the room. May. Mary Garth. When had she come? It was dark now. She heard George Gilmer also. They must have given her laudanum, for her mouth tasted coppery. It was nasty stuff. But better than the pain.

She came wide awake in the middle of a pain. It was light now in the room.

"Get her back down again," George snapped, "I can't see." At the end of a pain, he removed his hands from under the sheet. "See" was a relative term, unless he had eyeballs in strange places.

"What time is it?" she asked.

Thomas looked at his watch. "Seven o'clock," he said, stifling a yawn. She gave birth to another girl four hours later.

This one was blonde, weighing eight and an half pounds, with bright blue eyes and an angry squall. She didn't appear to have liked her scientific method of delivery, for her brow remained furrowed for days. When they were alone again Thomas asked the same question as before, "What shall we call her?"

This time she had an answer. "I know," she said, "Jane Randolph."

He smiled. "Yes. My mother would like that."

"Baby," Patsy said, pointing. She sat on Papa's lap on the bed.

"Yes," he said to her. "Patsy's baby, Papa's baby, Mama's baby."

"It no Mama baby!" Patsy insisted, poking her finger in Janey's eye. "It Patsy baby!"

"If you say," he murmured with a laugh. They looked at one another.

"Patsy," she said, "say 'Janey'."

Patsy shook her head, her auburn curls bobbling. "No Daney," she said, "Baby!"

And Baby is what she steadfastly called her from then on.

A few days later the grape vines were laid in on the southern slope of the mountain below the kitchen garden. They had Spanish raisins, scuppernongs, and muscadines. Mr. Mazzei's Tuscan vignerons came gladly to plant them, and to detail in a precise manner (which made her laugh and all George's sutures pull) how their plots were to be dug and cared for. It was Thomas's idea that if they were to be truly self sufficient—and this was their ultimate design—they should at least make an attempt to produce their own wine. Never mind they knew nothing about it. He could learn, he assured her. Mazzei would teach him. He had already planted olive trees come from Italy to the same purpose for their oil. That spring they began a fieldstone wall for the garden slope, which would preclude any such mishaps as had nearly befallen Patsy with the wheelbarrow. Overall, it was a time of much promise.

33

ℍlarums

Monticello, Williamsburg

Thomas went to Williamsburg for a few days for the General Court, though it had not been certain, given the political clime, whether there would be a court at all. He was back again by the twenty-fifth, calmly sowing peas and beets, and the radishes that had come from Tuckahoe, giving no indication that anything untoward had occurred while he was away.

They had an unaccountable cold snap early in May, with snow on the Blue Ridge and a killing frost. It was far late in the year for such weather and was generally attributed to the disturbance of their recent earthquake. Almost everything was killed: the wheat, rye, corn, many tobacco plants, and even large saplings. The leaves of the trees were entirely killed, and all the shoots of the vines that had just been planted. At Monticello near half the fruit of every kind was killed; and before this no instance had ever occurred of any fruit killed here by the frost. In all other places in the neighborhood the destruction of fruit was total. This frost was general, and equally destructive through the whole country and the neighboring colonies.

One blossom was not disturbed by this upheaval. For all her loud entry upon the world, Janey was not discontented as Patsy had been. She ate well, slept well, and never had a bit of colic. Patty fared as well, this time taking longer about getting up, and by the end of a month she was fit enough to insist that Thomas go about his business in Williamsburg and not fret over them, for there were ominous happenings there that wanted his attention.

The source of trouble close to home was that while Governor Dunmore had continued to prorogue the Assembly, the bill setting the court and other legal fees throughout the colony had expired on April 12. Another bill of like or different fees was required for the courts to be able to function. Whether this was merely an oversight on the governor's part, or a maladroit plot to bankrupt the colony was a matter of speculation, but public opinion was not in Dunmore's favor at this time, nor for long since.

He had proved himself to be against the general wishes of the people with the counterfeit crisis, for it became known that he had declared to Lord North, the prime minister, that the resolves to institute Committees of Correspondence were "so insignificant that I took no notice of them." Such haughtiness had not won him any hearts among the proud Virginians. Those of more sanguine temperament, George Wythe among them, argued that the governor may well have merely assumed that the fee bill would be renewed retroactively upon the next meeting of the Burgesses. But the hotbloods prevailed; why else, they queried, would he have continued to prorogue the Assembly to no purpose?

Thomas was late getting to town, largely because of the frost they had endured, and wrote to her on his arrival that:

> . . .on the 6th inst. RH Lee was assigned, in his office of chairman of the Committee for the Courts of Justice, the toilsome task of examining what laws have expired since the previous session, or are about to expire, that the committee might make their recommendations. the fee Bill is most conspicuously absent among the lists of reviewed laws, which bodes not well for us. even if the county Courts defy the General courts on this point, debts of over £10 may yet be brought before the General Court.

On the 11th he wrote that:

> . . .The House has overruled Colo. Lee and brought in a revival of the bill. this was presented by Mr. Bland. . . . the question now remains whether the courts have the legal power to fix their own fees, and thereby avoid a situation as has just occurred. if it proves they do not, then we shall face their Closure until a directive on this matter is received from England. i do not hold out much hope for such a Directive being handed down to us, for D__ appears not in a conciliatory mood. . . .

The general alarum which had drawn the Burgesses to Williamsburg was of more far-reaching import than the closing of their colony's courts, although they could not help but be aligned in the minds of the people.

Word had been received of the Boston Port Bill, which closed down that port to all trade, foreign or domestic, until the tea wasted in the so-called Tea Party of the previous December was paid for.

On the twenty-sixth of May, Thomas wrote:

> you will be pleased to hear that i have presented our entail Bill before the House, and that it has duly pass'd. now we may at last be rid of the annoyance of the Cumberland lands in favour of those in

Goochland. . . i will endeavour to give you word of the general alarum which has drawn me here: the port of Boston is indeed closed down to all trade, foreign or domestic, until the tea should be paid for. this, I hazard, would, were the loathesome Bill obeyed, take no little time, as i reckon the cost to be near £100,000, tea at present being at roughly twenty-two shillings per pound cost. no matter what one may think of the destruction of the tea, the Government's penalizing an entire colony for the rowdy-dow of a minority is insupportable. further, what, now that a precedent has been set, is to stop Parliament from levying such bills against any colony who dare to protest unfair measures? this is the great fear amongst us, that the menace which has swept down on Boston may soon consume us all, from new York to Georgia. . . our committee has put forward a resolution that our country abserve a day of prayer and Fasting in suport of massachusetts Bay. . . . summarily called into the prescence of Ld Dn'r and informed we are dissolved. . . .

The next day he wrote:

my Telei— lest you hear from other sources some of our doings and think me fiddling while Rome burns, let me tell *mia dilettarsi* that the gambol of Her Excellency's was planned long ere, and was in any case tedious, for there was no one with whom to dance, without her presence in whom my heart delights. it is now but ten o'clock, a fact which i offer as proof of my earnesty. likely i shall be detained until the middle of next month, due to aforesaid developments. if you wish to know where to direct a letter, and i have been in expectation of the promised one this week, i would say that Westover or Shirley should be the place, as i am bound to travel thence later next week or the early part of the following. after that the usual place will do. it is imperative that i attend the Council this month, difficult as it is to be so long parted. φρομ μψ σωεετ φριενδ. but this does not give my colpetta leave to neglect her pen! on the contrary, as you know whence to direct letters i shall expect many one a week at least! every day would be preferable. at least until i return here. there is much to tell that cannot be written. for the moment i hope it may suffice that I send my regards to all—remember to kiss my sweet angels and tell Patsy her papa will be home soon—reserving for yourself, my heart's darling, that greater portion which you hold in my affections. i look forward with longing to when I may look on the dancing eyes of my beauty and hear your voice. there is nothing here to compare! i miss the comforts of your smile, the touch of your hand, and the delight of your rosy face in the quiet night. the nights are too long! o, write to me and tell me that they are for you, also! write to me and tell me a thousand things—you know what to say! i live by those words, and eagerly await a renewed acquaintence with them. know that until then, i remain,

Yr devoted,

Th: Jefferson

She was busy at Monticello during Thomas's absence. Not only were there Janey and Patsy to look after, but all the usual chores as well. Their Muscovy ducks, who had first begun to lay in March, did so in earnest in May and June, requiring constant supervision that they not secret away to lay their eggs in inappropriate places, such as the vegetable garden or in the parlor. This was not unlikely, with the doors open and uncovered as they were.

There were cherries and the first peaches to get in, and by the second week of June they had more peas than they knew what to do with.

Betty was soon to come with her younger children from Elk Hill and required house space and similar arrangements.

She sent to Mr. Mazzei's people at Colle a shoulder and middling of bacon. And she, Mary Garth, and Liza Reynolds worked every evening to finish the summer ration of clothes for the Negroes.

The day before Thomas came home, she once again found her clean laundry engulfed in silt and sawdust, as they were digging a permanent saw pit just down the row from her washhouse, and the entire set, baby clouts and all, had to be washed over. Thus she was in no mood to be sweet or soothing when Thomas complained of the letters he had received.

It was one-thirty in the morning, and she had just put the baby back in bed and was undressing to retire. She had been awake since before dawn, but he had been asleep nearly these two hours since.

"I have a bone to pluck with you," he said companionably from the bed. She hung up her gown in the clothes press.

"What's that?" she asked evenly, untying her petticoat. She looked up at him.

"You didn't write to me as you promised."

She said nothing for the moment, but removed her shift and placed it with the pile of others on the chair that wanted washing. A bath now would have been nice, even a cold one, but it required too much effort. She could hardly keep her eyes open. She pulled on her dressing sacque and went across the room, tripping up on Patsy's bed in the process. Oh, she would be glad when they had more space! When they at least did not have to share a room with the children. She sat on the bed and rubbed her foot. *What had he been talking about?* Her brain was fuzzy.

"Are you all right?" he asked.

"Yes." she said absently. Oh yes, now she remembered: letters!

She climbed across him on the bed rather than getting up again to go around, and flung herself into the pillows. How sweet it would be to sleep on in the mornings as she had done as a girl! Not to have to rise until nine or ten o'clock if she wished. Those were pampered days. But she had to write letters— No! She shook herself awake and sat up a bit, yawning.

"I did write to you when you were gone," she said, passing a hand over her face. "And by your replies you received at least one of them."

"One of two," he said glumly. He looked at her, putting his arm behind his head. "Did you write more?"

"No," she said frankly. She was too tired to be mollifying or apologetic. She wanted nothing more than to go to sleep, and sleep for days.

"You said you'd write every week," he persisted. "And I was gone four and an half weeks." Some part of her mind perceived that he was wounded, but at the moment it seemed nothing short of absurd that he should have expected her to write every week when she had so much to do. Looking after the children alone would have kept her well occupied. He was lucky she'd managed to write as much as she did. She shook her head.

"I simply didn't have the time." She yawned again, broadly this time, and mumbled half intelligibly behind her hand, "Excuse me."

"Look," she said, at his expression. "You know that if I'd had the time I would have written more; if I'd had the time I'd have written every day." She laid her hand on his on the coverlet. "I missed you very much and greatly enjoyed receiving of yours, but too often—" she yawned again, "I would sit down to write a letter in the evening and simply fall asleep at the table. I'm sorry. I meant no offense."

He made a grimace, laying aside his disappointment, and put his arm about her. "I know," he said quietly.

She laid her head on his shoulder and in a moment was asleep. He had to rouse her when Janey woke two hours later for a feed, for she didn't hear her at all.

The next day she set about distributing the summer's ration of clothes. She had stayed up last night to finish the sewing of those she had and could only hope that her two helpers had done likewise, for they had as many duties as she, and more children. But she needn't have feared, for when they all met at the table outside the kitchen, every last piece of clothing was done.

"If I never see another needle and thread, it'll be too soon," Mary said.

Patty nodded. "Mm." She tucked a pair of stones under either side of Janey's basket so it wouldn't tip over with her wriggling, for she was awake.

"I was awake until three o'clock this morning," Liza said, "and then the baby woke at five-thirty. I tell you, I'm like to collapse."

Patty laughed shortly, in sympathy, for even judicious paint couldn't hide the circles under her eyes. It was only the four cups of coffee that she'd drunk with breakfast that kept her alert now. Twice a year and again at harvest time, it was this way and never got any better.

"I don't see as how men can complain ever of being tired," Liza continued. "Lackaday, they don't know what tired is till they've been our round."

"Well, it does no good to complain to 'em," Mary said. She put her hand on her hip. "I tried that on with Mr. Garth the first or second year we was married, and all it did was send him drinking."

"Perhaps we should take to drink," Patty suggested merrily. "Then at least we'd get a bit of rest!" She jangled the keys in her pocket. Her companions laughed and May shook her head.

"Mrs. Jefferson, you are a caution!" she cried.

Of the distribution, she later tabulated in her accounts for the primary servants:

> gave orange 2 suits of clothes
> gave ursula 2 suits ditto (no aprons)
> gave marg 2 suits ditto   (one apron)
> gave siller 2 suits ditto (one apron)
> gave bob 2 pr of breeches & 2 white shirts
> gave martin 3 white shirts & one brown ditto
> gave Jupiter 2 white shirts & 2 brown ditto
> gave ursula & bet each a white shift
> gave ned & Jim pr of trowsers each
> gave Juno & luna each a crocus coat

When this was done she set to boiling soap and made fifteen gallons of soft and fifty-four pounds of hard, twenty of which she sent to Mrs. Mazzei at Colle, for they had none. She also paid Ursula a middling of bacon for the twenty chickens she'd sold her and noted that she was still due eight.

Later in the day she cut out new linens and began an inventory of their tableware not ruined in February's earthquake:

> cut of 6 tea towels of dowlas
> 4 halfe ditto crocus
> 2 dairy towels
> 2 crocus table cloths
> 10 Queens china dishes
> 29 shallow plates
> 19 deep ditto

She was interrupted in this enterprise by Patsy and Janey, for one woke the other, and they both wanted attention. She passed a harrying half-hour that seemed much longer with two crying, hungry, dissatisfied, crabby babies. She snapped at Patsy and bounced the baby rather more vigorously than was necessary, and frightened herself in the doing. Sweet mercy, she was a wreck, all burning eyes, fumbling hands, and rude temper. She couldn't go on this way; where would it lead? When the girls were more or less settled she sat down at the table and wept from sheer nerves.

It was then she resolved to petition for both more space and a permanent nurse, for she couldn't cope with things as they stood at all. She hadn't properly appreciated how easy her housekeeping was when at The Forest, for she'd taken for granted a convenient house, servants who knew their duties, and long-established outbuildings.

Oh, how heartily sick she was of the endless dirt and clutter; the cramped, makeshift quality of this place! She couldn't exist in such disorder and have any peace, and didn't know how Thomas did either. Yet he didn't seem to mind that they lived with the contents of four rooms in one, that nothing was ever clean for more than ten minutes altogether, that their parlor roof was encased in canvas, that the oilcloth over the doors and windows shut out any light and air, while letting in bugs and other creatures. If there was only somewhere that she could go, as she had with her distillery off the kitchen at home, and be alone with her thoughts for a few moments, to collect herself. But she had no such luxury here.

They had Edward and Elizabeth Coles from Ennicorthy plantation to dinner; and afterwards they sat in the parlor, with its dim, ochre light, and played music by the light of her new-made candles. It was only in the strains of Mozart's sonata, playing follow-my-lead with Thomas's violin, that she was able to relax and find some peace. It was true that in a short while baby Jane would require her attention, or there would be some other domestic crisis before supper; but for this one interlude she could give herself over to the music and her play with Thomas and love him, forgiving all those thousand wrongs she suffered which were not in fact his fault, but which she had attributed to him because they lived in an unfinished house. "Remind me how I love you," she had bade him. *Let time and distractions melt away my crossness;* thus the sonata did. In the quietude of the second movement, slow, peaceful, she could anticipate his thoughts, his feelings.

And when the music picked up again, spritely, playful, she could follow along with it in the proper mood. Her hands ranged over the keys of her fortepiano with delicacy, skipping carefree as a child. She didn't really need the music any more. They had played this piece many times, and the cadences of it were burned into her memory. They danced along, first one then the other, merrily, and she was diverted from her cares.

Thus she was in a far better humor than she otherwise might have been when they were alone again before supper. Thomas had retired to their chamber to work, but she followed him, on the pretext of looking after the baby, to put forth her request.

"Thomas," she began, once she had changed and settled the baby. He was standing at the bookcase on the south wall, pulling down legal texts.

"Yes, my sweet?"

She put the baby down in her crib. Patsy was off playing with the Garth children. "How long do you think it'll be before we have windows—in the parlor, I mean? "

He frowned a bit, thoughtfully, bringing the books over to the table.

"I hadn't thought about it yet," he said honestly. "Why? Is the oilcloth insufficient?"

She hedged a bit. "Not exactly. But—" She put the clout in the bucket. "It's so. . . oppressive. Dark and all." She put one hand on her hip and rested the other on it. "Sometimes when I'm in there I get the most *nervous* feeling, like I'm going to be sick." She sighed. "I know we can't do anything about the roof as yet, but I thought we might do with the windows. Some light at least might aid the oppression I feel."

He nodded. "I see. Very well." He drew a piece of paper from the stack. "I'll write Adams and have him get on sending us some from England." For the duty on glass had been lifted some months ago.

"Thank you," she said earnestly.

He smiled. "You only need mention your requirements, my dear. I'm afraid I can't guess at them all."

She smiled also, in better humor, and went to him, leaning her hand on the table. "Of what are you writing?" she asked, indicating his stacks of law books.

"Resolves!" he cried. "Resolves for our convention in August." He kissed her briefly and sat down. "But I will write to Adams first."

She touched his hair where it curled back, let her hand fall to his shoulder. By such amiability he made himself very easy to love.

"Thank you," she said again, and kissed his cheek.

34

Summer Complaint

Monticello

During the whole of July Thomas continued with his writing of resolutions, of which there were eventually twenty-three. He took little time out for the business of life—it was an effort simply to get him to eat—although he did ride in the afternoons, and she saw for the first time how concentrated his effort could be. As she moved in and out of the house in the course of the days, seeing to the children or some aspect of management, he hardly noticed. Even when Janey was howling with hunger he barely looked up, and then only absently, once the noise had abated. He kept his fiddle at hand, and whenever he was stalled in the writing he would pick it up and play some slow air.

She could see now how such unsociability would have irritated his mother at Shadwell, how it would have only added to their ill feeling. There were always guests of one sort or another, and it would have been expected of him to be present for their entertainment. In Thomas's mind such work took precedence over any houseguest. She didn't mind his closeting himself away, for it was better than his being gone, and he was accessible to her. She suspected therein lay the difference between herself and Mrs. Jefferson.

During this time she continued her list of their tableware and gave out the last of the clothing for the summer ration. They owned:

    11 pewter dishes
    2 doz. pewter plates
    6 deep ditto
    6 old shallow ditto
    6 old dishes
    12 water plates

She made more candles and cut out half a dozen bags for the kitchen from the crocus Thomas had brought from Williamsburg. She had a letter from Lisbet, and another towards the end of the month from Bathurst's sister Lucy. Lisbet noted that Francis had found, among their father's papers, a memorandum regarding a deed for 453 acres of land in their neighborhood for life by William Byrd and William Cole to their Dick or Jack, whomever should live the longest. Did she wish them to look it up, and see where the land lay? They'd be willing to part with some of it if she wished. She wrote back saying that she thought it better they keep the land about the house as intact as they may for the nonce, as Dick might need to divide it up amongst his children later.

Lucy wrote saying that her oldest boy was for the College this year, though there were hopes they might afterwards send him to Edinburgh to the divinity school; Sally, the older sister, was not well, being troubled greatly with a painful swelling of the legs which necessitated bleeding to remove the ill humors. She was neither doing well with her time of life, being much subject to headaches and giddiness. Meriwether, the surviving brother, was well as ever, if likewise reclusive. He was a monkish man, study being the principle joy of his life. If he could have been a cleric, Lucy believed, he'd have been entirely happy.

She wrote to Sally, condoling with her and wishing her a rapid improvement of health, and continuance of it. To amuse her, she related several of Patsy's exploits and the progress Janey made in health and liveliness. Despite the grave contents of the letter, she was glad to hear from Bathurst's family, for she had not done in well over a year and had begun to fear they had forgotten her. Though she was quite happy here with Thomas, yet was she loathe to relinquish that fond tie that had sustained her so in her mourning, for she truly loved Batt's sisters.

Her own health might have been better. She was yet tired out from waking with Jane in the night, and as the summer wore on the heat made her dull. She had no energy, but dragged about the day, accomplishing her tasks mechanically. She drank a good deal with the hot weather, but it was not refreshing for long. When George and Queenie lost their Archy to the summer complaint, she was unable to offer them any solace in their grief, so low of spirits was she. She took a tonic of George Gilmer's as July waned, and that helped some, easing the tenderness of her eyes and pain at bright light that she had suffered for about a week. She had to give over reading and sewing entirely and lazed about in her idle moments in complete dissipation. But by the time Thomas was due to leave for Williamsburg again she was improved, and afterwards was glad of it, for he soon had need of her strength in a fashion that she should have foreseen.

He set off with John Walker on the twenty-eighth, carrying with him copies of his resolutions to the convention. She had word from Dungenness in the middle of the next day that he was ill and immediately sent the carriage down for him. They had told her nothing of his complaint, but she knew at a glance it was the summer complaint. With Ursula's help she got him to bed and began the course which was to mark the tenor of their life for several weeks to come.

She dosed him with herbals, bathed, massaged him in sweet oil, and laid him under an anodyne fomentation. He could keep down no food, and was feverish and weak. In the first fortnight she had despaired of saving him, for he lost weight so rapidly and took in so little in broth and gruels, or lost what he did take. At length, she prevailed upon George Gilmer, who sent her up some Peruvian bark, and this, though he complained of its bitterness, finally broke his fever. By the time the week was out he was no more subject to the wrenching spasms or looseness he had suffered. Now he was only thin and hungry and tired. She breathed a sigh of relief. Dysentery was no easy disease to overcome.

During the long while of his illness she had kept Patsy and Janey with the Garths during the day, and slept on Patsy's trundle at night to leave him the bed. Not that she slept much. He had only to move and she was awake, leaning over him and murmuring in her soft voice, "It's all right, dear. I'm here. What do you need, Tom?"

The regular chores and nursing had stripped from her any thoughts but that he should get well. The intimacy of the sickbed produced no blush in her, even when he was improving, talking and cognizant of her moving about him throughout the day. She did not think of him in the old way, as a lover, and was therefore startled when he laid his hand upon her face one morning as she was leaning over him making up the bed. She stopped and looked at him, full of concern, but he was smiling his rare smile, and the morning light shewed the green in his eyes.

"You've been very good to me," he said. Her vision swam.

"I have a vested interest," she murmured, touching his hand on her cheek.

"But it's not been easy, or pleasant." He clasped her hand on the coverlet. "Yet you've always been my same sweet Patty. I'm grateful."

She sat down next to him on the bed and searched his face. She saw the gratitude plain in his eyes. What had he expected her to do? She shook her head. "You've no cause to be indebted to me. You've sat through two childbirths and several sicknesses, and I never heard an ill word or a complaint about the work or its unpleasantness. What I have done has been because I love you, and because I love you—" she felt a leap of joy and sorrow, "there is no disease, no situation whose necessity can render you distasteful to me. It is I who am grateful." Her tears threatened to spill over, and she dashed them away impatiently. "Oh, my dear Thomas," she cried, "there were days I was so afraid I would lose you! And then I don't know what I should do!"

She sniffed, wiping her eyes. "I have seen cases with the best nursing and the most potent medicines succumb, and that was my greatest fear." All her long hours were worth his smile now.

"You needn't worry over that, my sweet. I can't answer for walking across the room yet, but I can assure you that I am most vital nonetheless." He leaned forward and kissed her. "And I am grateful. To your skill, to your love, to merciful fate that spared me to you." He leaned back again, pale, tired out from so much talk, and she rose from the bed to continue smoothing the sheets and blankets about him.

They were blessed that he had his father's constitution, and not the delicate one of the Randolphs, who were always afflicted with gout or rheumatics or some other weakness of the system. His mother was positively a martyr to her rheumatic pains, and his sister Lucy was constantly beset by female problems. The only one of them besides himself who seemed to have inherited good health was Patsy. She thanked her lucky stars on his behalf.

It was a week before he was able to get out of bed and a further week before she would allow him up. By this time he was quite hale and spoiling for something to do. He'd read every book in the place, including his old lawbooks. One afternoon he determined to ride to Colle and would listen to none of her protestations against it, but put on his boots and Italian coat and called for Fearnought to be saddled. She followed him outside for one last endeavor.

"You're still much too thin, sir," she said beside him, conscious of the workmen beyond.

He waved his hand. "Oh, that'll soon right itself." He tapped his riding crop against his boot, looking up at the house. They'd begun the walls of the south wing.

"Well, please be careful," she continued. "You may not be as well as you think."

He laughed and put an arm about her, not caring who saw. "Would you have me shuffle about the house in carpet slippers till Christmas? I tell you, Mrs. Jefferson, I am as fine as ever I was, thanks to your excellent care." He let go of her. "Now, I shall return before supper, and you know where I am bound, so go about your business with an easy mind." He kissed her hand. "Good-bye, sweet, try not to fret." He began to walk away from her across the yard to the stables. "I will convey your warmest regards to our friend Mrs. Mazzei while I am there," he called.

She laughed now. "Oh, go on, sir," she smiled, "to be back the sooner."

"I shall." He raised the stick in a salute and sauntered off across the lawn.

It was just dark enough for candles by the time he got home. She had a cozy supper waiting in the little house and the little girls tucked up in bed. Afterward he announced his intention to write several long-overdue letters, but she coaxed him instead to play the fiddle. At last, they retired to bed and read Sidney together, as in courting days.

And as in those days, he watched and admired the way the candlelight gleamed off her dark hair so that it glowed a burnished auburn, and listened musingly to the cadence of her soft voice. It was rare these days that they could read together, and most of their private time was stolen from the small hours past midnight. In this she was at a disadvantage, for he had never required much sleep, while she paid for such quiet intimacies the next day.

He lounged on the bed, listening to the mellifluous roll of the antique words, toying idly with the fine ends of her hair as it lay on the coverlet near his hand. She sat in taylor-fashion facing him, her head inclined toward the book and the candlelight.

At the end of her poem he took the book from her fingers and laid it aside wordlessly. She looked up at him breathlessly and knew his intention by his languid gaze and her racing pulse. *Oh, my dear!* she thought, as the warmth stole over her. She had not minded chastity these last two months in her worry for him, but now it seemed forever. He slid his hand up her arm, over her fine shift, across the narrow, curving shoulders he had first and always found so delightful, and caressed the hair back from her face.

"My Diana," he said.

She inclined her head against his hand, with a wordless murmur. He sat up and leaned forward. "Patty." In her name he conveyed all the love he bore her. Her hand slipped down over his collarbone, trembling.

"Are you sure you're well enough?" she whispered. He gave an amused murmur. "Why don't you find out?" He wrapped her in an embrace, turning her about so that she lay beside him crosswise on their bed. It wasn't long enough from end to end for much sport.

"What about the curtains?" she asked after an interval. If the girls should— His glance brought her up short.

"Hang the curtains," he said. She laughed and gave over worry on the mundane.

They were wakened later by Jane. When she was fed and once more put to bed, Patty said into the companionable dark, "Thomas?"

He moved his face out of her hair. "What?" She turned in his arms so that she faced him. The matter had returned to plague her as she stumbled to the baby's crib, half in her shift. She ventured now, "When d'you think we might have some more room up in the house? Shall we have our chamber by next year, do you think?"

He shifted himself and threw a leg over her body so that she was enveloped.

"It's possible," he said, "tho' I wouldn't say certain. Much depends on how many adequate bricks Willis can have fired before then. Why, did you have something in mind for this space?"

"No," she said, smiling. "I was just thinking." She sighed. "Patsy will be too old to share a room with us ere long, and Janey'll soon be sleeping thro' the night. They should have their own room. We should have our own room. Then, too, you're always saying you need more space for books. You could use this room as an office, somewhere to get away from all of us and work. . ." She paused. There was a further reason. "What if we should have another child?"

He frowned a little.

"Is that an immediate prospect?" he asked her plainly.

"No," she said doubtfully. "Not so as I'm aware. But you must admit that trying to live us together with three children in this chamber would tell on all of us."

"What an unreasonable woman you are," he murmured.

"What—" she began.

"I can't imagine what you'll want next: a dependable well, a roof for the parlor, a proper weaving house instead of the cellar." He left off this sport at his own expense. "I will do my best," he promised her, and kissed her forehead. She settled herself against him.

"Thank you," she said. She was asleep in a moment.

Patsy's birthday was the next week, and she began the day with an altercation with Jane over her favorite toy, a rag baby with which she slept, that Janey seized upon as she sat on the little bed. Patsy pushed her hair out of her eyes and tore the kidnapped one from the usurper's grasp. "No, Baby!" she said fiercely. "Is not your doy, it's my doy."

Jane looked at her in surprise, then set up an indignant howl. Patty turned around from where she was turning down the bedclothes for airing.

"Oh Bat," she said sadly to Patsy, who sat clutching her dear toy to one side, out of Janey's reach. "Oh, don't be mean with Baby. Look, she's sad now, you've made her sad." She picked up Jane. "There, dumpling, it's all right." She knelt down. "Pats," she proposed. "May Janey have this toy?" She held up the long unused red knitted ball.

"No," Patsy said with a frown. "It's my ball, not Baby's."

"She won't keep it," Patty assured. "Just to make her happy again. Will you be my big girl and share with Baby?"

The child stopped to consider. "Will her not keep my ball?" She made a hard bargain.

Patty smiled. "No, love."

Patsy nodded. "Baby may play with Patsy's ball."

"Good." She wanted to encourage the child's generous impulses, for, like

Jack, she had the tendency to be forgetful of others' feelings. And she was genuinely sorry to hurt one's feelings when it was pointed out that those feelings were the same as hers. She was in essence a good child, somewhat intractable, but that was largely her age. It was hard to believe that she was already two years old.

She was tall for her age, and well-formed, rather precocious of speech and habit for a girl, but that could be toned down. She had already begun to lose her babyish look; she was thinner now and her middle didn't stick out quite so far. She was happy to run and play with the other children on the place and evinced a rash of freckles across her nose that no buttermilk could lighten. Bonnets, too, were useless, mostly because she lost them. She had a thick tangle of dark red hair down to her shoulders that refused to be tidy, and intelligent hazel eyes. She could pick out a tune upon the fortepiano, altho' the spinet was easier for her to reach, as it could be placed on a low table, and she didn't require a lap to sit on. She knew many nursery songs, which she sang in remarkably correct key, and knew her letters and numbers up to twenty. The latter was the result of Thomas's efforts, for he'd spent part of every day with her for the last six months, barring the time he was away or too ill, patiently teaching her such rudiments. He was quite proud of her quickness. "She promises a scholar," he said.

"She'll probably refuse to read aught but novels," she returned, to tease him.

"Oh, I don't know," he argued reasonably. "She did seem to have a taste for the Roman historians."

"Only because they were within her reach," she laughed. But she was glad of the child's quick wit, also. It would have been a grave disappointment to have a dull child.

Not that she found virtue only in learnedness. Thomas's youngest sister Nancy was uneducated at best, and one would be hard-put to find a sweeter young woman. She was not graceful, but that was due more to the isolation of her position than any inborn quality. She wanted only a season in Williamsburg to give her a bit of dash. She was nineteen, after all, and it was time for her to seek society other than that of her family.

In coloring and temperament, Janey reminded her of this aunt, for the child was yet blonde and her eyes were coming a shade of greenish blue-grey rather than hazel or brown. She had her Aunty Jefferson's good nature, too, for she hardly ever cried, save when she was hungry or if Patsy had taken something from her or pushed her over in a fit of pique. She was a dear, sweet, placid, angelic baby, and a joy to raise. She would go to any stranger, loved company, but would play by herself with equal happiness. At near six months, she had never caused a bit of trouble. It was Patty's dearest delight to cuddle that fuzzy head in the crook of her arm and look upon that loving little face with its violet-shadowed eyes and rosy cheeks.

Such moments were becoming rarer by the day. Janey was already rocking, hobby-horse fashion, upon hands and knees and would be crawling away before long. Then she would lose her peaceable baby to the insatiable curiosity evident in those little eyes. She would inspect buttons or clasps upon a garment, or any old thing she came across, with the utmost scrutiny.

And why not? She saw her Papa do it every day.

35

Mixed Blessings

Monticello, Fairfield

In October they received a letter from Edmund Randolph, bearing an account concurrent with John Walker's, of the reception of Thomas's resolutions to the Virginia convention.

"Mr. Speaker Randolph," he wrote, "laid it on the table for perusal. I distinctly recollect the applause bestowed on the most of them, tho' not all, when they were read to a large company at the house of Peyton Randolph. Several of your admirers, namely, Mssrs Pendelton, Bland, Henry and RH Lee, took it upon themselves to have the resolves printed up in pamphlet-form. I have secured a copy for you, and will relay it at my earliest opportunity."

This pamphlet, which bore the title of "A Summary View of the Rights of British America Set Forth in Some Resolutions Intended for the Inspection of the Present Delegates of the People of Virginia Now in Convention," though it did not bear his name, was published not only in Williamsburg, but in New York, Boston, and Philadelphia as well, and before the winter was over, in London. From Peyton Randolph, presiding at Congress in Philadelphia, they heard that the name of the author of "A Summary View" had been placed on a list of proscriptions.

The word set Patty's heart thumping in alarm. "What is this list of proscriptions?" she asked with a frown as she read his cousin's letter. He put down his bow, his eyes gauging her.

"The names of those whose works have been deemed seditious by His Majesty's government," he said frankly.

"But your name wasn't on the paper they published!" she exclaimed, sitting down hard at the table across from him.

"No," he said. "But as here, the authorship is no secret." He ran the bow across the upper strings of the fiddle and stopped to tune them upwards an eighth. His calmness at the sudden threat of danger baffled her, so she turned her anxiety upon those she deemed responsible. She turned the letter over face down. "They had no right to publish it without your knowledge or consent!"

"Perhaps not," he agreed. "But it wouldn't be the first time." He set to tuning the upper registers as he spoke, a measure of his unconcern, plainly hoping to show her by such that her fears were ungrounded. "Besides, they thought to be doing me a favor by their publication, and indeed, I believe they have. They'd have languished otherwise, being too—what did he say?—forward in tone to present to the king. But it needed to be said. And better me than some avowed radical like Lee or Henry. At least there is some hope of moderates or conservatives getting past the first page." He looked at her, saw her stricken expression, and put down the fiddle entirely, reaching across the table for her hand.

"Don't worry, sweetheart. There are a dozen others well ahead of me on that list. And I doubt it really means much anyway. Just a way to frighten us into submission to their tyranny. Don't let their bellow-weathering distress you, for it's no more than that."

She looked at him. "Do you really think so?"

"Yes," he nodded firmly. "Come here now and sit nearer to me, and I'll play you the Boccherini." She came and sat with her sewing while he played. Outside the wind had risen and whistled through the trees on the mountainside, but here before the fire all was peace. Concerns of the broad world melted away in the sonata, and they were, for a time, transported to a space where such harsh realities had no reach.

Early in November Richard Bland brought back a copy of the Continental Association that had been passed in Congress in October. These were fourteen resolves, much in keeping with the strong ones of nonimportation and nonconsumption of any British goods whatsoever that Thomas had advocated in his directions to the Virginia Convention. The Association was printed up as a broadside sheet and distributed in various counties, including Albemarle.

She mitigated her anxiety over the future by setting down precisely the minutiae of the present. In the middle of November she began a count of the household linen, intending to have a clear record of how much of each type they had at various places. This work continued for the better part of two days, during which they had their first hard frost. From then on, the days grew bitterly cold, and she drew comfort from knowing just how many blankets, counterpanes, and so forth they owned.

> 6 beds 5 bolsters 7 pillows 5 pr blankets
> (and one) 5 mattresses one cradle bed mattress
> sent to Bedford one of the 6 beds with a
> bolster 2 pr of sheets & two dutch blankets
>
> one
> a list of the house linen

12 pr of sheets 29 pillow cases
16 table cloths 12 damask napkins
12 diaper ditto 5 counterpains
2 pr of sheets for a crib
1 wool mattress 2 tow ditto 6 pr of brown
linen sheets 8 straw beds 1 green rug

The new nonimportation resolves meant that the windows Thomas had ordered in June from Adams were now restricted. They were detained for over a year, and Thomas finally was able to purchase them at auction, but by this time they had long since had window glass of Virginia manufacture.

About Christmastime, it became plain that something was seriously amiss with her pregnancy. Not only had she had cramps all along and a distressing brownish flux, but she was greatly enlarged over what should be expected at this time. She was troubled too by dropsy, which she'd never had before; by nervous headaches and dizziness; and a cold, tingling sensation of the hands. If it was twins, she had the assurance of several mothers of twins in the neighborhood, including Mrs. Jefferson, that she would have felt some movement before now. Yet she had not. She knew it was not miscarried, for she continued to expand in girth. George Gilmer was utterly flummoxed and went back home to pore over his medical texts in the hope of enlightening himself and relieving her anxiety. Something was plainly wrong; that much she knew by the all-pervading sense of foreboding that tracked her days and disturbed her nights. When enlightenment came, it was not from George's books, but from that creature within who shortly sought to make its true nature known.

The advent of January 1775, save for their one special day, left her with little reason to rejoice. They spent Christmas at Elk Hill with the Eppeses and the Skipwiths. Nancy was waiting her first child in a little over a month's time, and Lisbet, too, was in circumstances, though just. She envied them their security, for Nan's baby was small and Lisbet had the entire enterprise before her. Nevertheless, she enjoyed their company and the gathering of the family together. But the merriment of Mary and John Bolling's Twelfth Night celebrations was interrupted by Patty's illness.

Excusing herself, she went upstairs, and was not halfway down the quiet privacy of the upper passage before she was wrenched by such a cramp that she could only lean weakly against the wall. She had suffered some pretty severe nausea all day, she wrote to Lisbet later, but managed to keep above it by not eating anything except some white bread. In the hall the bright colors of the wallpaper danced before her eyes through silent tears.

Lucy Lewis and Patsy Carr came out of one of the rooms, chattering animatedly, and stopped when they saw her. They rushed over.

"Patty, what's wrong?" Lucy exclaimed.

"Are you ill?" Patsy said. She felt her head, and if it wasn't warm, she would be surprised, for she was trembling and drenched. They took her arms and she gave up her weight to them gratefully. "Please," she began, and had to wait for the agonizing cramp to pass. "Please help me to lie down," she said. "I think it's a miscarriage." But by the pain she had, she knew that it was. She had the tingling in her hands again, and they were stiff and cold. When she was reclined upon the bed in the tiny attic room, Patsy said, "I'll fetch Polly and tell her to send for a doctor."

Lucy wrung out a cloth and blotted her face with it, her pretty face all concern. The solemnity of the moment made a mockery of her trailing curls and paint. Patty could only nod.

Patsy was nothing if not discreet. Not wishing to alarm the entire household, she told only her sister and Thomas of the development. Polly sent a rider out immediately, and they were both up the stairs in short order.

When the doctor arrived, he made it plain that he considered husbands superfluous in such situations, for he did not mask his disdain when he said to Thomas, "You may go about your entertainment, sir, and not trouble yourself. We shall look after your wife sufficiently well." His 'we' was editorial entirely. But for all his gathered sisters and the pompous doctor, she felt safer and better attended by Thomas. She held out her hand to him. The room was low-ceilinged and not above eight feet square, so that it was now crowded.

"No, please, Mr. Jefferson—my dear—don't go. Doctor, let him stay—" She seized Thomas's hand and closed her eyes against her trial, marshalling her will not to cry out. She would not—not before this overfed leech who called himself a healer.

"I insist, Madame," he said, unbending. "I cannot work in such conditions." He glanced about the room in dismay, for with furniture and their trunks there was hardly room to turn around. Someone had already upset the ewer on the chest where Lucy had left it after pouring out the water.

In the end he won out, and only he and Patsy remained to help her. He produced some bitter tincture, sovereign to hasten matters, and after three hours of intermittent bleeding and almost constant pain the thing was produced.

There was silence in the room, and the doctor bent in consternation to look at the product. Patsy leaned across her, with the excuse of raising the bolster, that she might not see. Whatever it was, it was not a child, but a weird clump of clear globes and stringy matter. It bore a putrid stench. But they had no time to cater to their offended sensibilities over this, for she began to bleed almost immediately. She felt cold and sick and dizzy, and were it not for a strong dose of shepherd's purse she'd have slipped away entirely.

This medicament was continued for above an hour, during which time her feeble pulse returned and the roaring in her ears ceased. They had cleaned up the mess and stripped the bed down. The mattress was ruined, and another was brought in. She was carefully moved, for the slightest jostle set her to bleeding again, and at long last the doctor retired and Thomas was let in. Lucy told her afterward that he'd spent the entire four hours standing in the hall outside the door.

He knelt on the floor beside the low bed, and though she was very glad of him, she had no strength even to raise her hand or give any other sign of recognition beyond a look. He was as white as she was and looked stunned. Doubtless the doctor had told him in short order the outcome of the ordeal.

"Thomas," she said, and her voice was but a whisper. He cradled her hand in both of his.

"Hush, sweet, don't talk," he said.

"I want to go home," she said, anyway.

"You will, dear," he promised. "As soon as may be."

That was not for several days, and when the journey was made it was quite slowly. The day's journey took them two and an half, and at the end of it she was borne up their winding, rutted, dangerous mountain road on a litter carried by Bob and Jamey Hemings. Even so, it was exhausting, and it was another several days before she could dangle her legs over the side of the bed.

When she did, Janey got up from where she was sitting and crawled over the short way to pat her on the leg.

"Ma ma ma," she said. Patty smiled a little. It was good to see that life triumphed after all. She had been so melancholy and weak since their tragedy that she'd had no interest in what lay beyond her misery. She laid her hand on Jane's fine, blonde fuzz. "Janey," she said in return. "Who's my big girl now?" The baby smiled her delight in such praise and inclined her head as Patsy used to do. It was the best tonic and made Patty feel as though she could indeed get on with life again. Her health was uncertain for a good while yet but she was not depressed anymore.

She had a long convalescence. For several months she could not lift anything heavier than a loaf of sugar without feeling sapped, and she was often cold. When the first of the dandelions and nettles appeared, she took advantage of them and made them up as greens, but even that was not sufficient. In March she prevailed upon George Gilmer for his advice. He met with her in the little house and looked her over upon his arrival.

"Well, you're much too thin," he said straightaway, in his bold manner.

"How much do you eat?" He took up his bag and opened it on the table. She sat on the bed with the front of her gown unpinned, hands upon her knees.

She shrugged. "Not much. I'm not very hungry."

He turned, frowning at her. "Mmm. Do you take any sun, any exercise?"

She looked at him askance. "As when have I the time?" she asked with some impatience.

"You have Mrs. Garth," he insisted. "Take advantage of her presence. You work yourself much too hard. . . Are you very sleepy?"

She shrugged diffidently. "Only in the afternoons, but Jane is not yet weaned."

He put down his pinard horn in astonishment. "Good God, woman!" he burst out in a plain Scots burr. "Are you mad?" He shook his head. "That has to go," he said quickly. "That must end right now. You cannot continue thus when you haven't enough strength for yourself."

His bluntness forced her own. "I don't want to get pregnant," she said in a low fierce tone. "Not after *that.*" She shuddered at the memory.

He shook his head. "I will agree with you that it would not be wise. But did you never think of abstaining?" he asked plainly. "It generally works very well."

She felt herself blushing. But she could speak plain with this man as almost no other. "I wouldn't trust to know when or not," she explained. "I haven't had a flux since after January, nor did I at all after Jane. How am I to tell?" she asked desperately.

"Well, I'm not surprised," he conceded, "seeing how anemic you are." He came over to her and knelt, listening to her chest with the pinard. He pinched her in several places afterward, and ran his finger along her breastbone, shaking his head in disgust. "Eat!" he admonished her. Then he smiled a little. "You are too valuable to us, Madame, to let yourself waste away to a shadow. I will give you a tonic, and a physic I have to bring on your courses, since you so desire. But you must take all of it, and I warn you, it's not pleasant. I'll send it out to you when I get home." He made a gesture with the pinard. "Oh, you may dress yourself." She repinned her gown.

"I would like for you to walk some," he continued. "And that does not mean from the house to the dairy to the kitchens and back! If the weather is fine you should take the air for an half-hour a day. I'm sure you may find a willing companion in our friend.

"Now," he said digging in his case. "Lucy bids me give you these." He produced two jars of preserves. "For she thought your stock might be coming low, and to invite you all to dinner on the morrow if you are not engaged, young ladies welcome. They can play with our two hellions." Those were his sons Francis and Peachy.

She accepted the fruit and smiled. "We should love to. I know we are not engaged. And please to thank Mrs. Gilmer for these. They will be most appreciated. What are they?"

He was putting his things away. "Oh, apricot, I think," he said distractedly.

It was the wrong color for that, but she passed it over and rose to get her purse from the chest.

"How much do I owe you for this?" The fee would have to come from the household money, but she doubted Thomas would mind. He could not question her being overcharged in this instance, for George was nothing if not fair, unlike some of her other expenditures. In the first year they were married he had disputed what she paid for nearly everything. But she had triumphed in this last year, for in the summer she had bought seven pounds of hops for beer of one of the local farmers for an old Holland shirt.

"I'll write it up later," George said now, "and send it along with the tonics." He made her a bow. "Good day, my dear. We shall see you on the morrow—" His green eyes sparkled in a smile, "when I shall be able to see just how much you eat." He went to the door and then turned. "Oh," he said, looking about the room, "and bring your guitar if you would. Lucy has a new piece of music she wishes to share." For her birthday Thomas had given her a guitar to replace the one she'd left at The Forest for Nancy's use. It stood now in the corner of the bookcases in the far alcove.

"I will," she promised. "Good-bye, Dr Gilmer."

"Good-bye, Mrs. Jefferson."

When he was gone, she went down to the cellar by the north entrance below the dining room with Scilla to fetch the wine and beer for dinner. It was frigid in the dark space, as last week they had had a snap of cold weather and frosts every night throughout the whole area. This time the destruction of the fruit was total, as opposed to the late frost of the previous year. Every peach was killed, and apples and cherries; in short, any forward spring bloom. The beds of peas Thomas had sown last month were utterly wasted. This calamity was compounded by the small amount of snowfall during the winter, which meant that the springs nearby were inadequate for use, and water had to be hauled from the well, which was an annoyance. It was worse last year, with a mild winter and the well having failed.

She did not know how the present lack of water would affect their house building, but it had certainly affected her housekeeping in nearly every affect. She could not brew beer, for instance, nearly as often as they required.

They had fetched the claret and a small pitcher of rum and had moved on to the beer room when Thomas appeared at the door. She was dressed for work now, with her hair bound simply back under a plain ruffled cap, her skirts tucked up under her apron out of harm's way, and her sleeves twisted out of sight. She had a smudge of dirt on her left cheek. She was no longer embarrassed by her useful appearance before him, but smiled and said cheerfully, "Good afternoon, sir!"

She rose and said to Scilla of the beer and rum, "Take these up now and mind you don't spill any of them." The girl made to take the wine as well, and she said, taking it from her hand, "No, not that. I'll take that up with me. Go on, now, or Mrs. Garth will wonder where you've got to. She needs that rum straight."

"Yas'm," Scilla said, and went out into the dark passageway.

Thomas came over and wiped the smudge from her face and kissed her. "I spoke to George," he said, and she grimaced. "You should have Mrs. Garth down here, since's she so hot about the rum. What does she want it for, anyway?"

"She didn't say," she said abstractedly, taking his hand. "But she gave me fifteen pence, so I didn't argue."

"Nevertheless," he told her, steering the conversation back to its original subject, "you should be up at the house idling, not down here among the cobwebs." He took the cask bung from her and replaced it and the wine bottle.

"I had work to do," she reasoned.

"Nothing that couldn't wait or be done by someone else," he told her. "Come along now, and I'll see you off your feet. Did you receive Gilmer's courier?"

He took her hand again.

"Yes," she said with distaste. "And took his noxious concoctions. Mr. Jefferson," she said as they went out into the sunshine again, "what would you have me do? Someone has to manage things. I can't simply laze about like a French tart all day."

He stared in astonishment at her boldness. He could be so innocent.

"Well, I should hope," he said at last, "that there be some balance between incessant labor and such utter dissipation." She smiled, and he went on, "Besides, he only asks that you walk for a time during the day. Is that so much?"

"It is," she answered, thinking of his upcoming departure for Richmond and the Convention, "when I have letters to write, as I shall too soon."

He paused again, his eyes all dappled amber and green. "As long as you do," he returned after a time.

"I shall do my endeavor, sir," she promised.

He took her hand. "But meantime, Madame, would you walk with me in our woods?"

She looked up at him. "Until the very day."

36

The Tender Breasts of Ladies

Monticello, Pen Park

They went for a walk together in the woods after dinner and retired to the house while the girls had their nap. He said to her as she sat in the red chair, "My dear, you really should delegate more of the work out and spare yourself. It grieves me to think of you falling ill from lack of proper rest."

She smiled as she worked on her knitting, with one foot tucked under her in the chair.

"I would not grieve you for worlds," she murmured. "But we haven't so many servants that I can do that. Who would brew beer or dip candles or cook soap if not I? Who would see that the wash is properly cleaned and ironed, or the table to our satisfaction? There are a thousand other things I could mention without having to stop and think. It is my duty. I would no more shirk it than you would yours." She stopped knitting a moment and looked up at him. "You're a fine one to accuse of industry. You never loll about."

He put down his pen and came over to her. Laying her work aside, he took up her hands.

"Sweetheart. You must listen: while I am grateful of your industry and management, having things well run means nothing to me compared with you. They could all go to the devil, and it wouldn't matter so long as you were well and happy." He looked down at her hands and back again. "And I would say that at the moment you are neither." She blanched. "Please, Patty, for me, go easy on yourself. I want to have you around when those two—" he nodded his head in the direction of Patsy and Janey asleep on the trundle, "are grown." He shook his head, and his voice was soft and hoarse, "Please, for my sake, follow George's strictures to you!"

She sat wondering before him. What had George said to him to upset him so? Did Gilmer know aught that he was concealing from her? She frowned. She was tired, yes, but no more so than any other lady running a house. Why should Thomas think her an exception to that, or too frail to endure it? What she did at Elk Hill in his absence could scarce be considered taxing. But she took in his pleading expression and knew she could not send him away to Richmond in such a state.

"I will," she said, "for your sake."

The next day they put the girls into the carriage and went over to Pen Park. The Rivanna was somewhat swollen, but not nearly as much as in former years, due to their light winter snowfall. They met the Gilmers in the drawing room where they were gathered with their two boys and infant daughter Mildred. She greeted Lucy with real affection.

"Dear Mrs. Gilmer, how good to see you!"

Lucy smiled. "And you, Mrs. Jefferson!"

Lucy Gilmer was about her own height, with a mass of curling black hair and merry grey eyes. She was three years younger than Patty and had been married for five years now. Her sons were four and two and the baby just four months. She was a perfect doctor's wife, having been a doctor's daughter, for George had studied with her father, his uncle, before going to Edinburgh. She was patient, gracious, and kindness itself. Her gift of preserves was just one of many small niceties she showered on her friends.

"Thank you for the preserves," she said. "They're wonderful."

"Oh, my pleasure," Lucy said.

"Well," George turned to her with an appraising eye. "You look better today, I declare," he said.

"I think I am," she agreed. "Mr. Jefferson saw to it that I spent the whole day at leisure." She gave Thomas a warm smile, for he had laid by his work to play music with her.

"That's just what I like to hear," their host said, taking her arm. "I only wish all my patients were so docile. Come, come and sit down. I see the children are already engaged."

So it was. Patsy had gone over to peep in at baby Mildred in her welter of bedding in the basket, and Jane was toddling over, her arms outstretched, to the pile of blocks Francis and Peachy were playing with.

"I saw your mother yestere'en on my way home." George said to Thomas as they sat down.

"And how is she?"

"Complaining of growing old. I could find nothing wrong with her beyond a bit of rheum. I gave her a bottle of Turlington's balsam and she seemed satisfied."

Thomas crossed his legs. "I daresay she wants the attention as much as anything."

"Mr. Jefferson," Patty chided. "What an unkindness."

He frowned at her in confusion. "What? I meant no unkindness by it. She is old. You heard her yourself say last week that she felt superfluous." He turned to George. "I told her she should stay with my sister Lewis instead of out at Shadwell. She is cut off there. What do you think? Might you convince her for reasons of health?"

George laughed. "I'd be hard put to convince that lady of anything!" He exclaimed ruefully. "She is of a most firm mind in most regards."

"Aye," Thomas agreed shortly.

She turned to Lucy, folding her hands upon her knee. "What is your new music?" Lucy rose, her face alight. "Oh, you must let me show it to you! "she exclaimed. "It's the most wonderful piece, but difficult." She went to her box of music on the buffet table and rifled through it.

"Here it is," she said, holding it up. She came to sit again, this time next to Patty's chair. "It's by Giuliani," she said, pronouncing the name with three syllables. "Now, it's to be played in several parts, but the guitar solos here–" she turned the page and pointed out a line of music, "–and here are so complex that I can't keep up with them." She paused and looked at her with an expression of despair. "You play so well. I thought you might be able to help me."

"I see what you mean," she said, looking over the music. "The tempo change here would make this trill difficult." She glanced up. "Do you mind if I try it?"

"Oh please!" Lucy entreated.

She had her guitar brought in, and they retired to the opposite corner so not to disturb the gentlemen in their conversation. Leaning over her guitar to the music on the table, she played out the piece until the first change in tempo and paused.

"Now, on this 'F' here, how do you play it?" she asked, pointing out the chord.

"*De capo,*" Lucy said, shrugging. She tried it thus, and the notes all came out muffled. She shook her head.

"Do you see what I mean?" Lucy asked.

She thought for a moment. Her present guitar had a narrower neck than Nancy's or, she suspected, Lucy's, and she had never been able to get her hand around it as this chord required. Thus she had always compensated by a seeming more awkward fingering of individual strings. She tried it now as she came up to the change again. This time it was smooth.

"How do you do that?" Lucy said in amazement.

She smiled. "I always have because my fretboard was too wide for my hand." She flexed her fingers. "It does take some strength or you get a cramp." She put the instrument down and shook her hand. "Which I have. I'm not up to my old form, I'm afraid. Mr. Jefferson may have a better suggestion."

"What's that?" he asked from across the room. He was quite comfortably lounging on the sofa now. She got up and brought him the music. "This change here–" She pointed it out. "What would you do?"

"This is a guitar part?" He squinted at the music.

"Aye."

Lucy came over.

"Let me see."

She gave him her guitar, and he picked up the part a measure before the change, ranging the board dexterously and making a simple span of the strings across the sound hole. The notes were easily plucked, and the piece progressed into the cello part. He made it look very easy.

"Violin," he said, smiling at them. She took her guitar.

"I told you he'd have a better idea," she said to Lucy. "Thank you, sir." She made him a mocking little curtsey.

"Glad to oblige," he said, going back to his conversation.

Now they had three different ways of coping with the same section of music. It was up to Lucy to decide which suited her better. She picked up her guitar and tried both to her dissatisfaction. The discord was furthered by baby Mildred's fussing. Just as Lucy was about to get up, one of the nursemaids appeared and picked up the child. Patty pressed her guitar on Lucy.

"Try it with this," she said, "it may be the neck." She rose and went over to where the nurse was crossing the room with the baby.

"Let me see this sweetheart," she said, and took her from the girl. Mildred stared at her with bright blue eyes, her fussing ceased. "Well," she said to the baby, "look at you. Here's a face you don't recall. Look at those great blue eyes you have, and those plump cheeks." She bounced her a bit.

"You are a fat little miss, aren't you, yes. Ah, come here, sugar, now don't cry." She put the baby up on her shoulder and patted her, and in a moment the child brought up a bit of wind. "Oh now," she murmured, "that's better, isn't it?" She turned to Lucy. "Oh, she's sweet!" She gave her back to the nurse. "And so much hair," she said to Mildred, with a caress. Nurse and baby departed, and she went back to her chair. "How's the neck?" she asked her hostess, laying her arm on that of the chair.

"Much better!" Lucy declared. "I believe it was the trouble. Do you know, I've never been bothered by that before. It's most curious."

Patty smiled, leaning over and looking at George. "Yes," she said pointedly, a trifle loudly to catch his attention. "Now you'll have to buy another, won't you, my dear?"

"What's this?" George said. "Spending my money?"

"Our money," Patty said. "You've seen enough of the Jeffersons this week, for one reason or another, to afford a new guitar. She does need one, sir. Listen to how much better it sounds with mine. Go ahead, Mrs. Gilmer, show him."

Lucy played the piece and George nodded, impressed. "I can't tell the difference," he said. But they knew he was teasing because he played the cello himself. The Gilmers smiled at one another, but before they could indulge in any repartee the bell was rung for dinner.

After the cloth was removed, the conversation ran to political matters. George was recently elected to the Burgesses as Thomas's alternate and had placed before the body, before its dissolution, a resolution for the proper distribution of Crown lands. For in its charter every emigrant to the dominion was promised fifty acres of the public lands, and this lately had been bought up by companies whose members were Crown agents, Lord Dunmore included.

"We should have seen from the first that he was a tyrant and a dastardly coward," George said.

"I would that he were the worst of our problems," Thomas remarked, setting down his wine glass. "At least we know what to expect of him now, in general, if not in detail."

George leaned forward. "What do you mean? What's happened?"

"Oh." He waved his hand in disgust. "Friends of ours are now changing their minds about the wisdom of the Articles of Association, and the word is that they've refused to send any new delegates to Congress."

"Who?"

"New York," he said shortly. "It's all for the shilling, you may be sure. They have a very conservative legislature, from what I've heard. They were willing enough to enter into our committees when it looked as tho' their ports may have been closed immediately, but now that that danger's past they're covering their tracks like a man pursued." He shook his head. "I wrote to Peyton Randolph, but I doubt anything will be done before we convene. There simply aren't the funds. Cary and Col. Harrison have complained to me the same. I don't know what we'll do. If New York is allowed to slip away thus, the entire confederation is for naught."

Lucy rose and excused herself.

"Can't it be borrowed?" George asked, pouring out more wine. "Surely there must be someone among those lowland barons who could afford us the monies. What about Mr. Attorney General?"

Thomas smiled a little, musingly, although the rift in the family gave him some sharp anxiety. He should not like to see them diverged into political camps. "No, not John," he said. "He has withdrawn himself from our process since the last convention."

"That must be quite a house, with the father on one side and the son and brother on another." George looked up as Lucy came back. She had in her hands her carved cherrywood jewel box, and she came round the table and laid it in Thomas's hands.

"I can find no better use for these," she said, "than to aid our cause." Her eyes glittered tears. "Please take them."

He glanced at her in surprise and then opened the lid. He was silent a long moment, and his face was pale. "My dear lady," he said, closing the lid again. "I couldn't deprive you and your family of such treasures."

He made to hand the box back, but she murmured in a low, fierce tone, "If you do not, sir, I shall simply find someone else who would." Her face became soft again. "I believe they will better aid the future and safety of my children used now than mouldering away in a box for a score of years." She drew a breath. "If I wait there may be no future for which to preserve them." She pressed the box on him, and this time he accepted it.

Thus accomplished, she signalled Patty that she wished to retire, and she followed her into the drawing room once more.

They played Giuliani when Thomas and George returned, with George playing the cello part. It was a beautiful composition, soaring, intricate, neatly balanced between the prominence of strings, and when it was done Thomas laid his hand on her shoulder. She looked up and saw that he too, had experienced the thrill of concorde a good piece of music could produce. Since she had taken the minor guitar part, it most often directly led into and countered a song from the fiddle. It was in such dialogue that they had moments of the most sublime perfection of communication. There was little else that could surpass it; a poem could do betimes, or a woodland hunt for flowers, but only their most private intimacies bore the same intensity of feeling. She smiled and clasped his hand on her shoulder.

"Well," George said, into the void. "I think we make a passable string quartet."

"Only passable?" Patty returned in mock-offense. "Sir, you do us injustice! We were superlative. Signore Alberti and his band would be outdone."

Thomas laughed. "Well, wouldn't go that far. Maestro may pack up and leave us if he feels bettered in this outpost."

For Maestro complained that the only culture he experienced was amongst his own students; he had no liking for jigs and reels and lower sorts of music, and the hunting horn left him shuddering. He was a cosmopolite through and through. It was only his friendship with them and other students in the neighborhood that kept him there, for he preferred Williamsburg, or even Richmond. Here, he said, he had to put up with Mazzei and his Tuscans.

"We should be sorely tried then," Lucy said. It was at Maestro's insistence that she had taken up the guitar in the first place three years before when he came to Albemarle. "I am not nearly proficient." They all expressed their difference with this modesty and Lucy blushed prettily.

They spent the rest of the afternoon at play, with Haydn and Corelli, Vivaldi and Purcell, and one exquisite little song from Lucy called, "I Lo'ed Na a Laddie But Ane," that brought to mind all of the poetical passages from Ossian.

37

Let Me Be Buried on This Spot

Elk Hill

They travelled to Elk Hill the next week, and she saw Thomas off to Richmond. At Elk Hill she could enjoy herself, having few responsibilities. They rarely had guests at this retreat, or if they did, they were neighbors only whose visits were short. She could dandle Nancy's new baby, romp with the girls, lie abed, read, or play music all day if she chose. Here she could keep her word to write, with the small details of their lives, and she wrote every day:

17 March
My darling Thomas,
This is after the post, so you shan't get it till next week, but I would not have you Reproach me again for not writing. Pats has been sad since you left us and asked me this Morning when she would see her Papa. Soon, I told her. Janey still has her eruption, but I think it a trifle after all, for she has no Fever &c–tho' I am as puzzled for a cawse as anyone.
We went for a walk with Nan this afternoon, the first she has been Out since her confinement. The Crops are much desolated, and all the fruit trees down so far as the River are blighted. Mr. Skipwith says the Island is similarly afflicted and we may not expect any return from that quarter. 'Tis most Distressing to see. There is not a single flouer that was spared above the roses, and they sickly. Nannie put out some four-o'clocks yestere'en but she does not hold out much Hope for them.

Saturday
. . .A letter from Rob came by R_d Rand. this morning, as he was passing on his way from Louisa. He has promised to give you my letter and what news of our friend he has. . . . Janey was suddenly suspicious of poor Mary when I was holding her, she seems to Believe that she has been Displaced. . .

Sunday

. . . Tis a week and more 'til I shall see you again! I have missed you sorely. I scold myself that it has only been three Days, that we have endured many such longer Separations &c—but such thoughts are no relief. You are ever in my thoughts, my beloved. How absence does make me realise the deerness of my heart's Darling! May the business of the Publick trust be swiftly despatched, that I may once more know the night's sweet cadence of my lover's breath. I do not sleep without it.

Monday

. . . I grow weery with idleness! I am no better than the children in my restlessness and I think worse! They have the Excuse of not being able to read or sew whereas I am without Any. To illustrate to you the Extent of my boredom, I have taken up my French again, with a View to getting thro' all of Moliére ere your Return. . . . Patsy sends you Kisses, with which I enclose the same from Your loving

Ma J

Tuesday

We have heard a Rumour that Jno. Randolph is to quit the Country. Can this be true? If so our Family shall be the Less for his Abcence. . . . I saw some blue Bells in the woods today, so it seems Nature is not utterly bereft. . . . Janey has made Friends with the dairy Cat and her Kits. I shall be hard Put to persuade her to Leave them behind.

Wednesday

. . .Patsy has added her Petition to the matter of a Kit coming home with us. I told her she must wait on your Decision. Six days until I see you again; Let them pass quickly!

Thursday morning

My Leander,

I have but a moment to pen this to you, as the Post Rider waits on me. Oh, that this were not the last I may write you! It has been my solace that I've had at least this Communion with you this week gone.

May our Hermes sprout him Wings indeed and bear this to you with all haste.

A thousand kisses to my best beloved deer, from his loving Hero.

She laid down the pen and folded up the sheet with the others, sealing it and addressing it with haste, for Betty waited at the door to whisk it downstairs, and not patiently. She pressed a fervent kiss upon the thick packet and handed it over. Betty shook her head.

"I never seen such a carry-on," she said, and smiled a little. "You wouldna known you all been married three years. Even Mist' Henry and Miss Nancy have more decorum. . ."

"Oh hush," Patty declared, "and go fetch it downstairs before that fellow leaves." She wasn't wroth, for she was used to Bett's ways long since, but the words brought a flush to her cheeks. Did they carry on? She didn't think they did; she tried not to before servants and company, but how could she erase all signs of her affection for him? She couldn't halt the blushes that came nor the straying of a fond glance. She may as well be expected to cease breathing as that.

She sighed and looked about the room. Clothes, books, and toys were heaped everywhere. Her guitar lay upon the table. They were no better here than at Monticello. The girls could be heard running down the hall clamoring for their breakfast, and she was yet in her dressing sacque, with her hair flowing round her. It was already half-past seven. All her careful discipline was gone for naught, even with herself. Well, today she would make progress with Moliére. She went to the press and took off her dressing sacque. Patsy unlatched the door and tumbled in, with Jane behind her. They were dressed at least. Bett had seen to that. All that wanted was their hair brushed. Nannie and Henry wouldn't mind if they were late to breakfast.

"Mama," Patsy cried, "may we go to the Island today?" She was putting her sacque away in the press, and turned.

"Oh no, dear," she said, and was sorry to see the crumpling of that little face, "the Island is not nice yet." She went over at Patsy's threatened tears and smoothed her hair. "Mayhap the next time we are here."

"Oh—" the child exclaimed, beginning a fit. She held up a hand. "I said no. Now none of your carry-on." She relented then. "Oh Pats, it smells bad there," she explained, "and all the flowers are killed. You don't want to go there for that, do you?"

"No," Patsy muttered darkly.

"Good." She smiled a little. "We'll go out and feed the ducks if you like."

The child's face brightened immediately, and she was in raptures. "Oh yes, Mama, the ducks!" And Janey began clamoring behind her, "ducks ducks ducks!"

She held a finger to her lips. "Hush, sh, gently. Quietly. You too, Pats." But it was plain she was to have little peace in any wise that day from them.

When Thomas came home she was down in the straggling garden with Nancy picking through the herb plants for those which might be saved, either by care where they grew or by bringing indoors. Janey stumbled after them in the grass in her unaccustomed slippers, and Patsy was off by herself, bending over a milkweed plant at the edge of the meadow. She wore long clothes now, a plain gown and apron, and was very sweet with her tangled curls hanging down the back from under her cap. She loathed having her hair brushed, would do anything to avoid the daily torture, but it was, like her own, so curly that if left alone even half a day it became an unmanageable knot. Caps now helped some, although she was but little better at keeping them on her head than she had been with infant bonnets.

She heard her cry, "Papa!" and looked up to find her running toward the house. Thomas stood there, sunburnt, with a face of delight. He caught Patsy up as she came flinging herself on him. Patty caught her breath and snatched up the fallen baby, hurrying as much as decorum would allow, no better than Patsy. "Mr. Jefferson!" she cried. "We didn't expect you till tomorrow!"

"I couldn't wait," he admitted. "it being so near." He kissed her, and Janey, who kept up a babble, "Papa papa papa—"

"Hello, sweet," he said to the child, laying his hand on her hair. It had finally begun to grow in earnest, curling at the ends, and was a beautiful golden color.

"I'm so glad!" she said. "Did you get my letters?"

He put down Patsy and took her arm. "I did." He lowered his voice. "And I liked them well, especially the cyphers." She blushed down her neck. "They stayed me when I would otherwise have fretted. You look so well." He let his gaze wander over her figure, that she might not misunderstand. "Nancy and Henry have taken good care of you."

She raised an eyebrow. "It is some of my own doing, too, sir!" She gave him a sidelong glance.

He laughed softly. "And how is Moliére?"

"Burlesque as ever." She glanced away, saying lightly, "I had forgotten how natural the French could be." She gave him her provocative look, her eyes all sparked with autumn tones. He laid his hand upon her back above the stays.

"Yet they have no arts that you do not own, Madame," he said softly. She melted. It had been a long fortnight.

Nancy came up, interrupting their wordplay. It was just as well. It could only be frustrating at this hour, for it was not dinnertime yet.

"Thomas, how good to see you," Nancy said, and blushed, holding out her hand, for she had abandoned the garden basket to a servant. "We were hoping we might yet see you today, but didn't think it very likely. John Peterson was past and said the road was a mire from yesterday's rain."

He kissed her hand. "Nancy. It's good to be home, if I may be so bold as that." She smiled. "As for the roads, your informant was quite correct. You never saw such a sticky, sucking mess as the Richmond road. On my way here I met a carriage that was mired in it, with the occupants all out in the road and most cross. I offered mine assistance, but they told me there was nothing for it, and they were waiting for another pair of horses from Westham. If they're on their way by nightfall, it would surprise." He glanced at Patty. "Happily, no such troubles befell us, for we took a path through the wood after that."

"Well," her sister said, clasping her hands, "that was providential! We're glad to have you with us the extra day." She smiled slyly at Patty. "Come inside and take your ease before dinner. Henry is in his office, but I'm sure he would welcome the interruption."

They came into the parlor with its windows facing the river. It was not a large room but gave the impression of spaciousness by the arrangement of furniture and draperies. Against the interior wall was a plain mantle, painted in pale tones so that it resembled marble and melted into the general color of the wall. A pair of sofas stood back-to-back, dividing the space of the room. On its stand by the doors, the cover closed now so that it resembled nothing so much as an occasional table, was the unfretted clavichord Patty had practiced upon when she lived here with Bathurst Skelton. It had belonged to some relative of his who died and was left as a part of the house furniture. In addition to this there were several chairs and a small desk with a hinged lid. The floors were sanded and painted with a thin wash of milk paint. Thus the whole room had an airy quality that was quite refreshing. If it was unpretentious, not possessing vaulted ceilings and actual space, it was yet comfortable and charming. The summer covers had lately been put on the furniture, so there was no bar to letting the children run about the room. It was bare of bric-a-brac.

Janey and Patsy climbed up with Thomas as he sat on the sofa, Patsy on his lap and Janey standing beside him. Patty sat in one of the chairs, smiling at him in amusement. It was admittedly his favorite posture, with their brace of nymphs, as he called them. He endured all their attentions in good humor. Janey put her hands on his face and patted him firmly.

"Papa!" she said. "Kiss!" and she gave him rather a wet kiss. "Janey, kiss," he returned, and kissed her. Patsy laid her head on him and said in a mournful voice, "I missed you, Papa. You were gone for days an' days."

"Well, you know you're loved," she said, laughing.

"I wouldn't have it else," he murmured.

Nancy came in with Henry behind her. The plumpness of his early youth had given way to a definite roundness of body and feature. He did not yet approach Peyton Randolph in that regard, but it was plain that he some day would. And like Randolph, his amiability was equal to his girth. Marriage suited him. The comforts of a wife and home were all that he'd needed to finish his personality.

"Henry!" Thomas was prevented from rising by the girls' sitting on him.

"Thomas!" Henry returned, smiling. "You're warmly welcomed, I see."

"Quite, thank you." Henry settled his bulk into the arm chair opposite, resting one foot upon his knee.

"Our legislators must have acted quickly after Mr. Henry's speech," he said. "For we didn't expect you 'till tomorrow."

"You've heard about that already?" Thomas asked, moving Janey's hand away from his mouth.

"Aye, Peterson was here and told us of some rousing thunderation. Strong men swooned was the way he put it, I believe." Henry's eyes twinkled at them, for Nancy stood by her chair. "We haven't the stuff of it, of course, for he wasn't present, only the rumors circulating the town—"

They had heard all manner of rumors, including that they were at war, which alarmed her considerably. For his part, Thomas was cool, toying idly with a resilient lock of Patsy's hair in the room, while the nurse brought baby Mary in her basket. When the girl was gone, he said, "He has called for a general and immediate founding of county militias to defend ourselves in case we are met with anything as has occurred in Massachusetts Bay."

She clutched the bottom of the chair. Dear God, it was true, they were at war! What would—

"Oh, do you think they will send soldiery to be quartered on us?" Nancy exclaimed beside her. Thomas looked their way, and she saw in his glance kind dissembling on their behalf.

"In Virginia?" he said. "No." He was shaking his head. "I don't think that an immediate prospect." But when he met her eyes she knew he believed far more than that possible. He put Patsy down on the floor. "But it may be for others, and I believe Mr. Henry spoke for a compact among us like unto the Committees of Correspondence, that an outrage to the rights and liberties of one were an outrage to all. . . . I grant you, it was quite impressive, but to my knowledge no one indoors swooned," he said with some humor. "Tho' they may have done out; it was rather humid."

"So we are to be prepared, is all," Henry said, "for what may be."

"Aye."

Patty picked up the baby and buried her face in the folds of the blanket, to all intents merely nuzzling the sleeping bundle, but she met Thomas's eye across the room and would not hide her anxiety.

War, dear God! Her mind ran to all the Wayles family stories of the civil wars, and how her great, great grandfather had stood by the king against his own brother. It was by such loyalty to the crown that he had lost his honor and his fortune, for they had been landed baronets before that. And when the Lord Protector came to power he claimed all their lands forfeit and all tithes and rents pertaining thereto. Their branch of the family became known as Wayles, took up root, and fled to Lancashire to become merchants.

Wealthy merchants, but in the eyes of the rest of the Morys family of Ynys Mon, mere tradesmen.

After Charles II was crowned, many families regained their old lands and titles, but not the western lords. It was a means to keep control of rebellious Wales. Her great grandfather compounded the misfortune by supporting the Duke of Monmouth in his rebellion. It was only through the influence of his wife's family at court that they had managed to maintain any public standing at all. So it was that war, in her estimation, led to nothing but misery. And now they were poised on the brink. . .

It was not that she was not patriotic. She wore Virginia cloth and eschewed tea as any right-thinking Virginia lady. Her window glass was of Virginia manufacture. She would stand by Thomas, and Henry and Francis, in whatever measures they chose to undertake on behalf of the liberties of free Englishmen. That was her privilege and her duty. But she could not in her heart countenance the spilling of blood on its behalf, for if there was one lesson that her father's compulsory history and philosophic lessons taught her it was that, at the end of such wars, often one was worse off than when one begun.

The whole talk that evening was politics. Aye, with its philosophic ramifications, but politics nonetheless. She became annoyed with the repetition, as neighbors came and went; of details of Mr. Henry's speech and the furor it caused, for it reminded her all too well of civil strife. It was in her family far back and closer now, amid the Randolphs. . . . Until Thomas said to her privately when they retired, "I did not tell you what Page said to me after Henry's speech."

She paused. "What was that?"

He leaned his head on his arm above the bolster, his eyes far away. "I shall never forget: he clutched my arm in a shocked way, and when I looked at him he was white as ashes, and he said to me, 'Let me be buried on this spot!'" He looked down at her. "He has a fine sense of historicity, does Page, and I did not until that moment realize in fact how very much Henry's words had changed our course. For from that moment, whatever action a man takes, he will fall to one side or the other of his appeal. . ." He smiled a little. "I cannot call it an argument, for he is too passionate."

The words rolled over her. If peace-loving men as he and Page approved of such girding, then they were surely on the road to war, for what was to restrain the bloodthirsty? The thought was a worm of fear in her bosom.

In spite of Thomas's presence she could not sleep that night. She endeavored not to disturb him, curled as they were together back to front in the bed, but she was restless and could not lie entirely still. At length he stirred and draped an arm about her. "What's wrong, love?"

"I'm sorry," she murmured, and turned her head. "I didn't mean to wake you. I just can't sleep is all."

He kissed her above the ear in the dark. "What are you fretting over? Not the girls' kitten or too much spent on writing paper?"

This teasing brought a bubble of laughter to her voice. "No!" She reached for his hand where it lay under her bosom. "Tom," she said seriously.

"Yes, my love?"

"*Do* you think it will come to bloodshed, the conflict with the Crown?"

He sighed. "I don't know, Patty," he said frankly. "I hope it will not, but fear that it will." He paused. "I'm afraid that we will be allowed no other course." That prickled at the very bubble of her anxiety.

"But allowed by whom?" she asked. "By Parliament or by firebrands such as Mr. Henry, or that Samuel Adams of Massachusetts Bay? What do those men really want? They don't strike me as candid for all their fire."

He tightened his embrace. "Well-spoken, my devious one," he said with affection. "As for what they want," his tone grew sober again. "What they want is independency."

She frowned in the enveloping blackness, her mind ticking off the possibilities. All seemed equally possible. "From what?" she asked. "From trade restrictions, from Parliament's rule, from the king's rule?"

He laughed. "All of the above!"

"Well I don't see how they should hope to gain that by spilling our blood!" she exclaimed tartly. "Killing one another, ruining the lives of hundreds of thousands for an ideal which either exists or does not in the minds of the beholders." The civil wars began to seem positively simple by comparison. At least the means and manners of the rule of kings and the rights of Parliaments was a tangible matter. It was those very subjects that had engaged their country these last ten years, and that was well. But what was independency that it could be agreed upon by all?

Thomas disentangled himself from her, fumbled in the dark for flint and steel, and lit a candle. She looked up at him in bewilderment. "What's the matter?"

He shook his head. "You are the most extraordinary woman."

She smiled her dimpled smile. "I thank ye, sir, and kindly, but wherefore am I extraordinary now?"

"For putting the finger on just my disturbance since Henry's speech." He leaned up on an elbow and traced the narrow line of her nose. "I spoke in favor of his resolve, did I tell you?" She shook her head. "Well I did. But even so, it troubled me. I am not fond of violence," he mused. "I suppose it's why I'm so staid as you say," he smiled at her. "Not hunting or wagering on bear-baiting or cockfights as the rest of them," he made a gesture, for even Henry and Francis were known to indulge in such pastimes on occasion. "I have no stomach for it. And in this case it would be for a belief either held or not." He settled back against the bolster and pillows piled against the wall. "Ah, but I suppose it is the way of mankind to come to war over intangibles. Look at all the wars fought over religion." He looked at her. "And we have no proof but our own spirit to tell us of a Creator! I think independency is at least somewhat more tangible than that!" He smiled.

"Yes, perhaps," she conceded cautiously, "but 'twould be simpler merely to declare the matter and settle it out as a point of law. Chalking up the victor as the one who has killed the most for an intangible strikes me as preternaturally stupid. For defence of home and hearth, perhaps. But not for independency. Why should the depth and breadth of our people suffer for that?" Her dark eyes regarded him earnestly.

He sighed, putting an arm about her and raising her up a little so that she rested against him. "I don't know, sweet." He kissed her. "But all this may be moot. It may not yet come to that. We can hope." He smiled a little, echoing her long-ago words, "If we do not expect. . . . For now, I'm weary of such lofty matters. Come settle yourself with me and I'll put out the candle. You know Patsy and Janey will be abroad at dawn."

She was easier now that she knew his mind, for she trusted his judgement. As he directed, she fitted herself against him again and was asleep almost immediately.

38

Caractacus

Monticello

They spent April in tending the garden, the crops, and the servants. It rained a good deal, so that the soil became a bloody mire, sticking to everything and drying to the consistency of fired brick. In the damp, the meats in the smokehouse took on a puffed appearance, not spoilt yet but swelled and the fat white as the salt absorbed the wet air. She had the hams, bacons, and fowl removed to one of the cellar rooms where a dry fire was set up likewise, for at least the stone walls were a better insulation against the damp than the wattle of the outside smokehouse. Laundry was entirely impossible. They were reduced to hanging it inside the hall and parlor. Woe betide them if they should have guests for dinner or overnight, for not all the clothes would fit into the out-chamber or the busy space of the kitchen. Unplanned-for guests would have to take things as they found them.

There were outbreaks of influenza among the cabins in such weather. It was of a dry sort, luckily for the spread, for there was no vomiting or flux of the bowels, only a lassitude and marked fever, lack of appetite, and restlessness. It had to be watched, though, for this was the sort that frequently settled in the lungs. It became expected that they should be startled from sleep by an insistent knocking, to be greeted by an equally insistent voice, requesting that the mistress come see to so-and-so, who'd come down powerful ill.

Why, Patty wondered as she clambered into a petticoat blear-eyed by the light of the lamp, did they always become ill, or have babies, or choose to die, in the middle of the night? Never in the hours of daylight was one called away to such an emergency. She fumbled with the strip of hooks down the front of her gown and found they wouldn't fasten. Going closer to the light, she discovered why; the thing was on wrong side out. Once she was decently dressed she knotted her hair at the nape of her neck and stuck a couple of pins in it. With a cap tied on anyhow she was ready to face whatever awaited.

"Do you need anything?" Thomas said from where he sat on the bed. It was a thoughtful but ridiculous question. It would have taken him longer to throw something on and fetch whatever she required than for her to get it herself. But she smiled a little as she shook her head, thankful for the courtesy.

"I have everything." Her voice, quiet tho' it was so as not to disturb the sleeping girls, was hoarse. They had only been properly asleep for about an hour, enough to make a laggard of her. Her arms felt like lead. She went over and pulled her bag down from the shelf, for she had taken to leaving it up there at night to save crashing about in the dark downstairs. The weight of it dragged on her shoulder, and she set it down beside the bed.

"I'm sorry," she said regretfully, leaning a little to put her arms about Thomas's neck. She kissed him, lingering a bit to ruffle his disordered hair with affection, ignoring the anxious fellow outside, needing some brace against sleepiness and the ordeal that lay ahead. After a time he took her hands away and kissed the palms by turns.

"Go on," he said.

She was more awake now. "Aye." She sighed, took up the bag and the lamp, and went out, closing the door behind her noiselessly.

The night air was cool, but not cold, heavy with the promise of rain. The woods smell was thick and pungent, assailing her, bringing her awake more than anything else had. They were alone but for the sound of crickets and the occasional tree frog. The night was black. She handed the lamp to Goliah. "Let's go."

They laboriously skirted the debris in the yard, Goliah holding the lamp aloft and she carefully picking her way behind him. She turned her ankle once on a pile of loose scantling, but before she could fall was caught under the forearm by a large black hand.

"Thank you," she said shortly, recovering her balance.

"Sorry, ma'am. I didn't meant t' be rough." This great field hand was nearly as tall as Thomas and twice his size. He matched Great George stone for stone, and had hands the size of platters.

"No."

They wended their way down the north face of the mountain and the wind came up, cold and sharp. Goliah and his brother Hercules shared a cabin down near where the third roundabout road ran across the north spring on the northeast of the mountain. The road was hazardous enough even in daylight, but the trails connecting them were impossible in the dark. In the end they only arrived by Goliah's resolutely tucking her hand under his armpit and treading slowly and carefully.

When they came to the log house they were greeted by no light within. Why should precious stuffs be wasted on a delirious man who wouldn't know the difference? This bachelor's establishment had few of the amenities of the married people's quarters, and the two plainly had no inclination to spend their little spare time on Sundays in housekeeping. The only saving grace was that they had so few belongings to scatter about. They did have the necessary pot and fireplace, however, and the spring was nearby.

The place had a reek of sickness. Though she had been assured, by close questioning, that Hercules was not subject to vomiting, still there was an odor about the fevered body that was unlike a healthy one, whether they sweated or no. She gave the sick one a cursory glance and handed the pot to his brother.

"Do you please fetch some water," she said, and sat down on her heels, uncorking the jar of tansy vinegar. It was good for one thing and another. At the moment she required it as a fumigatory, or she would be sick herself. She considered the man lying restless on the pallet before her. His skin was burning and dry, and he panted lightly like a dog on a summer's day in his disturbed dreaming. Plainly she couldn't move him herself, so taking his shirt off was out. Biting her lip she rummaged in the bag and came up with linting. Soaking it in the vinegar, she laid it on all the exposed parts of his body that she could reach; temples, neck, chest, wrists. He protested some, for it was cold from the jar, but she stilled him with a hand and a murmur in his ear, "Hush now, it will make you well."

Goliah came back with the water and she set about mixing up quantities of herbs under his watchful gaze before the embers of the fire. He stood, ill at ease with her crouched on the floor of his small house, his wrists hanging out of his shirtsleeves uselessly.

"Would you make up a fire and boil that?" she asked conversationally, gesturing toward the water. He nodded. "Not all of it," she cautioned, for he had brought about a gallon. "Half."

"Yas'm," he said anxiously.

She moved out of his way and laid out as many of her supplies as she could on the bag, for she knew it to be reasonably clean, and changed the linting, wringing it out first onto the floor. The sharp, bitter odor of tansy wafted up in the semi-darkness. It couldn't do any harm on an earthen floor, and might kill a few things as well. For having lived her entire life in the presence of them, she was not fond of bugs, and Virginia had her share. It was worse here in the woods than in Williamsburg, and she was always shaking down the beds from some uninvited guest. She probably should have taken it as a mere fact of life, but the creeping dirtiness unnerved her.

Once she had the infusion poured out she made up a couple of tablespoons' worth of elder and currant jelly with water and dribbled it down the prostrate man. She was not fond of the mustiness of elderberry herself, but wasn't prepared when he knocked the spoon from her hand and sent her rolling backwards in the process. She rubbed her hand across her eyes, and Goliah helped her right herself again.

"You a'right, Ma'am?"

"Yes," she said wearily, more annoyed than hurt. "Hold him down so I can get this into him," she directed, picking up the spoon and rinsing it off with a handful of water. If Hercules was thus disposed to taking a sweet medicine, heaven knew how he would react to the bitter forthcoming. It promised to be a long night.

So it was. Dawn was streaking the sky roseate when she went outside to relieve herself and stretch her cramped legs. Her back ached, and she had a sore place where her stays had been poking her in the thigh, but they had held her up at least. It promised a fine day, she thought as she looked out across to the Southwest mountains. The early gusts of wind had cleared the clouds, leaving only white springtime puffs to float along serene. The balance of the sky was azure above the green-black of the surrounding forest hills.

At this early hour only the birds were abroad, and there was a tender stillness to the world that made life seem new-created. Thus, before the bustle of the day began, she could reflect on the beauty of this place, and despite its many inconveniences, what a well-chosen spot it was for a house. Most of the time she was too busy, weary, or preoccupied to care. Most of the time she had more concern for her water supply, the state of the new-starched linens, or how she could tactfully keep the children from murthering each other to notice larger details. If there was mending or brewing or plastering a scald to be done, who cared what color the sky was, so long as it wasn't raining?

She stretched her neck, rolling her head from side to side, feeling the bones crack in exquisite relief. She had a headache from the close, smoky dimness and constant bending of her head. And yet for Hercules there was no relief. That was ironical. Here he was, a big strong man, worthy of the name, laid quite low by a womanish fever. If it had been a great sweating, vomiting, purging fever, with shakes and such it would have been better fitting, somehow.

He must be made to break into a sweat or the evil humors would never escape, and yet he failed to do, in spite of herbals, blankets, hot stones, and a very close room. She shook her head. They'd put enough liquid into him. La, he hadn't even pissed properly. She'd have to try more dandelion.

Resolved and marginally refreshed, she turned about and stepped back into the cabin, the mingled odors less offensive this time for their familiarity.

By the afternoon he was no better, though it was plain that the bladder was nearly bursting. She hadn't the tools at hand to syphon it off and had run out of herbs. When Scilla came down with her dinner, she gave her a list, written hastily in pencil on a scrap of paper torn from her herbal, to give to Thomas and a request to send for George Gilmer. If Hercules hadn't turned by her ministrations by the time he arrived, at least he might be able to suggest something more efficacious.

When the girl left she stood with her hands on her hips, frowning at the sick man, flummoxed. She was alone in the room now, Goliah having gone off to work. She was not especially hungry and couldn't have eaten inside in any case. To her surprise, Thomas himself appeared about a quarter of an hour later when she was sitting glumly on the stoop, the basket of food beside her untouched. He bore another with the items she required.

"What are you doing here?" she asked in astonishment.

He smiled. "Now what kind of greeting for your husband is that? It must be grim going for my vixen to be so surly."

"Sorry." She smiled sheepishly, rising and holding the hand he proffered. "You know that isn't what I meant."

"How does he do?" He nodded toward the man within. His tone had sobered considerably. She shook her head.

"Not at all well. He's utterly dry."

"I thought as much," he said, glancing down at the basket he held, "given what you asked for. I sent for George."

"Oh, good." There was considerable relief in that.

"You haven't eaten."

"I'm not hungry."

He put the basket down and took her shoulders in his hands, tho' gently. "Patty!" he cried in exasperation. He regarded her earnestly. "Would you fall sick as well? It will do no good to have you so when I am away at Philadelphia and unable to look after you—" He stopped, and flushed, plainly saying more than he intended.

"What?" she said stupidly, in disbelief. "When is this?"

He was still red, and he looked away from her, through the trees to the mountains beyond. "Oh, June or July," he said offhandedly. "And only if Peyton Randolph is called back to the Assembly." He looked down at her again, and his face was grim. "They need another delegate for Virginia," he finished lamely.

Because of her exhaustion her temper was short, and she thought of all the times he had accused her, affectionately or no, of being devious. "And when were you going to tell me?" she said rather tartly, echoing him in such instances.

His mouth twitched a little, ruefully. "I suppose I deserved that." He put his arms about her now, since they were alone. "I did mean to tell you before, but with this sickness, and one thing and another, I forgot about it. I'm sorry."

His tone was that of an abject small boy who fears a scolding, and she was well-disposed to give him one in any case. It occurred to her then that the Burgesses were meeting next month, and that if he was supposed to go to Philadelphia in June, he would have to leave from Williamsburg; she wouldn't even get to see him before he went away for an undetermined amount of time. Her brows knitted.

"I won't even get to see you!" she complained.

His hands were on her back, and his eyes amber-green and coaxing. "We have all of this month and part of next."

"Aye," she said shortly, not willing to concede even to his massaging fingers easing the knot under her shoulder blades. "This half gone and less than a week of the next! Thomas, how could you not tell me?" She raised her arm in a frustrated, helpless gesture, tears springing to her eyes. "I don't know how long this sickness will run, or if we shall be cursed with it too! So how much time have we, really, a few days at best?" She shook her head, overwrought, and took refuge in the ruffle of his shirtfront, burying her face in it.

Some part of her mind recognized that he was truly distressed by this blunder, that she should be easy with him over it, but she was too tired, too dispirited at the moment over her charge in the small house to be very logical or rational.

"Shall you manage while I am gone?" he asked earnestly, setting her from him a little.

"I rather shall have to," she said frankly. He winced. It had been in her mind to say that she had managed things well enough without a husband before but thought the better of it at the last moment. He would not like to be compared to a dead man, and in any case Batt was not an entirely easy subject with them, at least so far as matters of the heart were concerned.

"Patty," he pleaded. "Sweet, I am obliged to go!" He touched her cheek, lifting her face, and that gesture along with his distress undid her. Nervous tears ran down her face.

"Oh, I know," she burst out, miserably. "I only wish I'd had some warning, or that it was some other day; that he," she jerked her head toward the house, "would make some change; that I'd had some sleep— Oh!" She brushed angrily at the silly tears. She hated to cry over trifles.

"Come here, sweet," he murmured, and gathered her into an embrace. He rocked her gently in his arms, and she was soothed by the beating of his heart and the familiar scent of him. It was lulling in the warm air.

"You know I would never be so cruel as that on purpose," he said above her head. His cheek was against her hair, for she had lost her cap some time ago. "You know I wouldn't go if I wasn't obliged, or leave you without a good-bye if I could help it." He held her away and smiled a bit. "I wouldn't forfeit a kiss from my dear girl so quick as that." He kissed her now, slowly, gently, a courting kiss, and embraced her again.

"I think you need some rest," he said. "Duty does not demand that you exhaust yourself thus." He moved away again, and traced under her eyes with a finger. "If you can wait a little here, I'll send down Betty to sit with him until George comes so you can rest. Mrs. Reynolds is minding the girls."

She smiled at that, for he liked Liza Reynolds. He had once called Mary Garth a slut, and she wasn't any too sure which meaning he meant.

"As you wish," she acceded.

He held up a warning finger. "But first you will eat, Madame, desire or no." He turned her about and made her sit on the stool he dragged out while he sat on the stoop and fed her.

In an hour's time, she was gratefully tucked into her own bed with the shutters drawn, washed and decorously dressed in a shift and nightcap. She was never so glad of feather pillows, even if she had set the goose. She yawned in Thomas's face when he bent to give her a kiss. "Sorry."

He touched a wisp of curl on her forehead and kissed her lightly. "Sleep well, sweet. I shall not be far if you can't," for he was working at the table. But this was once when his familiar embrace was not required, for she was asleep practically as soon as his back was turned.

Hercules recovered eventually, after five days of dry fever and some rather large doses of nitre salts from George Gilmer. He apparently had some kidney stones, unrelated to the general fever about, and she felt better knowing that she had done all within her power to help him and that it was not her ignorance or ineptitude that had prolonged the trouble. She was advised to keep him on her regime of herbs and jellies until he was mended properly. He was not back to work until June.

They had an anxious time over another of the inhabitants of the mountain that season, but this time the outcome was anticipated joyously. Allycroker, Thomas's sorrel mare, was about to be foaled sometime in early May, and he was anxious that he should be there for it. This was not only because the dam herself was getting on, being seventeen years this spring, but that the sire of this foal was his own favorite Fearnought, and he hoped that the cross would prove as successful as it had in Allycroker's earlier foal, Cacullen. The mare certainly behaved as though she was getting close to term; she didn't venture out much when in paddock but stayed close on by the fence, as if to be within range of her stall when the birth commenced. She was restive besides, pawing and stamping in the box as if she didn't know what to do with herself.

"I've felt like that," Patty laughed, as she watched the mare tramp about the box. She had come down with Thomas to the stable on his invitation, seeing as they were both mothers, to observe and offer an opinion. She knew better. He was laying up the odds in his mind whether the mare would be foaled before he left. He looked down at her now curiously.

"Have you—did you?"

"Yes," she said emphatically. "Tired of lumbering about, wishing the whole business were done. If I had something with four legs and hooves roiling about inside, I'd be restive, too. A baby is uncomfortable enough at the end."

She smiled at his playfully wounded expression. "But worth it," she said, patting his hand. "Now, Mr. Jefferson, if my services as a seer are concluded, I should like to get back to my dairy." They were making butter and wringing cheese today. The latter was a laborious process that required both a strong arm and encouragement. She doubted anything had been accomplished in her absence.

The next day in the middle of dinner Martin came back into the room unexpectedly and leaned over Thomas's chair. He immediately put down the napkin.

"What is it?" she asked from the other end of the table.

"Allycroker," he said, rising. It was as if he had been touched by a lightning rod, for he was flushed and visibly excited. He bowed to the Madisons. "I beg your pardon, but we've been waiting this foaling for several days. If you'll excuse me?"

James smiled, for he was a horse man himself. "Of course." Thomas was out the door in a trice. By the undignified whoop he gave, it was plain he had not bothered to go and change first.

Patsy and Janey exchanged startled looks, and Janey piped up, "Silly Papa!"

Patty told them, "Shortly, my dears, Allycroker will have a brand new foal. And if you're very good, after pudding you may go and see it."

"Is it a filly or a colt, Mama?" Patsy asked.

"We don't know yet, Patt, but soon we will." She exchanged a glance with Eleanor. "Horses aren't long about their business."

"No, indeed," James agreed. "I've never seen a horse take much above an hour's time to foal." She refrained from remarking how fortunate that was, as the Madisons themselves had no children though they had been married nearly ten years. She knew Eleanor would have gladly endured days of childbirth if it meant an end to their barrenness. Even so, she had been a patient listener to the cathartic tale of many a woman's difficult childbed, including Patty's own. Playing confessor seemed to go with the position of being a minister's wife.

The cloth had scarcely been removed and the wine laid out before Thomas came bounding in again, his sleeves rolled up and his face all aglow.

"She's done it!" he cried, and poured himself a glass of wine. "A fine bay colt with legs a mile long. He's the spit of Fearnought."

"How's the mare?" James asked.

"Splendid! Up on her feet and hale as ever she was. Will you come and see?" The reverend pushed back his chair. Thomas asked her, "Are you coming?"

She shook her head, having no desire to be compared to such a stout birther. Besides, they could better engage themselves without the presence of ladies.

"No," she said, smiling. "I'll go down later."

Patsy was out of her chair. "May we go, Papa?" Her hand was on his sleeve.

Patty would have said no, but Thomas could not bring himself to deny the child anything, whether object or experience. He smiled down on her, laying her hand upon her head.

"Come," he murmured, inclining his head. Patsy gave a most unladylike whoop and raced out of the room while he picked up Janey.

"Would you like to see a new horse, my Joanna?" he queried her. She jumped up and down in his arms. "Horse horse!" she cried. They all went out together, Thomas and Janey and James, and Patty shook her head to Eleanor.

"We are the victims of enthusiasm."

Dark-haired Eleanor cocked her head, fiddling with the stem of the wine glass. "Would you rather go?" she asked curiously.

"Not at the moment." Patty said truthfully. "I'd like a quiet moment and a breathing space. I can go down later when some of the excitement's died down." She smiled. "Besides, now I can put my feet up on the chair and not feel utterly unmannered. I've been standing all day!"

"Ah." Her friend's dark eyes gleamed. "I begin to perceive the true reason!"

Patty blushed. "'Tis best not to let on to Mr. Jefferson. For while I am not lacking in feeling, he might take it so if he knew."

"I shan't say a word," Nellie promised, drinking some of the wine.

She did go down to the stable later with him, as the sun was setting. All was a warm hush in the salmon-touched quietude of twilight. The day's heat had begun to rise from the ground, so she took a coat along, for it would be cool on their return. Watch was still kept by the stable boys over the new mother and her offspring. A lantern was hung over the stall where sorrel Allycroker lay in the hay with her fine bay colt. He was piebald along the rump, but they were the sorts of spots to fade with age. His ears, tail, and one fetlock were nearly black in color. She leaned over the gate, and when the colt rose at a bit of coaxing she saw the reason for the excitement. He had a perfect conformation. Already he was quite steady upon his legs and stepped in the proud dancing way of the thoroughbred. His intelligent brown eyes with their long lashes regarded them solemnly.

"Oh, he's just beautiful!" she burst out. The animal came to her, and she laid her hand upon his pale velvet nose, then leaned so that her face was against his and they breathed the same air, that he might know her to be friendly. Thomas put his hands on her waist.

"You're going to fall in," he laughed.

She leaned back again and looked up at him. "What have you decided to call him?" His eyes gleamed in the yellow light of the lantern, and he was silent for a moment, his eyes all full of distant dreams. He put his hand down then, fondling the seeking muzzle. "His name shall be Caractacus."

Caractacus. It was the Roman name given to one of the proudest and most honored of Rome's enemies. For Caradoc ap Cunobellyn had been a Welsh prince, leader of the tribes of Dyfed, who rose in rebellion against Roman misrule. After his capture he spent his life as an exile in Rome, much honored for his charming manners, his learning, and his skill in tactics. Even in captivity he bore himself like a prince and would bow to no man save Claudius. Already yon Caractacus had a reputation to live up to. But, looking at him in the warm light of the stable as he stood now beside his mother, there were few doubts that he would do so, and more.

39

J Covered Me with Steel

Monticello

The evening that Caractacus was born Thomas spent a good deal of time draughting a letter to his old teacher William Small, now in Edinburgh. The Madisons had retired to Pen Park, where they were visiting with the Gilmers, and there was no other company. The nights were still cool enough that a fire was required, and Patty sat before it in Thomas's red leather armchair, stitching a rip in one of Patsy's aprons and doing other odd mending while he worked. The girls were asleep in their trundle at this late hour, for it was past nine o'clock, and the kitchen was quiet and dark below.

It was sweet to sit and savor the delicacy of his profile, bent as he was at the table to his writing. Though he was now in the beginnings of middle age, at thirty-two, she thought that he should long retain his youth. It was not merely the fair, moist quality of his skin that bade it so, but the ever-brimming enthusiasm he had for life would keep him vital when others were crabbed with age. One should be so lucky. With his mother it was not so; Mrs. Jefferson looked every day of her fifty-three years, and Polly Bolling was no blossom anymore, either. Oh, she loved Mary and would never say aught to indicate that she had noticed such aging, but it was a lamentably plain fact that women simply did not wear as well as men.

Look at Cousin Peyton. There was a man who ate and drank, if not to excess then to plenitude, who rarely took the air, who suffered from gout and other infirmities of the moribund, yet save for his occasional bouts was hale as a man half his age.

Her own father was a prime example, too. She knew how much he had consumed in food and drink, because most of it passed literally through her hands. He had never been known for abstemiousness, yet he had worn out three wives and was never sick a day she could remember until his final illness. Why was it that men could lead such reckless lives and never bear the burdens in the way women did?

Were women essentially the weaker vessel? She didn't know. Certainly they didn't have the brute strength of most men, but she didn't know many men as could endure the long hours of childbirth or the rigors of running a house. Why, Thomas Garth just yesterday had come to her in agonies because he'd had a splinter in his hand go putrid, and begged her would she dig it out and give him something for it? Ha! She gave him a mess of dandelion greens and told him to take a gill of rum for his pain. He wasn't much amused.

She took tiny stitches in her mending, running a neat line along the angled tear that would be sturdy yet nearly invisible to behold. The fire before her snapped and popped, sending sparks drifting upwards in the chimney. She moved her foot away from the heat, tucking it behind the ottoman. The clock on the mantle chimed quarter-past the hour precisely as the one on the chest did. She smiled a little. Such precision was Thomas's doing. He liked mending clocks and had gone to a great deal of trouble to set the one on the chest to working and in sync with the other, for their winding schedules were different. The mantle clock ran Sunday to Sunday, but the chest clock ran only three days and if it wasn't wound on the right day it would be off by as much as two minutes. And there was nothing worse than two clocks off time in a small room.

She looked up at Thomas again. He was writing quickly, the pen scratching loudly on the paper. The pen would want sharpening at that out. . . . He wasn't like Garth. He'd cut himself with a spade one time last spring and calmly as you please went about stitching it. He was a bit pale, granted, but that was small price for the fine work; his hand didn't even have a scar now.

He was annoyed with himself for his carelessness when he discovered that the stitches pulled when he tried to play the fiddle, so he'd had to give that over for a week, but such accidents were rare.

What would this Caractacus be like? she wondered. It would be years yet before they could tell. He wouldn't be saddle-broke for a year. Then he had to go through his pawky period. Would he settle into a quiet dependable animal? Cacullen had not. Oh, he was a bold fellow, all right, a bit too so for her comfort, going down the mountain in winter. He had plenty of go, but he lacked any natural fear and was stubborn nigh unto impossible, especially when he wanted his mouth. That horse one day was going to rue that he ever crossed wills with Thomas. She looked at him writing and smiled a little. He could be intractable, too. He would have his way. He got that from his mother. Patsy, too. She acceded to his wishes in most things because he was generally correct and to do so avoided scenes, but she would not with Patsy.

The child was too self-willed for a girl, too impassioned. She knew from her own experience what such a temperament could bring. She would have Patsy be quieter if she could—if not inwardly then outwardly. It behooved a lady to be mild. It was expected. She could not rage about as men did, giving vent to every little feeling. Not when the lives of so many depended upon her. It was ludicrous to envision any other life for Pats than that of the mistress of a house. Even if she married a city man, there would be a country house to manage, as well as servants and tradespeople in town. Decorum befitted such a position. It was hard. In her own self she was not often easy, but she could see at first hand the deleterious effects of a lack of self-government in Maria Byrd's relations with her servants. She was sorry to say they did not respect her, and why should they, pray, when she went on no better than they? She finished her mending of the rent and laid the apron aside for the wash.

She was reaching for another piece from her basket of mending beside the chair when she felt Thomas's eye upon her. Looking up, she saw that he'd laid down the pen and was regarding her speculatively, his hands folded into a little tent on the table.

"Aye?" she queried, her hand still on the shift. He smiled a little, ruefully.

"I was wondering. . ."

"Mmm?"

"How busy you are."

She sat up in the chair, feeling the blood come rushing into her face. "Not especially, not determinedly." She paused. "Why?"

"I was wondering if you'd like to read with me."

She smiled now, laying the sewing goods aside. "I just believe I would. What had you in mind, sir?"

"Ossian!" he said decisively, rising from the chair, and she laughed.

"Somehow, I rather had guessed it might be that."

"I can't think why," he replied innocently.

He retrieved the book from the shelf, and when they were tucked up in bed with the fire banked, he opened it to the fourth book of Fingal. Quoting the poet Ossian, he read in a clear, soft voice:

> Who comes with her songs from the hill, like the bow of the showery Lena? It is the maid of the voice of love! the white-armed daughter of Toscar! Often hast thou heard my song; often given the tear of beauty. Dost thou come to the wars of thy people? to hear of the actions of Oscar? When shall I cease to mourn, by the streams of resounding Cona? My years have passed away in battle. My age is darkened with grief—

He went on, but she fell to wondering if he had told his old teacher of their troubles. Dr. Small would be most aggrieved to learn the news that had been heard two days before: a little over a month ago, regulars had gone out into the Massachusetts countryside to seize the powder stores of that colony at Concord and had been met by militiamen in the little hamlet of Lexington. Under no orders to fire, merely to stand their ground, they had been brutally shot down without provocation upon the green. How curious it was that about that same time Governor Dunmore had seized the powder in Williamsburg, determined upon it for their "safety," as he said! These actions had raised a general alarum, and the common mass of people were suddenly flinging themselves upon the bosom of Liberty as a protecting mother. This news, coupled with George Gilmer's speech to their own volunteers, gave her dreadful pause for the future. And now Thomas, too, spoke of war, albeit veiledly. Was there no way to turn from this wrenching course? Was there no balm to be had save bloodshed?

His voice came back to her, harsh now, and a bit strained in the reading, intense:

> Oscar met Dala the strong face to face, on the field of heroes. The battle of the chiefs was like wind, on ocean's foamy waves. . . Three times I broke on Cormac's shield: three times he broke his spear. But, unhappy youth of love! I cut his head away. Five times I shook it back by the lock. The friends of Cormac have fled. Whoever would have told me, lovely maid, when then I strove in battle, that being, forsaken and forlorn, I now should pass the night; firm ought his mail to have been; unmatched his arm in war.
>
> On Lena's gloomy heath the voice of music died away. The inconstant blast blew hard. The high oak shook its leaves around. Of Everallin were my thoughts, when in all the light of beauty she came; her blue eyes rolling in tears. She stood on a cloud before my sight and spoke in a feeble voice! "Rise, Ossian, rise, and save my son; save Oscar, prince of men. Near the red oak of Luba's stream he fights with Lochlin's sons." She sunk into her cloud again. I covered me with steel. My spear supported my steps; my rattling armor rang. I hummed, as I was wont in danger, the songs of heroes of old. Like distant thunder Lochlin heard. They fled; my son pursued—

His voice broke, and she continued, reading,

> I called him like a distant stream. "Oscar, return over Lena. No further pursue the foe," I said, "though Ossian is behind thee." He came! and pleasant to my ear was Oscar's sounding steel. "Why didst thou stop my hand," he said, "till death had covered all? For dark and dreadful by the stream they met thy son and Fillan. They watched the terrors of the night. Our swords have conquered some. But as the winds of night pour the ocean over the white sands of Mora, so dark advance the sons of Lochlin, over Lena's rustling heat!

The ghosts of the night shriek afar: I have seen the meteors of death. Let me wake the king of Morven, he that smiles in danger, he that is like the sun of heaven, rising in a storm!"

Fingal had started from a dream, and leaned on Trenmor's shield. . . . The hero had seen, in his rest, the mournful form of Agandecca. She came from the way of the ocean. She slowly, lonely, moved over Lena. Her face was pale, like the mist of Cromla. Dark were the tears on her cheek. She often raised her dim hand over Fingal and turned away silent eyes! "Why weeps the daughter of Starno?" said Fingal with a sigh; "and why is thy face so pale, fair wanderer of the clouds?" She departed on the wind of Lena. She left him in the midst of the night. She mourned the sons of her people, that were to fall by the hands of Fingal—

She stopped and caught her breath, the immediacy of the words too poignant for comfort.

"I can't read more," she cried, and looked up at Thomas beseechingly. How could he stand it? But she saw that there were tears in eyes also. He nodded and took the book away, folding her into an embrace. How safe the world from this vantage, with his heart hammering beneath her ear! But what refuge was this from that which was to come? How would she shift when he was so far away from her? Oh, not in ordinary actions, for she could run her house whether he was there or no, but in emotions. She knew herself well enough to be acquainted with despair.

"Oh," she said, almost to herself, "if we could but turn back time and undo what has been done!"

"No," he said thoughtfully and kissed her hair, his arms tightening round her. "This is needful, like a bloodletting to purge evil humors. Much as I regret that." He smiled a little. "You know how I feel about bloodletting!" His face sobered again after a moment. "But my concern lies in that it will not be a clean wound. How can we be certain that it will not bleed overmuch or go putrid?" He sighed. "I fear that others besides soldiery shall bear the burdens of this war." He moved away and looked down at her. His eyes were so close they filled her whole vision, beautiful, loving hazel eyes. "You, for instance."

She tried to ease her sense of dread with humor. "Are you planning to go for a soldier then, my Lysander?" she asked, smiling.

He raised an eyebrow. "Me? Not likely! I've no stomach for bloodshed and no craving for glories. At least not that lie that way. No. You know what I mean. Not only inconvenience of dear goods, but the whole burthen of conflict looks to be placed on our shores. If what has occurred in Boston is a prophecy, then there shall be many a woman to lament the sons of somebody."

She frowned. "Then what's left for it? Do we pitch in to conciliations?"

He kissed her nose. "You're sounding like your father. No, my sweet, we do not, as well you know!" He sighed. "It would appear that we have no course but the one set. God help us."

They were silent together for a long time. She stared at the red glow of the banked fire beyond Thomas's shoulder. Even their personal future immediately was uncertain. The Congress in Philadelphia could sit for two weeks, two months, or two years, or be broken up altogether as an illegal assembly and the participants taken off to hang, especially those on the proscribed list. . . . She shivered a little.

"Are you cold, sweet?" Thomas murmured. Ever attentive, warm and considerate: how could she have asked for a better mate if it had been decreed by fate? She made no answer but looked up at him. And the fear and uncertainty, the love and tenderness she bore him rushed up, and she wanted nothing more just then than to forget the world, to hold for that immortal second the spark of perfection that was dearer than life because it was shared with him. She reached up and kissed him. They had no time but now, and she was determined to seize the moment.

"Oh my dear." She breathed against his beard-roughened cheek when they paused for air. "Oh Tom, I do love you so, and I'm so afraid that—" He stifled her anxiety with a searing kiss.

"My sweet Patty, my darling girl." He lifted his head away from her a bit, and his eyes were an intense green. "You hold my soul in your hand. I love you better than any person that breathes. We shall weather this storm, my sweet, my lovely maid, for I shall hold thee safe and warm."

What but that could she have wanted in all the world, to be thus enfolded in the arms of her dear love, whose eyes spoke the truth of his words. The promise made she believed with her whole heart because it came from him, and she knew he would execute it. But how was she to know then the dearness of its cost? She knew nothing of that, only melted fear in the present's warm lineaments. They stole a moment from great Time's clock, and she knew some peace then, enough to linger while he was away.

Lord Dunmore, to his own purposes, indeed summoned the Burgesses that month, but not until it was nearly half gone, and not to sit until the beginning of June. That esteemed gentleman remained out of reach on shipboard until he had proof of their good will, that he would not be dragged from his residence in Palace Green and tarred and feathered by them or the mob. It was a nice piece of cowardice that did nothing to win him friends or support.

At Monticello they made the best of their meager fruit supply not killed in the general frost of March and pressed currants and elder and whortleberries from the woods. Some of this was cooked down to jelly and syrup, but the rest was set up with several loaves of sugar and yeasted bread to make wine and cordial. If they couldn't have their own wine from grapes, they could at least drink something. She made two casks of beer and paid for cider. There was a heat spell after Allycroker foaled in May that made useful work difficult. But the walls were up in the hall and stairwells and taking shape in the south wing. There were hopes of a permanent roof for the lower floor before winter, so all was not desolate. They went visiting round the family in the third week, and she proposed to Thomas during their pause at Shadwell that his mother should come and live with them.

She was doing poorly, even with Nan's help, and Randolph was so often gone to the Fluvanna property or on the roads between Snowden and Shadwell that depending upon him was chancy. Not that he wasn't dutiful or attentive when he was there, but farming and the militia took up a great deal of his time. Charles and Lucy couldn't take her in, for they were expecting another baby and Lucy was dropsical. John and Polly Bolling, on the Hardware river, were too far away for Jane's liking, so Monticello it must be.

Even so, he took some convincing. With the past warily in his eye, he argued the matter with her in the bedchamber in low tones, "I should not like to leave you ladies all alone on our mountain while I am away. Here at least the neighbors are within easy reach."

"And so are Mr. Garth and Mr. Reynolds," she said calmly. She had, in point of fact, never seen Mrs. Jefferson other than collected. She could be testy, it was true, and often spoke her mind with no soft dissembling. But that did not indicate mania, for there were old ladies aplenty who did the same. "We should not want for protectors."

"You know what I mean," he murmured. She lifted her chin. "I do, and I tell you I have no fear of your mother. . . ." She sighed. "She's old, Thomas, and rheumatic. She needs us—"

By such reasoning she convinced him, and the two ladies came to Monticello. They kept their beds in the parlor, with as many personal items as could be managed in the chest in the passageway between the parlor and hall. It was cramped and makeshift, but if something should happen, Mrs. Jefferson was within a reasonable distance. It certainly wouldn't be the first time the parlor had been used for such affairs; it had been so since it was anything like habitable.

Thomas didn't leave for the Capitol until his mother and sister were properly settled, but he was waiting for another settlement as well. She knew that he had business that he would rather have attended to before the Assembly met, and several times in the fourth week as time stretched out, she bade him not fret over her and go, but he would not. He must leave by the twenty-ninth to get to town on time, and he should not be late.

"I can write to you whether or no," she reasoned, one afternoon.

"If I leave on Monday, I'll be there in plenty of time," he said, not to be moved. "That'll be three weeks. And even you have never been eight weeks between times, to my knowledge."

She put the sleeping Janey down on their bed. She was getting big and heavy now, for she was nearly fourteen months. She walked and ran with her sister and the others, a placid, happy child. She had tired herself out chasing after the children in the garden and was regular enough to like her nap at a particular hour still. Patsy, on the other hand, she had to fight tooth and nail to take a bit of rest. She had nervous energy to spare, but it bore itself in a bad temper in the evenings if she got overtired.

"What about after her?" she said, tucking up a crib sheet about Jane so she wouldn't roll off the bed. "I didn't have a single flux the whole five months."

"That was an aberration."

"This may be, too."

She wasn't at all certain how she felt about the possibility of another child, truth to tell. January's disaster had scared her. She didn't want to begin another pregnancy only to have it fail so spectacularly. On the other hand, everyone she knew, it seemed, had a new baby or was about to: from Ursula and Liza Reynolds to Nancy, Lisbet, Lucy Gilmer, Lucy Lewis, Fanny Page, even Maria Byrd. The only woman that wasn't in such a circumstance was Mary Mazzei, and that was understandable. She was quite above such an age or amorous inclination. And it was pleasant to hold a new baby, to revel in their smell, their fuzzy heads, their wriggling, mewling, endearing helplessness. Yet every time she had pause enough to wonder why her course was so late, fear would be choking that some misbirth had occurred again and her life would be all grief again.

As it happened, they were coming back from the Gilmers on Sunday evening when she was seized by such a cramp as she rarely had. They never did know which it was, an early misbirth or a very delayed flux, but by the great relief she felt, she knew the time had not come yet for another child.

40

Housewifery

Monticello

In the morning they bid Thomas farewell. He would not be long in Williamsburg, being due in Philadelphia on the fifteenth, but he promised to write from there anyway, as he usually did. He kissed the girls good-bye as she was tying up their hair and slipped an arm about her waist. "I'll miss you," he said in her ear, and gave it a kiss.

She put down the hairbrush and let Janey climb down from the table. She thought it would be easy, bearable at least, when it came to this, but her throat ached so that she could hardly speak. She flung her arms about Thomas and kissed him soundly. "Be careful, my dear!"

She moved back a trifle, sniffling, and saw in his eyes all the affection she could ever wish for. Her eyes were brimming but she was resolved not to cry. He took her clenched fist and loosed the fingers gently, one by one, then placed a single kiss upon the palm. "Write to me," he entreated. She nodded blindly. "You know I will!"

He smiled a little. "There's my girl."

He touched her face with a soft caress and lifted her chin with a finger. He kissed her forehead and her mouth, and she closed her eyes, willing herself to remember with all her senses the particulars of this moment, in case it should be the last they ever had. She would remember how his fingers felt on her face, the roughness of the callused fingertips; the lean strength of his tall body; the clean, familiar smell of bergamot intermingled with an indefinable masculine one; the beating of his heart that she could feel through her clothes. Love's heart beat there. All these things were hers in a bare moment. She opened her eyes and found his searching, a little troubled, green in their depths, but mostly amber today, framed by their dark lashes, long as a girl's. Her heart was hammering again. How could she say farewell?

He cleared his throat and she saw the pulse beating there, as so many times that none could tell. She blushed, and was glad to see it answered in Thomas's face.

"Well," he said softly. "This must be adieu." He touched her face again. "I could say a thousand things to you, but I think you know them all." He kissed her again, softly, softly. "Adieu, sweet Hero. Keep my lamp burning."

In the love-name, in their private mythology, she too could bear to speak the words. She clasped his hand. "Adieu, my Leander. Be swift, be bold, and come you back to me." Her voice broke on the last syllables.

He nodded without a further word, pale and with burning eyes, and then was gone.

She would not watch him go. The girls ran to the far window, but she busied herself in turning down the bed. When they came back to her she turned about, forcing cheer into her voice, and clasped her hands.

"Well, my dears, shall we go down for our breakfast now? Who'll be the first to the door? I sa-y—" She drew out the word. "Janey!" Janey laughed and ran for the door with Patsy soon after, but the little one couldn't reach the knob to turn. Patty picked her up and they all see-sawed across the maze of the yard, singing "Heigh Down-a-Down." The combined effects of Grandmama and the smell of breakfast drifting from the next room was enough to keep their minds off their loss. Would that she herself could have done so thus easily.

She was cheerful in her greeting, kissing each of the ladies per usual.

"Good morning, Mother; good morning, Nancy." Blonde Nancy put down her netting and returned her kiss with affection. Mrs. Jefferson said simply, "Good morning, my dear." There was a pause, and then she said, over the heads of the children, "He's gone, so? He came here to say farewell."

"Aye," Patty said carefully, but she was not careful enough to evade the notice of those sharp brown eyes. Mrs. Jefferson reached over and patted her hand.

"We'll shift, my dear," she said in sympathy, "all we ladies together. Many's the time I had to do so when Mr. Jefferson was away on his surveys." She sighed a little and said lightly, "Aye, and I worried, too. But I had my cousin Randolph to cheer me, so 'twas bearable." She meant William Randolph's wife, whose house she had so long shared at Tuckahoe. "Then, too, my son is a writing man, and his father rarely was." She looked at Nancy. Nancy with her father's fair hair and features. "Well, come along, my girl, and to our breakfast." She took her daughter's arm, for she was something troubled this morning with rheumatics. At the door to the dining room she turned. "You are airing linens today, Patty?"

"Yes, Mother."

She was appraised with a keen eye. "Well, you bring me down that quilt that wants stitching, and I'll set it up for you. I always was a fair hand at quilts. And we'll have a nice drawl."

She smiled. The mending of the quilt was only the old lady's excuse to be kindly. "I will, Mother."

When the breakfast was done she sent the girls to play under Liza Reynold's watchful eye down by her house with her two children and the

Garths, and herself went back to the kitchen to order dinner. She found Nan and Ursula washing ware while with Scilla, Sukey laid the kettle on the fire. It was a job for two strong girls, for the iron cauldron weighed fifty pounds empty. With water in, it could easily outweigh both of them. Queenie usually did it, but Queenie was pregnant and forbidden to lift heavy objects.

"It's too hot today for roasting anything, Suke," she said to her agile little cook. "I think we should just fry up a mess of the chickens and call it done. How's the bread?" She went to the oven near the outside door and with a towel wrapped about her hand opened the iron door and peered in at the individual loaves of wheat and corn bread that were the day's ration. They were just turning a pale gold now. "The cornbread will want removing in a moment." She closed the door so as not to let out too much heat and turned back to Scilla.

"Run down before dinner and fetch up some of the long beans and both kinds of peas and we'll make up a salad. That and a custard and some wafers should do for pudding."

"Yas'm," they both said.

She nodded her head at Scilla. "Come along with me and we'll have the chickens."

"Yas'm."

Two days before they had killed an half-dozen of the birds and preserved them in the cellar in pepper and saltpetre. In her game cellar there were other fowl hanging—geese, muscovy ducks, a pair of squab caught in the woods, an early turkey. Most of these had been smoked, but the chickens had not, for she intended that they be eaten quickly. She climbed up on her stool and cut four of them down now. They had no plans for company at dinner, but anyone could come along. She handed them down to Scilla, who laid them in her apron, and jumped down again. "There we are." She wiped her hands on her apron and followed the girl out again.

Swinging the heavy door closed, she took out her keys and locked the fowl securely into their prison again. It was rather like a gaol down here, dark and damp-smelling. On her way out she stopped at the wine cellar and brought out three bottles of Madeira and one of Mazzei's Tuscan varieties. She rationed out, too, the day's cheese, a great wedge of creamy-pale, medium-hard stuff that they had made themselves.

She could admit to great satisfaction in her industry and their resultant self-sufficiency, for the fowl were her domain as well. Rearing them herself, tending them, feeding them, she also saw to their slaughter, their setting, and their preparation. She had to oversee the boys in her fowl yard, for they were not always diligent. Many's the time the ducks or the geese had escaped to trouble Stephen Willis and his brick lads, or John Reynolds and his, laying a floor.

She spent most of her days in constant motion between one task and another, between one servant and another, for just this reason. They could not always be trusted to do their jobs. Oh, the kitchen staff she could trust implicitly now, but they were the only ones. Even the laundry women were slothful if not prodded from time to time. They had been known to spend an entire morning on a single pair of sheets. But all she had to do to get them going again was walk in the room and ask to see the product, and they were busy as bees, for they knew that no excuse was accepted save childbirth or actual illness, and she was experienced enough to see through a sham of the latter. She expected a certain output every washing day, for she knew how long such things should take. Besides, a job well done was likely to be rewarded with a sweetening of several pence or some small object, so it behooved them to do well.

Going across the lawn with Scilla, she met John Reynolds with his swinging walk and apron pockets full of nails. They were finishing the main joinery in the hall, the door and window frames, wainscoting and such today. He was tall and sinewy with hanging brown hair and a pleasant visage. She never saw him scowling, not even when her charges ran afoul of him.

"Good morning, Mr. Reynolds," she said, smiling. She couldn't help the dimples showing, for she liked him well.

He nodded his head. "Good morning, ma'am. "His blue eyes were twinkling. He had great large, blunt-fingered hands, the skin much broken by his rough work, but in manners he was not rough. He was gallant as a courtier. She could believe Liza that he had been something of a rake, in a mild way, in his early youth; he too liked to charm.

"We'll have the woodwork finished today," he said, knowing how pleased she would be.

"Oh good!" She laughed. "Now all we need is a roof!"

"Stairs first," he countered.

"Ah, yes. I suppose a ladder would be a trifle inelegant." Though they would not be the first people to have such as a stopgap measure. The Mazzeis had lived with a ladder for well-nigh on five months. John Reynolds's own house down the mountain had a loft ladder in the manner of the early settlers.

"Hard going on a lady," he said. She blushed.

"Indeed." She dropped her eyes, unwilling to this rake's progress. He was nothing less than polite, and implied no disrespect, but there was an indefinable air about him that made her conscious of him in a way she should not be. Granted, she had always found his sort of man attractive, for artisan or not, he could probably hold his own with a girl as well or better than more gently born beaux. He was warm and personable, with no false tricks or fashionable manners to hide behind.

"Well, I'm away," he said suddenly, and she looked up. He nodded again. "Good day to you, ma'am."

She bowed her head in return. "And to you." She turned to Scilla. "Come along, and we'll get this all to Suke." They parted company with Reynolds, who went on his way around to the front of the house with his swinging walk, his pockets full of nails jangling about him like the noise of a tinker's cart.

Once the receipts were given out for dinner she went upstairs and brought down all the blankets and quilts for the household. Some of them merely wanted an airing and others, like her white quilted counterpane, a mending. Mostly this was bindings fraying or coming loose, for this was the area of hardest wear. Those for airing she took down to her laundry women.

The laundry was between her smokehouse and the joinery shop, about three-quarters down the row from the Garth's small house. Both were placed here for the convenience of the spring nearby, but the work done sometimes conflicted. Between sawyer's dust and the steamy damp from outdoor boiling of wash, it was a wonder that it didn't come more often to blows. Today, however, 'twas all indoor work, for the heavy bedding would be cleaned with fuller's earth to preserve its life and the hanging done in the orchard. And all the men from the sawpit beyond were up at the house helping in the joinery there.

"Take them down along about suppertime," she instructed Juno and Lena. "I'll come down for them afterward."

"Yas'm," Juno said.

"Oh, yes," she said, turning from the door, "and see if you can get the stain out of Janey's coverlet. If not, it should be boiled." She looked outside. "But I doubt she'll need it this night," for it was quite warm, "so not to worry if it doesn't come out today. It'll hold till tomorrow."

"We'll do our best, ma'am," Lena said. "You gel—" she called to her underling, "come fetch this'r quilt with me out onter that table—"

Patty went out, leaving the mending on the bench outside the door. She wanted to collect the girls from Liza's house, for they could have a sewing lesson while the mending was done. Janey already liked to take needle and thread to scraps of cloth. Mostly she managed to tie it all up in a wad, but she must start somewhere. Familiarity was the key. And Patsy was beginning plain sewing. The last mending day she had sewed four lines of good even stitches. They were broad yet, better suited to basting, but they were even; she had the idea.

Walking back along the row, she went down the stairs by the paling fence and traversed the vegetable garden until she came to the little steep path into the vineyard and the orchard beyond. She might have taken the roundabout road, and would do later with the girls, but for herself she liked the tramp through the woods. It was not ten o'clock yet, but the day was already warm. Even here under the trees it was no longer cool. A dark humidity gave the woods a womb-like quality.

Carefree for the moment, she stuck her hands in the slits of her skirts and jammed them into her pockets among the goods she carried: keys, handkerchief, a folding lancet, a stub of pencil, six pence and two half-pennies, a button that had come off Janey's frock and wanted sewing on again. If anyone had been about she would never have walked so boldly with her hands in her pockets like a man.

She had been taught that ladies did not do such things, nor stand with arms crossed or hands clasped behind like a bashful child. All the things that were normal and natural were trained out. She had a tendency in private, and sometimes among the servants if she was agitated, of laying her right hand on her hip and resting the other upon it. This was supposed to be sluttish, or pert at least, and it did call to mind the shrewish harangue of common females, but it gave her a way to hide her impatience or express her disapproval.

She removed her hands from the pockets and danced down the hillside, touching the trunks of trees as she went, skipping along, tempted for a giddy moment to toss her cap off and run through the woods. That would never do. She'd have to put her hair up again before she got to the Reynoldses, and it would spoil the fun. But O! the longing was there! She turned around several times in a clearing instead, breathing in delight the live, warm smell of the glade. Beside her a clump of Virginia creeper grew, tendrilling its way along the ground and up the tree trunk. Plum-colored cranesbill and nodding violets greeted her still, kept in bloom by the isolation of this place. There was trailing arbutus lingering too, though fading some, and she stooped to pick some of these, for their fragrance was heavy and sweet, a delight if preserved in oil. Now she merely tucked them into her bodice.

Far from holding her initial dismay at the wildness of the surrounding countryside, she had come to love it as much as Thomas did. It was strange and wondrous to behold the changing aspect of the seasons and the weathers. Sometimes, from the cozy safety of their little house, they would stand at the windows and watch thunder or snowstorms come rolling in from the northeast or across the Blue Ridge, until at length they too were enveloped. It was exciting. And even now, every little crook and turn in the woods held new wonders she had not discovered before, from unknown solitary flowers to new birds in spring. She felt at home here now. It had become as much hers as his.

She wondered where he was now. Was he as far as Point of Fork? Had he come to the ford and the tangle of trees along the western shore of the

Island, whose sight had greeted her every day for nigh on two years? Or was he farther still, past Dungeness, bearing on toward Louisa Courthouse? She felt the ache of their disappointed hopes and missed him with a pang. He had been very sorry yestereve, and distressed, when she had gone to bed with a compress at half-past nine. It would be a lonely few weeks until she adjusted to her single state again. Letters, welcome as they were, did not fill the gap of having no one to turn to with her concerns. The burthen of decisions rested solely and squarely with her. It wasn't that she felt unequal to her task, for she knew she could manage any crisis that arose with a sufficiency of level-headed calm, but rather that she felt the lack of her confidante. She could keep a journal, but for whom would she write it, and when would she find the time? She hardly had the time to dash off the occasional letter to Lisbet or Nan, let alone anything more introspective. Thomas found the time only because he required so very little sleep. He could write until one or two in the morning and rise at half-past five or six, but not she.

She passed along the spring and came on Liza boiling her laundry at the back of the house on a level space that John had cleared. "You're washing also, I see," she called. "I have a mess of quilts and blankets up at the house getting done."

Liza straightened, pushing back a lock of fallen brown hair. "Take this," she said, giving her paddle to her general girl, and came over. "Good morning," she said, and embraced her.

Patty laughed, with an exaggerated glance about. "Where're the little ones, or are you cooking children soup?"

"I'd like to, sometimes." Liza grinned. "No, they're up in the house playing at draughts and supposedly minding the baby. She's asleep, so I thought I'd set this up. You've come for your two?"

"Aye," she said, "and Mary's if you want to get shut of them. She had her house airing last I saw and was putting out the carpets. I can't feature that they'd do much harm with the furniture all awry."

Liza bent her a droll glance. "That lot?" she asked in a low voice. "They'd wreak havoc in hell if it was to be got. Come and I'll fetch your little ladies." They went into the house.

Eight little faces, the baby's included, greeted them. Young Joanna played with her toes in the crib while the others took turns scattering draughts pieces about her bed. The Garth children looked uneasy for a moment before they realized that they were not to have a reprimand. Janey came toddling over.

"Mama Mama, up. Up!" she demanded. Patty picked her up.

"Come along now, children. It's time to go back home. Help put away the draughts, all of you, and thank Mrs. Reynolds for letting you come." She shifted Janey to the other hip. Patsy did as she was bidden, but the

Garths were somewhat more truculent; they lagged behind and let the others do the bulk of the work. She watched as Patsy made a neat curtsey to Liza and said all in a breath, "Thank you very kindly, ma'am, for letting my sister and me come and play."

Liza nodded solemnly. "You're quite welcome, Miss Patsy. I hope you'll come again soon." She glanced at Patty with a rolling eye. It was only then that the young Garths piped up in unison, "Thank you, Miz' Reynolds!" To her credit, Liza accepted their embraces about her legs with affection, patting their scruffy heads rather wistfully. They so plainly wanted to be loved, noticed, and approved of, that it was impossible to be short about their manners. They had not been trained to politeness. Their own mother was as like to holler at them as praise them for right actions, so was it any wonder they were backward? Still, Patty could not believe that they were willfully unkind, as Thomas maintained, though she did allow the girls to play with them only in the company of others now, to appease him.

They all clasped hands outdoors and in a queue scattered themselves ragtag along the roundabout road, singing rhymes as they climbed their slow way back up the mountain. Janey had to be carried the whole way, for her legs were too short still to walk very far, but they made it back at the overseer's house before eleven o'clock.

"Thanks," Mary said diffidently for their safe passage home. She turned from the door. "Go upstairs, you lot, until I'm finished getting this floor scrubbed—" She turned back again. "It's good weather for cleaning out."

"So it is," Patty agreed. She lifted her arm whereon the quilt and blankets rested. "I'm seeing to these today." She laid her hand on May's arm. "Come by this afternoon if you're able. I would welcome the company."

Mary raised an eyebrow. "What of your mother?"

"She and Miss Nancy usually take the air after dinner, if there's no company. Besides, we've not had a proper visit in ages." Her glance was entreating. "Please, May, if you're able. Bring Betsey. She and Janey can play together."

She saw in the melting glance the truth she sought. Being harried herself, Mrs. Garth was hard on everyone. Lacking the ability to ask for sympathy, she set herself up for a difficult situation. Mary Garth nodded. "I will, so."

"Good. Now, I'm for my mending. My mother Jefferson promised me that she would help with this." She plucked at the white counterpane. "Good day, my dear."

Mary smiled. "Good-bye, Mrs. Jefferson."

41

A Man Like His Father

Monticello

She found the ladies in the dining room, each at their work.

"It was too noisy in the parlor," Mrs. Jefferson explained. "All that hammering."

"Aye," Patty said. "But Mr. Reynolds told me they would have the joinery finished today, so we'll have some peace for a little. At least inside." As soon as the exterior walls were completed on the south wing the pilings would go up again, this time for the second floor. There was the north bow room to finish, which meant they would lose a wall to the dining room for a time, but that was not in the plans until the spring.

"Well, that's good news," Jane said acerbically. "I declare, I don't know how you live with it. This endless building would try the patience of a saint."

"Oh, but it's worth it all," she said, unable to keep a note of tenderness from her voice. They ate, slept, and breathed the house plans, and in her mind's eye she saw clearly the lofty, chaste beauty of the Palladian orders in their high-ceilinged, plastered rooms. Soaring, light, and delicately balanced, they would be the perfect frame for the views beyond, the perfect foil for their books and music, their convivial evenings.

She was not a visionary, an idealist as Thomas was, being too well trained to rational, practical reality, but he had infused her with his enthusiasm. By his endless gadgets and draughts he had made her see the practicality of the place where, when she had first heard of it sitting on the bench in the chamomile in Peyton Randolph's backyard, she had seen only the difficulties. But once completed, their manor house promised to be a most convenient place, in any sense of the word. And though she had her moments of frustration and despair now, she yet had that vision of what it would be, which Mrs. Jefferson and visitors of a like mind to hers did not share, could not know. They all thought Thomas was mad as a hatter. Build a house on the rise of a hill, yes, but not a mile high and miles from any reliable water source.

"As you say, my dear," Jane said, with a look. "Now, let's see this quilt of yours." Patty gave her the quilt and fetched her sewing basket from under the chest in the corner of the parlor.

"It's not so bad," Mrs. Jefferson said when she returned, examining the rip in the lining through her narrow spectacles. "It's just been worn, see?" She looked up at her daughter. "Nancy," she said, "fetch me a swatch of that holland I cut yesterday."

"Yes, Mama."

"We can't have something like this gone to ruin for want of such a simple mend, can we now?" she said pleasantly.

Patty shook her head and took a chair, removing from her own workbasket needles, thread, and scraps for the girls.

Drawing on one of the oblong strips of drugget in a small dotted pattern, she called to Patsy, "Come here to me, Pats."

Patsy came away from her grandmother's side.

"Do you see these marks here?"

Patsy nodded solemnly.

She handed her the needle. "I want you to stitch in between them. Here, I'll show you." She took a few stitches, about an eighth inch wide, and looked up. Patsy's face had the intensity of a witness to a miracle. Her expression was absorbed, and she looked so much like her father at that moment that Patty had to smile. "Do you think you can do it?"

"Yes, ma'am," the child said.

"Good. I'll fetch you my embroidery scissors, and you go sit in the window where the light is best; and when you're done come show it to me." She gave her the delicate gold-handled scissors and watched as she examined the stitches.

"Janey, come here." Janey smiled a broad smile and came toddling over. "Would Janey like to sew like a big girl?"

"'Es!" Janey crowed. Patty gave her a tapestry needle and a bit of crewel wool without a knot and a swatch of huckaback. "There you are!" Janey plopped herself down at her feet and attacked the cloth with the blunt needle joyously.

Jane, who had been watching this interchange, was smiling. "You're wise to do so," she said, nodding at the child. "It keeps them away from the stuffs they're not allowed."

"Aye," Patty said placidly. "My stepmother did the same." She picked up the Dutch blanket and repinned the loose binding. Mary Cocke was an excellent teacher, whatever her faults may have been as a mother. Her father had been so often away at his practice in those days that they were thrown wholly upon one another.

She remembered the time of Lisbet's infancy, having been fascinated with this new little being in the house who was so much more lively than her dolls. She remembered, too, the nervous, hovering mother who was anxious lest she do some mischief upon the babe. But she had never wished to hurt Lisbet. Lisbet was her own doll baby, and when she began to walk it was even better. She remembered a day in the nursery when Mother Mary was anticipating Tibb, walking round and round the perimeter of the room with Lisbet following behind singing, "doe doe doe" and rocking side to side as she walked, while the nurse looked on. The ribbon round Lisbet's wrist was not cruelly intended, no matter what her mother thought, for she had seen Betsy toddled about by lead-strings often enough. Babies needed them.

But Mary Cocke had taught her well those household arts she would need in future life. She was an excellent embroideress, and her work in gold and silver was breathtaking to a young girl. She was equally skilled in preserves and preserving and knew the best way to tie a fowl for smoking.

Oh, she and her sisters had been well taught. They could do plain sewing as well as the lady by the age of nine, could weave and embroider neatly if not perfectly; they could dance and sing and play simple tunes upon the keyboard or harp. Nothing had been left out. . . except, perhaps, in Patty's case, that full measure of affectionate attention that her spirit craved. Lisbet, Tibby, and Nannie had been showered with motherly kisses and affection to their hearts' delight, but such times were rare in Patty's memory. There was more when her father was about, but he was so often gone!

Once, in a period of rebellion she had threatened to go to him with this truth, but the threat did not produce the hoped-for conciliation, but instead a rather painful clout on the ear that was·remembered to this day. Because of that she had never so struck servant or child, no matter how furious she might be. But neither did she broach the subject again, and to her knowledge her father had never been the wiser of this rift in his household.

Then Mary had died, carried off by some female complaint, and Papa had married Elizabeth Skelton. She should be grateful to Mother Elizabeth, for it was by her brief presence in the house that she had come to know Batt, but she was even less cordial to a quartet of half-grown daughters than her predecessor had been to one toddler. They were polite to one another but never affectionate. Instead, this common enemy in their household had bound the sisters together in a manner that even death could not break. Tibb had not been forgotten. Every autumn mementos were sent for her grave, and letters between Lisbet, Nancy, and Patty did not infrequently allude to some shared memory of the lost one.

Patty glanced from her work to her two daughters: Janey with her golden hair escaping its cap, and Patsy, absorbed in her plain work by the window. They fought more often than she remembered doing with Lisbet—though Lisbet teased that this was because she was a tyrant and would brook no opposition—and she hoped that they would become one day the dear friends that she and her sisters were. What a blessing it was to share the female bond with women of one's own house! She shared things with them that no other females knew, nor would ever. There lay a trust and security, a reciprocity that time and distance could not touch.

She turned the edge of the blanket over and took up her needle on the other side of the binding, startled when Mrs. Jefferson spoke up into the silence. "My children were always a comfort to me when their father was away," she said as a presage to some speech.

Patty blushed. "Aye?"

"Oh, indeed," Jane continued at this invitation. "Sometimes he would be gone for months at a time, and I would think that I should forget his face were it not imprinted upon so-and-so's, or the manner of his walk or laugh if not for another. It was a great comfort. And now," she patted her daughter's arm, "so's my Nan in my widowhood. She's just like all the Jeffersons in her way, quiet and deep. They'll never tell you what they're thinking, but they won't blether your business about the neighborhood either. It's not a bad way to be."

She stitched complacently for a moment, then continued, "My son—now there's a man like his father if ever I saw. Tom has the same restlessness, see. Mr. Jefferson was ever about doing things when he was home. No, he was never one to idle, one must give him that. He had a thousand ideas to implement. He was always designing something. Do you know that butter churn I have, the odd-shaped one? He made that with his own hands, the best churn I've ever had, and sturdy into the bargain. He knew a mort of things, my husband.

"But I will tell you, aye and without a blush, I believe my son surpasses him. All the esteem of his fellows it took Mr. Jefferson half a lifetime to garner Thomas has now. I am proud of him, I don't mind saying."

Patty smiled wistfully at the words. If only Thomas himself could hear them, how glad he would be! He still labored with the notion that his mother disliked him, and how far that was from the truth. Why could these two, so frank and warm with others, never bring themselves to speak the words they both craved to hear? From an early time, he said, his mother was distant from him in a way that she wasn't with the others. Patty's own experience gave her compassion with this suffering, yet she questioned now the truth of his perception.

"You could not help to be," she said to Jane. The depth and breadth of his knowledge and enthusiasm was astonishing, and she herself stood in awe of it. It was so even now, when she knew him so well and shared many of his interests. But he could match and sometimes surpass her knowledge in some areas and was not shy of asking questions where he was ignorant. Feminine mystery was impossible with him, for he was curious about every aspect of her life. She had no doubt that should she be stricken ill or, heaven forbid, were to die, he could manage this place and the children as well as she, and it was not a comfortable thought. She stopped short of feeling redundant only because she knew his heart, the need he had for her.

"Do you know, my dear," Jane went on, "I was quite unfair to you early on; I don't know if you realize how. I wondered what you could want of my son when you were so young and wealthy in your own right. My daughters tried to make me see, but I was long too proud to admit it."

Patty stopped her sewing and held her breath at the words and the frank, brown gaze.

Jane regarded her levelly. "Well, I'm not now, when I can see how devoted you are, with all the goodly virtues I could hope for. I've discomfited you," she said, reaching out her hand, for Patty felt herself blushing hotly. "But I'm an old woman and must speak frank: I could not have picked a better helpmeet for Thomas had I searched myself." Her voice faltered, and her eyes grew dim with fond tears. "He is dear to me, quite dear. How could he not be, and him my eldest son?" She paused. "I have been hard on him betimes, I know, but for his own good." Her voice sharpened again. "I haven't long now, and I shall die happily, knowing he has you, who loves him so dear."

The gnarled, bony fingers on Mrs. Jefferson's once-elegant hand clasped hers, and Patty couldn't speak for sentiment. She shook her head, her eyes blurring tears, and reached into her pocket for her handkerchief. "Oh, ma'am," she murmured, and wiped her eyes. Looking up, she found a tenderness there that she'd never see before. "Thank you, ma'am. I am most sensible of the honor."

"Pah, honor!" Jane snorted, going back to her work. "Plain regard is all, and well deserved, Patt." She knotted the thread and spread out the quilt.

"There now," she cried. "I say it's sturdy enough to last out the wear of the piece. It'll be a petticoat before it's a rag, I vow." She gave it to Nancy.

"Fold this up, girl, and lay it on the table there out of the child's reach, and we'll see to this other binding. . . ." So the old lady's peace was made. They continued their mending together in companionable silence until it was time for dinner.

42

Tansy Pudding

Monticello, Blenheim

Later in the day, when she was down at the little house, Mary Garth came by as promised. Aside from mere pleasantries to exchange, there was the matter of the Negroes' nursery to discuss. Belinda was due to lie in shortly, and a woman must be found to do her work and to nurse her for the fortnight of her confinement. A midwife was no trouble; Aggy or old Jenny were equally skilled at bringing babies, but Belinda was likely to need a bit of extra care afterward, for she'd had some trouble after Iris last year. And she needed to know also which of the nurses might be ready to train for another position or go to the fields, for girls were generally only kept as nurses until they were eleven or twelve.

May's sharp rap upon the door stirred Janey on her trundle, and Patty laid a stilling hand on her from the chair.

"Get the door, Pats," she said softly to Patsy, "then you may go to practice your music. I'll be along directly, tell Aunty."

"Yes, Mama." Patsy said, and went over to the door. "Good day, Mrs. Garth," she said breathlessly. Mary smiled. "Hello, Patsy."

"I'm going to practice," Patsy said solemnly, and went out.

May laughed. "She's so serious! But a good child. Would that I could get Lila to behave such a little lady."

"It isn't difficult," Patty said, rising. "They just want to proper inducements. As for Patsy, she has company manners. I will not speak for the private ones. Come in, come in. I've just made up some coffee." She went to the coal brazier with its pot warming atop.

"I saw Mr. Willis and Mr. Garth talking outside your place after dinner," she said as she poured out coffee. "Did you get your cleaning done?"

"Near enough for today. Thank you." May accepted the coffee bowl. "I'm setting the girls to the inside windows tomorrow, and Mr. Willis has promised some of his boys to do the outside."

"Ah, so that's what it was about."

"Aye." Mary looked around the room. "I declare, how do you keep your house so tidy and you with two children here? We have four rooms with the children in their own, and it always looks like a cyclone."

It was hard to believe that their little house crammed with stuff as it was could look tidy to anyone. Granted there weren't dust curls roaming the floors, but that was only due to a daily sweeping.

"If it looks so," she drawled, "it's only because we're never in it! Actually, it's better since Betty came from Elk Hill. She's excellent at prodding the girls to their work and feels it her bounded duty that I should not be forced to raise my voice. She's quite a treasure."

May's eyes narrowed. "She's that mulatto woman with the green eyes?" Patty nodded.

Mary blew out her breath. "She gave one of my girls a telling out t' other day for leaving a broomstick in the path that would done credit to my old nurse! I never saw the lazy creature move so fast in her life. I must mind to thank her for it."

Patty laughed. "Bett's good at running things, and people. She had charge of my sisters and me. She was supposed to be our servant, our waiting maid, but somehow we always managed to find ourselves doing precisely as she wished. I wouldn't have it else, tho'. She's a mort of common sense." She put down the handleless blue bowl. "Speaking of common sense, I wanted to ask your opinion on who we should get to see after Belinda when she lies in. I thought maybe Bella or Fanny since they live near to her."

May waved her hand. "Oh, don't get Bella!" she exclaimed. "She's awful for that. Too busy mincing about making herself important to be of any real use. Fanny would be better; she's more settled, and she likes babies."

"You'd know better than I—" There was a knock at the door. "Come," she called.

Martin appeared with a bow. "Mist' Edward Carter's here, ma'am," he said, "and wants to know if you'll see him."

Oh bother. She glanced at the sleeping Jane. Well, she couldn't very well receive him here. "Yes," she murmured, rising. "Tell him I'll meet him in the parlor. Excuse me a moment," she said to Mary, and went out.

He was just coming up from the stable when she settled herself on the sofa. Mrs. Jefferson and Nancy were out on a walk along the roundabout, and Patsy sat at the spinet in the corner practicing her piece. She wondered what on earth he could possibly want of her, as he likely knew that Thomas was gone. Perhaps someone was ill. He entered through the glass doors on the western front, the only entrance to the house at the moment. He was wearing riding clothes, and his face was flushed in the heat of the day.

"Good day to you, Mrs. Jefferson," he said with a bow.

She gave him her hand. "Good day Mr, Carter. How do you do?"

"Passing well, ma'am," he nodded. "'Twas just on that head that I came here. I was on my way to Charlottesville and bethought you may have need of something there that I could bring you in Mr. Jefferson's absence."

"Ah," so that was it. She smiled. "How kind of you, sir, to be such a good neighbor. But I fear I have no demands to make."

"You get on well then?"

"Tolerably well." She smiled a little. "But then my husband is just gone this very day. I cannot speak the week or month or twelve-month, if he be gone that long." Patsy's halting rendition of Bach came wafting to them.

"Oh, I doubt it shall be that long." Edward put his foot up on her cushioned stool. "At least not altogether. They rarely sit so long to my recollection."

Patsy had stopped now and she glanced over. The child flexed her fingers and continued. She looked up at Edward Carter. "I thank you for that confidence, sir, and your prescience in stopping on your way." She inclined her head. "But I would not detain you sir, with idle talk, from your important business."

He harrumphed and took his foot from the stool. "Well, ma'am, there is in fact another matter which brought me here. . . ." He colored from more than the heat.

"Indeed, sir?"

"My good mother bids me enlist your aid in a private matter of one of her servants." He took a letter from his waistcoat and gave it to her. "She instructed me that it was most urgent and to plead that we may have your answer when I return from town." He colored again. "Please forgive the haste, Mrs. Jefferson, I. . . um. . . know it is unseemly, but believe that I would not press were it not urgent."

She raised an eyebrow and broke the seal of the letter, blanching at the contents written in the light, even hand. It was blotted in several places, suggesting the haste with which it was written.

"But why does she not ask Mr. Hall or Dr Gilmer to see to this?" she asked in bewilderment, unwilling to mix herself in such matters.

"She wants some privacy to it, as you may understand."

She gazed at him levelly. "For what did you travel to town, if I may be so frank?"

"Ipecac."

She shook her head. "That won't do it alone." She rose from the sofa, handing him the letter back. "I have some stuffs which are efficacious, and I will bring them. To wait would only suffer her end. I shan't be but a moment. Would you be so good as to have my horse brought?"

He looked thunderstruck. "Not the coach?"

She shook her head at him distractedly. "On our road? Mr. Carter, even the Thoroughfare would take long with the weight of four horses and the coach. I've travelled across the open country before," she said, recalling fleetingly their retreat from this man's house on their first journey, "and can do so again. But come! We are wasting precious time!"

She went over to Patsy, murmuring, "Darling, Mama has to go visit someone ill at Mr. Carter's. When you've done, wait here for Grandmama and Aunty Nancy and tell them thus. Can you remember it?"

"Yes Mama," Patsy said, with round eyes.

"Tell me."

"Mama had to go to Mr. Carter's to see someone ill," she parroted. Patty kissed her forehead. "There's my good girl! You mind now, while I'm away. I shan't be long."

"Yes, Mama."

She went out, hurrying down the slope of the mountain. By the spring there was a planting of cuckoopint which was said to be a sovereign remedy for poison and plague. She yanked up half the quantity of the purple-flowered herb by the roots and tossed it into her apron. Mary Garth stood outside the little house now, seeing some thing amiss.

"I have to go with Mr. Carter," she said as she brushed past her.

With trembling hands she unlocked her chest of medicinals and rifled through it for her bottle of syrup of ipecac. Holding it up to the light, she squinted in the dark glass to see the amount. Little over half a bottle. It would have to do. Snatching up her bag, she was out the door again, skimming across the lawn in her heelless slippers before the astonished Mary.

They rode overland as the crow flies, boldly fording the stream in the gap as though it were a trickle. Leaning forward over her leg, clinging to mane and reins, Patty thought she would be sick with each jolt. She hated riding, and only the thought of Edward's poor mother kept her going on. When at length they reached Blenheim she let Edward help her down, grateful for the steadying hands on her waist.

She half expected to find Mrs. Carter expired, but on going up to the bedchamber she heard by the lady's groans that she was not. She rapped twice on the door.

"Mrs. Carter, will you see me? It's Mrs. Jefferson."

The door was opened by an elderly serving-woman with grizzled hair. The mistress of the house lay abed, clothes loosed, writhing as if in childbirth. But she was not, being not in the way of such conflicts, and her gripe was plainly else.

Patty gave her bag to the old woman and went over. "Mrs. Carter," she murmured, smoothing the dark hair back. "It's Mrs. Jefferson. Your son brought me. You must tell me, what have you eaten? What has caused your trouble?"

The feverish eyes sought hers. "I think it was. . . the pudding."

"What sort of pudding, dear?" she asked, as to a child.

"Tansy."

Patty looked up at the old Negro woman, who went about her business, unpacking Patty's bag.

"Was it?" she asked her.

The cow-brown eyes, with their yellow eyeballs regarded her calmly. "I 'spect it was. I di'n't see it myself."

This truculence annoyed her. Doubtless some word of truth had filtered down to the old woman but she was unwilling to implicate her fellows. Poisonings did not often happen, but there generally was a great deal of ignorance among the Negroes when they did.

The internal workings of this matter, save those of the lady, did not concern her. It would be a simple matter to substitute ragwort tansy for the common stuff in a pudding, for they were both bitters, and say with truth that such was indeed tansy pudding.

"Fetch me that bottle," she said to the old woman, striving to keep an even tone. "And boil up that weed there. No, not in the kitchen. Here. Use the fire." She turned to her charge. "It's all right, Molly, we'll soon see you right. You are not sick enough to die." She wasn't any too certain of this, but the vomit and the stomachic together might effect a cure.

She picked up the glass on the bedside table and smelled it carefully. Not trusting that, she took a very small sip herself. Well, it was plain water, at least. She poured out a drachm of the ipecac and mixed it up.

"Up you come," she said, and forced the concoction on her charge. Edward came in in the midst of this. "Get out," he said shortly to the old woman, who was pottering about the fire. When she was gone he came over and stood beside the bed. "How are you, Mama?"

"No better," she said pitifully. She held up her hand. "No more, please. I'll be sick."

"That's the idea, dear," Patty said, and forced some more on her. She looked up at Edward. "Fetch me the pot, or a basin if there's one. By the look of her, we shouldn't have long to wait."

And they did not. It was not above ten minutes later that the poor lady began to retch. When it was clearly over she was dosed again with the emetic and the process was repeated. With Edward's help, the cuckoo-pint was decocted and strained through a shift, the only cloth at hand, and given to the lady in small doses. After an hour they sent for plain crackers and bread and fed these also. They kept the fire high in the room, though it was a warm day, to assist the sudorific properties of the herb.

"Can't we open a window?" Edward begged. He was pouring sweat as greatly as his mother. "It's awfully close in here."

She shook her head. She was no more comfortable than he. "It's what she needs, to sweat out what was not brought up." She reached for his hand across the bed. "She is plainly better, sir, see for yourself! Her breath is even and she has not the gripe she did. Please God, she will recover."

"Oh, thank God," he cried. "I shouldn't think what I'd write my father else!" His father was in Williamsburg at the Assembly.

"Well," she said, withdrawing her hand from his grasp. "You need had rather think what you are going to tell him about this. . . ." She paused. "Have you found the culprit?"

"Aye," he said grimly. "And 'tis the overseer's business."

She closed her eyes. "Not—" she couldn't speak the word. She'd never seen a Negro flayed in her life, and while this certainly warranted it, she was yet unwilling to such punishment. For who could blame the slave to chafe at his shackles, however softly made? Would not any person of sensibility do likewise if thus placed?

Mr. Carter avoided her gaze. "Yes."

She wondered what he would do with this servant. She could guess that it was one of the house or kitchen with some access to the mistress, else why the rancor. How would such a one fare in the field after a life of relative ease? Or to be sold with the brand of poisoner to follow ever after? She wondered but did dare not ask, for such was not a lady's business, and to do so would be pert. She confined her attentions to Mrs. Carter.

It was growing dark by the time she was settled on her horse with her escort of Edward's body servant beside her. It was good to be in the open air again. The temperature had dropped and the bugs were not out yet, so it was quite pleasant. But she was exhausted. Even the proffered glass of wine had not been vivifying. She felt dazed and stupid from the close warmth of the room she had occupied these five hours past and did not look forward to the ride home. They would travel along the Thoroughfare, which was reasonably smooth, but it was eight miles nonetheless.

As she rode home, her little grey Katie picking her way daintily, she was struck by what had occurred this afternoon at Blenheim. She had never felt unsafe among her own servants; indeed she had always felt respected by them. Certainly she had never considered the possibility of some complaint finding its outlet in tainted food.

Plainly, the guilty was a person of some wit to know the differences between one sort of tansy and another. The common or garden type was frequently used for abortions among the cabins, if a pregnancy came too soon for the liking of the mother. Any of the grannies could have given that. But even a small amount of the ragwort intermixt could make one violently ill. It frequently did cattle who unwisely consumed it. But why should anyone wish to harm Mrs. Carter? She was only the most gentle of mistresses.

Unless. . . . The possibility grew in her mind. Unless 'twere not intended for her. . . . Edward. Edward had not eaten it, being gone until after dinner. The amount taken was, upon examination of the tainted food, clearly not enough to kill, merely enough to belay one awhile. She sat back in the saddle in alarm. What ill had been planned that required the young master's absence for the space of a few days?

She shook her head, a shudder travelling through her. She didn't want to know. Raised her whole life with the trust of those about her, she had no wish to know the grim details of others' lives. Isolated as she was, how could she sleep at night, knowing some trouble may be brewing in their own sphere, unawares?

Thomas abhorred slavery and was most explicit with Thomas Garth as to how malcontents were to be treated, thus to avoid some of its grosser evils. If their difficulty could not be dealt with by rotation in work or locale, they were to be sold promptly. He would have no such trouble as occurred today. She knew from Mary Garth that corporal punishments were few at Monticello, and they had little word of trouble from Elk Hill, which they managed in the Skipwiths' absence, or any of their other farms. Plainly such a system worked.

She looked at the back of Carter's servant upon his horse before her. No, she would not be suspicious. Whatever he knew, what good could come to him in the harm of an innocent lady? But he was not one of her people, and she was not wholly easy in her mind.

She took in the view of the dimming countryside. They would be at Colle in a moment, and home was just beyond. She was no longer afraid of the wildness of the countryside as she had been three-and-an-half years before. Even in the lowering twilight she knew the landmarks now, and could have found her way home in the dark. They passed the Buck Island road, veering off to the right. The crickets were chirruping in the bushes beside the road. A hare darted out of the thicket, and on seeing them, paused, rearing up nervously, watchful until they passed. They came to the Mazzei's road on the left and moved on. Glancing up the hill she could just see the lights on in the house.

Oh, she missed Thomas! For how many months would there be no welcome face in the evening, no welcome smile to greet her weary from her toils, no welcome arms in which to rest? Her throat constricted. Aye, she may play at their pleasures for herself and what visitors she may have, but they would be empty. Life was empty without her sun. And thus he was. Her mind ran to the lines of Donne:

> *I wonder, by my troth, what thou, and I*
> *Did, till we lov'd? were we not wean'd til then?*
> *. . .But this all pleasures fancies bee.*
> *If ever any beauty did I see*
> *Which I desir'd, and got, t'was but a dreame of thee. . .*

If only public alarms and public duty did not require his absence from their haven! She did not grudge him the rightly held esteem of his fellows and the business of the public trust that came with their lauds (for that was the province of every gentlemen), merely the length of absence required and the danger to which he would be put. If anything should happen to him—a shiver went through her at the thought—oh, she would not wish to live! It would be worse than Bathurst's death, a thousand times so, if only for her knowledge of widowhood's losses. But there would never be a man to fill his place. His mother today had touched on his brilliance without apprehending it fully. Who was there to compare with him in the wide world, let alone their own country? All the Virginia men would seem pale shadows after her existence here.

She shook herself out of her gloomy presentiments as they began to wind their way up the mountain. There was no gain in such fancies, and to continue may tempt a capricious fate. *Be safe, my darling,* she bid him silently. *May this evening find you at some sweet repose, safe from harm. Aye, this and every one you sleep from my embrace.* He would be stopped at Richmond tonight, maybe, or Tuckahoe. Oh, how would she shift these next months alone?

Nancy was in the little house when she arrived, dirty, hot, bone-weary. She had put Janey to bed and was combing out Patsy's hair. Patsy jumped down from the table at the sight of her.

"Mama!" She came running and buried her face in her petticoats.

"Hush, sh, we mustn't wake Baby," she said softly. "Were you a good girl, my Patt?" She looked down at the little freckled face.

"She surely was," Nancy said, putting down the comb and rising. "And was very good at comforting Jane when she missed you." She laid her hand on the child's hair.

Patty embraced her. "Thank you, Nan, for looking after them. I'm sorry to have left so suddenly but there was nothing else for it."

Nancy's blue eyes clouded in worry. "All is well again at Blenheim, I trust?"

She nodded. "Aye, and what isn't will soon mend." Unless by the Carters' wish, she would not reveal what she knew, even to family.

She allowed Patsy to sleep with her this one night, recognizing the child's loneliness in her own. They sat together in the canopied bed with the curtains undrawn reading of Gulliver's adventures until Patsy grew sleepy.

In the candlelight, the little face was sweet, rosy-cheeked, earnest, and beautiful amid its cloud of dark curling hair. She was a big girl, tall and precocious, and it was easy to forget sometimes that she was not yet three. Now was not such a time. Her loving, earnest, tempestuous little girl snuggled against her like a kit to its cat, and it didn't seem so very long before that she'd been a babe in arms. Her eyes burned with tears of an aching tenderness, and she leaned across the child to put out the candle. She kissed the soft white forehead.

"Good night, sweet," she murmured, and settled down with her to sleep.

43

Draughtsman

Monticello

It was more than a fortnight before she received a letter. When it came it was a thick packet, as of old, pages upon pages of ramblings, jottings, endearments, and pleas of eternal remembrance, but none was so sweet to her eyes as that first salutation, "My darling Patt."

She read the letter, or parts of it, for it was four pages, every night, long after she had sent off her reply to his anticipated address at Philadelphia:

> 17 June, 1775. Monticello.
>
> Dearest Ulysses—
>
> Your little book of the 10th inst. safely came to hand, tho' a wonder it did not strain the Post rider. I am delighted with th' contents, such jest notwithstanding. Oh, my sweet! how deer to me are such Words! They are Air and Light, bread and Water to my soule. I tremble at the task of fulfilling such a Charge as equal words, not for want of Aught to say to my dearest love! but the cramping of my hand at the Attempt. But I will not Complaine of my only communication with my soul's twin.
>
> . . .I have done as you ask'd about the Far'ht temperatures, though as you may understand the noone Remarque is sometimes omitted. I have twice this week sent Nancy for its number. I hope what remains will be adequate to your Purposes. . . .
>
> . . .I was at Colle t'other day, on Mr. Mazzei's invitation, it being young Miss M's birth Day, and had the most Extra-ordinary conversation with Mrs. M that I must relate it to you, tho' it will probably not endeer her to you any More than she is at Present. Howsomever, it bears telling as an indication of her Character and Person.
>
> She turn'd the talk to the subject of Dress (and we no the lie of this Land) and commenced to induce me to her Opinion that I sho'd, in yr abcence, take the Opportunity to get for myself, as she put it, those fashionable artickles of Adornment which I had sorely lacked, which she herself Displayed, and without which no Lady of fashion

may call herself such. I was mightily perplexed as how to respond to this Invective, you may be sure, and was for some moments quite Speechless. I then endeavoured to explaine, perhaps fruitlessly, as you are thinking, that, in the first instance, I had no need of such gew-gaws, being quite able to make such my Self if I so desired; and in the second, that I should never think of being so perfidious as to order Goods without your noledge and Consent, &c. So what then does she say, in answer to this? In full hearing of her good husband I may add— "Well then, Madame, you are a fool." This may be the continental way of Goings-on, but my dear! I tell you, it brings tears to my eyes even now. I cannot imagine ever saying such a thing to a guest. I had rather receive two such insults as to offer one. Were it not for Mr. Mazzei and his quick response at seeing my distress, I'm sure I don't now what I would have done. . . .

. . .accepting every assurance of warm Affection fro

Yr Penelope

(She received afterward a note of apology from Philip Mazzei for his wife's behavior, laying it at the door of her poor response to the Virginia summers. It was delivered by one of the few remaining Tuscans, the others having sought employment elsewhere, not liking the atmosphere of the house. He waited while she wrote a reply, saying that apologies were kindly accepted but utterly unnecessary, that nothing could serve to dim her affection for him and his family, after having shared her roof with them and been the recipient of so much kind hospitality from them. The words were true so far as Mr. Mazzei and his stepdaughter were concerned, and there was never anything so very wrong with a polite lie for Mrs. Mazzei, if it kept the peace between friends and neighbors.)

In return she received from Thomas:

. . .of Speaker Randolph's reccommendations. it stands on the corner of Seventh and Market streets and from the windows of the chamber I have a fine view of the countryside beyond town. i see now, the reason for my cousin's insistence; for he, knowing my mind and temperament, could not fail to understand the effect such a view would have on me, who is too used to our wild mountains. . . .

. . .this evening I went with colo: Harrison and RH Lee to the house of Thomas Hill at the edge of town his wife is a Carter by birth, and she keeps a Virginia-style open House. gathered there i found all of our countrymen including Geo. Wash-n, who wore his company manners and did credit to the confidence lately espoused him. all of these you are entirely familiar with, &c. there were severall men also unknon to me but by reputation. among these mr Sam'l Adams and his Cousin, quite displaced in our merrie company, I thought at first. the former is deceptive in appearence, a Claudius, truly. he is not above medium height and exceedingly grey-haired, tho' he cannot have pass'd half-centennary, palsied, with a tic of the left side of the face, his cloaths much worse for wear, tho' plainly of good stuffs; withall he has the air of one failed in business, which by all accounts he is. yet when he speaks he loses ev'ry affliction and becomes as compelling as any that ever trod the public boards. the breadth of his knolege, even in conversation, is disarming in one so unreposessing. the reason for his sway over the people is plain. his kinsman is more voluble. nay, tho' he is brilliant, i would say he should not be missed in any company. neither is he of a remarkable Person, being likewise short, and rather fat. but his tones are more ringing than Lee's or Henry's. he is, or was, a lawyer by profession, and spent his time at the county Courts in piddling litigations, as he calls it. i take it that the general run of causes were not sufficient meat to his Appetite. i listen'd to his discourse for greater part of the evening, and have come away with an admiration of his talents. he shewed to me some of his Writing, a scrap, he said, and he is gifted in that way, too. mr Hancock I am promised to meet on the morrow. . . .

. . .is an aristocrat, more devoted to our cause by sentiment than necessity . . . but let me tell you of dr. Franklyn, who is but lately arrived from England. he has most kindly shared with me his draught for an Articles of Confederation, throwing open to me all the hospitality of his house. he there owns an astonishing array of scientific apparatus, in great part designed by himself. personally, he is posessed of great charm as well as erudition, the combination of which, i confess, I find irresistable. his dignity, earnesty, and learning are matched by the most exquisite measure of good sense; his observation of common events is no less than that of great. some of his humor i cannot relate to you, for it is of a hearty character, but this only serves to make him more like unto Swift and that whole School of English dons. imagine a combination of R.H. Lee, mr Bland, and your father, and i think you will have an accurate picture of him. . . .

. . .as to the purpose of my coming here, I will say that i've been much engaged in draughts, and in committees as formerly. i must consider the former a signal honour, being as much the junior member of our delegation. . . . I have writ Francis on what news i have of the late engagement, and will give you some of that, lest you hear exxagerated Reports and be alarumed.: our account sais we had between 40 and 70 killed and 140 wounded. The enemy had certainly 500 wounded and we suppose the same number killed, but this is not certain. the Congress have directed 20,000 men to be raised and hope to shortly dispose our enemies to treaty. thus, while our worst fears are most certainly realized, their full execution may not be necessary. i pray god that it is so, for no one abhors such Business more than I. . . ..

. . .let me leave off such unpleasantries! tell me how the children do, how Patsy does in her musick and what new thing Janey sais. tell me what you read and who visits, what they say and how you feel. i am not a month gone and i ache for such news. i ache for my blossom's lovely face and sweet voice. there may be diversions here, common friends, ever, but they cannot replace the one friend in whom my heart rests. write to me every day, no matter how little, no matter how trivial the subject. that you mended a shoe or stitched a new cap is not too feminine a report for my eye. tell me, *mia primula*, the thousand things I long to hear. . .

i have bought some new musick for you in the market here, and ribband of the modish colors, but you shall have to wait on both til i am home, for I do not trust the Post. 'twill give you something to look forward to. . . .

Patty received this last letter the next Friday, by which time she had already sent off another letter of her own. At this out, they would be crossing replies in the mail, and likely she would end up owing letters, but she did her best to fulfil her promise.

. . .I had a letter from the Eppeses along with yours, Nancy and Henry are visiting until the end of the month, after which they shall depart for the Springs. Twill be their last jaunt till spring as N is gone quite stout. They are all very Well. On that head, I have Lisbet's word to expect their increase the end of July rather than August, so the Harvest will be well in before we see you in September. They send their kind regards. . . Holly Hocks are stil in bloom, do. Gillie flouers, tho' the striped variety seem to be faring less well in the Heat. . . . Garth says the Hay is in. . . Juno does poorly, though in truth I think it but overindulgence in Water-melons than any Distemper. . . Belinda is off Work, and Aggey with her, but we should not expect any Thing that way for a week or more Yet. . . . I am quite hale, you will be pleassed to know, and sun-burnt from having spent most of the last two days out-of-doors. The Marygoulds and Lavendar wanted cutting and drying. . . . Janey fell down and cut her chin, on the stone Wall at the end of the Garden, and all was alarm for a time, but when clean'd and stitched it proved but triviall. She's fine now.

There was some wry humor in this for it was the selfsame stone wall he had built to keep the children from falling down the hillside. But she needn't point out this obvious fact; he was as aware of it as she. She continued:

> Lest you think by such a Catalogue that I have been to busy to think of you, let me say it is not so. Every day when I sit to write, or read the thermometre, or answer Patsy's thousand questions, I am put in mind of you I hear your mother talk of her then only boy and cannot help to smile, for I know that lurking, brown-eyed lad, I see him in my darling's eyes in summer woods and winter frolics, and recall his vulnerability in the most cherished moments of bare intimacy. My heart swells, and I cannot write, but that I love you deer—

She broke off and the letter was continued the next day.

> I worry for your mother, dearest. I fear she is not well. Dr Gilmer assures that there is nothing wrong with her beside age and a little Rheumatick complaint, but there is about her a withering Air that's naught to do with her Randolph heritage. I do my best to engage her in the Business of life, but she is content to sit and stitch or muse. That may be the privelege of age, but she has lost her spark. It is for that, more than else that I fear. Thomas, she is gentled!

And two days later:

> Yr sister Nancy and Mother have this morning gone to Buck Island for a few days, so we are alone. . . . Stephen Willis has begun to plaister the Hall, and oh my deer! it looks so well! Mr. Reynolds has begun the stairs, and has a mort of turn'd pillasters, but says that he'll wait on your Approval on these before laying them in. I can see no difference from the Drawings, tho'. . . . that Ewe of Molly Page's has some trouble in the Udder. The milk is quite off. We thought it may be what she Et, so penned her up, but it continues. Garth is as perplexed as I. It isn't worms, for we dosed her. Are sheep subject the intermittent or billious Fever as we?

He wrote back saying that she had afforded him a curious diversion, pondering the inner processes of sheep, which teasing she took in good humor, for the rest of his letter was filled with news of a less diverting nature.

> . . .this was duly drawn by mr John Rutlege of South Carolina. . .not accepted, the writing not being of the calibre desired. thus

i and mr. Dickenson of Pennsylvania were added to the committee. . . . it would not be untruthful to say mr Dickinson is an avowed conservative, to whose heart the courtesies of public addresses and the soft answer that turneth away wrath are dear; he is in great hopes for a reconciliation with England, and the notion of offending Crown and Parliament he has admitted is distasteful to him. . . when i laid my draught before him in our committee, he made some few corrections to the text and appended many queries as to the advisability of certain passages remaining, mostly concerning the history and theory of imperial relations. . . . i will confess to being unwilling to concede so much. . . and went back to my rooms to prepare another draught to lay before the committee of the whole. . . . i will say that I have no personal acrimony for mr. Dickenson he is an honest man, an upright man, and fair, howsoever, i cannot agree with him on this matter, and fear our paper shews our differing views.

. . .friend D__ has laid before the body of Congress a petition to the King, assurising our undying affection for his majestie's person, and pleading his indulgence and influence to release us from the horrors of civil strife. . . the warmer members of our company poured much scorn on this effort. . . . we have heard from Arthur Lee that the aforesaid resolution was recieved by the King with contempt. . .

Late in July, he wrote that he had been nominated:

. . .by our committee to draught resolutions on Lord North's conciliatory proposal, and it was accepted by the committee and Congress as a whole with only minor changes. . . that we are now obliged to act as a whole, and cannot consent to treating with the Ministry on an individual basis.

By the ninth of August, he wrote that all of the Virginia men save Col. Lee were returned to Williamsburg to the Convention; and on the last day of Congress's sitting, that she may expect him as soon as may be after the business at Williamsburg is concluded. Glad as she was of such news, by the time it was received she had other concerns which pushed joyful anticipation from her mind.

44

Jane Randolph

Monticello

There was a rash of summer colds among the children. The Garths were the first to have it, then the Willises, the Reynoldses, and finally Patsy and Jane. Patsy stood against it the longest of any child, being taken ill a full week after her sister, so that Patty at first thought she may not have it at all. Her case was mild, too. Some lethargy, a slight fever, a congested head, a touch of quinsy, and that was all. By the time she had it, though, some alarming signs were seen in the other households that this was no mere summer malaise. And then there was Jane.

It was the sad truth of such epidemics that the smallest and frailest must suffer most, and by the time Thomas came home on the twenty-third it was plain that she was gravely ill. A severe quinsy and dull fever lasted out a week. By the time September dawned white patches of evil-smelling stuff appeared on the child's throat. She could not eat and wanted warm liquids only. Patty didn't have to be told what was wrong with her.

Desperately she consulted her herbal and every person with the smallest knowledge of physic, and applied all reasonable remedies. She omitted, for instance, an application of dung because she was seriously doubtful of its efficacy, and it seemed a cruel thing to subject a sick child to. She dosed Janey instead with calomel and a strong anodyne tincture of skullcap and lobelia. The sores were washed in goldenseal and powdered myrrh several times throughout the day and night to try and stay the killing formation of membrane across the throat. This required constant nursing.

She would not leave the child but slept in the chair when she could, and had food brought in. Such devotion at her own expense caused one of the worst altercations she and Thomas ever had.

She had promised, in Betty's presence, to let Nancy nurse the child, for Nancy had had the throat distemper already, and to take some rest. Thus promised, Thomas went out on his rounds with Thomas Garth. She did try to rest, and perhaps could have done if the sickroom was not also her own chamber, but along about the middle of the morning Betty and Nancy were trying to swab down Jane's throat, and she was choking and crying so weakly and pitifully that Patty couldn't bear it. It only took the one word, "Mama!" to send her flying over to snatch up her baby.

"Hush, love," she murmured, cradling the child against her. "Hush, bud, Mama's here, Mama's right here. Hush, shh, sweet." She rocked Janey until she was quiet again, sitting on the edge of the trundle with her knees up to her chest. She moved away then and looked into the dull eyes of her baby, smoothing her tossed blonde hair from her face.

"Mama's baby," she said. "My Janey." She kissed her forehead. "I know you don't like the bathe, but we must do it, sweet, to make you better." There was no response to this from Jane. "Would you let Mama do it if I'm extra gentle, Baby? There's a good child." Janey winced, swallowing, and nodded. Patty kissed her again. "My good girl. Fetch me that linting," she said to Betty.

Nancy and Betty held Janey's hands and feet while she gingerly swabbed the child's throat and dosed her with calomel. This she promptly vomited up; and so the floor, her clothes, and the bedclothes had to be changed. Patty was just handing over the pile of sheets for Betty's removal when the door opened and Thomas came in.

She met his gaze over Betty's shoulder and saw the raised eyebrow and the taut jaw. She raised her head, though her heart was hammering at his expression. He crossed his arms. "Leave us," he said in a quiet, even tone to her servant. Bett nodded without a word and was out the door. Nancy had gone to see to dinner, so they were alone.

"What do you think you're doing?" He didn't raise his voice, but his words were more measured than usual, and there was about his eyes a hard greenish glint that quailed her.

"Seeing to my child." She replied as calmly. "She was sick, and I couldn't leave it to Bett."

He advanced a step and her courage failed her. She retreated several, until she came up against the end of the trundle. His eyes were narrowed speculatively.

"You were supposed to be resting. You gave me your word on it." Again, he did not raise his voice. It was not his way. But she had seen his transactions with errant stable hands who didn't cool down or comb out a horse properly after a hard ride, and she understood their vivid fear now. It was not physical violence she was afraid of, for he would never strike her, but words that could be harder than any blow.

"I know," she admitted. "I tried, but could not." She made a gesture backwards. "She— they—" She drew in a breath and summoned her courage. "They were trying to bathe her throat and she was frightened. They weren't gentle enough and she wanted me. Thomas, I couldn't let her cry for me when I was a dozen steps away! I couldn't let them go on; it was unbearable!"

"Did you think them incapable?" he asked, almost conversationally.

She faltered. "Well, no. . . well, yes, if you must! The child was terrified!"

He glanced over at the sleeping Jane, all flushed cheeks and dark circles. "Doubtless she was," he agreed, his eyes on her again. He advanced slowly as he spoke, and every word was precise. "But I have seen her struggle the same with you." He took her arms, gently but firmly. "Why must you think you're the only one who can do anything right, who can look after the children, the kitchen, or whatever other fool thing you get into your head? Come here and sit with me."

It was not a request. Purposefully he led her over to the far side of the bed before the window, her side, and sat her down. He did not release her arms, but faced her squarely. She trembled under his hands but he paid no mind.

"Patty, for the love of God, I thought I could trust you to keep your word on so simple a matter as rest for yourself. I thought I could trust you to do, if not for your own sake then for ours, because I asked you to, for honor's sake." He shook his head. "But you do it every single time. Why are you so stubborn and willful? Every time I turn around you're wearing yourself out over this thing or that, and the only reason you can offer is that no one else does it as well as you. Well, I'm sorry to inform you, everyone else around here is not incompetent! Some of us are capable of managing quite well if given half a chance, but no, you must be vain about your management and skills and take on more than you're ever capable of doing, and then complain because you are worn out. Truth to tell, I'm sick to death of it!

"You may ignore what nature is trying to tell you, but I have to look at you, and cannot. Can you tell me how many meals have gone uneaten and how many nights unslept since this sickness began? Likely not, but if you are too busy to pick up a looking glass and see the effects, I am not." He picked up her hand mirror from the stool beside the bed where her hairbrush and other small articles lay and put it before her. His voice was hoarse.

"Here, look on what you've wrought!" She would not. He went on, "You've not had this distemper, I seem to recall. You may think such sacrifice noble or pure or your bounden duty, but it's not! By God, I have no intention of losing you to this or a consumption for vanity's sake!" He tossed the mirror away and took her arms again, not so gently this time. "I've never been in favor of the old manner of marriage, whereby I am the master and you my humble chattel bound to do as I say, but good God, you force me to it! Do I need to say it? Do I, Patty?"

She stubbornly said nothing but stared at him grimly, breathing hard, struggling with her own temper. How dare he? How dare he? Let him say, then, and he'd have an earful of hard words himself!

A muscle in his jaw twitched, and his eyes were very green. "Very well," he spat out in disgust. "I forbid you to have anything to do with that child's care for the next twenty-four hours, and if I find or hear of you being anywhere near her, so help me, I'll take a horsewhip to you."

She wrenched herself from his grasp at last. Idle threat or not, she would not be threatened or dictated to. "You do so, and it's the last you'll have of me," she swore, rising. She was no longer cold. At something of a disadvantage, being hardly taller standing than he was seated, she nevertheless gave vent to her ire.

"Thomas Jefferson, you are the most high-handed, conceited, distracting man I ever met! Why do you think you know what's best for me and everyone else? No matter what I do, you've always a better idea about how it should be done or run or thought of. Do you think I haven't a brain in my head, or the common sense I was born with? I grant you, I may not have the faculties that you yourself possess, but I am capable of looking after things to a satisfactory degree! Don't you think I know when I'm too tired for something? I should know better than you! Don't you think I know when time is enough and I can do no more! I can tell you, I've seen enough of life and death to know those things. I don't need you nor anyone else to tell me how to look after myself. I am not simpleminded, woman though I may be.

"If I was half so soft and helpless, so idle as you wish, you'd complain then that I was incapable of order and wonder at my wits. You can't have it both ways, my dear!" She gazed at him scornfully, but even in her agitation managed to bite back the words that came to her tongue next. They would never be forgiven, let alone forgotten, and she had the presence of mind to halt.

He was livid, his face a cold mask, and when he rose, casually enough, a small thrill of fear went through her. He was better than a foot taller than she and outweighed her by five-and-a-half stone. Most of the time this was a comfort, that she was literally under his protection, but at the moment it was intimidating. She was forced to look up at him, for they were not five inches apart.

"I never thought we'd come to this," he said in a leaden voice. "You sound just like my mother. I never thought to hear such a harangue from you. I had thought you were sweet." He laid his hands on her shoulders.

"I would be sweet," she countered, "if I may be trusted to be intelligent. As to your mother, perhaps her harangue," she paused on the word, "was just because she felt her views discounted, and it was the only way to be heard."

She struck a nerve with that, for he drew in his breath.

"That's as may be, but it doesn't bear on us. I—"

"I think it does." She spoke the words quietly but with force. She met his gaze levelly. They had travelled this road before but she would not yield now. She would make him understand the effect his well-intentioned dominance had on her.

"What do you mean?"

"I mean," she said, striving for an even tone, "that you have let your rancor with her affect your view of how women are, or should be. I mean that you have too often told me my business, and I have allowed it without speaking up. But I will speak up." She made a gesture toward the girls. "I bore those two, at great peril to myself. I've guarded them and guided them to the best of my abilities. I am responsible for their lives in the most fundamental way. Do you think," she spat out the words, "that I will sit by a moment and watch them suffer when I might aid them? For the love of God!" Tears came to her eyes and she shook her head angrily. She would not break down now, not weaken her cause. "My baby's life hangs in the balance at this moment. How can you ask me to sit by and do nothing?" The tears spilled over, and she was unable to stop them. "Thomas, I would gladly exchange my life for hers! I would do anything, anything, that my sweet baby should be spared! It is my right, my privilege, not my duty, to do so! I owe her it. Ah, don't you see?"

Tears were pouring down her face and she was hiccoughing hysterically, for she had not eaten or slept much that day and was on the raw edge of nerves. He stood now, his face troubled, holding her arms, but gently now, as the hurt poured from her, long buried but deeply wounding for all that.

"You seem to forget," she hiccoughed, "that I have buried a child ere this, and I know that pain! Before God, I will not suffer it again, not if I have an ounce of strength to give! I have not forgotten Jack!" she hiccoughed. "I let. . . let that wretched man do his deed at my father's insistence, against every instinct I possessed, and he died before my eyes. I'd as fain have murthered him my. . . myself. You may order as you like; you may. . . you may threaten, nay do what you like but I will not yield one inch on this. What sort of mother would I be if I did? Oh, it's all as one to men! 'Tis but to get another and call it contended, but you do not risk your life for love to have it flung in your face as sel. . . selfishness!"

He was staring at her, dumbstruck, and she turned away, leaning her head against the bedpost. When he would have embraced her she waved her hand. "Oh don't!" she cried. "I won't be coz. . . cozened! "

"Cozened!" He spoke as one who'd had the breath knocked out of him. He pulled her away from her sanctuary, and she collided with him by the force.

"I can only think that you're overwrought to say such a thing," he said in low, fierce tones. "For I know you wouldn't otherwise call love and concern cozening." He lifted her chin. "Look at me!" She hadn't much choice, crushed as she was against him.

"What I've bade you I have done from the deepest feeling I have ever borne any human being. If your belief of that is so shallow as to cause you to think it conceit, then we have done one another and them," he nodded toward the children, "the most grievous wrong, for it has no remedy in this world or the next." He paused a long while, and she realized through her nervous haze that he was weeping with the most terrible, noiseless sobs.

"Don't you think," he burst out after a time, "that I have been as distraught as you over this? Nay, more so because I could do nothing but watch! It tears my heart out by the hour!" He clung to her now shaking, clutching her so tightly that she could scarcely breathe.

"And then to watch you wear yourself out before my eyes, to waste your fragile strength, and know that I may lose not only Jane but you too because of it—God, what anguish I felt! And you gave your word, your sacred, blessed, trusted word to rest yourself awhile, and I come back, only to find you looking ready to faint away! And then to be accused that I do not love you— Patty, I would die for you, you are my soul! God, do you really think so ill of me? I can't bear it!"

In some wise, they had come to sit on the bed again, and she found herself half in his lap. For a very long time they sat thus, embraced and silent, until the tremors stopped and they were calmer. Thomas raised his head. His hair was in disorder, and his amber eyes were red and inflamed. His mother's beloved son looked out from those eyes, seeking the assurance he needed as air to breathe. "Say you love me," he pleaded.

She looked up at him searchingly, not quite sure where they had been, but glad that they had found a shore. She raised her hand to his cheek and kissed him fervently. "I love you," she swore. "Upon my eternal soul, I do." She kissed him again. "Forgive me, dearest," she said. "It was all my—"

He put a finger to her lips. "Nay." He shook his head. "You'll not blame yourself," he said softly, and kissed her burning eyes. "We have much to discuss, you and I." He caressed her fallen hair from her face. "And so we will."

But they had no chance that evening, nor for a long time after, for just after midnight, Baby gave up her struggling against the throat distemper to join the angels in holy chorus. Alerted to the final throes by her gargling breaths, they stumbled from bed and removed Patsy from her place, laying her in their bed and closing the curtains. They called in no one, for naught else was to be done for the child, and they had little enough privacy. They sat on the little bed together, holding her in their laps, with Thomas tilting back her head trying to make some passage for air, but she was so small that it was in vain. The membrane was too thick. The clock had barely struck half-past twelve when she ceased her flailing and was quiet. Their Jane, their sweet Jane, was gone.

No more, bright cherub, would she dance her way among the summer flowers singing her tuneless songs to bring them some treasure she had found. No more dear little face to greet them with rosy cheeks of a morning, clamoring to be let up on their bed. No more petted Baby for Patsy's playmate to mother and scold in fond imitation of those around her. Their angel was no more.

She had never caused an hour's trouble in all her life, had never been anything but sweetly compliant and blessedly contented from the hour of her birth. Even in her sickness she had troubled them little, rousing herself only against the painful swabbing of her poor raw throat. Seventeen months was all she'd known of life, but she'd brought greater joy in that time than many another longer-lived.

Patty was disconsolate. She took to bed and remained there a week, too distraught to go to the funeral and so violent of grief that Thomas was afraid to leave her alone. He postponed his journey to Philadelphia, for he was due there on the ninth, and spent his time beside her, coaxing her to life despite his own pain, endeavoring to cheer her, to comfort her in some way, to drive that awful haunted look from her eyes.

She ate but by his hand, and that precious little, and grew thinner. She would have no comfort in poetry or flowers for a fortnight, and the sight of Patsy brought her tears afresh. Nights were worse, for the days brought distractions, and they spent many a night lying awake until dawn. He cradled her in his arms, smoothing her burnished hair and listening to her tales of other griefs until he saw starkly how fragile she really was. So much buffeted by life long ere they met and overmuch since, he began to see her stubbornness as a defence against the exigencies of fate, and forgave without asking the harsh words that had been spoken, for they came from her deepest fear.

He played for her on his cousin Randolph's dear-bought violin. His kinsman, Peyton's brother, had given in at last to his sense of honor about the impending separation of colony from mother country and departed for England, but not before honoring a bargain they had long ago struck; the precious, coveted fiddle was had for thirteen pounds odd, but her acquisition in such a manner was as ash in his mouth. But he played for her, for its compass was sweet, and the sound of her favorite pieces brought her a bit of cheer. He read to her in the evenings, from Spencer and Marlowe and Donne. The songs and sonnets of the latter she loved; she would not bear the eulogies, and when the time came that he must go, as it inevitably did, it was to Donne he turned to leave her some consolation.

It was much against his desires that public duty needs must call him away at such a time, but he was already very late and could not delay longer. If there was a way under heaven that he could have remained without forcing a scene with the sergeant-at-arms he would have availed of it. As it stood, she found a scrap of paper in her sewing basket the morning after his departure, copied out in his small neat hand:

> Sweetest love, I do not goe,
>   For wearinesse of thee,
> Nor in hope the world can show,
>   A fitter love for mee;
> But since that I
>   Must dye at last, 'tis best,
> To use my selfe in jest
>   Thus by fain'd deaths to dye;
>
> Yesternight the Sunne went hence,
>   And yet is here to day,
> He hath no desire nor sense,
>   Nor halfe so short a way:
> Then feare not mee,
>   But beleeve that I shall make
> Speedier journeyes, since I take
>   More wings and spurres than hee.
>
>   . . .
>
> When thou sigh'st, thou sigh'st not winde,
>   But sigh'st my soule away,
> When thou weep'st, unkindly kinde,
>   My lifes blood doth decay. . .
>
>   . . .
>
> Let not thy divining heart
>   Forethinke me any ill,
> Destiny may take thy part,
>   And may thy fears fulfill;
> But thinke that wee
>   Are but turned aside to sleep;
> They who one another keepe
>   Alive, ne'er parted bee.

45

Mortal Plague

The Forest, Monticello

September 30. 1775.
Philadelphia.
Sweet Hero—

this to let you know that I am safely arrived. my course in following the mountains brought me here a full day ahead of what i expected, and i encountered none of the Difficulties of my last journey. did you find my note? i had thought it's place not too obscure as you are ever at your Needle and with the idleness of the journey hoped you might take up that Emploiment. i pray it gave you some Comfort and indication of my sentiment, if indeed such avowals are required to us. i hope you are better now, and that the Journey did not prove too taxing. i will not rest easy until I hear from your own hand that you are well and begun some recovery of Spirit. let mrs Eppes and her charming new friend distract your mind, and the Comfort of childhood's home bring you peace. kiss my Pats for me and remember me to her often. i miss you both.

there is some news from out our northern Borders. you will recall the last we had from that Quarter, Arnold and his Troop gone after the battle at Boston to secure the safety of Quebec. there is word now, come down by Gen'l Schuyler's adjunctant, of a skirmish on the St Lawrence. according to the report, Colo-Allen's men made thier way sucessfully by boat to Lake Champlain, with a view to the capture of St. John's and Montreal. about the third inst. they reached the Fort St John's and during the attack Gen'l Schulyer was taken so ill from the arduous journey and bad food that he needs must turn over the command of the Enterprise to Montgomery. the latter prepared for seige and Schuyler was borne home to New York. we have no further word, but it is hoped that this show of arms may induce the French there, who patently have to love of English rule, to join our Cause and thereby distract the enemy with the necessity of having to fight on two fronts.

may tranquility attend my dear Patty-patt, and the belief that tho' distance may separate us and larger concerns of the world's Affairs occupy my mind, they are not of graver import to me than the happiness of my sweet girl and the Memory of the fire thro' which we have pas'd. all my love an affections are eternally yours alone, no matter what may transpire. believe me, love, that I am ever your devoted

. . .there is little of consequence going on here. believe me that I would prefer to be where you are. even the company of mr. and Mrs. Wythe is no balm, tho' they endeavour to draw me Out of myself, insisting i accompany them many an evening to mrs. Hill's.

And late in October:

why have you not wrote? have you taken ill yourself of the throat distemper? if that is so, i pray you may assign some kindly Lieutenant to let me kno it. i cannot bear not hearing from you. are you so low that you cannot write, do your eyes trouble you? i am put in mind of your complaints of them before I departed. mayhap delivering you to such a proximity of mrs Eppes' new Friend was not the wisest course, but i could not bear the thought of you all alone at monticello. . . i have wrote to every single person of our acquaintance for some word of you, but have not recieved a single reply from any one. i am begun to think all on my country are dead. . .

Then, on the twenty-second:

i was out at mrs. H__'s today for dinner with Speaker Randolph, the Nelsons, &c—when in the midst of the meal my good cousin, who sat beside me at table, paused in his speech and siezed Up. we thought him at first to be choking, but it proved a fit of apoplexy, and by eight aclock in the evening he was dead. O! that i sho'd have to write such words!

the Randolphs are stript from us as if by some mortal plague. first our Attorney General, who may as well be as one dead to us, for all there be three thousand miles of relentless sea between us, and now our beloved Speaker. what comfort can attend his poor widow and us, left behind thus bereft? i recall too many memories of him to lay them all on paper; they would encompass volumes. at the moment, i recall one memory, cherished to my heart, that were it not for his Invitation, i would not have met my sweet Diana. there is no repaiment of that gift, as there is no replacement of our fair friend. what next? my mind misgives. i can only hope this harvest is at an end. i have writ mrs Peyton with my condolences, and enclose them herewith, trusting that my gentle-hearted one will convey them to her by some means. adieu for now, sweet.

In the second week of November came:

> i have paid a visit to mrs. Byrd, lately arrived in town, hoping that she may afford me some word of you, but she professed not to kno that you were in charles City. as you love me, i pray you send some word to relieve the anxious mind of your poor courtier as soon as may be, if not by your own Hand, then by another's. i am in agonies here not knowing, and cannot think or accomlish the least work for worrying over your condition. please, please, my dear as you love me, send some balm of kindness my way!

In Charles City Patty was low, but not so low as she knew Thomas was fearing. She was having some trouble with her eyes again and for a fortnight was unable to endure any light brighter than evening's candles. She spent the day in her room with the windows curtained and shuttered, unable to read, write, or sew, enveloped with lethargy, spells of weakness, and irritability wherein the least noise would send her into fits of weeping. She couldn't fathom what was wrong and was weekly more depressed by the continuing letters from Philadelphia pleading her to write. She had Francis's assurance that he had written every week, with an explanation of her malaise, but there was yet no word that his letters had been received. At length, on the tenth, she was able to write her own letter, and prayed that it would be received:

> My deerest beloved,
>
> I would first seek to ease your mind about the Gravity of our Situation. There is a general rumour hereabouts that the Post has been interfered with by order of our friend Dnr. While whatever you may have there heard about the late Engagement at Nor folk are for the greater part true, in truth I know not what wild Rumours may have reach'd you, I will endeavour to ease your Mind that we here are all safe and well.
>
> Francis assures me that he has wrote you severall times with news of how we fare, but with the difficulties of the Post, I expect they have gone Astray. I will be frank that I have not wrote before this, but only because I have been incapable of doing so, being much troubled by my eyes and a malaise I can ascribe only to mourning. I have spent the better part of ev'ry Day in a closed room, unable to bear the light. Reading or sewing were out of the question, so I beg

my love's pardon for my remissness. My own *carus cariad* should know I would not *willfully* neglect him. I must close now dearest as even this Little has begun to strain my eyes. I will write more anon, of that you have my firm Promise. Patsy bids me send you kisses, so keep some of those also from yr loving,

Ma Jefferson

By the alarums of Lord Dunmore she referred to the late engagement at Norfolk and Hampton between the Virginia militia and Dunmore's troops, and to the reaction throughout Virginia to the King's proclamation of 23 August, printed in Purdie's *Gazette*, declaring the American colonies to be in a state of open and avowed rebellion.

In response to this, Thomas sent her a letter wrote putting forward a plan to get her and the family out of harm's way:

> i would urge you, my sweet, not from tyrany or conceit that i alone know what's best for you, for at this distance that would be foolish indeed, but from love and the utmost concern for your safety, to take yourselves, by stages if needs be, to Eppington or Elk Hill. i am aware of the probable necessity of having this journey made in short jaunts, a progress if you will, due to your own difficulties and those of mrs Eppes. but if you go by way of Varina and Ampthill you may lodge awhile with the Skipwiths and thereby avoid Richmond and the river. you could cross to Tuckahoe by way of Jones creek—it should not be swollen there at this date—and be at Elk Hill for Christmas. i could meet you there, you and the Eppeses, i mean, for I don't see as how we'll get a recess much before Christmas. this is the least arduous route I can think of, and would not require much in the way of ferriage.

When they arrived at Tuckahoe, she was passed a letter by Col. Tom from Thomas, saying that he was delayed yet at Philadelphia, so to not wait on him and to so expect him instead at Monticello. This brought her no cheer, for she had been hoping to spend their anniversary together. This would be the first they had missed, and it saddened her. Nevertheless, there was nothing for it, so she sent him a note when they came to Elk Hill:

> Elk Hill. . . Little cheared as I am by the prospect of missing you at Christmas, and the One Day, I am consoled that you shall not miss Twelfth Night. But I expect the loss to be made up for. . . . The gods speed your journey, my Leander, for we are most Impatient to see you. The lanterns are ablaize from the Island upwards. Do hurry, sweet. . . .

He had missed a good many anniversaries in the execution of public duties—Patsy's birthday, her birthday, Christmas, and now their wedding's also. But she understood the importance of his work, no matter that he complained of its drudgery. For out of his innumerable committees and drafting of papers, he was becoming known outside of Virginia, and letters were handed onto her from Mrs. Wythe and Mrs. Nelson and others, full of the praise of Mr. Jefferson of Virginia, from persons she had never heard of nor was ever likely to meet.

He arrived at the mountain in the failing light of afternoon on the third day of the new year, with his horse heaving asthmatically under him. It was bitterly cold, and as he and his servants took their ascent of the road it began to snow. There had been an early snowfall before Christmas, unusual for Virginia, which brought to alert minds the warning dusting of snow on the northerly-most parts of the Blue ridge back in September. It put to her mind also their wedding journey, but at least now there was a better welcome awaiting than a frozen dark chamber on a windswept summit.

They were heard before they reached the top of the road, and a shout went up from the stable lads. In an instant, frozen snow or not, the place was alive with people pouring out from every building. Patty snatched up her dark cloak and hood from the parlor chair and flung them on anyhow. Struggling with her mittens, she ran out also into the dark night to fling herself on him with a cry. He was here at last! "My dear!" Snatching her up, he swung her around in a glad embrace, and she murmured for his ears alone when he set her on her feet, "O Tom, I missed you so." He smiled down at her his rare smile, taking in every aspect of her face and figure.

"You look fine," he said with pleasure, taking her mittened hand.

They made their way to the parlor amid greetings on every side, and dear it was to see the house so, lighted up and welcoming against the lowering sky. The dining room, the only room begun on their first arrival here, was permanently articulated to the parlor and hall and south chamber. The final lines of the house were evident now in the reaches of the first floor. All that wanted was a roof to begin the second. In what to ordinary eyes looked the raw bare bones of a habitable dwelling, they saw as the melody of his symphonic piece. It lacked yet chords and grace notes, the niceties accompaniment, but those would come. The simplicity of the melody was haunting on its own: pure, chaste, forever fresh and beautiful.

In the parlor the company waited in the warmth for his arrival: his mother and sister and the Lewises with their children, a tidy little family gathering. This number had been lately added to by the advent of baby Charles, snug and warmly ensconced in his basket before the fire, plump and sweet as a plum duff. She pointed out with pride the new fireplace mantel, painted in trompe l'oeil by Will Reynolds, and their beautiful staircase with its turned pilasters made to his design. Lucy saw him squinting at the changes in the parlor and teased, "You'd hardly recognize the place, would you?"

"Aye," he agreed, looking about.

Though the house lacked yet its Palladian orders, it was by no means unadorned. She had hung the dining room, hall, and parlor in Christmas greens, and every door and window frame was festooned in holly and ivy and twining red ribbon.

"You should visit your own house more often," she murmured, handing him a toddy of arrack punch. She wore tonight the same blue silk gown and cherry petticoat he had met her in, looped up now without hoops, with the ends of the skirt pulled up through the pocket slits *a lá polonaise*, for hoops were quite out of fashion. She wore too the silver and garnet Randolph necklace.

"I had the receipt for this from your mother," she said, urging him to drink.

"Is it so, Mama?" he asked Mrs. Jefferson. She had not heard him call her that affectionate name in all their days. Not in five years. Jane sat on the sofa, cheerily toasting her feet before the fire and admiring her newest grandson. She turned her head. "Aye," she smiled, contented in the family gathering and its attendant memories of Christmas seasons past. "And she had the story of it, too, so she knows the price of her house."

He drank more of the toddy. "A song," he said to Patty.

"Aye," she agreed, looking up at him. "It echoes still." He laid his hand on her back above her stays in a discreet caress, speaking of others to come. She trembled at the contact and hoped fervently that it was not noticed. But she had missed him. Letters, even enciphered letters, could not make up the lack.

46

Under My Own Roof
Monticello

The snow continued to fall steadily throughout supper and the evening. By ten o'clock it was plain that travelling, even to Buck Island by the Thoroughfare, was out of the question. Getting down the mountain would prove a feat. Besides, it would be most unsafe to subject baby Charles to the rigors of the weather, for he was only two months old. The Lewises must stay the night. The instruments were put away and the hymnals closed from their pages of carols, while the extra beds were brought up from the cellar and linen from the chest in the passageway. The children were put down closest to the fire, and the company broke up, everyone willing to retire.

She hurried across the frigid expanse of the yard with Thomas to the little house. Hand in hand, dodging the snow-covered debris they ran, laughing at the shocking chill of the air, their breath blowing white in the darkness before them. Inside the chamber it was twenty-six degrees, with the embers of a fire glowing in the hearth.

As he laid more wood on the fire, he turned to where she was covering Patsy with an extra quilt. "I remember a night when this was our refuge from the snow." He rose and put the poker aside.

"Aye," she said, her heart racing. She went nearer him, recalling sweetly the wine and the strains of Pachelbel, and a better homecoming after. "And I remember the result," she continued softly, glancing down. She put her cold hand on his chest, and he covered it with his own. Such contact, after such an absence, made it difficult to speak. It would be too easy to play the hoyden. But then, O then, they would miss this awful tension; that was as much a part of the game as love itself. At such times, some other part of her mind put into play, and she could always find just the right witty or provoking words. It had ever been so, even with Batt.

"Do you think, sir," she continued, raising her head to meet his eyes fully, "that history may repeat itself?" They stood a few inches apart, and the space was magnetic. It was easy to see by the green in his eyes that he wanted to close it, but he would play her game.

"It may be so," he murmured, taking a step. "One has but to look at the. . . conquests—" He paused on the word and laid a hand on her hair.

"Of Alexander and Caesar. . ." She watched him, waiting breathless. ". . .To see that one may trod a former path to equal—" He swallowed and nuzzled his cheek against the softness of her hair. "Or greater. . . glories." He moved away a little.

"Don't you think?" he asked softly. She was undone.

In the warm light her color was warmer still, a fervent blush across her cheeks that crept downwards on her neck. He traced its line with a finger, along her collarbone. A pulse beat there, rapid as a bird's, and she closed her eyes a long moment. The hand he had held was no longer cold.

"Of course," he went on, "one must always test such . . . hypotheses. . . in a scientific manner." He bent and kissed her forehead and temple, where the small curls rebelliously sprang. She was trembling. "Don't you agree?" He lifted her chin with his fingers.

She gave a wordless murmur, and forfeited the game. He kissed her. Time melted away in that instant, and the three months of his absence were as nothing and forever. They closed two sides of the bed curtains, a compromise between privacy and warmth, and put an end to clever artifice.

"So, is your loss suitably made up for?" he asked her later. They were labored now under the weight of the disordered quilts. The candle burned beyond her on the stool. They had no idea of the time, for the view of the clock was blocked by the lining of the bed curtain. She laughed, a low sound in her throat, and regarded him with eyes flecked green and orange. "I would call it a beginning," she judged.

He shouted with laughter. "I should have expected that from you, saucebox," he said, tracing the line of her nose with a finger. He cleared his throat. "Well, now that you're suitably warmed to my purposes, I have a proposal for you."

Her mouth curled up on one side, revealing a dimple. "Sirrah? I had rather thought you'd have enough of that for the time."

He blushed. "It's not indecent!" he protested.

She shrugged a little. "As you wish."

"No," he said, his face sobering. He pulled the quilt up about her shoulder from where it had fallen and gazed into the past weeks of distance from her. "When I was in Philadelphia," he began, "I gave some thought to the matter of our misunderstanding and how we should resolve it, for—" He kissed her lightly. "We shouldn't pass it over, or labor under it either. For our own sake, we should know the other's mind, that we may not wrangle over a difference in temperament." He sighed heavily. "So, what I had in mind is that we could each state our cause and arbitrate it accordingly. Mmm?"

She would rather forget their altercation over Jane. She looked up at him. "Must we now?" she queried, settling herself against him. He moved her hand.

"If we don't now, we never shall," he reasoned. "Would you have us as my parents?"

Hardly that! She shook her head. "Nay," she sighed, and sat up. "Very well. An assize it is. Who speaks first?"

He bit his lip, smiling a little. "Well, I wouldn't dare to call who in this case is prosecution or defence, for fear of coming up the latter, but you may, as a lady's privilege." He shifted and moved the pillow better between his head and the frigid wall.

She bowed her head in acquiescence and thought a moment. "You know my history," she said at last. "And I plead that as excuse. Perhaps I was too well indulged, but from the age of fifteen years I was the mistress of my father's house, and all such decisions fell to me. You well may say that I was spoilt, and perhaps I am, but I was trained to such business and entrusted with free rein. Papa never questioned my actions or, to my mind, presumed to advise me of my business, trusting that I could manage. And I did! When I married Bathurst—" She looked up at him quickly, unsure of the safety of the subject, and he nodded. "He was so often gone from Elk Hill on his practice, or occupied with it when at home, that I never thought to trouble him with household matters. I grew used to doing things myself in my own way, with no one offering opinions. I felt secure in the trust of mine abilities. No one questioned how I spent my time, for good or ill.

"You must remember—" she sought his gaze beseechingly, "that I daily question our people as to their business that I may be sure it's being done to my satisfaction. . ." She paused. "And I know how exacting you are!" She faltered. "When you question me, or suggest a plan, or tell me I should manage things else, I feel you think I'm incompetent, and I know I'm not! It puts me on a level with the servants, or Patsy." Her look was rueful. "And I am too proud for that. I suppose I am spoilt," she admitted at last.

He caressed her face. "Nay, sweet, not spoilt. A bit headstrong maybe, but not spoilt." He coaxed a reluctant smile out of her. "Now, as for me—" He leaned back against the pillows looking into the distance of time. "I plead two things. First, my history too, sweet, is responsible for my actions. When my father died I was left as head of the family, and the welfare of every person in it was my charge." He held up a hand. "I know, I didn't take this on immediately but I felt it. And later, since I was back and forth to Williamsburg so much I was charged with supplying many concerns you may think out of my sphere." He paused.

"And there was my mother," he said at last. "It was *her* house, by right of my father's will, and she ran it as such— Oh, you know!" he burst out. She could say nothing in the face of his revelations about his mother. "It was an agony, her refusing to let me have any real responsibility, while intimating that I should; insisting I go off to my studies, then complaining that I was unsociable in pursuit of them. So when I built here I had an idea that I should know what went on in my own house, should not be shut off from its comings and goings. Do you see?" He gazed at her imploringly.

"I do," she said quietly.

"Secondly," he continued, "my reason is that I love you, and am concerned for your welfare." He smiled a little. "Oh, you may think it merely an aspect of the first, that I want to run everything you do, and it may be so. But—" He lifted her face and searched her warm brown eyes a long moment, willing that she understand. "When I see you working yourself into a state of collapse it tears my heart. If I lost you—" His voice caught. "If I did, I would be lost forever." He kissed her fervently. "You are my sun and moon, my guiding star. I—

"Before I met you I had a dream for three years in the summertime. I used to come here and study and sometimes slept rough. But I had this dream at Shadwell, too." He closed his eyes, speaking in hushed tones, "I could see. . . this house, unfinished, and I followed a woman from room to room, never catching her up. It was tantalizing, a game. She seemed ethereal, for no matter how quickly I followed, the distance between us remained. And she smiled. . . just that smile you have, that's not quite there. It was maddening. Afterward I could not recall her face but knew its lineaments in my heart." He looked down at her. She saw the pulse beat in his throat. "When I saw you at Randolph's it was like a shock, because I'd seen you before but never laid eyes on you. I know all this must sound pretty foolish, for who cares for dreams? But I swear by God that it's the truth."

She did not laugh. How could she, when she'd been subject to foreshadowing dreams herself? She frowned, "Did you ever have this dream since?"

He smiled. "Nay, not that one. Why should I? But plenty of others."

"I've heard those," she remarked drily. "And in truth, I wonder if they weren't a fancy to induce me to your design."

He laughed aloud now. "Since when did you ever need inducements?" he enquired. "I dareswear it was quite the other way round, and I, poor innocent, being lured."

She raised an eyebrow. "You, innocent! In fact, may be, but never in thought or intent. And there's an equal sin, or I much mistake St Paul."

"I still do," he said, with a look. "Married or no."

Her eyes were round with mock innocence. "Do what?" she asked, blinking.

He laughed and kissed her. "You minx!. . . Now, before I lose my wits entirely—" Her answer was a murmur, "What shall our arbitration be in our impasse?"

She pushed herself away from him, outraged. "You are the most wicked man! How can you be so cruel as to lead me along and then change the subject? I should go to sleep with Patsy!"

"You'd freeze if you did, for she takes all the covers," he said in amusement. "As for the other, it's only to keep you compliant, troublesome wench! But if you're nice," he murmured in a coaxing tone, "so will I be later." He gathered her into an embrace again. She caught her breath.

"That's blackmail, sirrah," she replied softly.

"Will you be cozened now?" he asked in a hush against her ear. Her answer was more of a sigh than affirmation.

"Oh yes."

"Hmm."

It would have been easy to ignore the needful matter, but he was long trained to discipline and continued after a time, "What shall we judge?" She stirred herself from him, rising to sit, and shook her head.

"I don't know. I would almost think it enough to know the reasons." She met his eye. "For my part, I feel ashamed for not intuiting yours. I should have known!" Her dark eyes glittered tears. "I will in future and will endeavor to remember it when I feel pressed. But as I said before, you must tell me, dearest, else I say what I will regret, as I do most bitterly!"

The shadow of Janey's death stood between them and their trouble, and while for the greater part, the anxiety over that oppresive event was the cause of it, there were yet basic differences that could only be allowed for, never removed. Grief had made a healing of their breach, but Thomas's orderly mind required a close to the matter.

He took her hands. "For my part, I am sorry, too, sweet. I know enough of your life to have been able to guess the purpose of your actions, and I should have been gentler. You shouldn't have to remind me of that. It was thoughtless of me, selfish too, after a fashion. I'm sorry." He caressed her hands with his thumbs. "For the other, I admit I do want to know what you're doing, but of curiosity only, and if I suggest a better way, it's only to ease your burthens and not because I think you incompetent. I will try to put my suggestions better." He smiled crookedly. "But I can't help making them! I welcome yours, too. The bow rooms, for instance, and the beer. I only wish it were feasible to move the laundry."

He sighed. "Oh, love, if we strive, we must do so together, not against each other! That way lies only distance. And I wouldn't be distant from my sweet girl." He leaned and kissed her, and while he did the clock struck two.

"It grows late," he murmured. She was weary, but his last words enlivened her. "I'm not tired."

"Hmm. Then put out the candle," he said fondly, "and close the curtains, for I have missed my sweet girl." She did as she was bid, and night descended on them at last.

Work on the plantation continued, however much she might have wanted for once to idle. There were hogs sent up from Bedford and a quantity of their own hogs and beeves killed and wanted rendering. A week after Thomas came home she recorded in her accounts:

> 15 hogs killed
> put in the sellar a jar that held 32 gallons of leaf fat two firkins & two iron pots of gut fat two stone pots of sauce fat and half a barrel of cracknels
> made 229 lb of hard soap 200 lb ditto soft

> to make rennet
> let the calf suck just before you kill it, then wash the bag & curd very clean, salt it and let it lie three days, put the curd in the bag with a little mace, and put the bag into a linen bag, when you use the curd boil the water, and let it stand til it is cold, then put the curd in, and let it lay twelve hours, then salt your curd and put it in the bag.

Some of this meat went to the workmen, but the rest was salted or smoked, made up into hams or bacon according to its manner. That which wasn't preserved they could keep because of the cold weather. She made a batch of candles as well as the soap but was too busy to record it. Her ewes in lamb gave forth their burdens, and so she had five new charges and a resultant plenty of sheep's milk. The ducks and geese, penned up against the cold, produced abundantly and went broody, and she allowed them most of their eggs, for there were plenty of chicken eggs for general use. Thomas bought a small herd of fair-tailed deer as a beginning of the long-planned deer park on the north side of the mountain. Ursula came back to work after the birth of her baby Isaac just before Christmas. In spite of the continuing winter blast there were signs everywhere that life was burgeoning.

History proved to move in twain. Late in February she found herself with all the familiar discomforts of early pregnancy, and this time was glad of them. Patsy would be four when this child was born and old enough to notice. She noticed already with some anxiety her Mama's tiredness and intermittent retches but was reassured that it was a small indisposition only. Nevertheless Patty was worried for such sharp eyes and quick wit, for what else did she notice that they would rather she did not? The child was getting too old to share a room with them. She purposed to Thomas, "Now that we have a roof, might we move into our chamber?"

He took off his riding coat—the dark, slender design he had copied from the Tuscans. "It's not even plastered yet, mrs impatience!" he teased.

She waved her hand. "No matter that, I don't mind it. But, my dear," she said soberly, "we have need of more space. Patsy has sharp eyes, and I don't think it fitting that she sleep with us much longer. She could have the dressing room, so would still be nearby, and we could close the door. I am not in favor of furthering her education that way, no matter how bright she is!"

Thomas had taken to giving her lessons in the mornings and afternoons. They studied mathematics, history, and Greek, and Patsy had no trouble with any; already she could add and subtract simple sums and write out all the Greek characters with remarkable clarity.

"I see what you mean," he said, frowning. His cheeks were scarlet from the cold air and exercise, and his hair was in disorder. He stood in shirtsleeves now, in the warm red flannel waistcoat she had made for him. "What would we do about the building?" Will Reynolds's men were already putting up scaffolding for the supports of the second floor.

"They wouldn't disturb our sleep." She picked up the linens again and took them over to the chest, laying them away amid the sprigs of lavender and thyme.

"It would mean little privacy though." They had no shutters for the windows on that part of the house yet, nor windows either for that matter, but relied on oilcloth as before.

"And we have so much now?" She closed the drawer and faced him again. "I would welcome it, my dear, if you're willing to it." She came over to where he sat on the bed pulling off his boots, and did it for him. "Not only for the sake of decency," she said, dropping one of the boots on the floor. "But because after four years I would actually get to sleep under my own roof. It's irksome that guests have done so long before me." She pulled up the heel of the other boot and it slipped off easily. She was left with frozen mud all across her apron, but it would wash and she was not disturbed.

"There's the rub," he said, smiling. "Thank you." He took his boots from her. "If you are so set on it, and in earnest don't mind living with wet plaster a few weeks, I can't think of an argument against you. Can you wait until it thaws a bit out?"

She clucked her tongue. "Yes!" She clasped her hands. "Oh, I'm so glad you said yes! It puts the sun in the whole dreary day." She took off her apron and exchanged it for a clean one.

"I need to go see to the soup. Could you herd that daughter of yours away from her giddy playmates while I do?" Patsy was down at the Willises' at the workmen's enclave on the south side of the mountain.

"I will. It'll give me an excuse to speak with Willis about the next firing."

The shift was made in the next fortnight and proved expeditious, for while they moved their things from the out-chamber to the south wing of the house, Nancy and her mother set up a permanent room there, which was easier on the old lady, as she now had some quiet place to repair to besides the dining room during the day. The hammering and knocking, the whistling and singing of the carpenters, sawyers, and masons, to say nothing of the disorder of the place, was hard on her nerves. Now she could sit before a solitary fire of an afternoon in contented peace, knitting or making lace as fancy took her, disturbed only by the occasional noise from the kitchen.

Mrs. Jefferson was slow these days, the late cold weather playing havoc on her rheumatic pains, and contrary to her former self, these complaints were borne gently and stoically. She seemed, Thomas remarked in some concern, like a clock winding down. Her decline was gradual with no marked sudden debility; nevertheless it was noted by her sharp-eyed son. He was gentle with her, where before he had been merely courteous, and allowed himself those marks of affection with her that he so freely gave to others, because she did not refuse or rebuff them. He called her "Mama" again, as he had not done since he was thirteen or fourteen years old, certainly not since his father died and she was so cold. He held her hand when enquiring did she require anything, and spent time reading to her or listening to her stories of her girlhood that he had had no patience for before—private, personal reminiscences of her father and grandfather; her mother and sisters; of England and the gently undulating green hills of the Thames valley that encompassed her earliest memories.

How much of life and love together had they two missed, Patty mused as she listened to Mrs. Jefferson's tales over her sewing. It saddened her to think that age and infirmity were requisites for bringing together the hearts of such loving souls, but she was glad to see some healing made before it was too late. She had not managed to do so with Papa. That troubled her still.

47

The Headache

Monticello

On Sunday, the thirty-first, Mrs. Jefferson, Nancy, and their servants made a journey to the new church on the Hardware, meeting Lucy and Polly there with their families. They offered to take Patsy along, but she didn't want to go; and Patty wasn't feeling well enough; and Thomas had work to do. Making no moue against this irreligiosity, Jane and her company went and returned just before dinner. Afterward, she complained of tiredness, so retired, leaving Patty and Thomas alone with George Gilmer and John, Peter, and Hastings Marks, who had come up from their militia meeting in town.

There was word from Thomas Nelson in Philadelphia of the routing of Arnold's forces in Quebec. At the time of his writing one battalion had already marched from Connecticut to support the General's beleaguered army, and others were leaving every day. It was hoped by these actions that the British garrison there might be persuaded to abandon their post before a relief force arrived with the thawing of the river. There was news, too, of dire threats from London if the hostilities lately commenced by the said colonies in rebellion did not cease immediately. But the general feeling was that what Britain had begun she should see out. Nelson had sent along with his letter, as he said, "2/ worth of Common Sense," being Mr. Paine's pamphlet lately published, and an address by the Society of Friends to the king and government, outlining their principles.

Lord Dunmore continued harrying the seaport towns, and the Pages at Rosewell were so anxious for their safety that John removed them to Williamsburg for the duration. There they would at least be out of harm's way from shelling. This move did not come at the best of times, for Fanny was due to lie in in April. Luckily no harm came to her, either from the alarm and vexation of being uprooted or the hazards of the roads.

To their favor, Nelson reported that on the second of February a ship had arrived carrying sixty tons of saltpetre, thirteen tons of gunpowder, and two thousand stands of arms for their troops; twenty-five additional tons of gunpowder were shortly expected, so last year's complaint about garnering funds and supplies for the making of saltpetre and gunpowder was somewhat relieved.

Their militia was shortly to return to Williamsburg, being here only for a refill of supplies and a call for further volunteers. Thomas promised, in his capacity of county Lieutenant, to draw up and publish the new list.

During this discussion Patty sat silent in her chair engaged in a piece of embroidery, a pair of slippers for Patsy, trying to quell her nausea and uneasiness at the news of the war. She was quite happy to have been forgotten by the men and frankly wished there was some way to excuse herself, as she had done Patsy, without being unpardonably rude. Decorum demanded that she sit and play hostess, even if this was only to make sure there was plenty of tinder at hand for the lighting of pipes.

As she was thinking this, Nancy came rushing in from the out-chamber, incoherent with alarm. She stuttered badly, as she did when agitated, and they could make no sense of what she said. Thomas went and put a hand on her shoulder and a glass of water was fetched for her. "What's wrong, Nan?" Nancy gulped water, was able to still her twitching, and finally managed to splutter, "It's Mama! She's had some kind of fit!"

George was out of his chair. "Fetch my bag," he said shortly on his way out the door, and was gone before anyone could reply. Thomas was ashen and distractedly handed Nancy over to her.

"Look after her," he charged her. "And whatever you do, don't come down. If you need me, send someone to fetch me."

She nodded, her throat dry with fear. "I will," she managed to croak. He bounded off after George. She didn't think even he could move so quick. She turned to her guests. "Please be at your ease, gentlemen. I won't be a moment."

Turning, she put her arm about poor Nancy who by this time was weeping, and said gently, "Come with me, dear. I'll take care of you," and made to lead her into the bedroom, but Nancy pulled away.

"I must go to my Mama!" She was amazingly strong for being such a slight girl, and Patty recalled to mind Thomas's remarks about Lissa. She frowned. Nancy was a bit slow on cyphers and not much inclined to read, but apart from her stuttering, was there in fact more amiss with her? Did she too bear the uncertain Randolph temperament? They'd had no sign of it ere this, but then Nancy had not been subject to such dire distress before.

"No, dear," she replied gently. "Let Mr. Jefferson and the doctor look after her. It is no work for ladies. Come, Nancy. I have some lavender water. It will ease your distress. Please." With a physical strength she rarely showed, she turned the girl and forced her from the room, all the while murmuring softly words of comfort. It was not so very different from dealing with Jack.

She made Nancy recline on her battered old chaise lounge, covered now in a soft striped damask, and fetched a handful of feathers and her bottle of lavender water. The former she burned and let the acrid odor waft under the girl's nose and the latter she applied to temples, wrists, and neck. With loving care she loosened Nancy's hair and gown and covered her with her white quilt, reassuring her that her mother would be fine.

But she doubted so, even as she spoke the words. She had an evil sense of foreboding that was borne out as time passed and no word came back from their out-chamber. She hummed a little tune and soothed Nancy from her agitation until she was drowsy in her cloud of lavender. Half an hour went by, then three quarters. The clock struck four. At a little after quarter past the hour Thomas came into the bedroom, closing the door to the parlor behind him. His face was starkly white, and he wore a numbed expression. She knew what had happened even before he spoke the words.

"She's dead," he said dazedly, and a shudder went through her. She held up a hand and closed the dressing room door. Wordlessly she went to him and put her arms about him tightly. She could offer no better comfort than her own body, for what was there to say to the loss of one's mother. Bending his cheek upon her hair he clung to her silently, the muscles in his arms and legs jumping nervously betimes. She rocked back and forth with him in her arms, listening to the agitated racing of his heart under her ear. Her poor dear!

She felt an aching grief for him, made more poignant when he lost his shocked hold on his emotions and broke down, weeping into her hair with great silent, shuddering sobs. She steeled herself for his sake, though her heart was breaking for his agony, and managed to disentangle herself enough to lead him over to the bed, uncertain if his legs would support him in his state.

He sat with his head in her lap, clutching her skirts in his hands, soaking her petticoats with his tears, his grief not silent now, but choking and hiccoughing like a child's. She wept for him and stroked his hair, loosing it from its queue, soothing as she would a child, with hushes and nonsense murmurs and loving endearments. It grew dark while they sat, and she prayed Betty had the presence of mind to look after her child, for she could not leave Thomas now.

"Oh, what am I to do?" he lamented to her. "My Mama, my poor Mama! God, she deserved better than I gave her, and now I have no way to make it up—"

She winced. "Oh no, love," she murmured. "She knew, these last few months. She knew how you loved her." She paused and took a long breath, remembering her conversation of June with the old lady. "She was proud of you, and she loved you dear, better than the others. She told me so. She would not think you ill now. You were her darling!" She stroked his hair, disentangling the thick curls with her fingers. He must not blame himself or think that he had done his mother a wrong, for plainly it wasn't so!

"But I wasn't!" he protested. "We said such awful things when Father died—" he shuddered, "—and when the house burned. My mother! and I never gave her the proper esteem she deserved, nor affection! E-even today! I should have gone with her, I knew she wanted me to, but I b-begged off! I should have seen she was not well, had George look after her—something!—instead of sitting about indulging myself in p-politics. She always hated politics, even with my father. I should have seen. . . ." He hiccoughed. "I should have known. . . . I should have loved her better—"

He gave over to fresh grief at this perceived failure, too miserable to see now as she could see from without, that their breach was not in fact so very great and had mended considerably in the last years, the last few months especially. But she could not say what was in her heart, for this anguish was the great one of his life, the fear of a sensitive child that he was not loved. She knew every lineament of that spectre's visage herself. Later he could listen, later he would be comforted by such words, but not now. Now he could only have her presence and warmth for his comfort.

She managed to induce him to take a nervine in some sherry, and after that he slept. She slipped out then to see to Patsy and found her having a cold supper in the dining room. George Gilmer was with her, sitting beside her solemnly, matching her eating custard spoonful for spoonful. She was astonished to see him, expecting that he would have been long gone. The Markses were nowhere to be found.

"Doctor, I had thought you'd be home by now," she said from the doorway. He looked up. "Mrs. Jefferson." He rose. "Excuse me, pud," he murmured to Patsy. She nodded gravely. George came and took Patty's arm.

"I thought you might require some assistance," he said quietly, steering her into the parlor. "I understand Miss Nancy's not altogether stable, and at the moment, no offence to the dear man, I wouldn't trust your husband on that score. How is he?" His green eyes were anxious. "He looked pretty badly the last I saw."

"He's resting," she said. "I gave him some lobelia I had in wine."

He nodded. "Good girl," he said. "You did right. And Miss Nanc—" Before he could finish, Nancy came out of the bedroom, her hair and clothes in disarray, plainly dazed from her agitation and long sleep. George clutched her arm, for the girl resembled none so much as Ophelia in her madness.

"Where's my Mama?" She came up. "Do you know, Patty? Is she well again? Doctor Gilmer!" she said in surprise. "You're here! Then she must be. . .well." She turned around in a circle, staring out the windows into the black night. "But it's night!" Her voice began to rise in hysteria. "It hasn't been—" She turned and rushed out.

"Dear God!" Patty exclaimed.

"It's all right," George said quickly. "I removed the body to the kitchen." She stared at him.

"It has the largest table!" he replied irritably. "I didn't think you'd want your daughter eating her supper over her dead grandmother!" His brutality shocked her and silenced any protests she might have made. "Excuse me," he said shortly, and dashed out after the girl.

George's foresight in remaining proved well founded, for poor Nancy became quite hysterical in her grief, and only a large amount of opiate could calm her down. When she was settled into her bed in the south chamber with her servant standing watch, Patty came out from putting Patsy to bed and helped him to see to the body. She had written out hasty notes to Lucy and Polly, and asked Charles Lewis if he could fetch Randolph from Snowden, whither he had gone briefly to see to his affairs in the lull of militia duty, and get word to Patsy Carr in Goochland.

It was past midnight when she went to bed, leaving Jupiter and Martin and Bob Hemings sitting up with Mrs. Jefferson. When she came in the room, she found Thomas sitting up on the near side of the bed with his head in his hands. At the sight of her he ran his hands through his hair, wincing.

"I have a most wretched headache," he complained. She nodded in sympathy and took off her gown, then went to him and put her arms about him. He leaned his head against her.

"I know a remedy," she said tenderly.

He looked up, his beautiful eyes all red, squinting in pain at the light.

"Let me fetch you some sherry first," she murmured.

Once again she made him drink while she carefully got him out of his clothes, as lovingly and slowly as if he had been Jack, fallen asleep before bedtime and roused late. Conscious of his nervous headache, she did not light any more candles than the one that she had lit when she put Patsy to bed, and that she extinguished soon after. Laying aside her shift and petticoats, she climbed into their ample bed and went to him where he lay curled facing the inside. His headache, when it came, always came on the left side and never the right.

"That's so much better," he said in a voice of relief of the dark.

"I know," she said. She put her arms about him in the darkness, knowing too well without light the lean contours of his body. His skin was burning, for she'd left him lying under a quilt. "Come here, dear," she said gently, and kissed him, his mouth, the sharp line of his chin, the warm place in his neck where the pulse went racing. This was one physic whose efficacy she well trusted. "Let me make you better."

They had run this road many times before. The reasons were a mystery, but when the headache came on him, such physical release could effect a cure. It was sometimes permanent, sometimes only a few hours, but it never failed to give some relief.

When he slept again, it was poignantly with his arms wrapped about her and his head on her bosom. She smoothed his hair from his face tenderly and admired the line of his back before she covered it with the quilt. Clean-limbed, sturdy but graceful, a straight-up man, she found him beautiful to look upon. The Randolph grace was plainly evident in the delicacy of his profile. God willing, that grace would bear him through this tragedy and out the other side without his family's difficulty.

"Rest easy, my love," she whispered to him. "For I shall not leave you." She closed her eyes and in an instant was asleep.

The burial was held two days later, allowing time for Patsy to come from Goochland. There was a fine rain as they walked down the hill behind the pallbearers. Thomas was silent beside her, grim. Today was his thirty-third birthday, and he was burying the woman who bore him. That morning he'd awakened with a recurrence of his headache, with lights before his eyes and sickness, and now even the dull light of the lowering sky was painful. Patty held his arm on one side and Patsy on the other, together making their careful way down the slippery wet grass of the hillside.

The grave had been dug beyond Dabney Carr's under the tree, whose own last repose had but been recently adorned with its memorial stone and copperplate. The stone had been made in Charlottesville of their native sand variety, but the copperplate he had sent for from London and nailed on the oak under which he and this dearest friend used to sit. On the two, he'd had carved or engraved:

Here lie the remains of Dabney Carr
son of John and Barbara Carr of Louisa County, Va.
Intermarried July 20, 1765, with Martha Jefferson,
Daughter of Peter and Jane Randolph Jefferson
Born October 26, 1743–Died May 16, 1773, at Charlottesville, Va.

> *Lamented Shade!*
> *Whom every gift of heaven profusely blest,*
> *A temper winning mild, nor pity softer,*
> *Nor was truth more bright; Constant in doing*
> *Well, he neither sought nor shunned applause.*
> *No bashful merit sighed near him neglected;*
> *Sympathising he wiped off the tear from sorrow's clouded eye*
> *And with kindly hand taught her heart to smile.*

To his virtue, good sense, learning and friendship,
this stone is dedicated by Thomas Jefferson,
Who of all men loved him most.

> *Still shall thy grave in rising flowers be dressed*
> *And the green turf lie lightly on thy breast;*

There shall the moon her earliest tears bestow,
There the first roses of the years shall blow,
While angels with their silver wings o'ershade
The ground sacred by thy reliques made.

Late though these testimonials were, Dabney's grave had suffered a better fate than Janey's on the opposite side, now hardly noticeable as a grave, with the fresh spring grass growing on it. They had not put up a stone yet there, nor did she know when they would. Would there ever be a time when they could bear to say "Here lies buried. . ." over poor Jane's remains? Mr. Clay waited for them to assemble and commenced his brief service.

In half an hour it was over, the coffin having been lowered by the ropes. Their Patsy came, sidling herself between them and clutching her father's coat skirt. Thomas bent and picked her up, patting her as if she were a baby, and with a look of grim determination went and scattered a handful of earth over the open grave. He was quiet—he had hardly spoken two sentences together all day—and very pale. He'd borne his grief stoically since the other night and even with her did not break down so far again. In view of his headache and its attendant illness, she was stunned that he was managing to conduct himself anything like normally.

She sprinkled her handful of earth and went around to the opposite side after Thomas, passing George Gilmer as she did. He pressed her arm sympathetically, as he had done with Thomas and she met his gaze dolefully. She could forgive him his brutality the night of the death, for she saw his expediency. She would tell him so; there should not be constraint between friends.

Patsy Carr caught her up as she began her ascent of the hill and put an arm about her waist, over the sacque back of her mourning. "Are you well?" she murmured, leaning near. The sympathy brought tears and she shook her head fiercely, silent, not trusting herself to speak. The nausea of her pregnancy and lassitude she had felt with the late nights of these last two days at the grave had overwhelmed her, and she had feared for a moment that she would faint. She still was cold and uneasy, trembling, but there were others with a greater grief than hers, this lovely caring woman beside her for one, and she refused to give in to her weakness.

"You're very pale," Patsy said, her grey eyes concerned.

"Don't!" she begged tightly, and Patsy desisted, clasping her gloved hand as they went up to the house.

48

Misbirth

Monticello

She endeavored a private word with George Gilmer in the dining room, under the pretext of assuring herself that he was well taken care of and that the table need not be refilled yet. When she maneuvered him into the corner, he looked down on her with his bright green eyes, and she felt a flush rise up her neck and face. But he was not scoffing or impatient now, but gentle.

"Aye?" he queried, with his hint of a burr.

"I—" she faltered. They had been in far more intimate circumstances than this together, but the social context now was mortifying. She did not know his private heart well enough to be utterly at ease. What if he should laugh or rebuke her? But decency demanded that she made some amends for her rudeness to him, so she forced herself to continue, "I am sorry for my ire at you the other day. I see now you only had concern for our ease at heart, and I beg your pardon." She looked down at her shoes. The buckles wanted polishing.

"Nay lassie," he said softly, and she stared at him. He had never been so familiar with her before. "'Tis forgot. You should not trouble yourself at all over it."

Patsy Carr called her away from the doorway. "Sister, I would speak a word with you—"

"Yes," she said automatically, and curtseyed to George. "Pardon me." He made her a silent bow and turned away again to the table.

She murmured to Patsy, "What's the matter, my dear?"

The grey eyes that met hers were sorrowful. "My brother complains of his headache and wishes your attendance. I told him I'd ask you to order up some broth." She took her arm and continued in a low tone, "Oh, Patt, please go to him! He looks like to collapse!"

"I will; thank you, Pats," she whispered in return.

She ordered the broth but was delayed in her journey by sundry condolers whom she could not brush off, and when she came to Thomas he was lounging on the bench drinking chicken broth from a teacup and saucer.

He'd stretched himself out crosswise on the bench with his legs on the floor and his elbow resting on the carved back of the seat. He leaned his head against the wall, leaving the cup idle in his lap.

"You look comfortable," she said. Perhaps the broth had eased his head.

He opened his eyes, and by the way he squinted and blinked at her she could tell that his vision was blurred.

"I don't feel so," he said frankly. "I feel as if I'm being hammered by devils." He sat up and made space for her, laying his head on her shoulder when she sat. "I needed to see you," he said, moving his cheek a little against the scratchiness of her black woolen gown.

"Oh. . ." she mourned in sympathy for him. "Is it so bad?" She removed the cup and saucer from his lap. He made only a murmur in reply and closed his eyes.

"Do you wish me to fetch George? He's still here—"

"Don't go," he said quickly, putting a hand on her arm. "I only want to rest a little with you. You can have something from George later." He raised his head. "Would you come sit with me awhile?"

"But I am sitting with you, dear," she said fondly.

"No, outside," he insisted. "I want to take the air."

She nodded and helped him up. It had stopped raining, and outside it was dewy, with a fitful brightness from drifting clouds breaking up. They went out the front of the house through the east door in the hall and wandered until they came to the northeast slope of the hill and sat, gazing out at the distance to where the mountains began. She sat beside him, calmly and decorously, in a welter of black skirts, the lappets of her black-ribboned cap fluttering against her neck in the light breeze.

He was silent for some time, plainly ill at ease at speaking his mind. She thought of how he often complained that the worst part of his headaches was not being able to think, and prompted, "Tom?"

He looked up at her. "I'm afraid, my dear," he admitted. She felt a rush of compassion flood through her.

"Why, love?"

He took her hand with its plain gold band. "For you, for us." He sighed and shook his head, "For our country, for this continent." He looked eastward across the sprawling vista of the low country where a war raged unseen, and a legislature struggled to keep order in the midst of ever-shifting tides of fortune. "As greatly as I believe that our cause is just, I tremble for what suffering this war will bring. Shall you brave it, my little one, my Telei?" He met her eyes, his own solemnly brown in the darting of the sun behind a cloud. "I am obliged to go, but to leave you thus—" He made a gesture toward their silent one, "and not to know if you are well, or if I may come when you need me. . . is more than I can bear." He shut his eyes tightly, laying a trembling hand on his brow. "And with this blasted headache I haven't even the time or strength to think!"

She took his hand down. "Thomas—" She massaged the aching side of his head with her fingers while applying a counter pressure with her hand on the opposite side. "There is time enough for fretting when needs be," she said gently as she worked. "We have a long time yet that way. Come now, my dear." She left off and took his hands. "So much sun isn't good for you. Come inside and rest. The family won't mind. Please, dear."

He was unable to protest, and under her care he walked back to the house to lie down in the bedroom with its windows covered in oilcloth, for it was dark and cool there. She procured a dose of yellowbark of George Gilmer and a linting full of ice from the cellar to lay his head on. With these reliefs at hand he soon slept and remained insensible to the passings of the world for the next twelve hours.

He was supposed to return to Philadelphia on the Monday, but the funeral and his headache prevented it. A week went by and it was still with him, and even George's Peruvian bark only took the edge off his pain. He would not take opiates. Thus he was reduced to a half-existence, invalided, unable to write or read for work or comfort, food tenuously held. He was, he complained, no use to anybody, least of all himself.

A week went by, and she was forced from her worries on his behalf by her own agonies. Early in the morning on the sixteenth she suffered a miscarriage. She had not been really well with this pregnancy, enduring worse sickness and exhaustion than she had ever done before, so that merely getting through the day was a trial. It was worse in the fortnight since Mrs. Jefferson's death. She should have been nearly over her complaints by this time, and yet they continued, to the point that she retched all day and had fits of weeping most unlike her. She had not put on weight as she should have and was not enlarged at all, as she had been with Jane.

She was dreaming of swimming. Swimming in the creek at Fanny Burwell's with a group of girls when they were fourteen or fifteen years old. But John Page came sauntering onto the scene and they all shrieked, and she was seized with a cramp—

She was wide awake then, shuddering in the dark. She had no idea of the hour, but the room was black as pitch. And into the darkness she wept her silent pain as the cramps came again and again, and she realized that she had swum not in water, but in blood. Dear God, she would lose this child too!

She closed her eyes against the dark, against the pain, against the hot tears of grief that poured out despite her efforts to calm herself, to stay them. It was a long time that she endeavored to stay above the rising wave of pain, but at last she could bear it no more. It hurt so bad!

She jerked poor Thomas from sleep by her sharp cry.

"What's wrong, what's amiss?" He was sitting up, but she could not answer. It hurt so bad, it hurt so bad. *Oh God, I can do nothing but lie here. I cannot move, it will kill me.* She was curled into a ball, and Thomas made to loosen her clenched hand from the sheet. She shook her head and gasped, crying again while he lit a candle and paused in horror. There was blood everywhere.

"Patty!"

She raised her head enough to beseech him through clenched teeth, "Please help. . .me!" It was an agony to lie thus; she laid her head down again and wept. *Let me die, oh merciful God, have pity on me, and let me die, I cannot endure, endure—* Thomas pulled her into his lap and forced a glass of burning spirits on her.

"No!" she cried at being straightened from her coil. She clutched her belly with one hand. It was better if she curled herself against it. Not better. Less agonizing. Not less; she could bear it. She wept again as Thomas tried to drown her in wine. She could never bear it. Only sweet death would ease her now.

"Please," he was begging her. "Please, darling. Only a little." His hands were shaking, and he spilled a good deal of the wine down her neck. She shook her head, coughing and spluttering.

"Stop, please," she implored in a small voice, as the pain rose again.

"Ah!" She clutched his arm, her fingernails, well kept and strong, biting into his flesh.

Much against her will he forced more wine on her, until she found that it did give her some ease. She was coherent now and accepted another glass without protest. She took a third and began to feel sleepy. She still hurt but the pain was rolling now, dreamlike. She could rest. Rest.

She woke to Bett and Queenie trying to move her, and all the roiling unrest from the wine churning her stomach. She was sick, and after that the pain was worse again. She began to cry. Was there no help? Why did they fuss at her so? Where was Thomas? Thomas. There was something wrong with him, but she could not remember what it was. Oh, where was he?

He was kneeling beside her on the floor.

"Thomas—" She clutched his hand.

"I'm here, dear," he murmured. "I won't leave again." Had he been gone? She clung to him through the strong pain that came. Baby. Baby. Baby. He would never be now. Tears welled up in her eyes. "I don't want to lose this baby!"

He smoothed her hair and kissed her damp forehead. "I know, sweetheart."

Ursula and Bett made to remove the linen.

"Leave it," he told them. "He'll need to see." They did as they were bid and covered the worst of the mess with a towel. He looked at her. "Can you sit up enough for me to change your shift?" Even the thought was unbearable. She shook her head. "It hurts," she pleaded, tears running down.

"All right, love," he soothed. "Sh, sh, I won't do a thing."

They gave her more wine, soaked in bread this time, and it stayed down. She drifted in and out of the room, happier to be out than in it, until some time after she heard a voice calling her. "Mrs. Jefferson, Mrs. Jefferson, it's George Gilmer. Can you talk to me?"

She opened her eyes and turned a little to see him, sniffling. She nodded.

"Good," George said. "First of all—" He put his hand on her arm, stroking gently. "I want to tell you, dear, that you're going to be all right. You shall probably lose your child—" He paused at a sob from her, "and there's nothing for that." He went on stroking her arm as he spoke, his voice quiet and gentle. "But we shall do our best to expedite matters and make you as easy as possible. I should like to examine you. Do you feel you could bear that?"

She stared at Thomas in fear and dread. *Tell him no! Please, please, as you love me,* she begged him, *tell him no!* He came over and held her hand. "He won't if you forbid it."

She groaned, caught up in another siege, and clenched his hand. *Anything was better than this!* she thought as it passed. If he might thereby tell her that she was but shortly from her relief, then she could endure it.

She said to George in a steely voice, "You may, if I might have more wine—or better, rum."

He smiled. "Oh, I think we may do better than that."

After a strong dose of laudanum the deed was accomplished. It was a genuine miracle that anything could be discerned solely by touch under the volume of a clean sheet, but George seemed satisfied with the result.

"It shouldn't be long," he said to Thomas afterward, "but she's bled a good deal, and I'd like to hurry things along. Do you have any of that Peruvian bark at hand?"

It was all she heard of their exchange, the laudanum having begun to take effect. She drifted from them and slept for a long time.

She was not out of bed for a fortnight. For the first week she could not sit up without a nauseating rush of dizziness, so spent her time reclined on the pillows against the wall. She was too heavy and stupid to read, let alone sew, and the days passed in a blur, one into another, and she hardly noticed. She was very depressed both of mind and spirit, her mind revolving on the enormity of her loss. She would never be able to have another baby again! Why had fate chosen to serve them so unkindly? Why should she be denied her dearest wish? It was wickedly unfair.

The next week she grew worse. Thomas was up and about, although he was still troubled with his headache and unable to work, and spent his days on a circuit between the dining room, parlor, and bedroom, restlessly. She watched him dully from the bed, unable to summon any strength or even concern for him in her state. She was feverish and giddy. In some part of her mind she knew this was a childbed fever, that this was a dangerous state, but she was in its power and could not fight back. She drifted in and out through the days, rousing at a sudden noise or when someone came to look after her, a docile patient, unknowing of all the worry that went on around her.

She was thus for a week-and-an-half before her fever broke. She wakened ravenously hungry and her throat parched. It was the middle of the afternoon, and she had been asleep for two days. She turned and found Thomas lying on the bed with his head resting against the cool of the wall. The plaster must have dried.

"Thomas," she said, and her voice was a croak. "Are you still so poorly?" She tried to reach out her hand, but it was too heavy. He raised his drowsy eyes, and she saw that they were darkly shadowed. He looked as if he'd not been sleeping. Suddenly he was alert.

"Oh, Patty!" She was seized up in an embrace, and he kissed her face. "O thank goodness." He smoothed her hair back. His eyes were very green. "My dear, I thought we'd lose you. . . ."

She could remember little of the last two weeks, only that the child she had wanted so very much was lost to her; and that she had bled a lot, which plainly was the cause of her present weakness. Four days later, she put her feet on the floor for the first time, insisting over Betty's objections that she would get up and use her own pot. It was undignified to be treated as an invalid when she could walk. But the few steps were an exertion, and she was glad of the enveloping comfort of the bed when she sank into it, for her walk left her dizzy. It was a slow beginning to a long recovery.

Thomas was obliged to return to Philadelphia shortly. He was already many weeks late; he had been meant to return the day after Mrs. Jefferson's death, but that event and his subsequent headache plainly precluded it. His headache was not gone yet, but was diminished enough that he could make the journey safely.

On the morning of the ninth he came into the dressing room where she was lying on her lumpy old chaise watching Patsy play at cat's cradle with a piece of string, and knelt.

"Oh, my dear," she said, as he bent his head and kissed her hand. "Are you well enough to travel so far?" The thought of his taking ill again so far away or perhaps en route, as he had done before the first Convention, was unbearable.

He smiled a little. The sun shone on his hair, touching it gold in streaks. His eyes were green only narrowly around the pupil today; his complexion was fresh and the shadows gone from his eyes.

"It's I should be asking you that. Should I not have writ Francis to expect you so soon?" He had written saying that she would be at The Forest in a week to spend the summer there. "Are you strong enough for that?"

She nodded, not wanting him to fret. "I shall be. By then I certainly shall be." She clasped his hands. "Write to me, won't you? I promise I shall do as well."

"Not if it taxes you, sweet," he insisted. "I'll accept Francis's word for your welfare. Or Betsy's. Don't push yourself for me."

She bent her head. "But for whom else would I do it—" She looked up again, "if not my dearest love?" She hated the uncertainty of these partings. It had been easier when he was going away for the courts or the Assembly. Then at least she had known the day of his return.

"Sweet Patty." He kissed her forehead. "This must be adieu," he said with regret. His voice was hoarse. "You know that though I go, my heart remains wherever you are."

She gasped against the ache in her throat. "Aye. I do know. I live on it." He regarded her a long moment. "Adieu, my sweet friend, my dear girl." As he kissed her the tears that had been threatening slipped over. He brushed them away. "Get well again, dear," he charged her. She nodded blindly as he rose and went to kiss Patsy good-bye. Then he was gone, around the bed in their chamber and out into the hall with his long stride. She fussed with the coverlet, unfolding and refolding the neat folds at her waist unnecessarily.

"Mama, look! Look at this." Patsy came over, her fingers tangled in the intricate game she had been trying to accomplish all morning. She held out her hands. Looking into the little freckled face with its halo of red curls escaping her cap, she saw every mark of the father in the child. She sniffed and wiped her face. Thank goodness for Patsy! "That's very fine dear. Very fine indeed. When your Papa returns, you'll have to let him show you another. You know all the ones Mama knows. . . ." She leaned toward the child conspiratorially. "But I believe Papa makes them up."

Patsy giggled, all pleased blushes at this confidence. She was allowed to climb up, and they spent the remainder of the morning reading her little primer that Papa had brought home for her from his last journey to the Congress.

49

A Separate and Equal Station

Elk Hill

Thomas wrote on the sixteenth:

mr Innis tells me Gwatkin's books are left with Molly Digges for sale. i have wrote to Page to send me here a catalogue of them; and in the mean time purchase two of them which i recollect he had and have long wished to get; Historie des Celtes de Pelloutier. 2 vols. 12 mo. and Observations on Gardening, and a box of books he has of mine which I am in hopes some of the military or commisary's waggons will furnish him with an opportunity of sending to Albemarle. if they arrive before you leave, it would be a great aid to me if you could please leave an instruction that they are to be left in their packing crate and covered with a cloath, that they mightn't be subject to all weathers &c.

. . . it is the wish of my heart to hear some small word of your progress, best from your own hand, but if that is impossible then by some deputy of yours. it need not be long. this would ease my mind in absence of my own observation. . . . my head ach has left me. i think the air taken during the journey effected a final cure; whatever it was, i am much relieved by it's absence. . .on the subject of a change of Air, I have a notion to repair with you to the Warm springs after my return, what do you think of that? i fear the Hot might be too debilitating on a sensitive system. this depends entirely upon your pleasure of course. . . i am shortly to quit this place. dear as the Randolphs have become, the stifling quality of the air in the midst of the city is more than i can bear, being used as I am to mountain wilderness. . . i expect i shall move next week some time, after which you may address any scrip you send in care of Joseph Graaf in the High street. it is a brand-new house and just at the edge of town. the rolling hills of the low country are just beyond, yet it is convenient to my purposes. . . . kiss my dear Pats for me, and let her know she is not forgot, as neither is my Diana by her devoted

Th: J.

Contrary to her intentions, Patty did not travel to Charles City in a week's time, nor even make it so far as Elk Hill. Without Thomas, the melancholy which had threatened since her recovery from childbed fever descended. She mourned her loss in sudden fits of weeping or irritability where the least noise would set her teeth on edge. She spent her days cocooned in the south wing of the house, grateful for the semi-darkness, for her eyes troubled her. She sent only the briefest instructions to the kitchen as they had few visitors, and those they had Mary Garth could deal with. In the middle of the month she sent a note to Thomas, dictated as he had requested, since it strained her eyes to read or write, to Liza Reynolds:

> I am riting this via Mrs. Reynolds's kind Offices. Do not be alarmed, I am not so bad as that. It is only that my Eyes trouble me some. I intend to speak with Mr. Bentsen about fitting up a pair of Spectackles with green Glass, which should solve matters and allow me to rite you my own Letter. Patsy is well. I expect to be at Elk Hill this Sen'night.
>
> MJ

But she failed at this endeavor also. She was bleeding again, and as it was difficult and painful, feared there was something amiss with her. The nine days were the longest of her life. She took Gilmer's tonic more faithfully after that, and it dispelled some of her weakness. The apothecary in town delivered up her spectacles, making it possible for her to bear the light. Her eyeballs still hurt, and any reading was difficult but at least she could travel now. She had a visit from Daniel Hylton's servant, for she had intended to stop at his house along her progress a week past. She and Patsy set out for Elk Hill on the seventh, sending a letter first to Philadelphia of this shift.

When she arrived at Elk Hill, she found a letter for her from Thomas, forwarded there from Lisbet at The Forest:

> . . .your situation lays me under great anxiety. I have only just now received a letter from Francis saying you'd had a visit from Hylton's servant. having nothing from yourself to the contrary, until I received this i was convinced you had come to some greater harm than that in which I left you. i am pleased it isn't so, but i can see that you are far from well. take care, my blossom, and do not endeavor too Much. if ever you are tempted to do more than you have strength for, remember that there is one who places your welfare above all other concerns, and would be aggrieved that you endangered it. let others do that which you cannot; they will not grudge it you. . . .

She worried that he had not received her note by Liza Reynolds. It seemed as though they would have a repetition of last year, with mails being opened or lost before they reached their destinations. But it proved not to be the case, for he sent her regular epistles from Philadelphia full of news:

> yesterday, on Friday, colo: Lee introduced our resolution moving for independency. debate on this was deferred until to day. . . .
>
> Monday: our debate on the resolution continued today, tho' voting has been deferred for three weeks at the request of new York, new Jersey, Pennsylvania, Delaware, Mary-land and south Carolina, that those legislatures might have time to remove their restrictions against voting for independency. they call themselves friends to the measure and admit of the impossibility that these colonies should ever again be united with great Britain, yet they remain against adopting it. . . . Pennsylvania is bereft of Dr Franklyn, who is confined to his home with an attack of gout, and there fore his colonys Vote is under the control of John Dickenson. . .now, along with Livingston and the Rutledge brothers he has laid out a long list of reasons for the caution against the measure. you see how we are Divided. . .mr Adams, R.H Lee, and mr Wythe argue warmly on its behalf.
>
> . . .mr Dickinson and John Adams are since our last sessions become mortal enemies on the floor, and none too friendly outside. mr Adams complains of laggards who would drag their feet and their country down the path of ruin in the face of clear attacks, while mr Dickinson confines himself to sneering asides to his fellow conservatives about the dangerous Air of the Bay colony.
>
> . . .i am presently engaged in draughting, at mr Wythe's request, a recommendation for our country's constitution. word we have had here of Ld Dunmore's flight, and that I had already had from Francis, disturbs me much, for i trust him not not to make some treachery Against us.

In answer to this, she wrote him of such news that she had from down the country, which was little as she had few visitors, and small details of her and Patsy's lazy days. The green spectacles were much an improvement upon her usual state of vision, and she began to grow impatient again with idleness. Thomas wrote back the next week:

> i was much gratified to have a letter from your hands, and am pleased the spectacles have proved so useful, that you are out in the sunn, &c, but i would not have you use them as an excuse to exert yourself unduly. i want to hear but that you are indolent, not reading

too much or doing any other thing, no matter it's pleasure, that would bring you any strain. with a view to that, i will keep this short, and detain you only to further say that your notion of declaring that which exists is implimented. it requires yet some fine tuning, but the deed is done for the most part. may a fidelity of purpose attend us. i would say more to you, but true to my promise i will not tire you. i leave this place the 11th of August, and you may expect me there about the 18th. Till then I remain your devoted
Th: J.

He wrote too, with news of the great world that sent her heart skipping a beat, though he modestly denied any genius or ambition in the matter:

. . .and a committee was called for to prepare a declaration, in keeping with the form followed previously. this is made up of John Adams, Doctr Franklyn, Roger Sherman, Robert Livingston, and myself, tho' Doctr. Franklyn is unable to participate actively in the committee, due to his malady, but has agreed to serve in an advisory capacity. Livingston and Sherman do not consider themselves pen-men, and Adams, remarquing his, as he calls it, admiration of my former work, has likewise declined in my Favour. thus my time, already limited by my work on our Constitutions, is further reduced, so I beg my Telei's pardon if my letters are here for a short while reduced in Length.

Thursday: today our declaration committee, minus Dr Franklyn, met in John Adams's rooms and reviewed the paper. they approved it with the exception of some minor changes, one of which i find curious. he struck out 'fellow subjects', substituting instead 'citizens'. 'It's as well to be taken for a sheep as a lamb,' he said to me. . . . i espy mr. Adams is not nearly so Dour as some would have him painted. . . .

At the time Thomas was thus engaged, Patty had a visit at Elk Hill from the Eppeses. They had made their journey by slow stages much as she herself had done from Monticello, for Lisbet was five months gone in expecting another baby. They arrived on the twelfth, with a plan to stay a week at least. Francis had intended to leave Lisbet and the children and travel up the country to Monticello to look in on her, and was quite surprised when she came to the door of the hall at their advent.

"She lives!" he exclaimed to Lisbet. "Cousin, you had us in an awful fright. We had no word of you, and then we heard from Mr. Hylton that you were for his house and when we did not see you, we decided to seek you out. When did you come here?"

"The day before yesterday." She raised herself on her toe a little and kissed him. He was not a tall man, but he was taller than she. "Welcome." Blushing for her state of dishabille—for she was dressed in a light gown, but her hair was unbound and she wore a pair of old mules hastily slipped on at the sight of them—she embraced her sister fondly.

"You do look well," she said.

"That's a kindly remark given the state of the roads," Lisbet said. "The horses kicked up such a heap of dust that we were choked in our carriage, but thank you, Patt."

"You might always have ridden ahead with me," Francis teased her, "or postilion." His brown eyes twinkled.

"I think not," Lisbet said drily. She called to her son, "Dick, come here and say 'how do you do' to your aunty."

"Yes, Mama." He muttered obediently. The boy came away from the horses with a reluctant, shambling gate. He was tall and willowy now, being nearly seven years old, with an unruly shock of brown curls tied anyhow at the back. He looked rumpled and irritated, doubtless at having been called away from his freedom after hours in the carriage.

Lisbet put her arm about him. "Where's Jack?"

Dick shrugged. "Out with Tessa, I expect." Tessa was their nursemaid.

"Well, say hello, and then you may go and play."

The boy glanced at her shyly, for they had not met these six months, and that was a long time in the life of a child. He made a neat little bow.

"Good day, Aunty Jefferson," he said, and colored.

She smiled. "Hello, Dick. Are you enjoying your holiday?" He was home from his grammar school until the Assembly.

"Oh yes!" he exclaimed, his face beaming. "I've been fishing in the river and swimming in the creek, and Matt Brown taught me to make a nail, see—" He dug in his pocket and produced it. It was about three inches long and flat at the head end, undistinguishable from the hundreds of other nails she had seen.

"It's very good," she said, handing it back to him. "Do you know, Patsy's down the kitchen helping Nana make ices for dinner. I'm sure she'd like your company." She looked at Lisbet. "Is that all right?"

"I don't see why not," Lisbet smiled. "Take your brother along," she told Dick as he raced out the door. She shook her head. "Boys," she said, rolling her eyes.

"I object to that," Francis said in a mock-wounded tone.

"Not you, sirrah," Lisbet returned, "but then, if you gadded about the like of your son, I might say the same of you, too. He never sits still," she told Patty.

Patty smiled. "Neither did Jack, do you remember?"

"Aye!" Lisbet laughed.

"And—" she looked askance at Francis, "I seem to recall a certain coz who did his share of that when young. Wasn't it you, sir, who was in disgrace for sliding down our bannister rails one Christmas and upsetting Mary's decor?"

Francis colored. "I don't remember that!" His protest was not very convincing.

"Come, let's sit down," she invited. "You must be tired after your journey." She went into the parlor and took up her place again on the sofa. She had had the furniture rearranged so that one of the sofas was under the window, looking out toward the river. "How far did you come?"

"Turkey Island." Francis said.

Tessa came in with the baby.

"Here's our bud!" he exclaimed. Mary smiled at him, all dark eyes and wispy curls. He took her from the nurse. "How's my charmer?" He bounced the baby on his knee. "She creeps about now, you know," he told Patty. She smiled at this boasting.

"Francis dotes on her," Lisbet said fondly. "I vow she's going to be quite spoilt."

"The first daughter usually is," he said, with a wink. If they had come to cheer her, then they were accomplishing their objective. These two were always a tonic.

50

Debates and Declarations

Elk Hill

Having grown up but across the river from The Forest, Francis was as familiar to her as if he had been a brother, for theirs was a close family. Even after her mother died, her father maintained his ties to Bermuda Hundred, out of friendship as well as kinship. It had never occurred to her that Mary Cocke might have resented the constant reminders of her father's first wife, and she did not know if that had occurred to Papa. But as she looked on it now, there may have been some cause for the enmity she was borne as a girl, for she was as like her Eppes cousins as if she had been one of them. As with the Randolphs and the Pages, there was a strong familial resemblance that marked them all.

It was only proper, being such close neighbors and kin, that Lisbet should have married Francis. It was expedient to keeping within the family control large tracts of land; there was also the matter of temperament. Patty was lucky where Thomas was concerned in having found someone without her own circle so suited. The Tuckahoe Randolphs certainly were not similar; they were a loud, passionate group of strong opinions and uncertain tempers. She did not find meals there an enjoyable experience. Oh, they were loving enough toward her, but she was used to a gentler existence than such eruptions afforded. Yes, it was much better to be among her sisters and the family, and at Elk Hill it was best of all.

The house had become the family retreat. Owned in fact by Henry and Nancy, managed by Thomas and Patty, it was shared by all as a gathering place equally. Thomas and she sent the surplus of goods to the Skipwiths, but accepted as their payment for stewardship a quantity of wool, corn, and animals every year. This year they had finally begun the recovery from the killing frost of '74, for last year there had been no excess to send or to keep after the people were provided for. Now young lambs and calves gamboled on the hillsides and on the Island, and there was a quantity of preserved fruit and vegetables in the cellar. The wheat crop rose to its full height with nodding golden heads full of promise. And the Island was once more full of flowers.

Every morning she had the view of it from her bedroom window, downriver from the tangle of trees at Secretary's ford and the Point of Fork.

It was a lovely green oasis in the slow-moving brownness of the river, a delight to the eye. Even the mill had a certain charm about it, standing ruined and idle on the farther shore.

Such had been her view every day for nearly two years when she was mistress of this place, and she never tired of it for it was ever changing. It was strange to be here now in this familiar place and realize how much her life had changed the last ten years. Her days as a new bride here with Batt seemed to be from another's life. There was not a single aspect of it that remained the same since that time. She never could have envisioned all that had transpired when she was here then, young and full of hope.

She sat idling, looking out the window at the river. Lisbet was resting and Francis had gone down to Dungenness. The children were out in the grass, playing a game of blind man's bluff, and Dick was careful not to catch the little ones too quickly. She watched him lurch his way around the tree after Patsy, who was squealing in delight, and the sight of his curly head brought another's to mind.

Jack would have been nine years old had he lived. Nine years. Would he have grown straight and sturdy as this cousin, to be a gentle, bright boy as Dick was? Bathurst had been so. She sought his dimming memory in the reaches of her mind. She had only impressions left now rather than the close reality of daily life. They had had so little time. . . . His image took shape in her mind. Jack had been so very like him, with the same golden hair and fair complexion, the same plumpness, too, although Jack was thinning out when he died. And temperament? He was bright, with an aptitude for languages and mathematics that his father had owned. But Batt was gentler and never subject to the passions that Jack displayed. No, in that he had been her son, and she had watched his torments and soaring joys with a sympathetic eye. Life was easier when one did not bound so from pillar to post and back.

And Patsy displayed them too. It was not that she was a bad or difficult child, for she was sensitive for all her enthusiasm, and a hard word or even a disapproving tone could send her to tears. But she must learn temperance, for her own sake, must learn to govern the passions of her soul before the whole world. Such ingenuousness would not serve her well when she came a young lady. . . . Patty never thought of her as her oldest child. Her oldest daughter, yes, but never the oldest child. How could she forget her first baby? He had changed her forever.

"That's what I like about this place, too," Lisbet said from the doorway. She was dressed again, in a loose sacque coat and petticoats. Patty smiled, holding out her hand, and Betsy came over to stand by the window with her.

"What's that?"

"Being able to sit and look at nothing." Lisbet looked down at her. "I don't get much of that."

She nodded in agreement. "Though we both do now. What?" Lisbet was staring at her.

"You're not wearing the spectacles!" she exclaimed. "My goodness, I've grown so used to you in those silly green things that I don't even notice them any more. You're better so?" She took up a chair and sat down on the opposite side of the window, her long brown hair stirring in the breeze that wafted in.

"Indoors," Patty said, looking down to the river and the Island. "I'd like to take a trip to the Island this summer, take a picnic. I used to enjoy that."

Lisbet leaned over and clasped her hand, her quiet face all sympathy. She had a heart soft as butter, did Lisbet, and no hint of melancholy escaped her notice.

"Poor Patt," she murmured. "It must be difficult for you here after having spent so much time before."

"Only sometimes," Patty admitted. She looked out the window again, leaning her arm on the sill and enjoying the cool breeze that met them. This had always been her room, and on days like this it bore a thousand memories. She didn't want to look now.

"We were happy here, Bathurst and me," she said softly, and hesitated. "I miss him sometimes, still, and that troubles me. It was one of the things I asked Aunty Randall when Tibb and I were in Williamsburg, whether it would trouble. I wonder was it different for Papa," she mused, glancing at her sister. "I never heard the least word from him of it, but he told me things sometimes of my Mama, when Elizabeth was alive. Lisbet, you are so lucky!" she burst out. "You knew your mother, while I am reduced to lamenting a shade." She toyed with the fringed edge of the white curtain beside her. "It's that way with Batt," she said without looking up. "Someday I shall forget him entirely. He is the less real to me by the year, and some day I shall have nothing." She sighed. "On the one hand, it seems fitting I should forget, for while he does not often intrude upon my peace, yet he does betimes, and I am troubled that he should. It seems. . . disloyal somehow.

"But it makes me think of others I have lost—Jack, and Janey, Papa—and I wonder, will I forget them too with time?" She shook her head. "I shouldn't wish to." She looked up, out into the distance again. "It would be dreadful to be passed away and forgotten forever by all one loved, no more substantial in their minds than if one's life had been a dream. . ." She heard her own voice, plaintive and distant, and stopped, blushing up her neck. She shook her head. "I'm sorry," she said, laying a hand on Lisbet's arm. "'Tis the weather, I expect, it makes me mopish. . . Here you come in for a pleasant chat, and I pour my dark murmurings all over you."

"I am grown used to your meanderings long ere this," Betsy teased, "else I would have throttled you years ago." She looked about. "Would you like to change rooms with Mr. Eppes and me? One room's as like another to me, and the change might ease your mind." They had the opposite front room across the stairs. It was the mirror of this, save that it had a small antechamber connecting to the upper hall.

Patty considered this. "No," she said at last. "'Tis better that I learn to shake myself from these spells when they come on than muddle in them. Besides, I wouldn't want to make you shift yourselves at this date. Keep your room, but I thank you for the offer."

Lisbet clucked her tongue. "'Tis ever like you, Patt! You're too stern with yourself. Well, but I will not argue with you, for I know what good it will do me." She paused and looked out the window. "How now, I think that's Mr. Eppes—" Below them the children went racing for the distant horseman coming up the road. "Shall we go down and see what news there is from Dungeness?"

After dinner Francis leaned back in his chair and drawled, "Well, my ladies, what shall we do with ourselves this afternoon? I hope you won't say music, for it's too hot to play. I feel as lazy as an old pig."

"Which would have nothing to do with Mr. Randolph's hospitality," Lisbet said with a sly smile, for Francis's excuse for nearly missing dinner was the necessity of finishing off a bowl of punch. She wasn't upset, though, for Francis's excursions that way were rare. He bore her a baleful glance and shook his head.

"What of whist or landerloo?" Patty suggested. "Have you wits enough for that?" They stared at her.

"By God, cousin, I've not heard you advocate a game of cards in many a year!" Francis exclaimed. "Is it the weather affecting you?"

Patty regarded him primly. "I have not, sirrah," she said, soft-voiced, "because my husband dislikes cards, and it would be exceedingly ill-mannered of me to suggest them with such knowledge. However—" Her glance slid to her sister. "If you'll recall, we played often enough at home."

Lisbet nodded, leaning forward. "We did, so. But tell me, if it's not too impertinent, why does Mr. Jefferson dislike cards? It's true I've never seen him play, have you, Francis?" He shook his head. "What argument can he have with them?"

Patty considered. "The dissipation, I think, is one reason. 'Tis too easy, he said, to gamble away lands and goods with nary a thought. There is a kinsman of his who did so, and I believe it affected him much. As for other reasons—" She smiled a little, "it may not be a challenge enough; he has other more active occupations; it is not productive. For myself, I have no quarrel with idling away a few hours with good friends in the manner. We used to play for buttons, didn't we, Betsy, between ourselves?"

"We did," she agreed strongly, "and you won all my most fetching ones!"
"I gave them back."

"If it suited you," Lisbet complained. "But I seem to recall half-a-dozen pink mother-of-pearls I never saw again but on a gown of Nancy's."

Patty smoothed her skirt. "At least I didn't keep them for myself," she murmured. "Besides, they looked excellently with that gown."

Lisbet harrumphed. "I don't argue that, simply the manner of their getting there." She shook her finger. "You are too sly, Ba, for your own good."

"I don't know if I want to play cards with you after all," Francis told her in mock alarm. "I hadn't realized what a sharp player you were. Why," he looked down at the rows of buttons on the legs of his breeches. "I'd be most embarrassed if I was to lose heavily to you." There was his devilish twinkle in his brown eyes.

Patty waved her hand. "Oh stop, or I shan't play anything with you but take myself upstairs and play goose with Patsy."

"Very well," Francis laughed. "I say 'loo, then, for I haven't the diligence at the moment for whist." This required some memory of what cards had already been played, and a deal of concentration, hence the name, but landerloo was quick and straightforward. It was the single most popular game of Virginia households. They used carved counters, belonging to Henry and Nancy, instead of buttons and played cards beside the open windows until nearly suppertime. At the end of their game, no one was the poorer, for it was all for sport. They hadn't even kept track of wins or losses, although Francis claimed that he was ahead of Patty by four hands. This led to a friendly dispute that continued intermittently through supper until Lisbet put an end to it. They spent the evening with the children, sitting out in the hall, until dusk fell too far to see. Such was the tenor of their days in this house, and it a welcome respite for all. At the end of their visit she promised to be at The Forest in a week.

But once they had gone, the heat brought on all her old complaints. Her eyes troubled her, and she was plagued by dropsy, her fingers ached, and she grew melancholy. She spent her days lying on the sofa in the sunny parlor, brooding on her afflictions and being exceedingly short-tempered with poor Patsy and the servants, so that they were nearly all in tears. She could not write and could read only with difficulty the quantity of letters Thomas sent:

> our declaration was read en committee by mr Adams, and whilst he did so, I could not help but to think how he must have Thundered in the Courts during his law practice, for he is a notable orator—mr. Thompson afterwards called for requests for changes, and upon my soule, you may think me Vain, but I truly expected there to be none, as our committee had put forth so very few, and i was, i will admit

quite dumbstruck as a sea of hands arose, along with a babel of voices with a mass of changes ready to hand. I cannot properly tell you how angry their tampering made me. it became nigh unto impossible to sit and listen to their dissection.

. . .since i wrote you Last, the onslaught to which I have been subjected continues. they question every thing, from my reasoning, to my facts, to my reason, I would go so far as to say. O! where is colo: Lee, our fair Demosthenes, when he is required! i tell you truly, were it not for the ready tongue of mr Adams there shall have been worse indignities created against my work. he is our, and my, greatest advocate. blessedly, he is not the only one, but his is the most frequent and most passionate voice in favor of the pristine text. i cannot bear to speak for it my self. in the first place, i profess no skill at public speaking, and in the second, i am so overcome by the length and tenor of the disputes that I may scarce trust myself to speak anything but an impassioned outcry at their mutilations. howsoever, I doubt me such an emotional appeal would avail much.

. . .they are like jackals at a carcass, only the carcass in this case was living when they came upon it, and they have slowly killed it with their teeth; it is half-dead now, and i fear for it's life entirely if this wretched business is to continue another day. it must not continue, for what will there be left of it once these bloody-handed surgeons are thro'? they have left it half-hearted, where before it was bold.

happily, our committee is steadfast as ever. mr Adams argues with zeal and great ability, and without his advocacy our cause would be much the poorer. mr Sherman condoles with quiet words of god's hand in such matters, and i have no doubt that he beleives it sincerely. mr Livingston has left us to attend some private affairs in new York, but we are in daily expectation of his cousin who, we are assured, shares his sentiments perfectly. dr Franklyn today was sitting by me and when S. Carolina rose again for the fourth time, i was unable to be peaceful, and the Doctr. left off his emploiment and told me this little story:

"i have made it a rule," he said, "whenever in my power, to avoid becoming the draughtsman of papers to be reviewed by a public body. when i was a journeyman printer, one of my companions, an apprentice hatter, having served out his time was about to open shop for himself. his first concern was to have a handsome signboard with the proper inscription. he compased it in these words, 'John Thompson, Hatter, makes and sells hats for ready money' with a figure of a hat subjoined. but he thought he would submit it to his friends for their amendments. the first he showed it to thought the word hatter tautologous, because followed by the words makes hats which show he was a hatter. it was struck out. the next observed that the word makes might as well be omitted, because his customers would not care who made the hats. if good and to their mind, they would buy by whomsoever made. he struck it out. a third said he thought the words for ready money were useless, as it was not the custom to sell on credit. everyone who purchased expected to pay. they were parted with, and the inscription now stood, 'John Thompson sells hats.' 'sells hats!' sais his next friend. 'why nobody will expect you to give 'em away. what then is the use of that word?' it was stricken out, and hats followed it, the rather as there was one painted on the board. so the inscription was reduced ultimately to 'John Thompson' with the figure of a hat subjoined." now this story is likely entirely apocryphal, in fact I would wager that it is, yet in my present frame of mind cannot be reconciled to it's humor; I'm quite afraid that our paper will be reduced to "these colonies, with the King's pleasure, are independent states."

51

A Sacred Obligation

The Forest, Monticello

She was late in going to The Forest because of her eye complaint. On the Thursday after her arrival, she and Lisbet received a call from Maria Byrd. She was on her way up-country to the Warm Springs to spend the sickly months and couldn't pass up seeing them on her progress. Lisbet called for tea and cakes in the parlor, and their guest was shown in. Her gaggle of girls remained outside with the other children, far more interested in playing down by the creek than sitting stiff and silent listening to ladies' talk.

After the tea was brought, Maria settled herself more comfortably on the sofa and peered at Lisbet with an appraising eye. "Well, Madame, I swear you look fine for one in your health!" she exclaimed, crunching one of the sugar wafers. "Not a bit of dropsy about you. That's lucky. I'm plagued with it, fairly plagued. Isn't that so, Patty?"

Patty made a moue of agreement and sipped her tea, knowing better than to interrupt Polly Byrd when she was launched on a subject.

"Not that it's a hazard any longer, thank God," she went on. "Oh, I declare, I do oftentimes miss Mr. Byrd, but his absence has its compensations."

Lisbet opened her mouth to speak, but not soon enough. She exchanged a glance with Patty.

"I had heard that Fanny Page laid in," Maria said. "Is it so? You both are good friends with her; what have you heard?"

"She has." Patty raised her head. "In March." She frowned a little, remembering her own turn in the middle of April, "I think it was about the eighteenth."

"She did poorly, the last I heard," Lisbet added pointedly, reaching for a biscuit. "She had a difficult time."

"Difficult, tush," Maria scoffed. "She's a frail little thing, then reads too many books, I expect. Difficult!" She clucked her tongue. "Why, 'tis no more than a jog of the elbow."

Patty felt herself go numb. The teacup clattered in her nerveless fingers.

Lisbet looked up. "Sister—" She put her cup down. "Are you well? You're positively white—"

She waved her hand. "Aye," she said, hardly able to hear her own voice through the roaring in her ears. "I'm fine. No matter." She put the cup down in her lap.

"Well," Lisbet said to Maria, "it was more than that for her, for she nearly died. She took the fever after, and they feared for her for some time."

"Eh?" Maria left off nibbling the biscuit she held. "Well, then," she said in a softer tone, "I'm sorry to hear it."

"We have heard nothing dire, "Lisbet continued, "so we may hope she is better."

Patty had to get out of the room, away from Maria who was so cavalier, who couldn't care if she had another baby at all, who had never had the least trouble and no sympathy with women who did. She had to leave before she said something indiscreet. She put the cup on the table beside her and rose abruptly. "Excuse me," she said. "I need some air," and she hurried from the room, but not before hearing Maria Byrd's puzzled, "Have I said something—?"

Yes, she thought as she fled for the coolness of the hall—too much, and with too little thought! She sought the hall bench before the stairs and sank onto it, gulping in the cool breeze that wafted in as if she were drowning.

Oh, she would not weep, for she had wept enough over her barrenness, but the pang of April's loss swept over her afresh. She would be farther gone than Lisbet now, nearly to the end of term. O, how could Polly Willing be so cruel, with her passel of girls, not one of them more than a year apart in age. How could she make light, even if she had never suffered, when the tragedies of others were regular enough? Did it not touch her, wound her heart for the sufferer's grief? She was friends with Fanny Page. How could she so abjure that friendship with her flippancy? Hers were not the words of a friend. Not Fanny's friend, nor her own either, for if she was any sort of friend she'd have known what such things meant to her and not made light for her own sake.

The brilliant sky beyond sparkled more through her tears. Oh, she wept these days too easily! Some of it was the glare on her delicate eyes, but mostly there were genuine tears that she could not shake. Not even when she was pregnant was she so unsteady in her emotions as she'd been these last three months. She tried her best to put her tragedies behind her, bravely, but they loomed up on every side with too many reminders. She had always thought Maria Byrd was too forward a woman and put it down to her being a foreigner from the North, but she had surpassed even herself today.

She must go back inside. It was rude to loiter in the hall thus. Maria must think she had offended her, given her precipitous exit. Well, she had, but it was bad manners to discomfit a guest with knowledge of their shortcomings. She rose and stood looking out through the trees, at the slope of the hill to her right that ran toward the river. From the parlor they could see Bermuda Hundred. Had her mother chosen that, she wondered, or her father for her, that she might have the sight when she sat and sewed? She had never asked, though often wondered.

She was better now and took a few settling deep breaths before turning around. She'd behave as if her departure was nothing more remarkable than a call to her closet. She walked the few paces to the parlor and opened the doors. Maria stopped talking and looked up, her eyes sharp, but Lisbet was serene. Not even the ribbons on her cap fluttered with the change of air. But when Patty sat next to her, she pressed her hand under the cover of her sacque coat. It was fortifying against the further visit of this friend from Westover.

She was in low spirits for the rest of the week. She had intended writing a letter for Francis to send, but was not in a humor for it. She spent her time instead doing small things for Lisbet about the household and wandering in the woods with Patsy and the children. Even this didn't bring a balm, for she was struck with how wrecked had come all their hopes since the days she and Thomas wandered in the woods together. Only Patsy remained to them. She was not ungrateful for Patsy, most assuredly not! But her number was inadequate. She wrote to Thomas on the twenty-fourth:

> If it was within my power, I would go Home again to wait you, as we had lately planned, for there is nothing here but a misery to me. I do not mean my deer sister or mr Eppes, but Vistas, Objects and my own remembrances. Every Thing reminds me too well of hopes that are gone. I am in such a melancholy that I cannot rouse myself from it, tho' I have tried. I fear I am an unganely guest. E and F are to kindly to remarque of course. I miss you dredfully, my dearest, and no but you return and I shall be improved. I tell myself that it is onley a month til you are home, but it may as well be a year for all it seams to me. . . . I'm sorry I have not wrote, but what is there to write but more of this sighing to trouble you with? I have read your letters but cannot think of a thing to say to chear you save that Patsy is well, and looks forward to your return.

Thomas sent a note to Francis on the twenty-third that reinforcements had been called for out of Virginia, and adding at the end a personal aside:

> I have received no letter this week, which lays me under great anxiety. I shall leave this place about the 11th of next month. give my love to mrs Eppes, and tell her that when both you and Patty fail to write to me, i think i shall not be unreasonable in insisting that she shall. i am, dear sir, Yours affectionately. . .

In the middle of August she received the distressing news that he had been outmaneuvered by others of their Virginia delegation wishing to come home, that he would be delayed. This letter did not find its way to her hand until the Friday after it was expected, by which time she was home again. She had spent a day with Henry and Nancy in Goochland and another with Patsy Carr, and had taken an entire week to make the journey so that she would have little time to pass alone at Monticello. Had she liked Colonel Lee the less she would have cursed him, for as glad as she was to be home, the place was empty without her dear, and even nine days was an eternity.

> August 4, 1776
> Sweet Patty—
> I am counting that the post will not be delayed, and that this finds you ere you depart for Albemarle. i have only yesterday received by express word from colo: Lee that he will be unable to come here any sooner than the 20th inst., which necessity delays me that much longer. you must know dearest how it pains me to write this to you, after your letter reached me. you must know that only the difficulty of leaving our country unrepresented here would detain me a moment. i beg you to stay where you are until then, i would not have you travel more in the sickly months, when there are so many on the roads for the Springs. make a slow journey when you do, my dear, and tho' it may be longer, it would be worth while to you and relieving to my mind if you went by Ordemond rather than Elk Hill. it would be well for you besides to have a visit with mrs Skipwith. i wish i could be with you, above all that i could honor the promise i made you. every day that i am detained is a year! please, for god's sake my darling, take care! i shall be there as soon as i possibly can. this you must believe as a sacred oath from your devoted
> Th: Jefferson

The house had come along during their absence. The north bow room was built, with the dining room window now a doorway. It wanted plastering yet, but the woodwork was finished. The lower part of the library walls were up to about knee-high, and the connecting anteroom stairs were in. This would be the only access to the room, for Thomas did not consider his books for public consumption. They remained in the south out-chamber in their cases stacked everywhere anyhow, for he had been sending some back with those delegates who returned to Virginia, and the others were those that had been purchased at estate auction for him by John Page.

The room seemed bare by comparison to its former appearance. A lonely bed, an old chair, a chest, a stand, and the books were all it held. As soon as the library was up, even the books would go. It actually was not a bad little room and must have been quite adequate to Thomas as a bachelor here. It would be perfect for guests.

The garden had produced in abundance this year. Mary Garth gave her a written account, not complete, she was assured, of the numbers and items of produce. "I couldn't keep up," Mary said in exasperation of her lack. "There was just so much!"

Ursula's baby Isaac, born in December, was fat and sassy, crawling about the kitchen and making himself such an annoyance that Ursula intended to put him in the nursery. Betty was just out of childbed. Her son John had been born in July. He was very white, with blue eyes that looked to stay so, and it was the general gossip that the father was John Nielson, their master carpenter. Be that as it may, Bett was as hale as ever she was, and more than willing to take up her old duties toward her and Patsy. Baby John was carried about in a basket behind his mother as she went about her tasks by her knee-baby, Sally, who was tall for three. Patty was resolved to find her something more useful to do meantime than stand about. She could remove candle stubs, pick out basting, or any small thing that would not remove her from her mother's reach.

There was a barrel of flour used up entirely in her absence, and three loaves of sugar. The beer was gone, and not being inclined to make more, Mary had been sending to town for cider, which bill she presented for remittance. There were plenty of butter and eggs, and new cheese had been made the day before yesterday, so there was no immediate need that way. But something would have to be done about the beer. The next day she went down with Mrs. Garth and oversaw the making of two casks. They would still have to drink cider for a few days, but there was no help for it.

As it happened, Mr. Lee delayed even longer than expected and the leaves had begun to redden on the trees as September dawned before Bob Hemings came racing up the mountain in advance of his master.

52

Toleration

Monticello

On that Monday morning she was down in their flower garden on the north side of the mountain with Patsy cutting flowers for the dinner table. She stood with shears in hand, looking over the amaranths they'd chosen while Patsy held out the expanse of her apron for the blooms. These had been coaxed from the woods last year and appeared to be doing well, for there were flowers in abundance on every plant. The day was fine now, though the sky was low with thunderstorms earlier, and there was a translucent blue-white haze across the valley to the Southwest mountains. Charlottesville below them was wrapped in mist, but by dinner time it would burn off. The air was warm already up here. They were quiet as they worked, with no songs today, enjoying the peaceful stillness of the air, the smell of the woods, and the warm, vibrant colors of their autumn garden.

"We shall have to put these in the red-flowered vase, don't you think?" she said to Patsy. "Won't they look pretty?"

"Oh, yes, Mama!" Patsy exclaimed. "The one with the little arms!"

She laughed, for to a four-year-old her fan vase must look like it had arms. "They're not arms, goose," she said affectionately, "for if they are, where are the hands? But it was a good guess. . ." She cut several more flowers.

"How many are there?"

Patsy counted. "One-two-three-four-five— "She looked up. "Five."

Patty nodded. "And do you recall how many 'arms' are on the vase?" This recollection took somewhat longer.

"Seven?" the girl said at last.

"Correct." She stood up and laid her hand on her hip. "So how many more do we need?" Patsy knew this immediately.

"Two!" she cried happily, blushing.

"Very good." Patty cut another stalk and laid it in the outstretched apron.

The nodding little blood-red flowers were scattered like dainty bells in their white pool. "We must be gentle with them now," she told Patsy, putting away her shears, "for they're fragile. D'you know what that means?"

Patsy shook her head solemnly. She took her daughter's arm as they started up the hill. "It means, Miss Patt, that the flowers will fall off if roughly handled, so we'll have to walk very carefully, won't we? Like a lady at a ball with a fine gown and a long train. Come."

Stepping behind her, she took up the back of Patsy's looped up gown. "Gently now," she said. "Oh, Pats, are you a duchess or a chambermaid?" Patsy giggled. "Gently. . . good! Very fine! What a lovely day; we'll just glide along easy and slow. Ah, mind the step—good." She gave Patsy's head an affectionate pat. "What a great lady you are!"

They were nearly to the top of the hill before they were interrupted in this game. Scilla, who was usually decorous these days, came tearing across the lawn with her skirts clenched about her knees.

"Ma'am, Ma'am. Oh, Mrs. Jefferson," she was shouting. "He's here; the master's home!" She descended on them like a whirlwind, heaving breaths from her run, dancing up and down with excitement. "Davy said that Bob Hemings just came up stables," she puffed a little. "He runned t' tell us—oh, Ma'am, can we come to see?"

Patty's heart was thudding in her ears, and it was only warning sense of decorum that she didn't throw off the basket and join the groups that were coming out of buildings all over the mountain and hurrying towards the north road. She had heard hoofbeats a while ago but had thought them from the Thoroughfare, for they were distant.

"Yes," she said to Scilla. "You may go." She turned to Patsy, who was struggling between her important duty with the flowers and her excitement over her Papa being home. She fidgeted back and forth nervously.

"Papa's home," Patty cried to her, when Scilla had gone, and she couldn't keep the joy from her voice now. "Here," she said, going behind Patsy, "you give me the flowers, and I'll take them up to the kitchen. You may run along to the stable if you like and meet Papa there, but don't get underfoot."

Patsy barely waited to wiggle out of her apron before she too was racing away as fast as she could go in a tangle of pale green skirts and white petticoats. From the easy playfulness of their gardening, Patty suddenly felt as taut as a bowstring, anticipation sharpening her movements as she hurried across the lawn, skirting the scantling and bricks that Scilla had leapt over. Thomas was home. Thomas was home! After so many weeks of delay, he was really here!

In the kitchen there was a ferment. Baby Isaac, upset by all the confusion, was wailing. Joe, the turn-spit boy, had burned himself and was whimpering in the corner. Nan was scolding him because he wouldn't hold still for linting and butter, and Ursula was talking to herself about the fuss folks got into. Only Sukey was calm, bending over the fire stirring a pot of vegetables.

"Queenie," Patty said, to devil her, "when Martin comes in, tell him to set an extra plate. I hear Mr. Jefferson is home." Ursula left off her kneading of dough, staring at her open-mouthed, and she couldn't help but to laugh. "Oh, I'm sorry, Queenie," she smiled, "but you looked so earnest."

She found a quick bucket for the delicate flowers and flung off her own apron. She would go round to the front door and wait. As she passed through the parlor and the hall, she gave her hair a glance in the looking glass and wished it were not so fuzzy today, but it had rained earlier and the air was damp. There was nothing for it at the moment, and she would not delay to brush it out again, or Thomas would think she did not care to meet him. And that was most certainly not so!

She would have liked to sit on the bench to make a pretty picture when he came up, but she was too agitated. Even standing still was difficult, and she forced herself not to waver back and forth, to hold her hands before her properly. Every nerve was quivering, and she could not still the racing over her heart. When he appeared on Mulberry row from the stable, Patsy beside him, she could restrain herself no more and picked up her skirts. Skipping down the path, she slowed herself to a hurried walk when she came upon him.

"Mr. Jefferson, welcome home!"

His face was all smiles, sunburnt from the road, and his eyes were dancing, green in their depths. "Mrs. Jefferson," he laughed. "I saw you up before the house. You look well, my dear." His gaze, as always, said far more than his words.

"I am, sir," she murmured, smiling with her dimples. They exchanged a proper kiss before all the company. It was not enough; oh, it was never enough. She took his arm as they walked to the house, with Patsy on his other side.

"You see, my dear," she said, with a wave of her hand toward the scaffolding on the second floor. "You nearly have a library. And the bow room is finished off the dining room, and the floors are all done in the chamber."

"That's fine work," he agreed, looking at her. She caught her breath and blushed at his next words, "It's always good to come home to such improvements."

There was a wealth of gifts arrived home with him. Mostly they were small items, but treasured and dear for all that. Volumes and volumes of books came out of the saddle bags after dinner when they had retired to the parlor. There were children's primers, a bestiary, and watercolor drawings for Patsy; there were French and English novels, a cookery book, a bound sketchbook, and an herbal of scented waters for Patty; and many, many volumes of history and law for himself. Yet he had not neglected the garden, for he included James's garden book, and already it was bristled with slips of paper, brimming with ideas.

Of a more material sort, there were reels of cotton in several colors, lengths of calico and drugget, one precious length of shimmering blue-green silk, seven pair of gloves, two of shoes, stockings with clocks embroidered, a handsome needle case, a dozen handkerchiefs, pins, and an half pound of real black tea in its own tin. Upon uncovering this last, Patty threw her arms about Thomas's neck with a cry.

"Oh my dear! Tea! Oh, real tea!" She set the tin down in her lap and kissed him several times. "Thank you, oh, thank you! How I've longed for tea!" She pulled off the lid and up wafted the most delicious odor she had ever smelled in her life, deep and pungent, faintly smoky, the small curled black leaves of Ceylon that were a restorative even in their dry state. It was heavenly, heavenly to sit and contemplate a cup, or a whole pot of rich, beautiful, real, amber tea awaiting her at breakfast. She liked coffee well enough; its necessity did not work so great a hardship on her, but tea was an evocation that coffee could never be. "Oh, how splendid!" she said in a small voice of delight, closing the lid again lest the magical stuff somehow escape like the treasures of Pandora's box.

"I was hoping I might share some with you," Thomas said with amusement. She looked up at him in confusion. "What? Oh." She put aside the tin. "Well, of course!" She blushed. "I didn't mean that you should think—."

He laughed heartily and put an arm about her shoulders. "Save your explanations, sweetheart," he said, smiling. "I'm only teasing." He looked across her lap at the bag. "I believe you've missed something there. There should be another packet."

"Mmm?" She opened the satchel again, and pulled out a small paper-wrapped parcel.

"No," he said, "that's for Pats." He took it and handed it down to the child where she sat at their feet beside the sofa, playing with her new doll.

"It's bigger than that, but soft," he directed. She came at last to the right bundle and this, when unwrapped, proved to be a lovely tippet of dark blue silk with long fringe and dainty embroidery. Lined in a like fabric it was plainly only for evening, for show, for it would never keep out a winter's chill.

"Something for visiting in Williamsburg," Thomas said, and his voice was musing and warm. "You are coming with me?"

She looked up at him and saw that his eyes were very green. She had missed the changing lights of his eyes these four months, forgotten their intensity, their effect. "Oh yes," she replied a little breathlessly.

"Good." He was full of humor. "It'll save me insisting, for I wouldn't have you gone from me again if I could avoid it. And this separation we may avoid." His eyes were a warm caress, though he did not touch her, and she felt very warm of a sudden.

"I would go anywhere with you," she said earnestly. He made no reply but that loving glance, and it spoke more than any words could have done.

"I'm so glad you're better," Thomas said to her in a tone of relief when they were alone later in their curtained bed.

"Am I?" she asked lightly, with a provocative glance, and laughed at his expression, settling herself against him again companionably under the white quilt.

"I was worried, you know," he said seriously, tracing her nose with his finger.

"I know." She rolled her eyes. "I'd begun to wonder if you'd received any of our letters at all." He moved away to look at her.

"Did you write many?"

"Three," she admitted. "But Francis wrote nearly every week."

He leaned back again. "I received two from you," he said broodingly, "and one from Mrs. Reynolds. I didn't know if I could trust Francis. One week I have from him that there's nothing wrong with you, and the next I have your letter from Charles City." He shook his head. "After that, I was certain he had written what he had only to pacify me." His fingers, hardened from hours of contact with fiddle strings, moved in a light caress across her temple, below the frill of her cap, and though she could not see it she knew his face was pensive. "The only other word I had was from Pendleton."

She nodded. "Nannie wrote that they had a visit from him a few days after I left." She turned that she might see his face in the dim light from the candle burning on the stand outside the bed. The curtain was open at the headboard by a hand's breadth. "You needn't fear for me any longer, dearest," she said earnestly. "As I told you, now you're here I am an hundred percent improved. You make me well, better than any of George's tonics, as you make me happy just by your presence." She kissed him and settled herself into his embrace again.

Thomas sighed. "Oh, my sweet Patty," he murmured. His voice was thick with emotion, and his arms tightened about her. "How I do love you."

They had three gloriously peaceful weeks at home with few visitors before they were obliged to make their journey to the Tidewater. Thomas spent most of his time closeted away among his books in the out-chamber writing, for he had many bills and resolutions he wished to present to the General Assembly at its succeeding meeting. The most primary of these was a disestablishment of the Church of England, a matter which for many years now had been of great concern to the large numbers of dissenters in the colony. In June, the legislature had countenanced limited toleration for dissenters, and there was every signal now that the time was ripe for complete toleration, for in the Declaration of Rights they had stated "that religion, or the duty which we owe to our Creator, and the manner of discharging it, can be directed only by reason and conviction, not by force or violence, and therefore all men are equally entitled to the free exercise of religion, according to the dictates of conscience; and that it is the mutual duty of all to practice Christian forbearance, love and charity, towards each other."

Others less secure in their affections might have complained at gaining a husband only to lose him again, and one did in the person of Mrs. Mazzei, but Patty was contented to have Thomas nearby again, within her sphere, at hand whenever she desired or required, and did not beg the constant attentions Mrs. Mazzei espoused. Every day, he took a break from his work to take a ride; every evening they spent together reading or playing music, or visiting with guests if there were any; she was not without his companionship. Her day was filled with duties of the house and yard, as it always was, and preparing for their stay in Williamsburg, so that she hardly had time to think that she was being ill-used. Such a notion never entered her head, and when Mary Mazzei voiced it she was shocked, for by that time it was late in September, and she had begun to suspect that her hopes would not go forever unanswered after all.

"Oh, no, Madame," she hastened to assure her guest. "I had rather Mr. Jefferson were here and working so hard than away in Philadelphia where I may have no knowledge of him for days or weeks. The posts are so bad, I think it a wonder I ever received any word at all from him when he was there. I'm sure if it was your situation you would feel the same. Imagine not being able to follow one's husband! I count Mrs. Washington very lucky and very brave indeed to endure such hardships to follow the army and the General!"

"Mph!" Mrs. Mazzei choked on her tea. It was not the black tea Thomas had brought from Philadelphia, for that was shared only between themselves and very special guests, but huckleberry.

"Mama—" Peggy Martin was out of her chair. She had grown tall this last year and was a sweet, gentle-hearted, endearing young woman of good manners—though it was a vexing question who would marry her with such a mother as she had and not a penny to her name. A considerate parson was about the best she could hope to do. Patty thought she would make a very fine parson's wife, but plainly her mother had other ideas. Peggy now thumped her mother on the back as she coughed into her handkerchief.

"Stop, child," Mrs. Mazzei managed at last between coughs, "or you'll collapse a lung."

Peggy desisted demurely. "I'm sorry, Mama." She sat down again with a blush.

"Are you well, ma'am?" Patty enquired. "I could fetch your servant. . ."

The lady waved her hand. "No," she spluttered, gaining some control. "I'm fine. Thank you." She shook her head. "My dear Mrs. Jefferson, do you mean to say that were you in Lady Washington's place, you would uproot yourself from your home and country to be a camp follower?" She gave the phrase a vulgar meaning. Patty raised her head.

"I would so, Madame," she said quietly, "if it meant I could thereby ease my husband's mind about my circumstance, or be of any consolation to the brave men in the field."

"You are a patriot then?" Mrs. Mazzei asked with an unconcealed sneer of disgust. Patty thought of all the papers Thomas had written and the bills he was draughting now in their out-chamber.

"Under the circumstances," she murmured with no little irony, "I could hardly do else. After all," she continued, gossiping for once for Mrs. Mazzei's benefit, "if poor Lucy Gilmer could give over all her family jewels to our cause then I should surely follow my husband."

Mary's pinched face was thunderstruck. "Did she?" She was all amazement at this now quite old news.

Patty nodded solemnly. "Aye. I saw her deliver them up myself."

The lady shook her head, completely undone. "Incredible." For one of Mrs. Mazzei's turn of mind, doubtless it was; she who had married Mr. Mazzei for her own security only without a speck of kindly feeling towards him. But that was unkind, and she should not think such things in the presence of their object, for her reflections might show on her face. She composed herself better and offered another of Ursula's sugar wafers to Peggy.

The next day she gave Patsy her music lesson. They had left off their practice for most of the summer, but once they had returned to Monticello the presence of the spinet and the pianoforte made it easy to take up their old habit. Before they left for town the clavichord arrived from Elk Hill, as Patty had requested, since Nancy and Henry had bought a new harpsichord, and soon Patsy was practicing on this instrument, as it was small and could be removed from its stand and placed on a table within her reach. The child was now playing chords and trills with some grace, though the swifter changes caught her out sometimes. She learned Vivaldi and Haydn, little songs out of Clarke, and such English tunes and hymns as were thought suitable. Thomas even taught her several of the latter that he had learned from his mother and sister Jane that were, he said, amongst his earliest memories. For her part, Patsy was quick to learn new pieces, and these simple sweet tunes, cherished of her Papa, she begged the words for. She would sing them afterwards in company, in her clear, thin, childish soprano, and thus became acquainted with one of the requisites of life: that it was not enough merely to be entertained, but that one must in some wise entertain as well.

53

Paris Beckons

Williamsburg

By the time they had begun their journey to town at the beginning of October, the certainty of the new pregnancy was as fair as it would be before grosser signs gave their evidence, and it was for that reason they travelled slowly. Every bump and jounce of the carriage along the road made Patty feel ill, so that virtually all she could abide from the horses was a quick trot. Thomas made no complaint against this pace; indeed, it was by his insistence it was undertaken after he discovered how poorly she was at an afternoon stop the first day. They were thus en route five days, rather than the usual three.

She had not brought Betty Hemings with her, as Bett's child was still too small to travel. Instead, for a waiting-maid she had chosen Betty's young daughter Nance. Nance was now fifteen, well over the age to be a nurse. She had been working for the last two-and-an-half years at divers occupations to test her skill and inclination. She had already served some time in the dairy and the laundry, the smokehouse, the vegetable garden, and as a seamstress. Of late she had served as a general maid, dusting the floors and furniture (no little job in their house), and overseen the smaller children such as her younger sister Sally, who were learning to make themselves useful at small chores. Thus this needful elevation was a natural one. If she proved quick and skilled, she would be carried along on journeys, obviating the necessity of removing Betty from her young children. It was for this same reason of family that Thomas had taken to leaving Jupiter behind at the mountain and taking Bob Hemings as his personal servant on journeys. Knowing too well the pangs of separation themselves, they were unwilling to inflict them on their people without good cause.

They were not in town two days before an express rider came from Philadelphia with news for Thomas of his appointment as Commissioner to France, along with Dr. Franklin and Mr. Silas Deane. Apropos of their situation, the resolve ran:

> . . .The Ballots being taken Mr. Franklin, Mr. Deane and Mr.
> Jefferson were elected. . . Resolved, That an Express be sent to Mr.

Jefferson to inform him of his Appointment. . . and that he be requested to inform the President at what Time and Place the Vessel shall meet him.

> By order of Congress John Hancock
> Presidt.

"Are they ordering you to go?" Patty asked, peering dubiously at the paper. The express rider had been sent away for the nonce until the matter was settled.

"Not as such," Thomas said. His face was as pale as the paper he held, and pensive. "But it's quite plain that a refusal was not considered." He dropped his hand to his side. "Oh, damn," he muttered, running a hand through his hair. She stared at him, for he almost never swore. "Why did this have to come now, when I'm in the middle of the law revisal, and you—"

"I can go with you!" she said quickly, clasping his hand. His answer was a smirk, but not unkindly. "Oh, my brave dear." He touched her face. "You are sweet. But I would not risk you, not even for France."

She tossed her head. "I'll manage!" she cried, with more conviction than she felt. It was plain to see that he was torn. He did really want to go, had always longed for Europe, and she did not wish to be the impediment that stood in his way. The colony—or state, rather—of Virginia was another matter and she could not answer for it, but she would not have herself be a burthen of any kind.

Thomas raised an eyebrow. "Six weeks at rough winter seas with your indisposition? I think not, Patty-patt." He clasped her hand. "Come sit," he entreated. "I need to think." He led her over to the sofa under the window and sat with her, knee to knee, his face a shifting mass of emotions. Into the silence the clock on the table ticked loudly as seconds passed by as moments before he spoke. When at last he raised his head, his eyes were a pure clear amber, unmarked by green, as earnest and guileless as a child's. The summer's freckles, hitherto fading with the cool of autumn, stood out in relief across his nose, against the unaccustomed paleness of his face.

He shook his head. "This is a great honor of trust to be elected to this post, and one which I cannot lightly turn aside. If it is refused, I can't say whether I would ever again be given the public trust, for doing so would give them reasons enough for caution. It is important work that I would relish doing even if it were not in Paris. However, there is work here, too, which is of great importance, perhaps not to as many as the other, but certainly to many dearer to us: friends and family, and unseen progeny far in the future." His eyes were far away, gazing into the middle distance. "It means much to me to have a hand in molding that future. So you see, I am torn." He glanced at her. "And this says nothing of you and the children." She felt a shiver at the words. "I could name an hundred reasons there."

"I can go with you," she insisted. "It would not harm me to stay below decks, if needs be, that long."

He shook his head. "No, dear," he said gently but firmly, caressing her hands. "You are valiant to suggest it, but I will not take the gamble."

She saw another avenue, wrenching as the thought of such a long separation was. "Then I could wait, Thomas, until the child is born and old enough to travel. Six months only—"

He laughed a little. "That would be a year and odd months. The middle of January! Are you so hardy that you would brave a winter sea with a small baby?"

"I would go anywhere, do anything, to be with you, you know that!" she exclaimed recklessly. If she had been able to give the matter better thought than a moment's notice, in truth her heart would have quailed at the prospect, for she feared the sea more than horses. Though it might be the most economic and convenient mode of transport in these colonies, yet she would prefer the more arduous overland travel to a sea journey. Unfortunately, in going to France that was not possible.

"I have no doubt you would," he said affectionately, with a chuck behind her left ear. "But," his tone sobered, "we both know the difficulties that lay ahead, whether here or in France, and quite frankly, I'd rather I was here than in Paris with an ocean between, not knowing how things went with you. I'd be useless to myself and everyone else for worry. And I know your propensity for writing," he teased at last.

She blushed. "I would rather you were here than in France, too," she said honestly, for though she had steeled herself to her difficulties in childbed as a necessary particle to achieving her desires, they were not looked forward to with relish. "But I would not detain you either!"

He leaned back on the sofa, lounging as was his habit, and drawling now in exasperation. "Mrs. Jefferson, you are really a most vexing woman!" he said, shaking his head. "Do you earnestly believe at this out I would put any public duty above your welfare or happiness? Has all our discourse on this head passed entirely by you, or are you being deliberately self-effacing? I know that tack, madame," he intoned, echoing the villains out of plays, "and by my faith, such low, female trickery will work no way with me. You'll not lose me that easily."

She looked behind her at him and saw that he was smiling, but the effort at humor was entirely for her benefit. Obligingly, she smiled a little, though she did not feel it, and he sat up again, taking her hand as it lay in the lap of her dark woolen skirts. "Better so," he said; "I did not like your frowning." He kissed her hand. "It was not my design to make you uneasy with my remark, believe me. But that is the primary reason I would decline this offer."

She looked up into the close intensity of his face, troubled by this offer that forced them to choose so unfairly. Then it crept into her mind that perhaps the ill-timing was more her own fault than the Congress's, for should she not have expected that they would lay such an honor as this at his feet? If not this, than a reappointment to Congress that would take him away or some yet undreamt-of post. Was it she who was unfair to hope for a fulfillment of her desire for more children as soon as may be? It was true that she did not need inducements to make it possible, and had flown in the face of George Gilmer's sensible advice to wait until she was stronger. Had she been selfish? Was she, in fact, to blame for the tearing indecision she saw in Thomas's face? It was a dreadful thought, not to be worthy as a helpmeet, to be an impediment and willfully so. He had called her that in anger and in jest, so it must be true. She knew in some respects it was true. Was she devious? Had she worked her will in this against his own? It was a muddle.

"Oh!" she cried in distress.

"What's the matter?"

She bowed her head. "I don't want to be a burthen on you! You should go." She looked up again quickly. "I will wait, if it's what you desire, and I can wait another few months beyond until spring; it—" she faltered. It would be eighteen months or more apart. It was a daunting prospect, nearly two years of absence. She gazed at him helplessly for a moment, then gathered her courage. "You should go," she repeated in a steadier voice.

"It is a grave duty, and you should not miss Paris. I can stay with my sisters. We shall all be well." She saw his eyes change and clasped his hand. "Oh, my dear love, I would not stand in your way."

Thomas made no reply but took her face in his hands gently and kissed her forehead. Rising, he went and stood in the broad nook of the window dormer looking down into the garden where Patsy played under Nance's eye.

He was silent a long while.

She took in his countenance, mixed as it was with yearning and sorrow. Her poor dear! He should not be put to such decisions as this! Whatever her own situation, her first instinct, far beyond duty, was to make him easy. She rose at length and laid her hand on his arm. He started and glanced down at her, then bid her a wordless greeting, his mouth turning up a little at one side, and put an arm about her. They stared out the window together a long time.

He dithered in his decision for three days, keeping the messenger at hand because he didn't have the heart to send him away. The day after the arrival of the news and letter from Mr. Hancock, he sent her to the doctor again, this time to ascertain whether she would be strong enough to make such a journey, for they'd spent most of the night before discussing such a possibility. She had managed to convince him, she thought, of the allowability of the measure, but in the cold light of day he voiced doubts again. She'd seen Brydon in Charlottesville before they left at his insistence. This visit too, was to ease his mind. But in spite of William Carter's positive recommendations, in the end he summoned the messenger and gave him a nay.

So was France lost to them, and perhaps any further hope of such honors from Congress. But Thomas averred that to his mind; the loss was more than justified in the lack of anxiety he would suffer over his family's welfare. There was important work before him in Virginia to make up the loss besides. He took up the business of life once more and his vision of the changes he wished to see effected in the laws of Virginia.

The laws were not the only things changing in Williamsburg that season. There were new faces amongst the old, including one which bore the lineaments of familiarity; young James Madison from Orange, cousin of their friend the reverend, now president of William and Mary, was newly elected to the General Assembly and made his first appearance that autumn. He was a lively young man, twenty-five years old, and soon became a welcome part of their evening company for his wit and acute observations. He was a small man, hardly taller than Patty, with fair hair, eyes of a deceptively mellow grey-brown, and the same delicate features as his kinsman. But for all his unprepossessing appearance, he had a brilliant mind and charming manners that would have done credit to the greatest prince in Europe.

There was comfortable society that season. The Pages had been living in town since John took over Governor Henry's duties in the summer, and all six of their children were with them. The Madisons, too, were always at hand. Thomas Adams and his wife had come from their place up-country for the season, with a view to remaining until Christmas. There were the two French gentlemen, M. St. Aubin and M. de Harrincourt, the chevaliers for whom Page had not been able to secure a troop from Congress. It had been Thomas's opinion that, given the general feeling of Congress at the moment towards Frenchmen—for they were pressed on every side by requests for commands from those countrymen—these two gentlemen would do better to remain in Virginia, and thus they had. They remained through the season and past Christmas before travelling north to seek their fortunes with the army. Their presence brightened the season considerably, and gave Patty and Thomas some balm at having missed France.

The Chevalier St. Aubin was a small, dark, Gallic fellow with great expressive eyes and a pockmarked skin. He walked with a slightly rolling gait, due to being somewhat lame in one leg—a keepsake, as he called it, from one of his adventures. He delighted in Patty, his manners toward her being excessively graceful, and she blushed to hear how remarkably she put him in mind of his wife, Minette. She too, he said, was such a woodland flower, too shy and sweet and rare for the garden bed.

She found such hand-in-glove flattery a trifle overwhelming, but she had fended off less subtle and more unwelcome advances ere this. She had been the recipient of a rather pointed admiring remark of Richard Henry Lee's at a party during the brief period that he was widowered, which she could only attribute to too much punch, as he was normally most circumspect with ladies. Now to the chevalier, she smiled her dimpled smile and murmured that if such was the case, he must be a most anxious man, being away from his wife so long, as even wildflowers were susceptible to cultivation, at which he laughed and made a bow. They were friends, equals, and such a jesting half-courtship continued as long as he was in their company.

His companion, M. de Harrincourt, was far less bold, for he had been a soldier of necessity and less accustomed to the charms of the salon. According to his friend, his family, though noble, had suffered in fortunes for the Huguenot faith of an ancestor. He was a shy man, over-sober for his years, with fair hair and notably broad shoulders. He was taller than St. Aubin by nearly a foot. Being acquainted with the passions that often lurked unsuspected in the bosoms of the reticent, Patty sounded him out in a casual way on various subjects and found that he was a cellist and an avid music lover.

"Oh, Monsieur!" she cried in delight. "Then you must speak to my husband. Mr. Jefferson has quite a collection of music and plays the cello passing fine. I believe he has some music for it with him. If you like, I will ask him to bring it to you. . ." De Harrincourt's round face glowed. "I should like that, Madame," he said, bowing his head gravely. But there was about his countenance a pleasure that the formal words belied. Thomas gave him several pieces of cello music.

Early in November they took up a temporary residence in Mr. Wythe's house on Palace Green, the rented rooms being too small and inconvenient for their use. It was impossible to host dinners, suppers, and salons in the cramped space, and such impromptu entertainments were an annoyance to their hosts. They needed a place until more suitable lodgings came free. The Wythes' house, built by Mrs. Wythe's father Richard Taliaferro, was ideal, and only too gladly lent, as they were assured by Mr. Wythe in a letter received later in the month.

Being made of brick, the house was a typical Virginia mansion house reduced in scale. The rooms were smaller, but it yet possessed the familiar suites of rooms separated by a central hall and staircase. In the back of the property were all the elements of a plantation house: kitchens, dairy, laundry, smokehouse, a formal and a kitchen garden, the latter of which ran parallel to the churchyard next door. For their chamber they occupied the southwest bedroom, which overlooked the gardens on two sides. Situated over the study and part of the parlor, it was the most commodious of rooms, warm and sunny for the better part of the day.

She spent her time while Thomas was away at the business of the Assembly, stitching in the chamber, strolling in the gardens with Patsy, playing music on Elizabeth Wythe's spinet in the parlor, and receiving guests. It was understood that she was not well enough to go out, so many of the ladies called on her instead. She had a visit from Sylvia Drummond, Thomas's old friend; and Molly Digges, who had secured several books for him when Richard Bland died; as well as from Fanny Page, Elizabeth Adams, and Eleanor Madison. Her sisters came in for a week that November, and together they paid a call on Aunty Randall, who was doing too poorly with rheumatism these days to pay calls.

In spite of this, Patty found the visit vivifying, for she'd not had an opportunity to write in some time, and the proximity of her sisters meant that they fell into their old familiar easy pattern. Nancy was now the mother of two children with another anticipated, plumper than she used to be, but far less shy. When her children would have joined in the mischief of sliding down the stair rails in Aunt's quiet house, she went out into the hall and called them off it in a still, firm voice.

"Jack, Polly, you will come down. It is not how we play at Aunt's house. Come and sit." She was kindly, but would clearly brook no opposition, and her children offered none, instead coming to sit and munch a biscuit until their chagrin was forgotten.

Lisbet was concerned that she had several teeth loose at the back, and wondered aloud at the efficacy of Dr. Baker and having them out.

"Oh, but then I shall look gaunt and have to wear plumpers like old ladies, and it would be ever so drear!" She paused and colored, glancing at their aunt, who regarded her with amusement. "Your pardon, aunt. I did mean no offence."

Elizabeth laughed. "None taken, pet. I still have all my teeth! 'Tis a product of being childless, some would say, tho' I doubt not that my taking tea may have weakened them. They do plague me when it's cold outdoors."

Patty ventured, "If your teeth are a burthen to you, sister, I would seek out Dr. Baker, for he is equal to his reputation. I saw him several years ago now about an abscess that troubled me, and he was able to fit a replacement to the tooth." She turned her head a little indicating the place. "You can't even tell the shift."

Lisbet frowned, considering. "Of what manner is the stuff?"

"Oh, ivory or hippopotamus, I think," she said. "I don't rightly recall. 'Tisn't wood or plain bone, for we paid extra. It's wired in, and I've never had the least bother from it. It would be worth your while."

Betsy nodded. "Let me see."

"What?" Patty asked blankly. Lisbet inclined her head at this stupidity, and she understood. "Oh, the tooth! Come here." She opened her mouth for Lisbet's inspection.

"It's never troubled you?" she ascertained when Patty closed her mouth again.

"Not a bit. I'm hard put to believe sometimes it's not my own."

"Hmm." Betsy sighed. "Well. I shall certainly speak to Mr. Eppes."

54

Domestic Disturbances

Monticello

It was about this time that Thomas's committee brought forward their bill for the removal of the capitol to some place farther inland. Virginia was not the only state struggling with the problem of long-established coastal towns being endangered from naval attack, as well as no longer serving the best needs of their far-flung citizenry. The most likely towns in Virginia would be Fredericksburg or Richmond, and Thomas made extensive notes on the reasons for removal to use in debate. The rights of the western people, he declared, were equal to those of the eastern as members of the legislature, and over an hundred years of experience had proved that Williamsburg could never be great, for she had not risen any more from her position held since Nicholson laid out the town from the Middle Plantation in 1673. Norfolk was more populous six times over. All his careful calculations and illustrations went for naught in the end, for the bill went defeated by a vote of 61 to 38. But he was not daunted. He merely tucked the paper and notes away to save for another time.

On Thursday, the fourth of December, they took lodgings with Mr. Pinkney at the far end of town, but their stay was brief. By the middle of the month they were home again at Monticello, having achieved their object of avoiding being caught in the first snowfall. Two days before Christmas, she made a note in her accounts book, which had lain fallow for close to an entire year:

> Dec 23 6 hogs killed to make Cream Cheese by mrs Adams to two gallons of new milk warm from the Cow, put a pint of cream mixt well with the milk, three or four spoon-fulls of rennet stured in, cover it till it wheys, then turne it into a cloth over the vat, till all the whey is drained of, then put it into the vat, & put in the sop, and increase the weight in the sop every hour, bare & into a cheese cloth every half hour, let it remain in the vat till the nex morning, if their should be any whey in it, rub it over with salt night & morning, fit to eat in four or five days.

They had their first real snowfall the next day, and the weather set in cold. It had snowed on the twentieth, but that had only lain a few hours. Now, from Christmas night onwards, when the snow fell two feet deep overnight, they were gripped by the severest winter cold in local memory. It was unusual during the whole of January 1777 for the temperature to rise above thirty-five degrees in the middle of the day, and even February did not produce much warmer temperatures.

During this time, she busied herself with the usual winter tasks of slaughtering and dressing the hogs that came from Elk Hill, Bedford, Poplar Forest, and their own herds. On the first day of the new year, thirty-one hogs were killed. Eight days later there were seventeen more, and after three weeks there were sixty-eight beasts worth of hams, bacon, and fat set up in the smokehouse or the cellar. She was getting large now and was anxious to have her house in order before the child came. In the middle of February, she noted in her book:

> a beef killed   66 lb of tallow in ye cellar

The rivers were all low that spring, so that it was impossible to have any navigation above the falls of the James at all. Their well was dry as bone, and water had to be hauled up the mountain by hand, for the springs too yielded little. Early in March Patty was busy with her household in spite of the drought and its inconvenience, and the discomforts of her increasing bulk and general weariness. On the fifth, she noted that there were eleven dozen and two candles in the cellar; on the eighth, she made an hundred pounds of soft soap, killed two geese, and made an inventory of her linens:

> 7 beds 7 bolsters 10 pillows 7 pr of blankets
> 5 matresses one straw bed 6 counterpains

She later made more soap, both soft and hard, and more candles. Thomas planted peas and broccoli, lettuce and radiccio in the garden, and three beds of strawberries. April came, and the peach and cherry trees were in bloom, turning the orchard into a faeryland of pink-and-white-skirted ladies dancing on the wind for Patsy's delight. Patty began to take stock of their clothes to see what wanted replacing:

> T. Jeff.   14 old fine shirts   9 ruffled ditt   12 new plain
> M. Jefferson   10 old ruffled shifts   4 new ones, not made
> 8 old ones ditto 9 night caps   6 fine linen Aprons
> 8 coarse ditto   6 pr of silk hoes   6 pr ditto of cotton
> Pattsy Jef 7 new shift   2 night caps   9 frocks   4 pr stockings
> 2 laced tuckers   2 hemstitched do

Thomas retired Young Fearnought that spring as his main riding horse, Caractacus now being two years old and dependable enough in his temperament to be taken on long journeys. He had waited until the animal was a yearling to saddle-train him. It might have been done sooner by one of the stable boys, but as he wanted to be known as the horse's only master, he put it off until he was strong enough to bear his weight. Now, though sometimes skittish, Caractacus was a fine mount. His playfulness and unfortunate high spirits he would eventually outgrow, and since a severe rebuke at the narrow turn of their road along the north side of the mountain where he had threatened rebellion, he was obedient and thoroughly attached to Thomas. With good reason! He was brought bribes of good behavior by his master every day after breakfast: apples, oats, a piece of sugar. Both had come to look forward to this pleasant ritual. One morning Patty needed to go down to speak with Mary Garth in the row anyway, so accompanied him to the stable.

The boys were shy in her presence, especially as she was great now with her child, but George was not. He took off his hat and grinned at her. "G' mawning, ma'am," he cried, delighted that she should pay him a visit. They liked one another.

"Good morning, King George," she smiled back, blushing.

"You Davy!" George hollered at one of the boys, who was leaning on the door of the box a few feet away, "Fetch the mistress a clean stool!"

Patty held up her hand, glancing at Thomas, who said nothing but smiled.

"Oh, no," she said. "I don't mean to disturb you that long. I just wanted to see how Caractacus was getting on." She leaned to look at Davy. "Please don't."

"You'll make them nervous," Thomas whispered to her, leaning down so that his face was behind her shoulder. He made to pick up a piece of straw. "They're afraid you'll burst. Accept it."

"Very well," she relented, and the stool was brought. It was convenient, as it happened, for with her present girth she could not get near enough to see over the box, so she used the stool to stand on. This was not calculated to make the hands any more confident, but she couldn't help that. Thomas kept his hand under her elbow the while, plainly not trusting her balance either.

They had sugar today, and at the sight of his master the horse advanced with alacrity. He wore the same intelligent, quizzical expression he had at his birth, rather comical now, with a forelock falling over his eyes.

"Hello there, my old fellow," Thomas said to him, with a caress of his perked-up ears. The horse nudged him. "Think I have something for you, do you?" He laughed softly in a familiar way, full of affection and delight. Patty looked up curiously. It was the same low-murmured chuckle she had heard when she protested his teasing. "Very well, now," he said. "Where is it?"

Caractacus nudged him again, at the very pocket where the piece of sugar was concealed.

"He can scent it," Thomas said to her.

"Mr. Jefferson, you're an awful tease!" she exclaimed, watching the horse stamp about in the box. He was like a child, dancing up and down for a treat. Thomas laid a finger before his lips, smiling a little. "He expects it," he murmured. "'Tis our game. It sharpens his instincts."

"For treats," she disparaged. He only laughed.

Taking the sugar from his pocket, he put it behind his back and shifted hands, ending up by holding both before him. "Where is it now, laddie?" Without hesitation, the animal chose the right, and Thomas opened his palm. The sugar was there. "Good boy," he said admiringly, with a friendly nuzzle of the horse's nose. Thomas walked with her to the Garths' after that, with a hand proprietarily under her elbow.

"We're putting in the potatoes today," he said, helping her up the slope of the hill.

"Irish or sweet?"

"Irish." He looked across the garden to Montalto. "Please God, we'll have enough water for them. How are those from last year?"

She made a mental tally of the contents of the root cellar. "Enough to last till July, I think. If not, we have plenty of swedes and turnips."

He grimaced. "Cattle fodder," he murmured. She laughed now, for she knew he was not fond of the vegetable.

"I didn't mean for us!" She paused at a twinge, laying a hand on her side. "Oh!"

"What's amiss?" The sudden anxiety in his face was endearing. After five pregnancies, most men would have accustomed themselves to a woman's every groaning complaint.

"It's nothing, just a twinge," she assured him. "You shouldn't make me laugh."

He took her arm again. "But it's one of my primary amusements," he said in a low tone. "It shows your dimples." She blushed again, thankful that Mary or the Garth children were not outdoors. "Mr. Jefferson," she chided him, shaking her head. She looked up at him and saw his mouth twitch a little as he suppressed a laugh. The sun shone on the gold in his hair.

"Very well," he acceded. "I'll desist." He rapped on the door for her. "Good day to you, Madame," he said with a bow, before the door should open. "If you require me I shall be down the garden." The green glinted in his eyes and he kissed her hand briefly and was away, his coatskirts fluttering

414

behind him. Just then, Mrs. Garth's servant opened the door. Patty started a little, not anticipating so short a wait. They were usually long at answering the door here.

"Good morning, Nell," she said belatedly. "Is Mrs. Garth abroad?"

"Oh, yas'm." Nell rolled her eyes. "Come in, ma'am, come in, an I just run to fetch her. . . ." She was shown into the common room of the little house and took a chair, clearing it first of clothing, a pocket knife, and several children's toys. From upstairs she heard Mrs. Garth telling out one of her children to comb his hair and was very glad for her peaceful little family.

She stopped by the kitchen before going into the house again, to give out instructions for dinner. Ursula was testing the oven for the baking; Nan and Scilla were washing the dishes in a tub on the dresser, stacking plates neatly as they went; and Sukey sat at the table polishing the silverware with a piece of baize and a solution of alum, strong lye, and soft soap. Sukey was now six months forward in her fourth pregnancy and spent most of her time seated now on a low stool before the fire. This was the first time her circumstance had advanced beyond the early stages and was a vast improvement upon her barrenness the first year of her marriage. She was now eighteen years old, not much taller than she had been at thirteen, and slender about the limbs for all her girth. Her demeanor had sobered some because of her losses, but not as much as many a white woman's. She was cheerful and calm, direct and hard-working, with a demonstrated cool head in a crisis. If there was a new dish to be prepared, Sukey didn't need to be told the directions twice, and they were never subject to unpleasant surprises in the dining room.

"Good morning!" she said as a greeting to all, and was met with returns of "G'morning, ma'am," on every side. Isaac clambered up to her, toddling in his wide-legged gait, to tug on her skirt.

"Why, hello, Izzy," she cried, peering at him over the mound of her belly. He fetched her a wide grin and toddled away again to play in the pudding molds he'd been allowed on the floor.

Before her Sukey was absorbed in her task, frowning a little in concentration, but there was about her countenance a distracted quality, too, that set off a warning bell in her mind.

"Sukey," she enquired suddenly, "are you well?"

"Yas'm." Sukey scrubbed a little harder at the serving spoon's minute blemish. She would wear it out, with such diligence. The girl did not meet her gaze but went on with her work. The others paid them no mind, though doubtless they were listening avidly.

"Are you certain?" she persisted. "You look queer." She saw the sheen of perspiration now on her cook's brow, though it was a fine day and she was far from the fire. Sukey said nothing. The room was still, with an echoing silence. Only Isaac's babbles punctuated the void. Patty would not let it lie. Sukey was her responsibility, and she didn't want her falling into the soup in any case. She pressed her lips together determinedly. "Sukey," she asked plainly, "have you a cramp?"

For a long moment the girl went on polishing and did not speak. She looked at no one, but took up a ladle embossed with Bathurst and Patty's initials, dipped it into her cleaning solution, and scrubbed. The ladle had not shone so in ten years. Sukey muttered grimly at last, "Yas'm."

That was all it took. "Queenie," she said to Ursula, who had turned from the oven, "take Sukey to her house. We may wait about dinner until she's settled."

"Yas, Mis' Jefferson," Ursula said.

"Nan, you finish up the silver; Scilla's nearly done there." She went over to her cook and laid a hand on her arm. "Suke, you must go with Ursula."

Sukey looked up at her with piercing eyes. She really must be in great pain, Patty thought. Well, we are not so desperate. She'll not lose this child on my account.

"I know you're frightened," she said gently. "But you have yet no cause for fear. Go with Ursie to your house and stay there. Lie down. All day. Don't fret about things here, for we shall manage. If you like, I'll fetch down Aggey or old Jenny to you."

The girl nodded briefly.

"Good," she said. "You go now. Everything will be fine." She patted Sukey's skinny arm as she went out with Ursula. Queenie was muttering comfortingly about how these things always work out, and young girls with their first baby fret so, and so on. There was another woman Patty would stand against any crisis.

Sukey did not lose her child. After two days of lying abed she came back to the kitchen with all signs of threat past, not to reappear until their proper time. Patty was, if not grateful for her own experience, then thankful it had provided her a necessary knowledge and compassion. She wrote to her sister Nancy:

> How far this difficulty may have been advanced I do not know, but on recognizing it I was determined to stop it. She is a stubborn creature, and if I had not contravened she doubtless would have borne her sufferings in the same stoic silence until there was no help for them. She is now made to understand the delicacy of her situation, and why half-labor was called for. Queenie is there to enforce it on her. Under a merciful heaven we may see this matter come to it's just and proper end.

Thomas left for Williamsburg and the spring session of the Assembly. He had promised to be back early, given her habit of early deliveries, and were it not for the pressing business of the law revisals he would not have gone at all. But she was well and cheerful, busy enough in her own regard that a short absence would not be unbearable. "I'll remember to remark the temperatures for you, and the garden yield," she promised. She sat on the bed, pulling a brush through her hair, watching while he packed his toilet box with its sundry bottles and brushes. It was only six o'clock in the morning, and the servants were not yet abroad.

Thomas smiled a little. "Thank you, sweet." He was absorbed in the task, distracted by his own thoughts, for he had much important work ahead of him; and she knew, too, that he was uneasy about leaving her alone so close to her time. When he had voiced this concern last night, she said, "But it is not for a month yet, and in any case George is near to hand. There is no cause for alarum. We shall not begin our business without you."

Now she put down her hairbrush beside her, another concern coming to mind.

"Thomas," she ventured. "If you could, would you make a visit to Mrs. Charlton's and see if she has my gown ready?" In accordance with their habit, she had a new gown as a celebration to wear once she had had her baby. This one, in grey, embroidered with pink flowers, had been fitted from an old measure in December.

He frowned a moment, not recollecting. "Oh yes," he said at last. "Of course I will." He leaned to kiss her. "At least you never present me with a list of impossible gewgaws as my mother used to do." He smiled a little. "I never told her that most of her requests were got by Mrs. Wythe or Mrs. Drummond." He colored. "I could never face Tarpley or Prentis again after a personal request in their store for four pairs of ladies' stays in drab colors. . ."

She inclined her head. "I seem to recall your mentioning a fondness for the business of ladies' stays," she teased. He flushed again.

"It was a trifle different when I was sixteen," he protested.

At a sudden shift from the baby she drew up, bracing her hands behind her on the bed to avoid being kicked in the ribs. The child moved from side to side, and the progress was plainly evident under her shift. Thomas left off his packing, watching these maneuvers with interest. When it was done, she sat up again gingerly, for alacrity had long since left her.

"He's getting impatient," she said.

Thomas raised an eyebrow, closing the box. "He?" His eyes were full of amusement.

She shrugged. "'Tis a convention. Besides, we may hope—"

"But not expect?" he finished, helping her off the bed.

"Aye," she said, pleased, and lumbered off to dress.

While he was away, she kept her tally of the weather and the plantings, as she promised, though she could get the temperature but once a day, and sometimes not until after dinner. She wrote out her observations of both on the loose sheets she used for her expenses.

> 12 french beans planted   sugar, & ditto matzeis,
> 19 a shoat killed made   17 candles
> sowed— pudding pease gallerance   ditto

> May 1- 8:30 A.M. 48   May 7- 2:30 P.M. 70
>   3:30 P.M. 52½   May 8- 8:40 A.M. 60
> May 2- 3:00 P.M. 53   May 10- 7:40 A.M. 55
> May 3- 9:00 A.M. 48   4:55 P.M. 58½

He was home again on the twenty-third, and not before time, for true to past form, her labor began about a week before it was expected. Once more it began in the morning on the twenty-eighth, this time quite early, but she was able to get through breakfast and having dinner ordered before anything was noticed. She was in the chamber with Betty, rotating all the linens since the laundering and starching of the day before. She knew that she would soon have to say something, for the pains were beginning to take her breath away, but she wanted this final task completed, for she would be several days abed afterward. She climbed up on the stool and reached toward the top shelf, and heard behind her, "Miss Patty, what are you doin' up on that chair! Get down from there! Are you trying to lose yourself this child too? Get down, I say! I can reach them sheets up there myself with no stool anyhow. Get down!"

She looked over her shoulder at Betty's carping. "O hush, Bett, I'm perfectly safe," she scoffed. "Besides, you'd put yourself in danger also, reaching high up like that." For Betty was well gone herself in another pregnancy. "I can manage perfectly well." She held onto the shelf of the airing cupboard and with her other hand took down the pile of pillowcases strewn in thyme.

Betty took the linen from her and laid it on the bed. She was scowling. "You make no mind about me, Miss Patty. After twelve chillerns I expect I know what I kin and can't do, but I ain't a dainty lady like you. Come down off that stool, sugar, there's a good girl."

Annoyance broke through her concentration of her breath. "Don't sugar me and try to wheedle, Bett— Oh," she gasped in surprise, for she had a deep sharp twinge suddenly and nearly toppled off the little stool. She caught her balance on the shelf below her and stepped down, grateful for solid ground. Betty was beside her in an instant, all her clucking, mother-hen fretting gone in the presence of a real worry. She took Patty's arms in her firm grip while she stood, silent and pale, closing her eyes against her onslaught.

"I knew'd you'd a have this chile today, lambie," Betty said, bending solicitously over her. "I had a feeling. You come and sit, and Bett'll take care of you. Come now."

Patty was usually scornful of such slop, especially from Betty, who was otherwise sharp-tongued and pithy in her caring, but in her present state she was happy to indulge it. She let herself be led away to put her feet up on the bed, and while Bett was gone, dragging Sally out by the hand behind her, she closed her eyes and leaned her head against the pillows on the wall, listening to the work of Stephen Willis's lads going on above her head. Out the windows the day was fine and warm and clear, with a hint of balmy summer coming on. In a week it would be humid, hot, and unbearable to carry a child. But in a week this travail would be done and her child beside her.

She listened, in a quiet space, floating as a fluff of down along the river, to the far-off birdsong in the woods, a thrush or woodcock calling to its mate. And she remembered that the muscovies had not been felt for eggs today. She would remark it when Betty came back. It was easier to wait through the pains lying thus, half-reclined upon the bed. Three or four went by in some quarter of an hour, to judge by the chiming of the clock on the mantel. She hoped this birth would not be as bad as the others. It was beginning gently enough. She had no sooner thought this than there came a great rush of the waters, and she struggled off the bed so as not to ruin her counterpane.

"Oh bother," she said aloud to herself, for she was wearing a new petticoat, and it would never come clean again.

Slowly, gingerly, she went about changing her clothes, for the cold clammy petticoat and warm, ripe smell of the waters were too disgusting and indelicate for her comfort. The pains were sharper now, though no more frequent, but she became anxious nonetheless, for it was said that dry births were harder to bear, and all of hers had begun as this. She knew too well what lay ahead and felt a thrill of dread at the thought.

Betty returned when she was treading on her new petticoat to sop up the mess, and she was put instantly to bed. "I told Juba to fetch the master, an' he told me he's down the Tufton lands looking at the tobacco." Juba was Jupiter's nickname.

"I know he is," she said calmly. "He told me he was going there this morning. Did he send to fetch him?"

Bett pulled the counterpane over her and she pushed it off. It would be too hot today for covers, even linen ones. Betty didn't fuss her about it. "Yes'm," she said evenly. "Great George, he sent Davy on Callista."

"Ah." It didn't really matter who was sent, for there was no great urgency as yet, but Davy was quick and Callista dependable. George was thoughtful in his choice.

55

A Son Born

Monticello

Thomas came in about an hour later, and she was playing a game of Goose with Patsy on the bed, her knees drawn up indecorously and her hair spilling about her. Patsy threw down her pair of dice when he appeared and leapt off the bed, scattering the game pieces.

"Gently, Patsy," Patty told her. Thomas came over and she took his hand. "I'm so glad you're here!" she said in relief, laying her cheek against his fingers. "Goose is become rather trying to my wits—" She paused, clutching his hand, closing her eyes against the pain that came sharply, steeling herself against it, saying nothing for Patsy's sake.

There was nothing so dear as the anxious, loving tenderness she saw in Thomas's face whenever he was called to such scenes. He was never brusque or callous or scornful of her difficulty, as she heard some were, enjoining her to bear up bravely to this just scourge of women. Maria Byrd told stories that made one question the sensibilities of the Byrd men, and grateful one was not amongst them. Doubtless such words had been uttered in a tone of comfort, but their message was otherwise. No, Thomas sat down next to her on the bed and held her hand in both of his, watching her with a cautious and discerning eye for a moment to see that it was over before speaking.

"Should I send for Gilmer?" he asked.

She shook her head. "Not yet. Not nearly yet. After dinner or so."

He touched her face. "Are you sure?"

She smiled a little, ruefully. "Ask me at dinner."

He sent Patsy from the room and removed the game from the bed, and spent a long while sitting with her with his arms about her. It was easier then, sweet to lie her head on his shoulder and relax. She could drift through one or two of the pains in this wise, without any sign but a sigh to mark their passing. But at noon Betty came in to make up the bed in her suit of childbed linen, stored in the chest in the out-chamber. When she was settled comfortably into his encompassing red leather chair, Thomas kissed her hand, murmuring, "I won't be a moment, my dear," and went from the room. He was indeed back before the bed was finished, and it was the only time he was from her side all the long while.

It was the easiest childbirth she had ever had. George Gilmer arrived at teatime, and she was yet lucid, talking between times with Thomas about sundry things, and easy. She felt a great heaviness when the pains came, as though she could sink into the bed and never move again, but little actual pain, for after a time the sharpness left them, and she could feel the bulk of the pressure moving upwards, like the gathering of a curtain on a string. Her child was born at ten o'clock that night in perfect peace and an echoing stillness. George never even took his fancy English instruments out of his bag. And she hardly bled at all. To crown the most glorious beauty of this gentle meeting was the most welcome of all sights: the child was a boy.

Tiny, perfect, for he was smaller even than Jack had been, he greeted them with a quiet mewling and a sneeze. He turned pink then, and all the room seemed to come alive with the rosy joy of his presence. When she took him in her arms, weeping for utter happiness, he gazed at her with his murky-dark eyes in searching curiosity, and it was as if she looked upon the face of an old friend. He was already dear.

"Oh, baby," she cried, cradling him close. "Baby, baby." She choked on tears and bent her head to rest near the little one. The fine blonde fuzz of his hair tickled her cheek. A son. They had a son! She met Thomas's eyes, not inches from her, warm and glittering amber, their green lost in the darkness of candlelight and emotion. After such loss and grief, their misfortunes were past them now. They had a son, from an easy birth, who was well and sound and perfect. She smiled at him, loving him better than she thought she possibly could.

"Mr. Jefferson," she murmured warmly.

"My dear." His voice was soft, the tone intimate, inaudible to George below her or Betty who hovered at the other side of the bed. She shifted herself a little, turning that she could face him better. "Here is your son, sir." She laid the baby in his hands. As she did, the tears slipped over and fell down her cheek. She closed her eyes against their companions at Thomas's kiss on her temple and his fervent whisper, "God bless you, darling."

For three days they were in bliss. The wild celebrations that went on in every nook and hollow of the property were met and matched by their quieter, more intimate, fervid ones in the privacy of their chamber. Joy buoyed them up, and delight was their constant companion. The first three days their little family circle was intimate, with only themselves and Patsy allowed inside. Work was suspended upstairs, and in the still peace of an afternoon with the baby asleep between them and Patsy at her nap at the end of the bed, they considered the most important, pressing question.

"What name shall we call him?" Thomas asked. The echoes of those words stretched back through time to the autumn of Patsy's birth. It was as yesterday and forever ago from this moment. She touched his face in a fond caress. The encompassing love she felt for him at the birth of their little one had not faded but grown, so that it was an almost unbearable joy. She trembled with it, longed with it, spoke it in an hundred ways a thousand times a day.

"I know one."

He kissed her palm. "Tell me."

"Oh, Thomas, what else?" She smiled, disbelieving he could really not guess her choice. He was only playing their game. As she had, he disagreed.

"Wouldn't that be confusing?"

"Oh, no," she said softly, sliding her hand in his with a murmur at his caress of her arm. "We could call him Tom."

He leaned and kissed her lingeringly, by the green sparkling of his eyes as caught up as she in this revel of love. "I like Peter better," he murmured into her ear. Her heart thudded, and the reaction let the milk down. She gasped. "Tom. . ." Things could get entirely too carried away.

As if in answer to her distress and the call of his dinner, the baby woke himself with a jerk between them. Thomas moved away, laughing silently, for they had encountered this trouble before.

"So you're going to be at this, too, boy?" he enquired of the searching, bewildered baby. But he was not put out. They couldn't have done aught but frustrate themselves anyway at this date. She picked up the baby and gave him his milk, his name still in dispute.

By the time he was six days old, they agreed that the child should be named Peter Field, for his grandfather and an uncle who had died an infant. Like his sister Jane before him, Peter was a placid baby of regular habits, who accepted what the world offered him without a fuss. But for his own part, there was a curious stillness about him. He was earnest. Where his sisters had smiled from the outset, he did not until he was a week old, and then it was coaxed from him.

She sat with him in the chair by the window in the morning, where the cool dappled light came dancing down from the copper beech tree outside through dust motes that swirled like Tatania's faeries at midsummer revels. She saw his fixed attention on these specks in his middle distance.

"What do you see, son?" she asked him in hushed tones. "Do you see the faeries dancing, Peter? Are they dancing for you?" At the sound of her voice his gaze shifted, and he stared at her a moment with his solemn dark eyes; and then to her delight, his face broke into the sunniest of smiles, as a flower opening its petals to the day. It was like looking upon the face of God to see his earnest little face dissolve in pleasure. Tears smarted in her eyes.

"Oh, baby!" she cried, lifting him up and cradling him to her bosom. "Mama loves you! My little Peter."

It proved to be a name of ill luck, for shortly after this their dear, peaceful, little blonde fellow began to have episodes of difficult breathing. Now she had seen enough babies in her life to know that they often had shallow breath and periods of seeming breathlessness to no harm, but this was different. Peter struggled, snoring and gasping, and turned an appalling shade of grey that sent her heart thumping in fear. All her insides turned to water, and she pulled the baby up from his bed and clutched him to her in mortal terror.

"Oh, baby, baby." The rising, desperate note in her voice was a strident call by the time she tore open the parlor door and shouted for Betty. Bett had left her not half an hour before that she might have a rest while the baby slept.

Betty came in from the hall, trailing baby John behind her, crawling as quickly as he could to catch his mama up.

"Miss Patty? What's troubling you, ma'am?" She eyed the snuffling baby then.

"Go tell Jupiter or Martin to fetch Mr. Jefferson, quick," she said sharply.

Betty took a step back. "They's all in Challotesville, ma'am," she reminded her. Patty turned away. She'd forgotten that Thomas was going to town today. "Oh God, oh God—" She took a breath. She must be calm. She must be. Peter depended on it. She whirled. "You send Martin down the stable," she directed. "Tell him to get two riders on the fastest horses in the place. I need Mr. Jefferson and Dr Gilmer back here as fast as may be. Tell him it's the baby. Hurry!"

"I will, ma'am." She didn't wait to see her go. She turned into the bedroom and slammed the door.

Peter was still snuffling. Snatching up her bottle of oil, she took him to the bed and untied the strings of his gown as quickly as she could, but her fingers fumbled in her trembling panic, and she was crying in fear and frustration by the time they were undone. He did not protest at this treatment nor did he cry in his distress, which made her frantic. Suddenly all his placid sweetness seemed a curse. She wanted him to cry, wanted him to fill his lungs with air, and live.

She rubbed his chest with the oil and that pinked him up some, but he was still struggling to breathe. By some instinct, all unbidden, she picked up the oil bottle with its curved concave bottom and pressed his chest with it. Over and over she pulled the seal away from his skin, leaving great red blotches on his tiny chest. But he ceased his struggling, dear God, and he breathed an angry gasp at last, howling that his dear Mama, who heretofore had only meant softness and comfort to him, should treat him this way. He wailed lustily for the first time ever.

The sound was music to her. She picked him up, trembling as he was, and sat down on the bed, hushing him in loving tones until he was settled and could take a comforting feed. Slowly, they calmed down together, she and he, taking and giving the warm life she had to offer. At length he slept, uneasily, twitching a little, but sleeping. She laid him on the bed and kept her hand on him until the door opened.

It was Thomas. His face was white under its red film of dust from the dry roads, and his hair was in disorder. His glance fell to the sleeping baby. "What happened?"

"Oh, my dear!" At the sight of him she melted in relief and flung herself on him, the tears coming now in trembling reaction. "We were resting, and I was nearly asleep when I heard the strangest noise! I looked over at him, and Thomas, he was blue! And making the most dreadful efforts to breathe." She wept against his dusty waistcoat. "I don't know what's wrong with him!" she cried, looking up at him beseechingly. "Oh, Thomas, our baby! Our little boy! I don't want to lose him too!"

"It's all right, sweet," he said, looking the baby over. "Did you call George?"

She nodded. "Directly when I sent for you."

He kissed her forehead. "Good girl." His eyes strayed back to the tiny body on the bed, and she was made glad once more that he had some knowledge of physic. "Can you stand?" he asked her.

She nodded reluctantly and he released his tight hold on her. Going to the stand, he removed his coat and gave himself a quick sluice with her heavy white soap. When he was done he poured her a glass of Madeira from the decanter on the chest and went to pick up the baby.

He was so little. He hardly weighed anything at all, and the compass of him fit in Thomas's arm. The child was peaceful now, if pale. She sat down on the bed beside him and watched anxiously as he looked him over under his loosened clothes.

"You did right, sweet," he murmured of her cupping, and bent his head to listen to the baby's heartbeat, but after an eternity he shook his head.

"I don't know," he admitted. "But George likely will."

She made a face.

"It is probably something entirely benign," he assured her.

She stared at him wide-eyed. "Thomas, you didn't see him! He was literally blue, and I had to nearly pound him before he would breathe! That is not benign! It may be a passing fit, but sweet mercy, it was not benign!"

"All right." He laid a hand on her arm at the creeping note of distress in her voice.

He walked with the baby, sleeping soundly now, until George Gilmer arrived half an hour later. George made his examinations, and Peter didn't even protest overmuch at being wakened. He mewled a little, but once he heard her voice soothing him, he was calm again. George sounded him out with the pinard horn.

"Ah," he said quickly.

"What is it?" Thomas asked. He uncrossed his arms and went over to the bed.

"Arrhythmias."

At the word, all the blood drained away from his face in a rush. It threw her into a panic.

"What's that; what's wrong?" she demanded, looking from one of them to the other, then at Peter.

"An irregular heartbeat, ma'am." George said. He rose and gave her the baby to dress. "It means in some cases that the chambers of the heart are not properly sealed yet. Blood leaks, in short." She felt the world recede away from her and sank onto the bed. Oh God, dear God, not another child to share Jack's fate! She went numb and hardly felt it when Thomas put an arm about her shoulders. She heard George as through water, "In some cases this is nothing—I have seen old men with this condition. . . . But sometimes the child dies. . . ." That broke through her wall of reserve, and she uttered a cry of dismay, short and sharp.

"Not directly," George hastened, "they may live for several years. But they are delicate and must be guarded against too-strenuous activity."

Dear God, it was all happening again! The vista stretched out before her: anxiously minding his babyhood, when every bump and fall would produce a black bruise; cringing in fear when he took his first steps—running— And all for naught when in childhood he would likely come to some mortal harm in an innocent fashion—

"I cannot live like that again!" she burst out, and turned her face into Thomas's hip.

"My dear," he said, to comfort her.

"Is there anything you can do?" she heard him ask their friend. She struggled up from her refuge and wiped her eyes with the heel of her hand.

"Would that I could undo the imperfections God has wrought," George said ruefully. "I would be out of business in a trice and the happiest man alive. Nay. Though they apprised us of this at Edinburgh they could not offer a cure. I would say that Mrs. Jefferson did well enough by instinct. I could recommend such massage, and cupping as she did; not to bleed, for it appears to circulate the blood sufficiently. You could try the baths at the warm springs, but all that would be in future. For the moment, I am at a loss. I have never seen such measures on a tiny infant."

"I see," Thomas murmured grimly. He held the baby against him, and Peter, all unknowing of his fate, sought his thumb among the folds of the blanket. Thomas moved them away from his face. The fine blond silk of the child's hair stood up, ruffled. His brow yet bore the worried furrows he had been born with. They were there with good reason. For how many, truly, were the number of his days?

For the next four days, the baby was watched every moment of the day and slept in their bed at night, rather than his own small one, at her insistence. Thomas did not raise an objection. The presence of their warm little one was relieving to both their anxieties. It was easier to sleep knowing that they could feel every movement the boy made, that they could know instantly when he did not, or struggled to breathe.

Peter grew worse as the days passed. He had another attack of breathlessness, and on the third day began to turn pale or grey-blue at the least activity. Even his feeds were a struggle and took hours, as he would have to pause and be coaxed back into breathing again before he could continue. But being still hungry he was miserable, and they both spent most of the day in tears.

On the fourth day he slept, quietly, easily, with none of the shuddering and twitching she had come to dread. When he was awake he was alert as ever he was, watchful and solemn, peaceable. He smiled at her once, when held by the window in the afternoon light, a joyous, laughing smile that lit up his entire face. She had hope, then, that his difficulty had passed, that George Gilmer was wrong, that his fits had been merely the transient mark of his change into life in the world.

In the evening, Thomas was at his desk in their anteroom, while she sat in the chair in the bedroom with the baby, humming a low tune. Patsy was long since asleep in her room in the dressing room. The clock had just struck a quarter past the hour, and Peter was at last asleep. She gazed on his quiet, peaceful baby face. At last he had found some ease from his difficulties. . . . Oh, George was wrong this time, my son. You shall be well now. . . . She sat for a time, to make certain he was genuinely asleep. The hands on the clock were reaching towards half-past ten o'clock. Time for a wee fellow to be abed. . . . She kissed his serene little face. And froze.

"Thomas!"

He came on the run, the crash of the chair in the anteroom bespeaking his haste, and was beside her in an instant. She wept; silent tears coursed down her face and fell onto the bosom of the peaceful baby. She bowed her head against his hand when he would have reached out and laid it on the baby's chest. She shook her head, her loose hair falling down her shoulder and across his hand. There was no reason to hope that some pulse of life yet beat in that fragile bosom. The Muse had fled. Their son was dead. Peter Field Jefferson had lived seventeen days, almost to the hour.

56

Diana and Endymion
Monticello

For two days she was numb. Beyond that first, spasmodic grief she had no tears. The enormity of the loss was too terrible, too painful to face. Until the burial. She had steeled herself when they laid him out, dressed in the best and newest of the baby gowns, gritted her teeth when the tiny coffin was brought in; but she could not bear it when Bob Hemings lowered it into the small grave. He was so tiny! How could he fare out here alone in the woods with the badgers and the wolves? Her baby! Her little baby! Then she wept, and had to speak her grief or burst.

"I had thought him sleeping," she said to Thomas that night. She leaned against him, her head pillowed at its accustomed place in the curve of his neck. She ached, and with more than grief. For two days now she had been in agonies, her breasts overfull of milk and no small helpmeet to ease their heaviness. "I thought at last he doesn't struggle so to breathe. Aye, well!" she murmured ruefully.

He stirred and kissed her hair. "Don't blame yourself, love. You could not know."

"He was so sweet, so peaceful," she went on, heedless. "He gave a sigh and was gone, as though he had done with his business here. I should have known, I should have felt it instantly. It was only when—" He lifted her chin and kissed her mouth. "Please don't," he begged her, his eyes glittering tears. His voice was hoarse. "Just. . . bide a space here with me." He tightened his arms about her. "I can't take it in right now," he said. "It's too close. Just bide with me and let me know there's some love in the world that may not be whisked away so. Oh God, Patty—"

He broke off with a sigh, and she turned to him fully, her cheek against his shoulder. It was a long time that they lay together, given over to their shared grief, until at last in the small hours all the pain was poured out and they were peaceful. The steady pulse under her temple was reassuring. The certain darkness of the grave receded a little. Life would go on, it whispered. Life would go on. This moment would pass without notice and become another, and pulse by pulse life would continue. Thomas buried his face in her hair, and she settled against him. And slept.

In the morning, the grey dawn came creeping through the closed shutters, spreading feeble light about their silent chamber. All was a hush yet. It was after five, and she was awake, but it was too dark to see the hour precisely. She leaned on the pillows, feeling the ebbing throb of well-run nature once again. This ache would end in a few days' time, as much she knew from Janey's weaning, but at the moment it was mortal.

Thomas lay sleeping beside her. He had passed a dream-tossed night and had not slept well. It was only now, in the cool, still peace of morning that he found true rest. Though a light sleeper, he was usually not disturbed so. He had been up and down once or twice in the small hours as well, hence this most unusual instance of the sun not finding him awake or abroad.

She turned on the pillow and braced her head on her elbow. It was rare she caught him sleeping. If she did he usually had a headache and was abed during the day. She gazed on him now, musing on the manner his loose hair waved as it fell across his brow. The ends were curled, and though at first glance it might appear of a rough texture to an undiscerning eye, she knew its silk-smoothness in her fingers without the touch. She moved the lock, smoothing it away from his forehead with a gingerly touch. Her dear. She smiled a little, remembering his needful, chaste, seeking embrace of her in the night. Her beloved dear. She was glad the delicate lineaments of his face were no longer marred by his wordless grief.

She bent and laid her cheek against his temple where the pulse beat evenly, swept by a choking tenderness. He stirred under the warmth of her hovering breath but did not wake. She bent and kissed his mouth, lightly, as she would a sleeping child, and started when his eyes fluttered open, drowsy-lidded, dappled amber and green, and he regarded her watchfully.

She drew back, but he stayed her with a hand, smiling his drowsy smile, and she gathered her wits. "Sweet Endymion," she murmured. "How camst to wake and brake my spell?"

His hand strayed to her hair, lifting it back over her shoulder from whence it had fallen. "Fair Diana," he murmured in kind, his voice hushed with overtones of sleep. "'Twas your breath of love that woke me." He took her shoulders, his thumbs sliding up her neck. "My Diana, ever sighing." His words echoed to other times, and she blushed.

"I didn't mean to wake you," she said.

He raised an eyebrow. "Aye? Well, worse luck. Why are you awake so early then, if not in longing for my company?"

"Thomas," she complained, at his teasing, blushing further. He traced the course of it with a finger and met her eyes again. "I like your blushes, Pattycakes, uncommon well." He sat forward and kissed her lightly. "Thank you for your patience last night," he said, sobering. "I know I woke you."

She shook her head, the thrall of tenderness washing over her again.

"No need, beloved." She gazed fully into his eyes. They could never regain what had been lost, but they could go on, could endure. Whatever befell, they had each other, and there was nothing so wrong with the world as long as there was that. There was strength in the bond of their shared joys and sorrows that time or distance could never break. She saw the answering sentiment in his amber gaze and had no need of further words. The unspoken was deeper and richer than shallow, puny words could encompass did they speak all day.

He took her hands. "What say I fetch us a cup of tea? We can loll together then, since you've no mind for brisker sport."

She smiled at this and watched him climb off the bed and shrug into his dressing gown. As so many of his specific articles, this was red, a deep, crimson shantung, woven from cotton and the raveling of old silk stockings. It was dyed in madder, cochineal being far too expensive for such a large endeavor, and trimmed in heavy cord. The pieces had all been woven to the nearest possible shape of the cut to avoid wasting the precious fabric. It was a rich, weighty, well-made garment, representing nearly a year of work by herself and her weavers.

She watched as he opened the shutters, letting in the warming light of day, and in amusement as he went about the careful task of making tea from their brazier. Scooping out the smoldering embers from the fire, he placed them in their small box and breathed life into them with the bellows. Measuring out a precise amount of water from the ewer, he set it to heating in the fore of the hearth while he weighed the tea on his assay scales. Tea was not a happenstance with Thomas; it was a scientific endeavor, with all conducted in the most attentive manner. It must brew for exactly four and an half minutes, the time he had determined it came out best; not three, or four, and certainly not five. But in the fullness of time there was tea, and she accepted the cup he proffered without remark. The method to his painstaking was for efficiency and uniformity of result, and she appreciated that fully. Besides, she could not have dissuaded him from his experiments had she wanted to.

She sat tailor-fashion on the bed, sipping tea while he shaved himself. It was always his first task of the day once up from bed, and she could not remember a time when she found him unshaven. Even when he was in the throes of a headache this ablution was performed, if not by herself then by Jupiter. It was worth the wait to have him come to her again with a kiss, smelling enticingly of bergamot.

"Come here, my honey-sweet," he entreated, stretching out his long legs on the bed. Mindful of her teacup, she scooted herself up to lean next to him, rearranging the folds of her shift to cover her knees.

"My shy flower," he teased. "As though I have not seen your knees."

"Oh hush!" she exclaimed, blushing. He laughed. "Telei, you're a caution.

Now come here," he said, when she moved away in offence at his funning. "I don't bite. I promise I won't tease you any more, so smooth your feathers." She laid her teacup carefully on the bed, far enough out of harm's way, and sat beside him again.

"Now, give me a kiss."

She turned to face him. "You are full of orders this morning, sirrah!"

He was not put out. She had no idea from whence had come this sudden, playful mood. "Not orders," he reasoned. "Requests. . . hopes. . . desires, if you will. Fancies." His hand was tangled in her hair, just below her left ear. "Come now and kiss me, so I know you're not mad." She could see that she was in for a good deal of wheedling if she didn't comply, and she was not so indisposed to his plan as all that, so she yielded.

"No," he said, after a time, "still ruffled." She laughed and shook her head. "Thomas. You intended to have your way all along."

"I did," he admitted. He bent his head into her neck. "Is it so dreadful?"

"Not at all."

They might have come to some business, had he not rolled over onto her teacup and soaked the bed.

"Oh blast," he complained, fishing the cup out from beneath his shoulder. They made a dash for towels, but the damage was done. By the time the mess was sopped up, Patsy came out of her room. Thomas seized her and swung her up into a whirling embrace so that she squealed, as he used to do when she was smaller.

"You're getting too big for that, Miss Patt," he told her, sliding her down with a kiss. He ruffled her disordered hair, for she was yet in her nightshift. "Why are you abroad so early, ba? It's not half-past six."

"The sun woke me up," Patsy complained, looking into the dressing room with a betrayed glance. "It shines right in my eyes in the morning!"

"Well, we shall have to put him about his business, shan't we? Perhaps Mr. Neilson can put in the shutters today for you. Would you like that?"

Patsy was earnest. "Yes, Papa."

"Come here, Pats," Patty entreated, from the bed. She hoped it was only the sun waking her too early, and not undue noise from them. She gave the child a kiss. "There's my sweeting. Now that you're awake, why don't you go in and pick out a frock you want to wear? There's my big girl. I'll be in momentarily to help you," she smiled, "since you won't wait for Bett, Miss Eagerness. But you can't gad about in your shift." Patsy's greenish eyes glowed with a new enthusiasm.

"I will, Mama," she agreed in a rush of words, "and I know just the one—" She went tearing away in excitement for her clothes press. Such ardor made Patty wonder what odd combination would afterward emerge, for Patsy had a rather artistic, not to say phantastic, sense of dress.

Life claimed them again by such ordinary means, and by the time the month had passed, they were beyond the worst of their grief. She felt perfectly well, full of energy and industry, and slowly their interlude with Peter became as a dream; half-remembered most of the while, but at moments possessing the ability to be recalled in infinite detail, with only a bitter-sweetness for its brevity.

During that summer, there was the annual doling out of the winter's meat that had been put up in the cold weather. This was the end of a very long, patient, and odorous process that began at the first signs of autumn. It was then the hogs were fattened up on corn for several weeks before being driven in from their haunts, for they roamed the woods freely for most of the year.

Once rounded up, by twos they were slaughtered, with a blow on the head with a mallet. The throat was cut immediately lest the blood congeal in the veins, and allowed to drain. The animal was singed then, and scalded, to remove the hair, hung up, and the cutting began. The backbone was removed; hams, shoulders, and middlings cut; the gut and leaf fat removed and tossed into pots for boiling down. The meat was immediately laid in salt tubs admixed with saltpetre to keep it from spoiling while it cured. The entrails were then removed, and the rest of the hog cut down for souse and hocks and lesser meats. The fatback was kept for cracknels, for it made good soap and better candles, being dense.

It was only in the spring, after a long curing and smoking till the crust was nearly black, that they were packed in pepper and sugar and capsicum and several other herbs. The smokehouse was a daily chore. Every morning she went to see to the fire, and that there was a sufficient smoke. Now, in the summer, the meat was rubbed in hickory ash about once a week, after being examined for putrid spots. Much the same process was completed with beeves.

With this valuable store, she was able to purchase other things she needed from the servants, the workmen, and their wives. At the end of June she bought eighty-odd chickens from Jupiter, Phil Shoemaker, and others, and paid for them all in middlings of bacon. In July, Thomas Garth had his payment of meat and killed nine hogs and one beef. Some of this went to Henry Gaines, to whom he owed a debt. These were salted quickly and eaten soon before the hot weather spoiled them. Four of the hogs were nearly shoats, they were so runty, so this modest quantity did not work any great hardship on them. In August she divided up their finished meats to make room for those soon to arrive. For their own use she packed up twenty-eight hams with bacon,· twenty-one shoulders, and twenty-seven middlings. For the workmen, there were forty hams and fifty shoulders, the middlings having been paid out in bacon throughout the year.

Late in July, Sukey and Jupiter's baby was born. After the threat of an early arrival, the infant arrived more than a week late, and when it did, she found herself prevailed upon to give aid.

It was about midnight, and the windows were open behind their closed shutters to let in the air, for it was stiflingly hot, and morning would be unbearable if they were closed up. The summer hangings on the bed were their only cover, and these did not afford much privacy, being of pierced muslin. They kept the bugs out, and that was all. Through her unreal haze, she began to perceive the discreet but insistent scratching at the door of the antechamber.

"Thomas," she whispered, into his hair, "the door—"

He raised himself a little, and kissed her. "I know, sweet. But it will hold." His eyes were glittering green, and his skin flushed down his chest. He smiled at her, drowsy-eyed. "Patty." He leaned to kiss her again, and she forgot about the door.

When he did answer it later, there was a low murmuring, and she recognized Jupiter's voice and knew instantly what the trouble was. Thomas came back, smiling a little, and reached for her where she sat on the bed. "It's Sukey," he said, in a tone of irony. "She wants you to come."

She thought of Jupiter standing outside the door in anxiety, at his laboring wife's bidding, being made to wait, and she blushed, for it wasn't the first time he had needed to wait.

"Don't worry," Thomas grinned, at her flaming face, "we have thick walls."

"Oh, don't!" she begged, in agonies. She should have been used to such disturbances by now, having been raised her whole life in the presence of servants, but some things were private and not meant for casual overhearing. "Why does she need me for?" she asked, even while she rose to dress. She pulled back the thin curtain. "Aggey can manage, or Nell, or old Jenny. Old Jenny's done lots of babies." But she knew why, and didn't really expect an answer. Sukey trusted her, liked her, and since her earlier threat, was grateful to her. She would go, even if she did nothing but sit by, because she was fond of Sukey and Jupiter.

The child was born in the morning, a tiny girl whom they named Aggey. Even though the child was not over-large, it had required some effort for Sukey to push her out. All her wiry strength was in her arms and legs; she could have run a foot race or pulled weeds or broadcast seed from now 'til Christmas, as she hefted iron pots and beat up a dozen eggs with a willow whip, but her baby was a trial. She did not complain. Even through the worst she did not cry out, only uttering a low, moose-like bellowing. All her suffering was in her eyes. Silent tears ran down from her frightened eyes in a way that was more wrenching than screams. But they were well, thank God. They were both well. There were extra rations and a new petticoat as a gift of celebration for the new mother and child.

Betty also had a girl, a big, fat sassy black child she called Lucy. She had none of Sukey's troubles, and but that she was gone from the house a fortnight, one could hardly tell she'd had a baby. Nance told the tale that Ma felt unwell after her supper and just laid down and had the baby while Critta, Thenia, and Sally all watched in amazement. They had Aggey in after that, but there was no need. Everything came right just as clean and pure as you'd want it to. She sent her some calico.

57

Chastisements

Monticello

The summer ration of clothes had been given out, and now that there was enough cloth arrived, from their plantations or purchased, it was time to begin cutting the winter supply. She no longer had Mrs. Reynolds' aid in this, for she and her family had moved on, but Mary Garth was glad to help for the company it gave her, and Nancy Willis was the most Christian of ladies and would offer her aid unbidden. She had not forgotten her gift of a pudding upon her arrival. It was signal of her kindly soul and had proved only the first of many such niceties.

In addition to cutting the winter ration, in September she took stock of her own family's clothes, continuing that which she had begun earlier in the year. It was raining that Tuesday afternoon, a fact which afforded her a perfect excuse to stay indoors. With Patsy and Nance Hemings trailing her about the rooms, unpacking linens and clothing from drawers and shelves, she made her inventory, and for once was not interrupted in it by some emergency. With everything laid out neatly on the bed and chairs, she went through methodically and wrote:

> 20 pr of sheets 2 pr of the 20 at bedford
> with a bed bolster & 2 dutch blankets and
> 2 pr of the sheets at Elk-hill with 5 beds bolsters
> and 2 pillows 5 pr of blankets 6 dowlas towels
> 6 linen table cloths was c mattress -
> 16 damask table cloths & 15 linen ditt at monticello
> 12 damask napkins 16 virginia towels
> 8 beds 8 bolsters 10 pillows 7 pr of blankets
> 5 mattress's one straw bed 7 counterpains
> and one bed quilt
>
> Pat7 shifts 2 pr of silk stockings 4 pr of cotten dit
> 6 old Jams 4 olds frocks 9 pocket hand kerchiefs
> 2 silk coats one flowered lawn coat 2 laced
> tuckers 5 hemstitched ditto 2 night caps
> 2 pr of pockets   arm cloths

9 ruffled shirts 18 plain dito 20 old cambrick
stocks 6 virginia ditto new 18 caps

She came to the next item and winced in disgust for the tatty state they were in—

                                                    15 old rags
of pocket hand kerchiefs 3 pr of english cordied
breeches 4 of virginiy ditto 6 virgia cordied
dimity waistcoats 2 striped ditto & 4 damascus ditt
2 Jeans dittt 13 pr of white silk stockings 6 pr brown
thread ditto 5 pr of indian cotten 2 pr of virginia ditt
2 brown holland coats one virginia ditto   11 cloth
coats 5 red waistcoats 2 buff 1 white flanel dit 6 cloth dit
4 pr of cloth breeches 10tten coat 1 black princes ditto
16 old shifts 4 new ditto 6 old fine aprons
8 old ditto & 2 rags 4 virginia pettycoats 5 linen
ditto 2 pr of dimity pockets   3 pr of old drilling do
2 pr of old dimity ditto   9 pr of silk stockings
12 pr of old cotten 3 night caps 4 striped muslen neck
hand kerchiefs 6 plain ditto linen ditto
2 sacks&coats   8 silk gowns 6 washing ditto old
& 2 new to make up 4 musin aprons 2 suits
of brussels lace one suit of worked muslen ditt
1 pr indian ruffles   2 pr of new black leather
shoes 1 pr green ditt 1 pr of calimancko ditto 2 pr
of old satten ditto 2 new clokes & one bonnet

The handkerchiefs got replaced immediately from a lot of leftover fine cotton; they were nicely hemstitched, and the effort, like the change, did not go unnoticed.

Sukey's Aggey was not as hardy as she first appeared. She did well in the warm days of July but was struck with a flux in the last days of August. The summer complaint often took the smallest, as they were the least able to combat its dread hold. But the loss of this little one, so hard won after much grief, was sorely felt. Jupiter was low, lacking his usual cheerful demeanor and wry observations; Sukey was silent. All her girlhood fled from her in that one instant. Her eyes were haunted. It was worse, Patty observed from watching her cook's bleak suffering, to be strong and stoic than give in to passionate rages of grief and have done. But she was sympathetic, being so lately removed from her own similar loss. There was nothing that would heal the wound but time, and she was not the mistress of that. She gave Sukey her space to bide, and did not expect much of her for that while.

October turned to grey November, and the leaves lost their fiery hues and began to fall. The air was crisp and cold, and for several days when it was clear, they could see snow on the farthermost reaches of the Blue ridge. The sheep and horses all had very thick coats, and they braced themselves for another bitter winter.

In the field, the army was beginning to show signs of strain. Earlier in the year they had been racked with smallpox; plague, if one believed the rumors sent to them from Richard Henry Lee. But Mr. Lee hastened to assure them this was not so, merely a British ploy to stop further inductions to the army. But he was wrong. General John Burgoyne was so convinced of the continental strength of force that he had called for reinforcements to his and the Baron de Riedesel's command. Nevertheless, after some four hours of fighting near Freedman's farm on the banks of the Hudson in New York, there could only be declared a draw. The English expatriate Virginian Horatio Gates, in whose command the continental forces were, afterwards relieved General Arnold, the hero of their Canadian campaign the year before, of his command for contravening orders: Arnold had rushed into the heat of battle and stunned all with his fury. It was whispered that he was not English at all, but Italian, or Spanish, and after the stories circulated of his recklessness, one could well believe it. In part because of these dashing heroics, Burgoyne lost nearly a third of his men.

One morning before they left for Williamsburg, she went into the dressing room to open the shutters and turn down Patsy's bed and halted in astonishment. The room was torn asunder, with clothes and caps, stockings and ribbons heaped everywhere in disarray. While it was true things had been rather untidy lately due to their packing to go down the country, yet there was no excuse for what greeted her save a whirlwind. And she knew what whirlwind. Patsy had, since she was now a big girl of five, taken to choosing her clothes and dressing herself entirely unaided, including her hair. She had an exceedingly discriminating taste of late, and changed her mind a dozen times, depending on her fancy. But heretofore her choices had been imaginary; she had not actually thrown everything from the cupboards.

"Patsy Jefferson, you will come here this instant!" she cried from the doorway. Patsy came from where she was playing in her jewelry on the floor.

"Yes, Mama?" she asked, in an innocent tone.

"What is *this*?" She made a sweep of the disordered room with her hand. Patsy looked confused. "My room, Mama," she said.

She caught her breath. *The child is not being deliberately smart; she is not. She could not be.* Patsy was sometimes rather literally-minded. "Yes," she agreed tautly. "And look at your room. Do you intend to leave it thus, with your belongings heaped everywhere?" she went on, not allowing the child time to speak. "Do you see me or your Papa leaving our belongings strewn about the house? Who is going to pick up these things?"

"Nance?" Patsy's dark eyes regarded her solemnly. *She was not being impudent. She was not, but if she thought that's the way the world was run, she would quickly learn otherwise.*

"No," she said firmly. She shook her head. "No. We may be lucky enough to have servants to look after us as some little girls do not, but we do not treat them so unjustly. Nance has better things to do than pick up after a thoughtless little girl. You will pick these things up, and you will fold them neatly away as Mama left them. You will do so quickly, and you will do so now. If you needs must miss your breakfast for your dawdling, then such will be. You may eat it later in the kitchen. But you will have this room to my satisfaction. And I will never see it in this state again, do you understand?"

Patsy was not looking at her, but at her hands. "Yes, Mama," she murmured in a teary voice. But she would not be moved. "Good," she said, quietly. "Go on, now." She moved aside to let the child in and closed the door behind her.

Thomas came in from the parlor with a puzzled frown. "What was all that?"

She was not disposed to be kindly, as Patsy was loudly weeping in the next room in a fit of pique. "I have ordered her there until she picks up her clothes. Thomas, you should have seen it! The room was in a state!"

"She's but a little child," he said reasonably. *She feared a moment he might go in and undo her lesson, but he only came near and put his hands on her arms.* His expression was regretful and entreating.

"Not so little," she declared. "Old enough to know not to throw her things about and expect someone else to pick up after her. Nance! Do you believe that when I asked her whom should see to it, she told me Nance—and she meant it! Sweet mercy, what sort of child are we raising? Is she so spoiled?"

He shook his head. "No, love, not spoiled. Thoughtless, perhaps, but not spoiled. Think of it from her view: she sees Betty or Nance putting away things all the time—" He raised his hand when she would protest. "I know, and you do, that they're clean, fresh from the laundry, but she does not. She has not begun to think that far. "He raised his head, and looked toward the dressing room in some sympathy. "I'm not saying you were wrong, sweet; on the contrary, she should learn the consequences of her actions, but I know your expectations of her." His eyes were warm as he regarded her. "Believe me, she will come to them in time. But go easy on her yet a little," he entreated. "Don't expect more of her than she can give. She wants so much to please you, and your disapprobation shatters her. Remember, sweet," he kissed her forehead, "what you have told me. She has that sensibility too, like us. Go easy on her, Patty. For me?"

She felt shamed in the face of his reasoning and could not meet his gaze, but nodded silently, swept by the burning memories of her own childhood's rebukes, and that they were often fairly given but not with a view toward her tenderness. As much as she wished not to visit such wounds upon her children she was compelled to words not of her choosing, and it was with great effort that she forbore their utterance. Only the warning of her own remembrances prevented it. "Aye," she said, softly. "I will."

Patsy missed her breakfast, as it happened, but was happy to eat it down the kitchen in the company of Ursula's boys, George and Bagwell. When she returned, they were as blithe as ever together and commenced a lesson in turkey work with a large piece of linen and red wool thread. For better than an hour they sat companionably in the pale sunshine of the parlor, stitching and singing little tunes, their morning contretemps forgotten.

But when Thomas came in and asked her if she wanted to go with him to Colle, she flung down her sewing on the chair and bounded up, ready to fetch her cloak and patterns.

"Yes!" she cried enthusiastically, her face all aglow. She liked to be allowed to go visiting with her Papa, and was a favorite of Miss Martin's amongst the neighborhood children.

Patty was appalled, and sat back dumbfounded. Had the child learned nothing this morning? She put down the shift she was hemming. "Pat-sy," she cried. "Fetch yourself back here this instant!"

Patsy turned about, bewildered.

The needle and scissors thrown anyhow on the chair were the last straw. What could she say if some unwitting guest betook himself to sit down there, or if one of the little ones found a fancy in the shiny objects and came to some harm? Her child stood chastened before her, and the words poured out before she could stop them.

"Pick up those things! Have you learned nothing today? It's not two hours since, but you were shut away in your room for leaving your goods lying about. Look at that there! It's dangerous to leave needles and pins on chairs. Did you never think of it? What if one should be swallowed? I'd have thought you'd have learned something with picking up your whole room. I'd have thought you'd remember for two mortal hours. Gracious, I'd never believe you were so addle-brained as that. Pick them up now and be off, and don't forget your mittens."

"Yes, ma'am," Patsy managed miserably before she burst into tears. She did go to the chair and very carefully folded the cloth and gathered the needle and wool into a small packet with the scissors inside. She felt Thomas's hand on her left shoulder. He leaned down a little and murmured, "My dear, a fault in so young a child once punished should be forgotten."

She knew whereof he spoke and the sympathy he had for poor Patsy, but for a moment the words only increased her ire. What did he know of her struggles with this child? What did he know of the struggles of any mother to properly raise a child to her own and society's expectations, particularly a girl? It was as well for him to stand by and be sympathetic, when he did not encounter Patsy's so-called forgetfulness at every turn, her too-willing tears that begged sympathy or leniency where firmness was needful. The child was a trial. She wanted to be soft and gentle with her always, wanted to see none but smiles on that little freckled face, but did she so, they would never have a suitable young lady. Patsy was too passionate. . . .

And yet— Her anger began to fade. If she had simply said to Patsy to put her things away, quietly, without rebuke for past misdeeds, she would not be in tears now. She had let her temper and her impatience and her expectations get the better of her, after so shortly promising to be patient and mild and light in her requirements! She was no better than Patsy and had far less excuse. She did know better. She bit her lip and reached for the firm hand on her shoulder. Thomas was perfectly correct, and she was wrong to be wroth with him.

"You're right," she said, with humble quietness. "Come here, Pats," she bade her sad-faced little girl. Patsy laid the sewing goods on the table beside her and stood silent, plainly not knowing what to expect. Her heart softened. The poor little dear! She held out her arms and Patsy sat on her lap, burying her face in her neck.

"I'm sorry, Batt," she soothed, smoothing the blue fabric over Patsy's thin back. "It was wrong for Mama to let her temper get the better of her. It's as wrong for mamas as little girls, and I am sorry." She felt Patsy's heavy sigh. "I should not have spoken to you so sharply. I know my dumpling's soft feelings, and I had no right." She held her away a little, to see her face. "For your part, you should have remembered without telling to bundle up your sewing. You know better than that, don't you, sweet?"

Patsy was on the verge of tears again at the sympathy, her eyes brimming. She nodded sadly.

"Ah, don't cry anymore, Patty-patt," she said, wiping the child's eyes. "We are both chastened. I'm not angry with you anymore, sweet." She tucked back a lock of the fallen auburn curls. "And I love my little girl very much. I always do, even if I'm angry. Do you still love Mama; are we friends, so?" Patsy nodded, breaking into fresh tears, and burying her face again in her neck. "There, sweet," she soothed, tears smarting her own eyes. "Come, don't cry anymore. You don't want to look so sad for Miss Peggy, do you? That's a good girl."

Patsy sniffled and sat up, and she gave her a kiss. "I'm sorry, Mama," Patsy said.

"I know, sweet. You run along now and fetch your wraps. I'll give you a treat to carry along for Mrs. Mazzei."

"Yes, ma'am." Not forgetting her sewing, Patsy left the room. Thomas knelt by her chair, his eyes frank and affectionate. She clasped his hand. "I'm a poor model," she admitted. "How should I expect her to be better than she sees?"

He smiled. "You are an excellent model! Humanity she will never learn better. She has your temper—" He traced her nose with a finger, "so its as well she learn from you its governance, or what to do if it gets the better of her." He kissed her hand and changed the subject. "What do you wish to send to Mrs. Mazzei?"

"Oh, I have some of the tomatoes put up that she asked for," she said distractedly. She shook her head. "I won't do that again," she sighed. The effort of the emotion was draining, a clear lesson in governing one's passions.

"Tomatoes?"

She laughed at the absurdity. "No, sir! Ah, no mind. Thank you, my dear, for your kind word. Patsy and I both would have been lost without it." He shrugged a little and made no more of it. Patsy came out then with her cloak and mittens. The ill effects of the altercation were soon forgotten, and they suffered no diminution of affection, but they neither of them forgot its cautions. Patsy was ever after carefully neat about her belongings, though her dress was yet apt to suffer; and she was circumspect to keep her temper with the child, remembering with a pang the tear-dissolved little face and Thomas's low-murmured, gentle rebuke.

58

The Price of Love

The next week they were in Williamsburg. She had intended to spend the remainder of the month in town, but after a week the noise and strange new crowds of men from the far west began to wear on her. She had lived too long in the quiet at Monticello to enjoy the crush and press overmuch. What would she have done had they gone to France? Williamsburg was a small town by even colonial standards, so Thomas said, in comparison to New York or Philadelphia, and they were dwarfed in turn by teeming London and Paris. She retreated happily to the woods at The Forest, where the only noise was that of Lisbet and Francis's children.

Francis's father, her Uncle Richard Eppes, had died in the last year, and the difficulties of being executor and coexecutor to so many far flung lands and responsible for so many debts had sent Francis to his bed with a rheumatic fever that lasted several weeks. It was only since the weather had turned that he was out of bed. He was thinner, a little weak on exertion, so that a ride down to Shirley was taxing, and his chestnut hair shewed signs of grey, but his spirit was recovered. His foxy face broke into as many sly smiles as ever it did. Francis was not a man given to lingering in melancholia.

The year of writing and research of legal traditions in which Thomas had been engaged began to pay off that autumn, for the bill against entails, over which passage he had been most anxious, was enacted. It made him an enemy in the person of Landon Carter, Senior, who was by this out comfortably ensconced in his lands in the Northern Neck. There was some irony in his vilification, for he was everything that Thomas was not: conservative, speculating, jealous of rights and property; he was as pompous as the old governor, but haply less a dangerous enemy. His harangue could not douse the bright spark of Thomas and Mr. Wythe's legal reform, nor could it rouse a party against them as had been done against the Lees. She remembered her young friend of long ago, namesake of her husband's enemy, and never doubted that she had chosen the right suitor. She could not have lived in that house and been happy.

For old Landon's fire, spectacular as it was, had turned smoldering and dark. John Page had complained of his dour face at his brother Mann's wedding the year before, as though he grudged anyone their joyful moments—while Thomas's quieter flame burned more steady and true. His focus was broad, rather than on his own personal interests and fortunes and those of his class. Landon Carter's young namesake she now found petty and irresolute, possessing all the faults and none of the virtues of the Virginia gentry. The knowledge was disturbing, for she could see now how he had borne the seeds of it in his early youth, and she had not seen it.

The only unfortunate result of her removal to the country was that it meant she and Patsy only saw Thomas for a day-and-an-half at the weekend. He rode out on Saturday evening to return on Monday morning very early. November passed in this curious way, and she went to town again in December with him for the beginning of the Christmas holidays. Christmas in town she enjoyed, for the hangings of greenery and the light-dappled windows. The crowds had abated, and she could enjoy herself. They went to church at Bruton Parish, and Thomas paid a tithe, and extra for charity. There was plenty to be grateful for; by Christmas she was well into another pregnancy, and no sign that it would miscarry.

There was glad news, too, from New York. John Burgoyne and his attendant foreign mercenaries, being badly repulsed at Saratoga, had surrendered themselves as prisoners of war to General Gates. That gentleman's old appellation of "Granny" Gates was now uttered with more affection than hitherto. Amongst the prisoners and their stores were one lieutenant general, two major generals, including the German de Riedesel, fifteen hundred stand of arms, forty cannon, and considerable quantities of clothing, all of which would relieve the continental army suffering in their winter quarters in Pennsylvania.

They spent their anniversary in town and went to a gathering at the Wythes' at Twelfth Night to drink a cup of wassail and sing the old songs. Mr. Wythe was now appointed as the chancellor of the High Court, a position for which he was eminently qualified. Thomas was bent that season upon enlisting his aid in convincing Edmund Pendleton, as leader of the conservatives, to advocate the reform of the curricula and chairs of the college. They agreed on the redundancy of the Indian school and of two chairs of divinity; they agreed that there wanted a school of law. But Pendleton was more cautious on the complete abolishment of the divinity chairs and the introduction of history and modern languages. Thomas was no more successful with his bill for establishing a public lending library at Richmond. Mr. Wythe said with wry humor and a twinkle in his grey eyes that Thomas would have to be contented for the time with his own.

One legal revisal which was to eventually prove a thorn to them, though they could not envision it then, was the proposal on the matter of outstanding debt to British merchants. The average planter, as John Wayles had well known from his personal experience and his business as agent to Farell and Jones of Bristol, was head-over-ears in debt. Differing—and now grossly depreciated—currency, bad harvests, poor storage of tobacco in passage, competition with small farmers, a depleted market where thousands of hogsheads of tobacco stood unsold in English warehouses combined with the stranglehold of credit and trade restrictions to make a situation of increasing urgency. Thomas's draught last year that the courts be reopened to settle matters of debt was highly voted down. It came up again in January 1778, modified by him rather, and this time it passed.

The scheme was this: property of British subjects in Virginia would be sequestered, as Dunmore's lands had been, and sold off to the advantage of the state; suits for debt between British merchants and Virginia planters were to remain as they had been before the closing of the courts in 1774, with deposits made by Virginians to a loan office in Commonwealth currency, with the state taking over any dispute of the matter after the war. Thus the planters would not be further indebted by interest and charges for nonpayment that had accrued during the war, and could pay off their debt as the money came available without fear of depreciated currency. The surety of their bond would be guaranteed with a treaty of peace. No dishonor was intended in this scheme, but it proved to be a very knotty problem indeed, for the merchant companies had little faith in Virginia currency or their former colonies' ability to wage, let alone win, war. They saw their entire investment, millions of pounds, gone for naught.

Once again, through a late January snow, they made their way westward home to Monticello. The winter had been mild, however, and spring remarkably forward, so that by the middle of February wildflowers showed their shy spring colors in the woods. Best of all, there was water in the well. Water after more than a year! Thomas had not been overmuch perturbed by its lack, but the daily nuisance of having to wait for water to be dragged up the mountain was wearing on her patience. And she had so little that spring.

She was not doing well in this pregnancy. The sickness she generally experienced did not abate until she was well into the fifth month, and she was listless and irritable. It was all she could do to get a sufficiency of chores done in the morning before she collapsed on her chaise until dinner. Her eyes hurt, and she could not write. As time went on she became dropsical, which she never had been before, and she got very large. She had headaches and nausea. When summer came, she could not bear the heat. She drank great quantities of beer and cider, even water, she was so desperate to assuage her impossible thirst. She lay on her chaise in the afternoons, listening to the brickmen above her head, wishing for quiet, wishing for cool autumn, wishing that her hands were not so tingling and painfully swollen. She felt terrible and was miserable, with no interest in life at all, though both Thomas and Patsy were sweet to bring notices of it to her attention. She wept and wept for no particular reason, save that she wanted her sickness and her confinement over. But then, O then, she should have the baby to look after, and she didn't have the strength for that. George Gilmer came out, himself much harried with militia business, and looked her over cursorily but could find no organic cause of her malady, save that she was in a family way. He told her to rest and gave her more of his foul tonic.

Thomas went to Williamsburg in the middle of June, during which time she was mostly ill. She was much subject to nausea and headaches, and although when he returned he tried to engage her interest in life's amusements—for there were natural diversions aplenty that summer—she could summon no enthusiasm. He saw firsthand now her complaint of two years before, and why she had not been able to write. She tried not to be unkindly or rejecting in her lack of enthusiasm for the news and observations he brought her, but it was clear even to her that her apathy damped his own enjoyment of the delights and wonders of the world, or the minutiae of building progress about the house, which gave her another reason to weep. In addition to everything else, she was now a dampe. Oh, it was simply too much!

In this wise the summer wore on. The house came finished toward the end of the season, in enough time for all hands to be called to the fields for the harvest. At last they had a permanent roof over their heads, and no more canvas or other makeshift. The floors in the upstairs bedchambers were laid and sanded, waiting on the cooling of autumn for their coats of varnish. There were too many bugs now. The stonecutter Rice, whose indenture Thomas had purchased in 1775, had been working paid nearly the whole of this year, and he had completed the columns for the front of the house. Heretofore, only one was completed, with the portico being braced on lumber.

At the end of July, even this finishing work halted for two days. In deference to her difficulty in her confinement, all the noise and bustle of inside carpentry ceased, and Rice and his helpers were sent elsewhere for the nonce. As all the others had done, the child came early, though this time it was more than a fortnight before expected.

Thomas sent for George immediately, but he left at the end of the day to come back in the morning. Finding little progress, he left again to see to some pressing business and then returned as it was falling dark. It was Sunday and his militia expected him at their muster. He did not leave again but waited through the long hours of evening and the night until at last, at half-past one in the morning on the first of August, Mary Jefferson was born. She was a large baby, and there had been some difficulty in extricating her shoulders, but she was well, and emerged howling at the indignity of George's cold instruments. There was reassurance in such vigorous life, for their Poll had a normal heartbeat and excellent color.

Patty did well for the first hour but then complained of feeling giddy and cold. Before they could respond, she fainted away for several minutes. She bled a good deal after that, and it took until dawn was coming on for George to be certain that she would not relapse. Once again, she had bled a good deal, and lassitude that had plagued her during her pregnancy did not dissipate with the birth of the child. She was grateful to be through her ordeal, that the child was sound, but she remained weak and could not summon any joy for the little one. The overwhelming gladness that had encircled them after Peter's birth was most conspicuously missing. Signal of her difficulties, she had no milk and could not nurse the child, where with Peter and Jane there had been milk in abundance. Polly was given to Betty Brown, Betty Hemings's daughter, who had lost her own child in May and was still an able wet nurse.

This failure on her part only increased her melancholy. What sort of mother was she that she could not provide for her own child? She was pleased with Polly's health, but found nothing but disappointment in the fact that she was a girl. She had so wanted another son! A son to drive away the ache she felt at Peter's loss. She felt it keenly as the month drew on, for Polly was as fat and healthy as could be wished. She'd weighed nigh onto ten pounds and at a month's age was as round as a pumpkin.

She was a beautiful baby, with the same fine dark hair that Patsy had owned, and great murky-dark eyes. The hair underneath her straight black fuzz was reddish and showed the promise of a curl. From past experience Patty judged that her eyes would likely be brown or hazel. They had not a single blue-eyed blonde in their generations to take after Thomas's father. Even his namesake had had dark eyes. Slowly she began to reconcile herself to the child, drawn in by Polly's soft quietness and timid startles. She would quiver at unexpected noises, her little fat body going still and her eyes watchful. One afternoon Patsy dropped a toy with a clatter in the next room and poor Poll howled.

Rising from her chaise, she went to the baby's crib and picked her up. She was solid in her arms, real and safe, with her sturdy little heart thumping in fright like a rabbit's. Patty's heart melted and every loving instinct came rushing to the fore.

"Oh Poll, my Polly." She bounced the baby a little, covering the dark head with her hand. She went over to the window. "Hush, ba, husha baby. Look sweet, see the pretty trees? Look at that! Ah, there's Mama's girl, my darling. Husha, don't cry." She bounced her until her shuddering ceased, and then held her away to find the great dark eyes regarding her curiously.

She smiled. "Why, hello, *cariad!*" she said. "Who's my sweet Poll?" She took her to sit in the chair, balancing her on her forearm, looking her over in detail for the first time. She had not her father's nose, thank goodness, but a sweet little button one, well-shaped small ears, and the heart-shaped face of the Eppeses. Her eyebrows would be dark, for they were noticeable now. She looked like Mary and Anne, Lisbet's daughters, who were the image of Francis. She looked like the miniature of her own mother and her Uncle Eppes. She looked like what she could remember faintly of her grandfather. They were elfin features, fey, no matter that Poll was now roly-poly. She smiled at all this attention, kicking her feet, and startled herself. Patty laughed and sat her up better.

"You silly little puss," she said affectionately, and kissed her. "Well, you certainly are a creature unto yourself, aren't you? Come here, Poll, silly goose, and you can come play with Mama." They went to sprawl on the expanse of the bed, with Miss Polly all unwrapped. She was glad of her then and loved her dear, and was never after sorry that she was not the boy for whom she had hoped.

George Gilmer called in while Thomas was gone two days to Fredericksburg at his turn for the post in September. She had come to dread his professional visits, especially those that were unbidden. While she found his mild audacity charming in the drawing room, its translation into bluntness in his official sphere left her blushing and not a little annoyed. There were other men who were bold with a lady, making some highly suggestive remarks in dubious taste, but they were not waspish as George could be. She greeted him in the parlor and braced herself for his advance.

"Well, Madame," he said cheerily, flinging his bag and hat on a chair as he stalked through from the hall. "Good day to you." He made her a bow. "I trust you do well in your husband's absence?"

"Tolerably," she nodded. She glanced at Polly beside her in the basket and back at George over the tops of her green spectacles. "And yourself?"

"Oh, passing well," he admitted. "Though I see by those contraptions you are wearing that you're not as well as you might be."

She ignored this and picked up the baby, enquiring casually, "How does your wife? I've not heard from Mrs. Gilmer this month gone."

He smiled a little, not duped by her smoothness. "She sends her regards," he paused, "and her wishes for your health."

"They are kindly received," she murmured, betraying no annoyance, but she glanced at him pointedly.

"May I sit?" he asked suddenly. She was taken aback, for she was anticipating some remark.

"Please do," she bade him hastily and indicated the nearer of the two chairs. He drew up a side chair instead and sat before her. She blushed at this proximity and could not look at him directly, but inclined her head toward the baby in her lap.

"I promised Mr. Jefferson I would look in on you," he said, evidently as some preamble, for he cleared his throat. "He seemed concerned for your well-being before he left."

She opened her mouth to make some polite rejoinder, but he forestalled it. "As am I." He leaned forward in the chair, his elbows on his knees. "Madame, I would speak to you earnestly about your case, for I confess it has caused me no few late nights of pondering." He paused, his green eyes regarding her steadily, gaugingly, and she felt herself blush again, every small defect of her person suddenly before his intent gaze.

"Mrs. Jefferson," he said at last, reaching out his hand and idling with the stitched hem of Polly's blanket. "We are of an accord regarding the difficulty of your confinements, are we not?"

She stared at him, not able to guess the bent of his words. "Aye, sir," she agreed, bewildered. Her confusion was only increased when he leaned back, coloring. She had never seen a blush from him, not even in the most intimate moments of their acquaintance.

"Good," he said thoughtfully, looking beyond her while he gathered his words. "Good. I think you will agree with me that your health is poorer when you are in circumstances than not."

"Aye—" she said cautiously, beginning to sense the drift of his thinking.

He looked at her sharply then, beseechingly, and she felt a chill.

"You will understand then that I make my recommendation from not only a stand of professional concern, but from that of a loving friend as well. Mrs. Gilmer and I cherish your society, madame, and we should hate to lose it, even to so worthy a cause— Mrs. Jefferson, I must entreat you, however great your desire to add companions to this sweet little babe, I must counsel you from the wisdom of my profession not to do so. I doubt not that you would be willing to risk any ill for such an undertaking, but I tell you that it is dangerous!" He shook his head. "Such abstinence as would be required would be doubtless difficult for two of such warm regard as yourself and my friend, but madame, for your very life, I would counsel you to it!"

She felt her heart thudding in her ears, and the surrounding scene had grown dim about George's face. It was as the center of a dark pool, the single bright spot from which no light radiated. He was asking her the impossible. To live in such utter barrenness would be to die living, for her. Perhaps he had been able to convince Thomas of such necessity, for her life's sake, but she could never endure it. The love they shared was the breath of life, and she could not willfully stifle it. To hold such love and abandon its expression would kill it ultimately. Though at thirty she was in fact of middle age, her life was not yet so far over as to want to live in sisterly celibacy for the balance of it. If love meant the risk of her life, then she would risk it, and gladly. What person of decent sensibility could do otherwise? She was scowling, though until that moment she had been unaware of it, and summoned her dignity to say to George, "Sir, you presume too far!"

He bowed his head. "Believe me, my dear Mrs. Jefferson, I meant you no offense." He met her gaze again. "You must know from what concern I speak."

Her wrath softened then at his face, for she did know the depth of his personal regard, his friendly affection. "I do, Dr Gilmer," she said in a softer tone, "but you ask the impossible." It was on her tongue to ask him, if faced similarly would he take his own advice, but thought the better of that impertinence.

"I had rather thought you'd say as much," he admitted. He rose from his chair. "Having made myself unwelcome now, I will trouble you no further," he said, in a rare moment of humility. A thought occurred to her. "Wait," she bade him, laying the baby in her basket. "Please—"

He turned and the light shone on his brown hair, touching it gold in its undertones. He was not so fierce. She relaxed her grip on the arms of the chair.

"You have not spoken similarly to my husband?" she enquired boldly. To her consternation and relief he burst out laughing.

"No, Madame, I have not! How like you, sweet lady." He came nearer again and made her a respectful bow, continuing more soberly, "I had thought to speak to you first on it, as it is you who would be primarily affected. But if you are unwilling, then I have no right to insist, you are correct, and I beg pardon for our friendship's sake. I would not sacrifice that, for you are both dear to me."

The words were so kindly and sincerely spoken that she forgave him his presumption. It did not lay forgotten, however, for she mentioned it to Thomas when he returned. Not to interfere with their good will, but because she was mindful of his exhortation not to keep things from him, and it was a troubling concern.

"I had a call from Dr. Gilmer while you were away," she said casually one night when they were at ease on their pillows. She had spent the day with a sick headache on her couch, and it was only marginally better now. She had taken nothing but broth all day and was ravenously hungry. Polly slept, sighing beside them between the bed and the wall, and the soft sounds of her breathing were soothing to Patty's head. Thomas kissed her forehead on the aching place above her eye. "You did?"

She nodded, settling against him with a sigh. It was perfectly, blissfully dark in the room. "Aye." She said quietly. She could not think of how to go on.

"And?" His prompting came gently, but it did not ease her quailing heart. For some time she was silent, casting about her mind for a way to relate the trouble without painting George the villain, or intimating that she agreed with him either.

"He said," she went on at last, haltingly, "he said we should endeavor—" She paused and sighed hugely, "not to add to Polly's number if we possibly may." The words were out, and she hoped he understood well enough her feelings about them.

"What did you say?" His voice was even, casual, disinterested, betraying no reaction of his own.

"I told him," she said strongly, sitting up, "that he presumed too far! He had no right to interfere with us!" The effort and emotion made her head pound. She made a moue of complaint and was drawn back into his embrace amongst the bolsters and pillows.

"Sweet," he said, to mollify her. She felt the beating of his heart in the dark, his radiant warmth, and her senses were filled with it, and the smell of bergamot that had come to mean such comfort in the companionable blackness. He was a long time gathering his thoughts, but she knew that he was not asleep, for his hand stroked her hair idly.

"Don't mistake me, love," he said in drawling, hushed tones finally, "for I find such a notion appalling, but for your own sake I would agree with him." He lifted her chin with his fingers and kissed her mouth. "Had you but agreed, you would have had no argument from me. Since you do not," he sighed, "I don't know what we shall do. There are means—" A note of humor crept into his voice, "but they are not perfectly reliable. I for one can't say that I could always be counted on."

She did not mistake his meaning. She clucked her tongue at his low humor. "Tom," she chided. Some measure of spirit crept through her aching head and her dizzying hunger. "'Tis a knotty problem," she agreed. He groaned. "I would have said nothing on it did I know it would raise such a response from you," he teased. She saw the avenue to take their conversation from bad to worse, and did not follow it. Laughing would make her head hurt.

"I'm sorry," she said, and sighed. "O, I wish I was well!" she complained. "I want to do things, but I have no energy for them. I tried to sit up with Patsy and take her through her music lesson today and partway through I had to stop. It's so frustrating! Else this or I can hardly force myself out of bed for lassitude. It's no manner of life—"

Thomas put two fingers across her mouth. "Hush, sweet," he murmured, in gentling tones. "We expect nothing from you, the girls and I, only hope that you soon be well. Don't push yourself for our sake. I love you Patty, and I want you to be well, too, but it will only come with rest. I know it's hard for you to be so idle; I know, love. But it won't be long."

She could believe it when he spoke the words. Such hope and love sustained her through her bad days when she felt so low and lazy and undeserving, and those days were plentiful that autumn. She could not regain her strength and wondered in despair what was wrong with her. None of Thomas's many diversions had any lasting effect on her health, though they were interesting:

— He had from Philip Mazzei an olive tree, it being from a shoot grown off the roots of the trees come from Italy, which were totally killed in the long frost of the winter of 1775-76. It was the sole survivor of this misadventure, and according to Mazzei it would be another ten years before they would see olives from it. But he professed patience.

— He also had some Seville orange trees that were likewise fugitives from the killing frost. They were boxed in compost and kept on the sunny south side of the house until the cold weather began, when they were brought indoors for the winter and housed in the dressing room before the windows, to Patsy's delight. She was enchanted with the idea of having her very own trees, an idea that was disappointed when she was moved into her own chamber upstairs.

— He had made a survey of their roundabout walk, and the distance from the door of the house, past the first stone gate, the orchard gate, the Garths' house, the flood mark by the river, along their private road that ran past Shadwell, to the public road and down past the mill site along the river to the Thoroughfare; in all a little over a mile and an half. He planted poplar and umbrella trees, and Pride of China along the east face of the house. He calculated the stone or timber needed to enclose their lands on the southwest, and decided that it would be easier and cheaper to enclose the lands in fieldstone than waste valuable timber. And at last he placed his theodolite, purchased in May, on top of the house and measured the distance of the mountains from that place. . . .

His energy and enthusiasm were daunting to her and depressing. Additionally, late in November the sergeant-at-arms of the Assembly came knocking on their door to escort him to his duties at Williamsburg, so she had an entire month in which to founder in her illness, for it (and thus she) was the cause of that disgrace, too. The new year would be better, he promised. And she sincerely hoped it would be, for in truth, things could not be much worse.

59

Bon Vivant

Monticello, The Forest

With the New Year the Convention troops, those whose surrender at Saratoga in the autumn of 1777 had rendered them prisoners of war, descended on Charlottesville as their place of internment until further notice. There were four thousand assorted British and Hessians, and they had marched the long way from Boston to Albemarle after Congress refused to send them to England, as had been agreed in the Convention of 1777. Thomas was in favor of their placement there, as he wrote to Governor Henry in March, but the deplorable conditions of the barracks were so inhospitable as to be a perfect embarrassment. The complaints of officers and men alike moved Congress to consider placing them elsewhere. This would necessitate their being broken up, officers from men, which violated the Convention further, and the Germans especially were averse to this.

It was not difficult to sympathize with them, for the site that greeted them was on Ivy creek, on the windy northwest of town, a great windowless barn of a place yet unfinished, of green wood. There was a gross insufficiency of supplies; no bread stores laid in, and a quantity of blankets for fewer than half as many men. To heap coals upon the outrage, they were met with the severest winter weather anyone in the neighborhood could remember.

General de Riedesel, the German commander, had his wife and daughters with him, and by the time they joined him to take up residence at Colle in February he had expended some £200 to 300 of his own money on seed and other provisions for his troops.

The General and his family they did not meet until they had come back from Charles City early in March. The Assembly had met through the month of February, and Thomas was there for most of it, for she and the girls had come along as far as The Forest.

Polly was now six months old, and as round and healthy as could be wished. She sat alone and by the end of February was creeping about. She was a timid child, however, and was slow to warm to strangers. It took most of their visit for her to feel comfortable enough to go to her Aunt

Eppes, who was delighted when she did. Lisbet had recently lost her little Nan, who was just over two and felt the lack of a little one.

Patsy, now that she could write, received the gift of a seal marked in her initial from her Papa on one of his visits from Williamsburg and spent hours every day writing up letters to her aunts and cousins just so she might seal them up in wax with her very own seal. She was a bright child, well-spoken, and her hand was improving all the time, so that her letters, which Patty would correct for spelling and neatness, were often quite entertaining. It was her delight to find a reply from her Aunt Carr waiting for her on her return home. She truly was now, in her own mind, a big girl, for only big girls could write and receive letters.

Patty was improved from her indisposition of the autumn but not recovered. She was better during the winter, for while she yet tired on exertion there were fewer reasons to go out, and the mild weather had stopped her headaches and the pressure in her eyes. It was pleasant to sit with Lisbet in her private parlor and sew, with nothing to disturb their homely gossip save the sound of ice breaking up in the river. By the end of the month there was spring grass on the hillsides, and the weather was so warm that the flowers began to bloom in the woods. All the trees put out new leaves, so that it appeared better March or April than February.

She took a walk in the woods with Patsy and her cousins as she used to do with Jack, pointing out all the spring flowers and asking their names. Dick thought himself too old for such nonsense, but Patsy and Jack and Mary had a splendid time among the bluebells and touch-me-nots and Dutchman's britches. They would not believe her about gill-over-the-ground or butter-and-eggs. The girls gathered up heaps of bluebells and carried them in their aprons, skipping through the woods toward the house.

The sight brought a pang of childhood's memories, for it could have been herself and Lisbet there running. They had often done the same, to come home, as the girls would do, and deck themselves and every vase in flowers. Patsy and Mary were about as far apart in age as they were, with similar coloring.

She walked through the glade where the primroses grew and stopped to take in the wonderful smell, for even so early in spring their heady odor was wafting. She should ask Lisbet to preserve some of them for her in oil. It would make a nice addition to toilet soap.

As she passed by the familiar haunts, she felt a stir in the passing breeze coming from the Chickahominy and lifted her face. When she opened her eyes again, she found herself looking into the startled eyes of a deer. Their own deer at Monticello were so tame that she was not surprised at first to find herself so close to one, for this young doe was not fifty feet from her. But when she would move for a closer look it fled, leaping away through the damp undergrowth with the white of its tail marking its quick progress thither. Dick came up behind her.

"What are you staring at, Aunty?"

"A deer," she said, still bemused. "I looked up and found her watching me." She sighed. "But she fled. I have not seen a deer in these woods for some time, though when your father was a boy they were plentiful, for he used to chase them." She smiled at her nephew. "Did he ever tell you that?"

"Oh, aye," he said, offhandedly. "He and Mr. Carter."

"That's right." she said. She gave over her musing and picked up the basket of wood sorrel. "Well, come along, Dick, or your Mama will wonder what's become of us laggards."

"I'll race you, Aunt," Dick offered.

The thought made her sick. "Oh no, I couldn't." At his crestfallen face, she amended, "but I thank you for the offer. You run, and I'll watch you. Show me how fast you can run."

"I will!" he cried, and raced off with his hair flying out behind him from its neat queue. She watched him run up the hill to the house, his brown hair shining in the sun and his clothes a blur of brown and white. He would be back in school in a few days' time. It was good that he should get his running out before he had to settle down for a scholar again. She sincerely liked Dick, and he was for her something of a surrogate as she watched him grow, for he was not too much younger than Jack, and in this cousin's progress she could see what might have been, what might yet be if the fates were kind.

When they returned home they had a visit from the Mazzeis, who were shortly to leave for Italy, as their Florentine friend had been appointed by the state as an agent to raise funds for the war effort. Mrs. Mazzei was only too happy to be leaving what she called "this wretched country," but she was less enthusiastic about leaving her house in the hands of General and Madame de Riedesel, who had rented it from her husband. The last three weeks she had done her utmost to make them feel unwelcome, despite the good will the baron and his wife showed, for most tellingly, she had insisted they not share the house—for which they had paid upwards of two years' rent—but must lodge in the overseer's house.

Their young friend Miss Martin they were truly sorry to part from, for she was a well-mannered and gracious young woman now, the kindest of neighbors, but the respite from the Mazzeis was welcome; they were a demanding pair and their society was trying, though each for vastly different reasons. She had always done her utmost to help Mary Mazzei in any way she could, for she understood that she felt displaced; nevertheless she remarked to Thomas after they were gone, "I am not sorry to see the last of her."

He glanced at her. "Do you think 'tis the last? They are only engaged for two years." She could not tell whether he was teasing.

The de Riedesels had made many improvements to Colle, which doubtless had annoyed Mrs. Mazzei more, for the outbuildings had long stood unfinished or ramshackle during her residence. In carpentry alone the general had paid out vast sums of money, and an even greater amount went to provisions. Indefatigable German industry had prevailed in other arenas as well, for the barracks were quite transformed, entirely by the soldiers' own labor. They had finished the disreputable barracks that had greeted them, had erected adjoining mess halls according to their companies, and leveled ground to lay out neat vegetable gardens, each separated by tidy paling. They had sheep and cows for their disposal, which were cared for after slaughter in a more circumspect manner than the stinking carcasses that greeted their arrival; the excuse of the poorly cured meat had been a want of salt, but this was entirely an excuse for dissipation, as salt had been gathered and dried in the Tidewater this year or better, and its domestic production had greatly reduced the price, so that it was available to any one with enough gumption to send for it.

Thomas wrote a long and indignant letter to Patrick Henry after going to view these miraculous changes, for it was generally rumored that the troops were to be marched again, as supposedly they could not be provided for.

> . . .indifferent nations will charge this either to ignorance or to whim and caprice; the parties interested to cruelty. they now view the proposition in that light and it is said there is a general and firm persuasion among them that they were marched from Boston with no other purpose than to harass and destroy them with eternal marches.

An unfortunate happenstance of the de Riedesels' tenancy at Colle was the general's horses' fondness for the vineyard, for the Mazzeis were not a week gone before the animals had trampled all the vines into such a state that they could not be saved.

Such destruction proved a blessing in disguise, for not long afterward they had a cold spell for several days, which would have killed the vines anyway as it did those at Monticello. Much of the fruit that was in bloom was killed, and Mazzei's grapes were not so hardy as that. There was snow on the Blue Ridge, remarkable for so late in the year. Then just as suddenly the weather turned mild again until the middle of April.

On the invitation of General Phillips, they went to dinner at Colle to meet General and Madame de Riedesel and their young daughters. Thomas had made the acquaintance of the general previously when he went out to view the barracks, but he had not met the lady.

Madame de Riedesel was nothing like the Virginia ladies of Patty's acquaintance. Even the boldest of them were not nearly so forward in public as Madame. The Baroness Friederika Luisa von Riedesel was a woman of mythic proportions. Nearly six feet tall, with broad shoulders and an immense bosom, which she wore mostly uncovered, she stood several inches above her equally large husband. She was handsome for all that, in a gross sort of way, with soft brown hair, intense blue eyes, a clear fine skin, and a perpetually florid complexion, which might have led one to suspect that she overindulged in paint were it not seen to wash and fade in her animated conversation. Although she was quite fluent in French, her English was quaint at best and her forays into their language produced some fairly terrible gaffes, for she not only lacked the subtle nuances of it, but had a forthright manner and spoke her mind candidly on many subjects that Patty had been taught no lady should dare approach in the company of gentlemen. She rode her horse astride like a man, morning and evening, wearing jackboots and the most extraordinary pair of red flannel breeches under her skirts, and thus was the scandal of the neighborhood. But, as Patty was to find, she had a good heart.

Her husband, the general, was older than she by a good many years, more years than there were between her and Thomas, and was much troubled by their climate. He became asthmatic in the heat and increasing humidity and seemed to have difficulty with his digestion, for he ate very simply at his wife's watchful insistence. He openly complained at this coddling, spluttering, when she warned him off a favorite sweetmeat, "I am a grown man, Madame, and not one of your goslings!" However, it was plain that there lay between them great affection.

They had three daughters; lovely, charming girls who were the most refined and ladylike she had ever met for their ages. They could teach Miss Patt a thing or two on that head by their example. They were Augusta, aged thirteen, with rippling golden brown hair and her mama's blue eyes; Friedericka, who was eleven, more blonde than her sister, and shy; and the youngest was Caroline, who was seven, and she was the most vivacious. Madame told the tale that it was Caroline who had so charmed an unwilling hostess of theirs that she gave them all the bread she had, her best beds, and taught them English as well, for to that point they had been foundering along in French only, a language in a most backward state in this country. Caroline had large, soft, engaging grey eyes and beautiful hair of a foxy brown. She and Patsy quickly became fast friends.

They returned the invitation to dine a few days hence and it was accepted, but between times they were subject to severe thunderstorms, and the weather turned quite cold, with frost again and damage to the garden plantings. The trees on the surrounding hills and those on the lower slopes of the mountain at Monticello were totally blasted of their foliage, so that it appeared as bleak as late autumn when the leaves had fallen.

Madame de Riedesel did not like thunderstorms. "Dey are too loud," she complained. "Ve never have shtorums like dat at home. It break the vindow in our chamber, and fright me so I break the pot—"

James Madison, who had come for dinner along with the entourage of Germans, popped his eyes wide at this remark, and made a small noise as he tried to stifle his laughter. Poor Madame became flustered, her florid face becoming redder still as she scowled at him. "Vhat!" she demanded. "Vhat I say?" Geismar, her husband's young adjunctant, muttered something to her in German. "No!" she cried, scowling at Jemmy with her dark brows drawn together like knotted cords. "Not a chamber pot, sirrah," she rebuked him in French, "de vase, the ewer, the—ah!" She abandoned English in frustration. "Das krug!" she insisted, amid the howls of all the men. Mr. Madison was nearly in tears, and Madame looked ready to do murther on him. Such were the nature of her confusions with their language.

The officers of the German prisoners were mostly young men, whose military careers nevertheless stretched back as many as ten years. They were undeniably career officers, having chosen army life as a means of getting on, rather than noblemen doing a token stint, and had come with the general hoping to advance that career. But if they were professional soldiers, they were yet not without grace and accomplishments. They spoke French as easily as German, and Captain Geismar was a very fine violinist. Their lieutenant, John de Unger was a philosophe of some note. Rude recruits they were not, as, for all his amiable camaraderie, Baron von Riedesel was a refined man not given to find much pleasure in the company of toads.

Geismar was the youngest child and only son of a baron, a small dark earnest young man, intense in his enthusiasms and grave in his affections, concerned with protocol and doing service to the proper honors. He was formal in his manners and always called her Madame. He was much taken with Thomas's library, removed now from their out-chamber to its room upstairs, and spent many hours there, for in his captivity he had few duties to fill his hours. De Unger was more engaging. Tall, blonde and brimming with enthusiasm for science, especially botany, he found much pleasure in Thomas's company and was endlessly absorbed by his observations and devices.

The British commander, Major General Sir William Phillips, was as frequent a visitor, but less diverting and diverted. He was polite, but with a cool formality that made Captain Geismar's propriety seem like schoolboy maneuvers. He was a large, powerfully built man of above medium height but not as tall as Thomas. He had brown hair and rather watery blue eyes under unruly eyebrows. He favored short jackets rather than the grenadier's coat, and wore with this a long yellow dress sash wrapped about his waist. He spoke with a pronounced hollow drawl, different from the Virginia gentlemen's, as though he calculated each word before he spoke it. Though he was unfailingly courteous, always calling her "maum" in his peculiar way, there was about his glance a cold dismissiveness that she didn't like. She was only to happy to retire from his company after dinner, once a decent interval had passed.

His officers and men were not so stiff, and once without his influence proved to be quite friendly, as most of them were languishing for home-sickness. They were pleasant to sit with in the hall or on the front portico in the mildness of evening. Together they would sing the old country songs and regale her with plainly oft-told stories of exploits since coming abroad. It was all very innocent and dear, for they were touchingly respectful of her presence, amending their language from its accustomed roughness and practicing upon her other such rusty arts of gallantry.

Of their foreign visitors she had a fondness for the French, and the Chevalier d'Anmours was a favorite. Charles-François d'Anmours was the consul for Virginia and Maryland, but he paid them several visits in a social capacity as well. He spoke excellent English, but obliged her by always addressing her in French. He was nearly forty years old at this time and thin as a stick, but he retained the charming manners of the beau and made it easy to look beyond his physical ugliness to the beauty of his spirit. He was a wit and delighted in bantering with her in a light and harmless way. He taught her an English song he had learned, an amusing little piece he called it, greatly suited to her. He hummed her the tune and then sang it out in smooth tenor while she played it with great blushes for the words:

> Come again: sweet love doth now invite
> Thy graces that refrain
> To do me due delight
> To see, to hear, to touch, to kiss, to die
> With thee again in sweetest sympathy
>
> Come again that I may cease to mourn
> Through thy unkind disdain
> For now left and forlorn:
> I sit, I sigh, I weep, I faint, I die
> In deadly pain, and endless misery

Out alas, my faith is ever true
Yet will she never rue
Nor yeild me any grace
Her eyes of fire, her heart of flint is made
Whom tears nor truth may once invade

Gentle love draw forth thy wounding dart
Thou canst not pierce her heart
For that I do approve:
By sighs and tears more hot than are thy shafts:
Did tempt while she for triumph laughs

"I hope I do not appear so heartless as that, Chevalier," she murmured, when he was done. She looked at Thomas, lounging in his chair, and his glance was full of devilling amusement, that silent laughter that was more maddening for its restraint.

d'Anmours made her a small bow. "All women should be heartless, Madame," he said with a wink, "and for a beautiful woman it is essential."

She regarded him from under her lashes. "Indeed, sir, and why is that?" She raised her eyes in a friendly challenge.

"A beautiful woman, as you know," the chevalier said, "is subject to the most pernicious onslaught by admirers on every side. If she be not heartless, then where is the challenge to gain such a prize?" His tone was drawling as he leaned philosophically on her fortepiano, questioning the unornamented cornice across the room. "It is the fate of man to desire that which he cannot have, or that which others covet as desirable. I'm afraid that in the arena of the heart, Madame, man is as little advanced from barbarism as the most remote aboriginal: for he requires the hunt, the chase, and there is greater satisfaction to be had in that which is acquired through effort than through capitulation. The meat may be the same in either case, but the flavor is sweeter when 'tis harder won."

He turned and smiled at her, a conspiratorial smile. "So you see, it is intended as a compliment to say a woman is heartless, particularly if she is also beautiful."

She laughed. "You have made your point, Chevalier, and I cannot argue against it." She dropped her eyes again a moment. "Tho," she said, pausing with a glance for Thomas, "I would not 'twere said that I capitulate."

"It's by such means that our friend always charms the ladies," d'Anmours' companion, Colonel Mercer, complained good-naturedly. "All the arts of a beau monde haven't a chance against such dizzying intellectual capacity. A few well-chosen words on the fate of man, and he may write his own. Beware, Madame Jefferson," he cautioned with a smirk at his friend, "our friend monsieur le consul is fickle and leaves behind him a string of broken hearts." The others hooted at this absurdity, and Patty smiled indulgently, for she knew none of them was in earnest, and all the teasing was merely good fun.

"I'm afraid the chevalier will find no milestone here. I am quite impervious to such blandishments," she replied smoothly.

"What did I say, eh?" d'Anmours shook his head. "Hard-hearted."

Oh, she did like the Frenchmen very well indeed, for she was not considered by them to be beyond such attentions, as she was by her countrymen. It was delightful to match wits with them, still quite secure in her honor and their intentions, for all went on before Thomas's gaze, and he never made the least complaint against it, but seemed to be pleased that she managed so well. She knew just how far to go, and when to retire herself from the focus of conversation and leave them to loftier subjects.

In the night after one such visit, she heard Thomas's sigh of unspoken regret and climbed out of bed to encounter him in the dark room.

"I'm sorry, "he said. "I didn't mean to wake you, my dear."

"I know." She put her arms about him and laid her head on his chest. "One day we shall go, beloved," she assured him. "Sometime we shall go. I know it as I know my own name. When this war is done. You have the connection in the person of the chevalier, and Dr Franklin as well. Who's to say Arthur Lee won't want to come home soon?" She looked up, but could not see his face in the enveloping dark. He sought her face with his fingers and gave her a fond caress.

"It's why I love you, sweet," he murmured. "You always know the right thing to say." He bent and kissed her lightly. "Come, it's late; you should away back to bed. I'll be along momentarily."

"Aye," she nodded, though he could not see, and did as he bid her, happy that she could ease his regret in some small wise, especially as she had been the primary reason for its existence.

She learned, too, thanks to their friend the chevalier, that his good-natured indulgence of her playful exchanges had its limits, and that his early possessiveness was not entirely dissipated.

"It's as well, sweet," he remarked idly when she was at the edge of sleep, "that you're not moved by d'Anmours' flattery, or anyone else's for that matter, else I should be inclined to be jealous." He kissed her ear, and she was suddenly wide awake, for his words, though lightly spoken, sent her heart thumping in alarm. She turned in the circle of his arms to face him, though there was not much to see in the utter dark.

"Are you; should you?" she asked anxiously. She remembered all too well his bitterness over Philip Lee and others, the tone of wounded reproach and the cold anger over a silly thing like a flower given and received. "My dear," she hastened to assure him, "you should know that such exchanges are with me nothing more than an idle amusement of a guest. I should hope you would not think I seek to play you false, even in jest. I certainly don't mean to encourage anyone to wrong ideas. And d'Anmours, for heaven's sake! I like him well, but Tom, he's ugly as homemade sin. He looks like a lizard!"

He laughed now, softly. "Methinks the lady doth protest too much.' Be easy, sweet Hero. I am not accusing you!" He kissed her and went on in a more sober tone. "I merely would have you know that I'm not without feeling in the matter. I know your fidelity and am glad of so ready an avowal of it. But there is truth in the Chevalier's words. To possess that which others desire is to be naturally guarded of its possession. For treasures may be snatched without their will."

"I am not so green, sirrah," she said, striving to be light, "that I may not recognize a wolf at the door, however wrapt he may be in lamb and oily promises. I should be injured," she pouted in exaggerated grief, "to know you find me so simple. Even the commonest milkmaid knows the face of enticement."

He laughed in earnest now. "Oh, Patt, you are a caution! You make me think my instincts the basest folly and superstition. You're too wily by half, my vixen."

"Oh, hush laughing," she scoffed, amused. "You'll wake Poll. Wily? You're determined to add insult to injury, I see."

"Oh Lord," he complained, "What a hornet's nest have I stirred up?" He tightened his embrace. "It would be better had I said nothing, rather shown you my concern."

"Mmm?" He did not find her feigned ignorance convincing. "You know what I mean," he said, in dulcet tones that set her heart thumping for another reason. "But are you well enough?"

She closed her eyes against the dark, against the thrill of her quickening pulse. They had been too long from one another. She could hardly speak. "I might be disposed to accommodate you," she whispered breathlessly. He rose and lighted the candle again.

> *. . .To see, to hear, to touch, to kiss, to die*
> *With thee again in sweetest sympathy. . .*

60

Fortepiano

Monticello

Madame de Riedesel was not finding her residence in Virginia entirely easy, in spite of the convenient improvements they had made to Colle. She had trouble with her servants; trouble with the local merchants, who were not always kindly disposed to her and pretended to misunderstand her English. As the weather warmed up she suffered from heat sickness and fretted over the health of her daughters and the general, who were no more strong than she against the various fevers that raged through the countryside. She had trouble with weevils in her grain stores, and there were mice in the walls at Colle. To all these troubles, Patty listened in sympathy and offered what advice and aid she could.

They sat out on the front portico, sheltered from the blaze of the noon sun, watching the girls play with Polly on the lawn, and stitched. She was engaged in a piece of drawnwork now, a replacement for the heavy shirt she had been making when the ladies from Colle arrived. As she rolled it up to put it in her sewing basket, Madame enquired who such a rough garment was for, as it did not fit with her image of the elegant Mr. Jefferson.

"Our people," she explained, pushing up her spectacles farther on her nose. "'Tis for their summer clothing ration."

"You make all these clothes yourself?" Madame exclaimed in amazement. "But you have so many slaves!"

She smiled, taking out her fancywork. "I don't do it all myself. Our steward's wife and some of the women contribute a substantial share. But I do all the cutting. Come sit, Madame," she indicated the other chair, "and I'll call for some refreshment."

Martin brought them lemonade in her creamware pitcher and a plate of Queenie's sponge fingers filled with clotted cream and currant jelly. She eschewed this last, for such sweets always made her feel ill, but took some of the lemonade and remarked to Madame, "I will admit, Madame, a great admiration for your courage. It must have been a difficult thing to leave your home and family and follow the general to a strange country where you were not certain of a welcome reception."

Madame shook her head. "Tush, Mrs. Jefferson!" She waved her hand.

"I tell you, I have received a better welcome in your country than in Britain before we sailed. A whole year we were there, and when our poor Christian died there was not a single call of sympathy tendered us. And they were supposed to be our friends, our allies! Tush," she said again, "I will hear no more about welcomes here, for nothing was so bad as that!"

Patty bent her head, feeling a wash of sympathy for that loss she knew too well, and no little chagrin for having prompted its revelation. "I'm sorry, Madame," she said in a low voice. "I didn't mean to bring up painful memories. Forgive me." But the baroness was not offended.

"Ach, liebschen, don't apologize." She pressed Patty's hand. "You are a good friend, Mrs. Jefferson, a kind heart. How could you know?" Their eyes met, and some of her embarrassment subsided under the candid gaze. The baroness was not as gross of manners as she first appeared. She was forthright; of that there was no argument, but she was a tender mother, and a devoted if somewhat smothering wife. Her first concern always during their following the army was for the safety and comfort of her little girls, and she was not above asking for help. She had even once prevailed upon that iceberg, General Phillips, for succor in his camp and was treated most kindly.

Now her clear blue eyes were watchful, and saw far more than the surface presented. "I think you know that grief, yes?" she said cannily. Patty nodded with reluctance. "I think if we had you in our company, then we would not have been so lonely in our sadness." She sighed. "You have been so good to us here, Mrs. Jefferson. Nowhere else are the general and I met with such welcome. I am honored I may count you as my friend."

Such praise brought a pang to her heart. O, that she should be counted so worthy by such a lady, when she knew all too well that dark that lurked in her soul, the meanness and temper and selfishness she fought against. Please God it should never be revealed to this dear lady who thought so well of her, and whose affections she returned fullfold. She put down her sewing to clasp the hand that held hers.

"Oh no, Madame, 'tis I who am honored. You grace us, not merely our home but our country, by your presence. You are deserving of every accolade that may be sung for your warmth and your devotion. It shows, Madame, in every facet of your life. Why, look." Her eyes strayed to the lawn where the four girls sat quietly playing in a circle round Polly. They were perfectly dressed and coifed, perfectly behaved—even Patsy had improved her raga-muffin-gay appearance by their example—and joyous for all that. There was not a cross word from any of them. "The proof is before us. I have met those deemed great ladies by others whose children are untamed boors, the worst sort, but yet they cannot be blamed, for children learn but by example. 'Tis plain your young ladies have met with only the best examples. . . ."

As if in answer to her glance and her praise, Caroline looked up and then rose to come to them, her beautiful silky hair flowing about her shoulders, glinting red in the overhead sun. She did not run, but came quickly nonetheless, gliding on her heelless slippers like a wraith.

"Hello, Madame," she said to Patty, with a small curtsey. "Mama, may I have a biscuit?"

"Yes, liebling," Madame de Riedesel said. "One." Caroline did not complain, but took the one she was allowed and held it in her hand. She was studying Patty's work with interest.

"Would you care to come see?" It was plain the child wished to.

"Oh yes!" She came and peered at the cloth without touching, but her face was all a wonder for the dainty work. "What is that called?"

"Drawnwork," Patty said. "See how the holes are made?"

"It's beautiful!" Caroline breathed. "Would you teach me how to do it?"

She thought her a trifle young for such fine work but had not the heart to put her off. Besides, given the delicacy of some of her pieces, she might well be able to effect it. She glanced at the baroness. "If your Mama thinks you are ready," she murmured, "I should be happy to."

Madame nodded her assent and Caroline went off to share her biscuit with her sisters and Patsy before commencing. She earned, by this generosity, but a very small portion of her coveted sweet, but this troubled her not at all. She cleaned her hands on her mother's napkin, then sat down with a needle and a scrap of Holland to learn. She gained the technique quickly and was soon busily engaged in making rows of the filleted stitches, so fine that it was impossible to believe by the work alone that they had been accomplished by a seven-year-old. She sat for as long as they did, never fidgeting, never interrupting, happy to embroider and let their talk float over her head. From that day, she and Caroline shared a very special feeling for one another. She could have adopted this little girl with no hardship, were such required by fate. Happily it was not, but the love she felt for the sweet child was as great as she felt for her own.

After dinner Polly was put down for her nap and the older girls went upstairs to Patsy's new room to play, leaving the adults to recreate themselves. Thomas suggested some music, and Geismar took out his violin and sheets of foolscap, only too ready to oblige. They played several duets together, then Thomas gave over his violin for the cello, and she joined them in one of Bach's Brandenburg concerti, playing the spinet rather than the fortepiano.

It was rare these days that Thomas played the cello, but it was a welcome change to hear Geismar at his violin, for he was an instinctive musician and admitted to having learnt to play by ear when he was but three years old. He was possessed of an exquisite sensitivity, soaring and delicate in its expression of nuances that brought tears to the eyes and a thrill to the soul. One could not ask such an artist to play second fiddle.

On the strength of his admiration for him, Thomas had prevailed upon Richard Henry Lee to do what he could in Congress to procure an exchange on behalf of William de Geismar, for only recently had that quiet-spoken gentleman received word that his father, a quite elderly man, was gravely ill and like to die. The urgency of his plea was due entirely to the fact that if the baron died while his son was in America, the baronial lands and other capital, if not the title, would become forfeit. Thomas was not in favor of anyone being so cheated of his patrimony, particularly for so flimsy an excuse. Such a situation did not speak well for the present condition of the German states, an observation with which Geismar, Riedesel, Unger, and the others heartily agreed.

"The princes would have us in thrall once more if they could maneuver it," the general said. "The taxes are already crippling." He shook his head, unwilling to verge upon politics. "But you know enough about that."

Madame was entreated later to sing, and there was some discussion at the piano over what she would sing. When at last the piece was agreed on, they took their respective places. Madame had quite an astonishing voice, a bright, rich mezzo-soprano which would have done credit to the acoustics of any opera house. Her control of breath was perfect, her phrasing most timely, although how she managed to hear the music was indeed a puzzle, for even in the echoing of the unornamented room it was impossible to hear the piano above or about her rendition of Puccini. Patty was troubled even to hear herself play. Somehow they managed to finish in unison.

"Mrs. Jefferson," General de Riedesel said, when their duet was done, "you must favor us with a song. I insist. You have a sweet voice."

"Oh, yes," John de Unger urged, putting down the viewing box on the stand beside him. She blushed and inclined her head.

"Oh, thank you, but no, sir. I could not hope to meet the excellence of Madame's song. . ." She blushed further down her neck. Thomas uncrossed his legs and put away his wine glass, coming to stand behind her. "My dear," he murmured, for her ears only. She sought his hand on her shoulder, and she shook her head minutely, smiling at the general.

"But if you like, sir," she said to him, "I will play for you a little, if Mr. Jefferson would join me." Her dark glance slid upward, and Thomas smiled. He fetched his fiddle and together they played Corelli. The music of this long-time favorite composer was given a new and vibrant richness played on the piano. Madame de Riedesel was enraptured.

"Oh, such a lovely instrument!" she cried. "Such a charming sound! I vow I would never hear my old Flemish harpsichord again had I the choice. Don't you agree, General," she prodded her husband, "that it is lovely?"

"Oh, indeed," he agreed. "Most lovely."

"Then you should have it," Patty said suddenly. Thomas stared at her, and she knew they were due for words when their guests departed, for she was nothing if not jealous of her cherished fortepiano. She saw to its polishing with an exacting diligence, continually denied Patsy permission to pluck out a tune on it, and had spent countless hours painstakingly practicing fingering. As a piece of furniture it was not allowed the light of day, but when not in use was ever covered from light and dust by a thick-napped green baize cloth that she had embroidered with her initials in gold thread.

Madame gave an exclamation of astonished delight, but her husband was more cautious.

"Oh, but Mrs. Jefferson," he said. "We could not allow you to give it to us." He turned to his wife. "Could we, my dear? If you are so determined upon its gift to us. . ."

"I am," she said determinedly.

"Then you must allow us to purchase it, at least. I would not do you a wrong by its transfer."

She bowed her head, her blush fading. It was not the same if they bought it. "If you must."

"We must," the general said.

Later, when they were alone, Thomas called her on the impulse of generosity. He stalked about the room while she sat on the bed and pulled a brush through her hair.

"I confess I don't know when I've been so startled," he told her. "Your fortepiano! You won't let Martin move the thing to clean the dustballs out from behind it, yet you would hand it over on a moment's notice to Madame. I'm flummoxed," he admitted. He stopped before her. "Why'd you want to do it?"

She looked up at him with the dark eyes of a doe, soft and trusting. All their autumn fire was gone in the dim light, and they were mild, brown, pleading. "Oh, don't be angry, please," she begged, taking his hand. "I meant no remark on its dearness! You should know better than that. But Thomas, I couldn't help myself. I esteem her so, and I would she have some mark of it from me other than empty words, for I may say all day how fond I am, but it means nothing beside the token. You saw her face! Oh, say you understand! Don't be vexed with me. I thought you would understand, for I know 'twas in such spirit that it was given to me. My dear! If it grieves you, then tell Riedesel how it was come by, and I'm certain he would not press, but I wish you would let me do this one thing for them. For are they not as dear to you as well?"

He sat on the bed, looking at her a long moment. She saw the dissolution of his protests in the mild amber of his eyes. He touched her cheek. "I'm not angry, sweet," he said quietly. "How could I be angry with such an angel as my Telei? Madame should count herself blessed too, for such a friend." He nodded, sighing. "Yes. I can say they have brought as much joy to me as to you, and that I esteem them, too."

He took the brush from her hand and laid it aside, taking up her hands in both of his.

"I admit, I shall be sorry to see it go and shall miss its sweet song, but I cannot deny you to bestow your fortepiano on them to such a cause." He kissed her hand and was pleased at her happy face. "Let's say, tho'," he murmured, "to use the money for another of its kind. Let that be my gift, my soft-hearted one." She nodded, her eyes brimming, and he pulled her into his embrace.

"I had thought as much," he murmured as to himself. She stirred against him.

"Mmm?"

He shook his head. "Nothing, love." He put her away from him. "Come you now, it's late. Take your medicine and to bed with you, else tomorrow poor Madame will be in remorse for having made you ill with her singing." She smiled.

"That's better. Go on, and don't dally," he told her, echoing her words to Patsy. "We'll pack it up tomorrow, if you like."

She rose from the bed. "Oh, yes." It would make the transaction easier to bear if the instrument was properly crated up. She took a glassful of Gilmer's stuff in wine, gagging and pulling a face at the bitter, dirty taste, and afterwards Thomas welcomed her into the haven of their curtained bed. The next day the piano was sent to Colle, and he made a note on its sale in his account book. Riedesel paid them £100 sterling.

Two days later they again had a visit from the Riedesels, but this was to a much more melancholy purpose, for the next day they would make their journey to the Tidewater for the sitting of the Assembly. Thomas alone would be in town, while she and the girls stayed in Charles City. The visit of their friends from Colle was unmarked by any mention of the impending separation and passed pleasantly enough until it was time for the Riedesels to depart. They sat in the cool of the hall in the fast-dimming twilight after supper. The children had been called from their play at the clavichord in the dining room for their farewells.

Instead of her usual polite little curtsey in train of her sisters, Caroline came and laid her head in Patty's lap. The length of the Assembly's sitting being uncertain, she was already aware how long it might be before they saw these dear friends again; and if they should be removed from Virginia in the meantime, they may not meet again. Nevertheless she was not prepared for the little girl's words.

"Oh, Madame," Caroline said in her perfect French, with her grey eyes brimming dolefully, "I love you so. I don't want you to go away."

Oh! she caught her breath and laid her hand on the child's silken hair. Her heart was thudding in her ears. "I know, petit," she managed through her constricting throat, "but I must go, as you were obliged to come here with your Mama, because she loves you. But I shall not forget my little friend, I promise, for I love you too, Caroline." She kissed her rounding forehead. "And I shall return soon. Then you and your sisters may come again and play at my house. That's something to look forward to, isn't it?"

Caroline nodded, her large grey eyes the larger for solemnity. "Yes, Madame," she said, and made her pretty curtsey. "Good night, Madame."

Patty smiled. "Good night, Caroline."

Madame de Riedesel would not have her rise from her chair to bid her farewell but leaned to kiss her on both cheeks in the English manner. "You are a good friend," she said, in her low, fierce tone in her uneasy English. Her embrace was rib-cracking, smothering in its intensity but welcome. Welcome. "I vill keep the flies from our larder as you say," she announced, for Patty had earlier in the week given her a quantity of cheesecloth to hang over the windows and doorways of her outbuildings which had been plagued with summer midges and mosquitoes.

"Yes," she smiled. She looked over Madame's face fondly. She was as dear a friend as though she had been known twenty years. Friedericka. She did not feel bold enough to call the baroness that yet, though she had been bidden to. How many of the neighbors only saw the outré riding attire she sported and her sometime horrible mistakes in word choice, and not the fond lady that was beneath? She was forthright, but she could overlook such trappings of personality for the kind heart it bore. She had grown used to Madame's daily company or notes, and would miss her.

"Take care," she said earnestly.

"Et tu," Madame replied. "Et tu." She clasped her hand and shook it. "Get vell!" she admonished. She took her leave then. Baron Riedesel made a handsome bow.

"Mrs. Jefferson," he said, in heavy accents. With his whitening hair, rotund proportions, and florid coloring, he resembled none so much as a well-fed Father Christmas, and behind his elegant and formal manners he was just as sentimental. "You have made us very happy and velcome here. Ve shall never forget you, dear lady." He took her hand and made the proper grace with polished finesse.

"Nor I you, sir," she murmured sincerely. "Godspeed you, if we do not meet again."

He gave a blinking nod and turned to Thomas, who waited by the portico, framed in the violet light of early evening. Beyond him the whirr and hum of locusts and crickets in the grass sang a soft farewell, and the fireflies came out to light them on their way. The late spring warmth was rising from the surrounding woods, and the air was still and balmy. The baron's footman came up to the steps with his lantern after handing down the ladies to their coach, but he retained his respectful distance.

"Vell, my friend," the general said, looking up at Thomas. She could no more see his face, for it was shadowed by the lantern.

"Sir," Thomas murmured warmly.

"Ve shall see you again, ere long?"

She heard Thomas's smile in the tone of his voice. "In the summer, God willing."

"Have a safe journey."

Thomas made a bow. "Thank you, General. We shall write."

"I count on it." Riedesel bowed away and was gone. In a moment the wheels of their coach could be heard on the road, and the footman's lantern marked their progress along the roundabout. Patsy moved nearer to her and held her hand. When the last faint noise of the coach could be heard no more, Thomas turned from the steps and came inside.

"I shall miss them," Patsy said forlornly. Thomas put his arm about her shoulders. "As shall we all, Patty-patt," he said, sighing. "As shall we all."

61

His Excellency

The Forest, Tuckahoe, Monticello

In Williamsburg, the Revisal of the Laws was at last before the House of Delegates for approval, forwarded thither by Messrs Pendleton and Wythe, and represented some three years' work by Thomas, George Mason, George Wythe, and some half a dozen others. Some of Thomas's more radical revisals were not to see passage into law, but most of those dealing with crimes and punishments were passed intact. Public education and a public library were thought too progressive. In short, they would cost too much and require, so conservatives thought, too much effort.

John Page was yet harried in his duties as lieutenant governor and head of the Council of State, a melange of duties not made easier by the proximity of Mazzei in Williamsburg waiting to sail. Their Italian friend prevailed upon his company to a degree greater than he had Thomas' with similar, though more politely restrained results, for Page was likewise inclined to be talkative. He did, however, resent, so far as Page could resent anything, the removal from the company of his wife and children such attendance on Mazzei caused. Fanny had just had a new baby in March, and he was loath to be too long apart from them.

Much to their mutual amusement and annoyance, Thomas and Page found themselves as adversaries in the political sphere that spring, for the vote for governor had split between them quite closely after a first vote had failed to reveal a clear majority between themselves and Thomas Nelson. The matter of six mere votes stood between them for the office, and Thomas, though he was glad of the public esteem, would have been as happy to let Page have the office, for he did not relish the long hours away from his family and the endless paperwork.

When the vote was in, Page was called away to a previous engagement at Mazzei's house in town, and wrote out a hasty note, lest his precipitous departure be misunderstood:

> To: His Excellency Thomas Jefferson, Governor of Virginia
> Wmsburg June the 2d. 1779
> My Dear Jefferson
> I would have waited on you to congratulate you on your appoint-

ment yesterday had I not been under an Engagement to return Home with Mazzei. I attended at your Lodgings today as soon as our Board adjourned, but you were not at Home. I am unhappily obliged to be at Gloster Court tomorrow, and therefore think it proper, notwithstanding our Intimacy and Friendshtp, to inform you of this; lest till I can have the PLeasure of conversing freely with you, you might be induced to suspect that I am influenced by some low dirty feelings and avoid seeing you to conceal that Embarassment which might be the Result of them. I can assure you However that I have such Confidence in your good Opinion of my Heart that were it not for the World who may put a wrong Construction on my Conduct I should scarcely trouble you with this Apology. I sincerely wish you all Happiness and will do every thing in my Power to make your Administration easy and agreeable to you. As soon as Mrs. Jefferson comes to Town Mrs. Page will wait on her.

I am Yrs., John Page

The next day, Thomas sent his reply to Page's house before he went to the meeting of the Council, as Page would be absent:

Williamsburg June 3d. 1779

Dear Page—

I received your letter by Mr. Jamieson. it had given me much pain that the zeal of our respective friends should ever have placed you and me in the situation of competitors. i was comforted however with the reflection that it was their competition, not ours, and that the difference of the numbers which decided between us, was too insignificant to give you a pain or me a pleasure had our dispositions towards each other been such as to have admitted those sensations. i know you too well to need an apology for any thing you do, and hope you will ever be assured of this; and as to the constructions of the world, they only would have added one to the many signs for which they are to go to the devil. as this is the first, so i hope it will be the last instance of ceremony between us. a desire to see my famliy which is in Charles City carries me thither tomorrow, and I shall not return till Monday. mrs Jefferson i believe will not come shortly to town. when she does however she has too much value for mrs Page not to consider her acquaintance as principle among those circumstances which are to reconcile her to her situation. a knoledge of her sentiments on this subject renders me safe in undertaking that she shall do her equal part in cultivating a friendly intercourse. be pleased to present my compliments to her & add this to the assurances I have ever given you that i am, Dr. Page, Your affectionate friend.

Th: Jefferson

He had good reason to believe that Patty would not come to town before the end of summer, for in addition to being rather unwell in the heat, and from the effects of their hundred mile journey, she remained at The Forest for a closer reason: The week before, young Dick—Francis and Elizabeth's oldest son—had drowned while fishing in the Chickahominy, and the shock of this had sent his poor distraught mother to her bed, only to lose the pledge that might have assuaged her grief. Under this combined assault, Lisbet, who was not commonly given to melancholy, was stricken as she had never been before. Faithful to the strong bond of feeling they shared, she stayed in Charles City. Lisbet had come to her aid all too often before, and she could not abandon her for the cheerier society of town. She stayed by her dear Betsy, to offer her what comfort she could.

From Albemarle came other unhappy news. Being much subject as was his lady to the ill effects of their unaccustomed heat, General de Riedesel had succumbed to an attack of sunstroke in their garden and required some time to revive. It was Madame's proposition that they be allowed to travel to the warm springs at Berkeley in the hopes that this might restore his health. As they were technically prisoners of war, such permission was required of the governor for travel beyond a moderate sphere from their home. General Phillips wrote a laconic note reminding Thomas of this desire in the middle of June, though he was not likely to have forgotten the de Riedesel's need for removal and requested to be notified beforehand if his troops were to be relocated. Phillips also took the time to congratulate him on his post and thanked him for his hospitality.

In Charles City, Lisbet had begun to recover from her troubles and was up and about again, suffering no permanent debilitation from them. In the week after the accident she was severely dropsical, so that they feared she would be carried off by milk leg, but she was bled twice at intervals and after that was much improved. Francis was gone to Petersburg when Thomas arrived, being plainly confident of his wife's situation. Affairs at Eppington called him away, but even so he would never have ventured so far if his Betsy was still in danger.

Patty was well enough herself, although the heat made her tired. But it was her stint as nurse and companion in grief that sobered her. Not given by nature to reveal secrets, she was now even less inclined when they struck so close to home.

For Lisbet and she had spent every day of the last month together, and there passed between them such scenes as could be spoken to none. When Lisbet had begun to come out of her numbed shock a little, she said bleakly to her one morning, "I thought I sympathized with your griefs, Patt. I thought I understood your melancholy over them. I wondered why your Jack haunted you at such a distance, though. Eight years! But I know now."

She sat on the bed, staring hollow-eyed at the gently luffing window curtains, one of Francis's large handkerchiefs clenched in her hand. Her warm hair spread about her, waving down until it met the coverlet, disordered in grief and sickness. She was pale, pale as she never was, all her resiliency vanished. Patty took her hand and Lisbet continued.

"You would think," she said bemusedly, "that he'd be safe after nine years, that he'd come through the rigors and frights of childhood unscathed. . . . He knew how to swim! Dear God." She looked up at Patty. "Sister, I owe you an apology. I see now how you too must have thought Jack safe when he had come so far and knew to be careful. Yet betimes I thought you laboring in your mourning, for you always did like a good cry." She smiled a little here, her words hearkening back to their lazy afternoons of novels-reading, that shadow of reality and exquisite tumult of feeling in whose indulgence, had she been capable of foresight, Patty never would have revelled. Life held enough of griefs without turning to fantastical ones.

She shook her head. "You need not apologize, Bet. My sweetest friend and dearest sister should not feel herself chagrined. 'Twas an honest mistake, given me." She reached out and put her arm about her sister's shoulder, leaning her forehead against Lisbet's temple. They sat together thus a long time, rocking gently, saying nothing, and presently when Lisbet began to weep again, she put both arms about her and held her close, murmuring gentle nonsense of comfort, feeling the wracking spasms of her always strong sister's low misery with an ache. Could she but heal her grief, she thought, could she but bring back the smile and calm assurance to that countenance! But she knew no way. She could not find the way for herself but through the slow-moving distance of time. So she stayed and was her sister's ready companion.

Truth to tell, she had no elation at Thomas's election to the governorship. Oh, she was pleased at the signal honor tendered him by his fellows, but the drear reality of the office was not lost on her. The thought of it brought her a feeling of dreadful panic, for the executive was bound nearly hand and foot to the Council, the Assembly, and the perimeters of the town. If she followed her dearest wish, to be near him, it would mean a long residence in Williamsburg which, save for the company of certain friends, she did not relish; if she gave in to her wish to remain in the country, it meant a further burden on Thomas's time as he had to travel to see her. She did not wish to burthen him. There were also Lisbet and Francis to consider. They commonly spent part of their time during the year at Eppington, but would not travel thence if it meant leaving her alone in Charles City. It was with some relief, therefore, that she greeted Thomas's plan to retire to Monticello for the sickly months, for it would give her a little space in which to steel herself for the inevitable: she was bound to be in Williamsburg.

The move would be good for Patsy as well, whom she did not wish to grow up without those graces and experiences which society would afterward require of her. She was of an age that the learning of such polite manners as dancing and how to conduct oneself as a lady on a formal call were becoming important. She was seven years old this September, and it was time enough she begin to learn to be a young lady. She was very bright, quick to learn whatever Thomas set out for her in regard to her studies. She spoke passable French and had learned some German from the de Riedesel girls. She read aloud quite well, could add a long column of sums in her head without recourse to counting on her fingers, and was a neat sketch artist. But what she lacked in the realm of ladylike accomplishments could fill a book!

Though she was capable of naming the names and usage of the most far-flung garden flower or wood or kitchen herb, she had no ability to preserve them properly. The arts of pastry and timing of baking was thoroughly beyond her. She could not make the simplest pudding. Though she could sew a passable seam in plain sewing, more intricate work frustrated her, so that her embroidery was lumpy, irregular, and peppered with knots. Faggoting a seam was hopeless.

When Patsy would complain of this daily torture in learning the needle arts, Patty reproved her, "When I was your age, pet, I could hemstitch a seam to my mother's satisfaction, and she was most exacting. I quilted a coverlet for my dolls with no help, and though it was small, none could find a miss in my stitches. Look here." She pointed out Patsy's stitches, turning over the piece to the wrong side. They were making up a quilted jacket and petticoat for her for the winter. "The stitches do not all come through to the back. They must do, Pats, or there will be gaps left for the wadding to shift, and it will not wear well."

"But why must I learn all this embroidery, Mama, when I have no skill?" Patsy wailed, tears coming to her eyes for the criticism of her hard work. "There are seamstresses aplenty from whom I may buy it, and their work is so much better than mine!" She put down the sleeve in despair. "It's ugly; I hate it. . . ."

Patty put down her own work, sighing in sympathy. "Poor bud," she said, putting her arm about Patsy. "You must, sweet, because it behooves a lady to be capable at such things. It marks the lady from the common female. As to buying another's work, that is good for some pieces, but there is in one's own embroidery an embellishment that a stranger may not copy. 'Tis an expression of feeling as well as merely a strengthening to the fabric. Would you rely on others to supply beauty to your life or refreshment to your soul? Having Thenia or Critta or Nan go for a walk in the woods for you is not the same as doing it yourself, is it?"

"No," Patsy said uncertainly.

"No," Patty agreed. "They may tell you how warm the sun or gay the flowers, or how thrilling the sight of the deer, but you would not have felt those joys for yourself; to say nothing of the relief of a bit of exercise! They cannot stretch your legs for you, nor bring you the fresh air, mm?" Patsy was smiling now, with the hectic upset color faded from her face. "No, Mama. That's silly!"

"It is, so." She took up the child's work again. "It is the same with quilting or any other work: if another makes it for you, you have not the joy of looking upon it with satisfaction and knowing that you yourself created it. You know Mama's white quilt?"

"Aye?"

"Well, your Aunty Eppes and I stitched that together, oh, almost twenty years ago now. I was twelve or thirteen years of age. That bed quilt has been on many adventures and travailed all over Virginia. And I can tell you, puss, that it has made many a homecoming dearer for its presence." She smiled a little, for Patsy, anticipating a story, had fetched her abandoned sleeve and begun to carefully redo her hasty former stitches.

"When Papa and I first came to Monticello before you were born, you'll remember how Papa has told you how snowy it was?" Patsy nodded. "Well, it was not only snowy and cold, but when we came here there was no house yet, only our little chamber, and part of the orchard, so there were practically no trees on the top of the mountain either." Her voice took on a soothing, hushed, conspirator's quality. "It was quite late at night, far past midnight, for we had come all the way from Blenheim in the dark with snowdrifts up to your— mmm—" she looked Patsy over, "elbows."

"Elbows!" Patsy exclaimed, for she had never seen snow that high.

"It was a hard way up the mountain then, for there was only a narrow track, and we were so cold and tired and hungry! When we came home at last, there wasn't a single person awake, nor any light but the moon's. They had all gone to bed! Well, the house had been shut up such a while that it was very cold indeed, and while Papa went to see to the horses I was left all alone in that strange little room, and it so cold and dark and lonely. I remember how the wind howled outside. . . And just when I was ready to cry from disappointment, I looked about and what should I see to welcome me on the bed?"

"The quilt?" Patsy ventured. Her hazel eyes were round as saucers.

Patty smiled and gave her a kiss. "Just so, the quilt. And it reminded me of so many things: making it with your aunt when we were young girls together, how it had gone with me out the country, all the cold nights my sisters and I sat under it telling stories in the dark, how much I loved them and my Papa, how happy and excited I had been to pack it up for our journey when your Papa and I were married, and mostly how very much

I loved him and what hopes we had. That little old quilt made all my sadness go away, so that when your Papa returned I was quite recovered in my homesickness. Now, if that quilt had been made by some far-off stranger in Philadelphia or London, do you think it would have been as dear to me and evoked so many remembrances?"

Patsy's face was glowing. "Oh, no, Mama!" she said, enchanted with the romance evoked by a simple coverlet. "It would merely have been a thing."

"That's right." Patty nodded. "And do you know why I want us to make this set together? Not simply so you have a warm costume for the winter, for we could buy that, but so that you may look on it some day when you are grown and remember all your happy times, too. I want to make this with you not only so you'll learn to quilt, but because I love my Patty-patt, and I want this to be very special to you, as my quilt is to me."

Patsy threw down her work again and hugged her exuberantly. "Oh Mama, thank you!" she cried. "I love you too, Mama! And I shall do my very best on my set so you'll be proud of me."

No hard heart could stand against such praise and earnest avowal of intention, and Patty's was not where Patsy was concerned. She might be exasperated betimes by the child's incredible notions of the world, but she was not ever wholly vexed with her. She did try to please, most touchingly. She touched the loosened curls at Patsy's forehead fondly. "I am already proud of you, sweet."

When Thomas came on the Friday, she told him of their exchange. He looked at her curiously. "Were you so thoroughly miserable?" he asked with a small frown. "You never told me that."

She laughed and turned to him where he sat at the desk in their room.

"Now what kind of bridal would that have been, had I set about complaining about the accommodations? Besides, my dismay was short-lived."

"Our friend Mrs. Mazzei complained," he reminded her.

She rolled her eyes. "Well, what should one expect from a duck but a quack?"

He burst out laughing. "My friend must be better to be so pithy in her observations," he remarked.

She was not well for long. The first day of their journey from Charles City to Monticello that July was hot and exceedingly humid. Even the curtained cool of the carriage was no refuge from the enervating weather. Nance and Critta Hemings were along in the carriage with her and the girls, Critta as a nurse for Polly. Poll commonly sat on the floor playing with people's shoe buckles or oddments of toys brought along, and when she was bored with that liked to sit up and play with the window curtains. But this made her nervous, for it would only take one good jolt to pitch poor Polly out the window, and she did not wholly trust Critta. Not that the girl would deliberately hurt her baby, but she was not as watchful as she might be, being much given to daydreaming.

When they stopped at Tuckahoe for dinner she was quite sick, and instead of joining them in the hall went upstairs to lie down. They remained the night at Tuckahoe, and the next day got only so far as Dungeness before she was overcome. The jostling of the carriage was too much. She would be sick. They must stop. She could not go so far as Fairfield or Spring Forest, or even Elk Hill. She wanted to die, to be relieved of her agonies, but Joe and Bob went on and on, heedless. She wept against the door.

Nance was alert in an instant. "What's they matter, ma'am?"

She removed the handkerchief from before her mouth. "Oh, please, Nance, tell them to stop! I can't—" They stopped at Will Randolph's, and she was installed upstairs in a blessedly cool, dark room.

In the evening Thomas came upstairs to where she was lying face down on the bed. He sat down next to her and smoothed her disordered hair.

"How are you, sweet?" he asked softly. She turned and sat up a little on her elbows. She had spent the day weeping intermittently between bouts of sickness, completely undone. She had inadvertently left the last of her store of medicine in Charles City, which became known when they had searched for it last night at Tuckahoe, so she was without aid.

But not comfort. Thomas kissed her forehead now. "You haven't eaten all day. Would you like me to send for some broth? It'll probably be only salt pork at this hour, but it would fill you up, and you should be able to keep it down."

She was very hungry. It would be awful to eat and have it come back up, but broth might be tolerable, and she was very dry. She was willing to the risk. "Yes," she assented, her voice crackling. She sat up fully and pressed her eyes with the heel of her hand. "Could I have some water, meantime? I'm very thirsty. It's been so awfully hot."

He fetched the water and sent Nance off to the kitchen for the broth. "We can stay at Elk Hill the summer if you need to, sweet," he assured her as she gulped down water. The thought of staying here through September quailed her. There were too many memories, too many ghosts. She shook her head violently at this suggestion.

"Oh, no!" she protested, putting the glass down. "I want to go home. You want to go home. We should go. I shall be all right presently. Oh, I don't want to stay at Elk Hill!"

Thomas looked alarmed. "All right," he said quickly. "We shall go home, as you wish." He got her settled again, resting against the bolsters and pillows, before going down to supper. The broth helped, and she did feel better afterward, but even so consented to see George Gilmer when they got home.

But George was off with the army just then, somewhere between Albemarle and Williamsburg. The only medical aid in the neighborhood at the moment was a young medical student amongst the British, Lieutenant Hayer, who recommended bleeding. She was willing by this out to resort to anything that might bring some relief, and contrary to his avowed beliefs against the practice, Thomas consented. To her mind, the lieutenant had performed a miracle, for the next day she was able to be out sitting in the sunshine with Polly and Patsy, her lassitude gone. Her eyes were still tender, and she needed her green spectacles against the strong light, but she could bear it at least.

62

At the Palace

Williamsburg

For Thomas, the time at home proved hardly restful, for he was plagued by General Phillips's partisan efforts at close proximity. Henry Hamilton, the former lieutenant governor of Detroit, the notorious "hair buyer" of the frontier, had been responsible for stirring up unrest amongst the Indians and urging them to make war on the whites who had encroached upon them, thus commencing a bloody attack on innocent settlers in the Illinois. He had been apprehended in February of this year by Lieutenant Colonel George Rogers Clark, a neighbor of theirs from Albemarle, who two years before had been authorized to stake a claim for Virginia in Illinois county beyond the Ohio. Having captured the perfidious lieutenant governor at Vincennes, he sent him to Kentucky, thence to be transported to Virginia. On his arrival, Hamilton, considered a dangerous enemy of the state, and his cohorts were clapped in irons and holed up in Williamsburg gaol without privileges of communication from outside. They were not allowed a scrap of paper, nor pen or pencil with which to write.

Phillips unfortunately betook himself to champion Hamilton's cause and wrote Thomas endless letters, pleading that Hamilton be set at liberty as any other prisoner of war, for Mr. Hamilton would surely, thrown as he was into the dungeon of a common jail in the most inclement season of the year, beleaguered by chains and close confinement, and so forth, perish and die were he not immediately released. He declared that a prisoner on capitulation may not be put into close confinement. He not only petitioned Thomas in this way, but John Jay, the president of the Congress, and General Washington as well.

Congress was not sympathetic and voted that the affair of Lt Governor Hamilton was entirely an internal concern of Virginia's and that it would not interfere. General Washington, after much reflection and consultation, was of the opinion that it might be expedient for Hamilton to continue in his confinement if public sentiment warranted. In that case, Washington suggested that a specification of Hamilton's cruelties, whether by his own hand or by his tacit consent, be published that the world might feel and approve the justice of his fate. He noted that, in any event, Hamilton hardly warranted the extensive indulgence General Phillips advocated.

Aside from the horrors inflicted on the settlers in Illinois—women, children, the aged and infirm, without discrimination or mercy to age or condition—there was the matter of the scandalous treatment of American prisoners at British hands, which had a long history. From Ethan Allen's capture after his brave and valorous conduct at Fort Ticonderoga in 1775 down to the present moment, there were such authenticated accounts of mistreatment as to banish gentle feeling towards the enemy from the breast of any lover of liberty or friend of humanity. Officers and men transported to England or taken on the sea were kept in prison ships teeming with malignant disorders so as to cause their deaths in numbers up to ten a day. Wherefore then should they be disposed to kindness toward the nefarious hair buyer? Unkindness did not begin with them, but was practiced by their enemies on men whose only war crimes were to be common soldiers.

Phillips requested that he be permitted to send some relief funds to Williamsburg to Hamilton's cohorts, who according to their senior, were languishing in poor health due to their close confinement. They wanted adequate clothing and food, and Phillips had gotten nowhere with Colonel Bland. He asked this only because his troops had been unable to obtain in specie the value in exchange for the continental dollars they had been given by Boston merchants before their coming to Virginia on bills they had given those gentlemen. In short, they were without funds, as the amount was in the neighborhood of twenty thousand dollars, and Governor Henry had been unable to exchange them.

Thomas was moved by this latter plea, for the friends of his house should not be without their private funds for the lack of a horse and rider, and he sent to Williamsburg immediately.

In answer to this mercy, they received Phillips's invitation to a play at the barracks, with a seat in his box, but they did not go. Patty was ill again and had no liking for the general, in any case.

There were other troubles with prisoners of war. Before leaving Williamsburg, he had received a letter from Theodorick Bland, informing him of gross desertions amongst the Convention troops, almost exclusively British, this due to the urging of some of their officers, and when he arrived home he found the numbers to be no exaggeration. Some of them were intercepted and sent north, but others were put under house arrest at their old barracks and denied the privileges they had formerly enjoyed.

In answer to his query on behalf of Phillips's constant anxiety of having his troops removed at a moment's notice to parts unknown, Thomas received from Page the information that the Board of War had no intention of removing the troops until he returned to Williamsburg, which greatly relieved the general's mind, as part of the cause of his troops' desertions was fear that they could not be provided for in Virginia. This was entirely due to rumors circulated amongst them, and accounts of the difficulties of their fellows in Chesterfield, where they were in a severe want of clothing.

At length, Phillips and the de Riedesels were granted permission by the Council to travel to New York, which they intended to do once the weather improved. By that time, the harvest was begun, and the trees were turning orange and scarlet with their autumn dress. It was time, too, to return to Williamsburg and more active work, as Page was beginning to complain of his health, though obliquely. He had been too long in the executive chair without respite; his nerves troubled him. At this request, which they could not refuse, they once more made the long journey to the Tidewater.

On taking up his residence as governor in the palace, Thomas had ordered an inventory of the goods and furnishings. This was duly made up and submitted for his approval, and he now presented Patty with a copy for her household use.

There was a quantity of delft and creamware; redware ditto; a japanned bread basket; several dozen mahogany chairs, some with leather bottoms, the rest hair; a pair of gilt looking glasses; a pembroke table; four beds and bedsteads; one set of worsted green bed curtains wanting the valance; six leather water buckets; seventeen prints; and sundry items. They would want nothing for the formal functions, being quite well supplied with chairs and tables, but their private apartments were sparsely furnished, especially as regarded linens. But half a dozen sets had come with them from Monticello, so all they urgently wanted was a wardrobe press, which was quickly obtained with the help of Mrs. Wythe.

Patty was ill for several days after their arrival, the strain of long travel in uncertain weather having done her no good. She was not as badly as she had been earlier in the summer, merely weak and tired. But she was impatient with it, wanting to be up and about tending to her duties instead of languishing in boredom. As an antidote to her restlessness, she began a journal for Patsy when she was older, a little book of anecdotes and observations which might prove useful or illuminating to the child as she came to her womanhood. She hoped it might aid her in her struggle with her passions to see that she too had struggled with them. But the most intimate thing she revealed in her pages was her marriage to Bathurst and brief remarks about Jack, for she had never spoken of either to Patsy, not thinking it fitting material with which to entertain a child.

. . .Mr. Skelton was the youngest son of the Hanover family of that name, there being two elder brothers and two sisters also. His father was an architect, and was that Jas Skelton whose work the new Capitol was. He was possessed of a lofty and lively spirit, being much enamored of learning and poetry and the arts. He spoke French excellently well and would converse with me in that language about as often as in English. This much improved my capacity in that regard, a fact which has since come to stand me in good stead, tho' I cannot have known it then. What melancholy troubles did afterwards afflict our peaceable establishment! Could we but have forseen, we may have spared their occurance! But, as Donne would have it, man's soule is subject to foreign motions, and we no not what God would wrot. And there are other, sweet meetings which would, had the forgone not transpird, never done.

Mr. Skelton and I were married in November in 1766, and spent most of our time up the country at Elk Hill, for he had his practice in Hanover, Goochland and Orange, principally. His mother lived with us for part of the time. She was a gracious lady, but a little troubled by deafness from a fever. The next Year a son was born to us, whom we named John Wayles after my father. He was blond as Mr. Skelton, and as he grew took after him in other ways, for at the age of three he could read and speak French handsomely. But I progress beyond my compass of time... In 1768 I was left a widow, being in the nineteenth year of my age, Mr. Skelton having met with a most unfortunate accident. He was then twenty-four years old. We are bidden by holy Writ to accept such sudden transformations of circumstaunce as part of God's benevolent plan, but twas a bitter pill to take that my beloved was so quickly snatched from me! My heart was made heavier still by the grief that my little one, my only pledge and token of the fondness to which I was party, was sickly. This we did not discover until his father was near six months in the Grave. I cannot continue these melancholy lines, lest I give these pages a cast so douer as to render them fitt for no one's reading—

...My little son died when he was three and one-half years. By this time I had been engaged to Mr. Jefferson above half a year. My sorrow and grief was reduced considerably by his prescence and his loving and gentle manner. O, how much do I owe to his tender sensibility! Though he was grately engaged in business, yet he encouraged me in his regular attentions, drawing me out with plans for the future and our life, yet never hestitating to lend a friendly ear if I was low. I am perhaps too Close to the subject to be an impartial judge, but I can think of no man who stands as Mr. Jefferson's equal in the spheres of publick business and domestic harmony, for the paths of his genius are many and varied, and the little attentions he is by nature enclin'd to shew worthy of any Lover out of books or hero tales. I am proud to call such a great man my husband.

All this brings me to the subject of my present estate. I was no little astonished to find myself one day wife of the Governour of Virginia! Not, as I have said, because I thought Mr. Jefferson unworthy of such a signal Honnour, but rather because in former times the office was so very different from what it is today. In the days before our present war, it was a position appointed by the King as a mark of Favour for services rendered, held until death. The only Native of this state to hold the Office in those days was Mr. Thomas Lee, but he dyed before he took residence in this house. That it is now an elected estate I am thankful to Heaven, for the term may only run three years together. As the war had brought us to such a pass that our lives would become forfeit should the tide of Events be against us, I am grateful that our term of endangerment is of a fixt length. We are now endangered of entrapment between the enemy's Army and Navy—pity such a prelude to what has occured at Savanna and Chastn.!—and supplies for our own men are deer indeed; for our prisoners of war they are scarcer still. The poor men in Chester-field waited five months for cloathes and shoes, and then not all was provided. This was not for perfidy on our part, but the genuine difficulty of procuring Supplies. Nevertheless, it rents one's heart to think of them suffering so, far from home and uncertain of their ultimate fate. The security of our friends amongst them we are more knolegable of, having correspondence that way, but these are general officers only. Who will fret for the common soldeir as he shivers in the snows of our winters? Charitie is deerly given when shoes are eight-hundred dollors the pair, and people scrapple to find shelter in ever-increasing rents. Whither will this storm lead us, dear God? To a safe port is the prayer of my heart. God perserve Virginia and the united States.

These were not empty or pious sentiments on her part, for she had been truly distressed at the news of the Chesterfield men and of the companions of Mr. Hamilton in Williamsburg gaol. For whatever the crimes these men had committed, none was heinous enough to her mind to allow them to suffer rheumatics and pneumonia from lack of decent clothing and blankets in a cold dark cell. The tales of Mr. Hamilton's deeds were bloodcurdling, it was true, but by his own word it was his sincere wish that these men of his not be made to suffer for following his orders. Plainly he was not wholly without animating spirit, could he be moved to pity in such a way, for he spoke not of his own misery.

When she remarked the same to Thomas one evening when he told her of the move in the legislature to parole the former lieutenant governor of Detroit as other prisoners, he looked up at her from his desk, his loose sandy hair falling across his brow and his greenish hazel eyes regarding her thoughtfully. His hair had faded considerably from its copper hues in the last year so that it was almost blond, being now only streaked with veins of real red. It would not turn white; he had too much vitality for that. She liked the softening of its color, for it suited the quieter aspect of his nature. He was not inclined to quietude at the moment.

He smiled a little and raised an eyebrow, saying, "I daresay that if you ladies had been in charge of the war you would have conducted a treaty of peace several years ago this."

She clucked her tongue and came over from the bed where she was brushing her hair. "Don't tease me, Thomas, I mean it! They have paid for their deeds in their own suffering. Are they to be doubly punished because they were weak-minded enough to follow his inducements? They should not be made an example of for their countrymen's ill-judgement. . ."

He swatted her. "Desist, woman! Or I shall be induced to believe you are Phillips's secret envoy." He smiled then and laid his head against her bosom. "Come kiss me, sweet and twenty, for 'tis better occupation for thee than such fretful coils. You are too soft-hearted, Patty, but your father trained your mind too well! I forget sometimes its sharpness, and perhaps that's your endeavor." He kissed her, but she would not be sweet. She raised her head and looked at him askance.

"I do not like to be called devious," she said plainly. "I have no secret purposes. Every endeavor of mine is before you for your view."

"Once its plan is outlined," he added wryly.

"Aye," she agreed, less certainly. He was winning ground.

"Mind you," he continued, "I am not averse to such soft blandishments as yours, but they don't pass without my notice, as you know." He brought her into his embrace again. Her defenses were considerably reduced, and she had no will to call up reinforcements.

"As to our two beleaguered prisoners, for whom you so ably spoke, you'll be pleased to know that they are shortly to be paroled for just such reasons as you espoused. So you see, you and our notable Assembly are of a like mind. But yours is the more comely pleading." His eyes engaged hers, beloved, green-dappled eyes, speaking volumes without a single word, and he carried the day. "Come sit," he entreated her, moving the chair farther from the desk. "I have work to do, but I could use a respite." So she sat with him awhile, and they passed the time murmuring loverly nonsense that was far removed from the fate of prisoners or the gyrations of the wide world's turnings.

63

Old Friends

Williamsburg

Patsy benefitted considerably by their residence in town. That September she began dancing lessons with Mrs. Hallam and continued at them until they repaired to Richmond. The lady was a former actress, whose husband had been of the Virginia Company of Comedians. Finding herself abandoned by that gentleman, she took up residence in Williamsburg and cultivated the society of the ladies, with whom she became very popular for her spritely wit and her generous hospitality. She got on by teaching singing and deportment to young ladies and for a while operated a genteel boarding establishment, finally, succumbing to the pressures of her friends, opened a dancing school in her house. Patsy loved her, for in addition to the attractions of the lady and her daughter, the class was always a gathering of her friends. There was much praise from Mrs. Hallam for Patsy's graceful carriage, her striking height, and beautiful manners.

"Such a friendly child!" Sarah exclaimed, when they came for Patsy one afternoon. She laid her hand on Patsy's shoulder. She too was a small woman and not much taller than her pupil. "And so polite, Mrs. Jefferson. I vow, she quite puts poor Amy to shame." Amy was Mrs. Hallam's daughter, who was now seventeen. Patsy blushed.

"Thank you, ma'am," she said, in a low, clear voice. But she was smiling.

"You see? She's a pleasure to instruct." She turned to Patsy. "You'll come back and visit me before next week, won't you, if your mama agrees?" She looked up. "Sometimes I like to treat my young friends to tea outside of class, so they may practice what they've learned in a more natural setting, yet without feeling constrained. Wednesday is our usual day. I would be so pleased to show her off, Mrs. Jefferson, for she's quite the jewel."

How could she gainsay such a flattering request? She assented, with the proviso that Papa's permission must also be got, for this was the first time Patsy had been asked away by herself, and such an important decision must have his approval. This was well understood by Mrs. Hallam, and Patsy was not downcast, for she knew her Papa could not deny her so innocent a pleasure.

They met Fanny Page in her carriage before the house. She had come for Sally and Anne. They bowed to each other warmly.

"Mrs. Page."

"Mrs. Jefferson." There were dimples above Fanny's curving mouth. "How does Your Excellency?"

"Excellently, Madame," Patty replied in kind. "Shall we see you this evening, then?" For the Pages were among the guests invited to supper.

"You shall. We look forward to it." She leaned to greet her daughters, who were handed into the carriage by their footman. Patty made her a bow. "As do we," she said, smiling. "Good day, Mrs. Page." She stepped back out of the way.

"Good day, Mrs. Jefferson," Fanny returned. She moved from the window and signalled their coachman. Patty hurried to her own carriage where Patsy waited with Polly and Critta. She and Fanny derived great amusement from the formalities of their positions, for such requirements amongst close friends were absurd to say the least. All their obeisances had the air of diversion about them, even in the most formal settings, which, had an observant not known better, might have been mistaken for mockery. But their friendship forestalled that, and the elevation of one did not change the esteem of the other. Shortly, their roles would likely be reversed, and Patty doubted Fanny would then put on airs, for she was too fond.

In the carriage Polly was bouncing up and down on the seat, an activity not inclined to please her father much, for the brocaded turquoise upholstery was new and Polly lately wearing shoes.

"Poll, come here to Mama," she said, anxious lest they start off and the child fall. Polly turned and smiled at her, ducking her head, and backed up into the corner teasingly. She made a dear picture, with curling hair tied up in ribbon and the wisp of transparent apron pulled up to cover half her face. She peeped shyly over the lace, her long-lashed dark eyes coyly coaxing a response. Patty shook her head. "Little silly! Come here sweet—" They began to move, and she said sharply to Critta, who was sitting stupidly opposite, "Catch her! I can't reach that far!"

To rescue Polly she would have had to climb over Patsy's legs. Critta reached her just in time to keep her from tumbling to the floor and handed her over complacently. After the incident with the flowers at home—Critta had wandered off, leaving Polly to pull up all of Thomas's summer plantings in the northeast lawn—she began to think it was best to find Poll another nurse. Critta was acceptable when Polly was a little baby and not able to move about much, but she was running now and required close watching.

Polly stood on her lap and patted her face. "Ma ma ma," she said, with a smile.

"Poll, Poll, Poll," she returned.

"Kiss," Polly insisted. She obliged and Polly kissed her noisily.

"Good girl," she said, sitting the child in her lap. They were passing

Bruton church now. "You know Poll, it's not good for Baby to stand on the seats," she admonished. "You may fall down, and we wouldn't want our Poll to be hurt." Polly looked up at her, her mouth turned down at the rebuke. Her face crumpled and she began to cry.

"Ah," she said, sympathy welling for Polly's sensitive nature. "Don't cry, sweet. There." She picked her up and patted her until she was calmed. She would have to be careful of this one, if so mild a remonstrance could bring her to tears. "Don't cry, lovey, Mama didn't mean to make you sad. Look here, you may stand with Mama or Patsy helping you, but not alone. For you're such a little thing, you'll just fly about." It was true. She was much daintier than Patsy had been, with delicate, slender arms and legs and small feet. Patsy, on the other hand, could now wear her mother's shoes, a most distressing indication of her ultimate stature. She feared she would end up like Madame de Riedesel. There was nothing dainty about Madame. She was a fulsome, solid woman who would have done credit to a Roman matron.

They came up to the entrance of the Governor's Palace, and she stood Polly at the window. "Look, Baby, we're home. Wasn't that a nice ride? How'd you like to go with Mama and Pats to the maze and play in the box for a while?" She looked over at Patsy. "What do you think of that? We can play there until it gets dark, get your running about done, and then you can come in and practice your music before this evening. Would that suit?" There was in the garden of the palace an enormously tall boxwood maze that was the favorite of children and lovers alike for hiding in. The girls enjoyed losing themselves in it for an hour or so in the late afternoons before tea. Afterward, they were content to sit and behave themselves genteelly if there were guests or visiting to be done.

"Oh, yes, Mama!" Patsy said, her eyes glowing. She was not wholly given over yet to being a young lady.

"Good." They were handed down from the carriage with its blue-and-white coat of arms of the Jeffersons, and she said to Critta, "You may go on. Only fetch to me Polly's lead-strings and the pins before you do."

"Yas'm." Critta dug the linen tapes from her pocket and handed them to her in a wad.

"Thank you, Critta."

Critta bobbed a curtsey and hurried off toward the servants' hall, her brown hair bouncing behind her in its braid, pleased as Polly to be at liberty, for she was just ten years old and rather immature for that.

The guests for supper that evening were the Pages, the Archibald Blairs, James Madison, the John Walkers, Eleanor and Reverend Madison, and Jacquelin Ambler. These gentlemen were either council members or, in Ambler's case, on the Board of Trade. Rev. Madison, president of William and Mary, had recently returned from the surveying trip to settle the boundary between Virginia and Pennsylvania. Archibald Blair was the clerk of the council. Far from being a serious gathering of the governor's cabinet, politics were forbidden that evening, and the only edict was one of conviviality.

Half of those assembled in the room were members of Thomas and Page's old college club, The Flat Hat Club Society, as they dubbed it, which was dedicated to no useful purpose. They had gathered in the evenings to play chess and indulge in boyish pranks such as breaking in on their teacher William Small in the late hours or dousing the lamps about the college dormitory, but they never caused any real harm. Meetings were more an excuse to indulge in bad puns in hog Latin and make up unflattering, if telling, rhymes about their friends. The antics of The Flat Hat Club had sobered some with the turn of years, become more scientific in bent, but they were not entirely forgotten. Even now, when the mantle of grave responsibility for the ship of state had settled on them, a low-murmured phrase from those carefree days would set them reminiscing in perfect clarity as to its origin. They all had had their secret names, as befitted a secret society, but none had ever divulged his to outsiders; as much from embarrassment as fidelity, for they were invariably silly.

Of that old group, Ambler was the only married man attending without his wife. That lady, the erstwhile Miss Burwell, Fanny's cousin and Thomas's once-dear Becca, was now an invalid who had not left her home in Chesterfield for some years. This information she had from Fanny and her other great gossip, Polly Byrd. Being nearly in that way herself, Patty thought it prudent not to enquire on Becky's absence. To do so might be to bring up an antique rivalry that Thomas and Mr. Ambler would rather forget, if indeed Mr. Ambler was aware of it at all.

She did find it rather curious that they had all been in Williamsburg at the same time during the seasons of 1763 to 1765 and never met up in their ultimate pairing. Even before Batt had put himself in her way again, she had come to town for the parties and the dancing. Yet she could not remember anything remarkable about Thomas at the time. "Do you believe in the Fates?" he had asked her upon their first meeting, and it was her only explanation: that the Fates had blinded her eyes until the proper time should come. She was conscious of all that past as she sat, listening to Patsy play the spinet for them, all dressed up in her silk gown with its uncovered neck.

Patsy played her piece, "The Old Highland Laddie," admirably without a single fault and demonstrated her company manners at their best in accepting the praise her playing won. She bowed her head simply, blushed a trifle but not overmuch, and thanked the company with a neat curtsey. When she came to her chair, Patty kissed her.

"You did splendidly, Patt," she murmured. Patsy then bid all good night, kissed her father, and departed, without even the most clandestine plea to be allowed to stay. She was coming along at last. By such means she would be gradually introduced into society, that she might learn in the easiest manner what was expected of her when she did come out as a young woman.

She looked from the retreating figure of her daughter to Thomas standing with his arms crossed behind Page's chair. She had never seen him in Ambler's company, though they worked closely together in council. He had no lingering resentments against that gentleman, plainly. But would it have been different if Mrs. Ambler were not an invalid? Becky Burwell was not the sort of rival calculated to be on friendly terms. How different from Fanny! Fanny had been likewise a belle in her day, but she was first and always a steadfast friend. How different would this evening be if Mrs. Ambler were present? Would Thomas still look on her with regret?

She felt a spasm of unexpected jealousy at the notion. He had not seen her in years. He would remember her as when young and fresh. Did he think on her now and again in the privacy of his heart? He had never mentioned her beyond an unrevealing casual remark. The details she knew, she had from others.

She knew she herself had not worn as well as Lisbet, who had had her own difficulties in childbed. She was now thirty-one, middle aged, and her own looking glass told her that her complexion was less smooth, more papery than it had been, and her hair less glossy. There were lines about her eyes that would not abate, no matter how much cucumber she put on them or oil she smoothed in. After eight pregnancies, she was softer in places she would rather not be, though she was still slender. There were marks on her that proclaimed her a mother once for all. Generally, she did not mind these things, for one could not expect youth's bloom to last forever, but now they troubled her. She could not compare with an idealistic memory of a young girl, and knew it.

She listened to the ladies' talk with half an ear, preoccupied, grateful that it was not a manner of conversation that required great input from her. Thus she started a little when Martin came and bent behind her chair to murmur, "They supper's ready, ma'am."

She turned her head, but did not look at him directly, and said in a discreet voice. "Yes, thank you. We shall be in presently."

Page and James Senior were animatedly expostulating to Blair and Jemmy about their Society for the Advancement of Useful Knowledge, and why it was important that they chart the daily sunrise and sunset and the changes in the weather from day to month to year. They were still garnering information for David Rittenhouse's proposed ephemeris, which after ten years' time was not near completion. The meteorologic and ombrometrical observations, they hoped, would serve as a source for weather forecasts in future almanacs, thereby improving the timing of planting and harvesting crops, and by extension, the wealth and prosperity of Virginia.

During this, Thomas stood as before, with his arms crossed behind Page's chair, one foot before the other, with a bemused expression. Though he had eschewed hair powder, he had dressed for the company, in his black princess coat and new red waistcoat with the bright tambour embroidery she had made. With his proper ruffles and buff breeches, he could have been any wealthy aristocrat, rather than the much-beleaguered governor of a war-ravaged state.

Mr. Ambler had the sallow complexion one found in some of the French, with rather bulbous brown eyes and a long, sharp, curving nose. He was not handsome but had an engaging manner. He reclined in his chair, taking in the conversation with amusement. He too was used to Page's enthusiasms. He was a fairly tall man, above the middle height, and dark, although he wore his hair powdered tonight. He was dressed in old lavender-embroidered silks of a fashion plainly dating from his college days. Ostentation was acceptable if it was antiquated. Lavish display á la mode was frowned upon in these difficult times. It gave rise to whispers of Tory sympathies, for surely any patriot would dress in Virginia cloth and keep finer garments for private functions.

Patty glanced at Fanny, who rolled her eyes at her husband's dissertation and nodded slightly, encouraging an interruption. She rose smoothly. "Excuse me, gentlemen," she said, when Page paused a moment. "But I have been informed that supper is ready." She made a graceful wave toward the dining room. "Shall we go in? I doubt not, Mr. Page, that you and Reverend Madison may continue your conversation as comfortably with a plate and wine before you."

John's fair skin flushed at her teasing. "Was I monopolizing, Mrs. Jefferson? I beg your pardon if I've kept everyone from their victuals."

She bestowed on him her dimpled smile. "Not at all, sir. Come, please, and be at your ease." She looked about the room. "Who'll escort Mrs. Page?"

Jemmy Madison leapt from his chair. "I will, with pleasure!" he exclaimed, and hurried to take Fanny's arm. Soon everyone was sorted out but herself, and she had the choice between Jacquelin Ambler and James Madison.

She was conscious of Thomas's raised eyebrow as he stood by the door with Betsey Walker. His recognition of the irony of her situation raised a prickling warning at the back of her neck, and she hesitated only a moment. To choose Jacquelin Ambler would be to jar an old wound, which though healed might yet be tender in bad weather. Given her own fleeting jealousy, she was not willing to inflict that pain on him. She had little to say to Mr. Ambler besides. He would do better on the other side of Mrs. Blair. She took James's arm and followed the procession into the dining room, feeling relieved when her premonition passed.

They went out into the hall, past the winding service stairs and the grand staircase. The walnut-panelled doors of the ballroom to the north were closed, as they had been since Henry's investiture. There would be no more grand Assembly balls as had been seen in the old days under the Royal Governors, not ever again in this fine old house. Those days were passed away forever. The burled panelling gleamed in the light of the sconce that Martin held beside the dining room door, reflected the cool marble of the black-and-white diamond-laid floor. There were evenings when she had seen these rooms brimming with the crush of hundreds of people, but now all was a hush, the only noise the quiet rustle of the ladies' gowns and low-murmured conversation. About them in the unused rooms there echoed a cavernous silence that was as a curtain rung down on a royal play. Gratefully, she slipped into the warm-lighted dining room before the Reverend James and took her seat, unwilling to look any longer upon a derelict past.

The dining room was ablaze in candles. A three-headed candelabrum stood upon the table, and three or four other stands were placed about the room. They gleamed off the pearlized ivory of the ivy-figured wallpaper, reflected in the looking glass that hung above the mantle, a brilliant illumination against her dark musings. As she took her chair, it came to her that the light was not merely that of an half-dozen odd candles, but the warm glow of sturdy friendships. How right and fitting that they should be gathered here, who had kept the fire kindled in the stormy days of Dunmore's alarms.

John Page had been among those to officially welcome their erstwhile friend to these shores and had been a member of his council until that gentleman's true colors became apparent. He had served longer than most of the patriotic men, for he was conscious of his family's long tradition of service and was at the mercy of his own considerable sense of honor. Though he could easily have done without censure, John did not bow out of public duty by virtue of his manifold private responsibilities. He and Fanny alone now had ten children, and he was much concerned with their education. His brother and sisters also depended on him. This attention to duty had taken its toll on him in sickness betimes, and he was no longer the fresh-faced young man of Patty's first acquaintance. But he was steadfast, and she had long ago forgiven him for their early difficulties.

Mr. Blair, though conservative as a burgess, had proved a staunch supporter of the new regime and had taken over the burdensome job of clerk of the council when his age and health should have precluded such work. Every piece of paper that came to or emerged from the council passed through his hands and was summarily docketed and filed. He could search up a document at a moment's notice, such was his organization.

Reverend Madison was none short of a scientific man. Not only a divine, he was at once surveyor, astronomer, linguist, professor of letters, and an avid angler and horseman. He had thrown himself into their cause with all the zeal of a revivalist. Far from being a stuffy intellectual, he, like Page, was animated and witty, possessing the ability to put one at their ease. In the ten years she had known him, she had never heard him utter a cross word. He was always erudite, slightly wry, and charming.

John Walker was so familiar as a neighbor and friend that he was more like family. He and Betsey, either or both, were guests at Monticello at least once a week. Their children were Patsy's playmates. Jack was not the firebrand of his cousin George Gilmer, nor was he as brilliant as Page, but he too had served Virginia from an early age. Like his father and brother, he was a surveyor, a burgess, a legislator. It was he who had drummed up support in Albemarle for the building of the barracks to house the Convention troops. That the buildings were eventually poorly built was not his fault, but that of the committee.

Ambler she knew less of. But as part of the old set he was unwavering in his loyalty and affection. He seemed more reserved than the others, doubtless due to the situation with his wife. His manners were grave and courtly, and it was easy to see how such attentions would have swayed Rebecca Burwell. According to Thomas, he was possessed of a fine mathematical mind and had been one of the worst punsters of The Flat Hat Club, so plainly he had once been of a livelier sensibility than he now presented. His daughter Polly was shortly to be married to George Wythe's law student, John Marshall, though she was hardly fourteen years old.

Then there was Jemmy, Reverend James's cousin. It was astonishing to contemplate how completely he had become a part of their inner circle in so short a time. He was their constant houseguest in the summers in Albemarle and a trusted member of Thomas's council, so they had seen him nearly every day for the past two years. His sharp mind and sharper wit had propelled him thus far, fueled by his enormous industry and energy. He was now twenty-eight years old and had all the requisites for a brilliant career before him. All he required was a wife to smooth his occasional rough edges. But when the subject was teasingly broached, he colored and replied that he had no time at the moment to play the troubadour.

They lingered at table long after the wine had given out, and when the Blairs departed, adjourned to the parlor once more. Through the course of the lazy, pleasant evening she forgot the disturbing moment of jealousy over a ghost that had caused her such pain and self-doubt.

It was idle foolishness to suspect Thomas of comparing her to a fleeting love, no matter its intensity. Such ruminations were more worthy of Mary Mazzei. What matter that she was no longer the blossom he had called her in those far-ago days? Their love was not based on such ephemerals. It was of a hardier fibre than mere flowery tendrils, rather woven firmly from the cords of affection and shared experience. By his yet-lingering glance she knew that he would always find her beautiful, always love her, no matter how faded she may in truth become. There was security in that, a security she counted on as a solitary constant in the shifting world, for the war drew ever nearer their sphere.

64

The Soldier in the Road

Williamsburg, Monticello

In the summer, Virginia militia had been sent to Savannah to aid Lincoln, Moultrie, and d'Estaing, who had just come from a victory over the British at Grenada. It was d'Estaing's plan to lay siege to the garrison and the town, and accordingly, trenches were dug and artillery placements set out. But this action was retarded by an attack of about 600 of Colonel Maitland's forces, who had only lately arrived from Beaufort, South Carolina. Seventy men were killed or wounded in this show of force by the badly outnumbered garrison. Their commander, General Prevost, was determined to fight. Bombardment by the Continental forces commenced early in October, and a few days later they engaged the garrison.

It began with a false attack, and soon degenerated into a melee due to the eagerness of the troops and the difficult terrain. It was impossible to maintain ranks, for they were forced to traverse a muddy swamp full of brambles. Men were caught out at the head of their columns without support due to their own quick march and were cut down at the garrison's entrenchments by grapeshot and musket fire. They sustained heavy losses, nearly all those who had made the first push, and d'Estaing was shot in the arm before the redoubt. Lincoln ordered a charging of the gate, and his Polish reinforcements went forward into a blistering hail of fire between the two batteries. In the face of such staggering casualties, d'Estaing ordered a retreat across the swamp, unfortunately well within range of the garrison's muskets, and thereby was wounded again in the leg.

There were 1,133 men killed or wounded, most of them French. The several hundred dead were scattered over the space of only a few yards, and the cry of the wounded, lying in the sucking, sticky mud was rending even to the ears of the British. The cause of all this carnage proved later to be American information to the garrison about the time and manner of attack. D'Estaing, at the pleading of his men, retreated with his fleet off the coast, with another undisclosed musket ball lodged in his breast, while Lincoln retreated to Charleston.

In December, while General Washington was setting up winter quarters in Morristown, New Jersey, the British General Sir Henry Clinton, impatient with the lull in the war, was pooling his forces at New York, preparatory to making a push for South Carolina. Toward Christmas, he embarked with a large portion of the army for Charleston, intent on finishing what was begun at Savannah, for Georgia was utterly under British rule. According to the papers, none of his troops left behind in the North objected overmuch, for he was generally considered to be haughty, morose, churlish, stupid, and uncommunicative. His plan was to seal off Charleston, with Lincoln's men inside the city, by positioning his troops from the Ashley to the Cooper river, at the junction of which stood Charleston peninsula. Amid a welter of grim rumors Lincoln's men dug in and waited for the inevitable attack. It was said that Congress, to treat with the British and end the war, planned to deliver up the states of South Carolina and Georgia to the British. The men would have none of this; they would stand fast.

In Virginia, there were calls for more recruits to be sent southward, and Thomas duly authorized recruiting commissions, which specified the bounty and articles he was to receive from Congress and from Virginia. In addition to sundry items, at the war's end a soldier would be entitled to 100 acres of unimproved Virginia land, and those disabled to a life pension. Recruiting commissioners received $150 for each soldier enlisted, which was not the great bounty it first appeared, when a barrel of flour was $200. In addition, there was great difficulty in procuring men willing to fight. They saw the poor provender dealt the prisoner of war in camp and heard too many tales of the travail of the army, knew too well the difficulty of civilian life. Who would look after their women if they were sent away to die in frozen New Jersey or mosquito-infested South Carolina? The infamous lassitude ascribed to their clime and way of life, coupled with the sheer jadedness of nearly five years of war, gripped them as a malaise. But there was little that could be done to rouse them from this intermittent fever. As Thomas Nelson had so acutely remarked two years before, it was doubted whether anything short of actual violation of their homes would induce their lazy countrymen to fight.

Henry Hamilton and several of his companions remained obstinate in refusing the terms of their parole, the objectionable passage being that they might not say any thing against the United States, and so were yet remanded in Williamsburg gaol, but without irons.

An embargo was proclaimed on all meat and corn provisions going out of the state in any manner, so as to discourage racketeers from flourishing quite as they had been doing, and there were strict penalties for any person or agency found doing so. This edict was echoed by a later one from the Congress. Henceforth, each state would supply the troops within its borders, whether militia or continental, friends or prisoners of war. This put a great burden on the areas of conflict, but it eased the flow of supplies falling into enemy hands.

There was a letter from General Riedesel at New York, offering his warmest thanks for the friendship and hospitality his family received at their hands while in Virginia and for the assistance shown his troops in his absence. He sent along a packet of personal letters for several of his soldiers and officers and begged the indulgence that they be allowed to be delivered, as they contained nothing that could have any influence on the general cause, but were purely remembrances from friends, which would give the men great pleasure to receive. He presented his and Madame's great respects to Patty, with assurances that her friendship would never be forgotten by them, and that she would ever rank as one of Madame's particular friends. This news she received with a blush and asked to be remembered when he sent his reply.

There were letters too from Mazzei, and one very long and gossipy one, outlining the general feeling of the French towards America and their war, and of the king's in particular. The Queen called Dr. Franklin her Papa, and he was much esteemed for his learning and so forth, but that it would have been better to send a younger, more active, insinuating person in his place. John Adams was not well regarded. About this Mazzei was very superior, for he had predicted it based on Thomas's earlier account of him, and maintained that Congress had lost their best and ablest man when they sent him to France. He deplored d'Estaing's defeat for its disheartening effect at home and abroad, but reported that the accounts were much confused and contradictory. It was believed at first that the action took place in New York, but they afterwards received the proper information. They were relieved to know that the deserter who caused the rout came from New England, and not from among the Virginia men.

General Washington and others warned of the possibility of a British invasion of Virginia, given the dire situation farther south. They postulated it as part of a larger sweep to be made of seaboard areas.

In addition to these alarums, the army's lot was made worse by a bad harvest, followed by a most severe winter all over North America, the worst in human memory and written records alike. In Virginia, the rivers were blocked up to their mouths with ice for six weeks, and people walked over to York river at York town, which had never been done since the founding of the country. Regiments of horses with their attendant wagons marched in over the Potomac at Howe's Ferry, and over the James at Warwick.

Late in February, they went home briefly to Monticello. It was good to be home, to look upon their own peaceful hills, to hear the song of new birds in the woods, to watch the quiet browsing of the deer. They walked in the woods together, read some, went out to inspect the cutting of the new lambs, and tested the aging of the hard cider in the cellar. They took note of the first blooms in the garden and the woods, laughing at Polly's discovery of what creatures lay under rocks, shaking them from her hand when she tried to eat them. Life drifted on pleasantly. They investigated sundry matters, but the best knowledge was that here was a safe refuge that none could touch. They were safe from the war and the world's cares.

Thomas sent a group of laborers over to Colle with Mazzei's servant Anthony to try and repair some of the damage done by the winter and by Riedesels' cows and horses. As a replacement of several blasted trees, he transplanted other young ones from the nursery and set out saplings from the cutting of sour orange. But Mazzei's olives and vines were all gone.

There were other changes. Garth had had several trees felled on the south slope of the mountain to put up more housing. Anthony and Giovanni, two of Mazzei's servants who remained behind, took up residence in the house vacated by the Reynoldses, as John Neilson found it too large for his use.

On the last day they were home, she told Thomas she was expecting a child. How could such an affirmation of life be anything but good news at home? In the burgeoning spring, far from the concerns of the great world, their days were all delight. Too, Polly was a year and an half old, and neither of them had wanted as long a stretch between Polly and a sibling as there was between Polly and Patsy. At once, the future was full of hope.

But they were rudely awakened from this happy dream. The war encroached on them again, quite literally in the persons of several hundreds of General Woodford's men on the long march toward Charleston. They swarmed in the road, making passage difficult, for they were exhausted from their journey thus far on inadequate provisions and did not have the inclination to move much out of the way.

As they approached ferriage point at the Chickahominy, the road became so thoroughly clogged that they were halted entirely. Patty put her head out to ask Bob, "What's amiss; what's the delay?" Thomas was talking with one of the soldiers up ahead.

Bob shook his head. "I don't rightly know, Missus."

When they came to the ferry, she asked Thomas the reason for their delay. With a deep blush he told her in embarrassed tones of the soldier she had seen, who was far behind his company and had begged a ride only so far as he should be caught up with them.

"What did you tell him?" she asked, for she saw the man nowhere in this sea of humanity. "I refused him," he said miserably.

"Mr. Jefferson!" she exclaimed, shocked. She had not thought him capable of such cruelty. "That poor man—" She looked back down the road they had come, as if to see him lingering yet. He held up his hand to placate her horrified frown. "I know, I know," he said miserably. "I feel wretched. If he is yet to be found, I would like to go back and fetch him."

"I would hope so." She looked up at him, her dark eyes unfathomable with pity. "My dear, you must, we must! It is our Christian duty. The poor man. . . ."

They herded children and servants back into the carriage and the wagon and turned around. Thomas and Bob and Jamey searched the roads for over an hour, enquired after him, but the soldier was not to be found. Like as not, he had entered some small byway and collapsed. Poor Thomas was wretched for days.

In Williamsburg, there was a letter from General Riedesel, informing that Madame was safely delivered of a fourth daughter. They had hoped for another son, but were evidently pleased with the little girl, for they named her America.

Such reminders as they had of their pleasant interlude amongst the Convention officers now seemed as belonging to another life. The state of affairs in Virginia were quite dire. Regiments were being sent by the day southward to the aid of South Carolina, and there were constant rumors of an attack by sea being planned by the British.

On the seventh of April, the official date of the removal of the government from Williamsburg, Thomas received a letter from Page tendering his resignation. It had been long expected, as John's health was not good—he had suffered from a lung complaint in the severe winter—and his personal affairs were in a complete state of disarray. He wrote:

> I had. . .determined to send in my resignation to the General
> Assembly at the latter End of their last Session; but that the Report
> which then prevailed of an Invasion had determined me to wait till
> I might resign without incurring the Suspicion of retiring to avoid
> the Dangers which then appeared to threaten us. . . . you will be
> assured that nothing but the particular Situation of my private and
> domestic Affairs which have suffered extremely by a four Years and
> an half almost total Neglect of them could induce me to retire from
> the Service of my Country during the War; and that it gives me great
> Pain to do so at present, and particularly during your Administra-
> tion. . . .

It mattered not that there were competent men to replace him. The loss of Page's ability at this hour Thomas sorely felt. They knew the private causes that made his retirement necessary, better than anyone. His health was poor; his estate was in arrears; his crops perishing for attention; his children growing up without the guidance he would wish; Fanny was ill and expecting a child; and the position of his lands between the bay and the river put him at grave risk on an invasion. Thus they did not grudge Page his retirement. They would not ask lifesblood from the wounded.

Wounded, in truth, there soon were. From Charleston came to news of a rout that was worse than Savannah's and a crushing blow to the morale of patriots. In the middle of April, Clinton, receiving a refusal from Lincoln to surrender the town, began a bombardment. Lincoln kept open a line of communication with the countryside by having his cavalry traverse the area east of the Cooper river, as he daily expected more reinforcements from Virginia to enter the town this way, as 700 of them had already done. Clinton sent a detachment of 1,400 men under Lieutenant Colonel Webster to cut them off from Charleston neck. The advance guard, made up of Tarleton's Legion and Ferguson's Corps, surprised Lincoln's cavalry in the night at Biggin's bridge, thirty miles from Charleston, and effectively undid Lincoln's line of reinforcement. Only thirty men were killed at the bridge, but the stories that came of Tarleton's quarter made it plain that they were not killed honorably.

Lieutenant Colonel Banastre Tarleton was a dashing young man, reckless and brave, who should have been a credit to any army. But he was also ruthless, brutal, and not disposed to deal kindly with an enemy, even a dying one. Nothing was sacred to him. No rule of war besides destruction did he follow. Nowhere was there to be found amongst his officers or men noble conduct toward civilians, wounded, or prisoners of war. None was safe in his hands or in his vicinity. Such was Tarleton's quarter of mercy that his men regularly burnt houses and crops, carried off slaves and property, violated women, and committed such vile atrocities against the living and the dead that his name became a curse on the lips of mild men. It became no surprise to hear that in his final moments some officer endured the insults and small cruel wounds of Tarleton's privates. Those who mercifully survived often bore a superfluity of unexplained sword wounds in obscure places; several had ears sliced off.

By the twenty-seventh of April, Charleston was surrounded by Clinton's reinforcements from New York. Fort Moultrie fell, and Clinton intercepted and published a letter from one of the militia to his wife, which stated plainly that a British victory was soon expected. Lincoln and Clinton began to discuss terms of surrender, but Lincoln was obdurate, and the shelling continued for several more days. On the eleventh, Charleston fell and the British standard was once more raised over South Carolina as well as Georgia. Expeditions were sent out into the countryside to subdue the people. Tarleton's dragoons swept upon a retreating company near the North Carolina border. The flag of surrender they carried was trampled as so much cloth by the colonel's troop of horse. An hundred and thirteen men were killed in brutal fashion on the spot when they had offered no provocation, and a greater number were badly wounded. They bore, as many had before them, the sabre marks of Tarleton's quarter. Clinton went back to New York and the conquering army, under Cornwallis, was moving northward.

65

Appeal for Aid

Richmond

In Richmond they took a house from Thomas's Uncle Turpin, for eight thousandweight of tobacco the year. It was a two-storey wood frame house on the hill at the corner of Broad street, with the meeting rooms of the council adjacent. It stood on an half-acre lot, with kitchens and other offices at the back. Inside it was narrow and somewhat dark, and the stair rails wanted repair, but it was considerably better than some of the other, recently slapped up buildings in use by the legislature, a quantity of which were made of wood still green. Here at least they had a garden and space for their servants, of whom they had brought several from Monticello. They shared the space with William Wiley and his family, taking the whole of the upper floor for their use. Mr. Wiley ran a saddlery downstairs. His wife ran a bakery.

They went home for a hurried week of packing and settling home affairs. As the year before, the farm and gardens were left under the Garths' care, for which they were paid in advance, and the grounds under the eye of John Brock. They had had some problem lately with poachers in their deer park, as well as from wolves in the winter. Brock lived in the gate lodge down at the Thoroughfare road, a tiny one-room building of split hickory and daub plaster.

Nance Hemings came in her mother's stead as before, and Mary and Betty Brown accompanied them to help with the sewing and the girls' care. Jupiter and Sukey came together, and the Great Georges, and the Hemings boys with Martin. There was little of their regular staff left at Monticello, but they didn't anticipate a return for at least until after the new baby came, for Thomas had, contrary to his own happiness, accepted another term in office. She knew that he would do it, for the situation in Georgia and the Carolinas and the ever-present threat of invasion here in Virginia, dictated that he do so. As with Page, he could not abandon his post until there was no avoidance of it.

She was not well as her pregnancy advanced. Healthy enough once the first sickness passed, she had a short respite from trouble before the now familiar symptoms began to manifest. In the hot weather she was lethargic and nauseous. Her eyes troubled her, and she was dropsical again and could hardly walk for the tenderness of her feet. She had flashes of light before her eyes and headaches, and for the entire month of July was confined to bed. During this time, she received a letter from Mrs. Washington by the express rider. She sat with it unfolded for several minutes, and got as far as "Dear Madm." The longer she looked at the page, the more blurred it became. Her eyes clouded and she pressed her fingers against them in exquisitely painful counterpressure but they would not clear.

She felt a rising panic and angry frustration, tore the green glass spectacles off, and threw them on the bed, choking a sob. How long would this go on? Dear God, if she could not read then all her pleasures were lost to her! She could not teach her children, play music, or even give out receipts in the kitchen. She covered her face with her hands, weeping, but the state of her hands only brought her further grief.

They were mottled and swollen, tingling and painful when she closed her fingers. Her lovely hands that were always so fair and slender, so dexterous on the keyboard! They were ugly. Had she lost that pleasure, too? Would she never be able to fly over the keys of her spinet in transporting trills? She had played since she was Polly's age. How could she give it over? Oh! She laid her hands on her belly at the baby's violent kicking, at a sharp stab under her rib. How could she ever have wanted this again, to be sick and fat and unable to cope?

At a time when she should have been a support for Thomas she was no help at all—a burthen, in fact, for he feared for her safety, she knew. Sometimes, in the cool of morning when he thought she was asleep she would find him looking at her with a pensive, grieved expression that tore her heart. She suspected he knew what was the matter with her and would not tell. She didn't want to be a burthen when he had so many already!

The thought brought her back to Lady Washington's letter. There was a packet of enclosures which she couldn't read either, but since it was addressed to her as Her Excellency and came by special courier, the contents could be guessed at. And so it proved when Thomas came in late that evening after supper. She was sitting with her eyes closed while Nance brushed her hair, her glasses and the letter and papers on the stand. She heard his step in the hall.

"That's fine," she said, opening her eyes. "Thank you." She glanced up at her servant. "Yas'm." Nance put down the brush as Thomas came in. When she was gone, gliding out on silent feet, he leaned and kissed her forehead.

"How are you today, sweeting?" He looked her over.

She sighed. "Oh, middling," she admitted, without much enthusiasm. He sat on the bed and she laid her head against him.

"What's wrong?"

"Oh," she sighed again, willing herself not to cry. "I received a letter today from Mrs. Washington, some official correspondence. . . And I couldn't read it, not a word!" She looked up at him, tears spilling over, heedless. "Oh, Tom, what am I to do if I can't read? I thought it would be better, but it just gets worse and worse! Every time I'm sick I lose a little more ground! Soon I shan't be able to read at all, or play. . .or play—" She shook her head and buried her face in his summer coat, giving over all her disappointment of the day to his tender sympathy.

"Ah, love," he murmured, taking her into his embrace. "Oh Patty, my poor love. It's all right, dear," his hands were on her hair, on her back, lifting her tear-marked face to face him. The green shone in his eyes, and all the cares of his own day melted from his face. He was no more the much harried governor, but her own sweet lover, who valued her happiness above all other considerations.

"Don't cry, pet," he bade her with a kiss. "All will be well. You'll play again, once this travail is over, and read to me from Donne in the quiet of our woods on a summer's day like we used to do. This shall pass, sweet." He kissed her again. "It shall pass. And as for now, I will read to you and play for you, whatever you need or wish. All you need do is rest and get better. Once the baby's come, you'll be your old self again and will have forgotten all this sorrow. Come now." He sat up with her properly. "Let's see what Mrs. Washington has to say—" He reached for the letter.

"Thomas—"

He turned, the packet in his hand. "Aye?"

She smiled at him, for she was grateful for his efforts to raise her spirits. He was always sympathetic. Where he might with justice have been distant, preoccupied with work, or scornful of her perennial melancholia, he never was. She was first with him, and her concerns, small or great, weighed more heavily than the world's. "I love you very much."

His face dissolved in his fetching smile. "That's what I like to hear." He kissed her lightly. "Now, let's see to business, Madame." Acquiescing, she settled herself against the pillows and listened while he read out the letter.

"'Dear Madame, I have received of late th' inclosed packet from the ladies associations of Pennsylvania, New York and New Jersey'— Good grief," he broke off, "it's no wonder you couldn't read it, pet, she has atrocious spelling! She's worse than my sister Polly."

She raised an eyebrow at him, in imitation of his skeptical query. "You're a poor secretary, sirrah!" she teased. "Passing judgement on my correspondents, for shame. Just read it, if you please! If you stop at every sentence we shall never get through it."

He shook his head, his eyes warm and teasing. "Tetchy. But as it's official business, I'll comply with your request, Madame Tyrant." He cleared his throat and continued:

". . .emm, New York, New Jersey, ah! The ladies of those states being much affected by the plight of our poor soldiers who have risked so much in defence of their country and received so ill a return from the coffers of their countrymen, and the state of the army being at this time most desperate, they have organized themselves to committees to the purpose of soliciting funds on their behalf. 'There has been a wide collection of gold and paper money, watches and other trinkets as may bring a fair price upon sale in those places, and the general scheme has met with such success that our sisters in Mary land have recently taken it up as well. It is my sincere wish that you may undertake a similar endeavor in our country, for it appears to be the most effective way of wresting needed funds from hard hearts. Knowing that our Virginia ladies possess the warmest sentiments of liberty, I entrust the enclosed to your care, certain that the scheme can but succeed under your leadership in whatever fashion you choose to undertake it. I am, with respect, Madame your humble servant,

Martha Washington.'"

She sighed in dismay. Since her going to Williamsburg, along with Thomas she had collected small amounts for the militia, forwarding them to wherever they were needed most at the time of their collection, but this was another matter entirely. It would require far greater efforts than she was presently capable of, to garner enough money for the support of Virginia's regular soldiers. It was not that she was unwilling to the duty, on the contrary. Nothing troubled her more than the thought of their valiant countrymen ragged and hungry due to profiteering setting basic supplies out of reach, but she could hardly travel about to personally oversee collections when she was hard put to walk across the room.

"Oh dear," she murmured quietly. "What am I to do?" She looked at Thomas and saw his understanding of her meaning. They each knew the other's mind and sentiments so well that a misunderstanding was well-nigh impossible on this head. His face grew pensive. She smiled a little, for she could see his thinking written across his face: he could do it himself, if he wasn't so pressed in the same regard. What else? He raised his eyebrows.

"A general collection announced in the papers might prove useful," he suggested.

She bit her thumb. "Yes, but it would yet need direction, someone to take charge. If we leave it to the discretion of individuals we'll be no better off than we are now." She shook her head. "And I can't do that. Even if I had all the energy in the world, I'm too fat."

"I don't know," he shrugged, looking her over with a speculative eye, "That could prove most provoking: an appeal from a pretty lady in your circumstance. You'd garner more attention than Steuben." She clucked her tongue at him, rolling her eyes. General von Steuben was a great beefy German who smoked cigars.

"Such a gallant," she said, shaking her head at his teasing. "Besides, I should probably then have the child in the road somewhere, and wouldn't that be pretty? I'll warrant you, I'd garner a very great deal of attention then!" Oh, it was good to be able to laugh about her situation! They so rarely did these days. Pregnancy had become a gravely serious matter to them, in both its progress and its outcome. How far different from Patsy's confinement, when every little bump and jostle was a subject for humorous speculation.

Thomas was folding the enclosures away with the letter again. "What you need now is a lieutenant. Someone of some like prominence who could manage this for you. How would Mrs. Page do?"

She shook her head. "No. She's just had a baby. Besides, they're so busy at Rosewell, I could hardly ask her to take on an additional burthen. I'd ask Mrs. Nelson, but she's still up the country." This was the lieutenant governor's wife.

"Mm." He put the letter on the stand again. "What of Nelly Madison? She's in town." There was just the person! Eleanor was as fervent a patriot and as tactful and dependable a friend as one could ever wish.

"Yes," she said, nodding slowly. "I believe she would do it."

She watched as Thomas went to take off his coat and lay it away in the wardrobe. Compared to any other chamber they had occupied, this was the smallest aside from the south pavilion at Monticello. Possessing a single small window in the north wall, its only amenity was that it was newly painted, for the floorboards creaked, the window leaked in the rain, and the door swelled in the humidity, requiring brute force to open it. They had replaced the ropes in the bedstead, but it was without curtains, which meant they were subject to bugs at night, for the window had to be opened. The house was no very great bargain, and certainly not worth the eight thousandweight of tobacco it had been contracted for. She thought Thomas's Uncle Turpin the most avaricious man short of an open profiteer she had ever met. To treat one's own kin thus was a scandal; he might at least have told them the condition of the house.

"Do you wish me to write to Mrs. Madison?" he asked her now, turning from the wardrobe. The damp heat had made his hair curl more than its wont, and he ran his hand through it, taking it out of its queue. It fell over his shoulders and softened his face, making him look younger than thirty-seven. His animation and energy would ever make him seem younger than he was, as it did John Page. The difficulties of the last several years had put lines in his face where none had been before, but a stranger could not have guessed his age. That was part of the Jefferson inheritance, for his mother and sisters looked every day of their age. Even Colonel Tom could be said to look his age, but he had a fearsome temper and that told on him.

"No," she said. "I'll do it presently. But if you could write up the appeal for me now it would be a great help. We should get it out before long."

"Indeed. I'll do it in the morning before the council meets." He picked up his fiddle from the desk in the corner, plucked the strings experimentally. "I've been looking forward to this all day." He came and pulled the chair nearer to her. "What would you like to hear, my dear?"

She closed her eyes. "Mm. . ." The music floated into her mind, pristine and lovely, echoing holy songs. "The Bach hymn." When she opened her eyes, he was smiling.

"Scales," he teased, but played the piece.

As he did, she leaned back again and closed her eyes, her fingers moving on the coverlet as though on her keyboard, and she felt suddenly such a searing joy that it startled her from her musing. She needn't fear losing her music for an inability to read the notation; it was all in her mind and her soul and her hands. She could play in the dark, entirely by touch if needs be. She had only to hear the music to play it. She had copied the notation from several of Clark's operas from memory. What was the bar to playing wholly by ear if she could not read? This realization, that the outlet of playing music would not be lost to her if her sight worsened, heartened her immediately. "What are you laughing about?" Thomas asked, without a pause.

Her eyes flew open and until he said it she had not been aware of her beaming smile. "I can still play!" she cried. He frowned, and his hair fell forward across his brow. "Of course you can," he said. "It hasn't been that long."

"No!"

He finished the piece and put the fiddle down. "What are you talking about?"

She leaned forward and seized his hand. "I don't have to be able to read music notation to play! Oh, don't you see? I thought—" She put a trembling hand to her forehead, sighing. "I thought when I could not read Mrs. Washington's letter that I was done for. But it isn't so! It's all here, in my head; I can hear it, I can feel it. . . My dear, it would be as if a part of me had died if I couldn't play. You know what I mean! But it isn't so! I realized that when you were playing."

His expression was amused. "All for scales. Let me play you some real music." His smile was crooked, teasing. "Mayhap you'll feel the urge to compose."

"Oh Tom, don't torment me so," she scoffed. He took up his bow. "But I like to, Patty-patt. I like the color it brings to your face. Let's see what this does," he murmured, grinning at her, and began the first measure of Pachelbel's Canon. She melted, leaning against the pillows with a sigh. He teased her no more, but was as absorbed by the music as she.

He played for an hour or so and then retired, reading over the day's paperwork while she slept beside him. Her revelation did not make her well, but it buoyed her spirits that she was able to better bear her illness. She was no more despairing, and that was a definite improvement.

She wrote her letter to Eleanor Madison the next week, in the morning after breakfast when she felt energetic. She sat down in the parlor overlooking the offices, where she could see Patsy and Polly running in and out amid the squashes. Ostensibly they'd gone to help pick them for dinner; but they did more dancing about than choosing, and this was as well. If only Mrs. Wiley would not give them sticky buns so early in the day. Polly had a desperate sweet tooth and would eat from one end of the day to the other if allowed.

She tested the point of the pen, then dipped it in the ink, writing:

> Richmond
> August 8th 1780
> Madam,
> Mrs. Washington has done me the honor of communicating the inclosed proposition of our sisters of Pennsylvania and of informing me that the same grateful sentiments are displaying themselves in Maryland. justified by the sanction of her letter in handing forward the scheme I undertake with chearfulness the duty of furnishing to my countrywomen an opportunity of proving that they also partic-ipate of those virtuous feelings which gave birth to it. I cannot do more for its promotion than by inclosing to you some of the papers to be disposed of as you think proper.
> I am, with the greatest respect
> Madam
>
> your most humble servant,
> Martha Jefferson
>
> To Mrs. James Madison

The concentration was a greater effort than she anticipated, and the paper more blotted than she would wish, but she could not write another, and this needed to be sent. She took off her green spectacles and laid them by, pressing the fingers of her left hand against her aching eyeballs. There was a knock at the door and she straightened, turning from the desk to find Mary Hemings behind her. Mary was a tall, large, very dark woman, as quiet as her mother was voluble, but equally dependable. She had two children whom she had left with her mother and sisters at Monticello. She was cheerful, always beaming smiles and ready to do any little thing.

"Yes, Mary?" Patty rose from the chair.

"They's a lady here t' see you, ma'am," Mary said.

"At this hour?" For it was not ten o'clock yet.

"Yas'm. well I tole her you wan't receiving, but she ast me t' fetch in to you."

She sighed. It was difficult enough to get through the day's duties without interruptions from people calling at strange hours.

"Do you tell her servant I will attend her business in an hour or two if she'll come back then."

Mary shook her head. "She'ms hain't got a sarvant, ma'am."

"She can't be a lady then. Look, where's Martin? Why didn't he send her at her business?"

"He'ms down the cellar, Mrs. Jefferson, laying up the wine that come from Monticello," Mary reminded her. "The lady say she has money, but she wants to give it you proper."

She couldn't very well turn her away at that. If she had money then she had seen or heard of the announcement in Dixon's *Gazette*. "We must see her then," she said. "Show her up."

"Yas'm. "Mary bobbed a curtsey.

She took the chair before the unused hearth and settled her white jacket about her. She didn't wish to look so very pregnant. She was but six months gone and great as one about to lie in. Mary showed the caller up, and indeed, she was no lady but a plain woman with a basket over her arm. Patty bowed her head from the chair.

"How do you do? Please, come in. You'll excuse my not rising, but I don't prefer to stand long these days."

Mary retired, closing the door. The woman smiled, and it lit up her sallow, pockmarked face. She was tall and well built, with greying brown hair pulled simply back. She had no pretense about her, but when she spoke it was plain she was not ignorant.

"Yes, of course. Mrs. Jefferson, my name is Mrs. Cox. I was in Mr. Dixon's this morning, and he told me of your appeal. Now, I know money's supposed to be collected at church, but I may be called away and didn't want to miss my chance to help, so I thought to bring you this. "From her reticule she drew out a folded packet of bills. "It's only twenty-five dollars, all I had at the moment, but if I am able to get to the regular collection there will be more. My husband was a soldier, you see, and I couldn't pass up helping the others. Times are so bad."

Patty felt contrite now for considering not seeing this woman. "Indeed, they are," she murmured feelingly. She accepted the money and flicked her thumbnail across the edge of the worn bills. Some of them were tobacco bonds from before the war, peculiar for a woman of Mrs. Cox's station to have in her possession. She raised her head to find her guest's blue eyes regarding her shrewdly. "Thank you, Mrs. Cox. Your sacrifice is most generous."

Mrs. Cox nodded and shifted her basket to the other arm. "You'll pardon me saying so, ma'am," she said in a softer tone than before, "but you don't look well."

Patty stared at her.

"I'm a midwife, see," she explained. "And I see plenty of sick folks and ladies in circumstance. You should not be abroad."

Patty smiled a little. The mysteries of the money were explained. She supposed that it was not unreasonable to expect some unsolicited advice along with the currency. "I am only just up from bed this day, thank you, Mrs. Cox." She regarded her visitor a moment. "You are a midwife," she said, thoughtfully. "I have not been well since we came to this place, and this has prevented me from seeking any of your sisters out. Given that every doctor of note is called away to minister to our troops, I find myself in a difficult situation. Are you engaged, ma'am, for the middle of November, or would you be willing to oversee my lying in? I assure you," she added with dark humor, "that however reduced the government's treasury, the governor would not fail to pay you."

Mrs. Cox had lost all her unease. Her face took on rosy undertones, and she clasped her bare hands before her. She was not as old as she appeared. "Oh, Madame," she murmured. "I would be pleased to do it. If you require notice of me, I could send you it from several prominent persons in this town. I'm quite accustomed to serving the gentry."

"As I see," Patty said, indicating the bonds in her lap. "Yes, I should like that. Thank you."

Mrs. Cox made her a bow. "Very good. Thank you for seeing me, Mrs. Jefferson. I won't detain you further. I'll get the references to you on the morrow."

"I am not so rushed as that, Mrs. Cox," she said with a wry smile. She put the money aside to rise from the chair, but the midwife detained her.

"Oh, no, please don't; I can find my way out. You sit. Good day, ma'am." Patty, not being overeager to struggle up from the chair in the first place, did as she was bidden. "Good day," she returned.

When her guest departed, she counted up the money and calculated that, in the days before the war it would have amounted to about an hundred pounds sterling. One of the bills was signed by Peyton Randolph and was dated from 1769. It wasn't worth much anymore, being only three pounds, and she wondered at Mrs. Cox's fall in fortunes since the war. What a terrible thing it was to consider oneself at least comfortably well-off, only to be deprived of that comfort in middle life, to say nothing of losing one's husband, all for a war which it appeared now they may well lose. The baby woke and stirred, this being its usual active time in the morning. She laid her hand on her belly where the outline of a foot protruded, not at all certain for the future.

66

Forebodings

Richmond

The announcement she and Thomas had written together appeared in the next *Gazette,* after the appeal of a Philadelphia lady against patriotic lassitude and before world and local considerations. She was greatly pleased with its scope and its tone, though she could have forgone Thomas's use of certain grisly images, and felt it would appeal to ladies who might otherwise feel reticent about coming forward with money. It was her idea for the collection to be made at churches:

> Virginia: The sister state of Pennsylvania had the honour of giving birth to the foregoing _____ The unhappy fate of Miss Macrae, Mrs. Caldwell, and others, has proved that the murder of women is an object of war with British and Indian enemies. The Ladies of that state have shown their gratitude by ample donations to those brave men who are shielding us from the sword of the one, and the scalping knife of the other. Our sisters of Maryland are following the fair example; and it is not doubted but those of this state will give equal proofs of gratitude and patriotism. It is thought that in this extensive country the conveyance of our offerings will be facilitated by their being given in at places of religious worship, at which sermons suited to the occasion will doubtless be preached by the several Ministers of the Gospel; such notice being first given as may reach all those who may conveniently attend. As paper money may be easily converted into specie, or into such necessaries as the soldiery want, offerings will be as readily received in the one, as the other.

There came a motley collection of money, paper and goods from this appeal: watch chains, gold rings—including three from Mrs. Rebecca Ambler—diamond eardrops, half-Joes, guineas, pistareens, and great fat bundles of Continental and Virginia currency, amounting to nearly $8,400 and about 2,300. In Albemarle, from Mrs. Mary Lewis, wife of the county Lieutenant, there came 1,559.8 old Continental and state money, as well as four guineas, a silver dollar, and two pistareens. But when Thomas counted it up, he found a seven and a five dollar bill more than Mrs. Lewis had accounted for, so corrected her enumeration before turning the whole over to the Treasury. Their appeal was remarkably successful, for funds and goods continued to trickle in from time to time, unbidden.

In June, Thomas had established a line of express riders from South Carolina, each at forty-mile intervals, to the purpose of ensuring more reliable information from that quarter, for their intelligence from thence was most lamentably defective. It was his plan to have information from one end to the other in twenty-four hours by this device, and he promoted as his source of information in the Carolinas Colonel James Monroe.

This young man, only twenty-five years old, had been a student at William and Mary when the war broke out. Without hesitation he abandoned his studies and his family in Caroline County and joined the Continental Army. Being wounded at Trenton the previous winter and disgusted with the progress of the army, he had come home again to find a place in his state's militia. But the Assembly, like the Congress, were preternaturally slow about such affairs, and poor James was left languishing. His uncle had recommended that he take up his law studies again, but the young man did not know whether he should stay in Williamsburg and study under Chancellor Wythe at the College or follow Thomas and the government to Richmond.

He was not, by nature, a quick study, nor was he possessed of a sharp social wit like Jemmy Madison. On the contrary, for a man of twenty-five he was extraordinarily shy and backward in company, and required some drawing out. He was not unhandsome, being above middle height and fair-haired, with grey-blue eyes and a ready blush. He might have been a poet or an artist. At the moment he was at loose ends, so he became Thomas's protégé in law and government.

Not long after, Thomas announced his intention that they should pack up the household for a week's respite at Monticello. He had been greatly subject to sleeplessness and headaches, and she understood his desire to get away, even for a few days, but the prospect produced her old nightmare, and in it she was unmistakably home. Thus when he put to her the proposition of remaining behind at Monticello until the baby came, she was adamant.

"I will not indeed!" she exclaimed, laying aside the gown she had been folding for the trunk, her heart thudding in her ears. She tried humor. "What? Are you so eager to be rid of me?" But he would have none of it, and she gazed at him desperately. "Thomas, there's no one about but Aggey and Old Jenny for help, and what if I need help?" She put her hand on her hip. "Mrs. Cox at least has some experience that I trust. Besides, who knows how long it may be before you may travel home again. I'll not wait 'til the new year to see you! And what if all this talk of invasion is true? My dear, I would rather die than be separated from you so, not knowing what's become of you. It's seventy miles! I will not stay, even if you insist."

Anything, she would say anything to avoid being left at Monticello. She had not seen herself in this house, not ever, and perhaps by some miracle, if she was let to have the child here, her dream would not transpire. Behind him the clock struck six as he came and took her arms in his hands.

"But, sweeting, it's just for the reasons you state that I would wish you to stay at home: if there is an attack on us from the British, I would feel far better knowing you and the children are away home safe at Monticello than dashing about the roads heaven-knows-where." He smoothed her fallen hair from her face with the back of his hand, smiling a little. "As for me, I shall be safe enough come what may, and less distracted knowing where you are!" She frowned at this. He would not cajole her into giving up, giving in, accepting a hard fate. At her truculence, he exclaimed, "Patty, it's sensible! You have every comfort there, and Brydon's still in Charlottesville should you require him."

She clucked scornfully. "Brydon! He's an old woman. There's good reason Lucy Gilmer did not call him when she had her last baby, and it was more than loyalty to George. I would trust young Dr Walker, or even old Dr Walker were he available, but not Brydon. He's a sawbones and naught else. O, *please.*" She gazed at him beseechingly. "Please don't make me stay there away from you! It's home and I love it, but not when you are seventy miles away from me and endangered. I can think of a dozen reasons to come back here, but only one to stay home, and that is that you urge it. Please, my dear—"

He sighed heavily, and his eyes were like agates. "There was a time when such urging would have been enough," he said quietly. "Have we come so far from love and trust that you can't see I ask for your own sake—" His voice crackled bleakly, "and for the sake and safety of our children?"

The words galvanized her. After all that she had endured for his sake, he had the effrontery to call her selfish, to say she had not the proper concern for the children. Dear God, when she was struggling with him to preserve her very life! Well, perhaps that did not matter so much to him. Perhaps all her care and love and affection were all so much a convenience—

The thought was enormous in her mind, and she could not bear to be near him. Let it not be true, dear God, but she was so livid now she could believe it of him. How many times had she risked her life for him, for this! She pulled herself away from him, seething, breathing hard to control herself. He held out his hand. "Patty—"

She inclined her head. "Don't," she said shortly, and turned away, picking up the discarded gown and laying it in the trunk anyhow fashion.

"I didn't mean to say that you—" he began, but her gaze brought him up and he faltered.

"I am inclined to accept your proposal," she said in measured tones. She shook her head slowly. "But not for the reasons you espouse, sir." She closed the trunk. "Please tell Martin I shan't be to breakfast. Excuse me." She brushed past him and yanked her travelling gown from the clothes press.

"Where are you going?" he asked, when she was at the door, for she was not dressed. She paused, her hand on the knob. "To the devil if you care," she murmured, too low for him to hear. She slammed the door behind her and strode into the girls' room to slam that door too.

For the two days of their journey to Monticello she did not speak to him. When they arrived home on the evening of the second day, he went upstairs to the library and closed the door. *Just as you please, my dear!* She saw Patsy and Polly to bed and went to bed herself, without leaving so much as a candle burning to light his way.

She was assailed again by the nightmare and woke with a cry, trembling and cold. It was black in the room and Thomas was nowhere to be found. She fumbled with flint and steel in the dark and lighted a candle with shaking hands. Sitting on the bed, she wept her shock and fear and misery. Oh, he hated her now, he did! He had never closed a door against her in their lives, not that way! But he must understand, must intuit how she felt without her telling. Oh, where could they go from here, how could she live without his love, how would this child fare if he was so distant and cold, rejecting of it and her? *Oh, I'm sorry I ever came here! I should have stayed at The Forest with Jack and never gone out to Williamsburg.* Philip Lee would have been better than this, for she had not loved him. In not loving, she would not either be suffering now this terrible ache. The one person in all the world whom she loved better than life, and she had driven him away—

She could not bear the sight of the bed, the room, and all its memories and fled to the dressing room in her bare feet to stand shivering, staring out at the thousand million stars above Carter's Mountain, beseeching from them some signal that her fears were not to be made manifest. *Stars, O, stars, I know not even all your names, how may I address you then? Thomas would know— Thomas!*

She heard his step in the room and stiffened, not knowing if it was really him or some ghost conjured by her fancy. But when he came behind her and put his arms about her she knew that he was real and leaned against him gratefully. He did love her! *Oh, sweet mercy, my dearest love, I am sorry for all!* He laid his cheek on her hair, his hands on the hiccoughing mound of the baby. The clock in the bedroom chimed eleven. All would be well. All would be well. She sighed, but his next words brought her up, "It's good to be home."

"Aye," she trembled, for at that moment she watched a star fall rapidly towards the north. Dear God, they were cursed! Her mind was all tumult, when Thomas bent his head to her ear. "I'm sorry, darling," he whispered feelingly. "I did not set out to hurt you. That you must believe."

She gave a quick sharp sigh and turned in his arms. "I wish it were that easy," she said, and her voice trembled at the edge of tears. "I want to say it's all right, but it isn't, can't be— Not when you run roughshod over my feelings and tell me it's for my own good. But I won't be good, Thomas, I won't back down on this." She was desperate. He must understand! "I won't be sweet! I have a right to be with you. So do the girls." When he made to speak, she raised her hand. "You can't prate to me of safety when Madame de Riedesel followed her husband across Europe and an entire ocean to be near him." She nodded. "Oh, she too might have stayed safe," she spoke the word bitterly, "in Germany. She might even then not have lost her son. But neither would she have been able to give comfort to the general when he needed her."

"But you are not Madame," he reminded her gently, "and she has not your health to consider." He kissed her. "I would rather you were safe and well here than ill or in danger in Richmond. Because I love you! As tormenting as the separation would be, I would be mortified to know that I had caused your uneasiness by asking you to follow me."

He did not understand, would never understand! She tore herself away, stumbled in the dark over to the window, and leaned against it with her arms huddled about her, shivering. "But I'm better when I'm with you!" she cried. "As for danger, I have no care for that. I would endure any danger for you." She turned again toward him, her voice shaking, "Only please, don't leave me alone—" He came to her and took her arms.

"Patt?" He probed the unspoken terror as gingerly as a surgeon at a wound.

"I'm afraid," she admitted, curling herself against his chest. She was trembling violently. "I'm afraid to die! I've had a dream— Oh God," she choked on a sob. "Tom, please—" She clutched his waistcoat in handfuls, burying her face, "don't make me have this baby here alone! I don't want to die!" She dissolved in tears before him, her safe refuge, and did not see his face pale.

"Ah, no, sweet, no," he murmured softly, above her. He held her close and kissed her forehead. The baby was roiling now at her unrest. He moved with her to sit on her covered chaise.

"You shall come with me, sweet," he assured her, "if only to ease your mind. All will be well, my Telei; you'll see, you shall not die, my love." He stroked her hair. "Such dreams are only fears. They do not portend the future. All will be well, you'll see. You'll see. Hush, sweet, it's all right. I shall not leave you behind, I swear it." He rocked her in his arms until she grew calmer.

"That's better," he said at length, putting her away a little. In the dim light from the bedroom he wiped her eyes with his handkerchief. "That's my love. Come here." He pulled her over to lie against him on the chaise. "Come look at the stars with me awhile." She drew a shuddering breath. "I'm sorry, Patt," he said sincerely now. "Truly. But you never tell me these things at the time. If you had told me this on Thursday I never would have insisted." She stirred against him, and he went on before she could protest. "I'm not blaming you. . . Well, not precisely, anyway. I should not have said what I did, in any case. I honestly didn't mean it the way you took it. I would never be so cruel deliberately."

"I know," she said forlornly. "It's just," she struggled with tears and overcame them, "you never bother to ask my reasons, and it does. . . make me more stubborn than I would be." She sighed and shifted her head where it rested under his chin. "I don't like to admit when I'm afraid. I never have. I don't want you to think I'm weak, or a ninny. I don't want to be a burthen. You have so much more important things to give consideration to, things that affect so many people, that my concerns seem trifling."

He sat her up and faced her. "I've told you this before," he said fiercely, holding her arms, "and I shall tell you again until you believe it: you are the most important person in the world to me, and nothing and no one comes before you. I have never spoken anything to you with greater earnestness than that. You should never feel small or unimportant or a burthen. I am nothing without you and your love. I exist only in your measure. Believe that, Patty, for on my soul it is the breath of truth."

She looked up at him with brimming eyes, the words she craved too sweet to hear, to believe. "Oh my dear. . ."

He took her hands. "Please, sweetheart, let's not be closed against one another again. It is too unbearable. As little as I care to quarrel with you, it's preferable to the other. Do you forgive me? Oh please, say you do! My Hero," his voice broke over the words, "you are my life. These last few days, I've been afraid I'd lost you."

She nodded silently and came into his embrace. They sat together for some time. "I'm sorry to have been withdrawn," she said at last. The quiet of the house and the night sounds enveloped them. The war and the world with all its cares was a dim dream in this place. Here there was only the easy swell of breath to breath and the quickening of life. Nothing else mattered.

"Hush," he soothed, moving her hair from her shoulder. "I know. I know." The stars were slowly turning above them, and the clock beyond chimed the hour. It would be past midnight now, but they sat together yet awhile, and she was grateful for her narrow miss. It was late, but not too late, thank God.

67

Conducive to the Public Good

Richmond

The French had landed at last from Toulon, and there was word that they would make their winter quarters at the Chesapeake, for rumors continued that the British would carry their campaign into Virginia. Congress sent word to the states from New Hampshire to Virginia that the army was in the most dire state with regard to provisions—that they should soon be required to be on half-rations or none at all, which would inevitably induce desertions, or worse, amongst those new-recruited unused to such privation as were the old soldiers. They earnestly lamented this state of affairs, for when America stood alone against one of the most powerful nations of the earth, the spirit of liberty had seemed to animate her sons to the noblest exertions, with each man cheerfully contributing his aid in support of her dearest rights. Now, when a respectable fleet and army of their ally were arrived on their shores, that spirit seemed extinguished amongst them. Should it be said at this early date in their enfranchisement that America had grown tired of being free? The advances of the British against them would make it seem so, for indifference and stupidity reigned everywhere amongst their troops. They could not leave it to future generations to say that that Providence had put into their hands the most essential means of achieving their object and that it was lost for want of proper exertions.

On the heels of this chastising discourse came worse news and proof of its truth: Gates's army was severely beaten at Camden in North Carolina. The armies met at night, with each having the intention of attacking the other's encampment. Gates had been greatly deceived as to the numbers of the enemy. It was hoped that they might by their maneuvers outflank the British line, but on Cornwallis's first fire and subsequent charge, the militias gave way and scattered as so many rabbits in a field, and it was impossible to rally them. This gave the enemy an opportunity of pushing their whole force against the Maryland line, which was not able to stand them long, and shortly the whole was a scene of the utmost confusion and panic. A more complete defeat was not possible without a general loss. All eight or ten artillery pieces were captured, and with them every bit of ammunition, wagons, and baggage of the whole army. Gates's men retreated up the country for an hundred miles through a loyalist enclave, with the inhabitants taking and disarming the chief of their men. Many whose arms were not taken threw them down and beat a hasty retreat for home fields, preferring to take their chances with the wild woods than Cornwallis's army.

As he had done southward with James Monroe, Thomas established an express line of communication with d'Anmours, who was shortly to remove to Maryland. Monroe himself was back in Richmond, there being little point in remaining amidst the scene of such confusion. He wrote a very charming letter expressing his gratitude, which was poignant in its particulars, and maintaining that the state of his finances required that he now retire to his studies as they had been laid out for him. He would be willing to do anything within his power for his troops, who were to be taken over by Colonel Lawson, but he could no longer bear the expense of being away from his lands as he had done in the past. In closing he assured Thomas of his great sensibility of the aid he had been given.

Patty, in response to this admission of pecuniary difficulty, made Monroe their regular guest, with the understanding that whenever he was in town he was to stay with them, or at least dine in. To save him any embarrassment over the offer, she insisted that it would be beneficial to his studies to be in such close proximity to the governor. Once again, the young man's gratitude was effusive.

He sat on their sofa with his bad leg stretched out, for his knee troubled him in the turning weather, and clasped her hand at the information, blushes spreading all over his fair face.

"Oh, Madame," he exclaimed. "Oh dear lady, you are most kind!" He shook his head. "I shan't ever be able to express to you how—"

She smiled and extracted her wrung hand gently from his grip. "It is no more than any lawyer would do for his clerk, Mr. Monroe," she assured him. "I require but one favor of you, however, for its effect." Her eyes flickered up from her lap, teasingly.

"Ma'am?"

"You must look on us as your friends and not feel beholden for such trifles, for I confess it gives me much unease to be so loftily regarded." She glanced at Thomas sidelong where he lounged in the chair. "I may not speak for my husband, for he is long used to such approbations." She was rewarded with a smirk from him. She looked at James again. "Will you say it, sir? May we be friends and equals with no further ceremony?"

Monroe blushed further, and she was reminded how preternaturally backward he was with ladies. He was a handsome young man, and she found it unlikely that no giddy girl had ever teased him so, but his response was not polished.

"Oh, I shall, ma'am— Mrs. Jefferson, yes. I should cherish your friendship. As to ceremony," he gave a self-deprecating smile, "well, that may take something longer to eradicate."

When they went in to dinner she saw that he was limping badly. As he passed her in the upper hall she said compassionately, "It troubles you greatly, doesn't it, your knee?"

He tried to be bluff. "Only betimes," he shrugged, but the sudden whiteness of his face told a better truth.

"You should bathe it in camphor salts, sir," she murmured offhand. "It would bring you great relief." He met her gaze, his blue-grey eyes searching and a little troubled. Was there no female in his life to deliver him such ordinary kindnesses, no mother or sister to care for him? Good heavens, even camp followers were not bereft of compassion! However, given his shyness, he had probably avoided them in any capacity.

"I will, ma'am," he said gravely. "Thank you." Beside her, Thomas took her elbow, and she did not miss the small encouraging pressure he gave the gesture.

At the beginning of October they received a very disturbed and disturbing letter from Page, whose tone and sentiments were entirely unlike him.

> The particular Attention paid by the Executive to my Recommendations, and Informations could not but be flattering to me, it ran, but the Manner in which you expressed your Approbation of them, in your last Letter, greatly abated the Satisfaction I should have felt. But, should I tell you what I felt and thought on reading your Letter, you might think me either captious or Hypocritical for I must confess, I was much disposed to quarrel with you, for one of your Expressions, and to say in general, what might appear like Flattery, to you, and like mere Affectation of Modesty, of me. . . .

"Good heavens," she exclaimed, putting the letter down. "What on earth did you say to him?"

"I can't remember," Thomas said, pacing the floor abstractedly.

"Don't you have a draught?"

He stopped walking and frowned at her. "Of a letter to Page? Whatever for? No, unless it were an official correspondence, which this was not."

She bit her lip at that, striving to control her temper, reminding herself that he was agitated by John's ire, that he would not be deliberately rude or curt. She tried another avenue. "Well, have you a blotter copy, perchance? You should at least know what he's angry about."

This he took entirely wrongly. He stopped again and muttered in a very cold voice, measuring his words precisely, "I did not think it necessary at the time to go to lengths to preserve a mere friendly letter. It was not of national import."

She scowled. "Well, don't bite my head off." She picked up the hood she had been embroidering for Polly, and could not resist to comment sotto voce, "I'm not the one who has offended my dearest friend." If he heard this complaint, he made no reply, but went to the desk in the corner of the bedroom and began rifling through the neat drawers. She went on stitching until the light gave way, watching surreptitiously the pile of disordered draughts and dispatches grow on the carpet.

At length she rose and lit the candles, then went out to see that the girls were come inside from their play and ready for supper. When she returned Thomas was sitting on the end of the bed with a scrap of paper in his hand, bent over it, trying to discern the badly blurred blotter copy.

"I found it," he said, upon her entrance, and colored a little. "Thank you for suggesting it. I'm sorry I was rude." She went to him and laid her arm on his shoulder.

"I understand," she murmured. She peered at the sheet. "Can you make it out?"

"Not very well," he admitted with a sigh.

"Just a moment." She fetched a candle and held it above the paper between them, and they sat for the next half an hour painstakingly trying to discern the text. Only Mary's knock informing them that supper was ready called them away. They pored over the copy for the next two days, at last reconstructing from it and memory what was said. The offending passage appeared to be regarding Thomas's proposal that Page succeed him to the governorship, for he had been thinking to resign before the spring:

> . . .tho' we differ principally in many regards of public policy, i yet have no doubt that your usual good judgement would prevail and that you would effect measures more conducive to the public good than I at this hour am capable of. . . .

"Surely he must know I did not mean to say that his good judgement would prevail in spite of himself," Thomas said in distress, running his hand through his hair. She shook her head, concentrated as she was on the binding of the hood. "Plainly, it's what he did think. Although why he should believe you have lurking suspicions of him, I don't know." She knotted the thread and snipped it off with her tiny gold scissors. "You've never been anything but cordial."

She looked up as he flung himself into the chair.

"I believe he feels it keenly to have had to leave the government when he did," he said. "Any suspicion he may think I have is predicated on that only. I certainly never challenged his loyalty or ability."

She put down the finished work and went to where he sat before the desk. "Then you must write and tell him so," she murmured, putting her arms about his neck. "You should not come to grief over such a small misunderstanding, not you and Page."

He reached for her hand where it lay on his shoulder. "I know," he said. "I will later. Right now I have a word to speak to another friend. Come sit." He moved the chair for her to sit with him, but she demurred.

"I'm too fat," she protested.

He laughed. "My dear, even as great as you are, I still outweigh you by a good four stone at least. Now come here and don't be so coy." She came and sat, and when she had done so he kissed her.

"I know I haven't been easy to live with these last weeks," he admitted, and she stared at him. It was true he had been irritable since they returned from Albemarle, and it was all the more shocking for that, as at home, once they had sorted out their difference, he had been his sweet old charming self, with many a wry remark to amuse her. Now the lines were back in his face, and he was pale and discontented, too willing to quarrel over nothing.

"I'm sorry for that, little one," he said, bending his face momentarily into the folded volume of her neck linen. "But I am not the man for this job now. It wants someone of greater skill, greater drive. I've done what I could, but I cannot push men to war; I cannot rally forces left and right and charge heedless into the fray. This wants a military man." He sighed. "Good Lord, I can't even assure Gates of the most necessary supplies for our men. Those I have commissioned to obtain supplies are worse profiteers than the pirates they were meant to replace. Our perpetual bankruptcy does nothing to help matters. . . . I feel inept," he admitted and her heart went out to him, for she knew how capable he was.

"I do everything I can to improve our situation," he went on, "and at every turn we are thwarted. I can but believe that the fault must lie in leadership, and ultimately that devolves on me. I would do better to leave it to others—Nelson or Harrison—who know more of how to run a war—or Page, who has power and influence." He laid his head against her cheek, and his voice was bleak. "I feel as though everything I have done this last year has been for naught. Everything is coming apart and I don't know how to keep it together. Page is only the latest example." He looked up at her, his eyes a clear, pure amber, and she saw all the grief he had carried for this long while unspoken.

"Even with you, I am unable to be of any real help. I should have seen you were frightened; I should have known, given the past, but I was too preoccupied. You were right, there, and I'm sorry. Now I just want to go home and put us back together. It was terrifying to think I might have lost my sweetest friend. I could not live without love the way my parents did, tolerating each other. I need you, Patt."

She kissed him fervently, as if by that kiss all the hurt would dissolve as though it had never been. He was a proud and sensitive man, and did not take failure or criticism well. That the present situation was largely out of his control seemed not to have occurred to him.

"Oh, my beloved," she said in hushing tones, putting her arms about his neck. "Oh Tom, no. No, love, you have it all wrong, dear. It's not your fault! If it were, then every man from General Washington to the freshest recruit would be at equal fault. You cannot take the blame for every profiteer or lazy commissioner, every idiot who throws down his gun in craven terror before the enemy, every error of judgement made by pompous generals.

"You've done more than any other man would do in your place; you know it's so—you read what Jemmy Madison said of the general malaise of our governments. That cannot be said of you! I vow, there's not a more conscientious man in any government. Why should we need a military man for governor, pray? Why have we generals in the field, then? Let them do their business and let you do yours. It is difficult now, but it is so everywhere. We must only persevere."

She smoothed back his fading hair and noticed how much it had receded since his investiture. The office might be an honor, but it was doing him no private good in any regard. It was painful to see him age so suddenly. "As for me," she murmured, with a kiss, "nothing could ever separate me from the regard I have for you. No matter what may endure, I shall always love you, even to my detriment. Anything I forgive. I can't promise to be sweet always," she smiled a little, "for I have my own faults, but you need never fear I will forsake you in my heart. No matter what." She kissed him again.

"Do you recall that song about the highwayman my father had?" She meant the song they had sung together years ago in the parlor at The Forest, "Come unto this Bosom."

He frowned a little. "Oh," he said at last. "Aye."

"Well, think of that when next you're afraid I may take after your mother," she said with playful asperity. "What a malignment, sirrah!" She dropped her teasing tone for a softer, more intimate one. "After all the love I have showered on you," she chided, the words no more than a breath upon his ear, "you should know better." She felt his change of pulse and raised her head to look at him. By the languid quality of his drowsy gaze she knew she had taken his mind off his troubles to some degree. "Well, sirrah?" she asked in soft challenge.

He smiled, the beautiful slow-dawning smile she loved. "You do have a remarkable way of cheering a man up, Madame."

"Only one man," she assured him, with a kiss. They idled a long while in this manner before she rose and let him write his letter to Page, satisfied that it would not be the gloomy epistle it would formerly have been. She was well rewarded for the trouble taken, for Page's next letter was addressed with the salutation, "My dear Jefferson," a familiarity which had been missing from his correspondence for some time.

A few days later, on the second of November, she had a letter from the Chevalier d'Anmours, who was staying at their house briefly on his way to Maryland. It arrived in a packet of letters from that direction, including a poorly spelt one from Lucy Lewis, and an elegant, encouraging one from Lucy Gilmer. d'Anmours' was gossipy and diverting, a coy admixture of French and English. His observations were painfully acute, particularly in certain instances, but he clothed his waspish humor in the most detached language that it was impossible to be scandalized or annoyed. He was biting toward the hapless Signore Alberti, whose little band struggled, in the maestro's opinion, to bring culture to a virtual wasteland. The maestro considered the advent of the Germans a distinct improvement in the neighborhood, but the chevalier did not.

He was less humorous on the subject of a hospitality he had received lately, or rather, not received.

I may truly say, dear lady (he wrote in his cramped hand) that I did not properly appreciate your and Gov'r Jefferson's gracious hospitality until I was made acquainted with the alternatives. Being much used to the Courtesies of your grand houses, I was quite unprepared for what I should encounter at the house of Mr. J. Ellwood. I was warned beforehand by your good husband, whose Wisdom I would have done well to heed. Having been invited to an audience with him at the usual dinner hour, I came fully anticipating to be included at table. But when I arrived, the house was in such a state of disarray that my hopes were seriously weakened. Dogs, children, servants, all flying hither-thither as if Propelled by Devils. Nay Madame, I do not exaggerate; as you know I am above such mean Attempts at diversion. My host was no Where to be seen, and by the harried lady of the house I was informed at my reception that he was not expected to return until past Dark. She rather peevishly invited me to stay to dinner, if I did not mind that it would be delayed. I politely replied to the affirmative, whereupon I was left alone in the Hall of the house to find my own comforts as I may. Two hours later, all were called to table. One may blame the lack of Fare on the fortunes of War, but not the ill-cookery and worse company. Hardly three words were spoken to me the entire Time I was there. Justified you may say, if I was an unknown traveller merely come in hopes of sparing myself the Cost of a Tavern, but I had been Expressly invited to attend the absent Master. I departed as soon as

I could decently do so, and whom should I encounter on the road down but my host, weaving on his Horse and entirely forgetful of my name or our interview. He insisted it must have been made for another day, but when I showed him my pocket book, he grew very cross and surly and told me plainly to go to ____, after which I departed without further intercourse. The latter Remark I may only ascribe to Drink, as it was utterly unwarranted, I assure you.

To Thomas he wrote:

This is the only instance of inhospitality I ever met from virginians, and another proof that national virtues, as well as Rules, though ever so General, have their exceptions. I leave monte-cielo to day to Continue my Journey by Staunton and winchester to Baltimore, where I will be obliged to you to send me by the Expresses you send to the northward any Packets that might be Directed to me by your means.

68

Our Sweet Lucy

Richmond

She might have stayed at home after all, for George Gilmer was home from Williamsburg by the beginning of November, but they had no time to consider changing their minds. Before dawn on the fifth she was awakened with a low backache and intermittent cramps, whose purpose, by now, she knew only too well. The child's coming was a fortnight early, but she should have learned to expect that by now. Not a single one of her children had gone to the date she calculated. She lay awake in bed and watched the sun seep slowly through the shutters, drowsing now and then, steeling herself for what was to come, wishing fervently that it was done. It would be a long time. Oh, to be like Maria Byrd and have one's childbirth's be no more than a jog of the elbow, quick and easy! Polly was the only woman she knew with such luck. Neither of her sisters had it, nor Thomas's; even Polly Bolling's had been long, and she a great stately woman who took after her father. She hoped this child was a boy. It would be good to have a boy. It would take the awful shadow away from Thomas's eyes.

She looked at him. The lines etched in his face did not disappear with sleep these days, and it troubled her. He should not look so harried. He was not yet thirty-eight. As bad as it would be for his public esteem, for his own sake she wished he would resign. Not that she thought him incapable of the office, far from it. He threw himself into it too well, never allowing time for rest or play. He was always at the desk writing. Far into the night he would work on requisitions, on letters, on despatches. He drank too much coffee and fiddled too little. It was only by luck he'd not been brought low with the summer complaint; he did suffer from headaches, although they were not long lasting. She could only do so much to help him. She could not remove the source of the trouble. The war went on and on despite their beleaguered state.

She would do what she could. Rising with awkward gingerliness for her aching joints, she padded over to the fire in her bare feet and poked at the embers, laying tinder before adding a fresh log. Her cramps were still intermittent and mild enough to be of little trouble. She poured water from the ewer and boiled it on the hearth, making up a pot of coffee, though they had tea, because Thomas liked it. When it was made she drew up a chair before the fire and sat staring into the hypnotic flickering warmth, drowsing again, until she heard a voice murmur soft in her ear, "Good morning, sleepyhead."

She opened her eyes and found Thomas before her in his dressing gown. She smiled at him lazily.

"It's today, isn't it?" he asked. His hand was warm on her leg.

"Your perspicacity is amazing, sir," she teased, and yawned. "Do you read cards? Palms? The little bumps on one's head?"

"Minx," he said. He rose and came behind her chair, lifting her disordered hair back from her face and shoulders and winding it into a knot about his hands. When she was thus trapped, he kissed the back of her neck. "Are you well?"

"As yet," she admitted. "It's not happening very fast."

"Do you wish me to stay home?" He came around her again and pulled up at chair. She shook her head. He would only fret.

"No. I can't foresee any alarum until after dinner at least. There's no point in milling about; I know you have work to do."

He leaned forward and took her hands. "Are you sure, love?"

She thought of how much she would need him later. "Yes. But you might send to Frances Cox to expect it today. She's been anticipating the seventeenth or so. I should hate to discover at the last moment that she's engaged."

"I'll do that," he said, rising from his chair. She could not help but to laugh. "You'd think you'd never had a baby before, Tom!"

He turned from the stack of writing paper at the desk. His eyes were very green in the morning light, even from this distance. "I haven't, love," he said softly, his eyes suddenly sharp. "That's the point." He wrote out a note for the midwife and sealed it.

She didn't feel much like eating breakfast, but did at his insistence, and saw him off to the council meeting next door. Downstairs Mrs. Wiley was setting out her morning's wares and hailed her as she passed. "Oh, good morning, ma'am!" She took a long sniff of the crisp air. "Isn't it a fine morning?"

Patty bowed her head, pulling her cloak about her more securely. "Good morning, Mrs. Wiley. Yes, it's a fine morning. One may hope it will be an even finer evening. I'm sorry, you must excuse me, but I must see to my staff—"

The bakeress put down the basket of loaves she had taken up, her face dawning understanding. "Ah! Well, the best of luck to you, ma'am."

"Thank you." She hurried on toward the kitchen, avoiding the wet patches of the brick walk. She would ruin her shoes walking in the damp, but better that than a less repairable mishap.

Thomas came home at dinner, and in spite of her insistence that she was quite well, was determined to remain. He read to her from Donne and Sydney until teatime when she couldn't listen anymore and sent the children away. They had played in the room all day, the weather being too damp outdoors. He sent Great George for Mrs. Cox and had broth ordered from the kitchen for her.

"I can't," she complained when Mary brought her the bowl. "Please, take it away." She felt restless and irritable, her stomach in a thousand knots. If she ate anything, it was as likely to come straight up again. Dinner still sat uneasily.

"Please, sweet," Thomas urged, "for me."

"I can't," she shook her head, sick at the thought. The broth was left on the stand.

At suppertime the actual birth began. Frances had the room made very hot, which eased her difficulty somewhat, and gave her a dose of some foul-tasting herb that made her drowsy. Lobelia. It smoothed away the sharp edges of the pain without the debility of laudanum. She found herself sitting upright at the edge of the bed, with Mrs. Cox kneeling on the floor. There was a tremendous pressure but it hurt less than being flat on her back. Between times she floated, leaning against Thomas as he sat behind her on the bed, his arms about her shoulders. Mrs. Cox had taken some convincing to let him stay, for she was not in favor of men at confinements, but Patty's tearful insistence and her own practicality won out. They were paying her and could stand on their heads chanting hymns did they feel it aided Patty. There was no real harm in his remaining.

After three hours, at half-past ten o'clock, the child was born. At the last, Frances was glad of a pair of strong arms, and said as much, for she had not the strength to effect enough pressure on the tapes. Patty required a large dose of rum before she would let them try a final time before summoning a surgeon with instruments. When it had taken effect, Frances, Thomas, and Mary Hemings all maneuvered together, pulling and pushing from different directions on tapes and belly and slippery head. Lucy Elizabeth came howling at this rude entrance, unharmed for all her sore trial, weighing ten and an half pounds on Thomas's scale. The incisions George Gilmer had previously made gave way and Mrs. Cox had a long time repairing them. When she went downstairs to sleep with the Wileys, dawn was creeping over the horizon. Patty was weak, but safe. Her nightmare had not transpired.

They had no cozy interlude in which to revel in the safe arrival of this little one. On Monday, the sixth, Thomas was back in council meetings and sessions of the Assembly, for the British had been at Newport News for a fortnight now. The British amongst the Convention troops were removed across the Blue Ridge to Maryland, to forestall any possible communication between them and Colonel Leslie's troops. There were great alarums of the numbers of the enemy, but in spite of many landings on both sides of the river to secure beeves, they made no attempt to travel farther upriver. This proved a blessing, as the militia raised to defend Portsmouth were raw recruits, nervous and complaining. None of them had ever looked on the face of the enemy. As it happened, they did not need to, for the fleet sailed in the middle of the month. Leslie's intercepted letter to Cornwallis was proved correct: he was waiting for orders and had no definite plan to invade Virginia at that time.

They received a letter from Jacob Rubsamen, one of the Germans who had remained behind. He had lately married Theodoric Bland's daughter, so was now a permanent neighbor of theirs. He was presently across the river at Manchester. His purpose of writing was to forward a newspaper clipping to them he had received from Germany and translated, for it concerned them. Though the writer was not named, they knew as well as Jacob that it was Jean d'Unger's work. It was dated from The Barracks at Charlottesville:

> My only Occupation at present is, to learn the English Language, it is the easier for me as I have free Acess to a copious and well chosen Library of Colo. Jefferson's Governor of Virginia. The father of this learned Man's was also a favourite of the Muses. There is now a Map of his Virginia extant, the best of its Kind. The Governor possesses a Noble Spirit of Building, he is now finishing an elegant building projected according to his own fancy. In his parlour he is creating on the Ceiling a Compass of his own invention by wich he can know the strenght as well as Direction of the Winds. I have promised to paint the Compass for it. He was much pleased with a fancy Painting of mine and particularly admired the Paper Money brought in on the piece, and in Joke often rebuked me for my thoughtlessness to shew him counterfeit money for wich I Knew many had been hanged already. As all Virginians are fond of Music, he is particularly so. You will find in his House an Elegant Harpsichord Piano forte and some Violins. The latter he performs well upon himself, the former his Lady touches very skillfully, and who, is in all Respects a very agreeable Sensible and Accomplished Lady.

"You're famous," she teased, and laughed when he colored up. "We're famous," he corrected.

"Our ceiling is famous!" she continued, to amuse him. He laughed now.

"And the library," he countered. "Our house shall be a wonder for travellers."

She smiled. "It already is."

As a grace note to this pleasantly flattering letter, they had one from Geismar in New York, who was soon to sail. That very fine and sensitive violinist most kindly left his music behind with the British quartermaster in Chesterfield for Thomas's use, as a mark of his gratitude and esteem.

Others closer to home were not so gracious. Thomas's uncle Turpin, from whom they rented the house, wrote peevishly enquiring when he would be paid the ten thousandweight of tobacco they had agreed on, as he needed it for another purchase. Though he sent his regards and warm congratulations on Lucy's birth, it did not make up for the ill breeding and utter selfishness of demanding money at such a time. Kin or no, she would not hold her tongue on this, when Thomas hopefully suggested finding the money somewhere.

"Indeed you will not!" she exclaimed. They sat in the parlor before supper. Patsy played draughts on the floor with Peter Carr, lately come to their household, and Lucy was asleep in her cot beside the fire. Polly was upstairs, for she was not feeling well.

"He has no right to ask for it at such a time! He should know the state of the government, to say nothing of our own pocketbook! Good grief, ten thousands, is he mad? I can't believe you would agree to that!"

He frowned and crossed his arms. "I did not. But if it is the only way to appease him, I may well." He paced before her.

"Thomas, you're too good to be true!"

"He is family," he reminded her. His eyes were dolefully amber in the light of the fire. It would work a great hardship on him to pay his uncle now, and he knew it as well as she. The price of tobacco was exceedingly low.

She bit back a sharp observation on the fate of Thomas Turpin's soul, her cheeks flaming, and confined herself to remarking, "He is not deserving of such esteem. My dear, he is using you only. He did us no favors by renting us this place, and does us none now. He has no regard for family! Only for his own comfort. Why should you be made to pay from your own want? The government has always paid for the governor's house before."

He made a bitter grimace. "The government couldn't pay for ferriage across the river at the moment. I don't see as there's any choice."

"Then let him wait. He's waited this long. He only wants it because he has a deal to make. Let him find his dirty money elsewhere. Why's he buying property now, when every penny is needed for the army, I should like to know. You're too soft-hearted."

He sighed, putting a hand to his brow. "Perhaps. Perhaps. Oh, sweet," he came to her chair, "you do right to upbraid me, for I know we can't afford it either. But I can't ask the Council for it in the present situation, not when I contracted with him privately."

She took his hand as it lay on her shoulder. "Let be then, Thomas. You have more important considerations. He can hardly turn us out, after all."

He was silent for so long that she looked up at him, and found that he was smiling ruefully. "d'Anmours was right about you," he commented. "You are a most hard-hearted woman." He touched her cheek. "Don't change, sweet. I like your defence. Your father trained a fine lawyer."

She blushed at his teasing. "O, hush," she murmured. Martin announced supper, and she was spared any further discussion of Turpin and his money.

She was up from bed by this time, but not really well. She tired easily and had to put off many of the things she had wanted to do once the baby was born. Lucy was no trouble at all. Like Jane and Peter she was placid. She ate and slept and grew very fat; she did not have colic, though by rights she should have, for the enthusiastic way she fed. When awake, she was content to look out on the world without forever wanting to be held; she smiled at two weeks' age.

No, it was not her baby over whom she fretted that winter, but Polly. She caught a cold from the Wiley children which at first did not seem serious, but by the twentieth she was abed with a fever and cough. Docilely she lay in the big bed she shared with Patsy, her dark hair hanging round her poor hectic cheeks, dull-eyed. It was bitter cold weather out, with freezing sleet and a strong wind from the north that rattled the windows. Patty brought the baby's cot with her and half a dozen books, and spent the next four days sitting with her small daughter before a blazing fire, reading to her and administering such infusions as the child would take.

She made a sticky syrup of wild cherry and elm bark, and that was well tolerated, but Poll would have none of the feverfew or yarrow teas, and truth to tell she couldn't blame her, for they reeked and were bitter. Nothing could disguise their taste. They made do with cold cloths and broth from the kitchen, read Gulliver and Psalms, and she watched Polly's cheeks grow brighter, and her eyes duller by the day.

She was disconsolate. To lose Poll would be too much to bear in her state. Polly was a worrisome child, being as sensitive and fragile as she was, but she was sweet also. Gentle and ladylike even at her age, she required protection from the hurts the world could offer. She was happiest when with them, her Mama or Papa, when performing some small, helpful task, when being indulged in the affectionate attention she craved. One could not rough about with Polly, teasing or chasing, as they had done with Pat, for that would make her cry; but a quiet, softly told tale would make her happy for days. Beautiful things moved her easily, whether a story, a garden bloom, a shimmering piece of cloth, or a phrase of music. She was highly musical and could already play more complicated pieces than Patsy had done at her age. Oh, yes, to lose their angel would go hard.

Patsy was not sick. Patsy could play out of doors for hours in the bitter cold, sliding down the hillside with her companions on a piece of scrap leather, losing her cap, her mittens, her muffler, and never take a chill. She was hardy, and so full of life that illness could not touch her. She would spike a fever betimes in the evening, but a hot drink and an early bedtime would cure it. In the morning, it had never been.

When Polly slept, she nursed the baby, or simply sat looking into the fire, resting from the difficulty of reading. She brooded over being fat, for she was still not back to her former size. Gowns could be managed if she laced her stays very tight, but then she could not get through the day, for she commonly wore them tight enough. Thus she was reduced to wearing undress clothes for the most part, sacques and jackets that did not require firm lacing. But she was not happy about it. Would her daintiness be gone forever? She had had nine babies. She could not expect not to grow more stout because of it. Lisbet was no longer willowy, and neither was Nannie; Maria Byrd had never been, and Fanny disguised her softness by clever device. That would appear the only course. Much as she loved them, she did not want to look like Ursula or Mary.

She bent and picked up Lucy from her cot. "It's all your fault, greedy," she told the baby affectionately. Lucy smiled at her and reached out a hand toward her face. Her eyes remained blue, a clear bright color, sparkled radiant silver about the pupils. At last they had a Jefferson instead of a Randolph or Eppes. Because of her size, Lucy appeared much older than she was, and it was easy to speak to her candidly, to play with her in a more grown-up manner than with the usual tiny infant. She weighed a stone, and she was not yet two months old.

"But I couldn't give you over to Bett," she assured her. "Not my Lucy-lu. No, because you're too sweet, too sweet," she said again while the baby grinned, and then laughed. She walked her fingers up her middle to her mouth. "No, I'll keep my Lucy all to myself; yes, fuzzyhead, silly little fuzzyhead—and when you're grown up a little we'll dress you up in ribbons and bows." She kissed Lucy in the creases of her fat little neck. "For we can't do it now. We'd have to stick them to your head with gum paste." The child's dark hair had begun to fall out, and there remained underneath the fine sparse strands of truly red hair. These made a shadow only on her forehead under the bonnet she wore and were but a promise of glories to come.

"Would you like to see Patsy?" She rose from the chair and took the baby to the window. When the cloud was rubbed off, they peered out at the sloping hill beside the house. The children were playing a racing game from tree to tree. "See there, Lucy? There's Patsy, and Peter, and Bob and Will and Sally, and way up there behind—do you see that house there behind us? Way up at that house behind, do you know who's there? Why your Papa is there! Papa. But he should be home ere long to see his Lu, for it's nearly dinner. Yes. Well, 'tis always dinner for our greedy miss, isn't it, yes." She laid her again in the crook of her arm and went back to the fire. "We should feed you beforehand, because, no offence to you, missy-miss, but I should like to see your Papa without attachments. Come here now, sweet. Are you willing to a feed?" She unpinned the front of her loose blue taffeta undress gown. Lucy didn't need any other encouragement. She took her early feed and went straight to sleep again.

Thomas came in as Patty was putting her back in the cot. She laid a finger across her lips and rose to give him a kiss.

"What a charming scene," he murmured. He looked over at the bed, and his face sobered. "How's Poll?"

She shook her head, following him to the bed. "No better, I fear. She hardly took anything all morning." She watched as he felt Polly's face and neck with the back of his hand.

"If she's not better on the morrow, I think we should call a doctor."

"On Christmas Day?"

He regarded her seriously across the bed. "What choice have we? As you said, she refuses any medicaments from you."

She swallowed that criticism whole. She could not force herself on poor Poll in that way. "The fever will follow its own course. It's not dangerous high."

"No, but she's been three days now abed with it." He sighed. Between them, the specter of Janey's death arose, and she saw in his pained expression the memory of how helpless he had felt then. "We cannot let it go on and on."

"If we put out a bucket overnight we'll have ice aplenty," she said. "Let us try that first. Please, dear?" She paused and caught her breath, steeling herself against another memory. "I am wary of doctors and surgeons were children are concerned. They've already killed a child of mine," her voice broke harshly. "I could not endure that again." She looked up at him, her eyes dry and bleak. "Please? We can manage on our own, I know we can. She isn't so badly off."

He looked at Polly, with her flushed cheeks and disordered hair. She looked so little in the big bed. His face softened. "Very well," he murmured. "Let's try the ice. I can no more subject her to their frights than you." He reached for her hand across the quilts and pressed it. She felt a wash of relief. She had bought Poll some time, if nothing else.

The next day Polly's fever rose alarmingly, in spite of the ice. She slept fitfully, tossing and restless, to wake clamoring for a drink. She complained that her eyes were hot, that she didn't want covers, but when they were removed to lay the ice about her she shuddered with cold. In the evening the crisis came and she was delirious. Thomas sat with her, quite literally restraining her by wrapping her in a blanket and holding her fast in his arms. By midnight she was quiet again, breaking out in a sweat, and she slept. When he came to bed he was pale with haggard dark circles under his eyes. His quietness alarmed her considerably.

"She's not—" She could not speak the words.

He shook his head and passed a hand over his face. "No, I'm sorry. I didn't mean you to think— She's fine, sweet. She's only sleeping." He flung himself on the bed beside her and Lucy.

"Oh, thank God!" She clutched the baby tighter, glad of lusty life with all its demands. She looked at Thomas, leaning as he was on the pillows, nearly asleep himself.

"You should come to bed," she entreated.

"I have work to do," he murmured, without opening his eyes.

"It can wait 'til morning." She leaned with the drowsy baby and kissed him. He shook his head. "No," he said, opening his eyes and determinedly rising. "It can't." He heaved a sigh. "I'll take it into the parlor so you can rest." In the dim candlelight he looked about to collapse. She cursed the gratifying public whose approbations had driven him to this. He had worn himself out on their behalf.

"No, please, stay," she told him. "You shan't disturb me. It's warm here." She picked up the candle from the stand. "Take this. You shan't disturb me, really. I can sleep through anything."

He smiled a little at that and accepted the candle from her.

When she awoke in the morning he had put the baby in her cot and was himself awake and shaving before the scrap of mirror he used. It was hardly six o'clock, but by the signs he had been awake for a while. There was a fire laid, water boiled, and a pot of tea made and waiting on the stand beside her. He was humming a spritely Scottish air half under his breath, thoroughly engrossed in the business of the day. One could not have told that he had been up until all hours after nursing a sick child and dealing with all the petty frustrations of running a bankrupt government at the brink of invasion. His endurance was astonishing, and that was fortunate, for in the next days it was sorely proved.

69

Flight from the Enemy

Richmond, Tuckahoe

They had not finished breakfast on the morning of New Year's Eve, when Mr. Wiley rushed upstairs with a letter from Thomas Nelson. Thomas accepted the letter and gave a gratuity to Wiley for the express rider.

"Thank you," he murmured. "Have him wait a moment." He rose from the chair and had Martin fetch him pen and paper.

"What's the matter?" she asked in alarm.

He exchanged a glance with Wiley and cleared his throat. "Just a piece of intelligence," he said smoothly. But she was not fooled. He had received some word of the British; she could tell it by his face. He was too pale for true ease.

Martin brought the writing goods, and he scratched a hasty note to Nelson and his lieutenants and gave them to Wiley. When their neighbor was gone he sat again and calmly picked up the discarded fork. She could not bear the suspense.

"Thomas!"

He looked up. The children were staring at them, alerted by the tone of her voice. But he was nonchalant.

"Yes, my dear?" he enquired calmly. Her own heart was racing and she admired his cool demeanor.

"What's happened?"

"We may have company," he said obliquely and picked up his cup. *It was not certain. Thank goodness!* She gave a quick sigh and her hand clenched on the tablecloth, but she emitted no other sign of distress.

When the children had gone, she set on him for news.

"What did you hear? What's happened?" She followed him into the parlor. "Has Leslie returned?"

"Not Leslie," he said, closing the door. He looked down at her grimly. "Arnold."

Arnold. The hero of the Canadian campaigns had become discontented after his treatment at Saratoga by General Gates and had accepted the post of military governor of Philadelphia after the British withdrawal from that city. He had there formed an attachment with one of the Shippen family—Margaret, a cousin of Maria Byrd's. The Shippens were Loyalists, and this connection, as well as his own ambition and despair of America's situation, had led Arnold to shift his allegiance. His comrade in command of this venture against Virginia was none other than General Sir William Phillips, who had been traded as a prisoner of war. That gentleman was presently on his way from New York.

"If the ships are indeed British, then it will be Arnold, by my lights. They may not be. But in any case we must be prepared, for if it is not the enemy, rest assured that they will not be long in reaching us." His eyes were very green now.

"Is that your word from Maryland?" she asked. He nodded slowly, his gaze abstracted. "That is my intelligence," he agreed, and put his arms about her. "I shall do my endeavor to keep you all safe, but I cannot promise to be with you. Are you well enough to travel in this weather?"

She would rather have to be. She shrugged, striving to be cool in this crisis. "Whether I am or no, we shall manage." She touched his face. "But I am concerned for you," she said. "If you should be taken, I—" The mere thought was distressing.

He turned his head quickly and kissed her hand.

"I shall not," he insisted. "I shall not." He smiled, "I am a much better rider than they, and I know the country. I have a distinct advantage."

She was not amused by his levity. It was not a matter for sport. In apology, he bent a hovering kiss upon her mouth. "I'll be all right, sweetheart." He kissed her again. "Have I not my Diana's blessings?"

She smiled at the name. Not the fragile Hero he had called her, but Diana, fearless and strong. "Tom. . ."

"That's my dear girl." He straightened and clasped her to him for a moment, and it was only in that embrace that she knew his own uncertainty.

He went for a walk alone in the woods at the top of the hill after that, and when he returned he said to her, "I had a visit from one of Nelson's staff whilst on my walk."

"Did you?" She looked up from her mending.

"Aye." He clasped his hands behind his back, rocking on his toes a bit. "He wanted to know if I'd heard the British are coming."

She shook her head at the glint in his eye. "Thomas. . . What did you tell him?" He was smiling now. "That I had heard that intelligence. He was not amused."

"You are a wicked man," she said.

His face sobered. "I would hope not too greatly so, for I sent him to Steuben as an express rider. . . . He was hot for it. I tell you, sweet, it is well to find such hardy souls in this desperate hour. I had quite begun to think our candle nearly extinguished." She looked up again at this. There were tears in his eyes.

They had no further word that day, and in the quietude of evening they opened a bottle of wine to mark the occasion, their wedding anniversary, but neither felt much like celebrating. It was more a gesture of thanksgiving that they were yet at peace and together. How long that peace would last was known only to Providence.

At five o'clock on the third, a letter came from Nelson's adjunctant, stating that the British were at Jamestown, and a similar message came later in the evening.

Before daylight on the morning of the fourth, they were awakened by a thumping on the door and Martin calling loudly, "Sir, sir!"

The clatter woke poor Lucy, but lately asleep again, and she howled her own warnings as Thomas shoved his arms into his dressing gown.

"Just a moment," he muttered, and stumbled to the door in the dark. She endeavored to soothe the baby, squinting in the poor light to see who it was disturbing their peace.

"Frank—"

It was Francis, with his hat dripping and his clothes in disarray.

"Thomas—" He turned around. "Damme, where is your servant with the lamp? Come in here, man," he snapped at Martin, who hovered by the door. Martin brought the lamp in and retreated before her cousin's unaccustomed shortness. She wondered where Lisbet was, and the children. Francis did not wait for the door to be closed.

"Thomas, I've just come from Harrison's." He walked as he spoke, stripping off his muddy greatcoat. "Arnold's coming up from Kennon's." He tossed his coat on the chair before the fireplace and noticed her and the snuffling baby. "I'm sorry to rouse you so early, cousin," he murmured. Thomas poured him a glass of wine.

"Thanks. We were at Harrison's when we had word that they had passed Williamsburg early in the evening. The tide's up and the wind in their favor. I had thought to move my family up country in case they should land and thank God, for our men are all over our place. They intend it as headquarters, at least for the next day or so. I thought you should know."

Then Lisbet would be downstairs in the parlor, or in the carriage. She would be wet through in this rain. She rose and put the baby down in her basket.

"Good man," Thomas was saying, as he poured out another glassful of Madeira. "Thank you—" She flung on her dressing gown behind the open door of the press. "Do you know if they've passed Westover?" Where are my slippers? Why are they never where I left them? She found them under the press and put them on. Francis was shaking his head.

"I do not. I thought it best not to travel the main road here, to keep it open for militia coming in."

Thomas clasped his arm. "By God, you're worth a dozen generals, Frank! I wish every man had your spirit."

"They may also have this," her cousin said, moving into the light. His coatsleeve was torn at the shoulder and bloodied. She blanched. Had he been pursued? "It's not what you think," he said quickly, seeing their distress. "I got it caught up in a tree branch. But it's pretty damned smarting anyhow. I'd be obliged if you had something stronger than wine about the place." His face was covered with bleeding scratches. Thomas nodded. "Surely."

She brought the lamp over and set it on the table.

"Sit down, Francis," she directed. "I'll get some bandages." She flung open the door, calling for Martin.

An hour later, after hurried packing, the children and she were assembled in their room and ready to depart. Francis and Lisbet, their children and servants, had a few moments before they left for Elk Hill. She had cleaned and bandaged Francis's arm. The wound was not as serious as they had first thought, but he would not have the use of it for several days. She sent Betsy off with what supplies could be hastily gathered from the kitchen and her own clothing stores, for they knew not what was to be had presently at Elk Hill. In the interim, Thomas had induced William Wiley to send to the council for an emergency session at seven o'clock and wrote out an order for the immediate call for full militias to assemble. She watched them furtively as she flung clothes into her valise anyhow.

"Take this straight to Jamieson," he instructed, still writing out the missive. "And tell him to warn the Committee of Safety to be on their alert. I don't have time to rouse them now." He handed Mr. Wiley the papers. "Go," he said in a strong voice. "Go quickly!"

At the carriage, she gave the much-bundled baby to Nance before being handed in herself. Thomas had carried Poll hither, on the excuse of not wanting to waste time waiting for pattens to be tied on, and the child wrapped herself around him by arm and leg. Poor Polly, she was so timid; and, young as she was, she understood something of the danger they were in. How could she not? The early rising, the hastened dressing, cold stale bread instead of breakfast, and now to be deposited in the carriage at an hour at which she would normally not even be awake. Patsy and Peter were silent, round-eyed. Doubtless they were frightened, but they were well-trained enough not to clamor.

A thousand thoughts raced through her mind: what if the roads were blocked, or they got mired in the mud? Had she packed enough clothing? In the valise tossed up to Jupiter, she had laid away a single change of clothes, the rest being taken up in goods for the children, but that was no guarantee. She did not know how long they would be away or what to expect at all. Oh, would she ever see this house, all their things, the servants; oh, would she ever see Thomas again?

Through the opened window, he took her hand and kissed it. "I'll get to you when I can," he murmured. The words were orderly, but the light in his greening eyes spoke volumes. She touched his face with her gloved hand, wishing that propriety did not forbid a kiss good-bye, at least the sort of kiss she longed to give him. I may never see my dear again—

"Take care, my dear!" she bade him, and put all her love and worry into those words. He nodded, with a little smile. "I shall." She sat back then and he gave the word to Jupiter and John to be off.

They had got so far as the river road when she thumped on the ceiling. Inside, they were careening about from one end to the other, jouncing on the snowy, rain-guttered road. Lucy and Polly were screaming, with the latter clutching her sister in a death's grip. Patsy and Peter, for their part, were stricken but silent. Nance swerved about, trying to save the baby a bang on the head. Patty pulled the curtain aside. "Slow down!" she shouted at Jamey.

"Ma'am?" he shouted back.

"Slow down!" she repeated. "Tell them to slow down! You'll have us all in the river!" They bounded over a hole in the road, and she smacked her temple against the window frame. She withdrew and closed the curtain again, rubbing the sore place above her left eyebrow. She would have a delightful bruise.

They began to slow at last, and she said to Nance, "Here, give me Lucy." She took the fretful baby from her, unwrapping her enough to see her little face.

"Hush a ba, hush thee, Lucy," she soothed the shuddering baby. "It's all right; here's your Mama, Lucy-lu." She cuddled her against her shoulder. "There's Mama's baby. Hush, sh."

It was nearly twenty miles to Tuckahoe, and the roads were so bad that it took them until the middle of the morning to reach the sprawling, gracious house on Tuckahoe Creek, overlooking the James. The alarm had not yet spread this far, and thus their arrival caused considerable disturbance. Colonel Tom set out immediately on his horse to rouse the neighborhood, and they were shown upstairs by his wife Nancy.

Anne Cary Randolph was as calm and quiet as her husband was volatile. She saw to the drawing of baths and the making up of beds with quick, kindly efficiency.

"My dear," she exclaimed, when Patty took off her bonnet, "whatever happened to you?"

"What?" She had forgotten the jolt against the window in her relief to be before a fire. They had been subject to a sleeting rain shortly after taking to the road, which turned last night's snow into a muddy slush, and her skirts were sodden, for they'd had to get out twice to rescue the carriage wheels. She pushed back her dripping hair and encountered the bruise. "Oh, this." She made a face. "We made a rather precipitous departure, I'm afraid."

"You should let me see to it," her cousin said. "It's purple. I'll bring up some salves when you're out from the bath."

She nodded and handed her cloak to Nance Hemings for drying. "But I'd like to see to the children first," she said. Nancy waved her hand. "They're in good hands, Martha. Jenna's seeing to them, and she was my nurse. Don't worry. I've laid out fresh clothes, and they're all drying out before the nursery fire with a large dose of black treacle and tea. You just see to yourself and let us fret over them. I'll bring you some sherry in a moment. I believe Colonel Randolph has some upstairs here. . ."

"Thank you," she murmured gratefully.

"Oh," Nancy said, as she was hurrying out the door. "I've laid out my brown alpaca for you in the dressing room, so you shan't have to wait for the others to dry out." All their things had gone damp through the valise while waiting in the rain.

"You're an angel, Nancy!" she told her sincerely, but Nancy only smiled and closed the door noiselessly behind her.

It was good to sit in the hot bath drinking sherry, letting the warmth seep into her chilled bones. The screen had been put up behind the tub to retain the heat of the fire about her. She closed her eyes, but all she could think of was the children taking sick, and Thomas down at Richmond in a dangerous situation. Even the bath and wine could not unloose the coiled knot of that anxiety. She did not like to think of what would befall him if he was captured. *Dear God,* she prayed silently, *let him be all right!*

He arrived at one o'clock in the morning.

"Patty." He leaned over her in the bed and kissed her. She had not been asleep, only drowsing enough not to have heard his entrance, and she flung her arms about his neck with a gasp.

"Oh, Tom, thank God! My darling—." She kissed him soundly again and again, overcome with gladness that he was alive. "I thought I should never see you again!" He yielded to her dragging arms and collapsed with her on the bed.

"Well, here I am," he murmured, smiling in the dark, and leaned up on an elbow, "if briefly." He kissed her and buried his face in her hair.

"I want to take you all up to Fine Creek in the morning," he told her. "Arnold's bent on Richmond, and I would prefer to have the river between you. Patty—" He wrested himself from her embrace. "I'm sodden. I have to take these things off—the boots at least. They'll put Nancy's bedding to wreck."

She could bear to lose him again for only that short space of time. She gave a sigh of acquiescence, and he divested himself of his muddy clothes. In a moment he was beside her again, his lean warmth all gooseflesh from the wetting he had taken. He gathered her in a fierce embrace.

"Come here, dear," he murmured, and it was no sooner than she laid her cheek to rest in its usual place against his collarbone than he was asleep.

By seven o'clock they and the rest of Tuckahoe's inhabitants were on the road and gone in their various directions. Nancy took her family up to Dungeness, a few miles below Elk Hill, where Colonel Tom's brother Will was in residence. They themselves crossed the river, and she and the girls went up to Fine Creek, his father's old place now owned by his brother Randolph.

"I'll be there tonight if I possibly may," he promised on their parting. "And if not, I'll send a rider out. You shan't be without news." In spite of his sound sleep his face was yet haggard. She would bide well at Fine Creek, or anywhere here upriver, but was he at this moment equal to the task before him? What if he should be endangered by his worn state? Oh, it would be worse to hear all alone out here that he had been taken! She wished he had agreed to let them go to Elk Hill. At least there she had Lisbet for some comfort against bad news. But he desired the river between them and Arnold's army. . . . She inclined her head and said nothing. He bent and kissed her hand.

"Don't fret, sweet," he murmured in a low voice. "I shall be safe." Safe! How could he ever be safe; he was the governor! He was the first person they would look for! She looked up at him and was unable to conceal her concern.

70

Colin and Phoebe

Fine Creek

She spent the day settling the children in, and clearing out what furniture and provisions were to be had about the place. The chimneys were in dreadful condition, having been long unused and even longer uncleaned. They would not draw properly and filled the two lower rooms with smoke, which necessitated opening the windows and doors to the frigid air. This, after the stresses of the morning and day before brought her to grief. She retired upstairs for half an hour, leaving matters downstairs to Nance and Jupiter.

After a distance of ten or twelves miles in the rain and wind, they had reached the small frame house about the middle of the morning to find not a single soul in evidence, the house securely locked, and it had begun to sleet. She had sent Jupiter and John out in search of the steward and herded the girls back into the carriage. It was dry there at least, and they had the small comforts of Nancy Randolph's provisions. She had wrapped the girls in blankets and doled out to them a portion of the bread and cheese brought down from above. It was slightly damp, but better than nothing. They had not had a proper breakfast, and heaven knew what provender awaited them inside the house.

This house, which had belonged to his grandfather, was situated on a property which had been a 1,500-acre grant from old Governor Spotswood in 1718. It was a modest dwelling, not differing greatly in size from Shadwell, with the usual configuration of two rooms up and two down, with a central hall. There was a further loft under the steeply peaked roof, which could be reached by a ladder from the upper stair landing. The overseer, Mr. Bennet, appeared at last and was nonplussed at seeing them.

"There's not much as amenities for yourself and the young ones, ma'am," he admitted, scratching his head. "The colonel don't use this place but for summer stops and all."

"I know," she said shortly. "But it will have to suit. You have heard the British are come up the country?"

Bennet waved his hand. "Why shoot, ma'am! There was a rider come past yestere'en with that news. What would they want this place for, so small and off the river as it is? I daresay, ma'am," he said to reassure her, "that you'll have no cause for alarm here. And I'll do my best t' make you welcome."

She bowed her head. "Thank you, Mr. Bennet. I appreciate the sentiment." She raised her head again and glanced at him sharply, for he had not taken the hint before. "Mr. Bennet," she said, in her best calm, directive tones, those that she used with slow Negroes, "I should be much obliged to you for the keys, if you please. My children and I have been on the road since very early this morning, and I have a small infant who needs the warmth of a fire and comforts of a roof about her."

He colored and said belatedly, digging in his coat pocket, "Why, of course! Of course! Come along ma'am, Mrs. Jefferson." He held out his hand to help her down from the carriage, "and I'll have you and the young ones before a fire sooner than— as soon as can be," he amended.

She took Lucy from Nance's outstretched arms, nodding. "Thank you, sir."

Now she sat before the feeble fire in the dark-panelled parlor with Lucy, listening to the wind whip about the trees outside. She had no idea of the time, possessing no watch, but she had put the tired girls to bed in the chamber upstairs shortly ago. Their clothes hung about the room, drying out from the wetting they had again received. The baby drifted off to sleep, and she leaned her head back against the settle, weary, lulled by the rain and wind and Lucy's sighing breath. The clatter of hoofbeats roused her from her drowsy reverie.

But instead of the welcome and familiar step, there came a hammering on the door that set her heart thudding likewise. She put the baby down on the narrow settle, securing her with a pillow, and hurriedly hooked her gown together down the front with a shaking hand. It might be Mr. Bennet, but he was scarce likely to pound the door, rude of manners as he was. It might be a neighbor, come to spread some alarm. She was dread that it should be the news she had feared the last two days.

She opened the door to a wet and muddy express rider, and had she not been clenching the handle of the door she would have fallen, for her knees went to jelly.

"Mrs. Jefferson," the man said. By his accent, he came from across the Blue Ridge. She could not see his face in the dark.

"Aye," she managed. Her voice came forth weakly.

"I have this from the governor." He held out a slightly crumpled folded slip of paper, unsealed. She took it from his icy, ungloved hand, her heart in her throat.

"I— thank you." She took the missive to the fire. "Please come in," she said to the courier distractedly and unfolded the note.

7 P.M. Friday

I shall be detained at this place the night. our friends are at Westham, having burned the Magazine much good it will do them. i am unharmed and safe, and will be with you tomorrow if I possibly may.

She breathed a sigh of relief at the contents. He was well, and safe! At least as of this evening. She turned to the young man as he was stooped before the fire. His black hair was plastered to his skull. He was lank and light-eyed, laconic as most of his sort. "From where did you come?"

"Fleming's," he said, without turning. He probably had little society with women in general, and fewer with ladies. He would not look at her but chafed his blue hands continually, making a puddle on the bare floor. Her heart went out to him, for he had come a long way only that her mind would be at ease.

"What happened to your gloves, sir?" she asked him.

"Lost 'em." He slung back a lock of fallen wet hair and spat in the fire.

"Well, I'm certain the overseer will loan you a pair. You cannot be without any in this weather. . ." She faltered, wanting to help him more but having no means. "I haven't a penny to give you," she admitted, "or spirit either, but perhaps Mr. Bennet shall. Just a moment—" She could secure him a meal at least. She went out to the stairs and called up to Nance, who was with the children.

"Yas'm?" the girl said when she came down.

"Fetch something for this man to eat quick, won't you please? Mr. Jefferson shan't be in tonight, so when you've done that you may go to bed."

"I will, ma'am." Nance glanced toward the parlor, her green eyes uneasy. "Mis' Jefferson?"

"Yes?"

"Master's all right, ain't he?"

She smiled. "Yes, Nance, he is." She patted her arm. "You go on now."

"Yas'm."

She went back into the parlor to find the courier staring at Lucy as she slept on the bench. He looked up at her entrance. "She's a pretty baby, ma'am," he said nodding.

"Yes."

"I have a babe pert' near her age at home by this time, I reckon," he ventured reflectively. She did not miss the meaning of this admission, and the knowledge made her eyes smart with tears. He had left a wife and young family behind, uncertain of their fate, to fight for his home and country.

"You have not seen it?" she murmured.

"No, ma'am." He met her gaze, but she found no self-pity there, only a thoughtful reluctance. Plainly, his wife had kin about and could look after herself.

"Well," she said into the long silence. "My servant is getting you up a meal. Please feel free to remain as long as you like. I shall send to Mr. Bennet for some spirit, and gloves if he has any." To her surprise the man rose to his feet and made her a not inelegant bow. "Thank you, ma'am. You're a kind lady."

To this she could not reply, but nodded and scooped up Lucy with a blush. She retired upstairs until he was away, coming down only later to bank the fire. In spite of Thomas's note and her own weariness, it proved a long night.

They heard nothing the next day or night. The sixth was a bad day, with Patsy and Peter quarrelling over nothing because they were not allowed outdoors, and Polly being struck with a fever which would flare and subside without warning or reason. She had no medicinals here, beyond some patent nostrum offered by Mr. Bennet, which seemed to her taste to be mostly laudanum, and thus she was reduced to packing the child in poultices of snow, which set her howling. In addition to this, Lucy was greatly unsettled until past midnight. She would not lie in the strange bed, nor in the equally strange chest drawer which had been outfitted as a makeshift cot. But no sooner was she at last asleep and moved to her little bed, than Polly awoke screaming in the next room, frightening Peter and Patsy into nervous calls as well.

She tore out of bed, stumbling, her limbs all leaden, and collided with the dresser in the unfamiliar room.

"Damn," she muttered, and hastily massaged her throbbing foot. "Mama's coming, Poll," she called to the yet hysterical child and hobbled into the adjoining room.

Peter, Patsy, and Nance were all on the bed, huddled round poor Polly, who was struggling desperately to get away, crying, "Mama, Mama, Mama, Papa—"

She gathered her in her arms, feeling Polly's thin little body quivering with fear and cold even through the thick nightdress, and smoothed her hair. "Hush, love, sh sh, Polly. You're safe," she murmured. "Mama's here, Mama's here. You're safe."

"No, no, no!" Polly wrestled against her. "I want my Papa! I want Papa, where's Papa—" It was two hours before she could calm the child enough to lie down in the bed again.

She took the candle with her into the hall, for her foot still ached, and she had no wish to disturb it further. The distance between the two rooms was not eight feet; howsoever the flickering light threw shadows about her, and her anxious imagination created menaces as frightening as Poll's redcoats before her. She was nearly to the door of her room when a figure stepped out of the darkness. Dear God! She gave a weak cry of fright.

"It's all right," he murmured, stepping into the circle of light. "It's only me." Sodden, his greatcoat black with rain, it was Thomas, his face pale in the poor light. Substantial or shade, she did not know. She had seen ghosts before. . . His visage faded grey before her.

"Oh, Thomas—"

He took the candlestick from her fingers and laid it on the floor, catching her up with an arm about her waist. He was real, and his solid warmth brought her back to herself. "It's all right," he said again. "What are you doing abroad at this hour? It must be two o'clock."

Why was she abroad? Her brain was still a bit foggy. Ah! "Polly had a nightmare. I was just putting her back to bed," she murmured, looking up at him. He was exhausted, more haggard than she had ever seen him. He would catch his death in those wet clothes.

"She's well?" he ascertained.

She nodded. "Now she is. But it was two hours before I could convince her to lie down again in the bed. She thinks the British will come and take her, as they have done her Papa." So far as Polly was concerned, he was gone from the morning they had left Tuckahoe. "I tried to convince her that you were well, but she is little yet, and words don't mean very much. . . ." She wanted to know that he was really here, truly safe. "With that I'm inclined to agree. . ." Her hands were on his face, under his wet hair. "Oh my beloved, you're really here, and not my imagining— I received your note last night, but anything may happen in a day. And when you did not come, I thought—"

She broke off, raising herself on her toes to kiss him with such force and passion that he was taken aback a moment. Diana would claim her quarry, and he did not protest much.

"You're sodden now," he said when they parted.

The words had echoes to that other time, and she made no reply, but picked up the candle and they went into the chamber where there was the vestige of a fire.

"You'll take a chill," she murmured. "I'll not have you die of exposure." She smiled a little now, remembering his Holland shirts, and took the greatcoat from him. "I have an extra shift, and would offer you it, but I'm afraid you'd look silly." She could not resist speaking the next words, "You'll have to make do with the blankets."

"Patty," he chided.

She raised an eyebrow. "I am quite in earnest, my dear. You would do well to get yourself out of those things before I am forced to do it myself." *There's for you, my dear, not letting me undress myself!* They had no sweet malmsey, so Mr. Bennet's rum would have to suffice. She went to the dresser and poured some into a cup. "Here you are," she said, pressing it into his hand. "I'm afraid it's all there is, left over from your courier."

"I hate rum," he complained.

"I don't intend to be a widow twice," she murmured, not unkindly. "It grows early, sweeting." She took his other hand, and abandoned teasing. "I know you must be away at first light. Please, Tom. As little as you like it, 'twill do you good. Please. Have it down and come to bed. You look as though you haven't slept in days."

His eyes kindled. "As you wish," he murmured, and tossed back the raw, burning spirit. "Tho' I would reserve the right to undress myself, if you please."

She smiled and shook her head. Oh, no. This was a debt of honor. "Sit down," she murmured, "and I'll help you with those boots." He gave himself over to her care, and not long after was asleep in the warmth of her embrace.

> *Well, well, dearest Phoebe and why in such haste?*
> *Through fields and through meadows all day I have chased*
> *In search of the fair one who doth me disdain*
> *And who will reward me*
> *And who will reward me for all my past pain?*

71

Betrayal

Richmond

He was gone again by six, riding over the sodden ground to Britton's and Wetsham, to see what arms and powder had been salvaged there and oversee their removal across the river. It was still raining, though not as heavily as the night before.

From George Muter at Richmond was word that the town was in a state of the utmost confusion. There were looters whose depredations were worse, if that was possible, than those of the enemy. From John Nicholas at The Forest came word that Nelson had been repulsed at the courthouse in Charles City, and that he himself could not make a stand where he was without more horses. He was induced therefore to retreat to Malvern Hill, three miles upriver, and hoped to remain there if he could be reinforced. The next day was word the British were removed to Westover, and shortly thereafter they retreated down the country. Thomas sent word by an express rider to both her and Francis at Elk Hill, and she and the children made their way down to Richmond once more.

Muter's mild remark did not cover the half of the difficulties encountered from looting in Richmond. Shops of every kind had been broken into while the owners were absent, and goods carried away or destroyed if they could not be carried. Patrols were set up to halt this menace, and several looters were lodged in the gaol by evening. Nelson was at Holt's forge again, apologizing for not having been able to slow the enemy's approach due to the strong west wind.

At their own house in Broad street, very little was damaged, thanks to the quick thinking of Great George, who hid away all the plate in a bed tick and made other such attempts to preserve family property. For this loyalty he was, along with his family, Sukey, and the Hemingses, carried off by the British for the better part of six months.

They had the story of George's valor therefore only much later, but the Negroes told that, upon word that the British had seized the town, the Georges set about securing what they could. There was panic everywhere, women and children screaming, men running in every direction. They said that inside ten minutes of the alarm there wasn't a white man to be seen in the streets.

When Simcoe arrived with a party of men, he demanded of George the whereabouts of the governor. George told him he'd gone up to the mountains. The colonel then requested the keys to the house, and George gave them, with everyone in the place knowing that they would find nothing. The British were not half clever enough to think of looking in a box bed in the kitchen for goods. It was a great delight to them that "ignorant darkies" could so outwit an invading army.

Simcoe's cavalry made free with the house and stores for a few hours, but nothing in the house was damaged beyond a looking glass. Chests and drawers were searched, but the contents not otherwise disturbed. Only in the wine cellar and dependencies did they find any destruction. They lost about half the wine, most of the Antigua rum, and all of the corn and meat.

The servants were all rounded up and taken off, first to Westham where the magazine stores were destroyed, and then along as the British made their way up the country. The servants left at Tuckahoe and Hylton's were all taken, and the lot marched down to York. When the story came out, George and Ursula were given their freedom, though they chose to remain at Monticello. George had forty pounds as a token, and Queenie from then on was tithed seven dollars a month for her pastry and work in the laundry. Their loyalty and courage were not soon forgotten and were oft remarked upon at the house and in the quarters when anyone mentioned the dark days of Richmond's invasion.

When they had returned to town, Thomas was sent a note from Arnold to Major Dick by John Nicholas, wherein the general rather oilily suggested the the major come down to Westover under a flag of truce to receive such horses, goods, and Negroes as were required by the locals, if his terms were agreeable. This Thomas agreed to, loath as he was to encourage an intercourse with the enemy if Arnold was without discrimination of persons in returning property or slaves. This he did not think likely, however.

The next day Arnold's forces retreated, passing Burwell's Ferry. The militia was able to harry Arnold's forces enough to keep him at Portsmouth for the next two months. Then, late in March, Phillips arrived with 2,000 reinforcements. The Marquis de Lafayette had already come down from his fleet at Annapolis to consult with Steuben and the Virginia government about an expedition against Arnold and Cornwallis. Authorities from General Washington to Weedon, who headed the militia, saw Steuben's plan to reinforce General Green in Carolina as a master stroke that would likely terminate the war, but the times and the council were against them. Mild laws, a people not used to war and prompt obedience, a want of every sort of provision and means of procuring them rendered futile the entire business. The council could not agree to so large a removal of arms and men from the state, for it would leave the remaining militia powerless. Lafayette went back to Annapolis.

Were this state of affairs not vexing enough, Thomas also had to contend with the accusations made by Steuben and others to Maria Byrd that that lady had willfully given quarter to the enemy while they were encamped at her house, that she had indeed invited them there. Under laws passed in 1776, such an act constituted treason against the state, and Mrs. Byrd was most distressed that she should be seen in this light.

The accusations, she maintained, were entirely false and circumstantial. It was true that General Arnold was married to her cousin Margaret, but she had in no wise been apprised of his advance. She had received his officers according to her idea of propriety and felt herself entirely undeserving of the treatment she had received. Her property and slaves, like those of many others, had been confiscated. She was not aiding the enemy. She prevailed upon him not only as the governor, but as a friend, for aid in this matter. What she neglected to remark upon was the great volume of letters which had previously passed between her and the enemy, and the brandy, porter, linen, china, and broadcloth that had gone from Westover to Arnold's lieutenant's vessel at Sandy Point.

For her part, Patty would believe any such treachery of Polly Byrd after her unkind remarks about Fanny Page, but Thomas was merciful toward her and turned the authority for dealing with this over to Steuben, considering it a military matter. The general left it to the council's discretion. After the discovery of Maria's letters, it was decided that an investigation should be made, and several were scheduled, but none were ever held. March and April were taken up with more pressing concerns.

72

Reverberations

Richmond

She had not been well since the hurried flight up the country in January. She and all of the children had caught a chill in the constant wetting they had received travelling from one place to another. Peter and the girls—even Lucy—recovered from it fairly quickly and by March were as well as they had ever been, but she herself was still subject then to her old complaints of lassitude, nausea, and sickness. Nothing would stay down. She dropped a stone's weight, and as April advanced began to have trouble with her eyes. The entire catalogue began to unfold once more, and none of the doctors in Richmond could even procure the herbs recommended by George Gilmer since the invasion of the town; all the medical supplies had gone to the army.

April dragged on, raining and drear. They were likely to have floods if the downpour continued at this rate very much longer. The only advantage to it was that it kept the British away at Portsmouth. She wandered the house in intermittent restlessness, irritable at the depressing weather and her own lack of energy. She was tired but could not lie about anymore, looking at the too familiar objects in her room or the parlor. She wanted to be up properly, to be useful, not to be a further pall upon the inhabitants of the house.

It seemed as though the days would never end. Grey and dank, without even the enlivening diversion of a thunderstorm, they began and closed with the same unvaried scenes. The children became fractious. Patsy wanted to go out-of-doors and was petulant because she was only allowed so far as downstairs; Polly was frightened of the shadows that lowered about the hall and the budding tree branches scraping against the house in the wind; Lucy was teething and pleased with nothing. Thomas was gone from earliest morning until after supper, and when he did come in, was up half the night with paperwork, trying valiantly to secure troops and provisions to the army. He was not unsympathetic to her state, but she did not want to be a greater burthen by complaining more than she already was in being ill, so she kept her unhappiness to herself.

On the afternoon of the fourteenth, Lucy's crabbiness gave way to fever and lassitude. Her skin was dry and burning; she was dull-eyed and cried in a weak and moaning way, tossing about her cot, rejecting every effort of comfort that was shown her. On into evening, Patty tried to ease her by what simple means she could, struggling through her own sickness, and becoming more frantic and frustrated as the hours passed. At nine o'clock she could bear the situation no more. Overwrought and weeping herself, she called Nance in and pushed the baby into her arms.

"Please," she implored, sniffling, on the edge of nerves, "please take her a while! I can't— I've been walking with her all day! Please take her into the parlor for a little, Nance. I must rest!"

Nance took the baby away and she collapsed on the bed, her face buried in the pillows, sobbing in reaction to the long and terrible day. She wanted to be well, to be able and calm, without this constant sickness and weakness. She could do nothing for herself, so how could she be expected to look after poor Lucy? Lucy, dear God, how long must the poor child suffer of teeth! It had been a week already, but she yet felt no sharpness beneath the swelling lump of baby gum. Such fevers would subside when the tooth had come through, but her fever was so high! She would not suffer to be bathed in cold water as Thomas had suggested. Indeed, it made her scream worse. She could not abide that sound for long.

If only she were well! Then she could nurse Lucy as she needed to be and not have to content herself with half-measures. But all day she had been low, with a dull ache at the small of her back and an uneasy stomach. Breakfast had come straight back up, and she did not attempt supper at all. Her head ached, and her eyes were tender, and more than anything she wished that she could curl up and go to sleep; that she would find upon awakening that the nightmare of the last three months had been just that.

She was drifting on the edge of sleep when Thomas came in an hour later and laid the sleeping baby in her cot. She heard his step, but was too weary to rouse herself until he sat down next to her on the bed. She stirred herself then, reluctantly, for she felt as if she had been drugged.

"Hello," she said dully, and wet her dry lips. Her mouth tasted bitter, as though she had been taking laudanum, and her hand was heavy when she raised it to push her hair out of her face.

"I heard what happened," he said as she sat up. "You should have sent for me. I was only next door."

She shook her head, squinting at the light from the candle. "There's nothing you could have done. I didn't wish to disturb you." He took her shoulders in his hands.

"I might have aided you," he said strongly. She looked up at him stupidly and through her fog perceived that he was angry. "You're in no condition to carry on this way. We are not so desperate that I cannot spare you a little of my time! Good God, sweetheart, you should know that by now." He put his arms about her. "The world can never find a fitter love for me'—isn't that what your Rev. Donne says? When will you believe it?" He put her by again. His eyes were very green, and it was only now that she saw he was damp from the rain. "You must not be afraid to lean on me, Patty. It will not break me," he smiled at her coaxingly, "nor even bend me much, little one. I'm glad when you do." He touched her cheek. "Dictatorial as that may be."

"Thomas," she smiled reluctantly. "Don't tease me. I'm too stupid at the moment to be equal to it." She drew a shuddering breath. "How did you get Lucy to sleep?"

He shook his head. "I didn't. Nance had her thus when I came in."

The memory of the terrible day came flooding back. "Oh, Tom, she was so bad off—" she began, a note of distress rising in her voice. He smoothed her hair.

"I know, sweet," he murmured. "But you needn't worry any longer. I'll sit with her." He kissed her. "And you, too. Are you hungry? Nance's bringing up a tray. . ."

She winced and shook her head. "It would be wasted on me."

"Ah, now, bud, none of that." He rose from the bed and poured her a glass of Madeira. "You must have something," he said, putting the glass in her hand. "You've gone too thin. Come, come," he said, and the words had a thousand echoes, "'twill do you good."

She drank the wine reluctantly and such of the cheese and bread that he fed to her, afterwards sleeping while he worked at the desk. In the morning her head was clearer, but that day proved no better than the one just past.

They were at breakfast when Nance came in and leaned down to hiss in her ear, "I think y' should come, ma'am, an look at the wee miss. The'm's something gone quare with her."

All the blood drained away from Patty's face in an instant, and she was assailed by a roaring in her ears. By some effort, she rose from the table and went running down the hall with a choking cry for her sense of premonition. Thomas was on his feet, but she did not stop to wait for him.

In the bedroom, Lucy was in her cot, making quick, gasping little sighs instead of a regular breath. She had left her asleep, not easily, but asleep, only a quarter of an hour before. Her cheeks were scarlet, and when she picked her up she wailed feebly and arched against the contact, her face contorting in a spasm. All the muscles in her small frame knotted, and she began to twitch violently.

"Lucy!"

Her own half-strangled cry was hoarse and high-pitched, not her own voice at all. She clutched the baby and shrilled at Nance, "Fetch Mr. Jefferson! Something's wrong with Lucy—"

He was behind her, taking the baby from her with strong hands. His face was pale, but his hands were steady as he flung himself in the chair with the convulsive baby, one hand seeking the nerve in her neck and the other holding her head back to allow a passage of air.

"Go downstairs and tell Wiley to run for the doctor!" he barked to Nance. "Or one of his boys. Don't waste time!"

Nance fled.

"Keep the children out," he told her. "Close the door or send them downstairs." But she was too nerveless to move and could only stare at him, stricken, as he worked.

"Lucy, Lucy." He called the baby's name over and over, swinging her to and fro in his arms, having secured some abatement of the fit by manipulating her neck. The baby was breathless, gagging as if in an apoplexy, all her febrile color gone to a frightening blue-whiteness. Thomas roughly massaged her chest, all the while calling her name, and blew in her mouth intermittently. Though it was a cold and rainy day, he was as drenched at though it were hottest summer. That and his paleness were the only signs of his distress. She thanked God for his quick thinking, and quicker action.

Every fibre of her being and consciousness was focused on the struggling form of her baby daughter. It seemed an age that they had been in this room, watching or aiding her painful ordeal. At last, at last, blessedly, the baby gasped and turned bright red. But instead of the angry cry Patty expected, Lucy gave the most ear-splitting, high-pitched, and unnatural wail. The sound echoed through the house and turned all her vitals to water, for she had never heard its like before, but animal instinct knew the sound as a harbinger of death. Even Thomas was so shaken that he nearly dropped her. Their eyes met over the child's head, and her own alarm was at last mirrored in his. He sank into the chair again and pulled the baby to his chest, engulfing her in his arms, crooning her name.

She was panting quickly, shallowly, like a dog on a summer's day, her bright color gone once more into a chilling greyness. Where in God's name was the doctor, or someone, with something that could help their poor Lucy? Patty looked frantically to the door, but there were only Patsy and Polly, standing dumbstruck, their eyes round as saucers.

"Get out of here!" she shouted at them. "Patsy, take your sister away and stay there! Now!"

She had never hollered at them before in such a fashion all their lives. But she could think of nothing now but that they must not witness the impending scene.

It was too late. As she turned her gaze back to Thomas and the baby, Lucy gave a shudder in his arms and was still. There was no more struggling breath, no more heaving rise of the little chest. My God, oh God! Lucy was dead.

73

A State in Which I Would Not Wish To Leave Her

Richmond, Elk Hill, Monticello

Everything went dim around her. She fell on the floor at Thomas's knees with a cry, all restraint broken down by this one last blow which could never be borne. She wept incoherently, hysteria fast rising as the river of the last years' grief flooded out and overwhelmed her. She could not check it, but was swept along, sick and alone, clutching at, but not finding, a safe harbor or a friendly shore. She was blind, mad, insensible of any outside endeavor to reach her. There was nothing, nothing at all in the world but this tossing vortex in which she should soon be engulfed. She was drowning in it, in all the many losses that unkind fate had rained upon her. There was no light but a red-black glimmer of pain that passed overhead like the clouds of hell; no sound but the wailing lamentations of lost infants and children. Death she had given them, not life, eternal death in this place of misery that was no place but Dante's purgatorio made most terribly real.

She came to herself with a start and a cry, wracked by such a spasm that she knew from much experience it was but one thing. She was bleeding. Dear God, she'd had no course since Lucy's birth and now this—

"You're all right, dear," Thomas's voice was hushing in her ear. It was twilight outside the window, and she was safe abed beneath her own white quilt. She clutched the hand that held hers. "No," she whispered fervidly. She sought his gaze in dread and found his eyes a quiet brown in the dimming light. His face was haggard. And now she must heap greater misery upon him! She closed her eyes, steeling herself against the cramp.

"I'm bleeding," she muttered through clenched teeth.

He did not take in her meaning immediately. When he did he sat back in the chair, stunned. His face was ashen. "You're with child?" he murmured dreadfully.

"Was," she amended, with a gasp. Her voice was raw, a crone's, not her own.

Thomas sat forward again, and she forestalled his words. "I did not know it until this moment. But— Oh!— You know as well as I—" She shook her head violently, tears springing to her eyes. "I never have cramps like this—

God!" She clenched his hand and turned her face into the pillow, crying fitfully as the wave washed over her. It should hardly hurt so much as early as it was!

She did not know how far forward things were. It could be as much as three-odd months, or as little as a few weeks. She had been sick since their return to town. That told her nothing. She had not had a course since Lucy's birth, nor the merest hint of one. How was she to know? Lucy. She remembered something about Lucy.

Lucy was teething. Lucy was crabby. Lucy had a fever. Lucy was dead. She had lost not one child this day, but two.

The hysteria that had receded welled up in her again, compounding her agonies. She was lost in the long night, and had it not been for Thomas's constant presence beside her, she would have made good her declared wish to end them once for all.

It was clear by morning that her prescience of her situation was true. She was in no danger this time of great hemorrhage, thanks to Mrs. Cox's brew of herbs, but a large amount of clots were passed, giving circumstantial evidence.

Lucy was buried in St John's churchyard the next afternoon, where years before Thomas had sat with Page listening to Patrick Henry's inflammatory speech before the Assembly. Thomas went alone, and when he came home he was damp from the unremitting rain. He made a solitary entry in his account book for the previous day: "our daughter Lucy Elizabeth died about 10. o'clock A.M. this day"

They had no time for healing their griefs that desolate spring, for Arnold, with William Phillips' reinforcements, once again sailed up the country, this time to Petersburg. She was still sunk in her melancholia and illness when he sent her and the children up to Elk Hill. The journey was one she would rather forget. Two days in the rain and mud, with her spirits already damped, and not to know, once again, what would befall Thomas and Richmond. Would she come back to a burned-out house, as Phillips had burned Petersburg, and to a situation more agonizing than widowhood? If she had possessed any faith in a merciful God she would have prayed, but as it was, she could only stare numbly on the probability of a bleak future.

Lisbet was her calm and gently scolding self. She had bid Francis farewell four days before and held her own at the house with quiet assurance. The British would have a poor welcome if they came to this place, for Lisbet was staunch in her loyalties.

She accepted them, refugees once more, into the hall, and put her arms about Patty. "I'm sorry about Lucy," she murmured, too low for the children to hear. "We only heard yesterday, or I should have written. How are you, Patt?"

Patty raised her head from the curving shoulder and the welcome embrace. "I can't take it in," she murmured bleakly, not looking at Betsy. "It's just too much when I—" She caught herself and shook her head. "Don't let me begin that way, or I shall never stop."

Lisbet pressed her hand. "We'll have a good old drawl about it later," she promised. "Right now, come, take off your wraps, and I'll have you some tea made up in a trice." She smiled. "It's only strawberry, but it's hot. And with a little milk you can't tell the difference much. Come."

Nance took the girls upstairs and dried them off, and soon they were romping about the halls with their cousins, as blithe as if the tragedies and terrors of the last week had never occurred.

Betsy, for her part, was companion, nurse, confessor, and manager, cheerfully allowing none of the duties of the house to fall to her until she should wish it. After a week of this pampering, Patty began to come around. The rains had ceased, and she went out to view the new lambs and several colts lately born. They had a visit from Bolling Stark, on his way from Fairfield, bearing news of Thomas and the Bollings.

Lafayette had reached Richmond on the twenty-seventh, setting up camp on the heights above the town, and not before time, for Arnold once again was upriver from Westover, occupying Manchester from early in the morning of the thirteenth. Phillips was at Chesterfield courthouse, having moved further inland from Cumberland. General Muhlenburg, with a force less than half of Phillips's, retreated before him. It was this that prompted Mr. Stark, with whom Thomas had deposited the books and papers of state, to flee to his cousin John at Fairfield. Thomas was well, he said, when last he saw him, and the words were music to her ears. She murmured a prayer of thanks to her hastily abandoned gods, and sang with hope for the rest of the day.

The next morning the weather was fine, and she bethought to take a visit to Col. Harrison across the river, only to discover that all the batteaux, barges, and flats had been commandeered to carry grain for the army. Even their own small boat, that which Thomas and Henry had often used for fishing, was gone. Set in her mind for a day out, she expressed some sharp annoyance with this, which gave some amusement to Lisbet and Mr. Stark, and went out to wander the farm with the children.

With Patsy and Poll she fed corn to new-weaned calves, laughing at Polly's disgust of the mealy-wet mouths. They were much less dainty in their victualling than the deer in their park, or even the rabbits kept in Broad street. Polly much preferred the lambs. All was in abundance at Elk Hill and on the Island. Save for the annoying necessity of the boats having been commandeered, one could scarce believe there was a war.

Here the late spring sunrise sparkled over the pristine river, not clogged with warships, turning the sky and dewy fields gently from violet to rose to dazzling gold before the morning settled in decorously, and afternoons were a lazy long drawl in the mild sun before the cool of evening. From the upper windows one could watch the Rivanna come tumbling down from amid the tangle of trees at Secretary's ford by the home mountains, to join in slow-moving confluence with the James at Point of Fork, diverting itself at the Island to regroup sedately past Dungeness.

She did a lot of watching the rivers, as she always did when she came here. They were soothing in their coursing pulses, ever-changing and yet eternally the same, with one season as like its previous kind as could be—barring the occasional flood—reassuring and healing. Elk Hill was safe. Elk Hill would always be a safe refuge from the world's cares. This surety brought the life flowing back into her again, and she could have some hope, for though the news from the east was not good, yet there was not the one piece of bad news she feared hearing. Whatever his difficulties, Thomas was well and safe, and that was what mattered the most to her.

He arrived at Elk Hill well after dark when she was upstairs putting the girls to bed. She turned at the familiar step at the door, not daring to hope, for he had been expected that afternoon, and she had nearly given up on seeing him that night. "Oh, you're here at last!" she cried, and flew over. He smiled and kissed her before the children. "I was detained at Lafayette's. . . He talks almost as much as Mazzei." But he did not look put out. On the contrary, he was hale and vital, with warm color from more than the ride.

The girls came tumbling out of bed, clambering over their cousins, shouting, "Papa! Papa!" She put a finger over her lips. "Hush, shh," she murmured, smiling, "or you'll have Aunty Skipwith up here with her slipper to paddle you all." For Nancy had threatened the children into silence once before that evening as they cavorted about the beds. She never would strike them, except perhaps to throw the slipper at their heads, but she liked to play fierce. It was quite at odds with her appearance. For though she was no longer the willowy little person she had once been, there remained about her face a softness which belied any stern tone she might undertake to use. The cousins all knew this as well as her own children, but they paid heed to her threats on the outside chance that she may some time make good of them.

Peter and the girls were allowed an extra half-hour's indulgence beyond their usual bedtime. This made the young Skipwiths and Eppeses even more cantankerous, as Patsy and Polly's bedtime was later than theirs to begin with. But at last, after sufficient hugs and kisses and breathless tales of the last three weeks' adventures, they too were tucked up in the beds in the north room with their playmates, safe and happy in the assurance that Papa would indeed be here in the morning to take them home.

Monticello seemed strange without Martin and Sukey and the Georges about the house and stable. There were others to fill their jobs until such time as they should be returned: old Jenny in the kitchen; Scilla in the laundry; Jupiter waiting at table; but their places could not be filled, and everyone was most anxious that they be allowed to return from their captivity in York, where they had been since January.

Jupiter was particularly persistent in asking when his wife would be returned to him, as she had been in uncertain health after the loss of a child in December, and he was gravely afraid she might "catch something," as he said, at the British camp. This badgering went on day after day in the midst of more pressing affairs, until Thomas sent him out to the stable and told him to stay there. They could do without service at table and could certainly do with a little peace.

Finally, at the end of May, permission was secured for those at York to travel as far as Richmond, provided the governor would send someone to pick them up. The prisoners arrived home on the second of June to be warmly greeted by one and all. They were safe and hale, bursting with stories. Those, unfortunately, had to wait, for in the next few days other stories were garnered which would likewise be told and retold, amid the cabins and family alike.

74

The Chain of Friendship
Charlottesville

The day before the servants return, they all had gone down to Charlottesville, where Thomas was to bestow a desired medal upon the Kaskaskia Chief, John Baptiste Ducoigne, who had done so much to aid George Clarke and keep the peace in the Illinois.

The day was already warm when the gathering was collected and called to order at the new courthouse, though it was only midmorning. The heat and rising humidity appeared not to affect Ducoigne or his aids at all, dressed as they were in little more than fringed trousers. The chief was a tall man and possessed of a most noble visage: a high, bony nose, a straight, proud brow, and eyes of an eery steel-grey. His long hair was tied with shells and bits of beaver pelt, decorated with glistening black beads. He was magnificent, and bore himself with all the dignity of a patrician general. He confessed to an admiration of Thomas, the reason he had especially requested to receive an Indian Medal from his hand rather than wait on his successor. He had even named his three-months son Jefferson. The child was now peaceably asleep in an upright basket in the shade of the steps amongst the knot of women the chief and his men had brought along.

Patty found all of the Indians fascinating, never having seen any before, but she studied the women most particularly during the amenities before the investiture. While she had been presented to Ducoigne—he made her a fine English bow that surprised her with its grace—the chief's wife remained amongst her women. Only the greater ornamentation of her dress marked her as especial in any way; she was given no bowing deference.

The women were of every shape and size and condition of life. It would have been difficult to tell their ages, for they all seemed slightly weathered, yet none possessed white hairs or plainly missing teeth that would indicate middle age.

Their dress was simple, a gown of deerskin and short boots, but it was in their ornament that they shone. Ducoigne's lady wore a beautiful sash of glimmering fringed red silk, shot with silver and studded with hundreds of beads and carved buttons of mother-of-pearl. She wore as many jangling bracelets and earrings as Betty, and matched Bett's grandeur for mix of colors, for she had a sort of scarf knotted in her hair that was sea-green and spotted with marigold. In the center of each of these spots was a cluster of amber beads in a rosette pattern. The work was exquisite, and she could not help but exclaim. "Oh, Madame, you are beautiful!"

When her remark was relayed, the chief's wife smiled and nodded with as much charm as a young girl paid her first compliment. She was sweet.

For their part, the Indian women were as fascinated by her dress as she was by theirs. They smelled rather odd at close proximity, but it was no worse than Negro quarters on a summer's day, and she made no reaction to it while they fondled her lace and exclaimed over her shoes, and poked perplexed at her middle. They enquired of her in their own language, and she turned to the interpreter, who laughed. "They want to know how the English lady makes herself so firm like a birch tree."

Patty blushed and shook her head. "I couldn't think of how to explain corsets to them," she admitted, looking at her shoes.

"I can," he murmured, and told them a single word, at which the women all nodded sagely.

"What did you say?" she asked, not without some apprehension.

"Bones."

She was saved from further enquiries by the beginning of the ceremony and took her place again with Betsey Walker and Lucy Gilmer at the opposite side of the courthouse.

"What did they say to you?" Betsey hissed.

"Hush," she said, and put up her sunshade. "I'll tell you later."

Though Thomas was not commonly given to speeches, this one, marking as it did the end of his term and being on a subject very dear to him, went off splendidly. It was hardly so much read as recited, as a valued and familiar piece of poetry was recited, and he had about him all those marks of friendly animation that were his special charm. When the ceremonial matters of the exchange of medals and gifts and the smoking of a pipe were concluded, he began with a fondness in his glance:

"Brother Jean Baptiste de Coigne—I am very much pleased with the visit you have made us, and particularly when it has happened when the wise men from all parts of our country were assembled together in council, and had an opportunity of hearing the friendly discourse you held to me. We are all sensible of your friendship, and of the services you have rendered, and I now, for my countrymen, return you thanks, and most particularly, for your assistance to the garrison which was besieged by the hostile Indians. I hope it will please the Great Being above to continue you long in life, in health and in friendship to us; and that your son will afterwards succeed you in wisdom, in good disposition, and in power over your people." His glance fell to Ducoigne's wife, and to the small son lodged in the basket in the shade.

"I consider the name you have given your son as particularly honorable to me, but I value it the more as it proves your attachment to my country. We, like you, are Americans, born in the same land, and having the same interests. I have carefully attended to the figures represented on the skins"—he meant the four calf-sized paintings they had been just been given—"and to their explanation, and shall always keep them hanging on the walls in remembrance of you and your nation. I have joined with you sincerely in smoking the pipe of peace; it is a good old custom handed down by your ancestors, and as such I respect it and join in it with reverence." Ducoigne could not know what a reverence this truly was, for as long as Patty had known him and longer, if John Walker was to be credited, Thomas had eschewed tobacco in any form, not liking its giddy effects. "I hope we shall long continue to smoke in friendship together."

He looked down at his notes now, having deviated from his written course. "You find us, brother, engaged in war with a powerful nation. Our forefathers were Englishmen, inhabitants of a little island beyond the great water—" He succinctly traced the history of English settlement and that of the present conflict, continuing, "This quarrel, when it first began, was a family quarrel between us and the English, who were then our brothers. We, therefore, did not wish to engage you in it at all. We are strong enough ourselves without wasting your blood in fighting our battles. The English, knowing this, have always been suing to the Indians to help them fight. We do not wish you to take up the hatchet. We love and esteem you, We wish you to multiply and be strong—" He counselled them not to undertake a war for any but their own sake, if they had been injured by the English, the French settlers, or hostile tribes, and promised, "If you will make known to me any just cause of complaint against them, I will represent it to the great council at Philadelphia, and have justice done you."

He outlined such of their complaints as had already come to them and the reasons for their causes. He made promises to them for the redress of these grievances, which mostly concerned a want of goods. He bade them to be patient for yet a little longer. "—For the present, you shall have a share of what little goods we can get. We will order some immediately up the Mississippi for you and for us. If they be little, you will submit to suffer a little as your brothers do for a short time. And when we shall have beaten our enemies and forced them to make peace, we shall share more plentifully." He charged them to depend upon George Clark as an able and trusty warrior and Virginia's lieutenant beyond the Alleghenies, for he would advise all their difficulties and redress their wrongs, look after them in every way.

Thomas came to the last item in his notes, and one that was dear to his heart. Patty saw behind his amber gaze as he spoke all his childhood's memories of Indian visits to Shadwell and his father's many stories by an evening fireside. His face softened from the hard talk of war and became again the loving and amiable countenance she and other intimates knew well, suffused, eager, brilliant. She was glad that the last two years of overwork and worry should end thus, in honor and gladness and friendship. He deserved it.

His voice held, soft but insistent, casting a subtle spell over the gathering, and though they were outdoors, no one after complained of being unable to hear. "You ask us to send schoolmasters to educate your son and the sons of your people. We desire above all things, brother, to instruct you in whatever we know ourselves. We wish to learn you all our arts and make you wise and wealthy. As soon as there is peace we shall be able to send you the best of school-masters; but while the war is raging, I am afraid it will not be practicable. It shall be done, however, before your son is of an age to receive instruction.

"This, brother, is what I had to say to you. Repeat it from me to all your people, and to our friends, the Kickapous, Piorias, Piankeshaws, and Wyattanons. I will give you a commission to show them how much we esteem you." He paused, and his gaze rested upon the noble face of his friend Ducoigne, for his next words came from the heart. Softly, sincerely, he bade him, "Hold fast the chain of friendship which binds us together, keep it bright as the sun, and let them, you, and us, live together in perpetual love."

75

The Butcher

Monticello, Blenheim, Amherst

On the twenty-ninth of May, Banastre Tarleton and his cavalry were at Hanover courthouse. He and his legion of 500 green-coated horses had lately come from a humiliating defeat at Cowpens in South Carolina, and the lieutenant colonel was determined to make up his lost status and pride upon Virginia. He moved primarily at night, using that cover to his great advantage. Simcoe's cavalry, who had in January raided the house in Richmond, was at Point of Fork occupying Elk Hill as headquarters in advance of Cornwallis. The enemy's army was moving toward them once more, and on Monday, the fourth of June, it burst upon them at last.

They had entertained several of the councillors at dinner on Sunday, including Colonel Ben Harrison, Colonel Cary, Patrick Henry, John Tyler, and Jack Walker. When the hour grew too late for Walker to safely journey home across the river, he joined the others in the makeshift arrangements of beds abovestairs. All were retired shortly after midnight, and the house lay in peaceful quiet until the small hours before dawn.

Once again Martin, so lately returned home, came banging on their door in the darkness. She sat up in alarm, but Thomas had already lit a candle and was going to the hall door in the shadowy dark.

"Thomas—"

"It's all right," he said quietly, without turning. "I'll see to it."

He was a long time returning. She could hear nothing through the closed door, and the longer he was gone the more anxious she became. Had someone from down the country actually taken sick? None of them had appeared worse for wear yesterday. God, if Sukey did take sick, they'd never hear the end of it from Jupiter! The specter of camp fever rose before her, dreadfully, and when Thomas returned with the candle, she half expected him to speak the words.

Instead he murmured, in some surprise, "You're awake!"

"Of course," she returned, leaning forward as he sat on the bed. She didn't like the absorbed quality of his face. Something was seriously wrong.

"What's happened?"

He took off the dressing gown and rubbed a hand across his eyes. "Nothing, yet," he said cautiously, then turned to her fully. "That was Captain Jouette. He has just ridden from the Cuckoo in Louisa—"

"Louisa!" It was forty miles from that place to this, largely trackless, completely wooded and dangerous at night. Jouette, though, was a great bear of a man, a crack rider, and fearless. He had had three brothers in the Continental Army, one of whom had been killed at Brandywine creek. If there was any man to have accomplished such a ride, it was Jouette.

He held up a hand. "Because he there overheard Tarleton's men intending to make a raid on Charlottesville sometime today. As the Assembly are still gathered, he thought to come and warn us. They mean to capture the government."

The enormity of it struck her at once. They should have to flee as they had done that winter and spring. She had thought, now that they were home, that they were safe from such maneuvers. "Dear God," she cried in despair, "not again!" And then, "Tarleton!" The Butcher, who in Carolina had burnt and pillaged, leaving no crop standing, no man untormented, no woman in dignity. Sweet mercy, Tarleton was coming to Charlottesville! "Thomas, there aren't enough militia in the neighborhood to stand against Tarleton's dragoons! How shall we manage?" She clutched his arm. "What if they should come here? What's to stop them from burning this whole place and carrying you off?"

He smiled a little, grimly, and kissed her forehead. "You seem to forget I am no longer governor."

"I doubt the Butcher knows that!" she exclaimed. He took her arms. "Have no fear, little one. If they come I shall be long gone from here. As to the house," he sighed, "they can't do much to it, unfinished as it is. If they burn it, we shall rebuild." He shook his head. "I'm afraid we would have no hope for the farm. Even if he leaves the house, he's likely to confiscate our stores. His men need provision." He kissed her. "I'm sorry, sweetheart. I'm sorry to have to disturb you again."

"You're not to blame," she murmured. The blame lay with greedy quartermasters and lazy militia, who could summon no more love for their home country than half-hearted attempts at defence. They would be totally outnumbered and outdistanced now.

He did not reply, but gathered her up into an embrace beneath their light covers. They did not sleep again, but sat together silently until the sun began to creep about the shutters. She was uneasy in her mind, but Thomas did not evince the least concern for their safety or the urgency of the moment. He went about his usual routine calmly and cheerfully, somewhat more silent than usual, but otherwise not affected. From this measure, she drew strength and gathered up her own courage to face their guests and the day. She went upstairs at seven to dress the girls, only telling them that they would be going on a visit to the Coleses today. She brushed Polly's hair and helped Patsy secure her hemstitched tucker as she always did, spreading no alarm among them.

Breakfast was a casual affair, with nothing untoward to mark the day. The gentlemen had been informed previously of Jouette's visit and Tarleton's intentions, and spoke of sundry matters of state as easily as though they were to be together all day. Even Mr. Henry gave nothing away, though he was temperamentally incapable of containing himself. He thanked her for the hospitality of her fine table and excellent beds, then went upstairs to gather his things to depart. It was half-past nine o'clock when he and the others were seen off on their horses to a hasty meeting convened in Charlottesville.

Thomas came up from the stable and ordered the trunks brought up from the basement where they were lodged. He had already sent Caractacus to be shod and the carriage horses harnessed and made ready. Now all that remained were the trunks. They folded away enough clothes for a fortnight—for themselves, Peter, and the girls—and these were put on the carriage.

When she walked out onto steps of the portico with Thomas behind the children, all her hard-won calm deserted her, and she felt a choking panic that she should never see him again.

"Mr. Jefferson—" she began, and turned. He was directly behind her, and she looked up into the clear lovely amber of his eyes, and she could not speak the words she had intended. Her throat went dry as dust, and she could only stare at him anxiously, her heart thudding in her ears.

He looked down at her, calm, sympathetic, and she had never loved him better than then. He knew her fears for him, had his own for her and the children, but would not speak them into being. They were all as a puff of an half-forgotten child's dream, easily dissipated with tender regard. His face was soft and gentle, and he smiled at her with the slow-dawning sweet smile that was like the sun rising over the hills in the morning. "I'll see you at Carter's for dinner," he murmured, and kissed her hand. The touch was burning, making other words superfluous.

She swallowed. "I'll be waiting there," she returned, adjusting her hat.

"Up with you now," he said quietly. She went down the steps and was handed into the carriage by John. Thomas leaned in and said to Peter, "You'll look after them now, son. I'm counting on you." Peter's brown head nodded. "Aye, sir. I shan't fail."

"Good lad." Thomas stood away and gave Jim the order to start.

They were not out of the yard before Polly stood up on the seat in a panic and cried, staring out the back window, "Why's Papa not comin' with us!" In her face were all the terrors and uncertainty she had been subject to in the last six months. She put an arm about the child and drew her onto her lap.

"Sit down, Poll. It's all right," she said, with far more certitude than she felt, for her heart was still thumping. "Papa has some work to do, and then he'll come along to dinner with us. He shan't be long, sweet." She kissed the curly dark head. "He shan't be long." But as she looked out through the thinness of the summer hangings at the woods as they wound their way down the mountain to the Thoroughfare, she knew that the words were a prayer, and no more. Tarleton was abroad in their neighborhood, and the safety of no one was a certainty, least of all Thomas.

He arrived at Blenheim just before they sat down to dinner and told a tale of nearly missing the greencoats at Monticello.

"After Mrs. Jefferson retired," he said laughingly, "I spent some time sorting out my papers." He looked at her and she rolled her eyes. "I thought me safe, as I could see with the telescope any incursion the British made into the neighborhood. . . . Well, along about noon, Captain Hudson of our militia came riding up to inform me that the enemy were at the bottom of the Thoroughfare road out by Shadwell, and ready at any moment to make their ascent of our hill. 'I've left it too late,' I thought, and scrambled off for my crop and sword." He shook his head. "When I got down to the Thoroughfare, there wasn't a soul in sight, not even from the top of Montalto—" Carter smiled at the name, for before Thomas's purchase, it had been simply Carter's Mountain. But the proximity of Mazzei and his Tuscans at Colle had encouraged the change.

"So, in thinking Hudson to be mistaken in his alarm, I resolved to go back up to the house and bring along with me some of the more important papers. But on mounting my horse, I found that my dress sword was missing. Now, I grant you, it would be no great defence against a musket ball, but it would hold its own against one of its kind." He paused to eat some. "So I looked about and could not find it, and at last decided to look up on the mountain. And there it was!" The company was smiling, anticipating some exciting denouement, and Patty held her breath for he, completely heedless, was bleeding down his temple and into the folds of his neckstock.

"Whilst I was up there, I saw a flash of light from the town. On taking up the sights on the telescope, I found Charlottesville aswarm in greenbacks and a troop of them coming up our road. . . ." He laughed and made a swipe at the sword, which since his investiture with it as County Lieutenant eleven years ago had hung ceremoniously on the wall, the subject of many a jest. "Had it not been for missing this," he continued, "I would most certainly not have missed unwelcome guests!"

"Oh, did you meet them on the road?" Molly cried with a face of dreadful suspense, clutching her napkin. It was a question Patty wished an answer to as well. Thomas bowed his head to her.

"No, ma'am," he said with a smile. "I went through the woods past Lewis's Mill and around. I doubt they ever saw me at all." Plainly, he thought it a fine joke for their quarry to have been under their noses and the British all unknowing. Like the fox in a chase. . . . Before this, he had always scoffed at foxhunting. . . .

In the upstairs room where she had retired to stitch his coat after its brushing, Patty shook her head when Thomas discovered in the looking glass the bleeding scrape along his forehead that had been entertaining her all through the meal. He set to with Molly Carter's salves and milled soap to put to rights what his long blunder through the woods had undone.

"You do look a sight," she said. "Anyone would think you'd been pursued, dashing through the woods that way. I'm surprised you did it, knowing how Caractacus shies at shadows." Thomas was not taken in. Beneath her good-natured teasing was genuine relief that he was sound. He daubed at the wound gingerly with a flannel, wincing at the stinging soap.

"It could have been worse," he shrugged, taking the glass nearer the window. The wound did not dry up readily, but oozed upon application of the soap. "I might have been scraped off and broken my arm. He likes to do that, too. Mmm. I couldn't take the road for the chance Tarleton had put out men." He put down the glass. "Should I stitch this, do you think?" he asked, coming over to her.

She smiled. "Come here, my vain gallant," she said, putting down her sewing. "All it wants is a bit of pressure. Let me see." She took the cloth from him, and he sat before her in shirtsleeves tailor fashion on the floor while she mashed his skull between her hand and the cloth.

"Such a gentle nurse," he complained when she released him.

"Oh hush," she murmured fondly. "I stopped it, didn't I?" She had indeed. So well that it was more or less healed the next day, and never left the trace of a mark.

They spent the night with the Coleses at Enniscorthy, six miles farther west from Blenheim, on the Hardware river, and the next day stopped at Rockfish and Colonel Hugh Rose's in Amherst. On the seventh, Thomas returned to Monticello briefly to see what damage had been done, and when he returned on the tenth he had yet another tale to tell.

When he left Monticello on the day of Tarleton's raid, he had left Martin and Caesar storing plate in the narrow space beneath the front portico's floorboards. He had it from Martin that they were not finished in this task when they heard the jangle of harnesses coming up the north road. Martin had handed down her mother's wedding bowl and slammed the planking down on Caesar's head, and there he remained for the entire eighteen hours of Captain MacLeod's visit.

"Visit!" she sniffed. Thomas held up a hand, grinning.

"Wait, there's more: Martin says the captain was mightily impressed with the house and spent the better part of an hour wandering about, looking at things before he saw fit to search for me." His eyes twinkled. "He appears to have liked the Indian paintings especially."

She was not amused. "How much did they steal from us?" she asked tartly.

He raised an eyebrow. "Steal? Not much. Some wine was broken into. . . ." He rolled his tongue in his cheek. "But Martin was quaking in his shoes that they had dirtied up your linens and broken the reverse-glass painting in the parlor. He vowed to have Aggey launder them and find some way to replace the other. . . and begged me not to tell you."

"Oh, pooh." She waved her hand. "I never did care much for that picture anyhow. It doesn't match the chairs quite rightly. . ." She leaned forward and touched his arm. "But Tom, you're telling me they took nothing? No stores, no cattle, no horses?"

He shook his head. "Not a thing. They were under orders from Tarleton not to disturb the house, and I had removed the horses to Tufton, as you'll recall." She had not. It was a wonder itself, a genuine miracle, that they had been treated so kindly by that famously brutal man. The next day they made their way to Bedford, there to rusticate and wait out the invasion in peace, feeling very lucky to have been spared save a few bottles of wine and an old picture.

76

Matters of Public Trust

Poplar Forest

The house at Poplar Forest sat on a knoll in the midst of a clearing of plane, beech, and poplar trees. It was not remarkable in itself, being an ordinary, small frame house, but its situation amongst the trees and its isolation made it an excellent retreat. And it was cool. In the hottest summer all the house required was the front and rear doors opened to be heavenly cool. Being a working farm, there were few distractions to plague one as there were at Monticello.

Here she could read to the girls and sit in the sun, stitching some piece of fancywork, free from the cares of life, recovering her strength after a difficult winter and spring, and fret over nothing more than turning brown from being so much outdoors. Here, Thomas could give lessons to Peter and take him fishing; he could write up answers to the list of questions sent him from the French diplomat Marbois by Jack Ambler back in November, and spend the cool of the evening walking with her in the shaded woods hand in hand as in courting days. He played his fiddle for none but her, and they idled away time in plans for the garden at Monticello.

Then came news from John Innes, who bore a letter from Colonel Cary at Staunton that Elk Hill had been ravaged by Cornwallis, whose headquarters it had been for ten days. All the growing crops of corn and tobacco were destroyed, and every bit the same of last year's stored, except that which he took for his own use. He had slaughtered every sheep, hog, and cattle that could be used in that time and had carried off what he could not eat. Every horse worthy of the name was taken, and those too young for service had their throats cut. He burned every fence on the plantation and on the Island likewise, and took most of the silver and plate and not a few dishes, china and pewter, and blankets. In addition to this, he also carried off about thirty slaves from that place to York, where they were to suffer greatly from smallpox. The destruction was similar throughout the neighborhood, though it was the general belief that Cornwallis had gone particularly hard on Elk Hill, knowing it was, as he thought, the governor's possession.

In England, Cornwallis's character would have forbidden the belief that he shared in the plunder but that his table was served with plate thus plundered from private houses might have been proved by many hundred eyewitnesses. The whole loss to Virginia, in lands and crops, property and slaves, amounted to near three million pounds sterling. Much of this was irrecoverable.

Colonel Cary was also the forerunner with the news that the Assembly had seen fit to call for an enquiry into his conduct this last year, and since the first invasion particularly. Cary wrote:

> So Much for Assembly but I must give you one more piece of News respecting your Self. An Address was ready to be offered the Senat to you. What Can you think Stopt it? George Nicholas made a Motion in the House of Delegates for an Inquire into your Conduct, a Catalogue of omissions, and other Misconduct. I have not Seen the Particulars Your Friends Confident an Inquire would do you Honor Seconded the Motion. I presume you will be Serv'd with the order. As this Step was Taken I persuaded Winston not to make his Motion; I had heard something of this Kind was to be brought on the Carpit, and If I know you, it will Give you no pain.

Thomas was much distressed by this last piece of news. Elk Hill they could repair, but, as he said, not his reputation in the hands of Henry.

"How in the name of god can they be seriously induced to think that I did anything but my utmost for the country during my tenure?" he asked her rhetorically, pacing the floor in the parlor the evening of the letter's arrival. "Good god! They have only to examine the thousands of despatches and warrant orders I had wrote for men and arms, for provisions!" He ran a hand through his hair, shaking his head. "It's true, I was not willing to actually take men into the field myself—" James Monroe had intimated in his last letter that this had been an expectation.

"But short of that—" He began to stutter, and she looked up in alarm. He'd give himself an apoplexy getting so riled up. Who cared what Patrick Henry thought, my goodness! But he went on, heedless of her alarm. "Good God, when I recall how I rode up and down through rain and snow, night and day entirely alone, trying to secure the arms, trying to find Steuben— Ah," he gave a bitter cry, "they might have taken me then for all the aid I received from the government! And when I think that you and the children were left to founder—" She froze. *Please, please, don't say it!* she begged him, but he did not hear her silent plea. "And then Lucy, oh God—" She leapt up and flung herself on him, taking down his hands from where they were clasped under his chin.

"Thomas, please, darling, it's all right! Tom, please, Tom. . ." She pulled him down with her until they were sitting on the floor, and she rocked him in her arms like a child. "Hush, sh, my love, my dear. It's all right. They shall not trouble you. Hush, sh, my dear. Tom. Hush, there's my dear." She stroked his hair, kissed his face, soothing him as she had Poll, and slowly he began to calm down, until at last he drew a shuddering breath and sat up a little away from her. Her own hands were shaking yet, for here was witness to the nervous fits that had assailed his poor mother and sisters, and she could not bear the thought that he should be likewise troubled, if only for his own sake, for she knew he feared the Randolph madness.

"I'm sorry," he murmured, wiping his face with one hand. "I—" He looked lachrymose and ashamed, and in the lineaments of his face she saw her chastened Patsy. She took his hand and held it in both of hers. "No, love." She shook her head. "There is no need."

He brooded over Colonel Cary's letter for several days, saying little to anyone, all his joy at being released from magisterial bonds dissolved. He wandered gloomily about the house until she could bide it no more, and convinced him to take Caractacus out for a ride.

He did so, and she was pleased that he did not come back straightaway, until the hour grew very late. Evening was beginning to set in when he got back to the house. The locust and chiggers and lightening bugs set up their hum and swagger about the tall grasses at the edge of the clearing. The air smelled thick and green as the heat rose from the ground to meet the cooling breeze, making a pleasant haze over the landscape, and the sky to the west was a ruddy palette of streaming clouds that she saw beyond the frame of the door. When she looked down at her work again, she realized how truly late and dark it had become. Supper would be called in a moment. Where on earth was Thomas? Worried now, she took a stab at her work anyhow, her green spectacles falling down her nose, and stabbed her finger also.

She started and bit her thumb. Just then a shadow fell across the light from the front door. It was Thomas.

"Oh, my dear, I was beginning to wonder when you—" She stopped and peered at him. He was mighty dirty and unkempt. . . and pale. He held his left arm cradled in the other. His expression was dazed. "Thomas, what's happened to you?" she exclaimed, "you look queer—" She rose and went forward, reaching, but he moved his arm away.

"No please," he begged, sheltering it from her. "Caractacus shied. I was thrown. . . I think it's broken." *Oh dear, oh dear,* she thought in a brief moment of alarm. *Thomas, what have you done?* Then she took a breath and gathered her courage. "Come here," she murmured gently, and sat him on the bench she had vacated. "Mary," she called down to the dining room. Mary came.

"Ma'am?"

"Fetch a lamp. And close the doors, or we'll have all the bugs in the neighborhood in here."

"Yas'm."

The lamp was brought and the children instructed to have their supper and play upstairs, with the strictest decorum observed. There would be no running, shouting, pinching, tickling, or hollering. Warned by the tone of her voice, they did as they were bidden without complaint.

"Now," she knelt before him and unbuttoned his sleeve. His hand was mottled blue and swollen, the fingers curled and misshapen. If it wasn't broken, it was a very bad sprain. He looked about to faint away as he leaned with his head against the wall.

"I think before I do this you might be in need of some salubrious assistance," she said. "Don't go 'way." She went into the parlor and returned with the decanter of claret to pour him a large glassful. Taken strong, it would certainly put him in a way to allow her probings. The second large glass on an empty stomach made him a little sick, and he would have none of a third.

"I shan't hold it," he threatened, "and then you'll be sorry."

She looked up at him from where she was cutting open the seam of his sleeve. "I've cleaned up after men before," she remarked steadily.

He frowned in wine-induced curiosity. "Who?" Then he knew as soon as he asked. "Your father!"

"And Francis," she said evenly. "And George Carter several times. . . . " A memory came, clear and painful, of the one altercation she and Batt had ever had. ". . .And Mr. Skelton," she said abruptly, "but that was only once." She stared at him stolidly, seeing the questions written in his face. *Do not ask,* she bade him. *Do not ask. Not here, not now. This is bad enough.* After a moment his expression quietened, and she went on with her work.

"Here we are," she said, tossing the volume of his ruined sleeve out of the way. "Now, let's have a look." She sat on the bench beside him and took his arm into her lap, examining with deft fingers the state of each part with a light touch. Nevertheless, when she came upon the broken places, two on the outside and one part way down on the inside, he jumped involuntarily. She sighed, looking up at him. "I'm afraid it is indeed broken."

"Can you set it?"

She felt herself pale. Setting bones was never a task she relished, and certainly not with loved ones. "If you mean do I know how, the answer is yes," she said grimly. "But if you mean will I. . .I don't know." She bit her lip. "It would mean some pretty awful manipulations, as well you know." She looked up at him. His eyes were wide and green, dark from the wine.

"I promise to be good," he murmured.

She shook her head. "It isn't that. You know it isn't that."

He took her arm with his other hand. "Please try. For me. It hurts like hell. Once it's set it won't trouble me if it's splinted."

She couldn't bear the thought of him hurting now, but to set the bones and splint the arm would hurt far worse than she believed he knew.

"Thomas, I can't!" she cried. "I. . .I've set bones before." Her hand shook as she pushed her fallen hair away from her face. "I set a man's leg one time, with help. The great big bone. Sweet mercy, I never thought to hear a man shriek like that, and him with a gill of rum poured down him! I couldn't do that to you! I love you. I– please." Tears slipped over and fell down her cheeks. "Let me call a doctor! We can soak it in brine until then, or camphor salts if there are any; that should give you some ease. But don't ask me to hurt you!"

Her passion won out, and he acquiesced, letting her send for the doctor in Lynchburg. This man had no qualms about hurting him for his own good, and charged them 300 pounds for the privilege. His arm was set and splinted to the shoulder, which meant that Caractacus had a long incarceration in his box for his misadventure, for it was five weeks before the bracing was removed and he could sit a horse again.

He spent part of the time writing out what answers he could to Marbois's queries. But being away from Monticello meant that he was away from his books and notebooks, whither he had squirreled many curious facts of use to the Frenchman, which he might compare to the like on other states from which he had received replies. He claimed to be rather stalled, having to rely solely on his own memory, for he was wont to write things down rather than carry them around in his head. But by the end of the second week after his accident he had sketched out answers to half the questions and made notes on where to look up the others.

On the ninth of July, the post arrived and he was once again withdrawn. She suspected he had received some bad news but could not cajole it out of him. In the evening he sat sprawled in the tweed chair, sunk in a melancholy. Many times she tried to engage his glance and draw him out, but he would have none of it. She gave up the ruse at length and laid her book aside, going to drape herself over the back of the chair in which he sat before the empty hearth. Through the open windows, the hum of night creatures was a drone.

"What's the matter, love?" she whispered softly in his ear. He usually had few defences against such an advance, but now he moved away from her.

"Nothing," he said irritably. This matter of the enquiry had caused them no little private difficulties, and she was mindful of that, striving to be patient. It would not last forever.

He sighed sharply. "I'm sorry," he murmured. "It's– I–" He sighed again, blurting out baldly, "On top of everything else, today I received this letter from Lafayette and the Congress, congratulating me on having been appointed as commissioner to France!"

Her heart skipped a beat. This was his awful news? That they were to go to France! She skirted round the chair. "But that's wonderful!"

"It isn't!" he snapped. "I can't go with this damned enquiry taking place. I must stay," he said bitterly, "and answer to their charges of incompetence!" He clenched his fist on the arm of the chair.

The enquiry! Bother the enquiry, why should he care? The Congress plainly thought enough of him to offer him a post to France, again. She wished all the councilors speedily to the devil. Why should they obstruct their going to France when they had long so desired it, and until this day lost any hope of going soon!

"Why must you?" she exclaimed, folding her arm across her hip. "What a lot of jealous cowards won't think of, I don't know! Patrick Henry! What did he do with his own governorship, pray, but hide out in the country playing at illness, letting Page do all the work! A fine one for accusations. Oh he's grand at getting folks all riled up, but I'll warrant you he could never have done the things you did when Arnold came to town. If left to him, our papers would have been at Whitehall before you could say 'Jack Robinson'. What care has he for records of state? A man who studies at the law for six whole weeks and calls himself a lawyer! What does he know about anything but causing trouble! Thomas—" Her voice softened and she came to sit before him, avoiding his arm. "You mustn't think you need stay to answer to such scurvy men."

He looked at her, all the anger in his countenance faded. He reached for her hand as she sat between his feet on the floor. "Christ, sweetheart, my own friends have approved this! You heard Archy Cary: they are confident an enquiry would do me honor and seconded the motion. Dear God! I don't know any more who my friends are."

She laid her cheek against his hand. "They are who they have always been. Page would never desert you, nor Jack Walker, nor Mr. Wythe, nor even Nelson, though his position may be bad for friendship at the moment." Thomas Nelson, lately general, was the new governor. "They'll stand by you, love. Oh, Tom! And so will I. I think you need never fear being without advocates. You draw them to you by your goodness." She could not resist a teasing smile. ". . .As much as that might work to your detriment sometimes, it is always appealing. Let them speak for you, love. Or let the rumor-mongers latch onto some other prey. They'll find one soon enough! Let you go to France. You deserve it."

He smiled a little at this, brought round to good humor at last. "Let *us* go to France, you mean," he teased, and she blushed. "It did cross your mind."

"Well, yes," she admitted. "But how could it not?" She shook her head.

"It's not my primary reason for advocacy," she insisted. "That is the lovely green that the mere word brings to your eyes. I like to see that color warming there. It means you're happy. And that is my greatest wish. Why should you remain to be unhappy? For you will be, though they resound your name through the senatorial halls."

He laughed at her Roman image and its reality in Staunton. "They haven't any senatorial halls! If they're lucky they have a back room in the tavern clear of gamesters or drunkards."

She raised an eyebrow. "How would they tell?"

He shook his head and accepted her stealthy advance into his lap, resting his arm on the chair's, out of the way. "Oh, my Patty-patt, you are a wanton creature! What would all your admirers think if they knew how you really are? So cold, so heartless."

He bent his head and kissed that bare place above her plain round neckline. "Thank you, sweetheart," he murmured. "I needed you to cheer me."

"I know," she said, leaning her cheek against his hair. "I had only to know what the trouble was, but began to fear you'd never tell me."

"I always shall," he promised with a sigh.

77

Dreams and Realities

Monticello

In spite of her encouragement, Thomas announced in the morning that, futile or not, he could not live with himself if he did not answer the charges against him in person. His honor required it. He could not give over to others the task he must perform himself. At the very least it would give credence to their taunts of cowardice. Therefore, he must turn down the commission to France. When she was alone after breakfast, she wept with disappointment.

They were home again at the end of July, Thomas's arm having healed enough to remove the splinting. It was weak and looked rather shriveled compared to the other, but the doctor from Lynchburg made every assurance that exercise would remedy this quickly. He was delighted to hear Thomas played the violin, and recommended it as sovereign for returning strength and dexterity to the limb. He had from them his fee and went on his way.

Along their own route, they stopped at the home of Edmund Winston, Senator of the Bedford-Pittsylvania district in the Assembly. It was Winston whose address Colonel Cary had thwarted when the charges were brought up against Thomas, and he wished to thank him for his support if, as he remarked, he had no one else's.

They were home on Friday. On Saturday afternoon, Thomas went upstairs to the library to write a letter. She had a notion of a fitter occupation and, after seeing the children suitably distracted and herself divested of some encumbrances, went upstairs also to propose her plan. Six weeks was too long for chastity to her taste, and the endeavors while his arm was broken had been interesting, but not fulfilling to the soul's requirements, for transportation lay in more than the conveyance from one space to another.

She closed the door behind her silently and stole behind him as be sat at the desk chair, draping her arms about his neck. "Are you writing to Marbois?" she asked breathily. He started, nearly overturning the inkwell, and looked up. She smiled.

"No." He shook his head and laid down the pen. "Would that I were!"

He leaned his head against her shoulder. "Did you want something?" He took in with a smile the bare neckline of her light summer gown. "Or did you merely come in to distract me?"

Her glance was dark and provocative, glinting green and orange. "Yes," she murmured, with a bubble of laughter. By the greening of his eyes, he did not mistake her. He turned in the chair.

"Aye, Madame, and which is it? Or," he took her hand and kissed her fingers, "is it mine to riddle out the depths of your meaning?"

She inclined her head, blushing, giddy at his imaging. He was always so much better at this than she! "I daresay that might prove a pretty pastime, however unprofitable." Her cool, slim fingers worked their stealthy way up his shoulder to the clasp of his stock. With a nimbleness born of years of trills upon her keyboard, she had the three buckles unclasped between finger and thumb before he quite discerned what she was about. She bent a little and murmured in an hushing tone, "I've sent the children to bed or play–" She kissed his neck behind the ear, "and given word that I am not to be disturbed until I should ring. I told Martin I wished a nap, but in truth I had something more amiable in mind." She kissed him again, trailing as insidious ivy across his throat. His pulse raced against her cheek. She met his eye, her voice but a throaty whisper. "Are you so very busy, then–" her glance flickered toward the papers, "that it could not wait an hour?" She smiled hotly. "I promise you, the lack would be well made up, Mr. Jefferson."

In answer he put up his hands on either side of her face and kissed her as she bent before him. "Since you have ordered everything so well," he murmured to her, "what choice have I but to follow your course?"

He rose with her, awkwardly from the entabled chair, enthralled and bewildered when she slid herself from his seeking embrace to smile in her sidelong way at him. "Not here," she said, with a note of silver laughter. "Come." She held out her hand and disappeared around the door frame.

He caught her on the stairs, and for a moment she yielded to the advance, but then was dancing down the stairs with her elfin, secret smile, her buff-striped white gown floating behind her. He could not catch her up until they came to the anteroom, where she removed the key from the lock and laid it on his desk. She leaned against the chair, her hands braced behind her on the desk, regarding him in watchful delight.

He shook his head. "Patty–" He reached out for her. "I cannot say if you are real or my dream–"

She went into his embrace, vibrant, ardent, flesh and blood, yielding to the searching kiss he gave her willingly. "Tell me," she murmured, "if this is real!" He gave over talking and kissed her again. All the weeks of unhappy chastity were vanished.

Not intent on where they were walking, they bumbled into the dressing room, cool and dim now, with its open windows and closed shutters. She bumped her head on the door, and the collision broke them apart.

"I don't think my poor old chaise is equal to the part," she said, when she saw where they were. She remembered an afternoon tête-a-tête with one of the French officials, come unexpectedly when Thomas was at Charlottesville. She had been mortified at such unabashed revelations then—not to mention their plain purpose—but now she saw the humor, ". . .although I understand in Paris it is all the rage, in salons." Her glance slid up, teasingly.

He colored, to her delight. "d'Anmours told you that," he complained. Perhaps a little jealousy would be no bad thing at the moment. It might forestall their former concern.

"No," she said lightly. "Mercer did." Colonel Hugh Mercer was a large beefy man, known for his exploits with the ladies. He had been the talk of Williamsburg, according to Fanny. At Thomas's thunderstruck look, she took his hand and kissed it to distract him, and she was not disappointed. He closed the dressing room door behind him, so to discourage eavesdropping from outdoors.

"Well," he said, looking down at her, "here we are." She sighed. *Oh, be my love, sweet dear! Let it be well with us, I have missed you so!* His gaze wandered down her neck and farther, for the plain, low-cut gown she wore was no bar. She had not on so much as a tucker. *Oh, it would be well. . . all would be well.*

He encountered some difficulty with the laces of her gown and swore, "Why must you wear things that lace? This bloody thing's all a-snarl."

She smiled and reached behind her. "Aren't we impatient now?" she teased. "'Tis an old gown," she said, by way of apology. "I've had it since before I knew you. Laces were of a mode then." She untangled the knot and pulled up a loop of cord at the top for his ease. He kissed her neck.

"It is ancient then," he murmured in her ear, loosing the gown. "For you have been mine forever."

"Mm." He got through the corset strings with more patience. A hurry now would but delay later.

She turned to him in her plain shift and calimanco shoes with their high heels. The additional inches made maneuvers less awkward standing up. She put her arms about his neck. "Now, sirrah. I have me a business to attend, if you would but grant me a little patient assistance. . ." She kissed him, her hand falling to the buttons of his waistcoat. He gave over. "You make a fine body servant, Patty," he murmured, and she laughed. ". . .Better than Jupiter or Bob. . . ."

Three days later Patsy Carr arrived with all her children, as per their invitation, and put an end to such midday idylls. While they were possible with only the girls and Peter to divert, doing so with Pats and her other five children, old as they were, would have required considerably more planning. By that time, anyway, the ordinary matters of life had taken them up again, and they were less inclined to closet themselves away.

She took an inventory of the house linens, after their disarray by Captain MacLeod's men, making notations of those at Bedford and Elk Hill after Thomas came back from there:

August	Monticello
1781	15 pr of sheets 9 pr of blankets
	12 beds & bolsters 13 pillows 7 counterpain
	7 matresses 3 straw beds 8 pillow cases
	12 dammask napkins 5 new virginia ditt
	4 new virginia table cloths
	bedford
	3 bed and bolsters 2 pr of sheets
	one pr of blankets at bedford
	2 beds at Elk-hill & bolsters
	2 pr of blankets 2 pr of sheets
	Sent from monticello November 1781

With Patsy's help in August and continuing throughout the autumn, she made a tally of the spinning and weaving, the yarns and stuffs preparatory to making up the winter ration of clothes for themselves and the Negroes. John Kindred came from town to do the bulk of the weaving, hired on at a hundred dollars a month for however long his aid was required. By the time they left for Tuckahoe to spend the Christmas holidays, he had made up over five hundred yards of cloth, varying from coarse tow to the finest Holland and wool.

For all the worries of how to maintain Patsy's marriageable-age girls and educate her boys—the pecuniary difficulties arising from these being the reason they had invited her to Monticello—her presence was appreciated. She was cheerful, quick, and efficient, and had no complaint with taking over the bulk of the household duties when Patty's burgeoning pregnancy and its attendant illness forced her to give them up.

It should have been a happy time, graced as they were with the promise of life and grateful that Thomas's appearance before the Assembly had not only vindicated him, but produced a commendation from the entire body as well. Cornwallis had at last succumbed to the combined forces of Generals

Washington, Green, and Lafayette at Yorktown, and the British, humiliated by such a defeat, sued for peace. Edmund Randolph had, in September, tried to convince him to yet take the post in France, averring that, once the autumn session was concluded, he would have time get there by January. But by September they knew the impossibility of that move, for she was already ill.

The enquiry was postponed until the winter session of Assembly, and were it not for his sister Patsy's presence, he would not have left her at that time for twelve days in Richmond, even to answer charges, for she was in a bad way when he left, having great trouble with her eyes and intermittent headaches. While he was away George Gilmer came to see her and gave her a better tonic, and by Thomas's return she was improved. They passed a quiet Christmastide and went home by Elk Hill.

78

Spiral

Monticello

In February those of their Negroes who had not already died of camp fever amongst the enemy were returned to their former homes, either at Elk Hill or Monticello, and were received with sufferance or not, depending on the situation of their departure. Those that were carried off and were thus merely victims were obviously more welcome than those who had taken the opportunity to run off. There were several of the latter, mostly from Elk Hill or Shadwell, but one returnee to Monticello brought with him the effect of his sojourn amongst the enemy, and brief freedom. Barnaby was glad enough to return, for by that time he was mortal sick and died of smallpox when he was not three days home.

Old Jenny, being aged with no productive way to spend her time other than as a nurse, did so for poor Barnaby before his malady was recognized for what it was. By the time Barnaby died she was already caught in the throes of the contagion herself, and being old, succumbed not long after him. They buried her in the quarter of the graveyard where were already laid Jupiter and Sukey's small Aggey and a child each of Mary Hemings's and her sister Betty Brown's.

The day was cold and raw, after several that had been warm with the promise of spring, and above Thomas's objections she insisted on going down to bid a final farewell to this dear old friend. Jenny had been old as long as she could remember. She had no idea of her age. She might have been nearly an hundred, for she had not been a girl when she came from Bermuda Hundred.

She was melancholy after Jenny's death. Jenny was Jenny. Jenny would go on forever. So she had always thought. But now Jenny was dead, and another who shared her memories was gone from her. Would they all be stript so? Oh, she took Jenny's death very hard, for she was frightened already, and death seemed to loom too near.

Not even a gossipy remark about Colonel Mercer from the Chevalier d'Anmours for her, tucked into a letter to Thomas, could rouse her from her melancholy that bleak spring, for every day she lost some ground in her sight or her mobility. As March drew on the tingling numbness in her hands and feet increased, and her headaches became worse. She could not walk comfortably from the bedroom to the hall, let alone outdoors, for any pressure on her feet was painful. Were this not bad enough, her skin was dry and papery, and her hair began to come out into the brush in alarming clumps. She felt like a hag—ugly, enormous, and utterly burthensome. She wept a good deal at no particular provocation, save that she was miserable and debilitated. She wished she'd never had a baby. She had been so well before it.

George Gilmer was out to see her several times and was as alarmed as she by the disproportionate size of the baby. Her largeness was not merely due to a sagging or distention of the muscles after so many pregnancies, as Patsy Carr kindly suggested, but the actual dimensions of the child which could be readily felt, even by her unpracticed hands. These were frightening, for Lucy had weighed ten pounds, and this child could weigh that easily, and it was only the middle of March. She had another six weeks of growing time. To her fear thus voiced, George held out for her the one hope that she always had her babies early, and recommended that she take her ease as much as she could. It was not very encouraging. She began to have nightmares again.

There was some diversion to be had in overseeing the running of the house with Patsy. Everything Patsy did was first deferred to her in its mode of execution, and afterward in the minute detailing of its accomplishment. Her particular mode was sought for the smallest task, that the house might go on as little disturbed by her illness as possible, even to the way Thomas preferred his linens folded.

At this, Patty had to laugh, though it hurt her face to do so. "Oh, Patsy, come away from there!" she said to her sister-in-law as she stood at the clothes press. "Sit down." Patsy came to where she was lolling on the bed, and sat, her face all curiosity. "What's so funny, sister?"

"You are!" Patty said, with some of her old teasing humor. "Gadding about 'yes mem' and 'no mem' and 'how do you please' like a French chambermaid! We have known each other too long and too well for that!" She shook her head. "I really don't care how things are done, or if they are done, for the matter of that."

Patsy raised her eyebrows in perfect imitation of her brother.

"Oh, don't mistake me," she hastened, laying her hand on Mrs. Carr's. "I am most grateful that you are so willing to take over housekeeping for me! But I find the details tedious these days. Let you do as is most convenient to you, and not as I would wish, for you are the one who must bear the burthen of tasks. As to Mr. Jefferson's shirts, I dareswear that if he doesn't find your manner of laying them away commodious, he will put them to his preference with nary a remark. Be easy, sweet sister Carr! You need not work yourself so hard. We are not so exacting as that."

Patsy's grey eyes were clouded. "But I feel I must do something to discharge my debt to you," she exclaimed with real anxiety. "Not only for taking us all in when I know times are as bad for you as everyone else, but for all the times in the last ten years you and my brother have rescued us or shown us some thoughtful kindness that others missed. And now you are so poorly, I cannot but wish to ease you somehow as you have done me!" Tears threatened in the lovely clear eyes of Dabney Carr's beloved, and Thomas's favorite sister. Patty could not argue with the sentiment evinced there. She leaned forward and gave her a fierce hug.

"Oh Patsy, how I love you! You are an angel, a saint." Patsy ducked her head to hide her ready blush.

Later in the afternoon, Thomas came in when she was sitting in the dressing room with Polly, listening to her recitation of nursery rhymes. In the crook of his arm he bore a bunch of narcissus. "The first of the season," he said, depositing them in her lap with a kiss. "For my beauty."

She smiled at him. "Thank you, darling. They're very sweet."

He picked up Polly, who at three-and-an-half was getting too big to be carried about, and gave her a kiss. She wanted down straightaway, and he obligingly put her on the floor.

"May I go, Mama?" she asked, bouncing on her toes.

"Yes, Poll. But don't get into mischief."

When she was gone Thomas sat down next to on her lumpy old chaise. He looked vital for the sun he had taken, all gold-touched hair and fresh complexion. He smelled of earth and fresh air and horses. Comfortable smells, which she associated with him as much as bergamot or ink.

"You look tired," he said, with a caress of her undressed hair. "How are you?"

She shrugged. "Well enough." In truth she had had a headache since before sunrise, and dinner had made her want to retch, but she would not alarm him by reporting these symptoms.

"You should not have let Polly wear you out with her prattle," he chided.

She looked up at him anxiously. It would do neither her nor Poll any good if he limited the time she was allowed to come in to play. It helped to pass the dreary hours.

"But I like to listen to her," she protested. "She amuses me. It's so dull here all alone."

He colored. "I'm sorry, sweet." He took her hand, with its mottled, puffy fingers. She could not have played the spinet now, even did she have the energy. She had lost all her dexterity. Simply writing was a trial.

"You should have sent for me," he said. "You know I would have come."

She shook her head, though the movement was painful. "No, you have work to do. I would not keep you from it."

He laid her hot hand against his cheek, his face troubled. "You're more important to me than any crop, Patty-cakes. If you are blue, you cannot be well. That you are well means more than corn or wheat or damned tobacco."

She stared at him, shocked for the atypical roughness. That last year's crop had gone utterly for taxes, thanks to Cornwallis, she knew well, but this was the first intimation she had that this year's might go badly also. By his face, he plainly did not want to be reminded of matters of harvest, so she soothed him over instead.

"You're so good to me, my love," she said. "I can't think of anyone who has had more devotion than I have from you. Any little thing I want, you bring me without complaint. And some delights I don't ask for. Like the flowers." She touched the yellow blooms in her lap.

"Patty."

She looked up at the tone of his voice, to find his amber eyes regarding her seriously. His hands were cold.

"I will admit to you no little apprehension of your situation," he swallowed, his gaze intense, "and for my part I would have you know that I am most heartily sorry. If I had been thinking—not been so selfish, you would be well now, and not in the danger you are."

His words brought a chill through her that seized her headache away instantly. "Oh no, my dear," she hastened. "No. If there was one to regret any such action, it should be me, for I played the greater part in its commencement. And I do not," she lied fervently, because of the terrible sorrow she saw in his eyes. "I do not! As to the risk," she faltered a little here, for she could not deny her fear, "I would take any such risk for you—" Her heart was thudding in her ears. "That I could give you another son." She hurried on, rising over her own fear. "I know what such would mean to you. You can't deny that Peter leaves an ache." At the moment, she wasn't sure which she meant, their own boy or Peter Carr. Perhaps it didn't matter, for both would have been true.

"Not enough that would be filled by the loss of my dearest love," he said bleakly, and she saw the green come into his eyes as his face paled. He held her hands in a painful grip. "I could not live without my love," he declared. "I would be lost as on a stormy sea. I need you. I love you. And I am afraid for what I have wrought. If you were to hate me for it, I could bear that." He touched her tumbled hair again and went on, his voice hoarse. "But every day I see such love in your eyes that it reproaches me worse than hate. I have sacrificed nothing for you but would scarce make a drop in the ocean. And you would give up your life. You make me unworthy."

He was asking her to be less than she was with him. To ease his own heart by breaking it. But she could not do that, could not cast the blame upon him for her circumstance. She had entered into it fully aware of the likely outcome, desired it, with a deep, unspeakable craving.

"We cannot undo what is done," she said softly, remembering now all the times he had cast himself upon her bosom to reveal regrets about past actions done in haste and passion. "Lamenting what cannot be changed is only so many wasted tears." She saw her own great fault here, too. She had wasted too much of the precious present in lapsing after the past. She would do it no more. Whatever befell from this moment, there would only be the present, with no regret for the past nor anxiety for the future. She felt clear, and loving, and freed.

She touched his face, marked as it was by silent tears, loving him better than she had even thought possible in all their private hours.

"Tom." She kissed him. "My beloved dear. Whatever comes, let us not waste the time we have. Be with me, love me. With no regrets. That is the only sacrifice I have ever asked of you. And I have yet to find disappointment in its fulfillment." She kissed him again, fervently, her cheeks wet with his tears. His arms went round her, and they crushed the flowers. But she didn't care. She didn't care at all.

Her eyes troubled her greatly in the next weeks, though she did the best she could to disguise the effects, lazing about with the shutters closed in the dressing room and avoiding reading by having Patsy or one of the Carr girls read to her. But the evidence was clear enough in her accounts book, had anyone cared to look there.

> April 5th 1782
> now in the house unhackle flax & hemp
> 86 lb of course flax   31 lb of fine ditt
> 12 lb of fine hemp
> 70 lb of cotten in the seed   13 lb of picked ditto

She looked forward to the middle of the month, when by every past indication, she might begin to expect some sign of the baby's advent. It would be good to have the ordeal done with. Resolutely, she did not allow herself to ponder the possible outcomes. She would be cheerful. She would be cheerful, and well. And well. She accepted George Gilmer's new mixture for her gladly and did all that she was bidden by him, that she might be well again by the time of the child's birth.

By the end of the week she was somewhat better—less dropsical, any-way—and could walk outside again to sit in the sun, if she remembered to bring her spectacles. There was the diversion, too, of a visit from Rochambeau's erudite general, the Chevalier Chastellux, who had come from Williamsburg specifically to see Thomas.

Le Chevalier
Monticello

Jean-François, le Chevalier de Chastellux, had been expected since they received Carlo Bellini's letter of the eighth. This eminent adjunctant of the Commandant Rochambeau was far more than a military man. A fellow of the French Academy, he was versed in every art and science of that body: a surpassing linguist who could move with ease from one translation of the ancient authors to another. He was an avid architect and knew more than a smattering on the subject of horticulture. Withal, a perfectly diverting visitor. He arrived in the late afternoon with his cortege of lieutenants, who were taking the tour along with him, coming up the mountain at a leisurely pace, so that they were apprised of his arrival some quarter-hour before he actually appeared.

Thomas himself had only just returned from Charlottesville and must have just missed catching sight of him in the road, for he was hardly off his horse when word came up of a visitor. The chevalier, as it happened, had stopped at the mill at Shadwell to inspect the damage made there by Tarleton's dragoons, so narrowly missed his host. In the parlor, bedlam ensued, for she and Patsy Carr had been cutting and sewing for most of the day with Patsy's girls and Mary Garth. Shirts, towels, linen, and petticoats all were swept up and whisked away upstairs for the nonce. They scarce had time to compose themselves, that they might not appear as though they had spent the last quarter-hour in helter-skelter panic.

Thomas came through the narrow, white-painted hall with its unfinished ornamentation over the door ahead of the Frenchman's train, and his anxious expression melted at their peaceable calm. It was a measure of the sisterhood between her and Patsy that they could organize themselves on such short notice. At Buck Island, as Patsy often complained, it was bedlam continually. Lucy was a hopeless manageress, especially since Charles's mother died. Patty turned her gaze upon their guest.

Chastellux was a man of the middle height, with a broad forehead and the look of an intellectual. She was relieved that he was not a beau. Another Mercer she had not the health or wit to combat. Chastellux was all old-fashioned gallantry and soft good manners. He bowed before her, taking up her proffered hand. "Madame Jefferson."

She bestowed a smile on him because his brown eyes were so warm. "Chevalier, welcome to Monticello," she said in French and watched his eyes come alight. "I hope you will consider our home as your own."

He bowed again. "Thank you, Madame." He moved on to Patsy.

She was introduced to each of his five men in turn, none of whom spoke the least English, and they were all delighted that they could speak with her—with anyone new not themselves—and she was happy to oblige them.

Martin brought in wine, and they spent the time until supper first in listening to the chevalier's raptures of the house as he came up from the east and his overwhelmed impressions of its finesse once approached, and afterward hearing further in the same vein when Thomas had taken him on a tour of the house.

Chastellux's men were happy to tag along on a tour of the grounds and neighborhood the next day, but they begged off an opportunity to pore over the plans for the house with them, instead preferring to walk down to the lake at Tufton before dinner. They had been cooped up in Williamsburg the last five months and had had quite enough of indoors for the nonce. The smooth fields and rambling woods, the garden and the vineyards entranced them. Taking a servant along that they should not get lost, they departed, not to return until half-past five with the news that they had met with Colonel Lewis and had their dinner at his house.

In the evening after supper Patty was feeling rather tired, for they had finished the sewing left undone from the day before, and her eyes hurt. She had not been gone five minutes when Thomas appeared behind her. He put his hands on her shoulders as she sat at her table in the dressing room removing the pins from her hair. She wished she'd not sent Nance off to her leisure. Nance was always so good brushing out her hair. She could not ask Thomas now, with a roomful of guests beyond.

"Are you well?" he asked.

She looked up at him through the glass.

"Tired, but I know that's not what you mean." She reached for his hand on her right shoulder. "There's nothing that way, sweeting. Not the merest twinge. I should tell you if there was, believe me. Go on and enjoy our friends, and don't fret about me. I shall make an early night."

"If you're certain," he said. His color washed and faded.

She smiled, her eyes mild and brown. "I am. Good night."

"Good night, Patty-patt." He bent and kissed her, and then retreated to the parlor, but his gaze was still troubled.

In the morning Thomas was yet asleep when she awoke at half-past six. She shook her head, smiling. They must have stayed up very late. She should tell Patsy to have Queenie delay breakfast a little. Half an hour, perhaps; not an hour. That would make the children cross. She kissed Thomas, but he was far gone from her, so she pushed her hair back and rose to dress.

She was opening the shutters in the dressing room when he came in yawning at half-past seven. "Did I wake you?" She thought she had closed the adjoining door. He shook his head. She smiled at his haggard face. "Poor dear. . . What time did you all get to bed?"

He frowned a little. "Four, five? I don't recall. It was very early." She stared at him. Even for him, this was unusual.

"What were you talking about all that time?"

He ran a hand through his hair and raised a rueful eyebrow at her. "What were we not. . . " He came and put his arms around her. "But mostly Ossian."

"Ah!" The mystery began to fade. If the chevalier was a devotee of Ossian, she was surprised they had gone to bed at all.

"He made a quotation '. . .Our fathers met in battle, because they loved the strife of spears. But often did they feast in the hall, and send round the joy of the shell. Let thy face brighten with gladness, and thine ear delight in the harp. Dreadful as the storm of the ocean, thou hast poured thy valor forth; thy voice has been like the voice of thousands when they engaged in war. . . .'"

She knew the book, for they had read it often:

> *in peace thou art the gale of spring; in war the mountain storm*
> *take now my hand in friendship, king of echoing Selma!*
> *let thy bards mourn those who fell.*
> *let Erin give the sons of Lochlann to earth.*
> *raise high the mossy stones of their fame:*
> *that the children of the north hereafter may behold the place*
> *   where their fathers fought.*
> *the hunter may say, when he leans on a mossy tomb*
> *Here Fingal and Swaran fought, the heroes of other years*
> *thus hereafter shall he say, and our fame shall last for ever*
> *"Swaran," said the king of hills, "to day our fame is greatest*
> *We shall pass away like a dream. No sound will remain in*
> * our fields of war. Our tombs shall be lost in the heath. The*
> *hunter shall not know the place of our rest. Our names may*
> *be heard in song. What avails it, when our strength hath*
> * ceased? O Ossian, Carril, and Ullin! you know of heroes that*
> *are no more. Give us the song of other years. Let the night*
> *pass away on the sound, and morning return with joy."*

Thomas's voice came back to her, ". . .and none of his men know whereof he spoke." He shook his head, laughing. "His poor captain. . . Pouloud, took the worst wrath, for he is apparently from Armorica. . . my French is not so good, you'll have to ask him." Armorica. Old Brittany. Land of Geoffrey Plantagenet. . . and Launcelot. Ah! the connection came; they were supposed to be Celts. Fellows with Ossian, in spirit if not in blood.

"I will," she said, "after breakfast."

He let go of her to wander into the bedroom, but stopped at the door. "Oh, about that: I promised to take the general and his men to the Indian mound today." She cast a despairing glance out the windows. "But it's raining!"

He only shrugged.

He kept his promise and took the chevalier out to the burial mound when it cleared a little. Here he had found several hundred bones lying in every direction of the compass, some whole skeletons, but more in pieces. They were of small and large diameter, so plainly this was not a burial place of warriors only. There were skulls lodged carefully in niches in the close walls, indicative that it was neither the site of a hasty mass burial. There were few grave goods, such as he had been led to believe the Indians hereabouts had left out with their dead, though whether this was the result of robbery he did not know, for the mound had been broken into before his advent.

Chastellux's men professed no wish to go look at old bones, even aboriginal ones, and so it was that in the afternoon she found time to speak a word with the Breton captain; or rather, he found the courage to speak a private word with her.

He approached her as she sat on the sofa in the parlor, full of blushes. "Pardon, Madame." He made a little bow.

She smiled at him. "Captain. How fortuitous! I was just on the point of going to seek you out." He blushed further at this. He had a fair skin and face unmarked by life, though he was a soldier. He must be very young indeed. "Please," she amended, "do not be discomfited. How may I aid you?" He and the others slept out in the little house. Perhaps they wanted linen.

He paused. "May I sit?" She nodded, and he sat on the very edge of the nearest chair and regarded her earnestly. ". . .Madame, last evening your husband and the general had a book. . ." He shook his head. "I do not remember the name. Oh, Madame, might I trouble you to allow me to read this book, if only while I am here? I never heard the like of such words, and mayhap, I thought, it would help me to improve my English."

He was so sweet. She smiled at him. "I can do better than a loan of a book, sir, for I own a copy myself, which I would be happy to bestow upon you."

His eyes grew wide and he shook his head violently. "Oh no, Madame! I could not ask it! Not such a treasure—"

"You did not ask it," she murmured, with a little smile. "Please, I insist." She rang the bell beside her and Martin appeared instantly. "Martin, will you have Nance fetch a book to me? My father's *Poems of Ossian*. It's on the table in the library, I think."

"Yas'm." Martin bowed, but he rolled his eyes. She could see him thinking what a damned book it was, for breakfast had been an hour late after all.

When the book was brought, she took up pen and ink and inscribed the cover below her father's neat hand. *To Captain Pouloud from the Jeffersons, 1782.* She looked up at him.

"May I ask you a personal question?"

He blushed. "Madame?"

"What does Pouloud mean?" She shook her head. "I do not recognize it." He bowed his head, turning white and red. Finally he admitted, "It is Brezhoneg, Madame. Breton. . . . It means—" He paused and searched for the English word, "cook, I think as you say in English." He smiled a little, ruefully. "A bad cook." His hands made picture circles. "Lumpy porridge, you know, that sort of thing. . . But," he hastened. "I am not, nor ever have been, our cook."

She laughed. "I believe you, sir!"

The afternoon of the next day Chastellux and his men set out for the mountains and the Natural Bridge in Rockbridge County, about 150 miles to the southwest. Thomas rode with them as far as Rockfish to give them instructions on how to reach the bridge from Staunton. He returned home again that night tired from the ride but pleased for the interlude.

80

Gold to Ayerie Thinnesse Beat

Monticello

When she passed her typical week-early date with no sign of her confinement's onset, she was surprised but not overly concerned. It looked as though she might actually go to term with this baby. And since she had lost some of her puffiness, George was hopeful that the child might not be as large as previously feared—perhaps no larger than Lucy. Well, she had done that once. She could do it again.

She was feeling much better since the Chevalier's visit and was able to take up some of the sewing she had left off. On the first of May, she made a notation in her accounts book that Mr. Kindred had woven "5 yds of fine mixt cloth for a coat: mr Jefferson."

This, a lovely mulberry colored cotton on a linen warp, she cut that day and began to stitch to pass the time. She had already made up several shifts for Patsy, leaving the finishing work to her improving fingers, and had done her share of the mort of cutting clothing rations for the Negroes, for that was a task she could do sitting down.

She had nearly a week to wait before her labor began, by which time all that wanted on Thomas's coat were the buttonholes cut and buttons sewn on. It was a fine narrow coat of the Italian style with narrow sleeves and the skirts curving away from the front, and so slender they could scarce be called skirts at all.

In the morning of May sixth her labor began as it always did, this time after breakfast. She had naught but weak and gentle cramps, hardly pains, and she hoped fervently that this one might be easy as Peter's had been. The waters broke at noon, and suddenly things got very hard. All her hard-won courage and complacency rapidly deserted her, and she was frightened again for her life.

George was sent for, but he was away from his house on a call. Lucy sent a servant to round him up and hasten him along as soon as possible. That was about dinner time, by which time the house was in a complete upheaval, fetching in and out every ministration imaginable to ease her fear and pain. Patsy Carr suggested Madeira, or better, brandy, for it had eased her own confinements, and quickly that was brought. But it made her retch and was thus wasted.

Thomas sat with her while George investigated matters, letting her clutch his hands during the process and letting her weep on his shoulder after, when Gilmer unhappily announced that things were a long way from happening.

She was seized with fear and immediately broke into a fever which they were at pains to reduce. By evening George dosed her with Peruvian bark, and afterwards laudanum for the unbearable clamping down the former wrought. She wept between times and would not be diverted by talking or cool cloths or anything they endeavored. At some point, she gave over and slept from sheer exhaustion, only to be wakened from her peace by the dread reality of her nightmare coming true.

At the end of it this time, instead of her spiraling descent into an engulfing blackness, she had a vision of her mother, young and beautiful, younger than she. She stood with her arms outstretched in the midst of a grey fog that receded around her, smiling a beaming welcome that was more frightening than the blackness, for she knew what it meant. She awoke with a shriek in the middle of a pang.

Patsy was there, and Betty, bending over her, hushing, soothing her, like a child. The room was grey with the light of early morning, and Thomas and the doctor were nowhere to be seen.

"Please," she said, and did not recognize the croaking voice for her own.

Patsy held her hand. "What, sweet? What do you want, Patt?"

She closed her eyes again. "Mr. Jefferson. Where is he?"

"He's sleepin' lamby," Betty murmured in a soothing voice that she had not heard in 20 years. "Over in the'm next room. He was up wi' you all night. You's safe here wi' us, Miss Patty. We'll look after you a while."

"Mm." She swallowed but her throat was dry. "Could I have some water?"

"Sure, honey." This was Patsy. The water was brought, and this time she kept it down.

The long day passed once more into evening, and George returned to look in on her. She had made more progress, but still had a little way to go. She was so drugged that she hardly cared and was unheeding of the conversation afterward going on in the dressing room. They could have said she was dying, and she would not have cared.

From that carefree space, she was hurtled back into her body as by a siege of mortar fire. Every nerve was ablaze at the unexpected assault, and she pulled herself up off the bed with a strength she didn't know she had. She was suddenly bolt upright and wide awake, marshalling every force against the barrage that came with now cunning swiftness. It was half-after eleven o'clock, and the enemy made its long-anticipated foray out of the darkness.

As a siege, it did not last long and yet it lasted forever. George had given over the truce of the sheet and was sweating and swearing on her dainty footstool at her feet, a truculent general directing the advance and retreat of a force not at his command but mutinous, resorting to the use of entrenchments to seize the field. But to little avail. She shuddered under his blandishments, bare of help or aid save that of Thomas's arms about her as he sat behind her on the bed, literally holding her up through the worst moments. She tried her best to maintain her composure, not to cry out against the mounting pressure and considerable pain as her supposed deliverer forced from her that which she could not yield.

She was on fire. Everything was burning, and from a far distance she saw before she felt coming the final white-hot salvo that she could not stand against. It advanced with sickening slowness until it was upon her, engulfing her. She cried out against it in a shriek that rent the house, and fainted away.

She saw the scene as if from the outside and was at first confused, but became fascinated at George's maneuvers, never having see them from firsthand. She had no more of her former pain and watched the tumult in the room with a relieved sense of detachment. It was better than laudanum, for she was not fuzzy-headed.

"Patty!" Thomas cried, holding her in his arms. She wanted to tell him that she was well, not to fear, but she owned no power to speak to him.

"Get that scissors over here!" George was crying hoarsely to Betty for the blunt instrument he had cast aside. "Goddamn it, on the double quick! That there!" He took them up from her and wasted no time on niceties, for the infant's shoulders would not come. "Get out of here," he growled and didn't bother to see if she left. He spoke in terse sentences, all his Virginia softness gone in the brisk tones of Edinburgh.

"Jefferson! I need your help! Put her down, she's only fainted. Believe that I have a pulse. Damn it man, look sharp! I can't get the shoulder out— Would you lose them both? Push there when I say—" He reached in with both hands in an effort to loosen the upper shoulder from behind the pubic bone. The baby's head was purple and darkening. "Now!" But there was no dislodging the child. It was simply too big. He rubbed his face on his shoulder with his elbow upraised awkwardly, for he could hardly see for the sweat pouring. Death was scented in the room but he would not yield to it. Not one or the other if he could help it, and by God, he could. . . . How was it that she knew his thoughts?

"I have to break the clavicle," he spat shortly, glancing up. Thomas's face was ashen. "It's the only way!" he shouted. "Come here and give us a hand." In a moment he made some maneuver, the clavicle collapsed and he slid his fingers under the small armpit and pulled the baby out.

She was a long, big baby with a robust body, covered in sticky green-blackness and queer looking with the dragging shoulder. She gave a feeble wail at the cooler air, sneezed, and began to take on a less purple color. George severed the navel string and handed her over to her father.

"Bind that," he said of the shoulder, and turned his attentions to her body once more.

"Good God, George!" Thomas exclaimed in consternation. "She must weigh twenty pounds!"

So was Lucy Elizabeth born, at one o'clock a.m. on the eighth day of May, 1782. When she was weighed the next day, the tally came in at fifteen pounds and six ounces.

She came to herself very slowly. She had moments when she thought she might be awake, but all the room was so grey and blazing cold she could not be certain. She was swept along on the tide of the wind-blown ocean without an anchor, at some times more afloat than others. Hero was swimming valiantly towards her fast-fading Leander. But the Fates and the treacherous waters of the Hellespont appeared against them. She struggled onward, unwilling to submit, and at last such determination found small favor with the gods. Even so, it was a week or better before she finally reached the friendly shore.

June was nearly on them by the time she was well enough to sit up on the pillows and have a look at her daughter. Her first words were for Thomas, his the first face she sought, and his the first voice she heard.

"O thank God, darling!" he cried in her ear, engulfing her in his warm embrace. He rained tears and kisses upon her, and she was weakly grateful, bewildered at the response. He smelled comfortingly of ink and bergamot, and some part of her mind registered that he had been with her all along, only she couldn't reach him.

"What happened?" she rasped. "I feel so—" Her hand ranged slowly to encounter only sharp hipbone and she remembered. The baby.

"She's fine, sweet," he said to her. "Just fine. Bett will bring her in when you're better. I promise. Patty!" He kissed her forehead fervently. "Thank God the fever's broke."

Her mother had come to her, holding out her hands, smiling in all her young beauty. She had beckoned her, and now she knew why. But she had not died her mother's death. She slept again, safe in Thomas's arms.

Lucy was the biggest, fattest baby she had ever seen, and she could scarce believe that she was but three weeks old, let alone that she had given birth to her. She was as large as six-month babies! She had a shock of straight, fine black hair as Patsy's had been, enormous blue eyes, and a ready smile. Nannie brought her in rather than Betty. Nannie, who had been at the house a fortnight already without her knowing. Patty burst into tears at the sight of her. "O Nancy! O, my baby! O come and let me see you both!"

She made her reacquaintance with Patsy and Polly. Though it had been but three weeks, Polly seemed to have grown half a head and her speech was no longer babyish, but a young child's.

"Mama, you tell Sam t' stop teasing me! He don't listen to his Ma." Sam was Patsy Carr's middle boy, six years older than Polly.

She smiled, ruffling the dark hair. "I will, Poll."

Patsy was not to be credited. Under the influence of her Carr cousins, young ladies all, she had quite blossomed. She came into the room decorously, wearing a neat starched indoor cap and a frilly transparent apron, un-recognizable from the coltish, avid little girl she had once been.

"Why Pats," she declared in true pleasure, "you're beautiful! Come here, sweeting, and kiss me. I have missed my bud."

Patsy came and kissed her gently, her eyes full of tears. "O, Mama, I love you," she said mournfully. "I'm so glad you're all right!" She was old enough now to understand the tragedy so narrowly avoided.

But such gladnesses proved very temporary, for no sooner did June's hot weather dawn than she was stricken with her old complaint more virulently than ever before. Its course was swift and sharp, and within a week she vomited up anything they tried to feed her. She was reduced to broth alone, and sometimes not that. George's concoctions only made her sick, although they were forced on her with annoying regularity. When she tried once to get up, that she might not suffer the indignity of assistance at a chamber pot, she was so weak and dizzy that she nearly fainted. After that she gave herself over to her nurses' ministrations, more or less uncomplainingly.

Nancy left at the end of July, to be replaced by Lisbet. Lisbet brought her own baby from Chesterfield, for she was nursing her and would not leave her to a wet nurse. The baby, also Lucy, was but a week older than Lucy Elizabeth, and Aunty Eppes was more than happy to take over her feeding as well.

But her best nurse was Thomas. All through the turgid, painful summer he was beside her, never ranging farther than the confines of the house, and often not beyond their suite of rooms. He was a patient angel with all her many complaints and mortifying incontinencies. No matter the care required, he was never disgusted by her, as she was too often of herself. The sweetish envelopment of her sickness offended her. Yet he was ever-gentle, humoring her annoyances, coaxing her to take a bit of broth or tincture, amusing her dull hours, comforting her melancholia, loving her with a yet tender and lover-like devotion that she could only weep at for its anguishing memories.

August waned and the weather turned cooler, with thundery showers in the afternoons; Indian summer had returned. One day, late on in the month, she noticed that the copper beech outside the window opposite had begun its gradual change to a rusty scarlet. Autumn's herald. For seven years, the turning of this tree's foliage had meant autumn to her, and with it she remembered all their courting days, and especially one long ago on the banks of the James. Oh, how sweet was the memory of that crisp clear day when they had dallied carefree in the seed-sprung grasses! Life had held such promise then.

It was a promise held but not delivered by the exigencies of fate. Fate had been wicked cruel, laughing in the face of their dearest hopes, snatching from them nearly every pledge they set forth, robbing her of her strength, moreover of her will, for she had no heart to continue thus forever battling against bewildering misfortune. Lucy's birth had stripped that from her. As the life withered slowly from the tree beyond, so too she could feel her strength ebbing. With every day, that which she had done the day before was more difficult, more taxing, and she knew now that the days of her life ran short.

She turned her head and looked to where Thomas was working. For nearly four months he had not moved from their three rooms. He was always within her sight. Dear as that was, she knew he was spent. She regarded his clean, sharp profile. The Randolph nobility was there, graceful, delicate, speaking generations of gentle birth. She found him no less handsome now than the first day they met. But he was worn. It shewed in the lines about his eyes and his pallor. Where was that creeping, telling flush she loved so well, that told her better than words his tender regard? It was gone. It had been driven from him in the last troubling months, fretting over her. She felt a spasm of pity and grief for him.

"Thomas," she called, and her voice crackled. He was beside her in an instant.

"Yes, my sweet?" He sat beside her on the bed and smoothed back her hair. The familiar gesture nearly undid her. She held up her hand, laying it upon his cheek. He took it and kissed the palm. Tears welled in her eyes.

"Ah!" she cried, unable to speak for sentiment. She searched his face and saw all the old love written there. "Oh Tom, oh my beloved. . . ." Speech was an effort, and she paused. "How good you are to me. . . staying here thus. . . but you are wan, my dear. . . and I would not have you. . . fall ill. . . for my sake." She raised her head a little. "Look, see, the beech is turning!" She looked back at him. "Our autumn. . . . . Do you remember—"

"Yes!" he said instantly, softly, still holding her hand. "I do. How could I forget?" He smiled. "Every year I am recalled to it."

"You should go," she directed. ". . . You should go. . . and enjoy it. . . go for a ride. . . Caract—" She paused and took a deep breath, for the effort of speech had brought on her breathlessness. "Caractacus must think. . . you've abandoned him."

"I won't leave you," he insisted.

Tears spilled over and she wept weakly. She needed to cry, but could not, would not, in front of him. He was so patient and hopeful, so kind when she was thus helpless and disgusting to herself. She could not shatter that with the lamentations that crowded in her bosom against unkind fate. "Oh, *please,*" she begged, her voice raw with grief. "For my sake. . . It would please me. . . Please, my darling?"

She gazed up at him with brimming eyes, willing that he should say yes, that he should let her have the time to unburthen herself in grief without hurting him.

"Very well," he agreed at last, with a sigh. "But only for half an hour," he cautioned. "And I'll have Betsy come and sit with you."

She clasped his hand. "Oh no," she said quickly as she could, and he frowned a bit. "I'll just rest. . ." she amended, for she saw suspicion in his glance. "I promise." He acceded.

"Mind you do," he said with some of his old teasing spirit, "for I know you, my vixen." He kissed her forehead. "I'll be back before you're asleep," he vowed, and she nodded, watching him go to the clothes press for his boots.

When he was well gone, she turned over into the pillows and uttered a long, inarticulate cry, and gave vent to her anger and disappointment, her fear and sorrow, in choking loud wrenching sobs. She lost all sense of time or place and was at one with her grief. She wept, she swore, she pleaded with God for his injustice, and in the end lay sniffling and gasping on the pillows, for the outburst had cost her much.

The pain was in her chest again, the vague, burning pain that came on her with exertion, and she clenched her hands in the blankets against it, refusing to cry out. She did not want Lisbet here, nor Patsy neither. The burning grew until it was a vise-like constriction, and she arched against it. It was ten times worse than childbirth, for it came without warning. When it abated she was trembling, drenched in sweat, and disoriented.

She drowsed a little, and in that time, the words from Donne came to her, his valediction forbidding mourning. She woke with a start and reached for the book on the table. Thumbing the pages, she came to the poem, and read with difficulty through her unclear vision:

> . . .So let us melt, and make no noise,
>   No tear-floods, nor sigh tempests move,
>   Twere prophanation of our joyes
>   To tell the layetie our love.
> . . . Dull sublunary lovers love
>   (Whose soule is sense) cannot admit
>   Absence, because it doth remove
>   Those things which elemented it.

But we by a love so much refin'd,
    That we ourselves know not what it is,
Inter-assuréd of the mind,
    Care lesse, eyes, lips, and hands to misse.

Our two soules therefore, which are one,
    Though I must goe, endure not yet
A breach, but an expansion,
    Like gold to ayerie thinnesse beat.

If they are two, they are two so
    As stiffe twin compasses are two;
Thy soule the fixt foot, makes no show
    To move, but doth, if the other doe.

And though it in the center sit,
    Yet when the other far doth rome,
It leans, and harkens after it,
    And grows erect as that comes home.

Such wilt thou be to mee, who must
    Like t'other foot, obliquely runne;
Thy firmness makes my circle just,
    And makes me end, where I begunne.

She lay the book down on its face and wept a little, for it was truth indeed that the pain of leaving life was the pain of leaving Thomas. He was all her life: its course, its barque, its journey's end, and time was slipping away too fast. There was much she had never said, much they had never done, and oh God, she wanted it all back, all the days and hours of their life that were missed in sickness and separation, in wretched futile politicking where he was frustrated by public unregard. She wanted back their glad courting days and the soft, sweet hours that none could tell when they were alone and truly one. They would never come again, and she wept like a child for their loss. She did not want to die.

She full well understood now Yorrick's lament to his sweet Jenny. She breathed it, lived it, dear God. She was trembling and hiccoughing, but she reached for her pen and a scrap of paper, torn from the back of Donne, and wrote, with an unsteady hand:

time wastes too fast—every letter
I trace tells me with what rapidity
life follows my pen, the days and hours
of it are flying over our heads, like
clouds on a windy day, never to return—
more every thing presses on—

She dropped the pen, leaving the scrap of paper where it lay, and turned her face into the pillows, weeping. She could not finish it, she could not write the last words, she would not admit the end until the end came and she was too overcome to resist. Shortly she fell asleep, exhausted from the efforts of reading and writing.

81

Torn From Him

Monticello

A few days later Lisbet sat with her in the late morning. Thomas was asleep in the dressing room. It had been his habit, since the afternoon he went riding at her insistence, to sit up with her all night, not allowing his sister or hers to wear themselves out thus. It was raining and dreary, with the wind hastening newly decayed leaves from the trees. She had not the strength or sight left to read a book since Donne; the effort to concentrate was too great. All was a dancing blur before her eyes, and it made her eyeballs hurt. She spent her days drifting in and out, sleeping a good deal, and being plagued by memories when she was not. They gave her laudanum, which increased her fuzziness, but the pain in her chest had subsided, and the hazy half-world she inhabited was not entirely unpleasant.

She opened her eyes and said to Betsy, "Would you. . . read to me, dear?"

Lisbet put down her sewing. "What do you want me to read, Patt?" She thought for a moment. "The prayer book," she said at last. "Bathurst's prayer book. . . It's on the. . . table." She did not miss the paling of Lisbet's face, for Lisbet had been witness to the former scene, but she made no comment. The book was fetched and Lisbet opened it to the psaltery.

"Je suis sans la morte. . ." she read. Patty held up her hand a little.

"Not that," she said. "The blessings for the dead. . . . He wanted me to read them. I can't. . . now. Read them for me, Bets—"

Lisbet was weeping. "Patty, I can't—"

"You must!"

Betsy nodded and read, haltingly, and to Patty the words and the day floated back with perfect clarity. It was another September day, and the echoing phrases rang in her ears then as now:

> Hearken, O God, to my prayer; turn not away from my pleading;
> merciful God, who bestowed the gifts of salvation and everlasting
> life upon mankind. . . comfort this soul which you have created. . .
> at the hour of death. . . that. . . he may be brought by your angels
> before you. . . . Have pity on me, O Lord, for I am languishing. . . I

am in distress; with sorrow my eye is consumed; my soul also. . . my strength has failed through affliction. . . let my cry come to you. . . In God my heart trusts. . . my song I will give him in thanks.

O God, by your will the span of our lives is measured. . . accept the prayers we offer you in behalf of your servant. . . . Let your face shine upon your servant. . . have compassion. . . and strengthen him by your grace. May the enemy not triumph over him at the hour of death, but rather may he be brought to everlasting life in the company of your angels—

Lisbet broke off. "I can't read the rest of the page," she cried. "It's all blotted—"

"I know," Patty nodded, sighing. He would rest now, and so could she, having discharged the duty. She closed her eyes, her hand still in her sister's.

"Thank you, Bets," she murmured, and drifted off to sleep.

Three days later in the middle of the night she was awakened by the burning in her chest and a suffocating lapse of breath. Before retiring she had refused their usual dose of laudanum with such vigor that it was omitted. In her sleep she had slipped down so that she was lying nearly flat, and now the terrible constriction began with greater force than she ever remembered it. She broke out in a fevered sweat, nausea overcoming her, and her whole body revolted against this attack. She gasped, choking, feeling lost in a swirling, enclosing red-black darkness. She flung out her arm, but was unable to raise herself sufficiently to stop the giddiness. The pain continued, searing, encompassing, engulfing her, and she cried Thomas's name in a strangled voice before she began to retch.

When she came to herself again, Thomas's face swam above her. He held her in his lap in the chair while Betsy changed the bed.

"Tom—" her voice was hardly a whisper. He kissed her forehead.

"Hush, sweet," he murmured. "Rest." She closed her eyes again, feeling safe with him. Thomas would take care of her.

When she woke again the sun was up, and she squinted against the brightness and the cloud before her eyes. "She's awake," she heard someone say, and she looked up into Thomas's haggard face. Though its lineaments were indistinct to her, she was intimate with the heart behind the eyes, and she saw that he was suffering.

"What happened?" Her voice came out a croaking whisper. He smiled at her, a tender, intimate smile that she knew well from curtained beds and birth mornings. He smoothed her hair.

"Nothing, sweet," he whispered, and kissed her. "I love you, Patty." She was held close in his arms and felt his trembling. She remembered something having happened in the night, in a dream, but could not recollect what.

She smiled a little, her face feeling heavy. "I love you too, Thomas. . . I thought. . ."

She remembered what had happened in her dream, that it was not a dream. She had been struck as if by an iron weight and went away, to The Forest. She stood in the distillery and spoke to her father for a time, before being called away. She went down to the river, and over at Eppes's landing her mother was waiting for her, holding Jack's hand. But she could not secure a boat to cross. The army had commandeered them all.

"What, sweet?" Thomas's voice above her brought her back.

"I went away," she said, surprised at how difficult it was to speak. She'd had no trouble with her father. "But I couldn't. . . get a boat." He said nothing, but shook, and his tears fell as rain upon her face. *Why was he weeping?* They could do nothing about Peter. It was a gamble of fate, Dr. Gilmer had said so. They were not to hold themselves responsible. No! It was not Peter! She struggled up in fear against the knowledge that hit her like a blow: it was not Peter! They waited for her! She cried out sharply, but there was hardly a sound in the room.

"Thomas, I don't want to die!" She clung to him, feeling his heart pounding beneath her ear while he wept incoherently, rocking her in his arms. Sweet life! Her beloved dear! Why must she leave him? There was so much to do. *I want to go to France! I want to finish this house, to see our girls married, to have a son; I want to play my spinet, and dig the garden, and walk in the rain, and drown again in the depths of my lover's eyes when all boundaries between flesh and spirit are dissolved. I want to laugh, I want to run, I want to live!* She was weeping, but she had no tears left in her wasted body. Her grief was as a newborn babe's, and like a babe's it wore her out, and she slept in Thomas's arms as she had done so often before, safe and warm.

She fell to dreaming again, and was standing in the bedroom she shared with Lisbet as a girl. Mary Cocke, her father's wife, stood before her, her fair face ruddy with emotion, scolding her roundly for her stubbornness.

"You must go," she was saying, in strident tones. "You've kept your father waiting long enough with your nonsense, and I will have no more of it, do you hear?" She was shaken by the shoulders until her teeth rattled. "You are a willful, stubborn, sneaking, thoroughly bad child, and your Papa is well right not to love you!" She looked up at her stepmother, feeling the world dissolve around her. Great tears started in her eyes and spilled over.

"My Papa does not love me?" she murmured in a small, hurt voice. She cried, desolate, until she was hiccoughing, and promised in an unsteady, hiccoughing small voice, "I'll go, I'll be good, I'll go now. I want my Papa to love me! I'll be good, I'll go—" She ran to the door, flinging it open, and her father was standing there. She leapt into his arms, and woke, shuddering, to find herself in Thomas's close embrace.

"Hush, love," he whispered to her. "Hush love, my Patty. It's all right. Wake up, dear. I do love you. I shall always love you." She stirred. It was fully daylight now, and the light in the room was clear and warm. Her stomach felt acid.

"I—" she began.

"She's going to be sick," Lisbet said quickly and she was grateful for the attention.

Her head was much clearer after that, and the ringing in her ears had stopped. She leaned against Thomas's shoulder, watching the dust motes swirl in the middle distance. The girls. She needed to see the girls before her strength left her entirely and she was unable to speak. She roused herself a little.

"Please—" The croak that emerged was not her voice; it was rasping, ruined, belonging to a crone. She stopped in shock. A hand came into the field of her vision and removed the warm cloth on her head, replacing it with a cool one. It was much better, for she was burning.

"What do you need, dear?" It was Thomas's quiet voice, gentle, solicitous as always. Shadow figures moved about the room beyond her clouded sight, and she could not make them out.

"My baby. . . ." she said. "I want to see my baby."

"She's right here," she heard Lisbet say.

"I can't—"

"Bring her here," Thomas directed. She moved her hand a little, reaching for his in gratitude. He had always anticipated her every desire and fulfilled it. He was motherly in his care, not only of her, but the children as well. Lisbet came over with baby Lucy and held her low by the bed as she knelt. Lucy's dark hair was gone. She reached out her hand to the little fair head and found fine blonde fuzz. The great dark hazel eyes gazed back at her unblinkingly.

"My baby," she smiled. "My sweet Lucy. My little girl. I love you!"

Lucy turned her head and pulled her thumb into her mouth.

"No, baby," Lisbet said, and removed her.

"Please—" She took a deep breath. Her chest hurt again. "Don't. . . take her away. I shall not. . . see her again." The baby was brought back within her range of sight. Slowly, painfully, for it hurt to raise her arm so much, she ran her hand along Lucy's little arms and legs. She stroked her hair, her cheek, under her fat little chin. She wanted to hold her, but knew she could not, and the thought of Lucy's weight on her chest made it ache. Yet she had not held her, not in many weeks, and she wanted the feel of that soft little body against her own one last time. "Bring her near me," she said.

Oh, how sweet it was to feel the vibrancy of her little baby against her and to breathe in her soft, warm baby smell. She had not lost the smell of a tiny baby, though she was—what?—four months was it nearly now? Lucy began to squirm, so they took her away, but her face was replaced by Polly's great solemn eyes not six inches from her.

"Mama?"

She smiled. "Yes, Poll?"

"Why are you going away, Mama? Don't you love Polly no more?"

She burst into tears and wept with aching dryness. "Oh, Polly!" She coughed, turning her head minutely, caught her breath with difficulty, and said, "No, baby! Mama loves you more. . . than she ever did. Mama's just sick, honey. . . like old Jenny. . . . You 'member old Jenny?"

"Yes Mama."

"Well, you 'member. . . how old Jenny. . . had to go 'way? Mama—" she could hardly speak the next words, and they came haltingly. "Mama has to. . . go 'way too, that way. . . But Mama will always love her Polly. . . . Forever. . . and always—" She took several breaths with great difficulty, fear running through her that her time would come before she had spoken all she needed to, and was nearly smothered by Polly's firm, four-year-old's strangling embrace. But it was sweet. Her beautiful Poll. She was so gentle-hearted and kind. She would be a lovely woman.

She drifted awhile and came back again to Patsy's hand on her arm.

"Mama?"

She opened her eyes, but the room was grey, and she squinted, struggling to see. "Miss Patt," she said, smiling a little. "My big girl. My young lady." She felt Thomas's arms tighten about her. She thought fleetingly that he should get up, take a rest, take some nourishment. He must not wear himself out this way. She had been drifting thus for days.

"Oh, my Mama," Patsy sobbed, laying her head on her bosom. "My Mama, don't leave us, please, Mama. I love you, don't leave me!" She lifted her hand, very heavy it was now, to Patsy's head with its crisp, curling hair.

"Don't cry, sweet," she whispered, tears coming again. They fell no further than her eyes, though she was agonized. "I need you to be my big girl. . . . I need you to be brave. . . . I need you to look after. . . your Papa and. . . Poll and Baby. . . for me. Especially Papa. . . he needs you, Patt—" She broke off, heaving breaths and coughing. When the tightness subsided a little she said, "He needs you. . . to love him. . . for me. Won't you, Patt?"

Patsy was sobbing in Aunty Carr's embrace and made no reply.

"Patt?"

"I will, Mama," came the tearful reply, and she nodded, satisfied. Someone dear to him should be there for her poor love when she was gone. She could not expect Patsy Carr or Lisbet to fulfill that pledge.

". . .more every thing presses on. . ."

Her sense of time was disordered, minutes dragging as days and hours flying as minutes. She felt caught up in a vortex, swirling and shifting, and she lost all sense of the external world. Her only anchor was Thomas's arms about her, and his regular breath shifting her as a boat upon the sea. She hardly knew when she was awake or asleep. Either world was grey and dim and shifting. Once though, she heard Thomas calling her and it brought her out of her half-world and clearly into the room. It was nearly twilight now, and she asked for the candles to be brought in.

"Yes, love, we'll get them for you." he said. "Betty's here. Will you see Betty, and Critta and Nance?"

"Betty?" she said, and wept. "They should not have. . . sent her away."

A hand clasped hers. "Here I am, lamby," Betty said, as she used to do when Patty was a child and unhappy. Betty had always loved her, always been sweet and kind and listened to her young girl's torments. No matter how lonely or ugly or unloved she felt, no matter how superfluous the newest stepmother might consider her, Betty was always warm and welcoming, loving and affectionate. They should not have sent her away after Papa died. Papa loved her, too. He would have wanted her to stay in her old home where she was raised.

"Oh, Bett," she wailed, holding the dear hand to her cheek. "Tell me she's wrong; tell me he doesn't hate me! I didn't mean it! I was only jealous! You'll tell Papa, won't you Bett?"

"Yes, lamby." Betty was dissolved in her daughter Critta's arms. "I'll tell your Papa for you—"

"Ma'am—" A voice came through her fog. "It's Nance."

"Did you light the candles, Nance?"

"Yas'm, I did."

"It's still dark."

"I'se just going t' light more, ma'am."

"Good girl. . . . Nance!" Her voice came out, loud and clear, ringing in the room.

"Ma'am?"

"Fetch Mr. Jefferson quick!" Her voice rose. "Something's wrong with Lucy! *Lucy—* "She reached out her hand, but it encountered only cold space, and she remembered that Lucy was dead. Her poor little Lucy Elizabeth, harried all her pathetic short life, from pillar to post and back again, fleeing from Arnold's advancing army. It was no wonder she had convulsions!

She slept again, and woke with a start at a cold cloth on her forehead.

"No!" she insisted. She tried to reach up, but her arms were too heavy.

"All right," Thomas soothed. "We'll take it away." He was as good as his word because the icy chill was gone from her.

"Thomas?"

"Yes, sweet?"

"Is there an eclipse?"

"No, love, I don't think so."

"There must be. . . . It's dark. . . . You look and see. . . . I'll wager there is—"

"I will, Patty."

"Thank you, dearest." She slept again.

She woke in the middle of the night and was surprised to find that the lamp, left burning for her at night every night since her illness began, had not been lighted. She listened for the regular breath of her beloved and called to him quietly in the intimate, familiar darkness.

"Thomas—"

"Mmm?"

"The lamp is out—" The words were not half out of her mouth before the awful truth came rushing at her from afar, and she turned, reaching for him in the dark that was shadowy and strange, not at all her peaceful room.

"I. . .can't see!" she wailed. "Hold me, dearest! I'm so afraid! Don't let me fall."

"I won't let you fall. You're safe here, Patty," he said. "You're safe with me."

She felt his hands on her hair, on her arms, her back, and she was safe again from the sensation of falling into a void. She clung to him, though it was painful, for the muscles in her hands and arms were knotting. But she must not let him go, or she would fall.

"Promise me," she said.

"Anything, darling," he murmured, kissing her forehead. "Whatever you want."

"Don't make a fuss about. . . the burial. I don't want. . . all the neighbors. Just us." It was most important that he understand she didn't want all and sundry intruding on their privacy. The world had had enough of their privacy to last for two lifetimes.

"Don't, Patty, please," he begged, and she felt his tears against her cheek. "I can't bear it."

"I must. . . speak. I have so little time." She could feel the swirling wind rising up from the west, far across the Blue Ridge. It was a storm worse than the one that greeted them upon their first arrival here. She could feel its strength from an hundred miles distant. It would envelope her, and she must tell before it came upon her and swept her away.

"Give Nancy the clothes. . . they'll fit her, and my guitar. . . and the extra strings. . . don't forget the keys. . . are in the box . . . in the double chest. . . and my mother's wedding ring. Tell Lisbet. . . to send—" She broke off, gasping at a sharp pain in her side. "To send the pray. . .er. . . book. . . to Lucy Gil. . . Gilliam— Oh!" Her breath came in short, quick gasps and she could not get enough air. She couldn't die yet! She wasn't finished!

Please God, spare me, just a little longer, she implored. She tried to pick up the dropped thread of her thought, and wove back through the maze of encroaching fog. "It's his. . . he would want her to. . . have it. But mind, you keep the jewelry. . . for the little girls."

Oh, her poor little motherless girls! How would they fare? Thomas was as loving a father as any child could want, but he was not a mother, and he could never make up the lack. Her own father had not, tho' he had tried, through two wives, to give his girls the female direction they needed. Mary Cocke was bad enough, but all of Elizabeth Lomax's hopes had been pinned on the child she lost, and after that she was bitter. We tried, the four of us, but there was no pleasing her.

Thomas shook his head, looking at Lisbet. He had no idea what she meant. "Our stepmother," Lisbet said.

"You won't bring another in, Papa; I'd rather die!" she exclaimed. She would never forget the sorrow in his brown eyes as he looked at her.

"I won't, Patty. I swear I won't—" It was not a fair promise to ask of him, and she had not been able to ask his forgiveness for it when he died. She saw him standing with his fists on his hips as he always did, laughing at her, his brown eyes merry. His image came clearer and clearer into her focus. Forgive me, Papa! I didn't mean it! I ever only wanted your affection! But he passed by her, fading away, away, and she was floating in a void.

She saw Thomas standing in the sunshine of Bruton churchyard in his white coat. She saw him as he waited for her with Reverend Coutts to be married. She saw his drowsy eyes glittering bright in their private bower. She saw him going across water. France. He was going to France. She saw him a very old man, walking among his woods on the mountain. But he was alone, always alone. His true heart was always locked away, never to be shared again as he shared it with her, and she was saddened. He was not the sort to be alone.

"You shall not marry again," she said, with grief. She felt his tears on her face, but heard his voice as through water, "I won't, my darling, sweet, Patty. I swear it!" She tried to speak, to tell him that she hadn't meant that at all— But all was swirling fog and a rushing sound like the eye of a storm, and she could no longer reach him.

As suddenly, she found herself at peace again, the greyness yet about her, but it was peaceful. Everything would be all right. All would be well. . . Except—

Thomas appeared before her, unshaven, rumpled, with all matter of muck stained down him. She must have been sick. She regarded him fondly. Poor Thomas. He was always so caring of her.

"You cannot leave me," he pleaded. "I need you. I've always told you that! I cannot live without you, Patty; I'd sooner die myself!"

The words alarmed her, for she saw down the long vista of his days. He must not abrogate that for her sake!

"My dear, you must abide!" She took his hand. "You have so much to do! So much to do!" She shook her head. "And you know it was never the plan that I remain here so long. I have done so only for your sake." He nodded miserably, his beautiful eyes full of that painful truth. *Remember. Remember,* some part of them whispered. *Remember who you truly are.*

"I must go soon," she said. "But not forever." She looked at him, oh beautiful soul that he was! How had she never seen it so completely before this! She loved him beyond words or concepts and strove to find some way to convey that to him. "I will always love you. Forever. And you shall not be alone. I promise you that. Wherever you are, you need but call my name and I will be there. You shall not be alone, Thomas. We are never alone! And you have my love forever."

In the dressing room Patsy called out desperately, "Doctor, Elizabeth, please help me! I cannot rouse him!"

Lisbet looked up from where she sat on the bed with Polly, hardly having heard what was said. "But she's dead," she said.

Patsy implored, "Please! Leave the dead and come look after the living, or he shall be no more!" The words struck her in their full meaning, and she gave Polly to Nance. "I'll fetch Doctor," she called, and moved through the crowded room with alacrity.

She took his hands and kissed him. "You must go, my dear. Much depends on it. Believe that I am with you." She kissed him again and let him go.

With Lisbet he washed and laid out the body. As he moved through the drawers and clothes press, running his hands over the familiar things, he knew he could not use anything she had worn through their happy or difficult times. She could not bear his misery, so directed his attention to the box on top of the clothes press, whose contents were a gown she had planned to wear when she was thin again after Lucy. It was difficult to get him to hear.

The box, Thomas, she found herself nearly shouting. *The box on the clothes press!* Short of knocking it down, and she did not know how to accomplish that, she knew of no other way of reaching him. But at last he noticed it and climbed up.

It was in the new fashion, with a round neckline and long sleeves, in fine muslin of a pale blue-grey, the color of moonstone. It was an utterly plain gown save for muslin ruffles at the neck and wrists, pure and beautiful in its simplicity.

She was shocked at the body, and came down to look at it more closely. When had she gone so thin? And the lovely hair, about which she had always been so vain, streaked white like an old woman's? The skin was chalky, and the lips a grey-blue, not unlike the gown. They had taped the jaw shut with a strip of cloth tied up under the hair. As she hovered there, Thomas came and crossed the hands upon the breast, with a single offering of the last of summer's roses.

They had the burial the next morning, and as per her wishes it was small and quiet, with just the family and servants. They walked down the long path to the graveyard in the fine rain. The Hemings boys carried the coffin, and Lisbet and Patsy walked beside Thomas. He was composed enough until they started to lower the coffin into the grave by the ropes.

He turned away, into Lisbet's shoulder, with a cry. His poor darling! All she had of life was given to him, and in the end her life itself. But he had so much left to give her, and now he was alone, O God, so terribly alone! How could he support life without her? How could he pretend that all was but as it was, changed and blackened forever because of her loss? He could not live without his soul, and it robbed from him.

She tried to reach him, to comfort him, to remind him she was not gone, but he would not hear her. He had forgotten it all. He could only hear his grief.

She remained for a while. Days had no meaning nor time. Events floated together until they were an endless blur in her reality. She watched him write into his father's prayer book, wherein were recorded all the events of their lives:

> Martha Jefferson died Sept 6, 1782 at 11h. 45 a.m.
> aged 33y-10m-8d

He did not sleep, but paced the rooms endlessly in spasms of grief, and she could not reach him. Once she did manage to do so, but only because of his dire mental state. He was clearing out the room of everything that was hers, every article of clothing, every trinket, every scrap, and looking them over carefully one by one, touching, feeling, remembering. He came upon her copied lines from Sterne and was undone. She was anguished at his grief, but could only hover by in comfort, until the thought came to him to take up his razor. Then she was galvanized.

Thomas Jefferson, if you do that, you will have reneged on everything we were to one another! she shouted at him. *Thomas!* He heard this and looked up. She had his attention now, and would seize her advantage. *Thomas, if you love me, you will not do it! I need you there, to watch over Patsy and Poll, and poor Lucy. What would become of them, to lose us both? You cannot do it. I need you there.* Yes, she cried when she saw that he heard. *Yes! It's me! I love you! Believe it! I will love you forever.*

Not long after, he received word from the Congress that he had once more been appointed as minister to France. This time he accepted the post.

82

To Bid Adieu

Monticello, 1790

Autumn had turned the mountain russet when Thomas and Polly arrived in September, she from Eppington and he from Philadelphia, from whence he would be removed until the early part of November. It was good, good, he thought as he stood looking across the valley to the Blue Ridge the afternoon of their arrival, to be among his own hills again. The bustle and squalor of cities, even Philadelphia, was too great a pall on his spirit, and the duties as Secretary of State far less enchanting than grubbing in his gardens at home. He looked over to Edgehill, that much-disputed property, whose roofline was just visible through the trees. He was reminded that the matter of its ownership needed to be settled soon, preferably while he was home. This waffling on the part of Tom Randolph could not continue; both Patsy and young Tom were unhappy.

He turned from the window to his desk, where a pile of correspondence lay waiting his attention. Taking up the topmost letter, he sat and broke the seal. Inside was a letter from Edmund Randolph and an enclosure which fluttered to the floor. When he picked it up he did not recognize the name on it, for he had had no traffic with the person in some years: Jane Charlton, dressmaker. It was unlike either of his girls not to inform him of purchases, so he tore open the missive in some curiosity. There, in an even hand was written:

> Due against the account of Mrs. Martha Jefferson
> £ 4/16/2 gray lutestring 10 yds
> 1/13/0   labour for gray gown
>
> ———————————————
>
> £ 6/09/2 Due from May 20, 1777

He remembered that gray gown. It had been covered in pink stock, and she wore it with a ribbon round her neck that held the locket he'd bought for her in Philadelphia. . . Patty. Her face came vividly to mind. Eight years abroad, with sundry flirtations and one impassioned dalliance, had not erased its image. *Oh, my poor dear! My sweet Patty!* He crumpled the note in his fist, struggling to control the grief that came welling. Every moment spent with her came flooding back of its own volition, past the dam he had built for it. A thousand nameless, sacred things he recalled. They played in his mind like the movements of a dance, and continued though he closed his eyes against them. He did not weep, for that was long past, but trembled violently, silently, agonizing, sweet memories assailing him one upon another as waves of the sea. He suddenly had a violent headache. He gave a choking gasp and threw the bill on the floor. Just then there was a timid knock at the door.

"Papa?" It was Polly. He had not closed to door behind him, so she assumed he was available.

"Yes?" he cried in an uneven voice, rising and turning from the desk. She entered, her mild and pretty face all alarm. It was her mother's face, young and sweet, showing all promise of great beauty. Her dark auburn hair was swept away from her face in the French manner, and her ochre gown was of a simpler cut, but overall she was not very much different from Patty as she had been that first night at Randolph's. He was unable to speak, but looked at her with burning eyes. She scurried over, taking his arm solicitously.

"Papa, whatever is the matter?" she exclaimed. He patted her hand, endeavoring to regain some measure of emotional control. "Nothing, my Maria. Nothing really." He could never say to the child that she haunted him because she wore her mother's face. That would be cruel, and Polly was sensitive enough about her looks. "I am just. . . overcome to be back." He paused. "What did you require?"

"Patsy wishes to know if she might send a note to the Coleses asking their company this evening," she said in her soft voice. "She also desires an opinion of the wine." She waited with her hands folded and her head bowed politely, a relic of her days in the convent school. Yes, Polly would make a fine woman. In his present mood, he wasn't really desirous of company, but he would not deny the others a chance to celebrate.

"Yes," he said. "I should like to see them, wouldn't you?" he asked. "Tell her that they would be most welcome. As to the wine, I think there is some of the Montrachet chardonnay in the new shipment. That and the sherry for the ladies. You'll see to it, won't you, my dear?" He laid a hand on her shining hair.

"I will, Papa," Polly said. She looked up at him, her clear hazel eyes sparkling orange and green in their depths. Patty would have been pleased to know how well this daughter she had so fretted over had turned out, for Polly was as sweet and gentle as she was lovely. He smiled at her. "That's my good girl." She went out and he sank into his chair again, exhausted with the emotion and the facade.

He sat there for some time pensively before he roused himself and went to his chest. Beneath the third drawer, where on the face was a divider, there was a concealed compartment. He brought this out and laid it on the bed. In the shallow drawer were many mementos—locks of hair, watch fobs, the miniature Patty had given him for his birthday. This he drew out, holding it in his hand without looking at it. Seated as he was on the floor, he could only see the nearest treetops in the window. He recalled another time when he had sat gazing out this window. The house had changed since that September, but he could not change the view. He looked down at the miniature now, and scalding tears came welling. It was not a very good portrait; Marks had been an indifferent artist, but it was like her enough to bring forth a sob unbidden. The door was closed and he would not be disturbed, so he let himself weep as he had not done in eight long years. There was still anger there: with himself, for not caring for her better; with her, for leaving him rootless to find a new course without star or sun. He stayed there until dinner was called, and found the Coleses from nearby Enniscorthy arrived. He was blear-eyed and exhausted, but at least his headache had gone.

Later, when all had departed, Thomas went again into his study but this time to the closet, where in a cedar casket were stored all the letters he had written Patty in their twelve years together, and those replies of hers. She had kept her share of them carefully in this box, and when she died, the rest had gone there too. He had never looked at them. Now he did.

One by one, every scrap of paper he opened and read, in order with its chronologic companions, from his scribbled note that had accompanied the heliotrope spray—he found that preserved but crumbling in the first packet—to the lines she wrote out from Sterne in August before she died. On this last, he picked up his pen and finished:

> — and every
> Time I kiss thy hand to bid adieu,
> Ev'ry absence which follows it, are preludes to
> that eternal separation
> Which we are shortly to make!

The entirety of their life passed before him, all its joys and sorrows: their meeting, the wedding, Patsy's birth, the harried refugeeing from Tarleton's men, the terrible day in Richmond when Lucy died, and the last time she looked at him with her autumn-dark eyes and whispered, "I love you, too."

> Dear old friend,
> why comest hither, and why these demands?
> I shall bring all to pass for thee; I shall
> comply with all thy bidding. Only stand

nearer to me. For this little time
may we embrace and take our fill of tears.

A wisp of life remains
in the undergloom of Death: a visible form,
though no heart beats within it. All this night
the shade of poor Patróklos bent above me
grieving and weeping, charging me with tasks.
It seemed to the life the very man.

Dawn was streaking roseate toward the Blue Ridge before he put down his pen. The emotion which had stayed him through the night was spent, and he sat dully at the desk holding the paper in his hands. The bill which had thrown him lay nearby on the floor. He looked at it stupidly. What a furor it had caused! Please God, it was the last of such surprises, for he could not endure another. He put down the scrap of paper and laid his head in his arms wearily. Another hour or so and the house would be abroad. How could he face them as though nothing had occurred?

He drowsed a little, neither waking nor sleeping, and it came to him thus that the only way to prevent such torment in the future was to get rid of all that remained. The thought gave him a pang. Never again could he turn back time and bring her sweet face to life; never again would he be able to call up her silver laughter and dancing-eyed mischief. The only way to excise the mortal wound would banish her from him forever. He could rely only on his own memory, and as he knew from his father and others, the sharp edges faded, details blurred; he would be left with only bittersweetness, and not this terrible agony.

He raised his head and looked out the window. The sky was turning golden, brightening towards the interior. There was not very much time left. He rose and as he did every cold morning, laid a fire in the small hearth. When it was blazing cheerily, he took the box of letters in hand, and the miniature, and knelt before the fire.

It was difficult to lay that first note with the aged blossom upon the flames. He held it out unresolvedly for a long moment. Then he gathered his courage, swallowing, and murmured to his shade: "Understand what I do, my sweet." He laid the paper on the fire. The bloom caught quickly, dry and dusty as it was, and ignited the paper. Shortly—as shortly as their time together—there was nothing left but a blackened curl, rising heavenward toward she whose object it was.

Methodically, letter by letter, he consigned their life to the flames. Once before his life had been cut in twain by fire; now he did so purposefully. He might have merely dumped the entire lot onto the funerary pyre, but that would have meant his good-bye would be abrupt. He never had liked abrupt leave-takings from Patty. He was always too loathe to let her go, even for her safety. He came finally to the last letter, and dropped it in. Now, all that remained was the miniature. Painted on ivory, it would blacken and crack as charnel bones. He picked it up, caressing the filigree frame with a fingertip.

His determination weakened. Everything of her was given away but the letters and this. He owned not a single garment she had worn. Her jewelry was in Elizabeth's keeping for the girls. This, this mediocre portrait painted twenty years ago was all that remained. He stared at her face in the frame. Marks had not captured her beauty at all, for it was not merely exterior, but of the spirit, and he was not talented enough to convey that.

Thomas was trembling now, and the scalding tears slipped away heedless. "Good-bye, my love," he murmured huskily. "I will not forget you, though I live an hundred years." He held the miniature to his lips, one holy kiss, as upon a sacred relic, and closed his eyes. He could not watch this burn; she would die all over again. He tossed it on the fire and turned his back.

Dawn had fully broken, and the sky over the Blue Ridge was the color of a robin's egg, heralding another Indian summer day. The afternoon might be thundery, but now it was fine. He sighed and wiped his face with the back of one hand, then peered at his thermometer. It was forty-four degrees of Fahrenheit, forty-eight indoors, and there was a wind from the southeast. Today he would go down and see how the winter cover crop was being sown on the wheat fields. He yanked the bellpull and Jupiter came shortly. "Yassir?"

Thomas turned from the window. "Uncle Juba," he said, using the children's name for his old companion, "fetch me a bath."

"Yassir." Jupiter went, and he was alone again.

Never after to any living mortal did he breathe Patty's name, or hold forth very candidly on any subject that concerned her. He had locked her away in his heart, and his knowledge of their love and passionate regard would die with him, but for the single scrap of verse from *Tristram Shandy*—found, after he died, enclosing a lock of her hair—and his quotation of Homer upon her gravestone.

They rest now in the Monticello graveyard beneath a single stone, at one with the earth, with each other, in the place they loved.

> *Here it was once Leander crossed; here beats the swelling*
> *Straight that brought a lover—and her he loved—to dust.*
> *Here stands the ruined tower, that was once Hero's dwelling,*

Where of old she kindled the lamp that failed their trust.
Here in one grave together, they lie–still crying in vain
Against the wind that grudged them to each other's arms again.

To them this volume is sincerely dedicated.
Requiescat in pace.

Author's Afterword

"Thomas Jefferson still survives." The dying words of John Adams are as true today as they were in 1826. Martha Jefferson survives also, in spite of Thomas's attempt to preserve from prying eyes the "sacred intimacies of a lover" (to quote Page Smith) by burning their personal correspondence. Her ghost haunts the scenes of her life with as lively a passion as when Maria Cosway wrote in scorn to Thomas in Paris, querying whether the future would find him solitary and sad on his beautiful Monticello, haunted by the shadow of a woman. She is everywhere on the mountain, in Charles City–at Shirley, Berkeley, Bermuda Hundred, The Forest–at Eppington in Chesterfield, in Williamsburg, at Rosewell; she survives in the commentaries of friends and neighbors, of her daughter and granddaughters, and in the material goods left behind, from wedding salt-cellars to the lock of her hair Thomas wore in a mourning ring.

Like Thomas, I have been haunted by her shade my life long. From the age of five, when I first heard the name of Thomas Jefferson, her image has been before me, in intimate, indelible, and ordinary scenes of ringing clarity. The verity of these images has been confirmed in curious ways throughout the years, often from people who had no idea of the personal impact of their information. Invariably, I would emerge from such exchanges emotional, stunned and shaken, often in tears. It was all true.

By extrapolation, could I then say the irrecoverable elements of my knowledge were also true? And if they were not, why were those elements so persistent and consistent? This postulation has been the core of this book. What I can only call a strange sort of memory strikes me as true because the incidences are so commonplace–the ordinary elements of life. Are they my memories, a recollection of reincarnation, or part of the collective unconscious? I cannot say. I only know my lifelong experience and can allow the peculiar nature of the verifications to speak for themselves.

Of material culture, let me begin by saying that the first time I heard the *Pachelbel Canon in D* as a child, I had an image of Thomas and Patty sitting before a fire. Later, I found it in the Monticello music collection at the Alderman Library at the University of Virginia, and on a recording of the music of Monticello purveyed on the mountain at the Visitor's Center.

When I learnt to play the guitar at the age of eleven, my interest ran to classical pieces, and again, there was an image of Patty in my mind, bent over a guitar. No mention was made in popular books of that time that she played the guitar, only the harpsichord. But there are many references in Thomas's accounts to the purchase of guitar strings for Mrs. J., and Helen Cripe in her book, *Thomas Jefferson and Music* [1], details the guitars at Monticello, beginning with those owned by Patty before she was married to Thomas.

Likewise, in connection with Patty and music, there was an inexplicable resonance of Scottish songs. In the literature, I found no references. But in the Jefferson music collection, there is a folio of sheet music from The Forest, with examples aplenty of assorted Scottish tunes, including "The Ill Wife," an arch song about a troublesome jade, entirely in keeping with Patty's sensibility.

But the most uncanny elements were uncovered when I first went to the Visitor's Center in Charlottesville. This is an off-site free museum collection devoted to Jeffersonia–an anthropologist's dream. In the section devoted to the family, there were two items which rooted me to the spot:

One was Patty's music notebook, a copy of which I had secured on microfilm, which gave no hint of the size of the original. The original, memory said, was a small brown book, about seven by five inches. And there it was in a glass case, as memory saw.

The other was a note card which stated that the item, out for cleaning, was a "pin cushion", by family tradition made by Mrs. Jefferson when she was expecting their first child. My instinctive response was disgusted outrage. "It wasn't a pin cushion, it was a baby pillow!" Of the sort that are still made as keepsake tokens for babies. It was five by seven by two inches, embroidered in silks with a blue central applique on which was stitched the name Martha, and edged in gold fringe. I rang Kris Onuf at the Research Department on the mountain and asked her to read out from the catalogue a description of the "pin cushion." It matched exactly.

So to the incidences of her life:

There has been an idea among some scholars that Thomas did not speak French before his tenure in Paris. But I always saw them in conversation with some foreigners–d'Anmours, the Riedesels, and Chastellux, as it happened–and was delighted to find among Bathurst Skelton's books not only a French prayer book, but a ladies' French grammar. Plainly, Patty had some acquaintance with the language before she met Thomas.

When cogitating on her early life, I always saw her engaged in household business at someplace not Monticello, and leaning over a desk with a stoutish man with long grey hair–John Wayles. There is a family tradition that Patty was "trained to business by her father." In the land rolls and deeds of Charles City Co, there are better than half a dozen surviving documents franked by Mrs. Martha Skelton, as witness to a legal transaction between her father and a client, or standing as surety for a bond. The last one is in November 1771, hardly six weeks before her marriage to Thomas; it is the probate of Bathurst Skelton's will.

On the subject of John Wayles, I had the sense that he had been out of the country before her marriage to Batt Skelton, for an indeterminate time. In the aforementioned music collection, there is a much-used piece of sheet music, glued to the back of which is a page of the *Bristol Gazette,* dated August 1766; John Wayles was in England in his capacity as agent for the merchants Farell and Jones. There survives a letter directing that company to address any further concerns on a business matter to his brother Waller in Lancashire.

One episode stood out strongly in my mind, but it had no placement in time until I read Thomas's own account of the siege of Richmond, and Sarah Randolph's *Domestic Life.* All were in a small, leaky, musty room with a window that looked out on a sloping hill. In the first scene, it was dark, and Thomas was leaning over a desk. There was a feeling of great alarm. In the second scene, they were standing in the same room, he with a young baby in his arms, and she was weeping because the child was dead. Richmond. When Thomas died, he too went back in his memory to that ghastly scene, and according to Jeff Randolph, his grandson, sat up in bed and went through all the motions of writing, and told some person standing by to summon the Committee of Safety.

Thomas's governorship was significant to Patty, though not happily. Often and often, I saw her reclining, ill, on a chaise in an upper room, waiting for him to return from business. It was not Monticello. The room, I later saw, was what is now called the guest bedroom at the Governor's Palace in Williamsburg.

Her illness I knew only as a lassitude. Her eyes hurt, light was painful, her feet hurt on walking, and she vomited a lot. It was worse when she was pregnant. It was Thomas Fleming and Natalie Bober[2] who cued me in on all these symptoms as being diabetes. I was so excited when I read that in Natalie's book that I rang her in New York. She told me that both she and Fleming had described the symptoms to their doctors, and diabetes was the response. It was so abundantly clear that I set out immediately to prove it by surviving records. The result was a paper that was mentioned by Lucia C. Stanton, head of the Research Department at Monticello, at a conference on medicine in Virginia in the 18th century, as much proof as we can have at this distance of time.

Another instance of ill health in the family was a strong resonance of little Jackie Skelton's malady. The verification here came in the form of the peculiar, distinct name of the surgeon summoned—Mr. Harwood. Surgeons in those days were not necessarily medical doctors; more often they were simply "leeches," back country doctors with some medical training but no certification. There was a Mr. Harwood in the neighborhood, as I discovered courtesy of the library at Colonial Williamsburg Foundation: he was the cousin of Dr. William Carter, practicing in James City and Charles City counties. As the Wayleses by all accounts were close friends with several branches of the Carter family, the choice of Mr. Harwood was a reasonable one.

That Patty was close to her sisters, I knew from an early age. Two of them, Anne and Elizabeth, were particularly familiar. Nancy as a slight blonde girl was a regularly recurring image. How surprised I was to find that Patty did have a sister named Anne! Lisbet was always the brunette one, plumper, more serious, closer to Patty in age and emotion. They particularly were homebodies. All this was borne out in the prints of Francis and Elizabeth Eppes at Eppington, and Francis' words, quoted by the docent, how his wife loathed going to town, but preferred to stay at home with her children.

But Patty did not get on with Mrs. Jefferson, Thomas's mother. That I knew too from an early age. Mrs. Jefferson was cold, proud, and seemed to regard this daughter-in-law's family as upstart amongst the established Virginia gentry. There was something distinctly odd about Mrs. Jefferson. "Queer fits of temper" was the phrase that came to mind. Later, there was a persistent image of scenes that could only be at Shadwell between Peter and Jane, Thomas's parents; and of pillow talk about the situation between Thomas and Patty.

Years later, I read Patsy's account of her mother, which included the following concerning Jane Randolph Jefferson: "We all know what a delicate situation this is," intimating that there was enmity between Jane and Patty, well known to the family. I also came upon the piece of antique gossip from a neighbor whose family still lives adjacent to Shadwell, that she knew "perfectly well why Thomas Jefferson stayed just as far away from his mother as he could. That woman was as crazy as can be. She tried to burn the house down three times and she finally succeeded." It is ironic indeed that the only article known beyond the shadow of a doubt to have belonged to Jane Jefferson was a candlestick, which Thomas ever afterward kept on his nightstand at Monticello. On what sad scenes was that a commentary, a caution? Such an action was entirely like Thomas.

If I appear to be dragging unwelcome skeletons from the closets of Monticello, I offer that this is all well known to the family and to Jefferson scholars, and I offer it without malicious intent. On the contrary, the genuine pathos of the situation induces an even more profound respect for the domestic harmony achieved and maintained in the "ten years of unchequered happiness" of Thomas and Patty's marriage.

Patty's marriage to Batt Skelton and the loss of little Jack are often looked on by scholars as an unnecessary prelude to her subsequent marriage to Thomas, as if Batt and Jack were only vehicles to carry her to that place.

I would submit otherwise. The words "Bathurst Skelton" always induced in me a feeling of sorrow and horror, with one scene before me: a carriage in the Jamestown road, an accident, and a young girl's wild grief. She was only nineteen, with a child but a year old. I had no verification for this scene until I chanced upon a notice in the *Virginia Gazette* of September 1768 which publicized the death of Bathurst Skelton "of this town" several days previously in the Jamestown road. If Thomas was anything in the beginning of their acquaintance, then surely it was a balm to that grief.

Patty's character has, by some well-meaning historians, been described as rather bland, if she has been mentioned at all. Memory of an arch, passionate, sensitive, capable, well-read girl and a tender, fiery, sometimes willful woman has been borne out by what contemporaries said of her and what Thomas allowed to survive.

She was no milksop, nor, apparently, very docile. She lost, by Thomas's reckoning, over a hundred pounds sterling at cards at the Coles' house, Enniscorthy, in January of 1773, though Thomas himself abhorred cards and gambling. Her temper and vivacity are attested to by Patsy and her granddaughters in Sarah Randolph's book, as is her strong mind about child-rearing. Patsy in her recollections told of but one incident, where she had been scolded long for some offence, not once but twice, whereupon Thomas intervened with some gentle words.

But she was tender, too. Thomas told the very sensitive Polly (Maria) when she was grown that her mother had remarked, on being ill-treated by a neighbor, that she "had rather endure two such insults as to offer one."

She was a woman of her time, with all the graces and airs, yes, but the vanities, too. Can we blame her if she spent a little too freely at the dressmaker's in Williamsburg (as is instanced by a bill called for long after her death by Jane Charlton) or fretted over being replaced in her husband's affections too soon (the famous "death-bed promise" extracted)? She, like many women of her age, had seen so much of personal sorrow. She herself had three stepmothers, if we include Betty Hemings.

In the end, there is only one picture that lasts: a woman who loved. Her spirit breathed life into Monticello, so much so that her beloved could not bear to face it without her, had to change it materially, eradicate her strong image. He never did. Her laughter rings in the south pavilion, and the trills of her harpsichord echo in the parlor; her step sounds in the beer-room; her directing voice in the kitchen. Martha Jefferson still survives.

---

1 University Press of Virginia, 1974.

2 Fleming, Thomas. *Man on a Mountain;* Natalie Bober, *Thomas Jefferson.*

Primary Sources

The Jefferson Family

Jefferson, Martha. Household Accounts, 1772-1782, in *Cases Tried in Virginia Courts, 1768-9*. Jefferson Papers, Series 7, Vol. 1. Washington, DC: Library of Congress.

——. Music Notebook. Special Collections, Thomas Jefferson Memorial Foundation. Monticello.

——. Artifacts. Special Collections, Thomas Jefferson Memorial Foundation. Monticello.

Jefferson, Thomas. Jefferson Family Prayerbook. Special Collections, Alderman Library, University of Virginia, Charlottesville.

——. Memorandum Books. Typescript. Thomas Jefferson Memorial Foundation, Monticello.

——. Commonplace Books. Edited by Gilbert Chinard. Baltimore: Johns Hopkins Press, 1926.

——. *The Literary Bible of Thomas Jefferson*. Edited by Gilbert Chinard. Baltimore: Johns Hopkins Press, 1928.

——. *Thomas Jefferson's Library*. Edited by James Gilreath and Douglas L. Wilson. Washington, DC: Library of Congress, 1989)

——. *Garden and Farm Books*. Edited by Robert C. Baron. Golden, CO. Fulcrum Inc., 1987.

——. *The Papers of Thomas Jefferson*. Vols. 1-6, 15, 17, 18, 24. Edited by Julian P. Boyd, et al, Princeton, NJ: Princeton University Press, 1950.

——. *The Writings of Thomas Jefferson*. Edited by Paul Leicester Ford. NY, G.P. Putnam's Sons, 1892-99

——. *The Writings of Thomas Jefferson*. Edited by A.A. Lipscomb & A E. Bergh. Washington, DC, 1903.

——. *The Complete Anas of Thomas Jefferson*. Edited by Franklin B. Sawvel. (New York, 1903.

——. *Notes on Virginia*. Philadelphia, 1788.

——. *The Life and Morals of Jesus of Nazareth*. Boston: Beacon Hill Press, 1951.

Randolph, Martha Jefferson. *Reminiscences of Thomas Jefferson*. Edgehill-Randolph Papers. Special Collections, Alderman Library, University of Virginia, Charlottesville.

Wayles, John. Sheet Music. Jefferson Music Collection. Special Collections, Alderman Library, University of Virginia, Charlottesville.

Family and Visitors to Monticello

Chastellux, Marquis de. *Journal of Travels in America In the Years 1780, 1781, and 1782*. Edited by Howard Rice Jr. Chapel Hill, NC: University of North Carolina Press, 1963.

Fountaine, Rev James Maury. *A Sermon Preached at the Funeral of Mrs. Frances Page, Wife of John Page, esq. of Rosewell*. Richmond, VA: Nicholson, 1787.

Gilmer, George. Letterbook. Copy. Colonial Williamsburg Foundation Library, Williamsburg.

——. Medical Daybook. Special Collections, Alderman Library, University of Virginia, Charlottesville.

——. Papers, 1775-1778. Virginia Historical Society, Richmond.

Mazzei, Phillip. *Memoirs of the Life and Travels of the Florentine Dr. Phillip Mazzei*. Translated by Howard Marero. New York: Columbia University Press, 1942.

Page, John. "Autobiography," *Virginia Historical Register III* Richmond, VA, 1850.

Randolph, Edmund. "Essay On the Revolutionary History of Virginia, 1774-1782," *The Virginia Magazine of History and Biography*, XLIII-XLV.

Riedesel, Frederich Adolph von. *Memoirs, Letters, and Journals, during his Residence in America*. Translated by W. L. Stone. Albany, NY, 1868.

Riedesel, Friederike Charlotte Luise (von Massow) von. *Baroness von Riedesel and the American Revolution, a Journal and Correspondence of a Tour of Duty 1776-83*. Translated by Marvin L. Brown. Chapel Hill, NC: University of North Carolina Press, 1965.

Eppes Family Genealogy, Prince George County Records. Surry County Historical Society, Surry County, VA.

Charles City County Records. Abstracts. Sutro Genealogical Library, San Francisco.

Tax Rolls and Parish Records, Lancashire County, England, 1710-35, 1735-65. Sutro Genealogical Library, San Francisco.

Skelton Family Genealogy. Microfilm. Sutro Genealogical Library, San Francisco.

Skipwith Family Genealogy. Microfilm. Sutro Genealogical Library, San Francisco.

Virginia Gazette. Purdie, Dixon, Nicholson et al, Colonial Williamsburg Foundation Library, Williamsburg, VA, 1933.

Secondary Sources

History and Biography

Bober, Natalie S. *Thomas Jefferson, Man on a Mountain.* New York: Atheneum, 1988.

Brodie, Fawn. *Thomas Jefferson, an Intimate History.* New York: Norton, 1974.

Bullock, Helen D. *My Head and My Heart, a Little History of Thomas Jefferson and Maria Conway.* New York: G.P. Putnam's Sons, 1945.

Burstein, Andrew. *The Inner Jefferson, Portrait of a Grieving Optimist.* Charlottesville, VA: University Press of Virginia, 1995.

Dabney, Virginius. *The Jefferson Scandals.* New York, 1981.

Dumbald, Edward. *Thomas Jefferson, American Tourist.* Norman, OK: University of Oklahoma Press, 1976.

Faber, Doris. *Mothers of American Presidents.* New York: New American Library, 1968.

Fleming, Thomas. *The Man From Monticello, an Intimate Life of Thomas Jefferson.* New York: Morrow, 1969.

Hemphill, John M. II. "John Wayles Rates his Neighbours." *The Virginia Magazine of History and Biography.* 1958.

Kimball, Fiske. "In Search of Jefferson's Birthplace." *The Virginia Magazine of History and Biography*, Vol. LI, 1943.

Kimball, Marie. *Jefferson, the Road to Glory.* New York: Coward-McCann. 1943.

——. *Jefferson, War and Peace.* New York: Coward-McCann, 1947.

Long, E. John. "Shadwell- Jefferson's Birthplace." *The Ironworker*, Autumn, 1962.

McCord. T.B. *John Page of Rosewell, a Man of the Virginia Enlightenment.* Thesis Paper, Unpublished. George Mason University, 1975.

Malone, Dumas. *Jefferson The Virginian.* Boston: Little Brown & Co., 1951.

Miller, John Chester. *The Wolf by the Ears: Thomas Jefferson and Slavery.* New York: Free Press, 1977.

Peterson, Merrill, D. *Thomas Jefferson And the New Nation, A Biography.* New York: Oxford University Press, 1970.

——. *The Jefferson Image in the American Mind.* New York: Oxford University Press, 1960.

Randall, Henry S. *Life of Jefferson.* 3 Vols. New York, 1858.

Randall, Willard Sterne. *Thomas Jefferson, a Life.* New York: Holt, 1993.

Smith, Page. *Jefferson, a Revealing Biography*. New York: American Heritage, 1976.

Tucker, George. *Life of Thomas Jefferson*. London: Knight & Co., 1837.

Wills, Garry. *Inventing America: Jefferson's Declaration of Independence*. New York: Doubleday, 1978.

Wister, Mrs. Owen J. & Miss Agnes Irwin. *Worthy Women of Our First Century*. Philadelphia: Lippincott, 1877.

Life at Monticello

Adams, William Howard. *The Eye of Thomas Jefferson*. Washington: National Gallery of Art, 1976.

———. *Jefferson's Monticello*. New York: Abbeyville Press 1983.

Bear, James A., Jr. *Family Letters of Thomas Jefferson*. Columbia MO: University of Missouri Press, 1966.

———. *Jefferson at Monticello*. Charlottesville, VA: University Press of Virginia, 1967.

———. *Thomas Jefferson and his Unknown Brother*. Charlottesville, VA: University Press of Virginia, 1981.

Beiswanger, William L. *The South Pavilion, a Chronology of Design and Construction*. Unpublished. Research Center, Thomas Jefferson Memorial Foundation, Monticello, 1972.

Betts, Edwin M. and Hazelhurst Perkins. *Thomas Jefferson's Flower Garden At Monticello*. Charlottesville, VA: University Press of Virginia. 1986.

Cripe, Helen. *Thomas Jefferson and Music*. Charlottesville, VA: University Press of Virginia, 1974.

Dewey, Frank L. *Thomas Jefferson, Lawyer*. Charlottesville, VA: University Press of Virginia, 1986.

Kimball, Marie. *Thomas Jefferson's Cookbook*. Charlottesville, VA: University Press of Virginia. 1976.

Langhorne, Elizabeth Coles. *Monticello, A Family Story*. Chapel Hill, NC: Algonquin Books of Chapel Hill, 1989.

Lewis, Jan. *The Pursuit of Happiness; Family Values in Jefferson's Virginia*. New York: Columbia University Press, 1983.

McLaughlin, Jack. *Jefferson and Monticello, Biography of a Builder*. New York: H. Holt, 1988.

Mayo, Bernard. *Jefferson Himself*. Charlottesville, VA: University Press of Virginia, 1980.

Nichols, Frederick D. *Thomas Jefferson's Architectural Designs*. Charlottesville, VA: University Press of Virginia, for the Thomas Jefferson Memorial Foundation, 1961.

Quattrin, Kelly Neff. *Martha Jefferson and Diabetes*. Unpublished. Research Center, Thomas Jefferson Memorial Foundation, Monticello, 1992.

Randolph, Mary. *The Virginia Housewife*. 1824. Edited by Karen Hess. Columbia, MO: University of South Carolina Press, 1985.

Randolph, Sarah N. *The Domestic Life of Thomas Jefferson* 1871. Charlottesville, VA: University of Virginia Press, 1978.

Sanford, Charles B. *The Religious Life of Thomas Jefferson*. Charlottesville, VA: University of Virginia Press, 1984.

Stein, Susan. *The Worlds of Thomas Jefferson at Monticello*. New York: Henry Abrams, Inc. 1993.

Social Life and Customs

Arnold, Janet. *Patterns of Fashion, The Cut of Englishwomen's Clothes*, Vols. II and III. New York: Drama Books Specialists, 1972.

Blanton, Wyndam Bolling. *Medicine in Virginia in the Eighteenth Century*. Richmond, VA: Garret & Massey, 1931.

Breen, T.H. *Tobacco Culture; the Mentality of the Great Tidewater Planters on the Eve of Revolution*. Princeton, NJ: Princeton University Press, 1985.

Carson, Jane. *Colonial Virginians at Play*. Williamsburg, VA: Colonial Williamsburg Foundation, 1989.

Clinton, Catherine. *The Plantation Mistress; Woman's World of the Old South*. New York: Pantheon Books, 1982.

Darling, J.S. *A Jefferson Music Book*. Facsimile. Williamsburg, VA: Colonial Williamsburg Foundation, 1977.

Genovese, Elizabeth Fox. *Within the Plantation Household: Black and White Women in the Old South*. Chapel Hill, NC: University of North Carolina Press, 1988.

Jordan, Winthrop. *White Over Black*. Chapel Hill, NC: University of North Carolina Press, 1968.

Langhorne, Elizabeth Coles, et al. *A Virginia Family and Its Plantation Homes*. Charlottesville, VA: University Press of Virginia, 1987.

MacPherson, James. *The Poems of Ossian*. Boston: Phillips, Sampson & Co. 1851.

Millar, John Fitzhugh. *Country Dances of Colonial America*. Williamsburg, VA: Thirteen Colonies Press, 1990.

Playford, John. *The English Dancing Master*. Facsimile Williamsburg, VA: Colonial Williamsburg Foundation, 1933.

Wilstach, Paul. *Tidewater Virginia*. Folcroft, PA, Folcroft Library Editions: 1978.

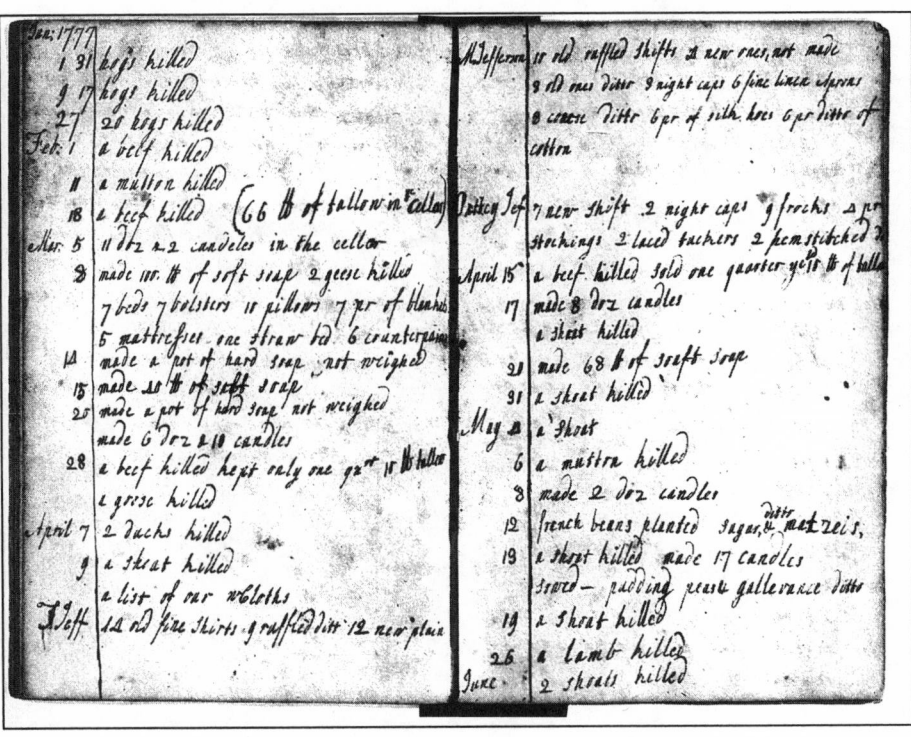

The third page of Patty's Accounts, in *Cases Tried in VA Courts, 1768-79, VII Series I* of the Jefferson Papers, beginning April 1775. Provided by the Library of Congress.

Madam   Richmond August 8ᵗʰ 1791

          Mrs Washington has done me the honor
of communicating the inclosed proposition of our sisters
of Pennsylvania and of informing me that the same grateful
sentiments are displaying themselves in maryland. justified
by the sanction of her letter in handing forward the scheme.
I undertake with chearfulness the duty of furnishing to my
countrywomen an opportunity of proving that they also
participate of those virtuous feelings which gave birth to it
I cannot do more for its promotion than by inclosing to you
some of the papers to be disposed of as you think proper
     I am with the greatest respect
        madam

                    your most humble servant

To Mrs James Madison   Martha Jefferson

Letter from Martha Jefferson to Mrs. James Madison,
Richmond, Virginia, 8 August 1791.
Provided by North Carolina Department of
Cultural Resources, Division of Archives and History.

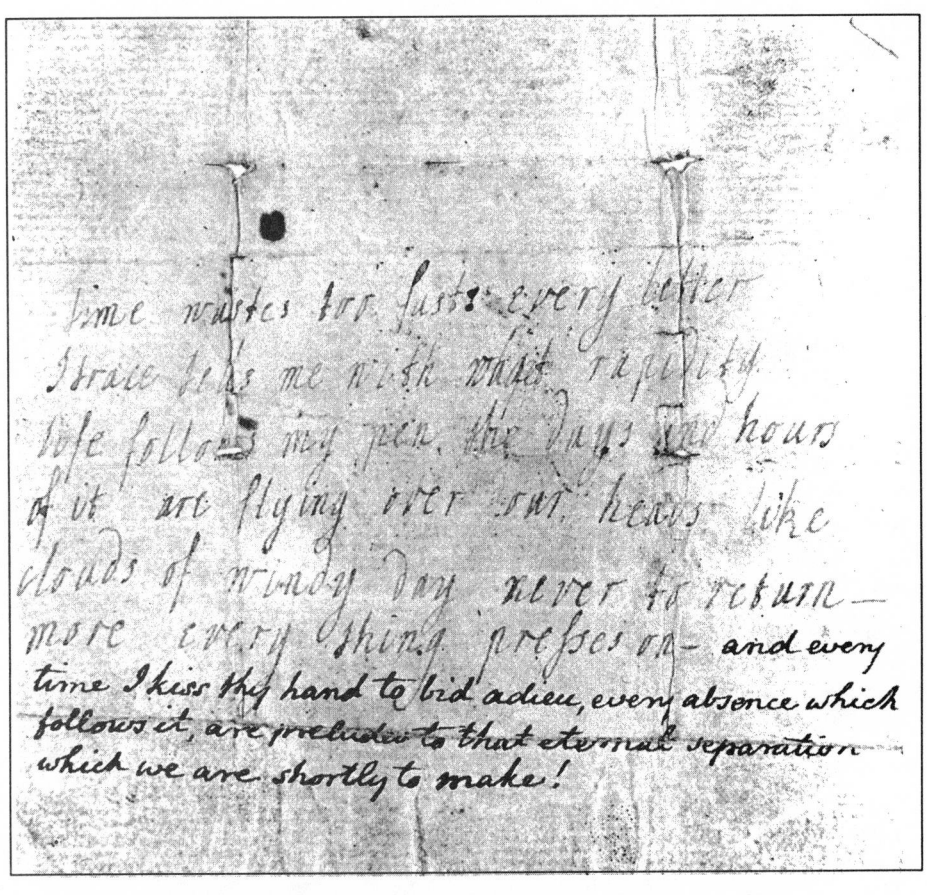

"Deathbed Adieu" by Patty and Thomas Jefferson.
Provided by the James Monroe Museum and
Memorial Library, Fredericksburg, Virginia.

About the Author

Kelly Joyce Neff has an interdisciplinary degree in Celtic studies which includes work in anthropology, history, language, and literature. A history and theatre buff from an early age, she has spent more than half her life performing, working both onstage and as a living history interpreter for the Living History Centre in northern and southern California, for the National Park Service's Maritime Musuem in San Francisco, and for the Colonial Williamsburg Foundation. She is a traditional midwife and herbalist and an active craftsperson. She lives in San Francisco.

Hampton Roads Publishing Company
publishes and distributes books on a variety of subjects,
including metaphysics, health, complementary medicine,
visionary fiction, and other related topics.

To order or receive a copy of our latest catalog, call toll-free,
(800) 766-8009, or send your name and address to:

Hampton Roads Publishing Company, Inc.
134 Burgess Lane
Charlottesville, VA 22902